. . . a novel that gives us a story of war in its most raw essence. It will lay claim as **THE ONE BOOK TO BE READ ABOUT THE AMERICAN WAR IN AFGHANISTAN.** —Kevin Nevisoll, *Denver Times-Intelligencer*

A perfect meshing of style and substance, **BLISTERINGLY ORIGINAL.** Avallone's prose is choppy and abrupt and acrobatic, and you can't pull your eyes away. Like his anti-hero ex-Marine Kyle Wolfe, Avallone plays by his own rules. . . . —*Orange Coast Literary View*

I left this book lying around for nearly a year unread because I had not heard of the author. Big mistake. Read it now! —Sebastine Jeünqer

For the 99.8% of Americans who know the Afghan War only from snippets reported in the lazy media, *Tattoo Zoo* will put you there personally, vividly, viscerally. For the .2% who were there, be prepared to relive it. —*The Green Beret Flash*

AN IMPORTANT NOVEL OF A FUTILE WAR. . . . Sit back and allow yourself to be swept into the expansive story told in brilliant simplicity in the language of the very generation we've called upon to do the fighting. —Peter Yank, *Houston Alamo Current*

Hard. Cold. Exact. . . . Avallone's voice is original, disarmingly casual, rough and streetwise to the point of giving an appearance of pulp fiction. That is the brilliance here. It is anything but pulp. It is literary. —*Book Me!*

. . . **MEGA-COOL . . . FEROCIOUS . . . SURPRISINGLY MOVING . . . THREE DAYS THAT WILL DEFINE THE AFGHAN WAR . . .** —Summer Elliott, *The Atlantic Standard*

In his debut novel Avallone does what Karl Marlantes did in *Matterhorn*, John Del Vecchio did in *The 13th Valley* and James Jones did in *The Thin Red Line*. . . Take note, *Tattoo Zoo* will be a classic. —*San Diego Palm Chronicle*

TATTOO ZOO

A NOVEL OF THE AFGHAN WAR

PAUL AVALLONE

ST. MARTIAN'S PRESS

TATTOO ZOO
A NOVEL OF THE AFGHAN WAR

Tattoo design and artwork by Tim Jensen of No Egrets Tattoo Studio, Clarksville, Tennessee.
Cover design by Renegade Filmworks.
Cover photographs by Paul Avallone.

Contact the author: AvallonePaul@yahoo.com

ISBN: 978-1-5053-6948-9

Fifth Printing, August 2020
St. Martian's Press

11 12 13 14 15   10 9 8 7 6 5

To the American and Nato soldiers who fought the Afghan War regardless that their senior commanders, civilian and military, were engaging them in warfare with mistaken assumptions about the enemy and no intent to vanquish them.

TATTOO ZOO

A Brief History Before Day One

Tattoo.

Zoo.

Two simple words.

One, permanent-inked body markings.

And, caged animals.

Tattoo Zoo is an Army infantry platoon.

Not Airborne, not Ranger, not Special Forces. A regular leg infantry platoon like any other in the Army, no better no worse.

Thirty-six soldiers today, Day One.

Nothing special about these guys, not as a whole.

The platoon leader and the platoon sergeant have their Ranger Tab, and Staff Sergeant Ketchum too, along with their paratrooper wings and air assault wings, as do a couple of the others, like Staff Sergeant Utah, who, along with the platoon sergeant, is sapper-qualified—but the thirty-some rest are just average-Joe off-the-shelf GIs.

Infantry.

Riflemen.

Grunts.

The only distinction here is the name, which came in Iraq two years ago when a couple of colonels were escorting five visiting congressmen through the platoon's barracks—

the soldiers mostly just in running shorts in the oppressive heat, nearly every one of them with tattoos on arms, legs, torsos, and Platoon Sergeant Travis Redcloud completely inked-out covered in them

—with the congressman from Connecticut trying to act like a regular everyday-one-of-the-guys himself by nonchalantly throwing out with a chortle, "What is this, a tattoo zoo?"

And the name stuck.

Who wouldn't want a cool nickname like that.

It aint a question.

Statement of fact: Who wouldn't.

Tattoo Zoo.

Ice cold.

Sharply clipped off the tongue, the hard Ts and Z, "*Tattoo Zoo.*"

Fahrenheit twenty-five below.

And even more awesome when others shortened it to just The Zoo.

Then next thing, they're even leaving out the The.

Zoo.

As in, "*What we got tomorrow, where've we got Zoo goin out on patrol?*"

Fahrenheit -50.

Then someone somewhere calls them Zoosters, and that sticks. As in today's patrol, "*Zoosters gonna be taking the HTT up to Wajma, they can scope out the lay of the land at the same time.*"

And Sniper Sergeant Rodriquez—

back then in Iraq just a nothing nobody corporal who'd enlisted back in '03 as a way out of 11/29 in county lockup for small-time drugs and everyday escalating petty gangbanger thuggery in the Bakersfield barrios where he'd inked tatts since he was a kid

—he drew up the *Tattoo Zoo* design, the skull and the roses and the single bullet hole right between the eyes for the first O in Zoo, and he inked the tatt first on himself right there in Iraq, on his own chest, using a mirror.

And others, if they deserved it, he inked them too.

On chests, shoulders, backs, thighs, and the wide arms of a couple of the guys who had weightlifters' ripped biceps.

And the tattoo became like the name, the coolest thing to have. In the company then battalion and the whole brigade. Guys wanted in the Zoo just for the tatt.

But the tatt's not for free, you don't get it just by being in the Zoo.

You've got to earn it.

Redcloud, Rodriquez, Ketchum and Utah and those few who've been in the Zoo since those nasty Iraq days, they judged who earned it back then and judge today who earns and gets it.

Preferably, if it's you, not posthumously.

As Pfc Holloway would say, "*Post—humorless—ly.*"

And not because he's a clever guy with a brilliant sense of comic irony, but because he just can't pronounce it properly.

Yeh, Holloway runs it all together, "*Post-humorlessly.*" And laughs *heh heh heh* when someone like Doc Eberly looks at him and just shakes his head and corrects him even though he knows it's a waste of time, "*It's posthumously, idiot.*"

And Pfc Holloway, he's going to go one better and answer that with *"Easy enough for you to say, Doc, sergeant college bookworm dork doofus."*
And laugh *heh heh heh* even louder and more insolent than before.

Day One, Late Morning

In Wajma Gorge

Three Zoo trucks—
two uparmored humvees and an Mrap between them
—are picking their way down the boulder-strewn stream in this narrow gorge that goes straight up in a steep V a couple thousand feet.

Just rock and shale. Pines and cedars and gnarly scrub oaks and thorned bushes growing out of fissures and cracks.

The gorge in shadow. From the bottom here in the stream you can see just a swath of blue sky way up top there on the ridgelines behind which the sun would be where on the maps it's etched as a border and labeled on the other side as Pakistan.

Down here in the stream it's Afghanistan.

"Affuckingstan" Pfc Holloway calls it, 'cause he heard it from someone once and loves saying it that way, always with his little *heh-heh* snicker, like he himself has just made it up.

It's *"The Stan"* to guys like Staff Sergeant Ketchum, who's been here before and is now a squad leader and next in line to take over if Platoon Sergeant Redcloud buys it. As Ketchum put up on Facebook before the Zoo deployed here four months ago, *"Stan #2 for me and the Zoo. See ya!"*

The first, Stan #1, being four years ago.

Pre Iraq for the Zoo.

Pre the cool nickname.

Pre the tatt.

And it's these four years later and Redcloud and Ketchum who were here before in the Zoo and the other guys who were here but in other units don't look at it as fighting a war to win it anymore. While the younger soldiers, like Pfc Holloway, who were hardly even teens back when this thing started after 9-11, even they all know now someone who's died here and guys who've lost a leg or fingers or nuts here, this time, this year, while they barely if ever see the enemy who blow off those legs and fingers and nuts with IEDs and distant ambushes and who they rarely if ever find the bodies of to count after the brief firefight, if there even is one.

For them, the younger guys, in the infantry in particular because they want to be warriors like Audie Murphy and John Wayne and Schwarzenegger and Eastwood, their attitude is exactly like Sergeant Rodriquez says often: *"It's a shitty war, 'mano, but it's the only one we got."*

Affuckingstan.

These days, now that Iraq's wound down to zilch, if you want to be an American warrior, a fighting man in combat, you can kiss off that place, there's no fighting there in Iraq anymore.

This here is where it's rockin'.

Affuckingstan. *The only one we got.*

Where these three Zoo gun-trucks are right now.

In the stream.

Down at the bottom of Wajma Gorge.

Two humvees and an Mrap between them.

Picking their way around the boulders, water up over their wheels, splashing up on the big Mrap's V-shaped hull designed to deflect the upward blast of the enemy's ever-bigger IEDs.

Mrap, or officially MRAP, for Mine Resistant Ambush Protected; pronounced for short simply *"M-rap"*.

Or, even shorter, like the humvee, just *"truck"*.

But about three times the size and heft of a humvee. Massive in contrast.

And cooler looking, sharp-edged boxy, futuristic, robotic.

The *mine* part of Mine Resistant, that's IEDs.

Formally, Improvised Explosive Devices.

Roadside bombs for short.

Just kaboom for really short.

That *"kaboom"* is only really when you can laugh about it later that day because it didn't get you, any of you, no one in the platoon, not that day. It's *"kaboom"* with a laugh because that's the way you try and ignore your fear, the way you try and pretend that you don't care, because you know every time you get into one of these trucks, no matter how good a soldier you are, no matter how proficient, how smart, how lucky, suddenly out of nowhere before you even know what's happening—

and it's probably the last thing you will ever hear, that one instant, and not even know it, not even hear it, really, except maybe later as a video-loop played back in your mind once you're in heaven, or hell

—that kaboom can come of a sudden and you can do nothing about it.

So, if you're a turret gunner or up front as driver or vehicle commander where you've got a good view of the roadway ahead, you try and see a telltale sign of irregular dirt, rocks overturned, or even a glint off an inch or two of bare copper wire left exposed. If you're a squad leader or platoon sergeant you demand that your drivers stay out of the well-worn ruts of decades of travel that make riding easy and instead take the roughest part of the road, where no one drives, because, simple common sense efficient practicality of the insurgent bomb-planter, the kaboom's going to be buried where everyone drives or is most likely to drive.

Either way, any truck any day can meet a kaboom. And the four or five soldiers in that truck, if the kaboom's big enough, have just earned their loved ones back home that big windfall SGLI payout of $400,000.

Serviceman's Group Life Insurance. Your family's winning lottery ticket, and it's only costing you less than twenty bucks a month, and then Big Army throws in a sweet bonus of a hundred grand on top just 'cause it's a swell organization. Totaled up, a cool half million, and all that's required of the guys in the unlucky truck is they've gotta not ever wake up or breathe a lick after the kaboom.

Which, with ever more skilled enemy bombmakers' bigger and better kaboom products, is all that ever much more likely.

And every guy in the trucks every day knows it and knows he can't shoot his gun back at the kaboom or charge through it or call in artillery or air on it, and that gives him a feeling of helplessness on top of the vulnerability because he cannot be a soldier and fight back, and he just secretly hopes that if there's going to be a kaboom that doesn't bring laughter afterwards it sure as shit had better be on the truck in front or the truck behind.

No kaboom of a roadside bomb coming here today, not to worry, you're in a stream.

No road.

No roadside.

Just water and boulders.

And the Americans have never come this far up anyway. They never come up here. No use wasting an IED on where the infidels don't go.

Nothing here. Just a running stream of water swirling around boulders.

And mountainsides so close you can almost reach out and scrape your gloved hands on the rocks as you bounce and jerk down the gorge.

Maybe a mile to go back to the village Wajma.

That's where these Zoosters in these three trucks will rejoin the rest of the platoon, after this recon they took up the gorge until it narrowed down to just a waterfall, impassable any farther, end of the line.

Back to Wajma they're headed, then from there later the whole Zoo will return the dozen miles switchbacking down the widening gorge to home.

Their COP.

As in Combat Outpost.

Just Cop for short.

A tiny piece of twenty-first century civilization surrounded by walls of Hesco barriers topped with razor wire, set down smack dab in the middle of nowhere.

Miles and many hours still from here.

Yeh shit yeh, get back to the Cop.

Wooden barrack B-huts with heat in the winter and AC the rest of the time.

Conex sit-down vinyl-curtained partitioned shitters.

Hot showers and hot chow.

And the internet. Email and MySpace and Facebook.

Porn, when you can get it past the Army firewalls.

Home.

Sometime this afternoon. If all goes according to plan.

If they don't throw an axle.

Or blow an engine.

Have a rollover.

Get ambushed.

Nothing but streambed and mountainsides between the village Wajma and the Cop.

According to plan.

The GIs in these three trucks've got to make it whole back to the village Wajma and the rest of the Zoo first before they can start thinking about home.

Which is why they're a good distance apart, these three trucks.

Thirty, forty meters between them.

Oldest lesson in combat, Rule #1:

Don't bunch up; one round gets you all.

Not really the case, one round, with these armored vehicles, especially the big Mrap, but then there's Combat Rule #2 to consider:

Separation makes for dispersed targets in an ambush. The more dispersed the better.

Unless the enemy insurgents are spread out themselves, dispersed hidden up high in the rocks, five or six or ten, each with a separate target, each with an RPG and four or five rounds.

Rocket-Propelled Grenade.

The Commie Bloc version of the old bazooka, ten bucks maybe wholesale on the international market. Shoulder tube, pistol grip, long snout-looking grenade sticking out the front. Trigger pulled, *paashoooop!*, the rocket's shot, fins flipping out, and flying just slow enough that if you've got focused vision you can watch its blur coming your way and you groan an *Oh shit*, pleading that it's not stopping to say hi but going right on by, thank you very much, better luck next time.

RPG.

Designed to go through things—exploding on contact, actually, and all its flaming power and its big and little bitty steel parts going through those things.

Like doors and windows.

And buildings and vehicles. Like armored trucks.

And the people in them.

An RPG will make hamburger out of flesh, bone and organs.

A half-dozen insurgents somewhere hidden up there with RPGs, they'll each aim his launcher at the open gun turrets. That's the most vulnerable spot from above, and the guns in those turrets are these trucks' only real firepower.

Insurgent Ambush Rule #1: *Take out the turret gunner.*

Might even get some of the guys down inside too on a good angle.

Which is why the three Zoo turret gunners here are alert.

Heads constantly in motion scanning.

Faceless and nameless behind the thick steel and glass of the turrets, and near impossible to tell one from another in their Kevlar helmets and bulky body armor, their ballistic-protection eyepro wraparound Wiley-Xs or Oakleys and their dust masks and scarves. Hands in $40 online-purchased gloves. Not a square inch of skin showing, except maybe a glimpse of the neck or chin.

Just the tops of their helmets peeking up out of the open turrets.

Not that any of that armor'll do any good against a direct hit RPG in the turret.

Which is why, again, these three Zoosters are alert on their guns.

RPGs, just call em rockets for short.

The first incoming rocket's most likely going to miss, but it sure increases your chances there isn't a second or third rocket if you've seen where the first came from so you can *slam bam thank you ma'am* pulverize that spot to really really *really* mess up the insurge's aim.

R.I.P not RPG.

Specialist Lee Tran is the turret gunner in the lead truck, a humvee. On his big .50-cal machinegun.

You put yourself in his place in that turret and imagine this very moment he's thinking there're Taliban up there hidden aiming their RPGs, he's not seeing a rocket coming his way, not the first one, it's not for him, it's taking out the gunner behind him, or the one behind him.

You start seeing that first rocket taking you out, you ask to get down off the gun, down inside, a driver or a dismount, and then there inside when you start seeing that rocket coming straight right through the window at you, you ask to stay back, sarge, man, please dude, you'll do anything, you'll even be the cook's helper, washing all those pots and pans breakfast and dinner. That don't work, they don't need another cook's helper, you'll shoot a 30-round mag off in the conex latrine at like 3a.m. to get sent asap, first chopper out, to the real rear, the big safe forward operating base, the FOB, or Fob, for a psych eval where, the better you can snowjob the Army shrink the better chance you'll land a job doing jack-shit in supply or the motor pool at brigade and wetting your dick every night in one of the chunky pfc and spec-4 soldierettes, white, black and brown, who get all hot-n-gooey just hearing your war stories from back where the RPGs and 7.62s fly and roadside bombs are always out there waiting just around the next bend to blow you to heroic smithereens.

You wish.

Not the kabloom blown to smithereens part. Blown by those wet pussies.

As in BJ blown.

Lewinsky blown.

You wish.

Those soldierettes, they're sluts, every last one of them, and more so, they're *"Worthless sluts!"*, you bet your frickin ass they are, every skanky last one of them, because they aint giving it up for you, dude, you kiddin? For you? Ha ha, what a scream. In your dreams. Wet dreams.

Fact is, odds are 10 to 1 they aint giving it up for anyone here in the Stan 'cause odds are they've got a husband and kids back home, and everyone knows that wives and mothers are far less hungry to give it up to just anybody, especially a zit-sprouting shitbird infantry goober.

If they're going to give it up, they're doing it on the side on the sly with someone a couple of ranks higher, guy or gal, as boyfriend or girl-friend, or with a married first sergeant or lite colonel as adulterer and mistress in double secret forbidden fornication.

Besides, there's but maybe one soldierette in a hundred who gets hot-n-anything hearing war stories, any more than there's one in a hundred who back home thinks date night at the movies means *300* or *Clash of the Titans*.

Rambo's for guys, *Twilight*'s for girls.

Die Hard's for guys. *Bride Wars* is for chicks.

And guys who dream themselves as heroes with blazing guns don't settle their asses down safe and comfy on a big Fob, not on your life.

Dude, if you've signed up for the infantry in this all-volunteer army, you're one of them, a Rambo dream-a-be, and unless you're a real head case, certified, wacko, nutso, Looney Tunes on Mars, you wind up back in the gun turret cuz you've begged to go back because you aint gettin no pussy or BJs even on the Fob and supply and the motor pool are boring do-nuthin snoozes cuz there's no fear and thus no adrenaline rush in either place, and when it comes right down to it all your buds are out there where the war stories might really happen, and that first round, rocket or 7.62 AK bullet, c'mon dude, you can't let it play mind games on you, you know cock-sucking good-n-plenty it's got the other guy's name on it, that cocksucker, your buddy in the other truck, it's always going to get him first.

You're infantry, a warrior, and you may think you want off the gun and out of patrolling period, a cook or in the motor pool, but it's a daydream, no more than wishful thinking in moments of stark unshaken anticipatory fear, and unless you really are shell-shocked wacko, you're never going to fire off that magazine in the shitter, because you belong out here not in the rear.

Because you're grunt infantry.

A warrior.

For real.

Down-n-dirty.

A flesh-and-blood warrior, like Audie Murphy and Sergeant York, not play-acting like Stallone and Schwarzenegger and Willis and *Top Gun* Cruise. Sure, cocky on the outside like them all, but on the inside tentative and sometimes scared shitless because it's human nature to be tentative and cautious and afraid when you can be killed out of nowhere from one moment to the next.

And you're in the turret now and tomorrow and the next day in spite of that fear, for real in person not in a movie, because a warrior pushes against the fear, won't let it overcome him, conquer him, enslave him, coward him.

That fear makes him realize his smallness, his insignificance, his vulnerability, and it humbles him underneath that cocky strutting, but he does not allow himself to obsess about it and allow it to bludgeon his own shame and send him crawling to the safe rear.

In spite of that fear, ever-present if only a nagging in the back of the brain, the flesh-and-blood warrior is here.

In Affuckingstan.

Right here in Wajma Gorge.

In the Zoo.

One of thirty-six of the Tattoo Zoo.

And if you haven't yet earned your tattoo, no one's going to give it to you back at brigade, back in the motor pool —

you've got to be way outside the wire, a million miles from that safe Fob, out in that nowhere Bumfuck Egypt, where war stories come out of nowhere, and are lived, and died.

That's where that tatt is earned.

Chill, dude, wake up from those wishful-thinking dreams wide awake born of entirely rational fear, it's etched in stone anyway:

The first round's going to miss by a hair or a foot, and if anything it's going to waste the other guy not you.

Your job's to save his ass before he's hit and everybody else's ass and then your ass too.

That's why you're up top.

Why you've got the big gun. Why you've kept it cleaned and oiled. Locked and loaded now.

Why you're alert.

Like Specialist Lee Tran in the turret of the lead truck. Behind his big awesome .50-cal machinegun aimed ahead downstream.

In the turret of the Mrap a ways behind, that gunner's got his Mark-19 auto grenade launcher aimed up the mountainside to his left. The Pakistan side.

Farther behind, the rear humvee gunner is faced backwards, aiming his M240-B machinegun upstream, where these three trucks just came.

Front, flanks, rear covered.

Oldest Rule of Combat #3.

Whether on foot or riding. On land, sea or air.

The three gunners each holding on tight to his gun and the turret, jerked and bounced as each truck splashes in the water slowly picking its way between the boulders, some as big as refrigerators.

A rock house up ahead just downstream, a hundred feet at least up the mountainside, built right into it. The only pretty color the faded teal blue wooden frames of the pane windows. Rough-hewn timber beams for a flat mud roof where a dozen kids—boys and some girls—are watching the approaching trucks.

A zigzag path goes down to the stream here.

Midway, two women are stopped, a plastic pail dripping water on each one's head, their backs turned to the approaching American trucks. Their colorful layered bulky clothing contrasted against the gray rock mountainside. Each with her shawl pulled around concealing her face.

It's what women do in Afghanistan. Shawl pulled around, backs turned. You aint going to see their faces. It's a Muslim thing.

Specialist Tran is happy.

Relieved happy.

Simple rule of thumb: *When kids are out in plain sight there are no Taliban.*

Or if there are, they're in the background laying low, waiting to fight another day, not today.

Tran waves to the kids.

All but the two older boys wave back.

And down below—

Inside this lead truck, this humvee, in the seat behind the driver, platoon medic Doc Eberly is looking out up at the rock house.

Wondering out loud, "Winters, how do they live up here . . . ?"

"They'll know in about a month." That's Kyle Wolfe.

Civilian contractor. Was Marine Corps Force Recon.

He's in the seat opposite Doc, with turret gunner Tran's legs and butt standing between them on the flat transmission case cover.

He's wearing a simple headset, like all in here. Plugged in for intercom and radio. Tiny earplug down below his ballcap in one ear, mic curved down across his cheek.

With the soldiers' earplugs hidden under their helmets. Just the curved mic showing.

Wolfe goes on, "This'll all be two foot of virgin white powder."

Driving, Pfc Holloway hoots out, "Woo-hoo, virgins! Gonna get Holloway a virgin!"

Doc Eberly, "Takes one to know one."

"I've got more beaver in a week, Doc, you ever had. Eight to eighty, crippled, blind or crazy. The Holloway Groove."

Again Eberly wonders aloud, "What do they do? How do they eat? What do they eat? How do they keep warm?"

"They're Afghans." From Redcloud up front.

He's the boss, Travis Redcloud. The platoon sergeant.

Sergeant First Class Travis Redcloud.

Seated right behind Redcloud, civilian contractor Wolfe jokes, "Dude's got ten acres of poppies down in Helmand, this is their vacation house. Fly fishing, white-water rafting in the summer. Skiing in winter."

"Like, right," from Pfc Holloway. "I don't see no ski lifts."

"They're Afghans." Wolfe this time, like Redcloud a moment ago. "Run up and down there like mountain goats. Barefoot in the snow."

Pfc Holloway, "Shit." The way he says it, *sheeeee-at*.

Doc Eberly taunts him, "You ever skied, Holloway?"

"Skiing's so yesterday. Last century. Your gran'pa skis. Snowboarding, that's where it's at."

"You ever snowboarded?"

"Gonna. When I get outta this place. Outta the Army. Gonna be the next Shaun White. Make a million bucks drinking Red Bull."

"Drive." Redcloud. Really saying *Shut up and pay attention where you're steering, Private.*

"Com'on, Sarge, I'm a multi-tasker."

Doc Eberly, "Can't even spell it."

"Your mama," Holloway spits back at Doc, and the steering wheel pops out of his hand in a sudden nosedive, water up over the hood, a geyser spraying Spec Tran up top, and Holloway fights the steering wheel, punching the gas, up out of the eddy hole—

Redcloud snapping, "What'd I tell you about getting me wet?"

A proud smirk of a grin from Holloway.

Just twenty, not quite three years in, no wife, no kids, no responsibilities, his whole life ahead, Pfc Holloway's got the world by the tail, can't nothing affect him.

"Aw, Sarge," he exaggerates a whine. "How'm I gonna see that hole? C'mon, you see it? You couldn't see it. I'm supposed to have Superman xray eyes?"

Redcloud, "You're bucking for cook, aren't you?"

"Sa-weeeet, no more patrols. Won't never hafta leave the Cop anymore! Chef Holloway in the Holloway Groove. Chef Boyardee Holloway!"

Shit yeh make him cook. He's got his Zoo tatt—three months with the Zoo in Iraq—no need now anymore to go out every day or every other day, each patrol upping the odds that much more of getting his ticket punched, even if it's just one leg lost. One leg, he thinks, he can live with that. *Not my balls, no way, no how, I aint givin up my balls.*

Doc Eberly, "Best rethink that, Sergeant. I don't want him in the D-fac. He'll muck up the chow."

Redcloud, "Good point. Considered. I send you to the mess hall, Holloway, it's gonna be washing pots and pans, not cooking."

Pfc Holloway, "Sheee-at, Sarge, I'll make you eggs t'order every morning. Omelet with everything. Steaks and lobster every ni-"—

"Drive!" from Redcloud just as

crunch! everyone's thrown forward by the abrupt stop, an unseen boulder run into against the front bumper.

And Tran kicks Holloway in the helmet, "Sonovabitch! Where'd you go to driving school, shitbird?!"

Doc Eberly, "Montessori."

Wolfe chuckles at that.

Kyle Wolfe.

He's not in the Zoo. Not in the Army.

No longer a Marine, with his week stubble of beard and his civilian clothes. No Kevlar helmet either. Just his ballcap—the *Sig Sauer* logo stitched on it.

Civilian ballistic vest and civilian ammo rack.

Army-issue M4 carbine, like everyone else.

Wednesday, the first day Wolfe went out with the Zoo, before leaving the Cop, Redcloud had asked him if he had a Kevlar. As in helmet.

Nope.

Why?

"Helmet's for wusses."

Okay, then what about his body armor vest there, that'd be for wusses too, wouldn't it?

"To carry this crap." The attached pouches of ammo and gear, like binos and GPS and first aid pack and Sure-fire flashlight and Leatherman. And *"Habit. Like a second skin. Putting on pants every day."*

And Wolfe had reversed it and proposed to Redcloud right back, *"If you wouldn't be taken down in rank to private for not wearing your Kevlar, would you, would you wear it?"*

Redcloud had thought a bit, then, *"Guess I'm a wuss,"* he'd said. With just the barest of a grin.

And right now Redcloud thinks of that, that moment two days ago, and he wonders if he'd toss aside this helmet that always pinches his forehead, a constant nagging ache. He wonders if he'd strip off this thirty-five pounds of body armor. Army says wear it, sergeant majors and colonels command wear it, he wears it. And he tells his guys they'll wear it all—Kevlar, body armor, eyepro—when they're outside the wire, *"Cuz the Captain don't wanna be writing home to your mamas your coffin's closed cuz you took a bullet to the head and there's nothing left of your pretty pale face but one big open scabbed-up bleeding zit."*

Holloway here, Redcloud thinks, *he'd toss his Kevlar in a second. Toss his IBA*—body armor—*run 'round in bermudas and flipflops.*

And Pfc Holloway now manages to get the truck up around the boulder.

A familiar voice comes from the radio, from one of the two trucks following. "That dumbshit Holloway driving? Guys bring your wetsuits? Life rafts? Seen the movie *Titanic*?"

That's Corporal Sandusky, in the Mrap, and Redcloud doesn't even answer. No sense encouraging Sandusky.

Sandusky's voice again, "Gonna hafta grow gills you keep letting Holloway drive."

Again Redcloud won't answer.

Seventeen years in now, Travis Redcloud has been Zoo platoon sergeant since just before Iraq and would be perfectly happy to stay it for the next three years, then at 20 he'll take it one year at a time, he can do thirty standing on his head, and they can put him permanent behind a desk back in the States for all he cares, and then maybe at least he'll get to go see his older kids' baseball and soccer games and be there every evening to sit down at the kitchen table with the three young ones doing their ABCs and 2+2s.

Not like no one sure had for him growing up.

But he doesn't think of that, not those years growing up, not longer than a millisecond, that past is long gone, dead, buried, it doesn't do any good to resurrect it but to haunt you to fill a two-gallon bucket of bile and piss.

The present's all he's got right now. Here, keeping these men all alive. He's confident in his experience, his knowing how to fight in real time, as the bullets fly overhead. He's confident in his knowing how to prepare to fight, how to feel one coming up, when to charge, when to wait and figure it out first, when and how to call in artillery and gunships and let them clean it up, and he knows the simple, inescapable and irrelevant truth that there's no conquest of victory here, not here in Affuckingstan.

Only his first obligation to get these men under him home alive and in one piece.

Not just these men in these three trucks right now, but all the Zoo. His platoon.

To real home. Stateside.

Where he can bury this 'Stan forever, make this his last deployment and year-in-year-out sleep in his own bed spooned up tight against Brenda every night. *Hmmmmm, spooned up against Brenda* . . . . No, don't go there, don't think about it, it doesn't do any good, you're half a world away and you won't be any closer tomorrow and the next day and the one after, and next month, or the month after. Count em off til the end of May, early June, got to make it to then. Worst case, June/July. And he blocks Brenda, the kids, home, all of it from his mind. He's in Afghanistan, or Af—F—istan, it's all the same, here, right now, nowhere else.

Going down this stream, which is widening a little here, as the gorge is opening up, that much closer to the village Wajma down around the next couple of bends maybe, which means that much closer to the secure bosom of the rest of the platoon down there.

"You want to be a cook, Holloway?" he says without even looking over. Eyes betray nothing behind his tinted Oakley wraparound eyepro constantly scanning ahead. "Blowtorch in the motor pool, we burn the tattoo off."

"The F you do."

"Wanna try me?" Dead serious. Now he grins right at Holloway.

Rare for Redcloud, a grin.

The thorn roses inked up his neck and along his chin and up his cheeks add a cynical hint to the grin.

Kyle Wolfe, "I love the smell of flesh burning in the morning."

Doc Eberly, "Acetylene torch. Six thousand degrees Fahrenheit. That's gotta hurt like a mother."

Redcloud, "Nothing but blue flame."

Holloway, "You got morphine, Doc. Shoot me up, burn it off, sheeeee-at, I don't give a flying fuck, I'll be tripping out in la-la-land."

"No morphine," and Redcloud is back to scanning ahead.

Scanning, always scanning, wary, got to look, they're not back with the platoon yet.

He can't resist, adding, "Six thousand degrees you say, Doc?"

"Six thousand two hundred. Or three hundred."

"What's a hundred degrees, give or take." A quiet snort. "Blue flame, Holloway."

"F you, Sarge. Due respect."

"Smart of you, PFC. Leave that part out" — that *due respect* — "have to write you up. Letter o' Reprimand. Take away that rocker."

Meaning, his rank, down from pfc to just pvt. Ouch!

Redcloud, first impression, you'd think that was an Indian name.

As in Native American Indian.

As in *woo woo woo woo woo*, the war cry.

And the first time a guy did that to him in Basic way long ago when Redcloud was just eighteen, Redcloud stepped to him slowly, calm, and whispered, "What was that again, paleface?" The big Bronx or Brooklyn dude laughed and again went "Woo woo woo," and Redcloud threw his fist into the guy's chin, sending him limp to the floor unconscious with a busted jaw and two teeth loose.

And Redcloud was left himself with busted fingers and a hand swelled up as big as a boxing glove, he couldn't salute properly for weeks, couldn't take apart his M-16 and flunked disassembly/assembly, and could barely pull the trigger on the rifle range, a pure natural-born shooter hitting six silhouettes out of forty and winding up getting recycled back into the next Basic class where, when a guy first called him Tonto, he ignored it and him, and when others called him Tonto, he ignored them too, simply pretended they didn't exist. And the guys stopped calling him that, he was just *"Redcloud"*, and he fired forty for forty on the rifle range, followed orders and kept his mouth shut, and months later on his final jump in Airborne School, like he'd heard as a kid so many times from his grandfather of his parachute jump into France the night of D Day, he too yelled *"Geronimo!"*

Redcloud to Wolfe, "You don't mind, Kyle," without looking around at him. "How's a guy go from Marine Recon door-kicker to bleeding heart social worker?"

"College. BS in anthropology."

"Yeeehaa!" from Holloway. "B-S, that for bull shit?"

"If for you, PFC"—Wolfe emphasizing the P-F-C in a derogatory tone. "One-sixty starting is bullshit."

Redcloud, "One-sixty a year?"

"Starting. First hundred and change tax-free."

"Where do I sign up? Doc, you've got college, you got a sheepskin. That's right up your alley."

Eberly, "Not anthropology. The other ology. The bio one."

Holloway, "I thought it was math you were in college for."

"The other math. The phi one. As in P-H-Y."

Wolfe, "Physics? Really, dude, physics?"

A shrug from Doc Eberly *No big deal.*

He won't mention, it was a double major.

Physics and biology.

3.9 GPA.

In four years.

At Cornell.

Enlisted right after, three years ago. Figured with two wars then being waged a guy shouldn't miss the opportunity to find out how much of a man he is for real where bravery doesn't come in *Top Gun* movies or Xbox PlayStation killing but from real bullets snapping by and splashing the dirt of the berm you're crouched behind, and if you don't rise up to pick out the enemy and take sure aim to return fire then you are a coward and you know it and will always know it, there is no hiding from it and never will be. Lord Jim. That challenge.

Yeh, Doc Eberly has read *Lord Jim*.

Tested two years ago in Iraq in Stryker brigade, he learned of himself that he would not run away, that he could be very afraid and still not run from the sound of the guns, yet off the battlefield, away from war, he's learned that a man again doubts his courage, needs to reaffirm it, become confident again of it, envies those who are in the midst of battle challenging themselves, feeling less of himself for being safely away from the battlefield, as if perhaps he was courageous in the past but would run this next time and the only way to be confident in one's own courage is to be tested, placing oneself voluntarily again in war, in spite of the first-hand knowledge of one's breathless, near immobilizing terror of the previous time. And ever such it has probably been, Eberly knows, back to before even the Greeks and their Battle of Issus—that warriors have felt the same, have needed to again and again reconfirm their courage. And Eberly understands now the old veterans dressed in their musty, ill-fitting uniforms on the sidewalks during the parades, that even in their physical and mental decay and infirmness, no longer soldier material, they still yearn to again test themselves, uncertain that they are still as brave as they long ago once had proved to themselves to be, dressed now again as soldiers as a visible, tactile reminder more for themselves than for others that they indeed once, despite their fear, went forward to the sound of the guns.

Yeh, Doc Eberly has read *The Red Badge of Courage*.

A studious geek since as long as he can remember—

chess club, science fairs, wrestling his sport, the individual one-on-one, not team play of football or basketball

—and with his college degrees he could have gone officer OCS but what he also wanted from the Army and combat was to know what it's like to live for a change not among bookworms and brainacs, the ambitious already headed toward med school or grad school or lab jobs on well-paying linear career paths, but with average-Joe grunt GIs making a crummy fifteen-hundred a month. GIs who Eberly knows wouldn't know adenosine triphosphate from deoxyribonucleic acid.

And don't give a shit.

And pretend to give even less a shit that you do know it.

Smirk scorn on you for knowing it.

Guys like Pfc Holloway.

"Beer U!" Holloway hoots. "I get out, I'm goin to Smirnoff State!"

Doc Eberly, "I thought you flunked out of U Tokem High."

"Sheeeee-at. We useta smoke homegrown in homeroom, wimp-ass Mr Lawson right up front. The Holloway Groove"—again, suddenly, he loses the steering wheel as the truck dives into an eddy, sending up a geyser showering everything, and Gunner Tran snap-kicks Holloway in the helmet harder this time, "Holl-a-fuckin-way!

"Jiminy Crickets, Holloway!" from Redcloud.

And Wolfe chuckles.

As Holloway now guns it up and out, Redcloud says it calmly, plainly, matter-of-factly: "Blowtorch. Blue flame. Six thousand degrees."

Doc Eberly, "No morphine."

From the radio, again Cpl Sandusky's voice, "You guys gonna put in for a Purple Heart, Sarge? You want, I can waterboard Holloway when we get back on the Cop."

Again Redcloud doesn't answer.

Holloway, "He's a asshole."

Redcloud, "Drive."

Pfc Holloway bounces the truck over some rocks, with everything in here all jerking so hard side-to-side that the guys have to grab or brace against something to keep helmets from banging the steel frame.

"They teach in your anthropology, Kyle," Redcloud asks Wolfe. "They teach why we have to always pick the most jacked-up places to fight our wars in?"

"Because the most fucked-up people live in these most jacked-up places."

Redcloud, "Just once I'd like the next war to be in like Hawaii. Fiji. Barbados."

Pfc Holloway, "Margaritaville!"

Redcloud, "You know how to spell it?"

"What, Margaritaville? C'mon, Sarge. M-A-R-"—

"D-R-I-V-E!" Redcloud's not playing. "S-H-U-T your trap."

Which Holloway does. At least for now.

"Kansas," Wolfe says. "Flat as a pancake. No mountains they can hide in. No rocks they can hide under."

It's simple to Redcloud. "No hajj in Kansas."

Doc Eberly, "Lucky they haven't figured out how to put IEDs in these rivers."

A quiet "Yeh" from Redcloud. "So far."

"In sh'allah," says Wolfe.

As in, *Allah willing.*

Doc Eberly echoes it, Americanizing it, "En-shall-aw."

Tattoo it in your brain: *Allah willing.*

Redcloud too, "En-sha-lah."

And Pfc Holloway hoots, "Enchilada!"

Which gets a laugh from Wolfe. "From the mouths of babes."

"You aint that much older'n me, Kyle."

"If ten years isn't old enough to slap the shit out of a PFC and make you call me Staff Sergeant Kyle."

"Screw you, I don't see no rank on you."

"Holloway!" from Redcloud.

"I know, I know. D-R-I-V-E."

Wolfe has to smile. Thinks, *This Holloway were a Marine, drill sergeant would be riding his ass sunup to sunset. All night too.*

He thinks of *Full Metal Jacket* the movie and instantly discards it because *Holloway's not crazy, he's no Private Pyle. He'd have the drill blowing his own brains out just to not have to listen to his shit 24/7.*

Three days ago, on Tuesday, Wolfe and his HTT teammate were dropped off by chopper into the Cop.

Wednesday they went out with the Zoo to a district center.

Yesterday they went out with 2nd Platoon to a village a few miles southwest of the Cop.

Today it's with the Zoo to Wajma. Tomorrow with 2nd Platoon or 3rd or the Zoo, whichever the company commander decides—it's a coin flip, a toss-up—to survey the settlements way up the gorge seven klicks or so to the southeast.

Wolfe's a contract civilian, which is what most HTT are.

Army-speak for Human Terrain Team.

Which in layman-speak is anthropologists.

Cultural scientists surveying and documenting the human terrain.

Human terrain, in everyday layman-speak, being people.

Situation: Afghanistan is a 13th century country made up of tribes within tribes within tribes within tribes—

like a carnival funhouse tent full of distorting mirrors

—about which America and its Nato partners knew very little after the initial rout of the Taliban around the beginning of 2002.

Problem: How do you tell the good guys from the bad guys?

Solution: Human Terrain Teams.

Process: Learn everything about those tribes, studying the human terrain, so to speak, down to the sub-sub-sub-sub-sub-sub tribal level.

Military assignment: Kill or capture the bad guys, give $ and lots of goodies to the good guys.

Result: Bad guys get captured or killed. Good guys get captured or killed. Bad guys become millionaires. Good guys become millionaires.

Conclusion: Everybody in Afghanistan is a good guy and a bad guy.

Effect: All Afghans like the $ and goodies they get but hate the foreign armies anyway, in particular these days, the Americans, no rational explanation necessary, it's just the way it is with the culture. For centuries.

Problem: How do you get them to love you anyway so that you can nation-build them into a 21st century democracy?

Solution: Human Terrain Teams.

Process: Repeat process above.

New emphasis: To know them is to know how to treat them and know what to give them so that they'll love you.

Endgame simplified: Knowing them will get them to love you.

Endgame in a nutshell: Oprah.

Human Terrain Team composition: Anthropologists.

Since the Army doesn't have anthropologists like it does infantry, artillery, MPs, truck drivers, xray techs, cooks, chopper pilots, mechanics, pay clerks and everyone else, the Pentagon's HTT brainchild became just another $100 million civilian contract.

Wanted: *Anthropologists, BS or PhD required. Int'l travel. Big pay. Food, lodging, transportation provided. Combat survival training/equipment provided. Medical/life insurance provided.*

Place of employment: The Stan.

A no-brainer for Kyle Wolfe, who'd had enough of the Corps and its regimented totalitarian order and little tolerance for creative initiative, doing what they say, when, where, why and how they say.

They say *"Jump,"* a Marine doesn't even ask *"How high?"* —he jumps as high as he can and keeps on jumping. Until someone tells him to stop.

Big Army wanted anthropologists, Wolfe would be an anthropologist, and get to hang and play in a war zone. Hang loose and play. Go where he wanted, when he wanted, wear what he wanted, eat when he wanted, and quit the whole thing when he wanted. On his terms, more or less, a lot more than less. For many times more than what he was making in the Marines, an E-6 coming up on the end of his enlistment.

Sure, a BS in anthropology after doing eight years in Marine Corps Force Recon, that's not your typical HTT applicant.

As in, Not - Your - Typical - HTT - Applicant.

First, that Force Recon thing.

Anthropologists don't do Force Recon.

Don't do Marine Corps.

Don't do Army. Not even the part-time once-a-month weekend thing in the Guard.

They're An-thro-pol-o-gists. Yeh, with a capital A.

Second, that BS from Arizona State is exactly to the letter what Pfc Holloway had said it was without even knowing he was correct.

BS as in Bull Shit. With a capital B and S.

100% pure angus bullshit.

If a Force Recon stud with lots of Delta/Cag time and a creative bend-the-rules streak can't counterfeit a reasonably authentic university diploma and accompanying transcripts to land an overseas government contract job toting a gun and starting at one-sixty a year—

mostly tax-free, remember

—what'd he waste those years attached to Delta for?

Audacious, Wolfe likes to remember, that afternoon in the DC conference room sitting across the table from the corporate HR exec studying his paperwork. Mr HR looking up over his glasses at him, and Wolfe knowing that he knows that he knows that he knows that Wolfe's two years of community college followed by eight in Force Recon then three for the BS from Arizona State don't add up.

Except to Pfc Holloway's version of BS.

A blind deaf-n-dumb HR intern could see that it's impossible to get an anthro degree from ASU when you are for most of those same three years—it's right there in the record—in Recon in the Stan.

With a chunk of that Recon Stan time on loan out to Delta, in a full beard, dressed in Afghani shalwar kameez pajama garb, MP-5 sub-machinegun and mags hidden under the full wool shawl wrap.

Which is what the snapshot photos right in front of Mr HR show.

Along with it all right there in the DD-214 Record of Service (not forged). Right there on the table with the fake diploma and transcripts and the USMC Pashto Language Qualification Test scores (not forged).

Mix the very real Corps, Delta and Pashto documents with scanned and Photoshopped college transcripts, and you've got the perfect candidate for HTT in warzone Afghanistan.

And Mr HR straightened up all those docs, paper-clipped them and smoothly slid them all back into the manila folder.

A wan smile.

Then, "Don't worry about your field analysis reports," Mr HR told Wolfe. "Just get some numbers, and no one's going to want to know how. They'll write the reports back here in the home office."

Wolfe couldn't even hold back his shit-eating grin.

"Win win," is what Mr HR later told the exec above him, who agreed.

A geek fresh-outta-grad-school anthropologist getting killed or wounded makes for a shitload more paperwork (not counting all the family lawsuits soon to follow) than a year's worth of a non-anthro ex-Marine's gibberish field reports having to be written or rewritten in the home office, accurate or not.

Bottom line, a highly experienced combat former Force Recon gyrine can decrease the odds of that nebbish geek grad getting killed or wounded, say ten-fold.

Rotate the newbie, pale, soft-palmed tenderfoot rookie combat-ignorant real college-grad anthros into operation with Wolfe for their first couple of months to learn firsthand combat survival in person from one who's lived it.

They can do the real anthro work for Wolfe.

And learn to stay alive for later on their own.

Win win win.

Wolfe's in his eleventh month.

Already signed on for another year.

He's on his fifth rookie. Like the first four, a real anthropologist. Their seventh week together.

She's in Wajma right now. With the rest of the platoon.

Probably on her fifth or sixth interview. Getting every tiny little detail just right. For those field analysis reports she writes up impeccably exact that tell the Army precisely who these people are in all these tiny villages so that the Army will know where to send the rice, beans, cooking oil, wells, roads, high-yield seed, electricity, schools, health clinics, bridges, and hydroelectric dams in the president's grand scheme of nation-building, hearts-and-minds, fighting a war as Santa Claus.

All of which Kyle Wolfe couldn't care less about.

He's in the Wild West, carrying a gun, in the open, legally, where there are people out there who want to kill him just to kill him, nothing personal, jihadist to infidel, making a ton of money direct-deposit right into his bank account and not having to touch a dime.

"Fuck me to tears," civilian contractor Kyle Wolfe would say with a grin.

And it's good tears, orgasmic tears of joy, because there's nowhere he would rather be than here right now, doing this, in the Wild West.

The Wild West of the Stan.

Af-fuck-him-to-tears-istan.

Platoon Sergeant Travis Redcloud is different.

All he wants right now is to get these three trucks back joined up with the platoon and the relative safety there in the village.

He glances quickly at the computer screen mounted right in front of him—

the live map image showing three tiny blue dots that are these three trucks and just a bit down around the bend of the steep contour are the six blue dots that are the other Zooster trucks.

Everything satellite-GPS linked.

It's called the Blue Force Tracker.

Blue Force are the good guys. Nato good guys—Americans and Euros. Yeh, the Blue part probably comes from the sissy blue of the Nato beret. Like as if powder blue puts the fear of anything into anyone. Whatever.

Blue Force Tracker's the computer program that does just that. Tracks.

Redcloud if he wants can scroll the computer map left and right, up and down, all over Afghanistan to find the blue dots of all the other Army trucks on patrol and actually bring up the unit designation of each individual dot. Send texts to any of them. Get texts from them.

21st century warfare, American style.

Through the windshield Redcloud checks out another rock house built into the mountainside and a cluster of kids on the path just up off the streambed.

He grabs up a huge plastic baggie of Tootsie Roll Pops and Baby Ruths and Snickers and calls out "Tran!"

He hands the bag up to Tran in the turret.

"Talk about touchy-feely bleeding heart do-gooder," Wolfe teases Redcloud.

"They send that stuff from home by the crate-loads."

"Let me guess. Churches. Elementary schools."

"Rotary Club. Girl Scouts."

Up top .50-cal gunner Spec Tran flings a fistful to the Afghan kids, who scramble among the rocks to retrieve the candy.

"Uncle Gunny Redcloud," Wolfe says.

Redcloud, "Wrong army. Gunny's you ex-gyrines."

"There are no ex Marines."

"Pardon me. Former."

"Uncle Sugar Sergeant Redcloud. They'll put your picture on the cover of the Coin Manual."

As in COIN.

Counter-insurgency.

Newly defined in the highly touted 21st-century field manual.

Boiled down, the Bible about winning a war with that hearts-and-minds Santa Claus stuff.

Less killing and lots more handshaking, hugging and handing over duffle bags overstuffed with cash.

Crisp, newly printed U.S. dollars.

Bundle upon bundle all in denominations of twenty, fifty and a hundred.

Wolfe, he'd put Redcloud's face on the cover of the Coin Manual just for shits-n-grins, print up a million copies and ship them straight to the nearest landfill.

Better, he thinks. *Print up the Koran in Pashto on paper soaked in bacon grease. Put a picture of Porky Pig on the cover and leave them by the truckloads in every village in this friggin shithole armpit of the world.*

He's thought it through before.

Extensively.

Some might say he's been here too long.

"It's not the kids' fault this is such a jacked-up place," Redcloud says. "Jacked-up people. Those boys there"—scurrying for another handful of candy thrown by Spec Tran. "Maybe they'll aim high in ten years when they're shooting at us."

Wolfe, "In sh'allah."

Pfc Holloway, "Enchilada!"

Doc Eberly, "Ten years more? Ten?"

"Fifty," from Wolfe. "It'll be like Western Europe, Korea. We'll be here forever. Except without the peace and prosperity. And they'll despise us even more."

"You'll be a millionaire," says Redcloud.

"In sh'allah."

And "Enchilada!" again out of Pfc Holloway.

"I've gotta get another driver," Redcloud groans.

"Aw, Sarge," from Holloway, "you've got the best. A-numba-one. The Holloway Groove."

Redcloud tunes him out, doesn't really care, there's sunshine ahead. And rounding the bend, coming out of the shadows of the gorge there's safety in numbers here, there's security.

It's all opened up into a valley.

A huge bowl ringed by the mountain range.

The Village Wajma

On the maps that's how this valley is labeled. Wajma.

This wide and long valley plateau of fields terraced by rock walls.

The fields are harvested barren now in October.

Walled family compounds of rock, mud and timber dot the far terraces.

Redcloud's truck climbs up out of the stream and heads for the six Zoo trucks spread out in a wide protective circle on the rocky dirt of the wide beach.

A Zooster in the turret of each truck, on his gun.

Close now to the safe bosom of the Zoo, Pfc Holloway speeds up, like a runner with a sudden spurt in sight of the finish line.

"One-sixty a year," Redcloud says to Wolfe. "And that's even before having a partner she could be on the cover of *Maxim.*"

Wolfe, "Robyn? Doctor Robyn Banks, make note. PhD doctor. Like, and I can't even spell anthropology. Let me tell you, she just turned twenty-four and no one has a PhD at twenty-four. You know what that is, Holloway? PhD, doctor of what?"

Holloway, "Means she's smart."

Doc Eberly, "Wicked smart."

Wolfe, "Way way outta my league."

Redcloud, "I thought college chicks dug stud-muscled Force Recon dudes."

Wolfe, "The dumb ones maybe. Drunk ones."

Redcloud, "That's her seat. No offense, going back to the Cop you're back riding in the lieutenant's truck."

Holloway, "Ditto that."

Doc Eberly, "Ditto on the ditto."

And Holloway smacks Tran's leg, yelling up, "Hey, Tran, you want Kyle riding with us back to the Cop or the smokin-hot babe Robyn?"

"Give me a hard question, would you."

Doc Eberly, "What's the square root of sixty-nine?"

"I hate math."

Wolfe corrects Doc, "There is no square root."

Doc, "Eight point three zero six six two three eight. Ad infinitum."

And Wolfe remembers the Montessori remark, and the one about acetylene flame's six thousand degrees, and the physics and biology in college, and thinks, *Now this guy's really no slouch, really no dumbshit.*

Up ahead where we're heading is the PL's Mrap —

where Platoon Leader Lieutenant Matt Caufield is leaning up against the big front bumper

— with Sniper Rodriquez seated right above him, on the hood. His ever-present Knight Arms sniper rifle across his lap.

That's Sergeant Rodriquez, of the very first Zoo tattoo, the artist. Of the truism *"It's the only war we got."*

Rodriquez, barrio punk made good, finding a perfect fit in the Army and winding up selected for Sniper School, where he'd have been Honor Grad, except for the written exams and their math by rote instead of instinct. Now he eats, sleeps and shits all things sniper.

No exaggeration, Sniper Rodriquez eats, sleeps, shits, shaves and showers with his Knight rifle right attached to him. It's his third arm.

The Mrap where Lieut Caufield and Rodriquez are watching is parked a respectful distance away from where Wolfe's HTT teammate Robyn Banks is on the raised area of beach where a half-dozen battered and rusted steel conex shipping containers sit in front of the first terrace rock wall.

She's got HTT terp Gulbarhar sitting with her on the ground with the lone village man they're interviewing.

Robyn's helmet off and on the ground, her Army-issue IBA body armor off as well.

Her Army-issue M4 carbine lying atop it.

It's all there in the Coin Field Manual:

Undressed for war means nonthreatening.

Nonthreatening means villagers will be more open.

More open means they'll be your friends.

Your friends means they'll turn in the Taliban among them.

Turning-in means eventual victory.

The corollary is why Robyn wears the head scarf—you've got to show them you respect their culture.

The only thing missing is a blue burka, and the scarf can't begin to hide that she's female, can't hide her attractiveness, her simple beauty, what Pfc Holloway had called:

Smokin hot.

Relatively speaking.

At Arizona State or any other university where Wolfe did not attend and did not receive a BS in anthropology or anything else, on a scale of 1 to 10, Robyn would be an 8 or 8+.

Makes her a 14 here where these Zoosters don't ever see real live American women in person in the flesh except if they were to make it back to one of the big Fobs, and that's only if they've been wounded and are still conscious enough to care about the pretty female doctors and nurses, or they've shot off a magazine in the latrine late at night, remember, for that psych eval/rec trip to the rear which they never actually do and never sent back for.

Robyn looks good, would look good anywhere. Out here real good. And that's in combat boots, cargo 5-11 pants like Wolfe wears and a guy's poplin shirt.

Without lipstick or eyeshadow or blush coloring or foundation or anything.

She doesn't do the *"Doctor"* thing either, tell people she's a PhD.

Wolfe knows it because, One, he's read her personnel file. Two, you don't not know things like that working so closely with someone for these many weeks, not in a 24-hour-a-day combat environment.

Like he knows about her longtime fiancé boyfriend, an MD doctor in his cardio-thoracic surgical residency, and how he told her that if she took this job and left him to come to Afghanistan he wouldn't wait for her. And he hasn't. When Wolfe found her that third week in tears over an email from a friend telling her that the MD was already hooking up with a resident radiologist, he wanted to take her into his arms, pull her to him and let her cry against him.

He didn't.

And wouldn't.

And if he tells guys anything about her—
infantry guys they're out in villages with, like these Zoosters today
—it's nothing private, nothing personal, nothing about her as a woman or a chick. Nothing about the douchebag surgical resident MD now ex-fiancé.

It's more along the lines of her having told him that she'd never held a weapon in her life before the HTT Indoctrination at Fort Leavenworth, and that was nothing more than *That's the M4, don't worry, you might carry it, but you're never going to use it,* and Wolfe gave her a full course of instruction, including time on Fob Salerno's range, and got her confident and skilled, consistently putting three rounds in a circle the size of an orange at 25 meters, then the same at 100 meters, then out to 250. The weapon's with her always outside the wire. Cleaned daily back inside.

To Wolfe, if she has a fault, it's not that she's too smart, or that she doesn't pretend to know what she doesn't know, or that she grasps new things and masters them so quickly.

It's that, to Wolfe, she takes this job too seriously, she thinks it matters.

It's not a dis on her.

It's her nature, it's a valued character trait. You take a job, you do it and do it well. Same as his job's teaching these egghead anthropologists fresh and eager with their important real diplomas how to survive in a combat environment and to be assured they can do it alone without him.

That's his job. And doing it the best he can. What he gets the big bucks for.

Teaching her the knowledge and skills and instincts to stay alive out here on her own.

Out of the truck now, from this distance Wolfe watches Robyn so single-minded in documenting in her notebook what their terp Gulbarhar is translating to her of what the village man is saying.

Redcloud directs Spec Tran to swing the big .50 off his aim at the collection of a hundred or more village men and boys hanging around watching from the concrete mosque down a ways on the first terrace—

"Com'on, Tran, use your brain. How you going to get them to love you like that?"

Wolfe laughs. "Take out the belt there, Tran, and load that fifty with those candy bars and Tootsie Roll Pops."

Redcloud, "Don't give the colonels any ideas."

"Yeh like they're going to listen to me."

They head over for Lieut Caufield's truck.

Pfc Holloway and Doc Eberly stay here in the hummer, doors all open, with Tran up on the gun.

Eberly already into a paperback.

Holloway mixes an MRE packet of grape drink powder into a bottle of water. "What you reading now, Doc?"

Eberly shows him the cover. *Slow Walk in a Sad Rain.*

"Never heard of it. Sounds like a real drag. Boooorrrrr—eeeen. Snoooooooze—ville. What's it about?"

"A classic. Vietnam."

"Ancient history. Make it into a movie?"

Nope.

"Why not? Say it's a classic? How a classic?"

Doc Eberly doesn't want to be bothered, wants to read.

"Sheeeee-at, Doc." Holloway shakes up his bottle. "Y'know, yer gonna go blind always reading."

Doc Eberly ignores him.

"You are. They're always saying jacking off makes you blind, but it's reading, reading all the time yer gonna go blind. Blind as a bat. Blind as a bat's got his face buried in a witch's deep dark black scabby cunt." And *heh-heh-heh-heh* at his own cleverness.

Holloway downs the entire bottle.

Lets the last mouthful fly in a spit for distance.

Then, "Gotta wonder, ever think, bats are blind, that mean they jerk off?"

Works his mouth, then spits a glob of purple loogie about twenty feet.

"Must be good. What's it about about Vietnam?"

"The platoon medic gets pissed at a private who's always haranguing him and beats him upside the head with his M-16 to a bloody pulp and stuffs his corpse in a body bag DOA."

Holloway laughs. "You're a real comedian, Doc. Get your own show on Comedy Central. Get a date with Snooki. She can break your cherry."

Doc harshly, "Nothing like the star you'll be in your own primetime show on Cartoon Network," and he gets out and goes around the back, pops open the lid and climbs up inside to get comfortable reclining on the gear to read unbothered in peace.

Redcloud thinks it's all too quiet, too peaceful, the calm before the storm, and he knows that's crazy because all those village men and boys around the mosque, and those few men together crossing that field, and those boys sitting on that wall down there watching, they're all watching, and they wouldn't be out, they'd be invisible, he knows, *If there were a storm coming. Storm of Taliban. Not today. It's TV time. Afghan TV.*

The American GIs are the one channel they're all watching. The only channel they get.

Exactly what Wolfe is thinking this moment. *Afghan TV. Those boys on the wall, like those kids on the roof of the house* back there up the gorge.

He remembers telling Redcloud the other day when they went out to that district center, same thing, same TV show. *"They don't even need a remote. No channel to change to. Volume, who gives a shit, they can't understand the English anyway."*

Wolfe remembers it's been this way since the first time he was here, a grunt Marine, in those first months of this war, Afghans wide-eyed at the "Creatures from outer space" a buddy said. "We're space aliens." Decked out in futuristic armor. *Starship Troopers* meets *Star Wars*. Kevlar and body armor and wraparound eyepro and little radio antennas sticking up out of pouches and short sleek little guns that spit bullets in one frightening stream of fire, and that's not even counting the fast-mover F-16s coming in streaking by just three hundred feet overhead at 500mph.

Couldn't lose the war then, Wolfe thinks now. *All those hajj up there at that mosque, they know different now, they know how this show's going to end, they just don't know when.*

"Afghan TV," Redcloud says now.

Wolfe, "All they're lacking's popcorn and a 32-ounce Coke. Five-dollar box of Milk Duds and some Junior Mints."

Redcloud's comfortable, at ease satisfied.

Because all his men are on or in or close right there to their individual trucks. Doors all open and, sure, guys smoking and eating—but the turret gunners on their guns, none of the guys out wandering over to the other trucks, his squad leaders Ketchum and Nell and Utah doing their job right, keeping their men tight. Ready for something and staying close right there to the thick steel trucks if that something comes, even though everyone knows nothing's coming today, *Not today, not with all these Afghans around. Watching Afghan TV,* Redcloud thinks. *The ANA, who knows it better than them?*

That's the two squads of Afghan soldiers, the Afghan National Army, along on the patrol today, as normal protocol is for a couple of squads from the half-strength ANA company sharing the Cop with the Zoo's company to always go out with the GIs.

These ANA soldiers are hanging outside their three standard-issue tan Ford Ranger pickup trucks, *Shucking and jiving,* thinks Wolfe. *Always with their chai, their freakin chai.*

ANA won't go anywhere, Wolfe'll swear, they don't bring their big chai kettle, their glass cups and a propane tank. *Screw the ammo, bring the chai.*

Time can almost stand still right now, tic toc tic toc . . . .

tic . . . .

toc . . . .

tic . . . .

So slow with nothing happening.

Principle of Combat #1:

99.8% of the time is sit-around-and-wait.

Pure quiet of nothing happening.

.2% is boom! Yeh, note it, not plain naked 2, but .2, Point 2.

Every once in a great while.

And most every last one of these Zoosters won't say it aloud but secretly craves that .2% — those electrifying adrenalin-rush seconds and minutes, just let it happen, today, right now, and these Zoosters to the last one is John Wayne for real. Each one imagines himself living through it unscratched, dude, then reliving it, retelling those moments with the others all the rest of the afternoon and evening and later back home stateside in the platoon rooms and barracks and dudes' houses over six-packs or a keg and years later at the American Legion hall with all the other middle-aged beer-paunch-gut triple-chin barstool vets.

Which ones of them are thinking it right now this very moment this very instant, craving that .2%?

Not Redcloud.

Even with all these guns, all this firepower, this widely spread-out circled-wagons perimeter, behind these armored steel trucks, it's over-whelming, and they can't lose, can't no way no how lose.

Not Redcloud.

He's been there.

Done that.

Got the tee-shirt.

Even winning, Redcloud knows, you can lose a man KIA, a couple WIA.

Been there.

Done that.

Packed up their tee-shirts in their duffle bags to ship home.

At Lieut Caufield's Truck

Redcloud shows Caufield on his map their route up the gorge.

"All kinds of goat trails snaking up, here, Pakistan side. Paki I-95. All that's missing's the median and white lines and guardrails and Cracker Barrels on every exit."

"Ratlines," Caufield says matter-of-factly, as if he has more experience than he does.

Ratlines. The routes the enemy comes and goes. Infil routes. Supply lines.

"Half expected to run into a donkey caravan carrying Stingers," Redcloud says only half-joking.

Wolfe, "Taliban version of the Ho Chi Minh Trail."

Just a nod from Caufield, like he knows this, nothing unusual, all part of this war, as if the Zoo isn't his first platoon and these aren't his first months in combat.

Which they both are. Firsts. But he's a quick learner, and this stuff isn't unusual.

A quick learner also in knowing that a first-time platoon leader makes his men confident in him if he projects calm knowing. Crate up and trash the braggadocio.

On the map Redcloud indicates the end of the gorge. "Waterfall, about thirty feet, water running so clear you could wash your newborn infant baby in it."

Slight nods again from Lieut Caufield. Nothing he can add. His five months as Zoo PL prior to the deployment to here and these four months here now, he understands his platoon sergeant, Redcloud, and will not insult him by patronizing him trying to impress him with a false superiority of experience or knowledge or military gut-instinct.

Redcloud, "Like drinking from a creek bubbling out of the mountainside high up in the Rockies. Cool clean Coors spring water."

Wolfe, "A picture postcard. Build a hotel up there, like Club Med, make it a tourist trap for yuppie trekkers. Make a killing, money up to your eyeballs. Sandals Afghanistan. Club Med Afghanistan. If these shitbirds could ever get their shit together."

Sniper Rodriquez spits a stream of chew. "Afghans get their shit t'get'er? What planet you livin on, Kyle? Disneylandia?"

"Hey, we're HTT. We can dream. By definition. Our job description."

"Dream? I dream of mi mamacita with tetas par' chupar sticking out to here, 'mano. Gonzo tits."

Redcloud, "Save it, Sniper, we don't want to hear your personal problems."

Wolfe, "Talk to the hand, Rodriquez."

Rodriquez, "Oh I'm gonna. Talkin to my hand. Be taking one chingada long shower t'night. Gonna say hola, comó estás, how you doin, wit' esa chica mamacita Rosa."

"What's this guy?" Wolfe asks Lieut Caufield about Robyn's interview. "How many's she done?"

Caufield shows four fingers.

First Lieutenant Matt Caufield.

Two years ago he was finishing his third year teaching Head Start after graduating University of Wisconsin, Madison, an English Lit major, when he shocked his friends and family—

and made his girlfriend cry and pound him in the chest and plead that he was crazy and didn't he love her?

—by enlisting for Army Officer Candidate, and he could only explain it away saying that the upper middle class college slackers like him as well as the rich-kid town-'n-country elites should serve in times of war same as the blue-collar trade school schlubs and the food-stamp ghetto thugs and hayseed dustbowl farmboy hicks.

That's his story and he's sticking to it.

Because it was the one rationalization, he knew, that the college educated and wealthy elites would understand and respect. Like his family, his peers, his community.

Not the other, his real reason, that there were two wars going on and someday they would be over and he'd be forty and entering middle age and he'd slap himself in the face, he'd be disgusted with himself, he'd be morosely regretful for having missed them.

For having not challenged himself in combat.

And he would always wonder if it was in the back of his mind somewhere, pushed away invisible, that he had avoided joining and going to war because he was afraid of being killed.

A coward.

Afraid of losing his legs.

Afraid of life in a wheelchair.

Losing his arms.

Who's going to wipe his ass?

Losing his nuts.

How do you live, what do you do without nuts?

Kill yourself?

In OCS he found himself with infantry- and combat-arms-branched young men just like him, that miniscule .001 percent of college grads who do join up. Young men who would never say it out loud but were thinking it too, that *Men go to war, they don't live to regret having missed it, having rejected the challenge of bravery and finding out if they have it or not. Men go to war.*

His family and friends might never know it, but Lieut Matt Caufield and most of those others in OCS are here because, as highly uneducated barrio schlub Sniper Rodriquez says:

"It's a shitty war, but it's the only one we got, 'mano."

But college-educated officers, unlike grunt GED guys like Rodriquez, they don't say it out loud.

Wolfe just asked how many interviews Robyn's done. Four.

And they're all watching her from this distance, not close enough to hear her questions to the villager.

"Indig interviews, who needs stinkin interviews?" Wolfe offers. "I could make up the raw data right off the top of my head, she could write up all the reports, and we'd never have to leave the Fob. Afghanistan for Dummies."

Lieut Caufield, "Idiot's Guide to Afghanistan?"

"Same thing. Number One, their tribe comes first, foremost. It's the tribe, stupid. Number Two, Islam, Sharia and all that shit. Three, what have you got for me, gimme gimme gimme."

Redcloud, "You got that right. No shortage of hands out. Can't blame them. You going to turn down the millionaire comes through town riding down Main Street throwing out hundred-dollar bills from the back of his limo?"

Lieut Caufield to Wolfe, "Number Four. You're forgetting the man-boy thing."

"Shhhhhhh!" Wolfe exaggerates. "Walking on thin ice, Lieutenant. They'll knock you back down to butterbar. Make you go to re-education classes. Put you in a pogrom camp. What's a little pedophilia when you've got a war to not win? First tenet of the Human Terrain System, wanna guess? Dictated down to each team. Don't ask about the boys."

Caufield, "Got to wonder whose brainchild it was. Imagine the clusterfuck of eagles and stars deep in the Pentagon conspiring to come up with a whole new military bureaucracy, Human Terrain System."

Clusterfuck, that's one of those words you'd never hear at UW Madison. Never use in Lit 320 Henry James. Not going to hear around the Head Start breakroom.

Wolfe jokes, "All part of St Claire's hearts-and-minds. You haven't seen St Claire's PowerPoint slide briefing?"

As in General Pete St Claire. 4-star. Credited author of that Coin Manual. Commander of the whole war.

Sniper Rodriquez pats the stock of his Knight sniper rifle. "Two in the heart. One in the mind."

Wolfe, "You, Sergeant, you're talkin court-martial there, you let St Claire hear you saying that."

"Oh yeh 'mano, he's gonna come down here where he's gonna get his ass shot up, wit' he don't got F-15s flyin cover. Apaches too. And's got his own Blackwater s'curity dudes guardin his puke 4-star culo. Hearts and pinche cabrones minds . . . "

Redcloud warns him, "Watch your lip, Rodriquez."

"Aw c'mon Sarge, la verdad es la verdad."

"General St Claire's just following orders. At ease with your tongue."

Sniper Rodriquez, "Orders from who, like from who? Aint nobody higher'n him, Sarge. Who's got more stars'n him?"

Lieut Caufield, "The President."

Wolfe, "Oh yeh, like it's going to get St Claire a fifth star."

Redcloud, "There is no fifth star."

"Exactly." Wolfe smiles.

Caufield, "Chairman of the Joint Chiefs."

Wolfe, "Not when he loses this war, he's not getting Joint Chiefs."

Caufield, "No one's ever going to admit losing."

Wolfe, "I'll give you that. First chapter, Politics of Command for Dummies."

Caufield, "You going to start a library with all your books?"

"Just one book. The Cliff Notes version. How to Not Win Wars and Not Influence People. It'll be required reading, colonels and above."

Rodriquez, "How's that, how you gonna do that, how you gonna win here?"

"Not win. Get the wax outta your ears, Sergeant. How would you propose winning, huh, c'mon you tell me."

"Turn the whole place inta glass." A grin from Rodriquez. He doesn't have to explain it, everyone knows the adage, but he does anyway, loving the sound of it coming out: "Nuke em til they glow."

"Young sergeant," Wolfe exaggerates his praise, "you belong in the White House. The very least, NSC."

Caufield, "National Security Council? Sniper Rodriquez?"

Wolfe, "Brief the president every day. Twice. Dawn and dusk."

Rodriquez, "Chingado, 'mano. They won't even let ese cholo take out the garbage."

Laughs all around.

Because it's true.

Redcloud asks Wolfe how many more interviews Robyn is going to want to do. "I'd like to get movin back out of here."

Unsaid, Rule of Combat #4:

Never go back the way you came.

The Cop to Wajma is one way in, one way out. Up the stream in, back down it out.

Today they've got no choice — going to have to break #4.

You know it, the enemy, if he's around, he knows it.

Oh, and he's around, somewhere, if only a watcher or two. With their little walkie-talkies up here far from cell service.

The less time you linger in the box, the less time you give them to get the word passed along on those walkie-talkies, the less time for them to get together — for that ambush.

Less is the better.

Wolfe, "She'll want to talk to the whole village, women too, if you let her."

"No way," adamant from Redcloud. "Been here too long already. We're not driving back through a shooting gallery, ping ping ping, and we're the sitting ducks going by. Taliban handing out kewpie dolls to the guys who get the most hits."

Lieut Caufield is less sure. "Captain said it's her call."

"My call," Wolfe corrects him. Then shows one finger. One more interview. "Lucky, remember? They haven't figured out how to put IEDs in water. Yet."

From Rodriquez. "They're buildin them in Pak'stan right now. Fact'ry crankin em out. They put a sticker on em, Made in Pak'staniland."

And Redcloud calls up for the driver to get out a case of MREs while he climbs up onto the hood, with Sniper Rodriquez scooting a bit to make him room.

Turret gunner Pvt Bybee here calls down, "Sergeant Redcloud," then tosses down to Redcloud an open case of MREs.

Redcloud, "Kyle, you hungry?"

Wolfe, "Chili mac. If you've got one."

He now glances around at Robyn.

Wonders what she's asking right now.

He could step closer to hear.

No need, he knows without hearing.

Multiple Choice. *If there is one thing your village needs more than anything else—one thing only—would it be: a health clinic; a water well; a schoolhouse; electricity; teachers; paid local police presence?*

Wolfe doesn't even think about smiling, but he is, knowing the answer that's always the same:

All of the above. "Everything, all of it, we need everything, we want every-thing. You give us everything. Yes, all, you give to us?"

"Wolfie," from Redcloud. "You're in luck," and he tosses Wolfe an MRE.

Wolfe checks it out, the markings. Yep, chili mac.

He plucks his knife from where it's clipped to his pants pocket.

Flicks it open.

Slits open the MRE bag.

Snaps the knife shut and slips it back down clipped to his pocket.

tic . . . .

toc . . . .

tic . . . .

toc . . . .

tic . . . .

Redcloud asks, "Is Robyn going to want one? She got a preference?"

Wolfe, "She's waiting for them to ask her to join them for lunch."

"No way, we're outta here, we are not sticking around for lunch or tea. No chai today."

"I'm just saying."

tic . . . .

toc . . . .

tic . . . .

toc . . . .

Sniper Rodriquez, "Greasy stringy goat? One bowl a'rice they all stick all their hands in all covered with all their shit wiping their asses? Robyn like gettin the screaming shits?"

Wolfe, "Hearts and minds, Sarge."

He sets the individual items from the MRE bag one-by-one lined up on the bumper.

tic . . . .

toc . . . .

tic . . . .

toc . . . .

Rodriquez, "Shittin green outta both ends for a week."

Redcloud, "Com'on, we're trying to eat here."

tic . . . .

toc . . . .

tic . . . .

"La Vengaza Montezuma. Here gonna call it Mohammed's Vengaza."

Wolfe, "That's what Cipro's for."

He holds his chili mac pouch up to the sky, an offering to the sun. A gift from the gods. He kneads it aggressively, mixing the contents.

tic . . . .

toc . . . .

Out with his knife again. He slits open the pouch longways straight and exact.

Flicks away the thin strip.

Knife folded back closed and clipped to his pocket.

Plastic spoon from the bumper.

Bites off the cellophane wrapper.

Spits it out.

Licks the spoon once—habit.

Just another part of his MRE ritual.

Spoon now dipped into the chili mac.

One spoonful into his mouth. Eyes closed loose in pleasure. Savors the taste and texture. Delicious ecstasy.

Swallows slowly.

Opens his eyes.

Rodriquez is amazed. "Shit, Kyle, you gettin yer rocks off?"

tic . . . .

toc . . . .

"Chili mac," Wolfe says. "Hot or cold, this, mi amigo, this is why God made MREs"—

tic—

Wolfe's eyes jump to something—

the man being interviewed suddenly hopping up to his feet—

another village man suddenly appearing from behind the conex shipping containers—

toc

"Robyn!"—Wolfe tosses aside his chili mac pouch—"Let's go, com'on we're going!"

—the second man flings the red bucket he carries, drenching Robyn and terp Gulbarhar and the ground around them, as the interview guy flicks a Bic lighter and it's suddenly all a gasoline explosion of fire—

And, M4 carbine snapped up to his shoulder, Wolfe fires *clack clack clack clack clack*, stitching the Bic lighter guy from neck to waist and immediately swings the rifle up to sight through the flames on the gas thrower who's not there, gone back behind the shipping containers—

as both Gulbarhar and Robyn are in flames, calling out, the ground around them afire, and they can't crawl out of it, with

Wolfe yelling at her "Roll! Roll! Roll, Robyn!" running to them, but it's a wall of flames, and he throws blurred scoops of dirt and sand at the flames, to no avail, and

Pfc Holloway is the first to arrive, with a fire extinguisher from his truck, and Wolfe snatches it away from him and shoots its ferocious cloud of white powder through the flames and onto Robyn.

And Redcloud is here with an extinguisher from the Mrap, spraying terp Gulbarhar.

Wolfe grabs Robyn under the shoulders and pulls her from the flames of the ground burning, and Doc Eberly elbows aside Wolfe, away from Robyn, and unzips open his aid bag.

Redcloud orders Holloway, "Litters. Ponchos." Orders the rest of the platoon through the handset clipped near his shoulder that runs to his small MBITR (Mbitr) platoon radio in its pouch low on his body armor, "Hold your fire, everyone. Eyes on your sector. Eyes – on – your – sector."

Sniper Rodriquez, standing on the roof of the Mrap, is sighted in through his sniper rifle scope on the gas thrower fleeing fast across the first barren field. "P'mission t' engage, Sarge!"

"Negative, hold your fire!" from Redcloud.

Lieut Caufield reinforces it. "I don't see a weapon on him, Rodriquez, do you?"

"Fuck that, L-T."

"Just hold your fire."

"Chingada, L-T!"

"That's an order, Sergeant!"

The entire Zoo is at combat alert.

Meals and cigarettes discarded.

Turret gunners sighting down their weapons.

The others behind their M4s behind the open doors of the trucks, each man sighted out on his sector.

While the village men and boys are scattering far from the mosque, sprinting away, toward the compounds up on the higher terraces.

And Wolfe steps to the Bic lighter guy sprawled, his back against the rusted shipping container, the chest of his white shalwar kameeze man-jammie garb soaked solid crimson blood red, his throat gurgling blood, his eyes blinking rapidly with hateful terror right at Wolfe coming near.

Wolfe says something in guttural, violent Pashto that loosely translates as *"See you in hell, hajji Mohammed,"* and he puts the muzzle of his M4 right over the guy's heart and *clack clack clack* puts three shots there.

Wolfe looks around at Doc Eberly tending to Robyn.

At Redcloud watching him right back.

Their eyes, his and Redcloud's, meet behind their tinted eyepro.

Redcloud with the exhausted extinguisher above terp Gulbarhar moaning on the ground. Not a hint of any emotion in him, nothing. Just a blank flatness at Wolfe's three-shot coup de grâce into the man. An action for which Redcloud knows any court-martial board would punish Wolfe with life without parole.

Nothing, Redcloud could be a statue.

Wolfe glances up at Lieut Caufield up in the door of the Mrap on the radio handset to call back to the Cop for a medevac. Like with Redcloud a moment ago, their eyes meet behind their eyepro. Just a slight wince in Lieut Caufield's upper lip. Slight, that wince, nothing more.

Wolfe gives a final glance down at Robyn.

What remains of her clothes is burnt tatters.

Blood already seeping through the purple-tinged white extinguisher powder of her exposed skin.

Burnt skin.

Black. Down to the bleeding muscle.

Her head, only patches of hair left.

Doc Eberly pulling an IV from his aid bag.

Wolfe senses the tragic sadness of Robyn's whole world suddenly completely radically changed. For the worse. *Worst. Worse to the max. Smokin-hot-babe Robyn Banks, next minute she's a burnt piece of toast. I shoulda seen it. If anyone coulda seen it, I shoulda seen it.*

And he calmly steps between the shipping containers and climbs up onto the rock wall.

He sights in his M4 carbine on the figure of the gas thrower a good three football fields' distance away climbing up over the terrace rock wall.

Settles the dark form of the man center on the peak of the chevron crosshairs of his Acog sight.

Calms his arms to absolute taut stillness.

Forces the carbine up even tighter to his shoulder.

Lets out his breath slowly, ever so evenly.

Fires *clack clack clack clack clack* and way out there the guy goes down, pitching forward. And doesn't move.

In the Third Terraced Field

A few minutes later, the gas thrower, his baggy, billowy pantlegs blood-soaked, is struggling to crawl away on his belly.

Wolfe's boot clamps down hard on his neck, pushing his face into the dirt.

"Where are you going?" he snarls in Pashto/ English mix. "Where are you running away to?"

The guy grabs at Wolfe's legs, and Wolfe kicks his hands away then kicks him over onto his back, and the guy screams in the agony of his legs shattered by the two of Wolfe's previous shots that hit.

Wolfe now puts the muzzle of his M4 right on the guy's forehead.

And the guy's eyes squint, focus sharply, and he starts ranting an indecipherable Arabic, repeated, fast, with Wolfe catching the many *"Allahs"*.

It's rote Muslim prayer.

"Yeh yeh pray. Pray," Wolfe tells him in English. "Lotta good that's gonna do."

And the guy keeps praying, faster, more urgent, eyes boring with hate straight into Wolfe's.

Now Wolfe pulls his M4 off the guy's forehead. In English, "Seventy-five virgins," he says. "Gonna get you some virgin tail?" He smiles.

Silence from the guy.

Wolfe in halting Pashto, "Seventy-five virgins? You want? Yes? Virgins?"

The guy's eyes soften. This Am'rican isn't going to kill him after all.

Wolfe says in English, "Shit yeh who wouldn't want a virgin?" He chuckles, and he puts the muzzle of his M4 right above the guy's groin, an inch away, and the guy is suddenly very very scared.

"Good luck with that," Wolfe says.

"Death to Am'rica!" the guy shouts in English, and

Wolfe pulls the trigger *clack clack* point-blank into his crotch.

Hello virgins.

Bye bye gonads.

Thirty Minutes Later

Just waiting on the medevac chopper.

Not a villager anywhere in sight.

Not one.

None.

Nowhere.

To Lieut Caufield it's *Like the whole village is deserted after a plague. The time of the locusts.*

No one here but for the Zoo.

And their two squads of ANA soldiers.

Both Robyn and Gulbarhar on litters set behind the Mrap. Ready to be rushed to the medevac chopper when it arrives.

Each wrapped in a poncho, with just their heads all wrapped in white gauze dressings showing. A slit open where their mouths are to breathe.

Pfc Holloway holding up an IV bag for each.

Wolfe on his knees beside Robyn. Words of comfort. *Medevac's almost here. Cash is just thirty minutes flight from here. I'll be right with you, Robyn.*

Cash, as in Combat Support Hospital.

Real docs, full-fledged surgeons, RNs.

The Cash on Fob Salerno these days is no longer a series of tents from the first years of the war but a concrete building, modern and well equipped, like a big-city trauma ward.

Get Robyn stabilized there and get a C-130 in asap to fly her up to the bigger hospital at Bagram, then maybe even by tonight a flight on a jet to the full US military hospital in Germany, and in as little as a couple of days she could be in the burn center at Brooke in Texas.

Gonna be in the hands of the best care in the world, Robyn. Gonna be alright, Robyn. All right. I got the sons-a-bitches, Robyn. Dead and in hell, Robyn, they're done with, they're taken care of. Just breathe. Slow and steady, Robyn. You're gonna be alright. I'm with you, Robyn. I'm here, I'm gonna be with you every step of the way.

Her lips move, and he puts his ear right to them to hear her whisper in her frightened stutter, "I'm – – cold."

"Cold's good, it's okay, they're gonna take care of you in the Cash."

"I – I – I – I don't – want – to – die – ."

"You're not going to die, no one's gonna die, don't think like that, Robyn. Best care in the world, lady. Have you back on Sal in thirty minutes. I'm right here and you're not going to die on me. We got you, you just hold on, hold on to good thoughts, think of your family. Your brother, your mom and dad. Your dog, think of Zelda, think of her. You're gonna be back with them, with them all, it's going to be all right. Going to look at this someday down the road as just a little bump in the road. We're here for you, all of us here for you. Chopper's on the way."

One of the ANA pickup trucks bounces up to a stop.

This squad had come over a while ago to see about the body of the Bic lighter guy, and no one had said anything to them or stopped them when the Afghan sergeant had his guys wrap the body in a white cotton blanket, and they drove it down and left it on the steps of the deserted mosque for the villagers to deal with.

This time they've got the gasoline guy in the pickup bed, wrapped in no white cotton blanket, he's alive.

And the Afghan sergeant hops out barking quick Pashto at Redcloud, which Zoo Platoon terp Nouri translates as a demand for medical treatment for the guy.

Nouri repeats it. "He says Cash for him helicopter take him. He goes to Cash."

Redcloud, so unfazed. So calm. Looks at the wounded gas guy in the pickup bed.

Looks right in the Afghan sergeant's eyes. They're close, within arm's reach. The Afghan sergeant's eyes burning fierce, angry. The man is tall for an Afghan, broad shouldered. He's Redcloud's height and build; Redcloud wouldn't have anything on him in a fight.

Redcloud says calmly, quietly, "Tell him, Nouri. Tell him . . . "

And that cynical grin of Redcloud's—deadly serious—and he pulls off his Oakley eyepro, eye-to-eye direct with the Afghan sergeant.

Unflinching.

Clear, concise, crisply exact.

No mistranslation going to happen here now.

Cold. Emotionless. Almost ruthless.

"Leave – him – for – his – Tal-eee-ban – doctors."

And he turns away from the Afghan sergeant, ordering Nouri, "Tell him, dump him, get his men ready to leave. The minute the medevac takes off, we're out of here." He catches Lieut Caufield's eye and cuts off Caufield's dissent with a fierce grimace that demands, *Don't even think of countermanding that.*

Sniper Rodriquez saw the look. Smiles. Thinks, *Roger that, Sarge. Let the pinche pendejo cabron die.*

He spits a stream of tobacco juice.

Pahumbang! from somewhere—

"Incoming!" and *"RPG!"* shouted—

Pahumbang! again, and *Pahumbang!*

Which were two fiery flashes from the windows of the concrete schoolhouse way far at least six-hundred meters up the beach, built right against the mountainside near where the streambed opens up from the narrow gorge upstream, and

the turret gunners of Ssgt Ketchum's three trucks facing that way open up with their .50-cal, M240 machinegun and Mark-19, and

their bullets hit high on the mountainside above the school, as three more rockets are fired in white flashes from the windows.

Paashoowoosh! of a rocket whizzing by twenty feet overhead, over all the trucks, and it explodes in the rocks down across the stream.

Passhoowoosh! of another rocket overhead, to explode like the other downstream.

Pahumbang! from the veranda of the school, and that rocket blurs in straight and explodes just in front of Ketchum's middle truck, showering it with dirt and rock. But the turret gunner on the Mk19 just keeps *plomp plomp plomping* out his grenades.

Pahumbang! from another window of the school, and that rocket *whooshes* toward one of the ANA pickups where, standing in the bed an ANA soldier is firing his PKM machinegun from his hip as another does likewise with his AK, and the rocket explodes right on the cab, throwing those two soldiers out of the bed and shredding the two inside, as

Ketchum's turret gunners have found their aim:

The .50-cal and 240 gunners sending their streams raking the school, all that ferocious volume of firepower shattering the huge wood frame windows and wood doors, splintering the concrete.

The Mk19 rounds plunking against the outside walls and right through the school veranda and in the windows.

There are explosions inside the building, with flames and now smoke billowing out the windows and up through the veranda.

The three turret gunners rain their violence against the schoolhouse from this distance.

No more RPGs are shot.

Standing on the roof of the Mrap, Redcloud commands the squad leaders through his pouched Mbitr radio, "Cease fire! Cease fire!"

He watches from this distance Ketchum get his gunners to do that, and it all so gradually grows quiet, to near silence.

Just the smoke and flames from the burning ANA pickup, and those soldiers there pulling their wounded and dead away from it.

Smoke and flames snake up from the distant school, from which there's now *Pahumbang!*

And Ketchum's three turret gunners again open up, as that rocket sails now over those trucks and explodes near Ssgt Nell's trucks on the other side.

When Ketchum's turret gunners' belts run out there's quiet. They pull open new cans of ammo, slap the belts onto their guns and slam the first linked rounds into the chambers.

Redcloud demands over the radio, "Status report. Casualties. Ketchum."

Gets a *Negative* back.

"Nelly?"

That squad the same, just some "Scratches, minor, not even Purple Heart worthy," from Ssgt Nell.

"All clear, we're good," from Ssgt Utah.

Redcloud likes what he sees, that no one in Nell's squad fired. Same with Utah's, they all kept their discipline, kept their eyes on their sectors, their backs to the school.

Guaranteed everyone took a glance or two to see the destruction rained upon the distant school, but they didn't fire, and that's good. Redcloud won't say anything now but it's not something he'll forget this evening, to compliment Nell and Utah back on the Cop when they get together to wargame the day.

Same with Pvt Bybee on the 240 on the Mrap here, and Spec Tran on the .50 back over there, good job, neither fired. Neither had to be yelled at not to fire.

No one sure had to tell Doc his duty, Redcloud thinks, as Eberly is sprinting with his aid bag toward the wounded ANA soldiers on the ground near their burning pickup.

An itch in the back of Redcloud's mind tells him to call Eberly off, let the ANA medic deal with them, *If they've even got a medic. And what's he got, a band-aid and an aspirin? Let them treat their own wounded.*

Except, *They're wounded, wounded are wounded,* that's Redcloud's better self. *Ours or theirs, they're wounded.*

He asks of Lieut Caufield, "Thought the ANA were supposed to check that school?"

"They did."

Wolfe, "They must of been hiding in the cloakrooms." It's not a joke. Said bitterly.

Redcloud watches the smoke coming up out of the school. "If they had cloakrooms."

"Then they'd have to have coats to hang in them." Wolfe again, and again not a joke.

Lieut Caufield, "The sergeant said, he said they checked it out and it was clear. No one, no kids, no insurgents. Nobody. Nouri! Nouri, what'd the ANA say about that?" The school. "ANA sergeant told you what?"

"No people in school. M-tee."

"He said that, empty?"

"Yes yes. M-tee."

Redcloud to Wolfe, "You're the anthropologist. What'd they teach you in college, what's that tell you?"

"Your ANA's either lazy or lying. Big Lima for L as in lazy or lying. Or both."

Lieut Caufield grabs his binos from inside the Mrap.

Wolfe continues, "Or they're working for the Taliban. Haqqani in this neck of the woods."

Redcloud, "They paid for it." The wounded ANA. "Taliban could of sneaked in around back."

"Nope," Caufield scanning with his binos. "Not possible."

The school is built right up against the concave mountainside which shelters most of the building.

Caufield, "No backside. It butts right up to the mountain there."

Wolfe, "Or they've got caves back in there. We should've checked it out."

Redcloud on the radio, "Ketchum, did you see anyone going into or out of that school building?"

And back from Ketchum over the radio, "Negative. Sarge, we was told the school was empty. My guys woulda said somethin."

From the school, a bright, loud explosion, with a surge of flames and streaming clouds of jet black smoke from the windows. Then a second explosion inside.

"Jesus Cristo!" from Sniper Rodriquez. "What do they got in there, a ammo dump?"

Wolfe, "I've seen, they store diesel in the schools. And clinics. District centers. Fifty-five gallon drums. Diesel and gasoline."

"AKs. RPGs," Rodriquez adds. "Fert'lizer they use in their roadside bombs. Prob'ly got cases of our claymores they rip off from the trucks comin in from Pak'stan."

Lieut Caufield, "It doesn't leave a lot of room for books."

Wolfe, "Books? We don't need no stinkin books." Not a joke. Again. Scorn. "I wouldn't build them any more schools. Clinics. Or mosques. District centers."

Redcloud, "Hearts and minds. You're the HTT, Wolfie."

At the corner of Wolfe's eyes, Robyn is motionless on her litter, wrapped up in the poncho, her head all white gauze seeping blood through. "F—double-U—double-C—double-K these people." At least, he knows, she's not hurting now, not with the morphine Doc gave her.

Even more guttural, he says, "Twice on Sunday."

Sniper Rodriquez laughs. "Yeh 'mano, you be the one, Kyle, you tell that to Gen'ral St Claire."

Wolfe, "I'll get right on that PowerPoint."

Redcloud cocks an ear, downstream, and there it is, the sound of a helicopter. An Apache gunship appears high over the ridgelines in the gap downstream, and it dives now screaming down into this valley.

Over the platoon freq comes the pilot, "Tattoo Zoo Platoon, this is Talon Three. Over."

Lieut Caufield answers, "Roger, Zoo Six here. Over."

Caufield's call-sign, Zoo Six. All unit commanders are something Six.

"What you got going, you got a barbeque cookout going on down there?"

Redcloud motions Caufield that he'll take it, and cuts in over his Mbitr radio, "Negative. Neg—ga—tive. All clear. Just a little test fire. Remodeling the little country schoolhouse. We've got two critical here for the medevac. Over."

"Say again, all clear?"

"All clear. This is Zoo Seven." A unit's ranking NCO is something Seven. "Calm as a kindergarten class at naptime. Repeat, two criticals for immediate evac."

A laugh over the radio. "Kindergarten what?"

"Kindergarten at naptime. You're in the protective bosom of the Tattoo Zoo. Bring in Nightingale."

"Talon's never been known to turn down any bosom. You hear that, Nightingale?"

"Roger that on the bosoms," is a second voice, the pilot of the Blackhawk medevac helicopter coming in fast now over the gap between the ridges downstream. "Give us a smoke, Tattoo Zoo. Where do you want us?"

"This is Zoo Seven. Center of mass," from Redcloud over the radio. And, "Nelly, you heard that? Toss them a smoke."

Over by his truck, Ssgt Nell pulls the pin on the grenade and heaves it with all his might, its green smoke billowing and the grenade bouncing close to the center of this wide circle perimeter.

Four Minutes Later

The Blackhawk is ascending, speeding forward, banking, to get out of here to follow the Apache gunship already climbing fast for the open sky above the gap in the ridgeline downstream.

Wolfe is left alone here.

Redcloud and the others jogging back for the Mrap.

Both ANA pickups bouncing back toward where the other pickup burns.

Wolfe's eyes following the departing Blackhawk.

Robyn is on it. Leaving. Gone.

He's not.

And there's a clenched fierce anger in his face, in his hands on his M4 carbine. Thoughts, feelings, he'd shoot off a whole magazine, thirty rounds, at that chopper. No—rather, turn and shoot up those ANA pickups. *Kill that hajj sergeant.*

They'd met the chopper as soon as it touched down, and they loaded Robyn and terp Gulbarhar inside, with Eberly coming in on one ANA pickup truck with their two wounded to load aboard.

The ANA sergeant came with the second pickup, with the wounded gas thrower, which had Wolfe going ballistic. "No fuckin way!" he'd screamed at the sergeant. And in Pashto/English mix, "Get him out of here, they are not taking him, he is going nowhere!"

But the Afghan sergeant, the gas guy in his arms, shoved right by him.

The rotors spinning in a loud blur right overhead and the Blackhawk twin engines screaming, Wolfe shouted right at the crew chief, "No, no, not him, he's Taliban! Haqqani Talib! He doesn't get on, he did all this!"

"Is he alive?" the crew chief shouted back.

"Who cares! He did that to her! He set her on fire!"

"Geneva Convention!"

"Geneva frickin bull shit! He's—not—going!"

"Tell it to your congressman!" And the crew chief blocked Wolfe from pulling the gas guy off then held him back from climbing aboard, "No pax!"

"I'm going with her to the Cash!"

"Overloaded!"

"She's my teammate!"

"Maxed-out weight! The altitude!" Final word, and the crew chief stepped back up inside then and slid the door shut.

Leaving Wolfe. Taking Robyn.

Wolfe motionless now. In the growing quiet as the Apache helicopter is gone and the Blackhawk is about to cross through the gap downstream.

Wolfe just watches the dark blur of the Blackhawk disappear.

Back at the Mrap Lieut Caufield asks of Redcloud, "Travis." It's an order, a question, a request. "We need to get a squad, do BDA."

Battle Damage Assessment. Check out the school. Account for the enemy dead.

BDA.

Getting numbers.

Higher headquarters likes numbers. All the way up, everyone likes numbers.

Numbers to affirm they're killing the bad guys.

Testament to a mission being accomplished.

With snapshot digital photo verification.

Numbers and pictures to make the battalion and brigade commanders look good, essential for eventual promotion. To give the generals a positive argument that they're winning, which gives the politicians protective cover to justify the cost. In dollars and blood.

The more enemy killed, the fewer enemy there are.

When you get it down to 0 enemy left, you win.

Tally up those numbers, scrapbook those photos.

Send it all up, and everyone along the way adds their own PowerPoint slides, until a final presentation at the White House shows the enemy on the run, on their last legs, and *"It's just a matter of a little longer and the Afghan Forces will be up to strength and in position to take over this war all by themselves."*

Redcloud over the radio, "Utah. Two trucks. Meet me over here for BDA."

He pulls from a chest pouch a small digital camera. Centers the burning ANA pickup in the viewscreen. Zooms in. *Click.* Moves the camera to get the smoking schoolhouse in the viewscreen. *Click—*

Pahumbang! from somewhere, and those here duck down behind the Mrap. They count four seconds, and the rocket explodes just to the side, showering the Mrap in dirt and rocks.

Pahumbang! of another, and Spec Tran has seen the flash and a puff of smoke from a compound way up in the terraced fields.

Pahumbang! another comes from there, and Tran opens up with his .50, as Bybee in the Mrap turret blasts his 240 machinegun.

And the second rocket sails *whoooosh* overhead, with the next exploding on the sand near Ketchum's trucks.

Redcloud advises Lieut Caufield, "You sure we want to stick around? It gonna be worth taking casualties? One in the hand, Lieutenant, count our blessings, get while the gettin's good."

Caufield runs his hand across his throat, doesn't have to put his *Nix on the BDA* into words, and

Redcloud orders over the radio, "Zoosters, frag-O. No BDA. Mount up. Now, asap. Ketchum, you're in the lead."

Frag-O, literally a fragmentation order, a change in an original order.

And word is passed on the radios and in shouts and gestures, and guys never move faster than when they know they're getting out of a place they no longer want to be, where maybe the next surprise RPG actually hits its target, like that ANA pickup burning, except *It's one of ours this time,* and *Damn straight we're gettin outta this shit-assed place* is what most of them are thinking, before it actually is one of theirs. *Hooah on the frag-O!*

Not so with Private Finkle, the pimply-faced eighteen-year-old Mk19 grenade gunner in Ketchum's truck. No hooah. He whines to Ketchum climbing in, "C'mon, Sarge, what's this shit, they're not doin BDA? I wanna see who I wasted."

"Next time."

"How we gonna know how many I wasted?"

"They're crispy critters –"

"Even more reason, Sarge!"

"Get back up on that gun!" And Ketchum motions driver Specialist Van Louse a pissed *Get movin behind our lead Mrap there* already moving out bouncing over the boulders heading for the stream. "Get your head outta your ass, Louie," he tells him.

Van Louse guns the hummer ahead, yanking the wheel to turn to follow. "I kinda wanted to see the BDA pictures too. How many you think we got? Dude, hadta be a shitload."

Ketchum, "What's it fucken matter?"

"Com'on, whaddaya think? Ten? Fifteen? That was one shitload of rockets coming outta there, Sarge. A shitload, you seen em."

Ketchum holds up three fingers.

Van Louse, "Three? No way. There was at least, I counted, I lost count, there were at least ten. Minimum."

Ketchum, "Three windows."

"Alright. And you got let's say three shooters in each one of them windows. Nine. Nine enemy K-I-A for the Zoo today. Kilo India Alpha. Big day for the Zoo."

"What's it to you, you think yer gonna get a attaboy from Colonel Pork-You-In-The-Ass? Yeh, in yer dreams."

"Notches. I wanna start puttin notches on her here." On this humvee's door outside. "Com'on whaddaya think? Skulls? Think I oughta do skulls? Skulls would be cool, don't ya think? Like the tatt."

Ketchum. "With beards. Turbines and beards. I think you got something there, Louie. Notches. Skull and crossbones. Sorry I ever tol' everybody yer a shitbird. Sorry I ever called you a lamebrain."

From the radio, Redcloud's voice, "Listen up, Zoosters. No horseplay, no relaxing. Keep a sharp eye out. We know now they're out there watching us."

Redcloud is at the open door of his humvee. Pfc Holloway revving the engine, anxious to get going.

Redcloud watches the Zoo trucks taking their proper order heading out, an order they know without thinking, widely spaced out.

Combat Rules #s 1 and 2: *Don't bunch up.*

Radio mic up close to his lips. "Enemy's out here. Itchy to play footsie. Get themselves an E-ticket to paradise. Let's not give em it."

Redcloud climbs in, cramped up in this tight space.

Motions Holloway *Turn it*, to take the tail end.

Cautions over the radio, "We're not home yet. So keep your eyes peeled. Ketchum, stay in the water. At all times. You gotta get out, go where it doesn't look like anyone'd want to ever drive."

Taliban know to plant their roadside bombs in the path the average-Joe anybody will instinctively take—the easy way.

"Stay in the tracks, Zoosters. Exact, right in the tracks of the truck in front. The bad guys are out here alright, aint no doubt they're watching."

And a final word, "Eyes like an eagle, men. Eagle that hasn't eaten since Sunday."

"Reminds me, Sarge," Sandusky's voice on the radio. "Speaking of eating and being lunchtime, think we can make a quick pit-stop at McDonald's? Or a Jack-in-the-Box?"

"What'd I just say about horsing around, Sandusky!"

No reply.

Nothing, silence on the radio.

For Redcloud, as it should be.

He points for Holloway to head for Wolfe, who's squatted on his haunches Afghan-style, unmoving, where the chopper left him. Like he's staying right here in Wajma. Alone, the lone American.

Holloway pulls up to Wolfe on Redcloud's side.

Redcloud drops his window. "Didn't want to ride with the L-T?"

Wolfe stands. Joyless smile. "He drove right on by. Like he didn't even see me."

Redcloud, "He's got a lot on his mind."

"Yeh," Wolfe pulls open the door behind. "Life's a bitch." Dry, dark, bitter.

"Sheeeeeee-at," from Pfc Holloway, and Redcloud shuts him up with a killer look that says *Shut — Your — Trap — Private.*

Wolfe climbs in into the seat behind Redcloud.

It's like it was before.

Up front, Holloway driving and Redcloud.

Doc Eberly seated behind Holloway, and Tran's legs and butt standing between him and Wolfe.

Wolfe in the seat that Redcloud had said was reserved for Robyn on the return.

Day One, Afternoon

NATO/ISAF Compound, Kabul

A handful of Nato countries is ISAF, the International Security Assistance Force.

Pronounced I-saf.

Spell it Isaf.

It's Nato, but it's really America predominant.

Predominant predominant, the gorilla in the room.

That's the way Kyle Wolfe had described it for his second anthropologist trainee, who could not seem to grasp the difference between Nato and Isaf.

"The nub, in a nutshell," Wolfe had explained. "Think of it as the U.S., plain and simple." The U.S. is the gorilla in the room and the rest of the countries a bunch of playful little chimpanzees, and they're all scampering around hopping on and off of the gorilla, tugging his hair, boxing his ears, checking his teeth, yanking his crank, and he feels like a big rich daddy having quality time with the kids after a stressful day in the corporate boardroom. "Not that I'd know anything about a rich guy coming home from a day at the corporate office."

Not that that second trainee or any of the others would ever confuse Kyle Wolfe with someone who could survive more than a few hours in any corporate office.

Isaf is Nato but really America, who's got ten times the soldiers in this war, twenty times the equipment, a thousand times the $.

Isaf is the boss of the entire war.

Isaf headquarters is this fortressed-out compound here in the center of Kabul.

It's a square chunk of three or four city blocks cut out and completely cordoned off surrounded by multiple layers of concrete blast walls fifteen feet tall.

Blast walls topped with embedded broken glass and strung coils of razor wire.

Video surveillance cameras mounted atop the wire every fifty feet or so.

Inside the perimeter, reinforced concrete buildings. Two and three stories tall.

Helicopter pad on the roof of the HQ Command building.

Blast-proof glass windows. Where there are windows. Few.

Modest-sized pastorally quiet quads of cut grass crisscrossed with cobblestone footpaths bordered with pines and cypresses.

Manicured ivy in clay planters along the concrete steps into buildings.

Homey.

Peaceful.

The quiet richness, the feeling of a scaled-down Oxford, Harvard or Dartmouth.

Rows of two-high stacked prefab conex officer living barracks.

For the many American, far fewer British, German, Canadian, Italian, French, Pole, Dutch, Dane and Norwegian officers running the war and their NCOs and soldiers making things run.

A few, officers and enlisted, seen today outside moving about. All in impeccably clean, perfectly pressed uniforms.

Trimmed, immaculate fingernails.

Not a speck of a smudge of black under them.

As it should be. This isn't Wajma. It's not the Zoo's Cop.

Those places, that's outdoors combat down there, grunting out the war, going outside the wire to find and engage it.

This here is where all that hands-on combat prosecuted down there is prioritized and watched over, with directives to the four regional combat two-star commands and from there to the full-bird brigades and shot down to the lite-bird battalions and then down to the mere-captain companies.

Principle of Combat #2:

The higher up the food chain you go, the greater your responsibility for the many more lives you direct below and the many more dollars you spend coming from above.

Corollary Principle: *With greater responsibility comes better living.*

Begrudged, of course, by just about every line-dog infantry GI, who all believe that soldiers back in the comfy rear should have it rough like them and don't realize that the colonels and one-stars and the four-star here can't be meeting with ambassadors and visiting senators and Karzai and *60 Minutes* dressed in filthy uniforms torn at the knees and crotch, hands blackened with gunpowder and grease, and brown grit embedded under hard-crusted broken fingernails.

Hard-crusted broken fingernails? Here?

C'mon dude, get real. There's a manicurist from Belarus who works in the salon/barber shop just over there the other side of the HQ building, next to the Tim Hortons.

In the HQ Command Building

Pete St Claire. Here he comes striding down the corridor.

General Pete St Claire.

Isaf commander.

Afghan War commander.

The four-star who Wolfe and the Zoosters were talking about before down in Wajma. The man credited with the gospel Coin Manual, that four-star.

Most four-star generals, you think they're going to be someone out of Central Casting. Tall, broad shouldered, ruggedly handsome, a bear of a man, commanding if only from a dominate physical bearing.

Think Patton, Schwarzkopf, Tommy Franks.

Think George C Scott.

Not General Pete St Claire.

5'9" at best. Wiry. Tight, sinewy. Precise in his movements. Precise and fluid. The physicality of a magician.

Short, thin, small, nothing but muscle, and in complete control of every tendon.

Ran cross-country in high school, ran it at West Point, runs five miles at 5:30 per mile today, and can do ten at 6:10/mile, has run the New York City Marathon four times, the last just two years ago, at age fifty-five, in 2hrs 52mins.

Pete St Claire has an elliptical and a treadmill in his office suite here, for the days there's no time for the short chopper hop over to Bagram for a run of the airfield perimeter there. Twice. Three times if he can slip it by his demanding schedule, with at least two of his young captain aides keeping up while huffing staccato notes into a mini-recorder and receiving operational updates and relaying directives on secure cell phones, voice and text.

Back in Isaf HQ Kabul in his office suite St Claire has weights for strength and tone along one wall.

A pull-up bar in a doorway.

A sit-up incline board.

Was the shortest, smallest cadet on the rugby team at the Point and made up for it by being physically and mentally all that much more aggressive.

Still takes to heart a lesson his father drilled into him as a boy: *Disciplined in body and disciplined in mind, can't have one without the other.*

And a second lesson from him: *More sweat in training, less blood in combat.*

St Claire's got footlockers of books in the backroom where he sleeps on an Army cot.

When he sleeps. In snatches, three, four hours, at most.

The books are mostly military and histories. Some go-down-easy popcorn fiction. Clancy and Grisham. Scott Turow. He leaves the Faulkner, the Mailer, the Cheever and Roth and Heller and Frazen and Dostoyevsky and Twain and Chekov for the literati snobs. He's already read them once—for familiarity and insight not art—no need for twice.

St Claire's nowhere near handsome but not overtly ugly either. Indistinguishable, forgettable. By his face.

A portrait artist studying him would instinctively relate that face to a mole's, maybe a chipmunk's.

Out of uniform St Claire blends right in, he could be the manager of a Walmart, the neighbor down the street mowing the lawn and trimming the hedges who you wave to but don't really know. The construction engineer of the town's new sewage treatment plant. The high school math teacher who coaches the wrestling squad.

The last guy Central Casting would pick for a general.

He's really no different from the next gent in the country club locker room, looks like the average 12-handicap duffer, but outside he'll shoot 18 holes two over par and beat you. That evening, upstairs at the formal dinner, when he strides in, in dress blues, a chest full of medals of every rainbow color, his elegant, quiet wife Margaret on his arm, every eye will turn his way. He's taller than his 5-9, he's General Pete St Claire and this is just outside Washington DC, or across country on the other coast at Torrey Pines while assessing the Marines at Pendleton. Every eye's on him because he's the one who's been entrusted with, in command of the Afghan War. He's the one, everyone knows, for whom unlimited fortune of whatever his choosing awaits after this war.

Unlimited political fortune, if he cares to go that way.

Which, as of now, no one knows.

And he's not saying.

Actually, always deferring the often raised question with a smile and *"I have a war to prosecute, that's my single duty and single objective."*

Earlier, throughout his career, from the highest cadet rank of First Captain at West Point and forward to three-star deputy commander in Iraq, he's led through his competence and confidence. Today he commands from his competence, confidence and his position, and knows that the last is the most powerful of the three. He knows as well that to misuse or abuse that position with incompetence, recklessness or over-confident immodesty is to lose it, to toss it away forever.

Gen Pete St Claire knows that if he were to lose that position, this position of master of this war, have it taken from him, it would mean throwing away that future limitless fortune.

He knows that he won't let that happen.

It's not who he is.

Another lesson from his father: *Respect the men below and those above will respect you.*

You don't command in the infantry from platoon through brigade and division and now theater over the course of thirty years from lieutenant to four-star by being limp, ho-hum, wet-noodlely.

You don't get that first star or keep it, or get another, if you aren't as smart as a brain surgeon.

As political as a senator.

As agreeable as a butler.

You don't get a four-star theater command of a war unless the president is convinced that you'll win that war for him.

Or make it appear that you have.

Or at the very least allow no one to rationally argue that your war is heading for the one word that must not be spoken.

Defeat.

At least never to be spoken in the short-term.

Long-term, in the history books, who cares, you'll all be long dead by then anyway, and generals don't get blamed for losing a war, political leaders do; look at Robert E Lee, he lost his war and he's a hero a hundred-fifty years later, haloed in biographies and film documentaries, and who the hell remembers anything about his feckless president, what's his name, that Jefferson Davis fellow?

In the simplest terms, you don't keep a four-star theater command unless the president believes you're doing him no harm.

In the short-term.

In increments of four-year chunks.

Election to election.

From St Claire's father: *You take a job, you do in one day what other men do in a week.*

And that work ethic, along with his brains, ambition and zipped-lips when prudent has propelled Gen St Claire to here, the most powerful man in Afghanistan, foreign or native.

Total, some 200,000 American and Euro-Nato soldiers and civilian contractors are under him, under his command. Add in de facto the disparate 300,000 Afghan forces, however ineffectual and rinky-dink.

That's a half-million-plus whose actions St Claire is responsible and accountable for.

Along with a few hundred billion dollars worth of equipment, from light bulbs to jet fighters.

A running yearly budget of ninety or a hundred billion dollars, no one's really that gung-ho about counting accurately.

And in the Op Center, listening to the radio comms of a Marine company in a firefight down in gates-of-hell hot Helmand or a GI scout platoon caught in an ambush up in the wicked mountain passes in Kunar or a lonely two-squad observation post getting rocketed on the border in Khowst, Gen St Claire is nostalgic to be the captain or lieutenant down there in the midst of it, where he never was as a captain or lieutenant— wishing to be leading men who he knows by their first names in combat where the bullets from your own gun actually directly kill people and their bullets can very much kill you.

Every true warrior officer in the Op Center listening to that far away fight in real-time wants to be in it, is envious of the low-ranking officer down there on the ground who is.

Every infantry officer worth his salt, regardless his rank, longs to be kneeling in the dirt directing his handful of men, his privates and sergeants, to kill the enemy just twenty meters away trying to overrun his platoon. Four-star and lower, the true warrior would trade ranks and places for a day to be that nameless lieutenant down there where real courage is tested and galvanized by the rounds snapping just overhead or splattering the rock beside you or splintering the tree you're behind, whacking your radioman at your elbow, two in his body armor, another that crushes his shoulder, and you're scared shitless, but you're in control of that fear, in control of the terror, no one sees it, you won't dare show it, no one knows it but you, and you're directing your platoon, grabbing that radio handset, reporting and ordering, making the instantaneous and correct decisions that are going to save the lives of most of your men and are right now effectively killing the enemy.

Just for an hour.

Maybe today.

For Gen Pete St Clair it wasn't to be as a lieutenant or captain because the only wars in those years after West Point were the tiny engagements in Grenada and Panama, and they were over in days and he was assigned somewhere else thousands of miles away during them.

He was a lieutenant colonel on staff in brigade op center for the Gulf War.

Was assigned to the Pentagon during that quick Somalia debacle.

Commanded a division as a two-star in Iraq after the fall, in '04, '05.

That's when that war had already turned vicious, in the streets, and he'd go on patrol with a random company, out into those streets, to the futile protests of his staff, just to be out there, out where his troops were being engaged and being killed and maimed.

Got a rep for it. The men admired him for it.

And it wasn't with a bunch of Blackwater bodyguards, no personal security at all, wouldn't Sniper Rodriquez be surprised to learn, but with his issue Beretta 9mm in a shoulder holster and a borrowed carbine on his lap, that's all, as he'd ride the backseat in a humvee.

Leaving command of the patrol to the captain or lieutenant—he wouldn't think to micromanage their company or platoon, but knew that his very presence would bring out the best in them.

He'd ride just to be there, in the streets, where the maiming and killing was being done.

Because that's what warriors do.

They, like St Claire, think that in any time and any place they would be Lieutenant Colonel Hal Moore—and they know him by his real name, as they've all read his book, more than once, and they visualize him and thus themselves as Mel Gibson in the film *We Were Soldiers Once*, as they've all seen the movie, multiple times, from lieutenants to colonels here, Americans and Euros, and countless have the DVD in their rooms here and have watched and rewatched it.

St Claire has a hardbound first edition of the book.

Signed.

Personally, to him, from Hal Moore.

In a footlocker here.

A warrior officer by definition of being a warrior imagines himself Gibson as Lieut Col Moore, seeing himself in the Ia Drang Valley, Vietnam, his battalion of 450 surrounded by 2,000 NVA enemy. In battle. Where you can die.

No one's going to die here in Isaf HQ Kabul.

Had Gen St Claire been born a dozen years earlier he might have been a first lieutenant platoon leader in Moore's battalion in the Central Highlands.

Born years later than he was, he might have been a Ranger captain fighting for his men's survival on the streets of Mogadishu.

Even more years later, he could be Lieutenant Matt Caufield taking his platoon back down Wajma Gorge right this very minute.

If he knew of Matt Caufield.

If he knew of the Zoo Platoon as anything more than a unit designation number on a status chart on an Excel spreadsheet.

You can't pick your generation nor your birth date or place. *It's what you do with what you're dealt*, he learned from his father. *Can't make your good luck any more than your bad. Confront the bad luck headstrong. Fight through it. Push it aside.*

Good luck and bad, an ROTC career artillery lieutenant colonel, his father was killed in Vietnam when an errant round from one of his own Central Highlands battery firebases on a hilltop four miles away made a direct hit on the outhouse latrine he just then happened to be taking a dump in.

Pete St Claire was in high school then.

It wasn't until years later as a lieutenant colonel in the Pentagon that he dug up the file with the dry clinical details, which didn't matter, didn't change his remembrance, his father was still a hero, he'd died in combat, in a war, like any war, where the most clear determinant of life or death was that random good luck or bad.

In war, where, despite his father's teachings, St Claire accepts that sometimes the bad will come so suddenly with such finality it cannot be confronted, fought through and pushed aside.

Sometimes. But so far never for him.

He's thought about it now and then, often enough. And he just knows, he feels it, he's confident that his good luck will hold out.

By anything other than its inconsequential numerical unit designation, and surely not by its nickname, as of this very moment right here right now in Isaf HQ, Gen St Claire has yet to hear of the Tattoo Zoo.

Here in the corridor, his strides long, sharp, St Claire's soft-soled boots make no sound on the polished linoleum-tile floor.

One's eyes automatically go up from the boots and zero in on the four jet-black stars one above another sewn into his uniform right down his sternum.

Four perfect embroidered black stars.

Power, ultimate power in those stars. In their perfect sewn alignment.

Your eyes jump across from those four stars over to the civilian man on the general's flank, stride for stride beside him—not even an effort keeping up. Abreast on line with St Claire, without being the centimeter or inch or half a stride behind that is the deference everyone seems to pay when walking with a four-star.

At 6'6" this man is a good nine inches taller than St Claire, a husky guy, huge-boned and still at least fifty pounds overweight.

Comfortably dressed in wrinkled, baggy slacks and a Caribbean guayabera shirt, pastel pink. Yeh, wrinkled.

No tie.

Of course no tie; you don't wear a tie with a guayabera.

Dreadlocks growing full and rich and long, bouncy.

Faded red-canvas laceless Keds, size fifteen or sixteen.

No socks.

All told, in appearance and deliberate disregard for convention, taste or neatness exactly contrasted to St Clair's physical and uniform perfection.

Twenty-plus years St Claire's junior.

That's right, junior. Young.

The only child, and a bastard, of an immigrant housekeeper from the Dominican Republic and a British Royal Navy aviator in Florida assigned on temporary exchange duty at the Jacksonville Naval Air Station whom this man as a boy never knew or knew of except for the bio-dad's own first and last names his mother gave him and his skin half the dark brown of his mother's and his superior intellect, a gift from his father, no more significant than his fierce self-assurance and his dogged competitiveness, gifts from his mother.

It was that superior intellect that from kindergarten on would separate him from his inner-city classmates in a culture that values above all else physical strength and aggressive pure hedonistic meanness on the baked asphalt streets and the dirt front lawns to the basketball arenas and football stadiums, all of which he shunned after having to just once use his towering size and strength, as well as an exaggerated wantonness, to with four unanswered punches break two ribs and smash the left side of the face of the top dog of a teen gang taunting him from out under a street hoop, *"C'mon, nigga, wanna show you aint a sissy-ass mama's boy out here"*.

No one ever taunted him again. Not on those streets.

Years later as a Yale undergrad he let the white ruling class elites around him assume he was an affirmative action ghetto token and didn't care when his performance changed their minds, and he shot through Princeton postgrad in eighteen months then a Stanford doctorate in sixteen, International Relations, Southwestern Asia.

On a map that's Iran, Afghanistan, Pakistan.

This man's fluent in Spanish and Brazilian Portuguese.

Fluent in Persian and Arabic.

Semi-fluent in Pashto and Urdu.

Recruited by the State Department in spite of his anti-Ivy League dress and Caribbean ganga dreadlocks, because the rising importance of a nuclear Pakistan made his doctorate rare and highly in demand. He then spent the mid- to late-90s in a back cubicle in the embassy in Islamabad where no one called him *"Doctor"* and his extensive reports about the threat of bin Laden and the al-Qaeda training camps just a stone's throw across the border went largely ignored.

Repeat: Where his extensive reports about the threat of bin Laden went largely ignored.

Until 9-11.

Since, he demands nothing of a title but everyone calls him *"Doctor"* anyway, and he had his own personal secretary and two assistants in the embassy here in Kabul until St Claire borrowed him after a first briefing from him just before taking command.

That was twenty months ago.

St Claire has yet to return him.

He is Dr Gene Hutchinsen, PhD.

"Doctor Hutchinsen" to everyone here at Isaf.

"Hutch" to St Claire.

St Claire's senior political adviser.

Only political adviser.

The prejudices and relative mediocrity of Dr Hutchinsen's Ivy League peers and profs and of those Department superiors who ignored him in that embassy cubicle have made him respect and accept only hard verifiable facts scattered in an airy gauze of political machinations while disrespecting and disregarding rank and position to the point of a baldly undisguised sarcastic scorn and flippant, irreverent, unapologetic insubordination.

Four black stars on the chest of a man a generation older merit no more of his deference than does the single gold bar on the chest of a young lieutenant fresh out of Officer Basic.

Which is why Gen St Claire keeps Dr Hutchinsen close.

For his blunt non-Machiavellian honesty.

For his encyclopedic knowledge and chess-master understanding of this Southwestern Asia, from language to history to culture to prejudicial religious mindset locked still in the 7th Century.

Like right now,

here striding the corridor together, side by side, equal.

Hutchinsen is saying, "In and out, Pete, all they're going to do is whine. District Governor Achmad, remember, with him it's going to be 'Why'd you give the road contract to whatshisname's brother?' Hello goodbye, ixnay on the frickin three cups of tea. I'll tell Achmad you have satellite imagery assessment showing insurgents driving past his district center in their Toyota Hi-Luxes in broad daylight daily stopping in for tea and a six-course lunch."

Interrupted, "General St Claire sir!" from an American Army officer — a major — hurrying up the stairwell from the basement.

St Claire doesn't even break stride.

Ten paces behind is one of his captain aides who are always near, bulging leather satchel in one hand, cell phone in the other, and he tries to stop the major, who simply snaps "Colonel Pluma" and proceeds to follow Gen St Claire and Dr Hutchinsen going out the doors.

Outside, the major catches up, keeping up a quarter step behind.

For that deference, remember?

He's on St Claire's flank opposite Hutchinsen, is tall like Hutchinsen, just a couple of inches shorter, visually balancing out and making seem diminutive Gen St Claire between them, but contrasted to Hutchinsen's casual, rumpled civilian appearance by the same crisp immaculate uniform and commanding carriage of St Claire.

He's Major Zachary Dove.

Quickly reporting, "Sir, Colonel Pluma thought you should know. A Human Terrain Team, in P2K, they took a hit, sir, about fifty minutes ago."

Dr Hutchinsen answers for St Claire. "And Dan thinks this is of such pressing concern precisely why?"

"R-C East is reporting, the anthropologist, a Dr Robyn Banks, female, twenty-four, from Maryland—. A villager doused her with gasoline and set her afire."

Gen St Claire still doesn't break stride, shows no reaction.

Has a single-word question, "Status?"

"We'll know when the dustoff arrives at Salerno, sir. It's still fifteen minutes out."

"Tic?"

As in TIC.

Troops in Contact.

Today's military lingo for firefight.

"Sketchy, sir. Not confirmed. R-C East isn't saying. Officially."

"Were there any embeds with the Human Terrain Team?"

"Sir? Embeds?"

"Find out."

"Yes sir." Maj Dove instantly knows the finality—that's all, nothing further—by St Claire's intonation and abruptly stops.

Can't help but admire the lightning speed and vacuum clarity of Gen St Claire's mind. *Embeds? Find out.*

Embeds, shorthand for embedded journalists.

Maj Dove watches St Claire and Dr Hutchinsen turn down the walkway to head for the meeting with district governors he knows the general has scheduled at the on-post mosque. Dove turns back for the steps of the HQ building.

Dr Hutchinsen is twenty-months accustomed to St Claire's speed and clarity. Matches it now with his own devilish, dark humor. "A female contractor torched like Joan of Arc." A sadistic grin more than a smile. "That kind of media, Pete . . . ."—

"Priceless."

Wow. Priceless.

Did he just say priceless?

It's enough to take one's breath away.

Not Dr Hutchinsen's. It had been his thought.

And Gen St Claire could say it aloud to him, but would never with anyone else, because he damn well knows that Hutch doesn't covet his four stars, doesn't want to be country chief, doesn't want to be ambassador, could not care less and has no ambition for position.

St Claire knows that all Hutchinsen cares about is winning this war, and he isn't even sure whether that's from patriotism or simply the challenge of winning under a strict counterinsurgency strategy imposed by stateside and global politics that limit the extreme violence and ruthless destruction here and in neighboring Pakistan that an acne-pus'd buck-tooth'd two-digit-IQ basic-trainee recruit could see would be the more direct course to victory.

Victory.

Back in the days when it still meant vanquishing the enemy.

Priceless.

Inside the HQ corridor Maj Dove is stopped by a female voice calling "Zachery!"

Immediate recognition, it's Vicky Marshall approaching.

Major Victoria Marshall.

American.

Medical Corps.

A nurse anesthetist.

By definition, in a Cash trauma center The Anesthetist.

Dove knows she's stationed at the hospital at Bagram Airfield, he's seen her around here in Kabul a few times already. First knew her from a Cash in Iraq, she's not someone anyone forgets.

For her looks alone.

She could melt the cover of a Sports Illustrated swimsuit issue, he thinks. *In uniform.* Burn your eyes out imagining her out of it.

Even more than her stunningly-natural physical beauty, her attraction is of a self-confidence in her intelligence and beauty and a reserve that signals to all that she's not giving it up to just anyone or everyone, and Maj Dove knows she's single—that's the word on her—and doesn't know if she's ever been married and doesn't want to imagine that she has been and can't recall that there's anyone she's ever been pinned to—that he's ever heard of anyone, *In all these Cashes she's been with since called up out of her reserve medical unit after 9-11 in all these combat zones. No one.* He imagines as if it's an ontological truth that *Major Victoria Marshall is the unobtainable woman,* the dream angel of all men's lust. And love. The woman walking the beach alone at sunset who you can't take your eyes off of and at the same time can't approach, feel too small, too lacking, to approach. A woman not deliberately hunted by men, but when glanced upon, stumbled upon, to be instinctively desired immediately and yearned for thereafter beyond anything rational. And never obtained. *She's never been linked to anyone, no other guy, not generals, not colonels, not Brits or Canadians, not special ops sergeants or gunslinger contractors.* Ever.

Not that he's heard. And he'd remember, if he'd heard.

"Are we going to see you tonight at Oktoberfest?" she asks as she comes near. "All that ballroom dancing you had to take at West Point, I hope they taught you how to polka."

All with a playful, innocent smile, and she goes right on by, continues down the corridor, doesn't even look back.

Maj Dove wouldn't be a heterosexual man, married with three kids or not, if he didn't allow his eyes to linger on her—

that backside, even under a uniform it's tight and enticing. With just the right, and not too much, feminine motion.

Locomotion.

Loco motion.

It drives you loco.

He now breathes in to smell her perfume, even if he's experienced wise and introspective enough to know that it's just his imagination—

but it's not—

Ah so much sensuality in that just bare scent.

A whiff, a hint, really, but with a siren note of ensnarling sweetness.

Expensive.

Feminine.

Maj Vicky Marshall knows he's watching her, knows that for just these few moments his eyes have lingered on her, is one hundred percent certain of it without turning to see, and she won't turn, she doesn't have to, not to remember him—his face is singed in her memory, from that first time, what was it?, three or four years ago, *When he came into the Cash in Iraq, he was a captain then,* she remembers, *twin bars on his uniform.*

A chunk of skin missing from his arm, and above his ear a scalp wound bleeding through the field dressing. Both wounds from bullets or shrapnel or both, but it was his three Ranger soldiers brought in on litters who everyone congregated over. One so bad he was brought straight into the OR, Vicky Marshall holding back then-Captain Zachery Dove, telling him, *"We'll take it from here."* Then seeing *His face watching through the little window in the doors,* and she doesn't remember whether the soldier died then, he wouldn't have in surgery, most likely, but perhaps later he did, that was daily then in Iraq.

She's as far down the corridor now as she was up it when she called *"Zachery",* and she knows he's no longer watching her, that he's moved on, down the stairs, down to the basement Op Center most likely, where he's just a lowly major with the other junior staff captains and majors among the seasoned lite colonels and the princely full-birds.

Zachery Dove should be a general, she thinks.

He looks like a general, like a general should look.

6'4" or 5", 220 and *All muscle, no fat, chiseled Hollywood good looks. Not that weasel General St Claire. Weasel-looking St Claire.* She thinks now of that one time in the crowded Cash tent in Iraq at Biap when the general was standing close and she felt he was just begging her to allow him to draw even closer, inching his arm closer, so that the sleeves of their uniforms touched, and she could sense the lust, feel it in the itch of her skin, that he was willing her to allow him to take hold of her in both his arms and pull her to him forcibly and kiss her—*St Claire kiss me?, even touching his bare hands on mine?* She shudders, *Never never ever—*

She's ruined it for herself, clouded over with the repulsiveness of General St Claire those very pleasant thoughts of Zachery Dove.

She brushes it off, too late now to change that. *Later, tonight.*

In Wajma Gorge

Zoo Platoon's trucks are making their way, spaced a good thirty meters. All nine in the water.

It's slow going, each picking its way around the boulders and rocks.

The gorge is maybe sixty meters wide here.

The second truck is Ssgt Ketchum's hummer. Pimply-face young Pvt Finkle up top in the turret on the Mk19 auto grenade launcher.

Inside, Spec Van Louse driving, asks Ketchum, "That Robyn chick, what was she doing anyway, what do we gotta come all the way out there for them for?"

Ketchum, "Army bullshit."

"Thought she was a civilian. That dude, what's his name? Fox I'm thinking?"

"Wolfe. Kyle. Sergeant Redcloud calls him Wolfie."

"Ex-Marine Corps isn't he, someone said, he's ex-Marine?"

"Former, there are no ex-Marines. You wanna call him that he'll be slappin you upside the head, don't you know nothin? Never ever ever call a guy was a Marine ex."

"What they doin way out here, with their own terp too?"

"Army bullshit, I told you. Census shit. Census takers. You know, when they go 'round and count up the pop'lation, like every ten years they do it. How many kids you got. Caucasian, black, brown, dumb Polack, spic, wop, chink. They wanna know do you jack-off how many times a week, you still beating your wife, you got a hard-on for the neighbor girl next door, she gets out back there on their trampoline, bouncing, bouncing, her little tight hard boobies in her tank top. Bouncing bouncing, y'know, in her shorts and doin splits in the air, her legs up, Louie dude, spread out like this, she's cheer-squad at the high school. All that kinda shit."

"Sarge, you're a sick mutha."

"Hey, you asked."

From the backseat, behind Ketchum, the Zoo's mortar man Sergeant Delmacha—

who everyone calls Slurpee because back in garrison in the real world he was always coming back from lunch with one and sucking it up hard and he'd go *"Brain freeze! Brain freeze!"*

—he simply says, like he really knows, like it's a cold hard fact, "They're CIA."

Van Louse, "Aw bullshit! Who told you that?"

"Ask um. Fact, Sar'ent Ketchum, it is. Ask um."

Slurpee's 60mm mortar tube and plate and five cardboard-tube-encased rounds are on the empty seat across from him.

He repeats it, "C – I – A."

Ssgt Ketchum, "You don't know shit, they're not CIA, the CIA's huntin the big dudes. Bin Laden. And they are not wastin their time puttin guys riding with the Zoo, for what, shit, when they got sat'lites, they got Pred'tors, they can count every cunt hair in that ville if they want to. They're not sending a skirt as god-awesome gorgeous, and that's with a capital G—they're not sendin her here, not the CIA, not today, not tomorra, not ever. Count on it."

Slurpee, "You see the way that Wolfe dude wasted that hajj, that first dude? Man, he had him blown away 'fore Sar'ent Redcloud even had his weapon raised up and off safe."

Ketchum, "What'd you see? You got telescopic eyes?"

"I saw him, he blowed him away. And the other dude, runnin, that hajj was at least five hundred meters and bamm bamm bamm bammmm he dropped him. Wicked-ass shooting, Sar'ent. C – I – A."

"Gonna put you, Slurpee my man, gonna put you in a rocket ship, blast you up into outer space, strap you up there lashed to a sat'lite, have you lookin down sendin back all the super-secret spy images 'n shit. Sat-tel-lite Slurpee gonna call you, yer eyes are so goddamn awesome spectac-tac-tac-ular, and that's with a capital S. Sat-tel-lite Slurpee."

"Maybe you oughta have your eyes checked, Sar'ent Ketchum."

"Check this," Ketchum flashes him the finger.

"How'd those two dudes get killed then if it wasn't him?"

"One's just wounded, and I'm not saying it wasn't him. He's not CIA, he's ex-Marine. And ex-Marines, every one of em knows how to shoot."

Driver Spec Van Louse, "Thought you can't say ex-Marine, Sarge?"

"Just testin you." A sneer. "Testin you, Louie."

And Van Louse to Slurpee, "Even a former Marine sniper, he aint gonna, no Marine, not a sniper or none of them's gonna hit someone at five hundred meters with a M4, no way, not a M4."

Slurpee, "Okay, four hundred meters."

Ketchum, "Standin still like a statue maybe, but was the hajj standin still or was he runnin like a jackrabbit scared naked of his own shadow, or couldn't yer bionic 20/20 vision eyes tell the dif'rence?"

"Running."

"Shooting prone, from the prone position? Kneelin? Standing?"

"Standing."

"Four hundred meters? Lucky shot. Nothin more."

And Van Louse, "Whaddaya think, Sergeant Ketchum, you think Sergeant Redcloud's gonna let me paint skulls 'n crossbones on here for our kills? Or you think he's gonna say it's destruction of goverment property?"

"I wanna see what yer skulls and crossbones, what they look like first, yer not painting nothin on here I don't see it first."

"I figure I'll ask Sergeant Rodriquez to draw me somethin. Y'know, put his tatt skull, then wit' pirates crossbones. Maybe, I'm thinking, have a snake coming through the eyes. With the tongue stickin out. Forked. How many we got for today? Five? Six, how many you think we can count?"

Ketchum, "Confirmed? Zero. With a capital Z."

An ANA Ford Ranger pickup is back a good distance behind Ketchum's humvee.

Next is the third Ketchum truck. Next after is the PL's Mrap.

Inside, the driver is a non-talkative soldier from Nell's squad.

Like Lieut Caufield who's sitting shotgun, silent. No words.

Caufield is just looking out his windshield and door window and occasionally at the Blue Force Tracker map on his computer screen mounted directly in front.

He's uneasy, he's disconcerted, he's bothered by what happened back there in Wajma, by this day's turn of events.

Not so much by the attack from the schoolhouse or the later one from the compounds far up—none of the guys were hit, none of the trucks damaged. He's bothered more by the image of Robyn burning, that she should be attacked so irrationally, so hatefully, insanely, there's no explaining it, and right under his very nose. Under his command and he could do nothing about it, nothing to stop it, had not seen it coming. He is the Zoo's platoon leader, she was his responsibility today and he had not thought, had not imagined, hadn't seen that anything like that could happen. *Where did that man come from? Why didn't I see him? He came out of nowhere. She's younger than me, I'll bet. What, maybe twenty-three, -five, -six? Her whole life ahead of her. What's her family going to think? Does she have a boyfriend? Think of the scars, the burn scars she's going to have. Who's going to want her now, how could you want to touch that?*

And that's not fair, he knows. *I hope she has a boyfriend who loves her already. Who'll be there for her. Who'll love her forever. No matter what she looks like. I hope.*

All the way to the rear of this Mrap where three hard-plastic seats line the walls on each side of the massive swing-out rear door, Sniper Rodriquez is harnessed in on one side.

Terp Nouri on the other

Facing each other.

Harnessed in because if one of these top-heavy trucks rolls over and you're not strapped down, you're going to wind up severely wounded or dead from multiple encounters with all the sharp-cornered hard steel here and the two-inch-thick windows that don't give.

Same with an IED.

Sure, the V-shaped hull's going to deflect the blast, but the truck's still going to fly and tumble and roll, and a guy sitting loose in the back is like a marble in an empty cookie tin batted about a ceramic tile floor by a couple of kittens.

It won't be pretty, and when they ship your body back to Dover, it'll come off the plane and there'll be a form letter pasted in a clear-plastic sheet protector on the lid of the coffin: *Dear Family, Do Not Open.*

Rodriquez has his Knight Arms sniper rifle lying on the floor, his boots planted on it, secure, he's not going to have it go flying around in here.

He's eating an MRE.

Thinking right now along the lines of Lieut Caufield up front there, except there's no regret, none of the lieutenant's questioning, just a wish that they had let him take the shot. He had the shot, it was an easy shot. He had the haji perfect in his sights. *One shot, not five like it took Kyle Wolfe.* One shot and the raghead'd be dead. *Dead. Muerto.* Not medevacced out of there.

And he can't help but see the flames. *Such a beautiful mamacita that Robyn, ay mí mamacita, pobrecita on fire.*

And he thinks that she should die, he knows it would be better if she died, better for her. *Who wants to be in the hospital for three years?, gonna have a hundred surgeries. Years in a hospital, burned charred like chorizo.*

He tells terp Nouri, "Yer some fucked up people, y'know that?"

Nouri meets his eyes.

Rodriquez repeats it. "Fucked. Up. Mo-fos."

He stabs the tip of his knife into the MRE pouch.

Grins.

Pulls up a thick ham slice.

"Yer all scrambled eggs, up here," his head, "and don't neven got a clue. Yer Mohammed don't know shit 'bout shit and he sure as shit don't know batshit 'bout the bes' part of life an' livin, you know what that be, you got a clue?" He bites off a chomp of the ham slice. "Niñas. Señoritas. La mujer. Womens."

And Nouri says nothing in reply. Looks away.

He doesn't like Rodriquez, hasn't from the very beginning when Zoo came here these few months ago. He wouldn't call it hate, though it is, and considers it a mutual feeling returned for what he knows of Rodriquez, what he's heard Rodriquez say and seen Rodriquez do. He knows that Rodriquez holds his people, his country, all Afghans in scorn and disgust and complete disrespect.

About Robyn right this instant Nouri thinks in his own native Pashto, *The woman did not belong here, it's her own fault. They bring her where a woman is not allowed, she does what a woman should not do, though she may not deserve it she should expect to be attacked, she should accept it.*

The very last truck way far back is Redcloud's humvee.

In it there's no talking.

Quiet. Just the rattling and jangling of everything that's loose and rattles and jangles from all the shaking moving down the stream in the rocks and boulders.

Not five minutes out of Wajma, Pfc Holloway had asked, "Whaddaya think, Doc, think she's got a pretty good chance?"

Wolfe answered before Doc Eberly could, sharply. "Pretty good chance at what, PFC?"

"Making it, I hope she makes it, she's a awesome chick. I'd like to know she's gonna make it."

"What do you know about Robyn or awesome or any 'chick', and who the fuck gives a shit what you hope or don't hope?"

"Yeah?! Yeah?! A guy can't care?"

"Care about what you know about, P fucken F fucken C," Wolfe said. "And that aint squat shit."

And Redcloud had given Holloway a direct look, even lowering his eyepro to do it. A look that said *Shut up and I mean it, and learn, PFC, learn when to talk and when to shut that trap up good and tight.*

And Holloway did shut up.

And knowing how to make it stick permanently with Holloway, Doc Eberly took it one step further, asking him, "Holloway, you've got two sisters, don't you?"

Holloway's helmet nodded *Yes.*

"Amber's the one in high school? Senior, right?"

Again a nod *Yes* of Holloway's helmet.

"I'll bet she's pretty, huh? Got to be pretty. Think of it this way . . ." And Eberly leaned up close to the back of Holloway's helmet, sure he'd hear it direct, mouth-to-ear, not just through the headset, and would understand every word. "Tonight at the football game a couple of the stoner dudes get sweet little Amber, y'know, she thinks for a sip of beer with them, underneath the bleachers while everyone's screaming 'cause the team's going down and they're on the ten-yard line and they're going to score a touchdown, and they push her down on the ground, surprise surprise, and she starts screaming and no one can hear her over all the cheering and stomping on the bleachers, and they're laughing, and they clamp their hands over her mouth and throat, and one of them starts burning her wrist with a cigarette and they pull up her tight little come-hither skirt—"—

"Tell him to shut up, Sergeant!" Holloway implored of Redcloud. "Before I have to shut him up myself, and I will too, Doc, I will!"

"Yeh, PFC," Wolfe had laughed. "Doc first, then come after me."

And Holloway hasn't said a word since.

But Wolfe said right then, to Doc Eberly, as if to shove a red-hot fireplace poker through Holloway's heart, with pure rhetorical cruelty, "The team score the touchdown, they win the game, Doc?"

And no one has said anything since.

None of them.

Which is fine with Redcloud, concentrating on this movement, his eight trucks in front of him, all in the stream, *Good boys,* taking it slow and careful, and it'll be another hour and a half at least back to the Cop, and that's alright too. Slow and careful and cautious. And he could not care less about the ANA, their two pickups, the front one way up there now turning out of the water to ride smoother on the dirt bank, *It's their lives, their choice.* And now the second pickup does the same, pulls up out of the stream. *They want to die, let em die.*

Life is cheap here, Redcloud thinks. *Four of their buddies dead or wounded bad an hour ago, and they want to ride high and dry. Life is cheap. What'd Robyn say? That was just this morning. Right there,* behind him in the seat where Wolfe is. *God bless her, God help her now, God save her. Lord Jesus Christ, look after her. What were her words, exact words?* "One out of four don't make it to five." *One out of four kids dead before even five years old.* "Twenty-five percent, and most in the first couple of months." *Just infant babies still.* "Mostly all preventable. Mostly all curable. Horrible nutrition, filthy water, no hygiene. Bugs, colds, flu, dysentery." *Redcloud snorts a trace of frustrated disgust. They there those ANA want to be blown up by an IED there in the dirt, go ahead have at it, numbskulls.*

Except he knows his Zoo will be left to police up the pieces.

Doc Eberly is perfectly happy with this quiet since he got Holloway to really shut up. Gives him a chance to read in peace, and it's hard enough in all the bouncing, but as a kid he learned to read in big chunks, to see whole blocks of lines at one glance and process it just a couple of milliseconds behind. So he can see the blocks between the bouncing, whereas otherwise it would be impossible to hold even a line in one's vision going word by word.

Still, he closes the paperback, leaving his thumb in as bookmark, and he now stares blankly out his window, as he remembers that he did not smell burning flesh and he should have. *Robyn PhD and that terp, there had to have been the smell,* and he doesn't remember smelling anything. Which means he must have blocked it, blocked it right then to do his job better. He'd gotten an IV running into her and one running into the terp, punched through the blackened, crunchy soft flesh, *How did I do that? How did I manage that?*

Seated right across from him on the other side of turret gunner Spec Lee Tran's legs and butt standing on the tranny box is Wolfe.

Cold killer civilian Kyle Wolfe.

Hasn't said a word since his angry, ugly ones at Holloway, and none before that.

M4 carbine muzzle-down between his legs.

His eyes search up through his window the near vertical mountainside. The crevices, the shadows between the rock, the shadows behind the shrubs.

He glances ahead through the windshield and sees way up there the ANA pickup riding on the dirt. Snickers, just a *heh-heh,* and sees the first pickup farther way up there ahead the same, on the dirt. *Heh-heh-heh. In sh'allah.*

He knows that *Asshole sergeant's in the first* and doesn't care if *They bite the big one,* and would joke and laugh and tell Redcloud *"Just drive on by, Sarge, leave them for the buzzards,"* except, *That hajj sergeant knows where every IED's buried and is going to scoot around them.*

He keeps his eyes on the closer ANA pickup, when it isn't blocked from view by the other trucks, and it might be that he's watching to see if it or the first will make that sudden stop and scoot, betraying they're hand-in-glove with the Taliban. Or to see that sudden flame explosion and its immediate billowing black and gray cloud and the pickup no longer anywhere. And even that, those thoughts, that imagining, that doesn't erase *Robyn sitting there on the ground and the man appearing out of nowhere and throwing that gasoline,* and "Fuck!" aloud Wolfe says.

Doc Eberly glances over.

Pfc Holloway throws a quick glance back.

Wolfe looks back up out his window, back up to scan the mountainside they're passing by.

Redcloud heard the *"Fuck!"* but didn't turn, didn't look, didn't need to. He's heard it before. Knows it's a man cursing himself, cursing his failure, wanting to go back to a moment in time and be one instant smarter, one second faster, and the *"Fuck!"* is from the realization this very moment right now that that can never be and will never be.

Riding in here, bouncing, jerking right and left skirting boulders, water splashing up.

Nothing but the sound of all the jangling in here.

Silent radios, all the other trucks are following Redcloud's orders from earlier as they were leaving Wajma. No goofing off, no horsing around, just concentrate on the enemy out there somewhere, gotta spot them first. You hope.

And Wolfe just wants back, to get back to the Cop, right now, and *Get the captain to get me a chopper, get me a chopper back to Sal. Gotta get to Salerno.*

To be with her.

He needs to be with her. She needs him. He thinks.

But because he's not delusional, he's a realist, he brings it one step further and knows she doesn't need him, *They've got her in the Cash now, they've got breathing tubes down her, she's knocked out so deep now, drugged already into a coma, she's not feeling anything, not thinking anything, she does not exist anymore, she has no consciousness, she's dead but for her body still alive,* like the only time he knows, when he was knocked out that time getting his wisdom teeth pulled, and he knows he's been lucky he's never been wounded, all this time in war and never wounded, never a patient carried into a Cash where he'd be knocked out, really knocked out, so he knows the death of anesthesia only from then with the wisdom teeth and you're counting *99 98 97* then you're waking up in a grog being led to the other room and you're aware you were gone away completely for a while, you did not exist, you were dead, you've lost how much time? *She's there now, gone, her mind blank, for good, they've got her not feeling a thing, not knowing a thing, she's alive and does not even know it. Oh Robyn . . . .*

And he still wants to get to Fob Salerno and be there. With her. *Beside her on the plane to Germany then to Texas to the burn center at Brooke Army Hospital, with her always, and meet her family there, who are they? They'll be crying, they will be crying. Grieving.* And he'll tell them how it happened. How he was slow, too slow to see it coming, too slow to stop it —

again "Fuck!" aloud, and he doesn't even know he says it.

Isaf, Kabul — In the Strategic Joint Operations Center

A darkened amphitheater.

Raised platforms in a semi-circle. Tiers, four of them, each three steps higher, where about thirty staff officers sit at their laptop workstations among the jumble of phones and radio comms equipment on the polished mahogany tabletops built curved along the front edge of each platform tier.

On the front wall, ten 60-inch flatscreen TVs showing Blue Force Tracker maps, live drone and jet-fighter feeds, weather imagery. One playing CNN, another Fox News, a third BBC World.

Millions of dollars of hi-tech, but who's counting?

The flatscreens controlled by the officers on their laptops.

Major Zachery Dove on his laptop at the front row center.

He's the American officer who brought the news of Robyn to General Pete St Claire.

The one who stopped in the corridor as Maj Vicky Marshall breezed by asking about Oktoberfest tonight.

On Maj Dove's laptop plays a news video that shows on the central flatscreen up front.

Gen Pete St Claire and Dr Hutchinsen standing in front of Dove's workstation. Watching that news video on the flatscreen.

On the screen is a collection of American soldiers hooting and hollering, celebrating, in their own sandbagged bunker Toc someplace lit with bare hanging lightbulbs. One soldier turns right into the camera and with a shit-eating grin growls, "That's the way you kill the bad guys. Can you hear me now? Reach out and touch em, before they get to your wire, with the premier number-one mortar crew in the whole F-ing U-S Army, pardon my French." The image freezes on his grin. A title appears: *A Film by Nick Flowers*. Then *The Times of London*.

Maj Dove directs his quiet voice to Gen St Claire. "That's his most recent, sir. In August the Christian Science Monitor ran two of his films from Uruzgan on their website and they both showed troopers of the Five-O-Two of the 101st in a positive light. Would you like to see them, sir? They're both about the same length, about twelve minutes each."

St Claire waves it off. "Wasn't it he, isn't Nick Flowers the one who made the film about you?"

"Yes sir, my 82nd task force, sir. He made the men look good, sir. He didn't whitewash anything, but he was fair."

Maj Dove's boss, Colonel Dan Pluma, is at his side. "Colonel Gray-Nance is checking with all the command PAOs, sir, but she says that Nick Flowers is one-hundred percent freelance and she's seen no negative feedback on him. This is his about umpteenth time here. Since September last year this embed."

PAO, as in Public Affairs Office. The military folks in charge of PR. Who run the embedded civilian journalist side of it.

Maj Dove flashes up onto the flatscreen copies of Nick Flowers' press credentials and US passport. "He's got over four years embed time just here, sir. Something totaling three years in and out in Iraq."

Col Pluma, "It's confirmed he's at Cop Valley Forge, but it's unclear whether or not he was out on the patrol. He's not on their trip ticket."

Maj Dove puts the digital file of Zoo Platoon's trip ticket up on the flatscreen.

That's the roster of all on the day's patrol. Names, ranks, SSNs, truck ID#s.

Dove explains, "But Nick, I remember, one mission we didn't have an empty seat and, sir, he's not one to take 'no'— he hopped up and rode in the back with the ASF in their Ford pickups."

ASF, for Afghan Special Forces. Soldiers multiple levels above the ragbag ANA, and trained by U.S. Special Ops Green Berets to work with them and select task forces like Dove's.

Col Pluma, "Rode with the Afghans, Zach, without getting blown up? That's a buddy now who I'd take with me to Vegas. One who's willing to ride in their unarmored pickups. Carry him in your pocket for a lucky rabbit's foot."

Maj Dove brings up onto the flatscreen a grainy black & white live video image from a Shadow surveillance drone. In the mountains, looking straight down, showing the length of the Zoo Platoon's nine trucks moving down the stream and the two ANA pickups riding out of the water on the dirt.

Maj Dove, "Shadow, real-time, sir. The platoon's still in movement back to Cop Valley Forge."

Dr Hutchinsen, "It would have been nice to have had Shadow up there two hours ago."

Col Pluma, "It wasn't requested, Doctor Hutchinsen. Zach?"

Maj Dove, "No sir, there was no request for 12-hour prior surveillance. There was no request for Shadow overflight."

Col Pluma, explaining to a silent Gen St Claire, "Previous overflights of the village have showed nothing out of the ordinary. No heat signatures coming down the ratlines from the border. Just one or two, a handful, on the goat trails, and that's normal for the local indig. Threat status, non-existent. When were they, Zach, the overflights?"

Maj Dove, "The most recent was 28/29 September. More than three weeks ago."

Col Pluma, again for St Claire, "This is the first incident from that particular ridgeline, sir. Database AARs show no previous Tics. That village Wajma's not registered as hostile anywhere."

AAR, as in After Action Report.

The official platoon and/or company document submitted after every operation, no matter how minor the patrol.

Dr Hutchinsen, "When's the last time anyone's been to that valley?"

Col Pluma doesn't know.

Maj Dove does. "In June, Doctor Hutchinsen. But not all the way to that particular village. At least, I haven't found any record, no AARs, of any patrols to Wajma village."

Dr Hutchinsen, "What have they been doing at Valley Forge, sitting on their asses playing video games?"

Col Pluma, "Alpha Company there has an Area of Operation the size of Rhode Island. With just a hundred twenty-six men. Look at the terrain."

On the flatscreen, the Shadow drone live feed. The stream and near vertical mountainsides. Inhospitable.

Maj Dove, "It takes them two hours to go ten miles, sir."

Gen St Claire has his priorities. "If this embed Nick Flowers is with them down there and he has film of Doctor Banks on fire, I want that film."

Col Pluma, "I've got two Blackhawks standing by, sir, at Salerno. Rotors already turning, for just that, to pick him up, sir."

From a row behind, a staff officer interrupts with an update off his laptop. "Cancel that, Colonel Pluma. Confirmation from Cop Valley Forge, Flowers didn't go on the patrol. He's back at the Cop."

Gen St Claire, "Get Salerno PAO in that Cash. I want video coverage of the HTT Doctor Banks from there to Landstuhl then stateside."

Col Pluma, "Done, sir. I had Salerno PAO out meeting the medevac chopper for coverage."

A nod of approval from St Claire, *Good job, that's thinking, that's initiative,* and he heads for the doors, Dr Hutchinsen with him.

An officer up on the fourth tier reports from a message on his laptop, "Salerno Cash, this just up. Robyn Banks: extremely critical. Third-degree burns, more than eighty percent of her body. All except for her feet and ankles."

"Hooah," from another officer, "on those Nomex boots."

Nomex, as in fire-resistant material.

Yet another officer reports, "Bagram Air Ops. C-130 Air Evac on the tarmac taxing right now to go pick her up."

Someone else, "I'll bet they wouldn't dispatch a C-130 for me."

And another, "If you looked like this they would."

And on one of the big flatscreens comes up Robyn Banks' Facebook page, and

at the doors St Claire and Hutchinsen stop and turn to look.

On the flatscreen, Robyn's Facebook is a slideshow of photos, clicked on the arrow one at a time:

college ceremony, PhD award, with mom and dad and her brother—

on the carpeted apartment floor with her border collie Zelda—

group photo, her and fellow Anthro HTT trainees at Fort Leaven-worth—

out at dinner in a TGI Fridays with a boothful of her girlfriends—

on the wooden patio deck of the USO on Fob Salerno, a group pose relaxed and playful with soldier friends, girls and guys—

her smiling face filling the open window of a humvee—

in a village, radiant warmth in her eyes and smile, standing together between a grinning terp Gulbarhar and an expressionless Wolfe, that she's captioned *Gulbarhar & Wolfie, my Guardian Angels.*

And it's now silent in here. Every eye on the continued slideshow of her snapshots. On the open, happy, attractive Robyn Banks.

No one says anything.

The joking's all done.

Gen St Claire meets the eyes of the officer who brought up the Facebook page. "Tag it. I want copies," he quietly orders.

Combat Outpost Valley Forge

A permanent encampment in the middle of nowhere high desert of dirt and rock.

Outside the encampment the shrubs and squat oaks and tall graceful willows grow only in the deep runoffs and along the stream meandering in the most eroded center of the half-mile-wide wadi up off of which Valley Forge sits.

Across the wadi are the foothills into which their own shallow tributary wadies become the gorges that run up into the mountains where somewhere way up top high on the other side lies Pakistan.

Cop Valley Forge is a 1200m by 1200m square formed by a perimeter of Hesco barriers.

Double-rowed Hescos.

Triple-tiered.

About ten feet between the two rows of three-wide, three-high stacks of Hescos. Each row capped with concertina razor wire and four taunt-stretched lines of barbed wire.

You're Taliban and want to set off a jingle truck full of explosives outside, you're just going to put a big rent in the first row of Hescos, which will bleed a small avalanche of dirt and rock and that's it, they aint going to collapse.

You're Taliban and you think on a moonless night you can sneak some guys like 'Nam sappers up to the first row of Hescos and up atop, they're going to get all mangled in the C-wire, and if the negligent, shouldn't-have-been-napping soldiers in the guard towers haven't seen them until then, someone's going to alert to their loud screaming *"yikes!"* and *"shit!"* and open up with his machinegun in the tower, and what of them that hasn't been cut up by the razor wire's going to be shredded by the 7.62 of the M240-Bs and the ANA's PKMs.

There's a wooden guard tower set high on each of the Cop's four corners just inside the interior Hesco row.

And a tower inside above the serpentine-mazed entrance gate that faces the wide wadi below.

All the towers are double-layer sandbagged except for the thick plexiglass awning windows all the way around. Slits in the windows from which the muzzles of the two machineguns in each tower can protrude facing out. Or, as on a hot day like today, the windows raised out horizontal and the whole machineguns in plain sight.

Two ANA and at least one American in each tower 24/7, there's never a break in that, that's not negotiable.

As in, not negotiable, period.

At least one American GI.

Regardless how it unashamedly screams of an American distrust of their Afghan allies. Regardless that the blessed Coin Manual preaches trust and instructs in giving America's *"indigenous partners"* a full responsibility in the conduct of this war.

Coin is theory.

Theory goes out the window when reality is what's been passed down from the first Cop Valley Forge commander a few years ago who accepted Coin as Truth and allowed the towers to be manned solely by ANA until on a random inspection one night after midnight he found the four guards of one tower under it smoking hashish and the tower empty.

Since then it's been at least one American per tower 24/7.

And no American here smokes hashish or any Afghan marijuana which is cultivated in the foothills of the more verdant provinces in fields thick and tall as an Iowa corn field, no matter that the ANA guys have always got it, are more than willing to share it, sell it.

It's not because the American GI is so vice-adverse.

The opposite.

You don't think guys like Sniper Rodriquez and Pfc Holloway weren't stoners back on the street?

Don't think that Ssgt Nell doesn't get drunk back home every Friday and Saturday night and most Tuesday, Wednesday and Thursday nights too?

Don't think that Ssgt Ketchum doesn't have a ritual every Friday afternoon stateside after duty where at his weekly squad blowout the guy or guys who missed one or more mornings of his Ranger-tough physical training or fell out of the Friday 8-miler at 7:30/mile have to provide the four cases of beer, iced down, and none of the lite shit either, and it better be Bud or Coors or his personal favorite, Sam Adams?

The US military's put alcohol, even a simple beer, off-limits to GIs anywhere anytime country-wide, and that's hard to skirt around because booze isn't readily found anywhere in this deeply Muslim country but for the few bigger cities, and it's near impossible to get even on the black market from terps' buddies bringing it in from Pakistan, and it's hard to hide anything from anybody on a small Cop.

But some of the guys have managed to get around it like GIs always will, having wives or girlfriends or brothers, whomever, box up bottles of heavy-duty alcohol-laden mouthwash, like Listerine, or fill 20-oz plastic soda bottles with gin or vodka or Southern Comfort and layer them all-protective in duct tape—extra secure around the caps—and ship them in Care packages of cookies, brownies, *Maxim* and *Popular Science* and biker and muscle magazines, deodorant, DVDs, moist flushable wipes.

The hardcore stateside drunks treasure and secret their contraband bottles like gold because the mail can be weeks or a month coming, depending on the availability of choppers. But other guys—guys like Holloway—they'll want to be cool and share with their closest buds their surprise gift from home the very day they get it.

But dope, that's different.

The military hasn't yet worked out piss-testing for booze, but every GI here knows that any day out of nowhere in total surprise a Blackhawk helicopter can land and out hops an MP/medical team with their little clear-plastic specimen cups that every GI from captain on down to Pvt-1 has to piss into and if the lab results come back hot, dude, that's pretty much it for you. Sure, you'll get out of the combat zone and eventually back to the states safe and secure out of harm's way—busted way down in rank, and if you're sergeant and above, busted straight out of the army.

Yeah, out of a job.

Kiss that easy paycheck goodbye.

Cop Valley Forge, like all the other Cops planted down in the moonscape of the scorching hot freezing cold Afghan Wild Wild West, may not be paradise or even a close approximation of the ease of life back on the block, but it's a bi-monthly direct deposit that the young unmarried privates and specialists are leaving untouched safe in their checking accounts to buy that big Chevy or Dodge pickup or street-racing crotch-rocket Yamaha or Kawasaki bike when they get back after deployment and the married guys are keeping their young wives and three-and-four kids sheltered and fed on right now and comfy with five hundred cable channels, cell phones for one and all, three nights a week of delivered pizza, garlic bread and 3-liter sodas, and don't forget every kid's birthday party thrown at Chuck E Cheese.

Which aint worth losing for a toke on a doobie from the ever-smiling, ever-pleasing ANA private more than willing, in the best Afghan generosity, to share his bounty.

In from the twin-rowed Hesco walls and the guard towers and the front entrance is a wide open area of large quarry-rock gravel—the helicopter landing zone. Or LZ. Big enough, in case of a dire emergency, for two Chinooks at one time squeezed in blade-to-blade a frog's hair apart.

Beyond that, Cop Valley Forge is all organized rows of wooden, tin-roofed little barrack B-huts, for both the Americans and the ANA, in separate sections.

Far up tucked into one back corner are the seven ammo storage conex containers that are triple-sandbagged on the sides and roofs.

On the opposite corner are the twin fuel blivets. Twenty thousand gallons each.

40,000 gallons total.

Restocked weekly overland by Afghan jingle trucks.

If snowbound in winter, restocked by Chinook. Full bladders sling-loaded in on pallets and set down close to the blivets from the hovering choppers a hundred feet up.

It takes a lot of diesel to run Valley Forge. Starting with Awesome Company's vehicles. The ANA's Ford Ranger pickups too. And a lot more to run the two monster 120kw generators and two other 60kw ones needed to provide the constant electricity that Americans can't and won't live without, and that the ANA sure like, especially since it's costing them nothing, not the generators nor the fuel.

Those generators supply the juice to the heating and air conditioning units for each B-hut, building and even the mechanics' maintenance tent.

The ANA sure like the high-velocity AC units as well. Except, every last one for their huts is broken, non-functioning. Parts missing, jerry-rigged, leaking, sparking, dead. None working, not a one. No heat, no air.

Don't ask why.

It's the culture, stupid.

Move along, nothing to see here.

Prominent in the Cop, the Tactical Operations Center is a sandbagged building, concrete, brick-and-mortar, walls and roof. Rocket- and mortar-resistant. A half-dozen satellite antennas scattered around the roof.

Inside, it's divided into four rooms:

The Op Center.

Internet room with 8 stations.

TV rec room.

Company medical trauma room.

The entire Toc is off-limits to the ANA or any Afghan unless escorted.

To the side of the Toc is the Hescoed-in artillery section. Two big 105 howitzers and the twin B-huts that house the artillery platoon assigned here with Awesome Company.

Off-limits to the ANA, the entire artillery section. Do Not Enter. No need for an escort—no need ever for the ANA in the arty section. Period.

What, don't think that jibes with Coin?

Yeh go ahead, let the Afghans play with the howitzers, and in a week both big guns will be busted and hajj-rigged with spit and baling wire, and they'll shoot alright, sure, and guaranteed not to hit anything within a mile of what they're aiming for.

Don't ask why.

It's the culture, stupid.

Move along, nothing to see here.

In the American barracks section with its fourteen identical B-huts, there are a Made-in-the-USA prefab conex shower and a conex shitter. For American use only. ANA, again, Do Not Enter.

In the ANA's section is their own wooden B-hut shower/shitter combo because that's the way they understand. Toilets are holes cut in the floor set over drums changed out only after overflowing. Showers are faucets with half the handles missing, the heads missing, just a pipe sticking out, and everything hajj-rigged, dribbling water all the time.

It's a lot like all the AC/heating units.

The first Americans here at Valley Forge a couple of years ago, following the Coin Manual as Truth, first let the ANA share their shower and latrine, to find the shower faucets busted and/or missing and nothing but shit all over the tops of the sit-down toilets, and they then made both off-limits to any Afghan, terps included, punishable by expulsion from the Cop. *DO NOT ENTER!!!*

Don't get it?

Follow the bouncing ball:

Not an air conditioner/heater functioning.

Big howitzer 105 sculptures of hardened steel shooting miles off-target from irresponsible negligence.

Shower faucets and heads taken for who-knows-what.

Sit-down toilets stood on and squatted upon to take a dump.

It's the culture, stupid.

Coin theory up on the Pentagon level says not to judge.

So no one judges. Not up there. Not down here.

At least not out loud.

Not written down, recorded.

Which down here will end a captain's career in a heartbeat.

American GIs will allow themselves to be transported ten thousand miles to live and fight for a year-plus in a dusty, barren, worthless 13th century land and people for nothing they can really explain rationally anymore, while accepting that they can't get drunk with their buddies after work a couple of nights a week and weekends and won't have a woman, won't even get to touch a woman not this whole time, if even see one in the flesh, but they are not going to sit their asses down on someone else's wet shit just to take a dump, especially not first damn thing waking up in the morning. And they're sure as shit not going to be forced to clean up those globs and smears of Afghan wet turds every single day before they can sit down to take their own crap.

Build them their own shitters, the ANA. Wood and tin and copper and PVC pipe is all American-bought and brought in, doesn't cost them a dime anyway.

And all live in happy peaceful harmony.

That's Coin.

On the Cop Valley Forge level.

A couple of soldiers step out of the Toc.

Followed by Awesome Company First Sergeant Eddie Kozak and Executive Officer Lieut Mike Frye. To stand here on the concrete steps looking way out there over the Hesco walls out across the wide wadi.

From their workstation laptops and one of the two mounted flatscreens in the Toc 1st Sgt Kozak and Lieut Frye have been watching on the Blue Force Tracker map the blue dots of the nine Zoo Platoon vehicles approaching close now down that tributary wadi across there.

Kozak now raises his binos to see the lead Mrap climb up out of the stream to ride on the dirt to cross the wide wadi, heading straight for the front gate here. A humvee appears following the Mrap.

Soldiers of the other two platoons and the artillery platoon are coming out of their barrack huts now. To see. Everyone's heard this or that, snatches, about Zoo's Tic, and they know that that hot civilian chick and her terp were medevacced along with some ANA. A couple of the ANA were KIA, they've heard.

Important, the only important thing, none of the Zoo, none of their guys, was hurt. No one from this Awesome Company to mourn over.

Everyone's curious. It's natural—one of the three platoons has been in a Tic, you can't help but want to know all about it.

1st Sgt Kozak and Lieut Frye know all the facts so far, all the real-time details from Wajma, as they've followed and relayed all the radio traffic since the initial attack on Robyn. They're out to meet the Zoo. No different than anyone else, they're curious about their own companion brothers coming in from combat.

Zoo's lead Mrap crosses the stream mid-wadi at a high point, climbs up onto the beaten path that is the cross-province road that Cop Valley Forge lies astride.

This Cop is the lone American outpost for about twenty-five miles in each direction. Call the beaten path a road, as it's been trudged on for two thousand years by nomads on their camels and donkeys, even still today in the 21st century, along now with the diesel-spewing jingle trucks laden sky-high with tarped loads and the random little Toyota pickups and Corollas used as your basic Afghan personal internal-combustion-engine transport.

The Mrap swings onto the road and stops, facing down the road, a threat to halt the single jingle truck approaching from down that way.

The humvee climbs up from the stream and takes a blocking position on the beaten path facing up the road. It's Ssgt Ketchum's truck, with Pvt Finkle in the turret pointing his Mk19 grenade launcher at the couple of jingle trucks just colorful blurs so far up that way.

In the Cop, embedded journalist Nick Flowers jogs the wooden steps up into the front entrance guard tower. Canon profession HD digital video camera in hand. He wants to get footage of the Zoo coming in.

Nick Flowers, whose film Maj Zachery Dove was showing Gen St Claire in the Isaf op center.

A fine arts major at the University of Iowa, Nick got into New York University's graduate film program on the strength of a single black &

white documentary he shot on a week in the life of a Des Moines junkie and her six kids by four or five men, none of them around.

That Tuesday morning September 11 he just happened to be carrying a beat-up video camera he'd borrowed from the equipment vault for a weekend shoot he wound up not doing—hey c'mon man, other things came up—and he was bullshitting with a couple of classmate buddies outside when the first plane hit the Twin Towers, and he took off at a sprint that direction and was close enough when the second hit to capture it on tape.

He caught the falling bodies.

Caught the firemen running in, the people swarming out.

Caught the first tower coming down, shot the panic, captured terrified and confused faces in close-up, filmed the emptiness of nothing but gray-white cloud, and its eerie silence. Cowered with a couple of strangers in the corner of a blown-out deli as the second tower came down. Thanked God and all the angels in heaven that he hadn't filmed all weekend and thus had three blank tapes in his pockets, and he shot all the rest of the day and into the night, right down there at Ground Zero.

He rough-cut edited it on his laptop all the next day and had it sold by midnight for a cool 50-grand to an Argentine distributor who quintupled his investment on the international market to anyone and everyone who wanted to show the real carnage and gore that the American media turned a blind eye to and would not even acknowledge existed on tape, no matter it was playing worldwide.

Nick bought his own Canon high-end videocam—the first of three in those pre-HD days, and he's on his third HD fully-digital one today. He was in Peshawar, Pakistan three weeks after 9-11.

Hitched a ride across the border in the back of a Datsun pickup with Afghans with guns, and spent the next six months hitching into anywhere combat-hot with anyone with guns who would let him tag along, from Afghans to Americans to Australians. He rough-cut edited his footage on-the-fly on his laptop and sold it internationally, and when the war petered out, won, with the enemy decimated, burning in hell, or escaped, chilling in Pakistan, and the headlines screaming out nothing but the run-up to the coming Iraq War, he came home, fine-cut a three-part 90-minute documentary which, Afghanistan being old news, no one wanted and he wound up giving away to PBS News Hour for free and they never ran.

He was back in NYU and bored out of his gourd, so he walked away from school, got embedded with the 101st Airborne and went with them into Iraq, where he stayed the next eleven months. Bounced back and forth to here, and when the war here really started kicking back up in early '06, he settled himself down here, as he's wont to say, *"To document this war for history because no one else is and someday someone's going to want to see it the way it was."*

Right now in this guard tower here Nick will get thirty seconds of the Zoo trucks coming this way, coming home after their Tic. He'll want to get one truck splashing across the stream.

He's pissed at himself that he wasn't with them in that village today, really pissed. It's like bile in his throat that he can't wash back down and still stings. Sergeant Redcloud had asked him last night if he was coming out with the Zoo today, that he had a seat for him and would put him on the trip ticket, and he'd told Redcloud he was going out with the 3rd, he'd been all day out with the 2nd with the HTT, Wolfie and Robyn, and it was the same-same, he's seen that shit before, Human Terrain touchy-feely makes for boring video.

You can't sell boring. *It's a lick on you,* he thinks. You pick some right, some wrong.

Out with 3rd today was a same-same nothing patrol, not five seconds worth of video. The Zoo on the other hand, to that ville, *Such a pretty woman on fire, talk about middle-American wholesome, and a brain on top of that, that's golden.* And he feels guilty for thinking it. Though it's true. That footage, he could have had it edited tonight and sent direct up to his agent in London on his own B-gan, zip, uploaded in cyberspace, *And imagine, just imagine, who knows how much it would bring.*

B-gan, that's a commercial non-military satellite service, and a B-gan receiver-transmitter, about the size of a laptop, is an essential part of his gear. The upload/download cost per megabyte is obscene, but it's 24/7 anytime anywhere and the Army aint shutting him down or cutting him off or restricting access or intercepting and spying on his stuff.

Or, for certain at least two out of three. Big Army probably is intercepting it. Just can't admit it. Can't reveal they're doing it.

Nick had been attracted to Robyn, who wouldn't be? Nothing phony about her, or distant or superior. She answered all his questions, was impressed that he'd been in NYU grad school. Though, "It's been so long," he told her, "they've probably thrown away my records." Then, trying to impress her—who wouldn't?—he couldn't resist trying to show off his independent rogue spirit by adding, "They wouldn't let me back in now anymore, not NYU. Not with all the schlock violent film glorifying war I've produced."

She's gotta be burned bad, he thinks. He'd thought to seek her out again tonight after dinner, talk, ask more about HTT, *yeh and flirt. Flirt, admit it.* Instead, tonight he'll edit a few minutes of her from the village yesterday and B-gan it up; with her burned hitting the wires, it'll be bought quick.

And he'll film this humvee now about to cross through the water, then he'll go down, outside the gate and get a low-angle shot of the last two, that Mrap and that hummer when they leave their blocking positions and bring up the tail, he'll get them coming at him then reverse angle and get them going into the entrance, focusing for sure on that sign.

The welded steel sign above the gate. **COP VALLEY FORGE**. Below it a plywood sign stenciled with a faded spray-painted **TALIBAN WELCOME – OPEN 24/7**. Hand-scrawled on it, **COME ON IN & GET YOUR VIRGINS!**

He's gotta edit that spray-painted sign into something sometime somewhere, it's gotta get out there, that's the shit the world's gotta see.

The dudes at NYU, *They think GIs are dumb stupid hick Cro-Magnum Man and wouldn't believe their gallows humor, man, some of these GIs could be writing for John Stewart. Writing for The Simpsons and Family Guy.*

Nick Flowers has been here at Valley Forge for about three weeks.

You gotta be someplace.

Bounce around from Cop to Cop, hope to get one that's hot, get the money footage.

It's a crap shoot, like going out with 3rd Platoon today and not the Zoo. *You screwed that one royal, buddy.* Like his first week here, that morning, preferring rack time to making the 0530 patrol and thus missing the ambush, roadside bomb and bullets flying, and only making it out with the follow-on QRF—Quick Reaction Force—too late for anything but footage of the medevac birds. *You choose sleep, you lose, scoop. Mathew Brady never slept.* Today Nick Flowers doesn't feel very Mathew Bradyish.

From the first here he'd asked the guys how the Cop got its name, why Valley Forge? No one knew. It's just a name, a Cop's a Cop, winter's supposed to be pretty cold up here.

And a couple of days later a bunch of them were hanging around on the steps and benches in front of the Toc. Evening, after chow. Bullshit time. Various Zoosters, with a couple from the other two platoons.

"It wasn't named after Captain Washington?" he'd asked, meaning their Awesome Company commander here. "You know, George Washington? Valley Forge?"

Nope. It was named Valley Forge long before they got here.

"Most of the Cops are named after guys who got killed," Nick Flowers suggested.

"That's a load of one-hundred-percent crap," Ssgt Ketchum said. "I don't buy that shit. One guy's killed, he gets a Cop, the next guy, he gets chickenshit squat. You got so many dudes've bought it now, what it is, a couple thousand, what you gonna have, gonna have a Cop out here set up one every mile? Be like a 7/Eleven on every street corner."

Sniper Rodriquez laughed. "Name one Rodriquez, means I'm dead, and no thanks, I aint plannin on gettin dead."

Redcloud, "No one's naming one Rodriquez. No one can even spell it. They'll mix up the S and the Z."

Rodriquez, "Can't spell it right, no Cop Rodriquez means I aint dead."

Lieut Caufield, "They'll just misspell it on your cross in Arlington."

"You just don't you be spelling it wrong, L-T. It's a Z. You make sure you spell it with a Z on my Medal of Honor cite-tay-shun."

And Redcloud told Nick, "The company here before us said the winters can be pretty tough. Like Valley Forge. But last year, they said, last winter it was the 4th ID here and they said they didn't even get a foot of snow all winter. I guess we'll see in a couple weeks."

Lieut Caufield, "You going to stick around, Nick? Get exclusive footage. Stalingrad."

Ssgt Utah threw in, "Stalingrad was a siege, and you think I want to be under siege here in four foot of snow and Taliban all around? Repeat of Stalingrad, no way."

Nick, "The Russians won Stalingrad. They had the Germans under siege."

Utah, "Yeh, a couple million dead, if I remember. And I don't want to be one of those couple million."

Redcloud, "Taliban's not attacking in four feet of snow or one foot of snow. The first snowflake falling, they're heading back over the hills, they're gonna be spending winter in front of the fire in their compounds with their Paki Army buddies drinking chai. You want a shoot-em-up fight, Nicky, you're going to have to go down to Kandahar to find it. Or Helmand."

Ssgt Nell asked, "You been there, Nick? Kandahar?"

Nick Flowers shrugged. Smiled. "I've lost count. The last time, it was December, December through . . . around the beginning of May. Mostly in Helmand. With the Marines is Helmand."

Sniper Rodriquez, "Ese muchachos are crazy. Loco maximo."

Utah, "Naw, the USMC just think they can win this war, like it's Iwo Jima, Guadalcanal all rolled up into one. They're always brainwashed, right starting in Basic, they're brainwashed they're never going to lose."

Nick, "Crazy, you want to know crazy? They walk every day. Everywhere, every day. Taliban are planting, you know how they've got big roadside bombs here and everywhere else, like thirty pounds of fertilizer, five gallons of liquid ignition, 'cause they're going to blow up an Mrap? They're putting little toe-poppers down there. Every day a guy's blowing off his foot. "

"No shit?" from Ssgt Nell.

"Get this. One day the second guy gets it, takes off everything from the knee here down, zap, it's like vaporized, it's gone, there's nothing left. Other foot's just hanging by a thread. Medevac comes in, and that takes maybe forty minutes, you know how that is, initial hit to dust-off. Then off we go again, la-dee-da, we're going through these grape vines, these grape orchards they have there all over, and not more'n a couple hundred meters from the first, boom, point this time. It's the guy on point, and his boot and foot are twenty meters that way and he's got his thighs, all up here, like hamburger meat."

Ssgt Ketchum, "What about his nuts, he lose his nuts? Fuck with losin yer nuts, and that's fuck wit' a capital F. Fuck that."

A shrug then from Nick. "What some of the guys are doing, and this is for real, this is jarhead ingenuity. You know the shoulder flap?" Piece of armor turret gunners wear. "They're, some of the Marines, they're rigging it up here"—in the crotch—"like with hundred-mile-an-hour tape. A little extra protection for their family jewels."

Sniper Rodriquez, "Bullshit, you can't be putting it here, 'mano, how you gonna walk?"

"Hey they do it."

Nell, "Talk about chafing you. It's going to chafe you, you wanna talk about turning into hamburger meat."

Utah, "I'll take chafing to castration."

"Hooah," from Slurpee. "Negative on the castration."

Utah, "They wear it inside or outside their uniform?"

Nick, "Outside."

Lieut Caufield, "Did you wear one?"

Nope. "Walked behind the lieutenant all the time. Slowly. Putting my foot in his footprints every time. And prayed a lot."

Utah, "Our Father who art in heaven"—

Slurpee, "Hair Mary full of grace"—

Sniper Rodriquez, "La virgen Mary don't give a shit you lose yer nuts. Es la virgen, she likes it better you got no nuts."

Ketchum, "Yeh, Rodriquez, like you're ever gonna be runnin with the Virgin Mary. And if you did, like she's gonna listen to your bullshit bar talk pick-up bullshit. 'Lookin good tonight ma—ma—seet—taw.' With a capital Mama."

Nell, "'What's a hot chick like you doing in a place like this? Dig the lambs and shit you got.'"

A kid private from 3rd Platoon sitting at the end of one bench got bold enough to enter the conversation. "You seen them, Nick, have you seen guys who've lost everything? Y'know, his stuff."

Ssgt Ketchum, "Dipshit, you can't tell out there in the bush that kinda shit. Dude's got his leg blown off, yeh. Has took a 20-mike-mike to the face, yeh. You aint lookin down at his nuts. Or maybe you are, shitbird. And you aint gonna be feeling around the ground lookin for em. 'Less yer a dick sucker. You a dick sucker, you like lookin at a guy's dick? Picking up a guy's dick?"

Redcloud, "Leave it, Ketch, leave him alone."

Ketchum, "Hey, Sarge, I'm sayin, all I'm sayin. If he likes dick"—

"Drop it."

And Nick Flowers was fair to the kid, it didn't matter he was just a private and these were his first months in combat. "It's in the Cashes," he told him. "That's where you hear about it. In Jaf, that's J-bad, Jalalabad, in the Cash there, this is '07, '08 when the shit was really hitting the fan up in Kunar and guys were really taking a hit up in those mountain passes up there, you'd see the dude'd lost it, in surgery. And the nurses after, they'd talk about it, but all kinda like real quiet."

Rodriquez made a quick sign of the cross, "Padre, Hijo, Espiritu Santo. Dios les benediga."

Nell, "Poor sons of bitches."

Redcloud, "Not to change the subject here, men . . ." —

Ssgt Utah, "Roger that, change the subject, Sarge."

Redcloud, "The snow hits in December, Nicky, if you want the action stuff, I'd be headin back to Kandahar if I was you. We're just going to be sitting here, can't take the trucks out in a foot of snow, it's going to be dead here."

Utah, "Cross your fingers, Sarge."

Ketchum, "You stick around, Nicky, we'll get you action shit. We'll roll up, make snowmen out in the wadi, put on em, put mop heads on em for beards, put em in man jammies. On their heads wrap up cargo parachutes for tur-bines" —

Nell, "Tur-*bans*, Einstein."

"Tur-*bines*. Take turns in the towers, man, pa-pa-pa-pa-pa-pa, waste em on the 240s. You'll have a 'Cademy 'Ward winner there. Call it Zoosters Wasting Ragheads."

And the conversation would go on until the sky lost all its color completely and it got so dark that all you could see was a couple of the young privates' faces when they sucked in hard on their cigarettes. And the guys wandered off little by little. Some back into the Toc. Others over to their barracks. Or to check on the guys in the towers. Black-out in the Cop, the barracks and all buildings closed up, with light only coming in those few seconds guys would open doors coming or going.

That was back a few weeks ago when Nick Flowers had first come here, and if the guys knew the history of the name they'd have told him, and they'd tell him today too. If they knew.

But Cop Valley Forge became that a good three years before Big Army even thought to slot Awesome Company and its Zoo Platoon into the rotation into here.

Long before Nick Flowers back last month would first hear about this wicked-cool-named Tattoo Zoo Platoon stuck in the middle of nowhere in a place called Cop Valley Forge which a PAO sergeant at Bagram thought that no embed had ever even been to.

"What's so special about this Tattoo Zoo?" Nick had asked the guy. "Are they like a super platoon hunting and killing Taliban?"

"Like, how should I know?" the PAO guy admitted. "Name's cool though, isn't it? And they've got this gnarly tatt of it. I've seen the tatt, a friend posted it on his Facebook."

Nick figured it'd be worth it just to see this tatt for himself and, since one Cop was the same as any other and no one'd ever been to Valley Forge, maybe he could get something saleable, unique. Get a story out of this Tattoo Zoo. If only for the renegade moniker.

As for the history, how this Valley Forge got its name, it began mid-November way back those years ago when a company of the 25th Infantry, stateside based in Hawaii, on an operation scouting a location to set up a Cop to control this chunk of the Wild Wild West, stopped to overnight here in this semi-barren wasteland.

The company set up their thirty-odd humvees, in the pre-Mrap days, in a wagon-wheel circle protecting from the injuns that wouldn't show that night, and the battalion radioed that brigade thought it looked like the perfect location on the map and said to make it permanent.

That night out of nowhere from the mountains to the north a storm system came in that not even the weather geniuses up in Isaf Kabul and American-Two-Star-Regional-Command Bagram could see forming on their computer models and dropped thirty inches of snow before dawn then another twenty inches all that next day. And the men all huddled in their humvees, engines running, heaters cranked, and every last truck would run dry and every last guy was bone-aching teeth-chattering shivering until their Day Three when the skies cleared enough to get big Chinook helicopters in to slingload down fuel bladders, water, MREs and extra ammo and wool blankets, along with rolls of C-wire to uncoil out on the snow the best they could as a temporary defensive perimeter.

Defensive against what, who the hajj-hell knew, there weren't going to be any insurgent Taliban tromping around in waist-high snow, and if it was three feet deep here, it had to be another couple at least up in the mountain passes, which, who didn't know, wouldn't be passable.

Yeh, those same mountain passes that otherwise in pleasant weather like today are busy ratlines. Talib Interstates between Pakistan and here.

The next day back then the Chinooks dropped snow shovels and ten-man tents and bundles of cots. It took two days of screaming on the radio back to battalion that half the guys were bordering on emergency evac for frostbite and hypothermia—

a conex of the company's cold-weather gear, including winter sleeping bags, having been lost somewhere between the port of Karachi and Afghanistan

—for brigade to chopper in three pallets of brand new gear, enough for two companies.

The company's conex, when it would finally make it to brigade four months later, would be empty, cleaned out down to the bare walls and floor.

Not unusual. Not unexpected. The men had been advised back stateside, as they still are, that there was 30% loss between the port of Karachi and Afghanistan of all cargo shipped by sea.

Which is why all weapons, radios, crypto gear and classified computers were to be hand-carried over, and *"You're thinkin yer gonna pack away in the conexes your personal laptops, iPods, family photos and your wife's panties to sniff on those lonely nights—don't"* the guys were told. Leave it home or hand-carry it, *"Unless you want some Paki hajj owning it and trucking it home and jackin off into mama's panties every night."*

Up there in the 25th Inf company's white world of snow that year, it was a couple of weeks later, along with the regular food, fuel and water resupply, the Chinooks dropped a case of sunglasses eyepro for the guys who'd lost or broken theirs and were going snow blind.

A couple of days later a Chinook sling-loaded in on a pallet three port-a-potty outhouses with four oil-drum halves for changing out and burning the waste, and the guys celebrated like it was Christmas. Until they realized there was no toilet paper, not a single roll. They'd just have to keep using their tiny little TP packets from their MREs.

As it had been more than a week since the last guy ran out of the rolls they'd squirreled away in the trucks for the initial three- to four-day movement.

Their first sergeant offered no sympathy to the men's whining. "Suck it up, you're infantry," he growled at them and refused to radio-request real toilet paper, but they got six cases of Charmin with their next food, water, fuel resupply, and the very next day after, a Chinook sling-loaded in a mobile-trailer field kitchen, and the company cook went absolutely apeshit with exuberance.

It wasn't just Christmas for him, it was a week at Disneyland and lifetime infield tickets at Talladega.

A second chopper dropped off two pallets of K-Rats and a pallet of frozen meat, and the cook had half the guys offering to help him, everyone chomping for the first hot chow in almost a month.

Of course, they had no refrigerators or freezers for the meat, but the air temp hadn't gone above 28F since that first storm and the snow was still . . . . snow.

When the meat was gone, totally consumed in four days, they requested another pallet and the next day received two.

The first week in January a Chinook sling-loaded in a 30kw generator and dropped out of its tail two pallets of electrical wire and combat fluorescent-light-tube fixtures. The Blackhawk chopper that followed dropped off two Kellog Brown & Root (KBR) electricians and one KBR carpenter and their big steel toolboxes, and another Chinook came down low to hover and the crew chief and gunners tossed out twelve-foot-long 2x4's individually, and the guys down below had to scurry for cover behind the humvees as the 2x4's were caught in the rotorwash and flung insanely anywhere, endangering life and limb—without benefit of a combat-related Purple Heart.

A Blackhawk picked up the KBR guys two days later, and the camp was by then crisscrossed with orange electrical cords strung from 2x4 tripods resembling naked teepees. The orange cords all running into a big junction box planted next to the 30kw generator.

And the long winter nights in the tents and trucks were no longer pitch dark.

Every last guy came out of the tents and the trucks one day when two Chinooks came sling-loading and dropping off a 105 howitzer each. You could read *What the fuck?* on everyone's face. Then a third Chinook follow-ed in low, tail dipping twenty feet off the snow, and dropped sliding off the ramp three pallets of artillery rounds. *What the fuck?!*

A quick call up to higher got the battalion commander's reassurance that an artillery platoon was soon to follow.

Two weeks later and still no platoon. Another week and battalion had to concede the arty platoon was nixed for the near future and ordered the company to keep the tarps strapped down tight on the 105s' muzzles and elevation/transverse wheels and not to fuck with the guns. *Do Not Fuck With The Guns.*

Yeh, tell that to a GI.

To a GI far out of sight and out of mind of battalion.

It took another couple of weeks, the two guns, tarps cinched down tight, sitting where they'd been dropped, both barrels pointing up at the 60-degree angle the guys had elevated them to before the *Don't Fuck With* order came. Both pointing straight west. Immoveable big green steel twin barrels. Pointing to the sky nowhere. Motionless big steel twins.

And one of the guys, probably a pfc sitting warm-n-toasty in a humvee with the engine purring out heat, said to the first sergeant who was enjoying the truck's warmth along with him, both looking straight out the windshield at the twin howitzers—

the guy said something like, "Y'know, Top. Look at em. They look like hard-ons that are always hard. They can't come down, like they took, y'know, like they've OD'd on a fistful of Viagra. And there aint a wet snatch anywhere for a hundred miles they can stick it in and shoot off their loads."

"Yeh," the first sergeant probably said.

"They've gotta have blue balls, don't you think, Top?"

"Purple." And the first sergeant thought for a little bit more, then he got out of the humvee into the iced cold. And he told the pfc, "Round up the platoon sergeants."

Twenty years earlier as a private-E-nothing the first sergeant had spent about five minutes in the artillery and he couldn't tell you then or now about aiming stakes or level bubbles or transverse or any of that, but he knew how to load a round in the breech and how to pull the trigger lanyard, and that day here he and the captain double-checked the map for nothing but mountains and desert straight west, at least to the edge of the map, which, hell, had to be farther than the shells could reach.

That afternoon the company fucked with those guns, oh did they fuck with the guns.

Every last guy who wanted to got a chance to load at least one round and pull the lanyard.

And they fucked with the elevation, lowering the barrels straight out level to watch the rounds explode on those mountainsides just over there. And raising them nearly straight up vertical to see the rounds sail so high out of sight and watch and wait and see how close they'd land without actually coming straight down into the perimeter.

They shot anything. HE, high explosive. Willie Pete, white phosphorus. Flechette. Illumination parachute flare.

They were more than mid-way through the third pallet when battalion called in a panic that brigade was screaming that Isaf was apoplectic because satellite imagery was showing visuals and heat signatures of a massive bombardment in the AO and *"What's goin on there, you under indirect-fire attack?"*

"Gee whiz," the captain responded in his deceptive good-ole-boy Oklahoma cowhand radio voice. "Peaceful as a bug in a rug here. Must be pixie dust clouding the satellites again."

But they stopped firing. Repacked the remaining rounds. Let the guns cool then dropped the barrels level and retarped them.

And the battalion commander said nothing further, never mentioned it ever later, not even long after when they were back at home-station in Hawaii. But he knew better then. He knew. Not by firsthand evidence, but by instinct and experience he knew exactly what the company out there in No Man's Land had been doing.

Yeh, a good battalion commander knows that when a GI's far away from the flagpole and he's got nothing meaningful on his plate 24/7 he's going to fuck with the guns.

And you've gotta let him. Can't formally punish him for it.

That was back almost four years ago, and nobody has carried on or spread all those stories of the first months of this Cop and how it was born that winter.

Nobody wrote them down.

Those 25th Inf soldiers are long gone, separated to the four winds in the Army or out. Some of those guys have their snapshots from then, but they're snapshots—dudes goofing off for the camera, washed-out because of all the brightness reflected off the snow, forgotten mostly, in digital zeroes and ones on hard drives of long-unused laptops and on CDs and thumb drives tossed into a shoebox on a bottom shelf.

If Nick Flowers knew of those stories he'd kill to have been here with that 25th Inf company. Footage to kill for. To be in the back of that humvee with the pfc's face in darkened profile, Canon HD camera running focused out the windshields at the twin big green 105 barrels up pointing west, and then getting the dude saying for real, live on tape, *"They look like hard-ons that are always hard"*.

Lines to kill for. Gone, forgotten. Never for the world to know.

Lost in the past, like that winter of nothing but snow covering everything as far as the eye could see, when that beaten path road out there in the wadi didn't see a jingle truck or a Corolla or a camel or a passing nomad tribe and their sheep and goats until the melt-off the first week of March, when Big Army could start trucking in the lumber and tin and C-wire and bundles upon bundles of Hescos and bulldozers and Bobcat skiploaders and two platoons of Engineers to run the equipment and supervise the Afghan laborers trucked in to build the Cop.

By September that year when the 25th Inf company turned it over to a company from 10th Mountain, the Cop was done, as it is today. A functioning, purring home to a company-plus of American GIs and a company-minus of ANA.

But it was way back then that mid-November on their Day Two when the place got its name. When one of the guys, or several, or all of them — tropical soldiers from Hawaii, remember — sitting freezing in their trucks running dry of fuel and conking out — and Nick Flowers, if he knew, would today have his eyeteeth extracted to have been there and shot it, captured it forever, as the guy or a couple of the guys or a dozen of them all said, shivering, *"This is f-f-f-fricken like Valley Forge"*.

That first winter it was Valley Forge.

The difference being those resupply Chinooks that kept it alive.

Nick Flowers hops up onto the hood of Ssgt Ketchum's humvee to sit and ride in through the gate, and he raises his camera to catch the line of Zoo trucks crossing the chopper LZ ahead, and inside Ssgt Ketchum yells out at him joking, "No unauthorized pax, Nicky!"

Nick flips him the bird back without looking, and Ketchum tells Van Louse, "Shake him off, Louie," and Van Louse yanks the steering wheel back and forth, slaloming the truck in the deep quarry rock, and Nick can't shoot and has to hold on to the big D-ring lift points just to stay on.

With Van Louse grinning like a fool and Ketchum cackling, Nick yells back at them in mock rage, "I'm going to edit you out of every shot, Ketchum! And I was going to make you the hero!"

"Gun it. Harder, get him off," Ketchum tells Van Louse, returning the joke, but Louie sees that Nick is just barely hanging on and chooses to ignore Ketchum and slow down, quitting the slaloming.

From his turret, Pvt Finkle yells down to Nick, "I thought you were gonna make me the star of your movie?"

"If you don't accidently put a grenade through my head, Finkle," meaning the Mk19 aiming right over him, but Finkle had already taken the belt out and cleared the gun coming through the gate, and now he throws a loose unlinked grenade at Nick, who catches it. Sniffs it. Licks it. "Needs a little salt," and he tosses it high and Finkle snatches it out of the air. Pretends to lick it. "Tabasco sauce," he jokes back.

The Zoo is all inside the double-Hesco-walled Valley Forge. Home. Safe.

No IED can magically suddenly explode under their truck.

No enemy can pop RPGs down at them suddenly from steep mountainsides.

The stress is gone.

They can joke and play around.

The trucks pull up tight outside the Toc, and Nick hops off, as Redcloud is out and pulling off his Kevlar then stripping off his body armor, as all the turret gunners are doing.

Redcloud shouts to be heard—all the trucks with their windows now lowered: "You know the drill. Refuel, vehicle maintenance, check"—

—and the guys shout it back with him, *"check all fluid levels, restock ammo, MREs, water"*—it's the same thing every time.

Redcloud, "And then and only then do I want to catch you eating chow and taking a shower. And don't let me know one of you's in there on the internet. Understood, Zoo?"

A chorus of half-hearted *"Hooahs"*, and the trucks take off up for the fuel point.

Nick Flowers is surprised to see Wolfe here. "Sonovabitch, Kyle, I thought you'd be on the medevac bird with Robyn."

An angry look *don't-remind-me*. Wolfe tells him, "You shoulda been out there. Could have used that camera. Show the world the misogynist savages here we think we can turn into Renaissance Man."

"I'm sorry, dude. For Robyn."

Captain Jashawn Washington has stepped out of the Toc to join 1st Sgt Kozak and Lieut Frye.

"Captain," Wolfe calls over. "What's the word from Salerno?"

Capt Washington's expression doesn't change—blank. A slight rocking of his hands, so-so.

Wolfe, "I've got to get to Salerno, did you ask them for a chopper, to send a chopper to get me outta here, they sending a chopper?"

1st Sgt Kozak answers. "They said no, Kyle."

"Did you ask them? Did they go through the regional manager there on Salerno?"

"They said no."

Capt Washington looks directly at Lieut Caufield and Redcloud.

The first words now from Washington.

Simple, emotionless.

With just a trace of command.

"Take a piss and a shit, get cleaned up, get something to drink. Then let's go over your eventful day."

With a touch of light irony in that *eventful*.

Forward Operations Base Salerno

The C-130 Air Evac landed almost an hour ago, swung its tail around on the tarmac, lowered the ramp and kept the four props turning fast, the doctors and med personnel aboard in back ready to accept Robyn Banks, at which time the crew chief would button it back up and the plane would take off.

Ten minutes on the ground max, they figured.

They had been sent to pick up two critical evac pax—both burn victims, Robyn and her terp Gulbarhar—but mid-flight they'd gotten word that the terp had died in the Cash.

He'd been anesthetized to near-coma, stabilized on breathing life-support and fluids, and suddenly the *beep beep beep* of the monitor just stopped.

The staff shocked him *"Clear!"* once, and nothing. Again, *"Clear!"*, and nothing. And again and again and again, nothing. And the trauma surgeon said aloud, "It's better," and quit, and he thought, *Induced near-coma and Afghans still know, they know when to give up the ghost, give it up to their Allah.*

Just outside the Cash trauma entrance, across the way, is the small graves registration morgue B-hut, and that's where Gulbarhar's body was carried on a simple litter.

Earlier, as the medevac Blackhawk helicopter had been leaving Wajma Valley, the pilots had called back the status of the dustoff patients. Seriously wounded, five.

One, female, Hotel Tango Tango. That's HTT.

One, male, Afghan local national, contract terp.

Two, ANA.

One, enemy combatant.

No mention of the two Afghan soldiers KIA left in the village.

The announcement had gone out immediately on the loudspeakers all over huge Fob Salerno: *"Trauma Black. Trauma Black."* Meaning, inbound four or more wounded. Meaning, all medical personnel—whether showering, sleeping, in the Dfac, in the gym, hanging at the basketball courts—to report immediately to the Cash.

When the medevac bird arrived, they were ready on the chopper pad and in the Cash.

Call it prejudice or favoritism—or American tribalism—Robyn was brought in first and immediately set upon by the ranking surgeon and ranking nurses. Blood-typed within minutes, she was the extremely rare AB Negative, and the call went out over the Fob's loudspeakers for it, and, from a lite colonel down to privates, men and women dropped everything and sprinted over to the Cash to line up to give, twenty-deep.

It hadn't been announced that it was for Robyn or an American, just *"Blood units AB Negative needed asap at the Cash"*.

Robyn was stabilized, near-comatized, on breathing and fluids, and they had quickly stripped her of what was left of her uniform, salved her and bandaged her, the surgeon admiring that the medic out there in the hills had done a pretty good job of initial first aid for the filthy field environment he had to be working in. *She's got a chance*, the surgeon thought. *Air Evac's on the way, if we can get her to Landstuhl tonight and Brooke burn unit within twenty-four hours, she's got a damn good chance.*

Word was relayed that the C-130 was five minutes out, the surgeon himself now carrying the portable life-support machine alongside out the doors where on the street they'd get her into the waiting ambulance, surgeon and nurse climbing in with her, then zip the quarter-mile over to the tarmac and then get her out of the ambulance and onto the plane.

On the concrete walkway, ten feet from the open rear doors of the ambulance is when the machine stopped going *beep beep beep*.

On the tarmac the pilots shut down the engines of the C-130.

In the Cash some of the female staff who'd showed no emotion while treating Robyn and the ANA just minutes ago now openly broke down, allowed some tears to flow. In these short weeks on the Fob, Robyn had lived with them in their barracks. Worked out in the gym with them, ate in the Dfac with them, drank iced-coffees in the Green Beans with them, watched DVD chick-flicks with them, talked late into the night with them.

Nobody didn't like Robyn.

Some in the Cash who were still treating the ANA had to pause, close their eyes for a moment, try to hold back the emotion, hold back even a single tear.

They carried Robyn on that litter straight over to the little graves registration morgue B-hut across the way.

The brigade commander, who also commands the Fob, was informed, and he discarded regs and normal procedures and ordered a *Fallen Comrade*, which until now had only been used for military dead.

It was announced solemnly on the loudspeakers: *"Attention on the Fob. Attention on the Fob. Fallen Comrade. Thirty minutes."*

Everybody who wasn't doing anything vital—soldiers, contract civilians, it didn't matter—started making their way over to the hospital, walking if close, in trucks and Gators if farther across the Fob.

Two ranks formed starting from the morgue, one on each side of the walkway and wound down to the street, one rank on each edge of the thin asphalt, and turned at the next street and went about halfway to the airfield fence at the edge of the tarmac where the silent C-130 sat.

Soldiers, male and female, civilian contractors, about arm's length apart, all standing facing in, rank facing rank, motionless and silent. And when someone would join, they'd shift a little to make room. There'd be a whisper, *"Who is it?"*   And a hushed answer, *"Civilian. Human Terrain Team. Anthropologist. Female."*

In front of the morgue the only movement was the PAO sergeant getting position with his video camera. As ordered earlier by Col Pluma's staff from Isaf Kabul, he'd made it in time to get the medevac Blackhawk arriving and them pulling Robyn's litter off, and he'd hurried, following them into the Cash and filmed freely in there. Now he figured to get the *Fallen Comrade*, that always made for emotional film, and he would DVD an extra copy and get it to the HTT director to send to the poor dead lady's family in the states.

At forty minutes the morgue doors opened from the inside and the first to emerge was the brigade chaplain, a solemn hard expression, cross held tight against his chest.

Next, the HTT regional director, Robyn's and Wolfe's boss.

Then Robyn's litter, carried by a strac, creased-uniformed soldier on each of the four handles. Hard emotionless expressions of profound serious purpose. Respect. American flag draped over the small bulge that was the unseen black body bag beneath.

The first few of each Fallen Comrade rank snapped to a salute, and as the litter was carried down between the ranks, those abreast snapped to a salute, to hold the salute a bit longer even after Robyn had passed, and on each side the salute was like a slow wave moving Robyn on the first leg of her final journey home, to the end of the ranks, pointing straight ahead to the airfield's edge.

Along the route, of the six hundred-plus in the ranks, those few who knew Robyn personally openly broke down, and their tears became infectious to some few others who, though they did not know Robyn, grieved now for those grieving.

The PAO sergeant sprinted out across the tarmac to get position to film the chaplain and the director leading the four soldiers and the litter alone across toward him, and as they came abreast he panned close in on the flag over the body and turned to film them heading toward the open rear of the C-130 where the brigade commander and brigade sergeant major were standing as lone tribunates at the foot of the ramp. The PAO sergeant zoomed in as the brigade commander and the sergeant major snapped a salute and held it as the bearer soldiers handed the litter off to the Air Force medics on the ramp, and then Robyn's flag-draped body disappeared into the darkness in there.

The colonel, sergeant major, chaplain, director and the four soldiers marched back toward the fenceline, and the C-130 ramp was pulled up tight, closing the airplane. The first of the four engines and props then kicked over, loud, with a burst of black exhaust.

The two ranks that had lined the way had completely dispersed, with the people going back to their work, whatever they'd been doing before.

The PAO sergeant stayed just inside the fenceline to film the plane taxiing then taking off, which he figured to edit in as the final ten seconds of the memorial video the family would keepsake.

Right now at this moment back in the Cash the trauma receiving area is mostly cleaned up and back in order. All the bloody linen and bandages that littered the gurneys and floor are gone.

A pfc med specialist is mopping the floor.

Another is restocking the shelves.

Behind the blood-typing counter two female specialists are watching *27 Dresses* on a portable DVD player. Neither one laughing, reacting. Just watching. Looking blankly at the small screen. Numbed.

Through the doors into the OR a surgical team is at work at each of the two stations. An ANA wounded on one. The gas thrower on the other, where they're mid-surgery.

A colonel comes in, holding a surgical mask over his face. The hospital commander. He asks in a whisper, "The insurgent?" A nurse points out the gas thrower. The hospital commander goes over there. He quietly tells the surgeon, "He's the one who set Robyn afire."

"What did you want me to do?"

Nothing, no response or emotion from the commander.

What could they do, pull the plug?

Down the corridor in the ICU the staff are silent, either at the monitors at the nurses island or tending to the few patients.

An xray tech Air Force sergeant walks the long corridor, and she remembers it couldn't have been more than three or four nights ago, in the USO with Robyn playing ping-pong, both terrible and both laughing at their terribleness, and Robyn saying she hadn't played since she was a kid. Robyn told her then that she was going out to Cop Valley Forge the next day, and the tech had joked, she remembers, *"Oooh ooooh, nothing but a bunch of horny soldiers."* And Robyn had replied lightheartedly, *"Naw, not really, no more than guys anywhere."*

The tech now enters the break/dining/kitchen room.

She pulls a honeybun from the basket on the counter. Strips it out of its cellophane wrapper, puts it on a paper napkin and into the microwave.

20 seconds, and she stares at it turning, and *bing*, done, and she remains staring, remembering telling Robyn, *"Yeh but, those trigger-pullers, hooah hooah, testosterone raging through the roof, who knows what they'd do if it weren't for Kyle there with you."* And Robyn had demurred, rejected that. *"It's just the opposite. It's maybe even better on those Cops, compared to here. It's their home, and they're family, close-knit, and you're their guest. They won't harm a guest. Not in their home."*

And the tech now pulls the honeybun out of the microwave.

A captain who's hit on her before and she doesn't like has entered and says to her, "Hey Jeanette. Aw c'mon, cheer up, wipe that black cloud off your face, you can't save em all. Win some, you lose some, life goes on."

And she throws the honeybun at him with all her might.

Combat Outpost Valley Forge

Kyle Wolfe is sitting on the concrete roof of the Toc, in one of the half-dozen fold-up nylon-fabric/aluminum-tube sport chairs scattered around up here.

The only other person here is Doc Eberly, in a sport chair away from Wolfe, reading now a different book from before earlier today.

Wolfe's got his feet up on the low lip ledge that circles the roof.

Facing southwest and the sun that's getting bigger and more orange by the minute as it sinks toward the cragged dark outline of the hills way out there.

He's doing nothing.

Staring out. His hands listless and numb-still on his M4 on his lap.

If you look closely you can see his chest rise ever so slightly in breath, a long interval between them, a heartbeat slowed way down to just above 20/minute.

He knows Eastern meditation, his first wife was into it and he learned it but could never completely wipe his mind clear the way they say you're supposed to. He can slow his pulse—*breathe in so slowly, hold it, breathe out slowly, repeat, repeat, repeat*—but he can never forget that he's he, can never escape the self-consciousness, can never leave himself completely. He may not see the sun right now directly, or may be seeing right through it, but he feels its remaining warmth on him, senses its slow movement away from him as it's falling down toward the horizon to what he clearly visualizes as a black night that will soon enough enclose him and wrap him in its own secure soulless vacuum.

At about the same time that on Fob Salerno the soldiers of the twin Fallen Comrade ranks were saluting Robyn's body carried past, the Zoo

Platoon had just arrived here and Wolfe heard twice from 1st Sgt Kozak that no, they weren't sending a chopper for him.

"Like hell they're not," Wolfe had said then and stepped up and asked Captain Washington calmly, "Can I get on your Sipper video link, please, can I, sir?"

A nod from Washington, and Wolfe followed him into the Toc, and the captain set him up on his secure link back to Fob Salerno, but Wolfe couldn't get the director or anyone in the office to click open, and he tried message-texting to buddies on Sal but all those non-secure connections were shut down, as brigades do immediately following KIAs.

Try and try, and after about fifty minutes his director came up on the video link.

"Kyle . . . ." is all the director said.

"I need you to get me a chopper, sir, I need to get over there, please, sir. How is she, what's her status?"

There was a pause and just a slight grimace in the director. Then, "We just put her on a plane."

"Good, I can meet her in Bagram and be with her on the flight to Landstuhl. I need a chopper out of here, sir, I'm going to need it asap."

"Fallen Comrade plane." The director let that sit. "I'm sorry, Kyle. Gulbarhar didn't make it either."

And Wolfe had held his stare on the screen for a few moments, then he'd clicked it off.

Capt Washington, Redcloud, Lieut Caufield, 1st Sgt Kozak, Lieut Frye and the couple of Toc sergeants had heard it. Saw it. Said nothing.

The room remained quiet.

And Wolfe stood up from the table, met Capt Washington's eyes, nodded a *Thanks* and then left.

It was then that the intel sergeant had said, "Battalion message board says brigade's reporting the Cash says she was burned over eighty percent of her body. Eighty percent."

1st Sgt Kozak, "Only the good die young."

Redcloud, "That leaves me out. Thanks, Top, I owe you. Boy Scout here," he'd lightly smacked Lieut Caufield on the shoulder. "It means, L-T, you're gonna hafta be extra careful. Wear double IBA." Body armor. "At the very least, double up on your ceramic plates."

Caufield, "I'll be safe if I just stay next to you all the time, Travis."

Lieut Mike Frye threw in, "Yeh, the bullets will go around Travis and hit you, Matt. It'll be like *The Matrix*, remember, in slow motion the bullets going and curving. Are you going to practice jumping, Matt? In slow motion, bending backwards a hundred-eighty degrees?"

And Capt Washington had moved to the front where one big flatscreen showed the map of his company's area of operations, or AO, and he now motioned over Caufield and Redcloud. "Here, give me the highlights. Run me through it. You know battalion's going to be screaming for your AAR like five minutes ago."

Right now on the Toc roof Wolfe can hear laughter of guys down below hanging out in front on the benches.

It's some of the Zoosters telling guys from the 2nd and 3rd platoons about today.

It's war-story time down there.

Yeh, there's Rodriquez's voice. Rodriquez, Mister Sniper Sergeant. Has got the military's newest, best-est lightweight medium distance sniper rifle, the M110 Semi-Automatic Sniper System. Rifle's a thing of beauty, a work of art from Knight Armament. Accurate easy out to 800 meters, *And my guess is he doesn't have one kill, not one sniper kill all this time and thinks he's a sniper god. He's got the M110 and aint never plunked a guy in the head with it.* Talks mile-a-minute, Rodriquez does, non-stop. Always loud, Rodriquez is. *A voice like he's screaming on a stage. To an empty theater. Mister Bullshit Extraordinaire.*

Wolfe hears something about *"Had the mutha dude scoped crosshairs right on his back, center of back, 'tween the shoulders here, dead-on gonna cut him in two, and Sarge and the L-T they wouldn't let me take the shot."* And something about *"Marine Sarge Wolfie it took'd him five shots. But that's wit' the M4 worthless piece of shit carbine I aint gonna keep if it's give to me free. Had t'be three-hun'red, three-fifty meters and the chingado he was beatin feet rapido muy muy rapido."*

And Wolfe thinks, *Was it four shots or five shots?*

He can't remember.

With Rodriquez's Knight M110, at that close distance, it woulda been just one, *I could of put one right through his back, straight through his heart.*

Feels good he'd put those two shots there point-blank in the guy's groin. Regrets he was selfish in wanting the guy to bleed slowly to death, to suffer, to *Know for twenty minutes that he had no more dick and nuts* and even if he lived and managed to not bleed to death to know *He'd never stick the dick he didn't have anymore in his wives again after beating them just for the fun of beating them because that's what hajj raghead woman-hating misogynists do every night to their wives.* And Wolfe now knows his selfish pleasure was wrong and he should have put another shot through the guy's heart and another through his eye right then right there and they would have never medevacced him and then there'd have been room for him on the chopper to be with Robyn.

Room for him on the chopper with Robyn, that's why he was wrong. He should have been on that chopper. Been in the Cash with her.

Earlier, when he'd left the Toc after the video link with his director, Wolfe had walked across straight to Zoo's command barrack B-hut where he's bunked. Outside was Pfc Holloway with the hood up on the hummer doing his daily maintenance. The other Zoo trucks were alongside the three squad B-huts, all back from refueling, guys taking guns off their turret mounts, other guys doing maintenance, restocking ammo and rats and water.

Inside Zoo command hut Doc Eberly was repacking his med bag.

Rodriquez was stripping his sniper rifle, down to the trigger.

Spec Lee Tran had the .50-cal broken down, cleaning it.

Wolfe had pulled his laptop out of his big Marine Corps rucksack, sat on his bunk, opened up Notepad and began to type.

An hour or so later he was done.

He saved the document as *Letter Robyn Family* and copied the file onto a thumb drive.

He'd then walked back across to the Toc, but the eight internet computers were all taken by guys from the 2nd and 3rd and the artillery platoon, and the whiteboard outside the door had a dozen guys slotted in line ahead of him, and it would right then be 7:00 in the morning in Robyn's family's home in Maryland and her brother would soon be leaving for school and wouldn't get the email until later if Wolfe didn't send it now, so Wolfe went into the Op Center room and asked Capt Washington if he could use his secure email.

"Here, use mine, Kyle," the intel sergeant had invited him over.

It took Wolfe maybe a minute to open his email on the sergeant's workstation laptop, transfer the file and cut-and-paste it and send it.

He'd left the building, and outside the few guys hanging out around the steps all said their *"Sorry, Kyle"*, *"Real real sorry, dude"*, which he acknowledged with just nods and a shrug of *Aint life a bitch, huh?*

And he then went around to the side and climbed the ladder to the roof.

Pulled the chair he's in now to near the edge, sat and put his feet up on the ledge.

This is where he's been since.

The first week Robyn was with him he had received an email from her brother, who apologized for writing, saying that he was a senior in high school and his sister *Robyn gave me your email address and I hope you don't mind me writing this but Robyn says so many great things about you, that you're teaching her so much about war and combat. And I just want you to know that Robyn is the greatest big sister that a brother could ever ever ever ever ever have and I'm glad she has someone like you with so much experience because I cannot imagine if ever anything bad happened to her. I know my friends would laugh at me for saying this so I don't tell them but I love my big sister. Please keep her safe.*

Wolfe didn't write him back then. But he told Robyn about it and she'd laughed *"That's my brother. He's so sweet."* And he figured she'd probably emailed him and told him *Don't bother Kyle, he's got enough to do, and don't worry, I'm safe and sound, and everywhere I go everyone I'm with, I know they're always going out of their way to make sure your big sister can always write her brother back that she loves him very very much.*

The letter that Wolfe has just sent opened with an apology that he was even writing and that maybe this was inappropriate and for Robyn's brother to *Stop reading right now, go get your mother and father right now and you have them read this first. This is not good news. Go get them right now.*

Wolfe wrote that his civilian contract company or the military, if they hadn't already contacted them, they would probably in a few hours, and he hoped *It would be in person like they do for soldiers and not on the phone, and I'm sorry I have to tell you this in email but you're so far away and I can't be there and Robyn was my responsibility more than anyone else's and I feel it should be me who tells you before anyone else what happened and how it happened. I am telling you because I want you to know because no one else will tell you that your daughter died because I failed her. I failed in her trust in me.*

He told what happened.

In precise, stark unemotional detail.

In straight chronological order. From the start of the patrol, driving out the Cop's gate at 7:35 exactly, to the medevac liftoff.

To his learning of her dying in the Cash far away.

He wrote it in short, concise, declarative sentences.

Without judgment upon others.

He wrote that if *Robyn had been a man this would not have happened. But the Afghans are different than us.*

He wrote that *The two enemy combatants who did this are dead. They will never harm another woman. Another American.*

He wrote that he hoped that knowing that would bring Robyn's mom and dad *Some little comfort at least.*

He wrote that these past weeks *With your daughter have made me a better man. Not because I am a better man, because I'm not, I'm not a nice person, I'm not a kind person, I don't really care about other people. No one who knows me would say that I'm nice or kind. Robyn did. She said once, she told me that I tried to make people not like me. She called it macho posturing. Even if it wasn't, she said it didn't matter. I am not a better man today, but if a woman as good as your daughter and as opposite me as she was in her heart and soul, if she could judge me not for my serious flaws of character and my uncaring heart and even still like me and respect me and treat me as an equal in spite of how and who I am, then I think that maybe someday I can be a better man. I have had women fall in love with me and marry me and they have very fast unloved me and unmarried me and it wasn't their fault. In these just two months I have known Robyn I am lucky that I now know that she is a woman who if I ever become a better man that there are women like her in the world and that there can be one who even likes me and that's the one I know is worth committing to.*

Wolfe used *is* in that last sentence and did not notice it when he wrote the letter nor when he sent it off nor does he realize it now. *She is a woman.*

The sun has disappeared, leaving a red-purple-orange half-curtain across the jagged tops of those distant hills, and Wolfe realizes a tear streaks down one of his cheeks. He wipes it off with his palm. Again, harsher, to remove all wetness.

He stands, flicks the chair around.

Doc Eberly looks up from his paperback.

"What you reading there, Doc?"

Eberly shows him. *The 13th Valley.*

Wolfe, "Good one there, that is. The company goes into that valley, line dogs, right?, spends a couple weeks lookin for the NVA headquarters dug into tunnels. The dude, the platoon sergeant, what was his name? War's in his blood. Fighting is."

"Egan. Danny Egan."

"Yeh yeh, Egan, yeh. The other's that prick asshole Cherry."

"Don't tell me what happens."

"I won't spoil it. How far are you?"

Eberly shows him. About a quarter.

Wolfe, "I've got a collection of Vietnam books. At my dad's house. They're his actually, he's got every book ever written about 'Nam. There're great ones. You read *Chickenhawk*?"

No.

"Gotta read *Chickenhawk*. Huey pilot. *Rumor of War*, you read it?" No. "How about *Dispatches*, that is essential."

"I have that here. Haven't read it yet."

"I read it again just before coming over this time, just to sorta get the mindset set right. Military insanity. Like *Catch-22* on steroids. The first time I read it, like in the seventh grade and my dad said, 'Don't read that one,' so you know, that's the one you're gonna read. And I didn't get like but a tenth of it. The first time. There's *The Killing Zone* and *Aftermath*. The same guy, he's a platoon leader, fresh young LT and in *Killing Zone* it ends he steps through a hedgerow and steps on a mine and loses his legs. The second one, *Aftermath*, it's even better. How you gonna remember all this?"

Eberly taps his temple, he will, it's already being stored.

"*Fortunate Son*, put that up there. Chesty Puller, you know who Chesty was? Only the most decorated Marine ever, they still tell stories 'bout him in Boot. He's a saint, I mean The Saint of the Corps. This is his son. In Vietnam. Un-believable. Un-real. Wanna talk irony? Son of the most famous Marine of all time and he gets both legs blown off."

"*Fortunate Son*? Fortunate?"

"You gotta read it, you'll see. Chesty Puller, Google him."

"Have you read *Slow Walk in a Sad Rain*?"

"That what you were reading before?"

"About a Green Beret camp. The guys are really crazy, they go and get mixed up with the CIA in playing both ends. They go into Laos."

"Yeh yeh yeh yeh yeh," Wolfe remembers. "Wild, that is a wild--assed freak-out story. They, like, they're interrogating this beautiful Viet Cong gook chick—I mean, number 10 hot—and she won't talk, so they shove a high-pressure fire hose up her cunt and turn it on."

A funny look from Doc Eberly. Huh?

Wolfe realizes, "I got that wrong? *Slow Walk?* Different book? *Slow Walk, Slow Walk. . .*" Wracks his brain, then, "Gotcha. *Slow Walk,* that's a cobra in a Cobra. A cobra, that flared head, comin up between that pilot's legs in a Cobra. That is one awesome, awesome book. Yeh yeh yeh, a mind-blow. *Slow Walk in a Sad Rain.*"

"Shotgun. Spaghetti. Quiet Voice."

"Right, right! They put one of em, I don't remember which is which, who's who, the names. They put one of them up like Jesus on a cross."

Nods from Doc Eberly, that's the book. "What's the other one, the Green Berets with the VC girl?"

"Whore, she was a whore VC spy. She didn't talk either, if I remember."

"What's the name of the book?"

"Aw . . ." Wolfe can't think it. "It was aw . . . It was aw . . . Guy was a mechanic. Guy was a truck driver. Over there. I remember. He took a deuce-and-a-half supplying out to some Green Beret camp, that's where they were doing it, where he saw it. Blew his mind. Had nightmares. My dad's got every book. Like a whole wall in his den. He's read em each more'n me."

"Was he in Vietnam?"

Yeh. A chuckle. "Never saw combat, didn't even carry a gun, he says. He was drafted, had a couple years of college, community college, and could type, could wail on a typewriter, and's always been a good speller, cuz he's a reader, so they made him a personnel clerk and he spent his all twelve months there at Division in Da Nang."

"Never saw combat?"

Nope.

"In the Army?"

Yep.

"Marine Corps. Force Recon." Doc Eberly meaning Wolfe, his service. "Sounds like overcompensation to me."

"Funny, that's exactly what Robyn said."

"Like minds." And immediately Eberly wishes he hadn't said it. It's not fair, not fair to her, she wouldn't think of him that way, *She doesn't know a thing about me, she didn't know a thing about me.* He hadn't said a word on the entire slow ride out to Wajma this morning, listening hard to every word of hers as she answered Redcloud's questions about HTT and

Holloway's *Dumbass questions like "Gotta tell you, Robyn, why would a pretty chick like you want to be out here in this shithole?" She could laugh at that, even with Redcloud telling Holloway to think before he spoke, or keep his big pie hole shut or Redcloud will stuff it with a knuckle sandwich.*

And Robyn hadn't minded, said she didn't mind at all. Had answered that her whole life had been studying and it was time to get out and experience the real world. And besides, there weren't a lot of jobs for anthropologists, *"Unless you want to teach, and I don't see myself stuck in that cloister of academe."*

Like minds, Eberly thinks, and regrets he hadn't met her in college, how could he have met her in college?—*Don't be absurd, where'd she even go to school? Ask her go ahead and ask her, why are you afraid to ask her?*

And he hadn't, hadn't asked, hadn't said a thing to her, the same way he hadn't asked anyone during his own four years at Cornell and could come out the virgin that he went in, and it was only at that advanced medic course at Fort Sam Houston that he met Cindy working at that Subway and she was so friendly and open and inviting and accepting of him as just him, boring reader Doc Eberly, and he fell in love those few weeks, was so in love with this girl who opened the world of sensuality and sex to him and broke his heart because he did not want to go out on Friday and Saturday nights to the bars and clubs, he hated it and said he could not, and he'd rather stay in and just watch movies with her or read, and she'd laughed at first and thought it was *"So cute, you're so romantic."* But then soon enough she'd tease him that real life and fun an' stuff wasn't in books reading all the time, and she'd go out without him, she lusted to party, and her memory is sweet to him even now and he misses her but *She sure isn't any Dr Robyn PhD, she sure isn't,* and

Wolfe has pulled one of the chairs closer and plopped himself down and, "You, Doc, you'll appreciate this, being a corpsman," he's saying about another book. "Army nurse in an evac hospital. '68 or '69, the heaviest shit of the war. Lynda . . . something. *Home Before Morning.* Look— . . . . I still get, look"—he shows his hand, makes it shake. "Get a shiver just thinking about it. Okay, so you got, Number One, and this is no particular order, just Number One, *Fortunate Son.* Chesty's son. Number Two, *Home Before Morning.*"

Now Eberly knows he's not going to remember, so he starts jotting them down on the inside cover of his book.

"Number Three, *Dispatches,* but you've got that. Four, *Chickenhawk.* Five, *Killing Zone* and *Aftermath.* There's a Marine, Bing West, famous writer. His *The Village.* It's the Coin thing, in Vietnam never mind, all the way back to 'Nam, hearts and minds back then, and every limp-dick general before coming here should read it. Should be forced to read it. 'Cause guess what? Just guess."

"It doesn't work."

"Exact-tow-mundo. Didn't work then, doesn't work now. And oh, now this'll blow your mind. It's heroes, real heroes like we all think we wanna be if we were one of them, and you're dropped into Laos, just you and one other American and four or five indig 'Yards. Like, reconnin the Ho Chi Minh Trail. And five out of six LZs goin in, five out of six LZs are compromised and they're waiting on your frickin ass and you're running for your life from the time you hit the ground outta that chopper. *Sog*. John Plaster, and he was one of them. One who made it back. One of the very few. Write it down. John L Plaster."

"Sog?"

"Capital S, capital O, capital G, you'll see."

"How do you remember all these?"

"I can see em on my dad's shelves. In the exact order, and don't you now forget and put them back out of order. I borrow a couple at a time, you know, to read again otherwise you forget em. And Dad always says, he still always says, 'Don't forget now, bring them back.' Every time, 'Don't forget, bring em back.'"

Wolfe now laughs a little at the memory.

"I'm just starting to learn about Vietnam," Doc Eberly says. "And it was sure a lot worse than this. 1969, like you say, I think it was like over thirteen thousand KIA just that year alone. Thirteen thousand."

"Every war is better than the one before. In Vietnam they thought, 'Shit, I'm glad this sure isn't World War Two'. In World War Two they thought, 'Shit, I'm thankful this isn't in those damn trenches of Verdun in World War One'. Can you imagine being in like *Braveheart*? Two armies charging each other across the field and clobbering each other with swords and maces? If this was like 'Nam, I'd of been dead a long time ago."

"You've read all those books, are you going to write one about this?"

Wolfe laughs. "Me? Write a book? I can't put two sentences in a row together that make sense. Wouldn't know where to even start."

"It was a dark and stormy night."

"You're exactly right, that's exactly how lame I'd be. The perfect book, six words. 'He came. He saw. He conquered.' I know you've heard what they say: 'Those who can, do. Those who can't, teach.' How about, 'Those who fight, fight. Those who can't, write.' Whoa, profound, dude, if I must say so myself. Look, I'm a poet and don't even know it. You know who said that, right? I'm a poet 'n don't even know it?"

Doc Eberly doesn't.

"Google it. Will surprise the shit outta you."

"Who? Do I know him, know of him?"

"Should. Google. Or Wikipedia. If I tell you, it's not the same, it won't stick. And you want ironic? Talking about 'Nam. He, it just so happened — he refused to be drafted and go to Vietnam, didn't skip out to Canada either. And did a couple of years in prison for it."

"Who? C'mon, who?"

"That's what Google's for."

Eberly asks, to etch it in memory, "I'm a poet and don't even know it?"

Bingo.

Down below in the Op Center, Redcloud comes in with two paper plates wrapped up in foil and a couple of cans of Mt Dew. Dinner for Lieut Caufield at his laptop.

"Not done yet, L-T?" Redcloud asks.

Meaning the After Action Report.

AAR.

Only a couple of other guys in here now.

Executive Officer (XO) Lieut Frye on personal email chat with his wife.

The intel sergeant at his laptop scrolling through Isaf random message traffic intel updates.

The pfc on radio-watch duty reading a gamer magazine in the signal corner with the five different radios stacked and a little flatscreen showing in rotation the four angles, 360 degrees of the cop, from the video cameras mounted on a twenty-foot mast atop on the roof above here.

And the artillery platoon leader at his laptop station doing Sudoku in a book in pen.

Lowered voice to Redcloud setting down the food, so the others won't hear, Caufield asks, "What about B – D – A?"

Remember, that's Battle Damage Assessment.

"Don't never give them nuthin to hang you on," Redcloud says. "You want to knot up your hangman's noose for them too? What have you got there, what'd you write? Don't even say BDA. Write, something, say, all you wanna say, 'The school building was totally consumed in smoke and flames and exploding ammo and we couldn't safely approach it without risking the lives of our men, and they started shooting rockets from up in the ville and we left.' Zipppp, what they don't know. . . ."

He pulls the foil from the plates. "I brought you one of each. Because I know, Lieutenant, you are a meat man."

One plate, beef slices in gravy with mashed potatoes and green beans and a stack of white bread slices. The second, two fat bratwursts, mashed potatoes and broccoli and a couple of toasted hotdog buns.

Redcloud pulls from his pocket and dumps out a bunch of mustard, mayo and catsup packets.

The Cop's Dfac is two B-huts side-by-side with a covered raised walkway between them coming from impromptu doors cut into their flanks.

That original mobile mess trailer from the first winter is long gone, probably scrap somewhere on Fob Salerno.

The first hut is the kitchen/serving line. The other has long plastic portable tables and metal fold-up chairs for eating, along with a back wall of coolers for drinks.

Permanently parked outside on the other side of the kitchen hut is a 40-foot reefer van. They all just call it "The Freezer". Its big fridge unit runs non-stop, sucking up diesel from a 55-gallon drum that nobody forgets to keep filled every day. The entire van, except for the fridge unit and the big doors, is skinned with two layers of sandbags, ground to roof and that too, with a wood/tin roof built over the length for cooling summer shade.

The Dfac means hot meals twice a day. Breakfast and dinner.

Big Army sends companies out to live on these Cops in the middle of this Afghan wasteland for twelve-month stretches, but they know the value of decent food on a GI's morale in that length of time, and they prioritize keeping that reefer van stocked, down to lobster and ice cream, and they send in by local jingle truck fresh veggies and fruit when possible.

Still, the Cops' menus can't begin to match those of the big Fobs and their KBR Dfacs that beat hands-down any big stateside post's and rival the best Ryan's and Golden Corrals. Easily.

There is not a GI on Valley Forge who isn't grateful for their two cooks' effort to put out two good hot meals a day, varying the menu, spicing up the food, barbecuing the brats tonight.

Not one would say about the meals, *"I guess it beats a MRE."*

Hell-yeh it beats an MRE.

By miles.

It's not a story much repeated or remembered anymore, and only 1st Sgt Kozak and a couple of others in the Toc that afternoon three months ago actually witnessed it, when head cook Ssgt Yglesias had just arrived, having been sent down from brigade at Salerno from his get-over job in the KBR Dfac there because he'd told the contract civilian KBR manager he didn't work breakfasts or get up before eight. Not ten minutes here at Valley Forge, Yglesias was pissed to the max to be in this outback hellhole a thousand miles from the chicks and the PX and the gym and the volleyball courts and the Green Beans and the USO and the only danger the seldom random rocket round that hasn't hurt a soul on huge Salerno since who-knows-when.

Not ten minutes, mind you, and Ssgt Yglesias made it clear, no words minced, right out loud through gritted teeth in the Toc to anyone and everyone, with Captain Jashawn Washington right there close at his workstation, that, cool, if they here at this Awesome Company wouldn't call in a chopper and send him straight on back to Salerno, it sure would be a mother trying to prove there wasn't now spit and piss and jack-off spume in the food, now wouldn't that be a pisser, huh, how about that? Cool, huh?

1st Sgt Kozak was there when Yglesias said all that, and he'd have taken him by the collar and smashed his head against the door jamb then kicked him in the ribs when he fell unconscious to the floor.

But he saw Capt Washington wince then just close up whatever battalion messaging he'd been reading on his laptop. Washington stood up out of his chair, folded his arms across his chest. Looked Yglesias in the eye. Told him quietly, "I'm going to let you walk that back, Staff Sergeant. Start fresh on a new foot. Pretend the last five minutes never happened. Go back in time. You don't have to go outside the wire. You don't have to man the guard towers. You will feed my men who do in the same manner with the same professionalism that you expect them to protect you when they're in those guard towers and outside the wire. If that doesn't suit you, I've got no problem with that. But you're mine for the next eleven months—mine, and you're going to stay mine. Get comfortable because this Cop is now your home away from home. If you would rather not cook, we can work that out. I've got any number of men here who would prefer staying back on the Cop as permanent cook. I can put you in a truck, on a gun right now. Your choice, Sergeant. Sleep on it. Breakfast here is 0630 to 0800."

That was three months ago.

Wolfe is in here in the Dfac now.

Doc Eberly is filling his own plate, but Wolfe is admiring the spread. "Brats with charred stripes on them, 'Lesias? Not boiled?"

Yglesias, "Yes, we boiled them first."

"I know, but you went to the trouble of putting them on the grill, they've got stripes, they're supposed to have stripes, do you know how many Cops, on how many Cops they do that? You know how many Cops I've been on? I've seen it all, believe me, it all. And nothing like this. Look, the broccoli it's not all soaking in water, it's not all just soggy, you've got melted cheese. You know how many Cops they put the broccoli in the oven with melted cheese? You're Number One, 'Lesias. Number One. Whoa, toasted brat buns? Toasted?"

A shrug from Yglesias, of course toasted, they've gotta be toasted.

Wolfe plops two open buns onto his plate. A brat now on each. "You know, if this is the last hot meal I eat, I'll die a happy man."

Yglesias and his spec-4 junior lay out two hots a day in the Dfac, and that's not just warming up Army standard rats and setting them out, it's actual cooking.

And the men know it, and if they complain about anything, nitpick anything, it's because a GI aint happy if he aint complaining. A GI would whine if he were hung with a new rope. Give him a million bucks, and he's going to ask, can't he have it in smaller bills. Give him a night with all the Kardashian sisters, and he's going to want the mom too and ask how come he can't have her and the pretty Latina housekeeper together, y'know, a threesome.

Nothing to complain about the mess at Valley Forge. Nothing that anyone takes you seriously about.

Make a mental note, in case you're wondering: The Dfac is off-limits to the ANA and the Afghan day laborers.

Do Not Enter.

Except for the terps, it's a privilege that sets them apart, and they eat most of their meals here.

The ANA have their own kitchen B-hut in their section. You wouldn't want to enter it. Even just to walk through. Tread carefully.

Weekly Capt Washington has to politely beg off entreaties from the ANA captain for food to feed his men, if only beans, rice and a little meat. *Oh and some bread too please. The white bread if you can.*

But Capt Washington is no fool. He had a company here in the Stan two years ago in Zabul, and he knows the drill. The US provides the Afghan Army with tens of millions of dollars to buy food for its soldiers, and those tens of millions go dribbling into pockets from the top down, until the companies are left with little.

"I am very sorry," Washington calmly explains time after time to the ANA captain. "My brigade provides me food for my men. Your brigade is to provide your food for your men. I would suggest that you should bring your concerns up with them."

Both Dfac huts and The Freezer are kept under thick padlock and chain when not in use.

That's Coin hearts-and-minds Valley Forge-style.

In case you're wondering.

As Wolfe follows Doc Eberly outside from the kitchen hut to the dining one, the eastern sky over the close mountains is nearly jet black, and the western sky has lost all its orange and is a gray quickly turning darker.

The chill is coming in.

The temp today topped in the mid 80s, but there's little to hold the heat here, and it's dropping now.

And the 2nd Platoon guys moving out to rotate into the guard towers know to bring along their Army fleece jackets.

Day One, Night

Cop Valley Forge

Nightly at about 20:30 on Valley Forge is the daily Cub.

Commander's Update Briefing.

Capt Washington and his company staff, along with the platoon leaders and platoon sergeants, artillery included.

Wolfe and Nick Flowers here tonight as well, standing in the back.

No Afghans. Do Not Enter.

Why?

Duh.

After the Cub, Lieut Frye's job will be to round up a terp and go brief the ANA. How many squads to prep for tomorrow's patrols whose destinations will not be shared with them. No use giving the bad guys twelve hours lead time in setting in their IEDs and/or ambushes by allowing the insurgent infiltrator or two in the ANA here a chance to get on their walkie-talkies and relay tomorrow's destinations to their buddies somewhere out there nearby.

The daily Cub is an info briefing, commander on down and vice versa. It's the Cop status report: personnel, matériel, activities.

"Down to ten day's bottled water," tonight from the supply sergeant. "This is my second Emergency Request and battalion says they're tracking it, but that's what they've been saying for a week now."

Capt Washington, "The minute we're down to seven day's I want to know. We'll shut down all external operations."

Someone, "Battalion's gonna have a shit-fit."

Someone else, "A shit-fit plus one."

Another, "I'll drink to that."

Laughter.

Redcloud, "Not for long you won't."

More laughter.

The daily Cub is a quick review of the day's activities. Patrols, events on the Cop, any issues. It's a more detailed outline of tomorrow's ops and an overlay view of the near and far future's.

Tonight, about tomorrow's ops, Capt Washington informs Lieut Paxton of 3rd Platoon, "You'll take the HTT patrol to Qazat Khel. Make it a 0720 ETD. Kyle, that work for you?"

Big thumbs-down from Wolfe. "What's the purpose, I don't see a reason. Unless you order me to go, Captain."

"It doesn't matter to me, HTT's your traveling road show. If they want my opinion, one village is the same as another."

Someone, "They're all friendly."

Laughter.

Wolfe, "Can I quote you on that, Captain. To General St Claire, one ville's the same as the next?"

Again light laughter.

Washington, "Quote me and I'll move you over to the ANA barracks and have the first sergeant there put you on permanent KP over there."

Exaggerated groans throughout.

Washington continues. "It's your decision about Qazat Khel. I'm not the one who has to answer to your boss."

Redcloud, "Either does Wolfie, Captain."

More laughter.

Wolfe thumbs-up Redcloud, *You said it man.*

Wolfe now to Capt Washington, "If it's alright with you I'll just stick around and wait on the next bird."

1st Sgt Kozak, "Could be a week, Kyle. Two weeks."

No difference to Wolfe.

Someone, "It could be spring."

Wolfe, "With your chow hall here it might be worth it. Sarge 'Lesias, he's the man."

"You got that right" and "Roger that" from guys, and, standing over against the wall by the door, Yglesias beams.

Washington tells 3rd Platoon they'll go to Qazat Khel anyway, HTT doesn't matter, they'll take a couple of boxes of HA.

That's not the ha ha ha laughter HA.

Just the opposite. It's Humanitarian Assistance.

As in, blankets, kids' clothes, tea kettles, sacks of rice, beans, cases of cooking oil.

Lieut Frye jokes, "And if they don't tell you who they are, those right there in the village, which ones are the insurgents—if they don't tell you, you pack it all back in the boxes and bring it all back."

Someone, "Might as well not even go then."

Redcloud, "Save the diesel."

Someone else, "It's not worth the risk of IEDs."

General agreement, might as well stay on the Cop, for what intel they're going to get about the Taliban.

Yeh, but everyone knows without Capt Washington even having to say it that 3rd will do HA to Qazat Khel tomorrow anyway, 'cause it's doing something, which looks good on battalion's update to brigade and brigade's to regional command and regional command's to Isaf.

Get the men outside the wire, the men out on patrol, the more the better, and on highers' stat reports those patrols become "Kinetic Operations", which up in the Pentagon translates to "Controlling the Battle Environment", which impresses the hell out of the White House.

Yep, 'cause the war's being won.

America winning is good news, and good news is no news.

So 3rd's going to Qazat Khel tomorrow, and Capt Washington assigns to 2nd Platoon the other patrol, up a wadi he traces on the map. "G-2 says they've got drones seeing lots of movement the past couple of weeks along all these ridgelines here and running down. Battalion wants it checked out."

Zoo Platoon will have Cop security tomorrow. Guard tower and radio watch rotations. A couple of guys supervising the day laborers in Cop clean-up, trash- and shit-burning, filling sandbags.

Capt Washington ends everything by asking Nick Flowers, "Who do you want to go out with tomorrow, 2nd or 3rd, pick your poison."

"Oh yeh, like I know how to pick, I'm so good at picking, I batted zero today. Which one of you's got more promise of some action?"

"I hope neither," from 1st Sgt Kozak. "Be careful what you wish for, Nicky."

Washington tells 3rd Platoon's Lieut Paxton, "Save Nick a seat. H-A's always good to show Big Army winning hearts and minds."

Nick, "Best stuff's when the mobs tear into those boxes, fists fly. I've got two grown men, gray beards, on tape, I forget where, fighting over one little kid's shoe. A four-year-old's sneaker with, y'know, the light that blinks in the back every time they step on it. Old men, gray beards down to here, throwing punches. And what are they gonna do with just one shoe anyway?"

Someone, "Their kid's probably got just one leg. Lost the other in a land mine, an old one left by the Russians."

Agreement, light chuckles.

Briefing over, the Cub breaks up, guys joking about their own HA stories here and there from wherever, and Capt Washington gets a *ping* from battalion on his workstation laptop and asks, "Men, men, a little quiet."

"At ease everyone!!!" from 1st Sgt Kozak, and the whole place goes silent. Most leave.

Over at the coffeepot Redcloud pours himself a cup. Another for Wolfe.

"Y'know," he tells Wolfe in a half whisper, "since you're sticking around on the Cop, you get bored at all, I can have my squad leaders add you to the tower-guard roster."

"Been there. Done that. Burned the tee-shirt. Shit, bad choice of words."

1st Sgt Kozak advises, "The Blue Ring Route's supposed to be Tuesday. But you know how the choppers go."

Wolfe agrees. "The brigade commander decides he wants a photo op somewhere in Timbuktu opening some National Police checkpoint that's going to be overrun in two weeks anyway, there goes all the available choppers for that day."

Redcloud, "Priorities, Wolfie, gotta have your priorities. Full-bird command is all about knowing the proper priorities. Which is why they're full birds."

Wolfe, "What, as opposed to partial birds?"

"As opposed to no birds," Redcloud says, meaning Wolfe, without rank.

Kozak, "As I say, you could be waiting two weeks for a flight out."

Capt Washington hurriedly waves over Caufield and Redcloud, where he's got the battalion commander on video link, a slightly out-of-sync image on his laptop.

Dragon Six. Awesome Company's battalion commander.

Washington, "Excuse me, sir, I lost you there for a minute, Colonel. What was that, something about Zoo Platoon's AAR, I lost you, sir. Can you repeat that please?"

Dragon Six on the laptop, slightly out-of-sync image, "Do you have me now, because you're coming in clear here?"

"Yes sir, Lima Charlie. Go ahead, Dragon Six."

LC, Loud and Clear. Radio talk, used the same in video comms.

"I was saying, Jashawn, there's a problem with your Zoo Platoon's AAR. I don't see anywhere in it how the insurgent received his wounds. Brigade is saying he's in the Cash at Salerno saying it was one of your men in your the platoon who shot him. Saying unarmed. He's saying he was unarmed and they shot him."

"I don't understand, Colonel."

"This is the interim report from the Cash." Dragon Six waves a print-out, even more out-of-sync and motion-blurred in the video transmission. "It says he was shot twice in the back—in the buttocks and the left thigh. And, with frontal gunshot wounds: quote, 'appeared shot multiple times in the groin. From the front.' End quote. His dick and balls, according to the surgeon, and I quote, he says, 'appear as if they were put through a Cuisinart'. Jashawn?"

"Yes sir, I heard you, sir."

"Why don't I see any of this in the AAR?"

"It's there. It's in the Zoo After Action Report. Leadership was providing first aid to the anthropologist and her terp, sir. Who were burned, sir, I believe the status report from Salerno said it was over eighty percent of their bodies. Zoo Six and Zoo Seven were not in position to see what was happening. Cuisinarting the nuts, sir, that sounds more like the sort of thing the ANA would do. ANA SOP."

Wolfe, "I shot him."

Capt Washington waves a hand *Shut up!* to Wolfe.

Battalion commander Dragon Six on the computer, "What was that, did I hear someone say they shot him?"

Washington, "That was Robyn's teammate, the HTT here, the other anthropologist. He said he wished he'd shot him. Quote, 'the mother-F-ing scumbag', end quote, he said. They were together a while, he and Robyn. A team. Have you had a chance to meet Robyn, sir?"

"Negative, negative. I've heard nothing but exemplary things about her though. Tell him, her teammate there, and I apologize I don't remember his name"—from the AAR—"but tell him I'm sorry for his loss. And I understand, I can surely hear where he's coming from. If that's the case, if it was your ANA doing the shooting, they did a pretty botched job of it. Maybe you ought to see about getting them some range time. Just kidding, Jashawn, don't go quoting me now."

Washington, "No sir, no problem, sir. Range time for the ANA, no problem, sounds like a good training Metl tasking we can apply. What I can do, what I'll do, Colonel, I'll question all the Zoosters. See if anyone saw anything, who what when where."

Dragon Six, "I know brigade is going to start asking questions. Even if it's your Afghan nationals, they can't be going into villages cuisinarting a local's nuts, insurgent or no insurgent. I want to be ahead of the curve here, Jashawn. You know brigade's going to start asking. And you know that AAR's going to throw big red flags up there. You have your Zoo Six send up the BDA photos. I didn't see them attached in the AAR. We need to confirm insurgent kills, Jashawn. A hard number with photo evidence. Another red flag from brigade."

"Roger, sir, I'll tell him."

"They've already got the AAR. I sent it forward because they were asking for details on the burning incident because Isaf's already sticking their noses in it. And you know brigade and everyone's going to want photos of the dead insurgents in that schoolhouse building. A picture says a thousand words. Lieutenant Caufield ought to know better."

"Roger, sir, understood."

"Out here," from the battalion commander, and the laptop video feed goes dead.

A moment of silence.

Washington, "BDA, I can't cover you on that, Matt."

Lieut Caufield, "My fuckup. We started taking more rockets, I just didn't think it was worth getting men killed over."

Redcloud, "It wasn't, Captain. Say we lose a soldier, the ANA already lost four, or we lose a vehicle, we lose even just one truck, just for BDA and a couple of pictures? Then the colonel's saying 'Didn't you have any common sense?' End quote."

Washington, "How'd you put it? 'The school engulfed in fire.' They'll have to accept it, we can't give them what we don't have. Can't go back and take pictures now. Send up your photos of the burning school."

Redcloud, "Rockets were coming from up in the compounds, Captain, and do you think if we called in here for artillery, you think battalion was going to approve it and risk how many civilian casualties up there in the actual village where the compounds are and they're all living? They won't even remember it by morning, sir."

A shrug from Washington. Too late now to worry about it.

Redcloud advises Wolfe, "I wouldn't be going around saying you shot the insurg. Or insurgents, multiple. You know the Roe."

ROE.

Rules of Engagement.

Among which, *You Can't Shoot An Unarmed Man.*

Addendum #1: *Especially not one running away.*

Addendum #2: *Thou Shalt Not Cuisinart His Nuts.*

Wolfe, "My bad, you're right. Nothing the big brass like more'n going after some poor sadsack on a Roe violation. They check it off their PC to-do checklist."

A chuckle from Lieut Caufield. "Do they send poor sadsack civilians to Leavenworth?"

Redcloud, "Can't dock you a rank, Kyle. Leavenworth sounds about right."

Wolfe, "Momentary lapse of judgment. I would have coup de grâc'd the dirtbag if I thought we'd be medevaccing him where he could start screaming 'Roe violation, Roe violation, Geneva Convention, I got my rights, waaaaaaahhhhh.'"

Capt Washington, "I'll pretend I didn't hear that. Matt, were any of your Zoosters in position to see what happened, they could swear on a Bible what they saw? What am I saying—screw it, forget it, I don't want to know."

Redcloud, "Captain, it'll all blow over by tomorrow, dust in the wind. Won't be anyone giving it a second thought. A Taliban insurgent had his privates Cuisinarted in battle, whoopteedoo one way or another, case closed, just another day in the Stan."

1st Sgt Kozak has stayed out of it. Now he teases Capt Washington. "There's just one problem with your theory. Telling the colonel. About the ANA the ones blasting that insurg's dick and nuts. Everyone knows if they were aiming for them they couldn't hit them from here to there. They were aiming for his head."

"Thus," quickly from Capt Washington, "the additional range time. Which, Eddie, I want you to take charge of. So let's have your lesson plans, training schedules, risk assessments, by, how about, 0800?"

Kozak knows it's a return tease, a joke, and he counterpunches. "I'll get right to them. Right after I fill out my retirement paperwork."

Lieut Caufield to Washington, "If you don't mind, Captain, I'd be happy if you give Wajma to 2nd or the Third Herd next time around."

Redcloud, "Better yet, leave them in peace out there, what are we bothering them for, they don't want to see Americans. Insurgents were right under our noses up there and we didn't even know it, the villagers didn't say one word. Isn't that the purpose of you HTTs, Wolfie? Aren't you-all supposed to get them to whisper there's a squad of Taliban hiding in the school? Why bother even going?"

Capt Washington, serious, "Even more reason. Hearts and minds. One village at a time. Maybe we do an HA drop there next week, Thursday, Friday. Winter's coming, around the corner. They're going to need blankets, kerosene, beans, rice. You know the way, you're already familiar with the terrain."

Meaning, The Zoo. Them, back to Wajma.

Stunned blank look from Caufield.

Redcloud just shrugs it off, *If so, so be it.*

Now a smile from Washington. Teasing, pulling their chain.

Redcloud, back at him, "Yeh, Captain, no problem, and how 'bout, I'll let you ride the .50 in my truck."

Isaf, Kabul

Major Zachery Dove is in his tiny room in the conex barracks. 6x8. No window.

Bunk against the wall. A double-door metal wall-locker for uniforms and gear.

A 3x2 desktop upon which there are stacks of books, a digital alarm clock that reads 21:35 and a laptop open and on, as he's seated cramped in the metal folding chair on video-chat with his wife.

"Love you, dear," he mouths, kisses his fingertips then touches them to her lips on the screen as she does the same, her fingers moving now out of the picture to be touching her own screen.

He clicks it off. Takes off his headset. Clicks out of the web browser, shuts it down.

Checks the digital alarm. Checks the digital watch on his wrist. The same exact time.

"Be safe" had been her last words to him, as they always are, every night here on chat. Impossible to be more safe, he knows, than right here on Isaf command staff. Hardly justifies the combat pay, let alone all his pay being tax-free. *Be safe,* that had made sense once, she would have been praying it every night back then when she wouldn't hear from him but maybe once a week, and most times less often, and always in just plain email, no chat then, no video, in particular not in the first year of the war here so long ago, when Dove was a junior captain with his own Ranger company.

Repeat, a junior captain with a Ranger company.

Consider this: Mostly it's majors who command a Ranger company.

Dove had been moved from Ranger platoon leader to company command two months after making captain, and that just doesn't happen, not ever, but that's the confidence his battalion commander had in him.

The same confidence that his next batt commander had when he kept Dove in that company command when they went to Iraq. And kept him there when they returned to Afghanistan.

In Big Army's wisdom of shuffling officers to give them an eclectic variety of experience, Dove was randomly moved to the 82nd, where he commanded a task force that operated in Kunar, Logar and Nuristan, then when he made major two years ahead of his peers he was suddenly snatched up back stateside onto the staff of the Special Ops Advisor, Pentagon, a two-star. He worked under Colonel Pluma on that staff, and six months after Pluma came here joining Gen St Claire's staff, he requested and snagged Maj Dove.

Of these eight-some years of war, five have been either here or Iraq, and his wife's *Be Safe* is perfunctory now, of that he's assured her. And she knows the military and knows that the next seven to twelve months here on Isaf staff will be followed by nothing but stateside staff time and grad school and the War College, and this war will be over by then, like Iraq, as the president promises, and there won't be any more command time for Dove until years down the road when he makes lieutenant colonel and gets his infantry battalion.

Years down the road.

If he doesn't screw the pooch somewhere along the line and get just one bad or minutely sub-par Officer Evaluation.

By the time he gets his battalion, maybe the wars will be Indonesia, the Philippines, maybe the whole horn of Africa, and he'll command a battalion in combat.

But that's way into the future.

He's in Isaf. Kabul. In this conex room. Hard to get much safer.

Be safe. I'm safe, honey, I'm safe.

Photos of her and the kids taped on the wall over the desk.

Kendra, 8.

Jason, 6.

Kristina, just 13 months.

I'm safe for you, he touches Kendra in one of the pictures. He does not ever want an Army officer handing to her a folded flag at graveside, as he did to that little girl streaming tears, and hard as it was for him he remained unbrokenly stoic then. *Jennifer she was. Eight, just like Kendra now.* Jennifer's father had been his first Ranger platoon sergeant years before. Then, those many years later, on the wrong chopper at the wrong time. All the Rangers on that chopper died. Maj Dove, on staff at the Pentagon, was honored when the family asked that he be the Arlington escort officer.

I'll be back, Kendra.

To his wife, *Honey, I'm a staff pogue, I'll be back safe to you.*

On the desk his cell phone vibrates. A text from a buddy here, a British captain. *BREWS R GETTING WARM.* Dove smiles, he knows what it means.

Vibration again. Second text, *YANK MAJ ASKING 4 U. 1ST COME 1ST SERVED. GOING 2 TAKE HER 2 MY HOVEL.*

Cop Valley Forge

The sky is a jet black all-encompassing void of ten thousand white pinpricks of stars. Twenty, a hundred thousand, you couldn't count them if you had all night and wanted to.

With the moon just a sliver, a micron of a sickle low in the southeast.

Redcloud stops short of the steps up into the Zoo command barracks B-hut for a long look, turning to take in this high ceiling of black and its hundred thousand stars.

Lord, it is pretty out here, he thinks.

Lord, you do make a beautiful and awesome universe.

As he always does first, he finds the Big Dipper, low right now but it will climb, rotating throughout the night. He traces it now to the North Star. Polaris. He thinks of how many times he used it alone in night land navigation, closing up and tucking in his compass, humping an angle to the North Star.

Throughout the sky he discerns the patterns. Constellations pop out. Maybe it's his seven-eighths Chickasaw blood, that's why he sees it all, and he thinks of his grandfathers' grandfathers' grandfathers two hundred years ago looking at this same sky. Now suddenly the dark is exploded by the stream of light from inside as the barrack door is pulled open and Corporal Sandusky comes out onto the top step. He pulls the door shut behind him.

Black darkness, and Sandusky remains motionless to allow his eyes to adjust.

Redcloud says, "What's up, Sandusky?"

"Whoa, Sarge, you scared me, didn't see you." Another flash of brightness as he lights a cigarette from his Zippo. "Sniper's started on Finkle's tatt."

Redcloud had figured as much. Earlier, at his meeting with the squad leaders he'd given the final okay on Pvt Finkle getting the Zoo tattoo. Finkle hadn't hesitated today on the Mk19, even when the RPGs were sailing in close, and hadn't ducked down in the turret, had kept firing, changing ammo cans, hadn't gone coward, hadn't panicked. Showed some grit, especially so young, such a kid still. Same as two weeks ago when that ANA pickup truck was shotgunned all to hell with that roadside bomb disguised in that bundle of firewood kindling and Finkle was on the -19 that day and hammered the blessed daylights out of that hillside across the wadi where the PKM machinegun fire was coming from. They'd laughed later at the bullet scars on the turret and side of Finkle's truck, but Finkle then hadn't hesitated nor ducked then when the bullets were hitting.

Cpl Sandusky steps down.

Redcloud, "Where's your weapon, Sandy?"

"Aw, in the barracks, I was only a minute."

"Where's your weapon?"

"In the barracks, I'm headin right now."

"Where's your weapon?"

"I know I know I know, Sarge," and he hurries off, but turns for one last thing. "Sarge? L-T was saying the B-C didn't have no attaboys for us today. That true, we kicked ass and he didn't give a shit?"

BC, for battalion commander.

"He took your attaboy away when he found out you're not carrying your weapon."

"Hooah, Sergeant."

In the B-hut Redcloud drops his M4 carbine onto his bunk.

A small group is over there at Sniper Rodriquez's corner where he's got his big Pelican case—10 drawers filled with guns, needles and inks—and he's right now inking the black of the Zoo tatt to spread above Pvt Finkle's left breast.

All the black tonight. Time for healing, then the colors in another couple of sessions.

Holloway, Wolfe and Nick Flowers the audience.

Redcloud calls over, "Rodriquez, you've got hajj detail. Utah and Nell and Ketch'll give you a man each."

Tomorrow's assignments.

"Roger that, Sarge."

"Holloway, it's you and Leonard on the radios. I don't care, you work out the rotations and dinner- and piss-breaks with him, and post them there, and I don't want to go in the Toc and not see one of you with your butt right in that seat there at the radios. Slurpee, where is Leonard anyway?"

"Internet he said."

"Captain wants you," Redcloud tells Sgt Slurpee, "to give 'Lesias a hand going through all the conexes and see if there are some pallets of water hidden in the back of them somewhere."

"Roger."

Redcloud, "Eberly," to Doc reading on his bunk, and Eberly takes out one iPod earbud to hear. "Doc Murphy's going to need some help on inventory of the med container."

A nod, *understood*, from Eberly.

That's it, assignments done.

Redcloud strips off his shirt and drops it on his bunk.

Long sleeves gone, just with his tee-shirt on, what jumps out are the colors and intricacies of the tattoos that cover both arms from the backs of the hands up.

Around his neck under thorned roses is a dashed line with CUT HERE under it on both the front and the back.

The right arm is inked with an intertwining of ivy and thorned rose stems. With religious symbols.

A crucifix.

Virgin Mary's face in halo.

Stone tablets.

Christ rising from the tomb.

A rosary winding along the elbow, and if the tee-shirt were removed, one would see the ivy and rose stems that cross the shoulder and upper back and Jesus on his knees in the Garden of Gethsemane across the right shoulder.

Barbed wire and twin snakes intertwine up the left arm. It's military.

Patches of units Redcloud has served in, from Ranger Batt to 82nd to The Big Red One.

An M-16, a hand grenade, a claymore.

A billowing parachute.

A bloody K-bar knife.

Were the tee-shirt removed one would see the barbed wire and rose stems abruptly end at the solid black edge of the Tattoo Zoo tatt that covers the back left shoulder. Just below on the inside edge of the lower rose is a tiny #2.

Redcloud's was the second tatt. Rodriquez's own was the first, without a number.

Pvt Finkle's, which is tonight only the rough design, will be #44.

Nick Flowers brings his camera out of a close-up of Rodriquez's hands jetting the black design and up to Finkle's face. "You want to tell the world exactly why you deserve this, Finkle?"

"Sergeant Redcloud and the rest said so."

"Yeh but why?"

"Killing Taliban."

Rodriquez, "No 'mano, it aint for killin, it's for doin your job an' not puking out. Shoulda seed him, Nicky. He put them Mark rounds, ya got RPGs flying outta there and he's cool as shit, palooka palooka palooka puttin them Mark rounds right in there. In through them windows, and they gotta be six hun'red meters min'mun. I tell ya, puttin a Mark round in a window aint easy, not neven from two hun'red meters, and we're talkin here six hun'red min-eeee-mun."

Pvt Finkle, "Just doin my job."

Nick asks over to Eberly, "Hey, Doc, what about you? What's this I heard that you don't want the tatt?"

Pfc Holloway pipes up, "He don't. Doc's too good for the tatt."

Rodriquez, "He's got the tatt anytime he wants, right, Doc 'mano? Nicky, Doc can have hisself the tatt three times if he be wantin."

Holloway, "He's too smart for it. Thinks he's gonna be some big important open-heart doctor at some big hospital and big important doctors don't have tattoos, and if he was half as wicked smart as he thinks he is he'd get the tatt just so he could get his cherry broke. The Holloway Groove, Doc. You ain't never gettin laid, never, gonna be like the 40-year-old virgin, you don't get some ink. The Zoo's guaranteed pussy. Zoo tatt, Doc, it's a round-trip ticket to Twat City. 'Course, less you don't care none 'bout gettin some."

Doc Eberly pretends he isn't listening, hasn't heard a word of any of it from anyone. Oblivious. Just reading. Ear buds in. About the tatt that he has been awarded and has chosen not to get, he knows that Redcloud's heard all this now, heard them talking, and Redcloud says nothing, doesn't interfere, but Redcloud knows that Doc told him back when he was approved for the tatt two months ago that, *No offense*, but he thought that the whole tattoo thing, in all society, not just the Army, was faddish, copy-cat, follow-the-crowd, unimaginative herd-thinking, opposite the individuality that the supposed rebellious act of getting a tatt purported to be. Beside, he'd told Redcloud, it's like he'd been told by his dad who had older brothers and their friends in that whole 1960s hippie thing, and would they today want to be wearing all those clothes from then, all that tied-dyed stuff, and their sandals and long hair and beads, permanently welded onto them. And would they today still want on their BMWs and Volvos the same bumper stickers they had then plastered on their VW Bugs? And a second time then Eberly had told Redcloud *No offense*. And he said that after the deployment he'd thought he'd make decal emblems of the Zoo tattoo and put it on tee-shirts for the guys, and them he'd wear proudly.

And Redcloud then had nodded his head and told him *No offense taken.* And meant it.

In here Redcloud has heard Holloway's ragging on Doc and knows that Doc's heard it and is only pretending not to, and knows that Doc doesn't need or want him coming to his defense, that Doc doesn't need that, that Doc's who he is and knows who he is and *Isn't like most of all the rest of us.* And that's good to Redcloud, and he wouldn't want to change it.

He grabs up his shower kit. Flicks a towel over his shoulder. "You shower yet, L-T?"

Lieut Caufield is on his bunk, on his laptop. "I'm thinking maybe sometime next week."

Redcloud knows he's joking. "B-O's a natural camouflage amongst the Taliban. Me, I'd prefer they see who's got them crosshaired in his sights." He takes his M4.

Caufield, "Going to splash on that Old Spice, huh?"

Redcloud, "In spades." He pulls open the door slowly, eyes focusing into the blackness outside gradually widening as he opens the door more.

Caufield is writing an email letter to his former girlfriend whom he first wrote just after coming here, hoping she would write him back. And she did. And it's been steady. He loved her before and didn't want to lose her and he still loves her, and now away from her for all this time in all the officer training and Ranger School and here he wants her even more and he hopes she still loves him, which she hasn't said yet in her emails, and he hopes that she is now understanding better his need to do this, to be in the Army in war, to challenge himself with the responsibility for all these men's lives.

When he finishes he'll drag the file onto a thumb drive, then way later sometime after midnight when there's always a few empty computers in the internet room he'll go over and send it. With his fingers crossed that there's already one from her waiting for him. Either way, he'll go to Facebook, and maybe she'll have some new pictures of herself posted, for her friends, sure, and of her and her girlfriends. Or just the old ones from before are okay. Either way.

And he'll check on the latest about the Wisconsin/Michigan State game tomorrow. A noon start-time back home means what, 2230 or 2330 here? And if no one's in the TV room already watching something and if Armed Forces Network is carrying it, tomorrow night late he can be rooting on his Badgers live.

Tonight after the internet and hopefully with something waiting from her, even just a short *Hi!*, then he'll go and shave and shower. Plenty of hot water then at that hour, he knows. Maybe borrow some of

Travis' Old Spice. Two splashes. *Here I am, Taliban, over here. Come and get me. If you can.*

Isaf, Kabul

In the clamshell gym a Polish polka band is playing on a makeshift stage under one of the basketball hoops.

Most of the court is the dance floor, and the Nato officers, male and female, all in uniform, use it. Europeans know how to polka. You want to see some polka, watch the Germans and Poles.

And the Americans may have court-martial rules against alcohol country-wide, but the Europeans sure don't. Beer is pumped from kegs by the pitcher and stein. It's Oktoberfest after all.

Fairness schmairness, Americans stationed down in the Fobs and Cops may have to smuggle via mail their booze, but not those here.

As Maj Zachery Dove has quickly downed one stein and now picks up a second. With the British captain who had texted him and who now considerately steps away with a *"See you, mate,"* as Maj Vicky Marshall is approaching, laser-like in on Dove.

A radiant smile from Vicky. "The cat drag you away from the Op Center? For what do we owe this rare treat of the gift of your presence, Zachery Dove?"

He shows her his stein. As if it's for this that he's come.

She takes it right out of his hand. Sips it. Slides it onto the table.

She invites him, "Now let's see how good you are"—on the dance floor.

He begs off with just a *naw, please no* shrug and smile.

"You must know how. Come on, one dance, Zach."

From his pant cargo pocket he withdraws a lime-green hardbound notebook that all American officers are wont to carry. He flips it open to show her the snapshot of his wife acetated on the inside cover.

Vicky is surprised and impressed. "I didn't know she was that pretty." She means it. "And ten time zones away. No harm in one polka, Zachary."

"A great philosopher once said, Plato or Aristotle or Dear Abby, I don't remember." His smile is genuine, easy. "The only effective way to avoid temptation is to stay away from it completely."

"That can lead"—she leans in close to his ear, to privately tease. "It can lead to a ruptured prostate from backed-up excess unrelieved pressure. We see it all the time in trauma."

He now answers close to her ear. "Mine's already backed up. And you're just too too damn attractive."

"I don't know to take that as a compliment or rejection. I'm temptation? Little ol' me?"

"With a capital T. And that rhymes with V, and that stands for trouble. Or temptation."

"Yet here you are. Did your Colonel Pluma give you the whole night free of Strategic Ops or has he and General St Claire tasked you with winning the war all by yourself? What if I told you that there's a great philosopher who said philosophers are only right about ten percent of the time?"

He'll play along. "Who?"

The attraction is strong between them.

To him she's unobtainable, the woman who no man has gotten near, yet here she is, *She can be mine.*

She plays it straight. "Descartes or Socrates or Dr Phil or Lady Gaga, I'm not really sure, one of them."

"If he or she were right, then by definition that would only be ten percent right. So, philosophers would be right ninety percent of the time. Which then would make your Lady Gaga or Dr Phil ninety percent right, not ten percent. Never-ending. It's like an Escher drawing."

Her eyes widen, delight. "What an interesting approach. A new twist. I suppose you have M.C. Escher etchings you'd like to show off?"

That's clever and suggestive, and there's no need for Dove to respond. Yes, she knows M.C. Escher, yes she would know him, of course she would, and *Would you like to come up and see my Eschers?*, she is someone he could talk with, talk Escher, talk Renoir perhaps, and she'd know Monet from Manet and could talk the Rolling Stones and Sheryl Crow and Duke Ellington, and Stevie Wonder verses Springsteen, and she's got to know the NFL, who's better?, Brady verses Manning, and Leno verses Letterman and the chemistry of anesthesia verses the pinpricks of acupuncture, an animal-based diet verses plant-based, the scam that is organic foods verses the addictive taste of Twinkies, and they could quiz each other like *Jeopardy!*, yes with the exclamation point, yes, she'd know there was that explanation point there, *Would I like to come up and see her Eschers?*, for just an hour of playful talk about everything that is not military, everything that is not this war, this unexciting white-glove safe staff job, and

Ten time zones, he's thinking, *oh to touch her cheek, oh to feel her lips, to touch them* with his own. No, *Better to heed the philosopher,* to avoid temptation. She doesn't have a place to come up to anyway here, she must be staying in the Visitor's Quarters, it was only a playful tease, a flirt, nothing more, and, "I've got a zero-five wake-up," he says. "I'd better go" —

Her hand to his arm stops him.

The whole world stops for him, and there's no polka band playing, there's no one else here, for an instant. . . . . . then there is again, "I'd better go" —

Again he's stopped, this time by a tightening of her grip.

"Come on, you must know, Zachary," she says quietly. Sensuous. Alluring. Charming and tempting. "In Mosul, it was a barely kept secret, three-star General St Claire and his protocol officer first lewy brunette. With perfect one-hundred-percent-natural Ds and an hourglass figure."

Dove knows what she's saying, though until now he did not know of the protocol officer, or any woman, any cheating on the general's part. He'd never thought to even consider of St Claire such a break in discipline, loss of self-control, breach of character. No, it can't be true. Can it? No, uh-uh, it can't, not General St Claire.

Vicky ties it up in a neat package now. "And he got his fourth star. One dance, Zach. And in ten years you'll still get your first."

He doesn't want to dance, that he knows. She doesn't really want to dance, that he knows. She wants what he wants, and it's not that crowded Visitor's Quarters she's in where everyone knows your comings and goings, but rather it's him to tell her, he knows, it is him, she wants him to tell her his conex barracks number. Upstairs, 2nd floor. Room 26A. His upstairs. Come up and see his M.C. Eschers. He wants to tell her to follow him in five minutes. He's never done it before. He hasn't, and he knows he should admit that, that can be his excuse to escape, to beg off. "I really wouldn't know what to do, Vicky, I really wouldn't."

"It's like riding a bike." She is certain now that he truly is one of the few good decent guys left. "I know you had a bike as a kid."

"Not built for two."

She laughs, naturally, both hands on his arm now, appreciating that that was so witty quick, amazing how quick that was, and so double entendre. And, even more, he is that rare good decent guy, she wants that rare man, *He really wouldn't know what to do, that's so innocent, this gentle modesty in a man of so much strength and intelligence and responsibility and ambition—*

"I really do have a zero-five wake-up," he's saying. "And"—

"I'm an early riser," she counters.

And that kind of immediate, sharp, double-entendre comeback stills him. Yes, she's quick. Witty quick. Wow. . . He draws in his breath. Slowly. Rationalizes, *I really wouldn't do anything,* no he wouldn't, except maybe *Just to touch her,* have her touch him, to *Lay beside her so enticing, so warm, open, with that laugh, that smile,* and he would love to touch his fingers so lightly on her smooth tight skin, feel her belly, run them up under her pert firm breasts, play them around them, swirl them over her hard nipples, wet his lips and slowly lower them to that pink nipple inviting him, and he realizes that Col Pluma is far across there in the entrance, eyes now catching his own, and immediately two fingers waving *Come here,* ordering *Right now.*

Dream zapped into thin air, temptation cut to the quick, a polite smile to Vicky, *Sorry, gotta go,* and she's seen Col Pluma and his beckoning but is still stung by the suddenness and finality of this rejection. Zapped herself, she grips his arm tighter just to hold him for a moment longer to tell him with a cold sting in return, "Your Colonel Pluma there. He's doing the Ukrainian twin stylists in the PX barber shop. And he gets his star when?—January?, February?"

A wince from Dove.

She is surprised, "You didn't know?"

No reaction *yes* or *no*, but he didn't know, and he gives her a polite shrug of *Regrets*, and his eyes convey the hope for *Another time?*, and he doesn't wait for an answer and steps away.

She's lost him tonight, she's certain. But maybe not. Maybe it's a problem that he can fix in ten minutes, *We'll see*, and in which case *he'll be back*. *Yes, yes* she hopes he will return.

Outside, Maj Dove meets Col Pluma, who has a knowing chuckle, "Hate to be the one to break up the party, Zach. Victoria Marshall, that's worth going Awol over." He steps off, briskly, and Dove alongside, on Pluma's left for deference. "I'd give up my first two sons for just one night with Major Vicky Marshall."

"She was in Iraq in the Cash when my company hit al-Yaqizi's bomb-making cell in Karbala."

"No explanation necessary. Bad timing, Zach, and I'm sorry. The shit has hit the proverbial fan down at Cop Valley Forge. Mass civilian casualties. On the order of whole careers could go down on this one. In that village where that HTT girl Robyn Banks was burned."

"Wajma? Mass casualties? As in more than five?"

"Exponentially. You'll see."

"From where, out of where, who's reporting it? Hearsay, sir, word of mouth? Witnesses from Wajma? You know how unreliable rural eye-witness testimony is."

"The Taliban. Direct from the horse's mouth. B-gan intercept. Approximately 1700 local. Genuine Taliban video. And they're either too stupid to know we're intercepting their satcoms or they're dangling it in front of us for extortion. Video in living color. Careful-you-don't-blow-your-chunks, that kind of living color. Doctor Hutchinsen is working the angles through Karzai, who's already being authorized up to twenty million dollars to work it out and make it go away if it is just extortion. Which we better pray to Jesus it is."

Maj Dove, "It's that bad? Sir, how could it be, how bad?"

"Cent Com's own words—you'll see. 'It makes Abu Ghraib look like a slumber party in a convent.' We have to hope that twenty mil can buy us four or five days and we can get a rein on it."

Pluma hands Dove a two-page print-out op order, which Dove immediately starts scanning in stride.

Pluma, "The blanks in there are to leave Cop Valley Forge in the dark."

Up the steps and in through the doors into the HQ building.

Pluma continuing, "We don't want to tip them off so they can get all their stories lined up, get their ducks all in a row. We're going to have to nail them solid. An L-shaped ambush, oh-dark-thirty, before they know what hit them.

"Just 1st Platoon A Company?"

"We bring in the platoon, and if the insurgents aren't playing ball for the twenty million, we release the videotape ourselves first, like we've got nothing to hide. Tell the media vultures, 'Here, we've uncovered this, have at it, boys'. And we throw the book at those 1st Platoon Alpha Company psychopaths, fast and furious. Then maybe, pray twice as hard to Jesus Christ and the Holy Trinity, maybe we can neutralize this."

"Zoo Platoon. The Tattoo Zoo, that's what they're called."

"They're a goddamn zoo alright."

"That's Awesome Company, they go by that. The C-O is a classmate of mine. Jashawn Washington."

"Is that going to be a problem? Because you're going to be point on this, Zach. We need a straight shooter with your impeccable credentials. A Boy Scout, Eagle Scout, Explorer, altar boy, church deacon. Who can give the media an all-warm-and-fuzzy, none of that bullshit Pat Tillman crap again, we're not going down that road, we all know where that leads. We're going to want to lay it all out, everything, from soup to shit, with dessert thrown in for good measure. With a cherry on top. Up front, all our cards on the table. And beat the enemy at their own PR."

He stops mid-corridor, confronts Dove for emphasis. "We'll get CNN, Fox, BBC, AP, Getty, even al Jazeera, all at Bagram for when the choppers land and those Zoo animals get off. In leg irons. We nip this in the bud now, Zach, the insurgents will be left with their thumbs up their asses. I wish I could say it was my idea. Doctor Hutchinsen. Thinking three levels in the 4th dimension outside the box in outer space beyond Jupiter and Uranus. He knows the devious, wicked Taliban mind, can read it like a kid's picture storybook. Leave them with their thumbs up their asses, limp dicks in their hands."

Dove, "Did Awesome Company get this yet?" The op order.

"As we speak. Shotgunning it to brigade, battalion, company. We want to limit the heads-up. For obvious reasons. Make that 1st Platoon and everyone else think they're executing temporary one-time QRF for us. That it's just another regular day in the neighborhood."

QRF, as in Quick Reaction Force. A platoon or company held in reserve at the ready to go in and rescue others who would have gotten caught in a jam.

Col Pluma finishes, "Just think L-shaped ambush. They're the dupes walking into it." And forward again, he leads Maj Dove a dozen strides further and in through the doors into Gen St Claire's office suite.

St Claire on the elliptical, legs pumping 5-minute-miles. In Nike running shorts, shirt, Asics shoes.

Dr Gene Hutchinsen seated on the end of the long teak conference table. Chair swiveled around, his back to the table.

Laptop in hand.

In front of the three 60" flatscreens on the wall.

The same paused video image on the center flatscreen as on Hutchinsen's laptop.

He tilts his head to indicate Col Pluma and Maj Dove to take the high-back swivel chairs on each side of him.

Behind them at the far end of the table, two of the general's captain junior aides. In the background, silent, inconspicuous, shadows.

Standard operating procedure for generals' aides.

Hutchinsen unpauses the video, and what plays is a rough-cut heavily edited version of the Taliban video that was satcom intercepted earlier. It is video of late morning in the village Wajma. It was shot from four different cameras at four different concealed locations using super-telephoto lenses and, as is the case with a camera from a peephole in one of the conex shipping containers, wide angle.

The video shows:

—Redcloud's three trucks coming up off the stream—

—joining the protective circle—

—shots of individual trucks—

—various turret gunners—

—different Zoosters hanging around their trucks—

—Redcloud, Lieut Caufield, Sniper Rodriquez and Wolfe talking at the Mrap—

Col Pluma explains for Maj Dove. "Cent Com sent it edited down from twenty-eight minutes total. This is the essence, they say."

"The Tattoo Zoo didn't see the camera?"

"At least four cameras. They're like a zoo alright. They're the animals and don't even know they're being filmed. Him in the civvies is the HTT. Ex-Marine. Force Recon. Kyle Wolfe. We're getting you his file."

As the video plays:

—Robyn and her terp Gulbarhar interviewing the Bic guy—

Col Pluma, "Doctor Robyn Banks. Watch here."

—the Bic guy standing—

—shaky images, blurred—

—the gas thrower flinging the red bucket on Robyn and Gulbarhar who are instantly aflame—

Dr Hutchinsen pauses the video on that image.

"This is it, this is our money shot, Pete. This was their mistake, this they should have edited out before they satcommed it. Their Achilles' heel call it. Worldwide this works to our advantage, Pete."

Gen St Claire pumping fast on the elliptical. "We had Daniel Pearl on tape worldwide. How did that work to our advantage?"

"He was a journalist. And a Jew. She's a woman. Worse, he looked like a journalist and a Jew. She's your girl-next-door homecoming queen. She works summers at the soda shoppe, Thanksgiving and Easter Sunday she volunteers at the soup kitchen. Saturday morning she rescues little kittens from up in the tree."

And he unpauses the video:

—Wolfe puts three shots point-blank into the wounded Bic guy—

—the distant gas thrower flees across the barren field—

—Wolfe standing on the wall taking aim and shooting—

—the gas thrower falling wounded—

Maj Dove says, "R-O-E, the insurgent doesn't have a weapon."

Roe, remember? Rules of Engagement. No weaponee no shootee.

Col Pluma, "It gets worse."

—Wolfe kicks over the gas thrower—

—shoots him point-blank in the groin—

Maj Dove lets out a breath.

Col Pluma, "It gets worse."

—the M240 turret gunner blazing away—

—the .50-cal gunner blasting—

—Pvt Finkle on the Mark-19 plunking out grenade rounds one after the other—

—flames and smoke pouring from the schoolhouse—

Maj Dove, "What are they firing at?"

Pluma, "Their AAR says they took rocket fire from that school building there. Multiple RPGs."

Dove, "I don't remember their reporting any casualties."

Dr Hutchinsen pauses the video. "Because there weren't any. Except the ANA. And the platoon could just as well have been responsible for those. Blue on Green. Their exacting vengeance for the HTT Doctor Robyn Banks."

Slick, Dr Hutchinsen. Reversing Green on Blue, which is the ally Afghan forces attacking their American and Nato partners.

Col Pluma, "Frankly, Blue on Green, really? I don't see that as a possibility. That would be pushing it, there's no reason for it, that seems awfully extreme."

"Frankly," Hutchinsen returns it, "you should clear the Mary Poppins cobwebs you have cluttering up the mushy brain matter between your ears, Danny. What are the possibilities, have you thought about that, that the ANA were assigned primary security for Robyn Banks and they allowed the insurgents entry, complicit or non-complicit, regardless, have you thought along those angles? That's not a valid reason, you don't see that as a valid reason? I'm sure you've seen such extreme retaliatory violence for far less. Does Fallujah ring a bell?"

Col Pluma holds his tongue.

Maj Dove asks him, "There's nothing in all twenty-eight minutes, sir, nothing showing the platoon taking rockets from the school building?"

Col Pluma, "We don't have all twenty-eight minutes."

Dr Hutchinsen, "Cent Com does and they assure us, 'Nothing'. No evidence, not one frame of insurgent initiation of any attack following the conflagration of our Human Terrain Team beauty queen Robyn Banks. Which, as I've said, the insurgents screwed up royally by leaving that in unedited."

He unpauses the video:

—flames and smoke coming out of the school—

—a full 30 seconds of Ketchum's turret gunners firing—

—continued flames and smoke from the school—

Maj Dove asks, "I assume the mass casualties are there?"

Col Pluma, "Coming up."

Dove, "If I might, a question?"

Dr Hutchinsen pauses the video.

Maj Dove, "If they didn't want us to intercept this or didn't know we would intercept it, why would they edit out their initial assault from the school building? Why edit it, what did the platoon say, the multiple RPGs fired from the building? If they don't know we're going to intercept it."

Col Pluma, "That's because you're assuming, Zach, and it's not safe to assume," with a touch of vengeful sarcasm, "now is it, Doctor Hutchinsen?—It's not safe to assume that the platoon was assaulted by any enemy fire whatsoever."

Dr Hutchinsen, "Assume better, Danny, we should assume, and this is precisely why the twenty million bait coming from Karzai will work. Assume their motive is extortion—it's the money. They wanted us to intercept it. That, Danny-Boy, is the only really practical, logical conclusion. For the money. Follow – The – Money. "

Col Pluma, "Then why leave in their setting afire the HTT? How's that make sense, if they're such freaking brilliant extortionists, they're going to be making that rookie mistake?"

A smile from Dr Hutchinsen. "They couldn't help themselves. They couldn't resist. They're jihadists, they hate us. Despise us. Their loathing is so deep…" His *loathing* drawn out, flavored with the feeling of hellfire, a forked tail and cloven hooves.

He continues. "It's jihadist porn. To rub our faces in it. To show us, to, shall we say, brag, to boast. 'In your face, infidel.' We think we can send our women out anywhere, our beautiful Rose Parade Queen feminists,

PhDs, MDs, a secretary of state, for God's sake. We put them out among them as equals. Equals and superiors, and they just can't resist the urge to retaliate. We're shoving their faces in it, 'Take this, Muslim jihadist misogynists.' They're going to rub our faces right back in it. 'How 'bout some of this, infidels!'"

Gen St Claire pumping his legs on his elliptical, listening and saying nothing.

Hutchinsen, "This is the degradation they have the power to shock us with anytime anyplace, that's what they're saying, why they couldn't help but leave it in. Anytime anyplace, at their choosing. Burning one of our beautiful young fertile women who we put out there flaunting our unholy sinful sexuality, flaunting it like nymphs, lascivious nymphs, to the point of begging any true-believer jihadist to strike back, he has no choice but to strike back. Women are not equal, it's in the Koran, right there in plain Arabic, it's the sacred word of Allah. And if they don't strike back, it's a sin, and worse, it shows weakness. Nothing, Danny— nothing in this culture, if you don't know it by now—nothing is more to be avoided than weakness or the most infinitesimal sign of weakness. There is no way, given the opportunity, no way come hell or high water that a faithful jihadist is not going to show us what he can do to our women, whom they believe down to their deepest core are all whores. Whores of the devil. Satan's concubines."

End of discussion.

No counter expected.

None offered.

Dr Hutchinsen unpauses the video.

Gen St Claire steps off the elliptical.

The video shows the burning school then cuts to the Apache helicopter skimming low over the beach straight for the school and pulling a sharp bank ahead of the school to climb alongside the mountain-side shielding the concrete building, and

—the Zoo trucks are leaving—

—the beach is empty—

—close shots now of the still smoking school—

—village men gathering below the steps of the school from which now only small trails of smoke rise—

—village men carrying bodies from the school—

Maj Dove does not blink.

—women and girls, mangled, bloody, shredded, burned—

—tiny girl babies—

—village men laying the bodies on the dirt out front—

—severed arms and legs—

—charred arms and legs—

Maj Dove in a whisper, "Can't be."

Dr Hutchinsen, "Is."

— panning down the line of bodies, more than a hundred —

End of video.

Gen St Claire takes his holstered 9mm from the conference table.

Maj Dove asks, "And the Zoo Platoon's BDA photographs."

Col Pluma, "Not included in their AAR."

Dr Hutchinsen, "Zoo Platoon?"

Maj Dove, "The Tattoo Zoo, that's what they're called. Famous for it in the brigade."

"Oh they're going to be famous all right. Makes it even better. Made for Hollywood."

Gen St Claire straps the pistol under his left arm. "The Alpha Company C-O, Zachary, this Jashawn Washington, he was a classmate of yours?"

Dove is surprised that the general would already be aware of such an inconsequential thing, but Col Pluma interrupts, to inform the general, "They're Awesome Company, sir. Of course, we've yet to see just how awesome." Pluma knows that St Claire despises this relatively new convention of discarding the traditional Alpha, Bravo, Charlie, Delta naming of companies from the phonetic alphabet for Able or Battle or Comanche or Dog or whatever they damn well please down there. Awesome? Pluma knows that a part of St Claire's scorn for the practice is his powerlessness to stop it because that sort of individual designation gives the troops an esprit de corps that no command wants to strangle.

St Claire repeats his question to Maj Dove. "This Awesome Company C-O Jashawn Washington is a classmate?"

Maj Dove, "Yes sir. Same company, sir."

"Friends?"

"Once, sir, yes sir."

"Close?"

"And competitors, sir."

"And he's still a captain?"

"He was sixteenth in the class ranking, sir."

"To your . . . ?"

"Twenty-third, sir."

"Where'd he lose his bearings?"

"Sir?"

"Sixteenth and he didn't beat you to major? Weren't you in the Regiment together?"

Rangers.

"Yes sir. Jashawn, sir—. . . He has a reputation for speaking his mind freely at times, sir."

"Speaking his mind, or insubordination?"

"Sir? No sir. There was an incident in Iraq"—

"I know," Gen St Claire cuts him off. Waves it off, unimportant.

And Dove realizes that the general would have already been briefed on Captain Washington and would know the whole history, that incident in particular that chopped the legs off Washington's career.

Cop Valley Forge

"This had better be good," Capt Washington tells Lieut Frye as they're walking from the huts toward the Toc in the pitch black.

1st Sgt Kozak is with them. Not pleased to have been awakened. "I was just starting to dream of Taylor Swift. It's a birthday party, I don't know for who, don't ask me who, one of my kids maybe, I guess, I don't know. And she pops out of the cake, and she's got balloons in both hands. Then we're in my man cave in my basement, it's just her and me, and you know once you're waken out of a dream you can't never get that dream back. You do know that, don't you, Lieutenant?"

Capt Washington, "Taylor Swift? That's statutory rape, Edward Kurt."

"Not in a dream it's not. If this is bullshit, Lieutenant, I'm sure I can convince the captain here to put you on shit-burning detail for a month."

Lieut Frye, "When it says 'For the C-O's Eyes Only' don't blame me. You want me to ignore it until morning and not wake you up?"

Capt Washington, "Yeh and tell me, are you going to swear on a stack of Bibles you didn't open the file?"

"I stand on the Fifth. Com'on sir, how many times do we get an operation order direct from Isaf HQ? CC'd to battalion and brigade, and you know they're probably waking the B-Cs there too. When's the last time you've seen a direct op order from Isaf?"

Up the steps and into the Toc building they go. "I was hoping," Capt Washington says. "Never."

Isaf, Kabul

Gen St Claire pulls on his Army green-gray fleece jacket. "Zachary, is your rucksack packed?"

Maj Dove comes up out of his chair fast, "Always, sir."

St Claire zips up his jacket. Four jet-black perfect stars sewn right down the sternum.

He motions Dove *Walk with me*, and out the doors he goes, Dove hurrying to join him. A quarter step behind.

One of the two captain aides trails a dozen paces, out of earshot.

Gen St Claire to Dove, "Big picture, Zach, strategically. Your initial gut assessment."

"Sir, I don't think there's anything I can add that you don't know already."

"Humor me."

"The prevailing omnipresent media narrative can greatly influence public perception. The photos from My Lai, sir. The photograph of the naked little girl running away burned from napalm."

"If I remember correctly we lost that war."

"Abu Ghraib only became Abu Ghraib because of the photographs, sir. The detainees in the pyramid. Lynndie England with the dog leash."

"Your assessment on that war?"

"I wouldn't call it a loss, sir."

"Good. Keep up the optimism. It helps."

"We prosecuted the soldiers. They were found guilty."

"Closing the barn door. Long after the horses."

Out the main entrance doors, and the polka band can be dimly heard from the clamshell tent somewhere on the other side of buildings.

Maj Dove ventures his opinion. "I can't see our troops wantonly firing on that school building, sir, not if they hadn't taken fire from it first. And not if they knew there were non-combatant women and children and babies inside."

"Meaningless. Irrelevant."

"The insurgents do know our troops are allowed to respond to lethal enemy fire without permission from higher. It was intentional. It was a setup, sir."

St Claire again, "Irrelevant."

Maj Dove knows it, shows the general he does by stating the underlying reasoning. "Because there is no way to get media video footage of the setup."

"That little Vietnamese girl running away. From the Americans. Did you see the photographs of the enemy in her village shooting at the American GIs and killing one or two of them not ten minutes before the GIs called in the napalm strike? Where were those pictures, Zachary? Or do you think there weren't any?"

"No sir. We never saw them."

"All anyone will remember is the dead women and girls and little babies. Killed by the American GIs."

"Which we counter with an open trial of our own, sir."

"With those Tattoo Zoo cowboys getting their legions of lawyers in a media circus dragged out for two years? We close the barn door, Zachary. Now. Immediate prosecution."

"They will lawyer-up, sir, and they will demand due process."

"You let me worry about due process. As Ranger company commander, did you ever knowingly and deliberately falsify an After

Action Report by failing to include BDA when you had even one non-combatant death?"

Maj Dove knows what the general is saying and offers a defense. "Is there any evidence, sir, that Jashawn Washington was with the platoon in the village?"

"He didn't have to be in the village. As Ranger company commander did you not know every action to the letter of your platoon leaders? Did you not know when they were lying to you? It's not rhetorical."

"Yes sir."

"Did you turn a blind eye to their lies and send forward their false AARs?"

"Sir, the Jashawn Washington I know, and have known—Jashawn would not attempt to hide or cover up an incident with so many non-combatant casualties."

"Assume for his sake incompetence in believing his platoon leader. Did you count the bodies in the film?"

That was rhetorical. Of course Maj Dove didn't have time to count the bodies. Nor had he thought of it.

Gen St Claire tells him. "One hundred and sixty-eight." He takes a sudden right onto the walkway that leads to the officer dining facility ahead. "Would you consider it incompetence as well that your classmate competitor Number Sixteen Jashawn Washington has failed to instill a sense of honor and truthfulness in his subordinate commanders that his Tattoo Zoo platoon leader would not even think to make mention of one of those women and children in that AAR? How many little Vietnamese girls were there, Zachary, in that photo running away from that napalm?"

Again rhetorical. St Claire well knows that they both know how many.

Just 1.

Not 168.

Cop Valley Forge, In the Toc

Capt Washington at his workstation laptop reading the op order from Isaf.

1st Sgt Kozak reading it over Washington's shoulder.

Lieut Frye watching them. Because, as the captain had basically supposed earlier, he's read it already.

Washington directs Frye, "Let's get all the Sixes and Sevens in here."

The platoon leaders and platoon sergeants.

"Tell Matt Caufield to give his Zoosters a heads-up. 0720 choppers. Pack for twenty-four hours. QRF. Light weapons. Heavy on the ammo."

1st Sgt Kozak is put-off. "Did you see it, I didn't catch anything, it doesn't say where. Or who. QRF for who? What kinda op order is this, all TBDs? What kinda dumbshits are they up there at Isaf?"

TBD, as in To Be Determined.

Washington, "You want me to send them an RSVP 'No'?" He sounds serious. "Better, I'll tell them hell no. All caps. HELL NO."

Call it black humor.

As in cynical.

Really, hell no? Like right, talk about an instant career killer.

Washington shrugs it all off. "Let's look at it from the positive side, Eddie. The Rangers are going to do a snatch somewhere here in the A-O. We're Quick Reaction Force for the Rangers."

Kozak, "Where's it say Rangers? Where's it say snatch operation? Snatches are at night. Why choppers at 0720?"

"Just speculating here, Edward Kurt. Getting into the mindset of an Isaf battle captain."

"Shit. . . ."

"The first sergeant is one of Travis Redcloud's old Ranger buddies from Batt, let's say"—

"Just speculating?"

"Speculating. And he figures there's no one more dependable, less bullshit. There's no one who can think without debate and hemming-and-hawing better than Travis. He made the request, he wants Travis for QRF. And you know that Rangers get what Rangers want."

Kozak, "Better chance they just picked 1st Platoon out of a hat. Bingo, guess whose day we just royally screwed today."

Washington snorts. Shakes his head, hopeless. "You really did think, didn't you?"

Kozak's look, *What, think what, what'd I think, huh?*

"That you were going to get yourself some poontang with Taylor Swift, didn't you?

Isaf, In the Officer Dining Hall

The Army cook unlocks the doors for Gen St Claire, and Maj Dove follows the general in, and the cook waits for the captain aide before locking the doors.

The place is empty except for the late-night staff, and up front at the serving counter awaiting St Claire are a toasted Rueben sandwich with chips and dill pickle halves and a tall glass of milk. He takes half the sandwich, bites into it.

The captain aide sets down his briefcase satchel on a table and opens it.

St Claire surprises Maj Dove by suddenly ripping Dove's velcroed gold oak leaf major rank from his chest.

Dove does nothing, offers no resistance. One doesn't question a four-star.

St Claire takes another bite of his Rueben and takes from his aide the proffered velcro black oak leaf lieutenant colonel rank and slaps it on level where Dove's major rank had just been.

The aide hands Dove a single-page Official Order. Promotion to lieutenant colonel. Dated the 1st of the month. Three weeks ago.

It's unexpected, it's impossible, it can't be real, but, again, one does not question a four-star.

The captain aide assures Dove, "It's real, Lieutenant Colonel Dove. It was lost in cyberspace somewhere."

Gen St Claire adds, "No one holds much countenance for majors. The clout won't hurt."

Another bite finishes the half sandwich, and he motions his aide who now hands Dove a three-page op order. The real one, the unabridged one. For Awesome Company at Valley Forge. That they haven't seen. And won't. Not yet.

St Claire starts into the second half of his sandwich.

Dove begins scanning the op order. Asks, "A Jag attorney and a video specialist?"

The captain aide answers. "They'll be on the helicopter from Bagram. Captain Laura Cathay. She said you know her."

Dove doesn't remember.

"Something about an Article 32 hearing. You were a witness, she said."

Dove remembers. Last year in DC, the Pentagon. "She was on the prosecution team."

The captain hands Dove a thumb drive. "The personnel records of all the main players. Secret No Forn. It's password protected in case it gets misplaced. LTC Zachary Dove. One word. Proper use of upper case."

Gen St Claire waits until Dove flips the last page of the op order. "Are you clear on your mission, Lieutenant Colonel?"

Dove, "I am assuming that the ideal outcome is, sir —. Is that I find evidence that the insurgents themselves killed the civilians."

"Ideally?" And St Claire chuckles. "Good luck with that. You find that ideal outcome, you bag it, you bring it back and you document everything on videotape. I want it wrapped so tight that Anderson Cooper, Lara Logan, and Matt fricken Lauer and Walter Lippmann himself can't even find the knot to start to think they've got reason to untie it."

St Claire drops the last bite of his sandwich onto the plate, takes a dill half and the glass of milk and heads for the kitchen.

Dove stands fast, until the captain aide motions him *Follow the general*, and Dove hurries and catches up in the kitchen where St Claire opens one of the big freezers that line one wall and pulls out three Klondike Bars. Two Heath flavors and an Original.

St Claire hands the Original to Dove and slips one Heath into his fleece jacket pocket. Tells Dove, "You'll see there," in the op order, "that the birds will pick you back up out there at 1300 precisely. 1300."

He unwraps and bites into the Original Klondike as he heads back, and Dove keeps up.

"It will be your decision, Zachary, yours alone, it will be all on you. You alone at 1300 will then either have that clear ideal all-exonerating evidence and return this Tattoo Zoo to Cop Valley Forge innocent of all charges. Or you will bring them back to Bagram for lock-up and prosecution."

Dove has in his hands the Klondike Bar, the promotion order, the unabridged op order, and the thumb drive of personnel files that he pockets.

"Understood?" asks St Claire. "Is that going to be a problem?"

"No sir."

Day Two, Morning

Cop Valley Forge

Near 0640, light and clear, but the sun has not yet crested the mountain range up there along the Paki border. All orange across the ridge there, lightening and washing-out fast.

The Zoo has been out here on the edge of the chopper LZ for about an hour, since it was still dark.

Hurry up and wait.

Guys all on the gravel sitting or laying back against their bulging rucksacks.

Helmets and body armor off, lying next to them.

Weapons lying across their laps or gear.

Plenty of time to get geared up when the choppers are in sight.

Some sleeping.

Yeh, get that sleep you lost when they got you up around midnight.

Some eating. Can't risk the choppers arriving early and getting caught at breakfast up in the Dfac, so head cook Yglesias a while ago brought down everything on the back of a Gator. Mermites of scrambled eggs, sausage links, hash browns, biscuits. A big green Army urn full of coffee, a couple of cases of Gatorade, a couple of pint orange juices and a few cases of off-the-shelf packaged goodies. Pop Tarts, single-serving cereal boxes, Otis Spunkmeyer muffins. Plastic plates and flatware.

"Hey c'mon," Spec Van Louse complained then, "where's the cups, man, how we supposed to drink this without any cups?"

"So you can have styrofoam flying all over the place when the choppers land?" Redcloud told him. "Use your canteen cup." And to everyone, "And I do not want to see one speck of litter, not one plate and not one fork and not one wrapper on the ground here. Understood?"

"Hooah," then from Zoosters, and from all Redcloud's years in he knows that GIs are GIs, and *They'll litter the Garden of Eden if you let them.*

The White House Rose Garden. St Peter's Square, The Sistine Chapel, their own front yard. The chopper'll come in, a Chinook with its two huge rotors front and rear blurring, and a hundred plastic plates and forks and little juice bottles and pastry wrappers will all be flying swirling everywhere.

Redcloud knows that even with the large plastic trash bags that Yglesias tied to the Gator the guys will leave their litter if you let them.

"You heard Sergeant Redcloud," Yglesias announced to all. "Cuz I aint pickin up all your crap when you leave out."

"Sarge?" Van Louse asked Redcloud. "Can I borrow your canteen cup?"

"What's wrong with yours? Yours got a leak?"

"Com'on, I don't have cooties."

"What, you leave yours back?" And Redcloud called out, "Sergeant Ketchum! Louie here failed to follow instructions, didn't you inform your squad to pack as if you're going for a week? Sergeant Nell, Sergeant Utah, listen up, everybody! I don't want to have to do an equipment layout. Make sure your men have everything. I find a man doesn't have his NVGs, it's on you, squad leaders. You-all know the bare minimum. So if any of you don't got it with you now—get it!"

Six or eight guys got up fast then and hurried back to the barracks to get what they knew they'd left behind, with Ssgt Ketchum kicking Van Louse in the butt, "What you making me look bad for?"

And right now Nick Flowers is filming. His camera at knee-level. Walking slowly in front of the Zoosters all sprawled out.

Coming across Pfc Holloway, Nick gets a joking middle-finger, about which Sniper Rodriquez berates the pfc. "Why you a'ways gotta ruin everythin, Holloway? Nicky, now yer gonna hafta start all over back 'gain."

Flowers, "Naw, it just reinforces the NPR All Things Considered snob stereotype view of the typical IQ-challenged redneck hillbilly GI."

Holloway, "Redneck hillbilly, Nicky? Who you callin redneck hillbilly?"

"No hills, he's from the concrete jungle," Wolfe corrects Nick. He's hanging out here, M4 carbine in hand but without any other gear. He's not going anywhere, especially not wasting his time on a mysterious QRF that he knows usually ends up as a nothing, dullsville. "California stoner skateboarder concrete-billy. You insult hillbillies, Nicky."

Holloway's answer: With both hands, a bird with each, he flips off Wolfe.

Wolfe, "You still in the seventh grade drawing dicks and cunts all over your schoolbook?"

"In yer basic training grad'ation pic'ure, Holloway," Rodriquez teases, "did you flip it off in that pic'ure too?"

Wolfe, "Too scared to, he'd have had the drill's boot up his ass. And enjoying it, asking for more. You like it in the ass, isn't that right, PFC?"

Holloway, "Ten thousand comedians out of work and you-all are cracking jokes."

Cpl Sandusky, "Like we haven't heard that one ten thousand times before, Hollo-weird."

And Nick Flowers continues filming on down to the two squads of ANA—twenty guys. And they've secured about half the Pop Tarts, cereals, muffins, orange juice and Gatorade, and what they haven't packed away in their small knapsacks they're chowing down with their chai.

The ANA sergeant from yesterday is in charge of these soldiers. The one who rescued the gas thrower insurgent and put him on the medevac.

If Wolfe noticed the Afghan sergeant, he couldn't care less. Again, because he's not going.

Nick Flowers is, wherever it is the Zoo's going.

When the op order came in last night Capt Washington cancelled the other two platoons' missions. They would stay back on the Cop, since the op order was nothing but a bunch of nebulous TBDs and Washington wouldn't know how long the Zoo would be gone.

It broke 3rd Platoon's heart that the HA mission was cancelled. No food and blankets for the poor Afghans villagers. Some of them wept openly.

Yeh right.

In another universe.

Flowers had asked Redcloud if he could go on the mysterious QRF, and Redcloud said if the CO said yes, and Capt Washington said the op order didn't specify no, so sure, have at it. Pack some warm gear and dry socks, Washington advised him. You never know—they could drop the Zoo off on a naked peak at ten thousand feet and forget about them for 48 hours.

As of now the only op order anyone's seen is the TBD one from late last night, not the unabridged one that newly-minted Lieut Col Zachary Dove was given.

All they know here is that two CH-47 Chinooks will pick them up sometime between 0720 and 0750.

That's why the Zoo was out here at 0545.

Hurry up and wait.

"What's that you're reading now, Doc?" Kyle Wolfe asks Eberly. "You finish *13th Valley*, no way, not already, how fast a reader are you?"

Doc shows his new book. *Dispatches*. Hardbound.

Wolfe, "What are you, a speed-reader, you take one of those speed-reading courses?"

A shrug from Eberly.

"Holy shit, Doc. You spend half your pay on Amazon? I'd think you'd have a Kindle, you don't have a Kindle?"

Eberly does. "It just doesn't feel the same as a book."

"I hear ya. Turning pages. Black ink on real paper. Like Gutenberg."
Eberly jokes, "Hard to picture all the titles on a Kindle on your dad's shelves."

Exactly right, thinks Wolfe. *Doc's nailed it,* and Wolfe visualizes the shelves, and his eyes scan down along the books and pick up random bits of the titles on their spines.

Cpl Sandusky, "That's a fact, Jack. You can't get this on a Kindle." He shows the double-page spread of a hot, barely clad up-and-coming unknown actress in his *FHM* magazine.

Holloway, "She can eat crackers in my bed anytime. In the Holloway Groove."

Sandusky, "Yeh, she's gonna wanna lay in your cum-caked sheets, Holloway, give me a break."

Ssgt Ketchum, "Cum-caked? Sounds like a cupcake dessert, Sandy. Holloway, you squirtin jism, making icing all over your mommy's cupcakes? With those little sprinkles all on top?"

Redcloud, "At ease! Com'on guys, it's not even seven o'clock, you have to talk sex already?"

Ketchum, "If we knew where we're goin, Sarge, who we're backin up QRF for. Enemy situation, friendly forces, terrain, weather. We don't got shit to plan for, you got somethin better'n cooch for us to be talkin 'bout? Give me a high school chick, in her cut-off shorts, dude, with her top tied up in a knot like this. Daisy Mae. I'm goin on a QRF for Daisy Mae."

Sandusky, "We're mushrooms. Kept in the dark, fed nothing but shit."

Redcloud, "You know everything I know."

Rodriquez chuckles, "It's the Army, Ketch. Worst, Isaf. Whaddaya wanna bet, gonna be a Isaf op an's gonna be like a soup san'wich. Watch, you see, gonna be Frenchies we gotta rescue and gonna be one big goat-rope, they don't speak no English, we don't speak no Frenchy shit"—

"I'll take the French," Ketchum cuts in. "They've got wine with their rats. That's all they're carryin in their canteens."

Ssgt Nell, "Hooah, I'm in, let's go! Par-lay voo fran-says?"

Ssgt Utah, "Don't listen to Ketch. You want to count on something, plan on being a blocking force for some flush-em-out operation, that's about all they're going to trust us with. A blocking force."

Ketchum, "You tell me when's a blocking force ever blocked shit? I haven't been on one we actually snagged one dude, not one."

Rodriquez to Lieut Caufield, "L-T, you're a officer, you know their thinkin. All them Isaf colonels, where you think they sendin us?"

Caufield, "Wherever the choppers dump us off."

Nell, "Emphasis on the dump."

Holloway, "Bagram! R-n-R for wasting all those insurg yesterday! Land of the PX and Burger King and smokin-hot Air Force chicks! The Holloway Groove!"

Sandusky, "You wanna bet your re-up bonus on that?"

"Re-up? That's for lame-ass lifers. Sheeee-at, you find me gettin set to sign papers to re-up, you just put one right here"—at his temple. "Save me the trouble."

Redcloud, "We gotta wait, Holloway?"

Laughter.

Others say this and that.

Joke.

Laugh.

Just bullshit.

Holloway asks Doc Eberly, "What you were reading yesterday, that *Walk in the Rain*. That four-eyed blind medic get court-martialed and sent to Leavenworth for killing that cool dude pfc?"

"You really want to know?"

"Couldn't sleep last night thinking about it. Honest, Doc. Honest. The dude get the 'lectric chair, get fried for it, didn't he?"

"He proved it was suicide and he got to escort the body home for the funeral, and the night before at the viewing he and the guy's sister they go into the back room there in the funeral home and they're doing it in one of the caskets and she's going 'Ooooh ooooh ooooh give it to me harder'. And he's pounding her, pounding her, I mean the casket's rocking, and she's going 'Harder, harder, Doc.' And he yells right back 'I'm pounding as hard as I can!—Amber!'"

Sandusky, "Hollo-weird, don't you got a little sister named Amber?"

Laughter.

Holloway, "You would know, Corporal Sandust-weird. Cuz I talked about her to your sister when I was boinking her the night before we came over here."

Wolfe, "P-F-C, that doesn't even make any sense. Say that again. You what to who when?"

Spec Lee Tran turns his ear. "Listen up, hear that? Choppers inbound."

Sandusky, "Where? Bullshit."

Rodriquez, "Way early, Tran."

Spec Tran listens harder. Can't discern it. Maybe they're right and he was wrong.

Sandusky to Holloway, "You couldn't of with my sister because I don't have a sister, and it was my big brother who was boinking you in the ass the night before we came over."

"Guys, guys!" from Redcloud. "Cool it, I said. Knock — It— Off."

Holloway, "He started it, Sarge. And Doc too, I didn't say"—

"Holloway!" from Redcloud, and a *Zip it!*

Peace, quiet, please, no more sex talk. Guys'll talk sex sex sex nonstop, Redcloud knows, until they haven't had any chow for a day and they're hungry, their stomachs are growling, in Ranger School *When it becomes meager rats and burning five times the calories humping patrol for 22 hours a day, it's food anybody thinks about, not sex, all kinds of food, and banquets, and just a big bucket of KFC and a Big Mac and fries and a shake,* until then when you haven't slept more'n an hour here an hour there for a week it becomes *Sleep sleep sleep, you want nothing but sleep, sleep and food,* and sex is nonexistent, then *In the freezing rain it's shelter, just get me outta this wet.* Food, sleep and shelter. Sex a way distant fourth. *We've got here the first three,* Redcloud thinks. Plenty of them, the first three, here in the Stan. But none of the sex. No possibilities even of the sex. Yeh they're gonna talk about it. *Until that first crack of that distant rifle somewhere.* Then, the instant of that crack, sex is out the window, and it's simply survival, to live another five minutes. And it's a rush better than sex. Scary.

Ssgt Nell offers the hope, "Maybe we'll get lucky and they'll cancel the whole thing and we can go back to bed."

Spec Van Louse, "And the Zoo gets over again. 2nd and 3rd pullin our cop security. Hooah."

Tran, "Shhhhhh, listen! There!"

Sure enough, the dim *whoop-whoop-whoop-whoop* of a helicopter somewhere.

Ears turn—from which direction?

There, from the north. A dark blip of something heading here way up the wadi and not fifty feet above the ground.

Closer, it's a Blackhawk. One Blackhawk alone.

Rodriquez laughs, "We aint all gonna fit in that."

Max capacity roomwise, and maxed-out weightwise, fully combat-loaded troops, eleven. No fudging those numbers. Nine's pushing it.

Redcloud checks his watch.

Lieut Caufield checks his.

Way too early for their choppers.

The Blackhawk fast approaches down the wadi.

And a second Blackhawk appears, up high, maybe 1200 feet. The wingman. No choppers fly alone in this war. There's safety in pairs.

Lieut Caufield to Redcloud, "The op order said Chinooks, didn't it?"

Redcloud, "Frag-O. Mission's scrubbed. It's General St Claire coming to pin medals on us for yesterday. And make you a captain."

Caufield to Wolfe, "You should have brought your gear down. If they're landing here, they could be your ride out to Fob Salerno."

Redcloud, "Or it's MPs for you, Kyle. I'd go hide in the hooch and we'll cover for you. We'll tell them you took a nomad caravan south."

Lieut Caufield chuckles, "Heading to Kandahar on a camel."

Wolfe sloughs it off, "I look good in stripes."

Redcloud, "And a ball-and-chain?"

"Keep in mind," joking advice from Lieut Caufield. "As they say in Special Ops: Deny everything and"—

Wolfe completes it, "And make counter-accusations."

"Serious," Lieut Caufield suggests. "You packed? We'll hold them for you if you want to go get your ruck."

Wolfe, "I was kinda looking forward to a second breakfast from 'Lesias. Denver omelet, some SOS, bacon and sausages."

"Wolfie," Redcloud laughs, "you're never leaving Valley Forge."

The lead Blackhawk cuts in from the wadi, crosses low over the Hesco perimeter, swings around, hovers and drops to the river rock in the center of the LZ, while the second one stays high and begins circling wide oval tracks, overwatch.

And all the Zoo is awake with all the engine noise and the rotor wash, but no one's gotten up or gotten his gear on, following the passive leads of Redcloud and Lieut Caufield remaining seated against their rucks.

A Blackhawk, a lone Blackhawk landing, it can't be for them.

Maybe if there were four. Five. And another two for the ANA.

The Zoosters watch as the door on this side slides open and first one soldier, then another, and a third get out. All three fully loaded under rucks and body armor, carrying M4 carbines. The third is a tall man who with his free hand pulls the smallest away out from under the spinning rotors, and the door is immediately slid shut from inside, and the rotors change pitch harshly, and the Blackhawk jumps up taking off, back over the Hescos, to now climb for altitude and now follow the other southwest.

Not even a minute on the ground. Even if Wolfe wanted on, he'd have never made it.

As the tall soldier, with longer strides, leads the other two, coming straight this way, sharp-eyed Redcloud can make out the black oak leaf insignia on his chest. He warns Caufield, "Rank, L-T. Lite colonel."

Caufield hops to his feet.

Twin black bars of captain on the smallest, the petite one.

Specialist rank on the short pudgy guy.

Caufield presents a salute to the approaching black oak leaf rank.

Lieut Colonel Zachary Dove comes up, returns it. Drops his rucksack.

Sheds his helmet and body armor.

Keeps his weapon. "Let's meet your C-O," he commands Caufield.

"Yes sir," and they step off.

The captain and the specialist drop their rucks and gear, shedding their helmets and body armor, and the entire Zoo locks eyes on the captain.

She's a woman.

Capt Laura Cathay.

Yessir, a woman.

Fresh and clean-looking and petite.

The opposite of rough. Smooth. Delicate.

Feminine.

Let it roll slowly off the tongue, Fem — in — ine.

Redcloud asks her, "Ma'am, excuse me. Can you tell me what's going on?"

"Sergeant First Class Redcloud, the Tattoo Zoo platoon sergeant?"

"Yes ma'am. What's all this about, a lieutenant colonel coming here?"

"I'm Captain Laura Cathay. Staff Judge Advocate."

"Jag? A lawyer?"

"We're here to look into the events of yesterday, with your platoon. In Wajma Valley. This is Specialist Howie. He's a video specialist. He'll be documenting our findings."

Redcloud turns away from her, and Wolfe is already stepping off quickly to follow Caufield and Lieut Col Dove for the Toc, and

Redcloud announces to his men, "Zoosters, listen up, listen up! Not one of you says one word to this lawyer captain and her choogie-boy specialist. Hear that? Not one word, the lieutenant or I'm not present. They wanna talk, you find me. Understood?"

"Hooah."

"Understood?!"

"Hooah!!!"

Cathay tells him, "You can't do that, Sergeant."

Redcloud just ignores her and takes off for the Toc

Cathay, angry, steps off after him, quickly, and Rodriquez calls after her, "Ma'am! Your weapon." Which she left on her gear, and she instantly knows her mistake. "It's injun country, ma'am," Rodriquez laughs.

Light laughter and snickers from Zoosters.

Capt Cathay retrieves her M4, tells companion Spec Howie, "Stay here," and hurries off to catch up.

All eyes eventually turn from her leaving to Spec Howie.

"Where you-all from, Specialist Chubby?" Sandusky asks. "You from Bagram?"

"Livin is good on Bagram," Rodriquez laughs. "No, gordito? La comida es muy buena, no?"

Ketchum teases, "Green Beans Coffee. Burger King. Pizza Hut and the KBR mess hall open 24/7."

Sandusky, "Mess halls, Sarge. There's three of em. Last I counted. I'd kill for breakfast right now in a KBR mess."

Ketchum, "Gonna hafta fight through Specialist Chubby here first. Be a drag-em-out fight with him, who gets the sausages and gravy and French toast and jelly donuts first. Like those, doncha, Chubby, y'like those jelly dough. . . .nuts?"

Laughter. And Spec Howie, pasty pale skin and soft hands, is scared of being here, scared of these guys, it's like he's just arrived on Mars and is met by ten-foot-tall crustacean aliens, and he says nothing, acts in no way in his defense, not even to laugh back pretending to enjoy the ribbing at his expense.

Ssgt Nell has some pity. "C'mon, c'mon, lay off him, all you-all." But not really. Adding with a snort, "Look, the poor headquarters pogue's already pissed his pants."

And Spec Howie looks down to check, even though he knows he hasn't pissed his pants, or should know he hasn't.

The guys howl.

Up on the steps of the Toc Capt Washington and 1st Sgt Kozak watch Caufield and Dove approaching, and Washington now realizes who it is.

Zachary Dove.

"Son of a bitch," Washington curses. "It's too early for this shit."

Kozak, "I didn't see any message traffic about visitors."

"Is that a black leaf, Eddie, or gold?" Dove's rank, unclear still from this distance.

Kozak squints. Makes it out. "Black."

"Son of a . . . . Zachary Dove an O-5. Wouldn't you know it."

"Do you know him?"

No need to answer, it's in Washington's angry look.

As Dove comes closer, Washington offers a flippant, disrespectful half-salute, and

Dove comes up the steps, returns a crisp partial salute and stops shoulder-to-shoulder next to Washington.

Each with an unwavering gaze into the other's eyes.

Two men of equal size.

Equal height.

Same age.

One black, one white.

One a captain, the other a lieutenant colonel.

Rank means something, and Washington gives in first. Asking, "You want to tell me what's the pleasure of this unexpected visit?" Said low, almost without moving his lips, his tar-thick sarcasm out in the wide open in the icky tone of his *pleasure* and *visit*.

Dove lets the moment pass, perhaps about to demand of Washington the respect of a *Sir* following that question. Then simply tells him, calmly, without anger, passion or dominance, "You'll want to get all your Sixes and Sevens, Jashawn." He looks to Kozak, "The Toc, First Sergeant?"

And Kozak points to the doors, steps there to lead, "This way, sir," and Dove follows him inside.

It took about ten minutes to get the other platoon leaders and platoon sergeants, including artillery, as well as Lieut Frye and a couple of others who'd pulled night shift and were already back in their B-huts.

In the Op Center Kozak invited Dove, then Capt Cathay, to help themselves to the coffee, and Dove did, but said nothing, just a *"Thank you"* to Kozak.

And no one said anything to him.

Or to Cathay.

The only speaking was just shared looks among the three staff guys already there on duty.

Capt Washington took his seat at his workstation. He'd wait, everything was now out of his control. The presence of a lieutenant colonel was serious. An unannounced drop-in by higher command, without even a *"We're five minutes out"* heads-up from the inbound chopper, never meant anything good. This had to be about Wolfe yesterday, what else could it be? So be it, what would happen would happen, it was going to happen, and Washington knew that he had temporarily lost command of his Cop, that there had been no smile from Zachary Dove, there'd been no *"How you doin, Jashawn?"*, that this wasn't an *"I was just in the neighborhood and thought I'd drop in"* impromptu get-reacquainted visit, not in light of yesterday with Wolfe in that village and in light of that mysterious TBD-overstuffed op order straight direct from Isaf Command no less.

Lieut Col Dove sat back against the radio bench up front, with the pfc from 2nd Platoon on radio watch pushing himself in his chair closer to the wall, putting distance from an unwelcome stranger lieutenant colonel.

Dove motioned subtly to Cathay to remain in the back of the room, quiet and inconspicuous.

Dove did not acknowledge the presence of Wolfe.

When Nick Flowers came in with Rodriquez, Nick gave a small wave of recognition to Dove who just nodded slightly back. Nick had spent three weeks with Dove and his 82nd paratroopers on the special task force two years ago and got a 30-minute film out of it that The UK Telegraph bought for its website and that he later sold to Australian, Canadian, and German TV.

As the lieutenants and platoon sergeants came in, they may have been talking coming through the hallway, but everyone instantly went silent in here. Lieutenant colonels don't just show up out of nowhere on a combat outpost and put out an order to get all the command elements together asap. And they don't just show up with what the word's immediately already been passed is a Jag officer.

Had been passed to Capt Washington in a whisper by Redcloud. *"A Jag captain's come too. Her, there. Jag, sir."*

This is not good, Washington had known. A female, an attractive female, on the Cop, that's one thing, it could make things seem a little brighter, guys would be more alert, out of their huts, out and about just wanting to see her and be seen by her. *Jag, female or male, nope, that's another thing completely. Not good. No one wants to see Jag, ever.* The good thing, Washington knew, *Kyle Wolfe is not in my command, is not my responsibility.* Cannot hurt his career any more than it's already scarred.

When Dove sensed it was everyone present, he met Washington's eyes, and Washington caught the eyes of Rodriquez nearest the doors, nodded, and Rodriquez pulled the doors shut.

Washington looked at Dove and leaned back in his chair, as if saying *Go ahead, it's all yours.*

Dove tossed Washington a thumb drive and told him to open the op order file and put it up on the briefing projection screen.

Dove apologized to Washington for Isaf having kept the company in the dark, but security was paramount. Then he went through the 3-page op order paragraph by paragraph.

The unabridged op order.

In a nutshell, Dove would be taking the Tattoo Zoo Platoon into the Wajma Valley to investigate yesterday's incident there.

Accompanied by two squads ANA, Capt Cathay and Spec Howie. The embed Nick Flowers was free to strap-hang if he so chose.

Infilling via two CH-47 Chinook helicopters.

Time on the ground: Approximately 5 hours.

Chopper exfil pickup in Wajma: 1300.

Risk Assessment: High.

Because of that High, on-station the entire time above Wajma would be two AH-64 Apache gunship helicopters.

Also because of that High, Valley Forge artillery was pre-approved. Attached map and sat photo indicated Artillery Free Fire Zone from the first terraced wall and all along the beach, across the stream and up that entire mountainside. Valley Forge's two 105s were to be pre-set on azimuth and elevation for center-of-stream.

Also, a Ranger platoon at Fob Salerno would be on standby as a Quick Reaction Force, with a Chinook dedicated their standby infil asset.

"If it seems excessive," Dove said, "since the Apache air cover should be more than enough to deter any insurgent attack, let me assure you all that this mission has the highest priority with General St Claire."

Further, he explained that General St Claire was taking no chances in Wajma Valley after yesterday's horrible tragedy.

Tragedy? All the Awsome Company officers and sergeants in the room knew by word of mouth what Wolfe did yesterday there in that valley and knew damn well that that wasn't a tragedy. The burning of Robyn, that's unfortunate, but not a horrible tragedy, and a couple of insurg being shot point-blank is the opposite of a tragedy — it warrants celebration. So, what, they all had to be wondering, what's this tragedy that has General Pete St Claire's panties all bunched in a knot?

"It's pretty straight forward," Dove said. "Shadow's been up since yesterday, and our drone image analysts assure us that there has been no unusual activity. No personnel movement in the mountains to speak of. No mass heat signatures. No one knows we're coming, not even our ANA coalition allies, so there shouldn't be any resistance on the air assault. If there is, that's what the Apaches are for. Any questions?"

And Wolfe immediately interjected, "I'll save you the time and the trouble, Colonel. Scrub the mission. Here, arrest me, I'm the one who shot the hajj."

Dove stared at him impassively, blankly. Said nothing.

Wolfe continued. "The Zoo had nothing to do with it, nothing at all. Number One, I didn't ask the L-T's permission. Number Two, I didn't get it, and Number Three, they didn't know what I was going to do and, Number Four, they couldn't of stopped me if they'd wanted to."

Still there was nothing from Dove. The whole Toc was so quiet you could hear the five radios' internal cooling fans humming.

Wolfe, "I'm the one you want, Colonel, take me. These guys don't have to go back out there, I killed the insurg. Or thought I killed him. Me, not these guys, they had nothing to do with it, no reason to go back out there, it's just another shitty Afghan ville."

"Thank you, Mr Wolfe," Dove said dispassionately. "You will have opportunity to give your complete statement later. Twelve noon straight-up a UH-60"—Blackhawk helicopter—"from Fob Salerno will pick you up here with your HTT regional director aboard and all your bags and baggage. And you will then be read your rights under the UCMJ by the two-man MP escort that will arrest you and then deliver you to Bagram Airfield. Understood?"

"Cool, Semper Fi, I'm all yours. Cancel the mission, Frag-O the op order, scrub the Chinooks and the Ranger QRF. A UH-60 at noon—hot dog! Passengers, you are free to move about the cabin."

A scattering of light chuckles from some, even as Wolfe wasn't finished. "I can't wait to get my say, I'll take my chances with a jury of my peers back stateside."

A couple of low and clandestine *"Hooahs"* around the crowded room. It wasn't ten minutes after the Zoo returned from the patrol yesterday that the word of Wolfe's actions out there had spread from Awesome soldier to Awesome soldier, artillery included, with nothing but high-fives for reaction, and fist-bumps and *"Wish it had been me."*

Wolfe grinned right at Dove after the *hooahs.* "Hear that?" Another low and clandestine *"Hooah"* from someone. "A jury of my peers, Colonel. Bring it on."

But Dove showed no reaction, no animation, utterly poker-faced. Pretended there'd been no *hooahs.* Nonplussed, deadpan, "You, Mr Wolfe," he said. He paused for effect. "In spite of your inflated narcissistic self-importance, you are a gnat on an elephant's ass. Consider it a courtesy that I've shared with you the status of your noon UH-60."

And he turned immediately to Capt Washington and told him to open the file folder *Images*. Then he pointed on the projection screen to the individual file *Wolfe #1*, and Washington opened it.

It was a video. Ten seconds without sound of Wolfe shooting the Bic guy point-blank three times.

Ten seconds and over, and it was so quiet in the op center that above the five radios' internal fans humming one could have heard a gnat breathe in and out slowly.

That was Wolfe yesterday doing what they'd all heard about. And there it was, right there, on video in living color. Real. Fact.

Dove then pointed on the screen for Washington to open *Wolfe #2*.

Video. Seven seconds. Wolfe shooting the gas thrower twice in the nuts.

Seven seconds and done.

One could have heard a gnat hold his breath.

It was Wolfe then who broke the silence. "Like I said, what'd I tell you, Colonel?" He chuckled. "Me," he reiterated, "not them. Here, arrest me, you arrest me right now, guilty as charged, save the Zoosters and a whole bunch of people a wasted trip for nuthin."

"Did you hear what I just said, Mr Wolfe? Need I remind you?"

"Gnat on an elephant's ass." Wolfe smiled. "Then what's the big deal, why go out there, what more proof do you need?"

And Dove tapped on the screen the file *School*.

Washington clicked it open.

Video. Like the others, without sound.

Fifty seconds.

Mangled and charred bodies of women and girls and babies carried from the school and set down in the dirt.

Severed legs and arms.

Fifty seconds and ended.

You could have heard a gnat die.

Then from Redcloud, no more than a mumble, a sad admission of regret, "Shoulda done BDA."

The first Apache came in low at exactly 0728 and buzzed the cop, followed by the first Chinook coming straight in without hovering and landing on the gravel with its ramp already down.

Ketchum's squad, Lieut Caufield and his radioman Holloway and terp Nouri and Doc Eberly, and half the ANA boarded.

Nick Flowers too.

And Capt Cathay and Spec Howie.

After them was Sniper Rodriquez, who would be the first out, first on the ground, aggressively itching to be out front to take on any possible resistance, fire up the enemy.

Lieut Col Dove boarded last.

And he remained standing on the ramp, looking back and pointing across to Capt Washington and Wolfe on the LZ edge, and he slashed his hand across his throat, *They were not to get on the second Chinook, they're not to come, they're not welcome.*

Just minutes before the Apache arrived, there had been white-hot words exchanged between Dove and Wolfe when Wolfe came down to the LZ in full ruck and battle-rattle and Dove told him, "If you're thinking what I think you're thinking, you're not welcome in Wajma Valley. Your helicopter is at noon, Mr Wolfe."

"Fuck you," Wolfe had said back.

"Noon. At which time, Mr Wolfe, you will be placed under arrest."

"I take that back. Fuck you and the Blackhawk you rode in on."

"Good luck with that if you think that F-you will be an effective courtroom defense."

"I'm turning myself in, I put myself in your custody. I'm your prisoner. You're going to Wajma, I'm going to Wajma."

"You're not manifested, you're not going to be manifested. These are my birds. Your flight is noon."

And Wolfe got right up close up into Dove's face, his hands on his M4 clipped to his body armor muzzle down, at the ready, and if he'd have thought it through he'd have to admit that his intent to go back to that valley wasn't to find a way to pull his bacon out of the fire but rather simply to see how and where all those women and girls' bodies came from out of that school building. "Add it to your list of charges," he hissed at Dove. "Failure to follow orders. Trespassing on your precious birds." He tapped the side of his M4 twice for emphasis, adding the unveiled threat, "It sure beats you leaving your commander stuck having to open a whole nuther set of charges, fratricide by double-tap."

Meaning, that Dove himself would be the double-tap fratricide.

Wolfe turned away, and Dove said nothing in return—what could he say?—he'd lost. How do you counter fratricide when you're going to be the one lying in the dirt with two neat holes in your temple?

Dove was then zero for two.

Just minutes before he'd had the same white-hot exchange with Capt Washington and had lost that one. Radio word had the choppers inbound seven minutes out and Washington had come down to the LZ with his RTO radioman, Sgt Akin, both all geared up to join the mission, and Dove had told him, sorry, neither Washington nor the RTO were in the op order nor on the manifest. And that wasn't him speaking, he said, it was "Straight from General St Claire, Jashawn."

"Screw the op order," Washington had told Dove. "And I'll reserve comment on the sexual proclivities of the general. This is my battlespace, the Zoo is my platoon, and if you and your P-C Coin bullshit General St

Claire's going to railroad my men, he can frickin court-martial me along with them."

"Don't make me give you a direct order, Jashawn," Dove told him then with soft caution.

"Order me," Washington taunted back. "And see if the Board of Inquiry respects a rank-hopper staff puke lieutenant colonel more than they respect my duty to my company in my battlespace to do all within my power to protect my men from harm. Both internal and external."

Dove: zero for two.

On the plus side, give him credit for knowing which battles are worth fighting for.

And which aren't.

Knowing which you're going to lose because you can't win because no one can win them.

Knowing that, shy of him cancelling the flights —

which would not be an option acceptable to Colonel Pluma and General St Claire, not under their time constraints which demanded the investigation happen now, this morning

— and calling Isaf to request an immediate MP contingent flown in to arrest Wolfe and detain Washington, he could not keep them from boarding the Chinook, either Chinook, verbal orders or slashed-throat commands or threats of disciplinary action notwithstanding.

Knowing that, as for Mr Kyle Wolfe, he's a loose cannon and would just as soon as not double-tap two bullets through Dove's head, plus two more into his heart just for good measure. And what's the harm in him coming along to Wajma now? What's the harm, what's the difference? Except as a defiance of Dove's demand that he not come. Except that body-blow to Dove's ego, his loss and Wolfe's win. On the other hand, it's not even a battle, but just an initial skirmish, irrelevant and forgotten in five minutes, in a battle and a war that Wolfe cannot and will not win.

Effective leaders adapt to changing circumstances. If Wolfe joined the mission to the valley, when they got there Dove would use the Zoo Platoon's satcom radio to call Isaf to tell them to cancel the noon MP Blackhawk to Cop Valley Forge, as Dove would be bringing Mr Wolfe back to Bagram Airfield under arrest with the rest of the platoon.

As for Capt Washington and that battle, that also had been but a minor skirmish lost by Dove, not the war. *Jashawn lost his war a long time ago,* Dove thought then with a sense of sad waste, remembering then in Iraq six years ago when then-lieutenant Washington blew up his career, stabbed a stake in the heart of his future, just to stand on the moral but untenable position arguing to command — first company then battalion — that his enraged platoon sergeant's pistol-whipping with the butt and muzzle of his M4 an 18-year-old Iraqi captured as the lookout of a cell that had just ambushed his platoon's sunrise urban raid —

1 dead, 3 badly wounded

—that that illegal assault, First Lieutenant Washington made the case to his command, could be dealt with on the company and battalion levels, without higher having to know and all the investigations and criminal prosecutions that would assuredly follow. And Washington, polite and respectful but still defiant, lost that argument then and there and further lost it down the road in a flat-line Company-level Officer Evaluation that hinted at *"situational ethics"* and *"borderline insubordination"* and was concurred by the Batt and Regiment commanders. Ensuring that Washington would never get a Ranger company, was fortunate to make captain at all, thereafter only assigned leg infantry commands, like this Awesome Company, and only being awarded those commands because the back-channel word on him was that he could run his company with minimum supervision, with consistent results that made the battalion look good, and that his soldiers respected him and trusted him.

The field-grades' grapevine word on Washington, indeed: His men trust him.

Anyone who has served or led in the infantry in combat knows that GIs may obey a superior from training, law, fear or habit, even while silently doubting and questioning his orders, but GIs will follow anywhere without question, even up a hill, charging into machinegun fire, a leader they trust.

And trust is always only first earned.

A trust that Dove knows, as his helicopter pulls up over the Hesco walls below, Jashawn Washington has earned because, just as that day those six years ago when he chose to challenge command to protect his platoon sergeant from what would be criminal judgment—

fourteen months lock-up and a dishonorable discharge, without benefits, for either the sergeant or his family

—it is that very nature, whether a character flaw or virtue, regardless, that now compels Captain Washington to shelter his GI Zoosters in horrible legal jeopardy.

Something that his Zoosters know without even thinking about.

Trust.

Right now Washington and Wolfe watch Dove's Chinook pulling up and banking over the Hesco walls. They had plainly seen Dove's slashed-throat command to stay back. And they have automatically discarded it.

Wolfe asks Washington, "Do you know that asshole?"

"He was a classmate at the Academy." More, he thinks but doesn't say, *PLs in Regiment together. He was at the hospital at the birth of our twins. Gwen and Bethany Ann, Dove's wife, they're peas-in-a-pod. BFFs.*

The Chinook rattles across the wadi to trail below the Apache to circle high above the Cop as

now a second Chinook comes in from down the wadi, with a second Apache trailing above.

Wolfe makes the observation, "Classmates, and you're a captain and he's already lite colonel?"

Washington has a slight grin. "You know how that goes."

"Yeh, whose ass is he kissing." It's a statement, not a question.

Washington shrugs. "Or I'm just another of those loser shitbird putz officers. Y'know, dime a dozen."

"I'm inclined to believe Number One."

Two Chinooks In Flight

Straight up the gorge.

The Apache in the lead and the one at tail are both at about 700ft above the ground.

The two Chinooks at about 400.

It's a thirteen-minute flight to the valley. What took the Zoo yesterday nearly two hours from there going home.

Dove surveys the troops here in the first Chinook. Ketchum and his squad are at the rear in the web seating along the sides. Sergeant Rodriquez standing at the half-raised ramp, ruck on his back like everyone in here. Lieut Caufield and Holloway plopped down on the floor.

No hooahs, no enthusiasm in these Zoosters.

Dove feels it, feels the passivity and apprehension of doom.

He assumes that word went quickly from the briefing down to the troops. Mass casualties yesterday in Wajma. Women and children. Shredded with Mk19 grenades and .50-cal.

Burned.

Dozens.

More than dozens.

"A shitload" is what soldiers were most likely saying and passing on soldier-to-soldier.

Dove knows it's 168. He didn't give out the number in the briefing. One thing at a time.

Silence among these Zoosters in here. Each in his own thoughts. Sure, screaming engines and rotors, it's deafening loud in here, but that's not why the silence and self-separateness.

All the Zoosters, down to the lowest privates, know that mass civilian casualties means trouble, big trouble. Heap big trouble.

The more experienced ones know that there's even more heap heap big trouble that those casualties were unreported.

By them.

Dove feels eyes behind tinted eyepro staring at him.

Sees Lieut Caufield's behind his clear eyepro avoiding him.

Nick Flowers is standing back here. Northface three-day backpack on. Camera in hand, held low. He'll exit right behind Rodriquez, filming, maybe it'll be a hot LZ down there in the village, and that's golden, most likely not, but it's good movement, motion, action shots anyway, soldiers sprinting from the back of a helicopter under the swirling, blurring rotor blades.

Good stuff when you can get it.

Yesterday was a total loss, but it was then, the past, yesterday. Today might be good for Nick Flowers.

Dove closes in up next to Flowers. Shouts in his ear. "You film whatever you want, Nick. No restrictions. My specialist is filming for me. All General St Claire asks—General St Claire would like you to return with us later today. To Bagram. Be advised, he might want to see your footage first. To ensure there's nothing released that might compromise our ongoing negotiations. Which I'm not at liberty to discuss."

A smile and shrug from Flowers, *No problem.* He leans close to tell Dove, "Good to see you again, Zachary. Wish it were a better place and time." A wince, regrets, *Instead of under these circumstances.*

Dove maneuvers his way between the ANA soldiers seated on the floor to get to Capt Cathay and Spec Howie who are standing at the front between the door gunners seated behind their mounted M240 machine-guns.

This is a first combat air assault for both Cathay and Howie, the first time either has been outside the comfy civilized safety of big Bagram Airfield, and Dove sees the apprehension and pale fear in both.

"When we touch down," he tells them, shouting. "Hurry out behind all them. Go straight six o'clock. Twenty meters. Hit the deck. I'll be right behind you. It's a cakewalk, Laura, relax. No one will be shooting at us. It's a cold LZ."

In the second Chinook Capt Washington tells Redcloud he'll push the stick from the rear, then makes his way between all Nell's and Utah's men and the ANA crowded in here to the front where he removes his helmet and grabs up a hanging headset to wear to monitor the pilots' communications, bending down just behind, between the pilots, to watch through the windshields.

Thundering up this gorge.

The mountainsides so close on each flank.

The first Chinook coming in and out of view as this bird comes out of banked curves and catches sight of the first just before it disappears around curves ahead.

Minutes ago, as Washington stood at the rear looking out over the ramp as this chopper banked away over the Hesco walls, climbing, with the entire Cop Valley Forge laid out below, leaving it, he'd felt a sense of pleasant comfort. *It's home.* His men down there, the few moving about, his two platoons all secure within the Hescos, as well as the arty platoon. He could make out the first sergeant heading back up for the Toc. His last words to Kozak had been to not let XO Frye screw up in the short time he'd be in command in Washington's absence. "Watch after him, Eddie," he'd joked, and Kozak had joked right back, "Shit, sir, I'm going back to bed." His Valley Forge below, receding, he had missed it already. *Home.*

Up front now the view outside the windshield is to him beautiful in an absolutely primitive, pre man-on-earth way. *As God made the earth,* he thinks. The dinosaurs could be down there, and he's flying above them, entering maybe the Garden of Eden ahead. And he thinks that he should have been a helicopter pilot, that he could have this view like this every day.

He could have been a pilot had he wanted to.

Up near the very top of his West Point class, he could have any Branch he wanted, and he debated Aviation, seriously considered it, but Infantry has always been where the true warriors go and where men go to be warriors, or so he'd reasoned then in his youth and knows now that a warrior isn't revealed in the Branch, it's in the man, regardless the Branch.

Infantry guarantees upon Academy graduation an immediate slot in Ranger School, and all true warriors, so goes the thinking of young stud cadets, challenge themselves to the max in Ranger School then cross their fingers to have that superior warrior officer status confirmed with an eventual Ranger platoon and even company command.

Things like that matter to a 22-year-old about to graduate near top-dog in a class of twelve hundred mostly alpha-males. To then follow Ranger School with a plum assignment as a butterbar platoon leader in the famed 173rd in Italy, and then use his superior performance there as a calling card to a coveted platoon leader slot a first lewy in the actual Ranger Regiment, where inexperienced butterbar second lieutenants who have never commanded a platoon do not exist.

It was in the 173rd in Italy, ironically, that his random meeting of a young American woman named Gwendolyn—

the cellist of the University of Georgia string quartet on a summer tour of Europe whose beauty so intrigued him when he saw her through the window of a bakery on a Saturday afternoon in Venice that he went in and went straight up to her and told her simply and quietly that he was enchanted at first sight, and wound up falling enfatuated that night in concert watching her play Vivaldi and Bach

—would deepen to love in the weeks and months that followed in their cyberspace long-distance relationship then to marriage and family once he was back stationed stateside as a Ranger PL.

It would then follow that the soft nature of this cellist, and her open-mindedness, and tolerance, and her playful imagination that can appreciate the inexplicable purity of a sonata born out of nowhere, would begin to crack his single-minded obsession and passion to be a warrior leading warriors, following warriors, and further erode his once unquestioned certitude in the Point's long gray line culture of the supremacy of fixed order and strict regimen, of command and career.

He feels a sense of rapture at this beauty, his flying right through it, and thinks that Gwendolyn would love to be here watching this, watching it beside him. And he recognizes that she would see it as a symphony, as the pages upon pages of notes, and hearing those notes flying through here, through this raw nature, and hearing it as the hundred instruments playing as one. She would be holding onto his arm with both hands, right here right now, close pressed side-by-side, and at this moment he suddenly feels the weight of this command, of this war, that he would so much rather be home with her, *Real home*, he thinks, *With her and the kids, not my Cop*, that's not home. What is he doing here, really? He'd trade it at this moment to be with them, *Home*, regardless this weightless gliding speed through this beautiful landscape of cragged mountainsides so close and that stream below, and he realizes that maybe this feeling of vacancy, of futility, it's from a sense of doom for his Zoo Platoon, that fate has played a tragic joke on them—on Matt Caufield and on Travis Redcloud who will now be court-martialed, which seems a foregone conclusion, *How could they not be?, how many bodies are there there on that video?* Bodies that were pulled from a school building into which Caufield's and Redcloud's Zoosters fired on their orders. *Travis*, he thinks, *An NCO who, were I a soldier in his platoon, I would want to try every day to emulate.*

Radio chatter over his headset tells that the first chopper, out of sight ahead, is touching down in Wajma. No enemy anywhere, they're saying. The few villagers up in the fields fleeing fast toward their compounds.

As his chopper goes through the narrow gap that is the door to Wajma Valley, Washington stares without blinking at the expansive majesty of the valley and its terraced fields and ring of jagged ridges 360 degrees around, and he imagines that Gwendolyn right here beside him catches her breath that he feels in the tightening of her grip on his arm, and he shakes his head hard once and blinks and now sees that

the first Chinook is pulling up off the wide beach where Washington can see the troops that were dropped off are in a perimeter, and from this distance they're tiny dead waterbugs splayed out flat on the dirt, and

the waterbugs quickly grow larger and larger, into human forms belly-down, weapons all pointed outward, then the chopper is flying directly over them, not twenty feet above them, then touching down, and Washington asks of the pilots over the headset, demanding, "Thirteen-hundred, roger?! You'll be back, 1300?!"

From the pilot on the right, the Chief Warrant Pilot, with a 9-11 NEVER FORGET decal on the back of his flight helmet—

the 11 being two silhouette towers

—an answer, "Roger, see you then," and a single stark nod of that flight helmet, and

Washington throws off the headset, grabs up his helmet and follows the Zoosters hurrying toward the rear and down the ramp onto the beach.

In Wajma

About one hundred feet in front of the school running from the edge of the stream to the first terrace wall is a short wide rock wall.

About three feet high, two feet wide.

Maybe a breakwater for the school when the stream runs floodwater high as a river. Except, the school building is itself solid concrete built up at least seven or eight feet with maybe a dozen concrete steps going up to the wide veranda.

No need for a breakwater.

No need for the rock wall.

Plus, the wall looks older than the school, which was constructed three summers ago with USAID money. So says the bronze plaque in both English and Dari on the schoolhouse wall at the now doorless entrance.

And until yesterday's Zoo barrage of 40mm grenades and .50-cal rounds, the school held its age nicely. Now it's pockmarked and blackened.

Nothing a couple hundred thousand more USAID dollars can't patch and paint up.

As for the short wide rock wall, why it even exists, who knows?

It T-intersects with the first terrace rock wall, and is at least as old as all the terrace walls, so maybe some overzealous young brick mason six hundred years ago built it just to show off to and win the heart of some beautiful maiden who had a thing for rocks and walls.

Or not.

It's Afghanistan.

If you're going to ask why about every little incongruity, you might as well just pack it in and go home and leave these people to their 13th century ways and call it a day.

But the Zoosters are here, in Wajma and in Afghanistan, and they're not going home stateside today or for a while anyway, and this rock wall was here long before they arrived, in both Wajma and Afghanistan, and no one thinks a second thought about it.

Except that it's a natural defensive position to set up on and along.

And that's what Lieut Col Dove has done, making his base here on both sides of it.

Primarily, Rto Akin and Pfc Holloway have their satellite radios and small flip-out antennas set up on the wall for comms.

Comms are always first. Establish comms with the rear because if the shit hits the fan, however slight or nonexistent the chance, that's where your support's coming from. Artillery. Air. Medevac.

Zoosters in pairs scattered about along the length of the wall.

The school building itself is a natural defensive position, and Dove left it to Capt Washington and Redcloud to establish primary security there on the flat roof. Which are three machineguns out front on the thick parapet around it.

Comms established and maintained via satellite by Rto Akin and Holloway.

Security by the machine-gunners on the roof.

Two Apaches circle the valley high overhead. Their constant drone is just background noise now, not even heard after this time on the ground.

When the platoon had just arrived and the second Chinook had taken off and followed the first downstream then out of the valley, Capt Washington had made his way over to Dove and told him, "It's your show, Lieutenant Colonel Zachary Dove."

Washington's mockery and disrespect so blatant in the exaggerated use of full rank and name, Dove had returned the insolence in the tone of an order. "Proper protocol, captain to colonel, is the use of the word sir."

"Good luck with that."

"Jashawn, we can do this the hard way or we can do it the easy way."

"It's your show," Washington had said. "You're the prosecutor, judge and jury. You've got your two court stenographers." He'd raised his hands in mock appeasement, "I'm just an interested spectator." Then he'd lowered his eyepro to look over the tinted lenses and directly meet Dove's gaze. "To ensure you don't manufacture your evidence."

And Dove had a memory flash of Cadet Jashawn Washington, nicknamed from day-one by his Point peers *"Jay-Sire"*, a recognition, which Cadet Washington found nothing wrong with, of his exaggerated sense of self-worth based on a very real confidence in his ability, leadership and correctness. *"Jay-Sire"* worked as 1 part mockery, 3 parts jealousy, 5 parts reality, 10 parts respect. It was the same ratio for Dove's cadet nickname, the Z of Zachery shortened to *"Zoom"*, ironic for his careful deliberateness and biting for what the deliberateness could not hide, his intent to race up the ranks.

Jay-Sire and Zoom, friends, competitors, equals. Both headstrong and sure, with Jay-Sire's upfront, unabashed, honest. Zoom's quiet, unassumed, veiled.

Jashawn's always been brazen, Dove thought. Always been direct, couched nothing, *Why should he be different now?* Equals as cadets, equals as Ranger platoon leaders, one jagged, the other polished, they could compete and spar as friends and be proud that their wives would become fast and close, like sisters, and each could recognize in the other the same promise and potential that would booster-rocket each separately to their general stars. Until the breech, that is, Washington's questioning of command in Iraq, that brazen defiance that exploded the booster rocket and sent his career tumbling, to eventually crash at sea, where it bobs on the shallow swells. The stars no longer even a dream.

It is natural that they would not remain friends. Nor acquaintances. The embarrassment of failure. The embarrassment for another's failure.

"To ensure you don't manufacture your evidence," Jashawn had said.

Your evidence.

And Dove sent the ANA along with Ketchum's squad in teams up to recon the compounds to ensure the village was insurgent-free and to bring villagers down to be questioned outside the schoolhouse where the rest of the platoon would set up base.

Separate teams of the ANA and Zoosters are now coming back, seen in the distance returning across the terraced fields. It was only the ANA who actually went into the compounds up there. Zoosters having stayed outside, apart, away, but everyone alert at the ready, with thumbs resting on their M4s' selectors, set to flick them off safe.

Again, the ANA had gone inside doing all the checking, Zoosters outside.

Respect for the culture, that sort of thing. Coin.

Can't have an American GI non-Muslim accidently get a peek at a woman stoking a cooking fire. Or suckling an infant.

Whoops, not that there'd be much of a chance of all that many women or infants still around after that little mass casualty incident here yesterday.

Oh well . . .

Then, lest one forget, wasn't it the ANA who supposedly checked out the school yesterday?

But who wants to quibble?

Call it fair play. The goose and the gander. Back on Valley Forge the ANA aren't allowed in the Toc, the Dfac, the showers or the conex shitter. Here outside the wire the GIs are afforded the same privileges.

Afforded the exact same respect.

Nick Flowers didn't go into the compounds, though he'd wanted to, and he'd tried at the first one, but an ANA soldier stopped him with the muzzle of his AK on his chest and a single word, *"Khazmony"*, which is "women" in Pashto and one of the various words for females, like "tani" and "janay", that Nick's bothered to learn simply by repeated hearing.

The same thing happens all the time to him out on patrols. And it never gets any better, always burns him up. He'll casually saunter over to go through the big steel-plate double gates of a compound, and an ANA soldier or a couple of them will stop him—AKs pointed, along with *"Khazmony"* or *"Janay"* or whatever, it's always "Women".

No matter how nice a guy he is, how non-confrontational, easy-going, it gnaws in his gut that these same Afghan soldiers who prize their women so much as to make seeing one punishable by AK 7.62 round to the gut, themselves go bananas drooling lust when they get one of the *Maxims* or *Men's Health* discarded by GIs or when they're watching over a GI's shoulder an American movie playing on the GI's little portable DVD, wide-eyed over the scantily-clad models and actresses.

It gnaws him still, gnawed him today when the soldier stopped him, *"Khazmony"*, and he didn't get any footage inside a compound. Couldn't get on tape Afghan homelife up close inside. He got a lot of that stuff in the early days and just a few years ago, when American soldiers would freely enter compounds, before the whole Coin hearts-and-minds deference for the culture thing became engraved-in-stone command policy.

Not that Nick holds it against the Afghans for protecting their women from the eyes or touch of the infidels. Shoot, it's just the opposite with the West, where women are displayed in all their naked sexual depravity in those magazines and those movies and MTV and billboards, everywhere.

Put them in a burka, Nick had emailed a NYU buddy who's working in Hollywood editing TV commercials. *Round up the publishers and all the film directors and studio heads and tar-and-feather them and string them up and gut them.* His buddy emailed him back, *It would make a great snuff film. Whip me up a treatment I can pitch.*

Nick had gone up to the compounds with Ketchum because that's where the action might be.

An ambush could be waiting.

Regardless of Dove's reassurance in the briefing that Shadow drones had seen no insurgent activity.

Regardless the two Apaches were flying cover right overhead.

Action's footage. Golden footage.

Not today, not this morning.

The footage he got of the guys coming off the Chinook was okay, but he's got that stuff from numerous other times, and if there's no gunfire, if there's no enemy waiting for you, it's B-roll filler shit. So far this morning for Nick this day's been a bust. This setting, this valley, it's absolutely beautiful, but it's something out of a NatGeo nature film, it's the pastoral backdrop of a Jane Austen novel, a British talkie film, and he's here shooting war.

Where's the war?

The only consolation for Nick is that he could be sitting back on the Cop and the guys there aint doing shit, not today. Boring. Where's the footage in tower guard duty? How many times can you film guys playing hearts in the TV room? Two guys throwing a football on the LZ?

At least it's a spectacular setting out here. And that school ahead, *Scene of the slaughter yesterday, maybe we'll get something.*

As for the other civilian along for the ride today, Kyle Wolfe, he couldn't care less about going up to search the compounds. He's stuck around with the command element. Here. With Redcloud.

And hasn't said much of anything.

Yeh, like Capt Washington he's just an interested spectator.

And he really doesn't know why he even came out here today, except for his curiosity about the dead bodies from the school. Not that he can do anything—not about them nor about his own two shot-up hajj. They've got him on tape, real live video, *Dead-to-rights shooting point-blank those two insurg killer bastards. That kiss-ass colonel doesn't even need to manufacture evidence* against him. He didn't even look insane on that video doing it. Temporary insanity, will that be his defense? He knows, military, tried in a court-martial, they'd lock him up and throw away the key. Civilian, it's *A civilian jury, of my peers,* and his defense will be Robyn Banks herself, who she was, the good person she was and how she was so *Violently, senselessly, savagely killed, burned to death.*

What's troubling, even with a civilian jury, they've got him on tape doing it, killing those two hajj, and *That's going to be hard to beat. How did they film it?, where were they?, and we didn't even know it.* Temporary insanity, he'll have to use that. Though he knows he wasn't temporarily insane, that he'd do it all over again today, except to *Make sure that second asshole was dead. And still anyway they'd still have it on tape.*

Wolfe could have stayed back on the Cop today and just waited for the noon Blackhawk. The MPs, they'd cuff him. Deliver him to whatever lockup brig they've got at Bagram. HTT is over. Everything is changed. He can't go back into the military anymore. Private security contractors won't hire him if he wanted to go that route. The Blackwaters. Triple Canopies. DynCorps. There goes the bank account, *Going to be cleaned out, going to go for the attorneys.*

He realizes that this out here today is going to be the last time in who-knows-how-long that he's out in someplace as wide open and unrestrictive and picturesque as this valley here.

He's on the school roof right now.

With Redcloud.

Standing at the parapet.

Funny, Wolfe thinks, he really didn't think yesterday how *Really landscape oil-painting scenic it is here.* He didn't notice yesterday. *It's something you see on a PBS travel show, makes you want to move to the hinterlands third-world country, live like a prince.*

He watches Ketchum's men and the ANA coming across the fields and notes that it looks like they've got three village men with them.

Earlier, below he'd heard Lieut Col Dove telling terp Nouri that when the villagers were brought down he would be terping for the Jag captain in her interrogations.

That fat specialist staff panty-waist would be documenting it on video.

Until then, right now Wolfe sees Dove indicate that the Jag captain and her fat specialist with the videocam are to follow him. Washington and Lieut Caufield as well. Up the steps below, inside here.

The school is built right up against the mountainside, in the shelter of it, with the mountainside caving up over half of it.

The building is standard USAID construction for a village this size.

80' by 40'. With the 80-foot length cut in the middle with the steps and entrance.

Wide veranda across the entire front. Enclosed by a waist-high wall interspersed with wide concrete support pillars arched above.

Capt Washington pauses at the top of the steps to survey the length of the veranda both ways. All the walls two-foot thick. Concrete, and what he knows would be solid brick underneath. Concrete, brick-and-mortar. Solid Afghan construction. *A natural fortress,* he thinks. *I could fight from this position.*

Three windows on each side of the entrance into the school.

From where the RPGs had shot yesterday.

What had been wooden windows and doors now just splinters. A thousand rounds of 7.62, .50-cal and 40mm will do that to a place.

Unpainted gray concrete, swaths of which are now scorched black. Chalk that up to the fires buring from inside yesterday.

Inside through the entrance it opens up into one room across the entire 80-foot length, half the building depth.

Set back centered is a wide concrete staircase up halfway to a landing then turning 90-degrees and running along the rear wall to the roof.

Capt Washington makes note of the exploded burnt twisted slices of 55-gallon drums strewn around in this front area.

Lieut Caufield remembers flames from yesterday dancing out the windows. *Diesel fuel or gasoline in those drums.*

On each side of the staircase is a classroom, sectioning this entire floor inside into just three rooms and the staircase.

The ceiling is high, maybe 18 feet. Concrete, a couple of feet thick, it's ceiling and roof. No signs of conduit or wire or light fixtures. *The villagers would have stripped it all out the week after opening,* thinks Washington.

Dove checks out the classroom on the left, and there are no windows along the back wall—just one on the side.

Same with the other classroom. Washington notes the litter of chunks of concrete and steel.

Lieut Caufield thinks, *No windows along the back, the side of the mountain is right there, what, a foot, two feet away? Did the Taliban sneak in the window there and we didn't see them? When'd they put all those women and kids in here?*

Washington is thinking, *They would have put the women and children in here before the Zoo arrived.* Insurgent watchers along the ridgelines on their walkie-talkies giving the hour-plus lead-time.

Dove is thinking, *Insurgents would have said it wasn't safe up in those compounds, not with the Americans coming, and to get all the women and the girls into the school.* Where they would be hidden from the American soldiers.

Washington thinks, *They would have told the villagers that the infidels can see through their women's clothes with our xray-vision Oakley eyepro.*

Dove thinks, *And the American soldiers would kick in their doors and take their women and rape them.*

Washington, *Rape the little girls too.*

The sad pity of uneducated ignorance, Dove thinks.

The ANA sergeant lied to me, Caufield thinks. *This wasn't M-tee. And not just the Taliban hiding in here. All those girls.*

If there ever had been school furniture here, there's no sign of it now. No desks, chairs, tables, not even in ruins. If USAID provided them, *The villagers hauled them away and sold them,* Washington knows. A long time ago. *Yeh, the week after opening.*

Afghan school kids sit on the floor on straw mats anyway.

It's the culture.

Like the electricity and light fixtures and copper wiring and a generator, Afghan village schools aint open at night, who needs em?

Who? The eldest village elder, for his compound, that's who. Especially the generator.

Repeat: It's the culture.

Cue laugh track.

When Wolfe came through here a little while ago with Redcloud to climb the stairs to the roof, he'd thought about the absence of desks and chairs and the absence of schoolbooks and writing tablets, and he thought that it wasn't the fire of yesterday, it was the culture part about Afghans selling what good ol' Uncle Sam was giving them, and he thought and had to laugh a little to himself and even feel a giggle of guilt for it that *Shit, what's it matter now, there aren't any kids now to go here anyway after yesterday.* And he'd visualized the video image of the torn and dismembered and burned bodies of the women and girls carried out and laid on the ground and thought *What the hell*, it was better, it really didn't matter, *Afghans are Muslims 99.999% and believe it's a sin for girls to be educated anyway. Ask Mohammed.*

In the classroom Dove kicks at some chunks of metal.

Washington does the same in the other classroom.

Dove picks up a jagged piece, half a curved cylinder chunk, about the diameter of a fire hydrant main. Picks up another. Exits the classroom and flicks one jagged piece over to Washington coming out of the other.

Dove closely examines the piece he kept with his high-intensity SureFire flashlight.

Washington examines his with his SureFire.

Washington knows what it is.

Dove knows as well.

Dove shines his SureFire back around in the classroom Washington has been in. Shines it along the floor. Hundreds of similar jagged chunks and pieces.

"Want to bet," Washington says. "Get CSI in here and they're going to find a trigger initiator. Going to find C-4 residue. Probably even lengths of copper command wire. Diesel residue in those drums that were here."

"Are you a fan of CSI, Jashawn?" Dove asks.

"Gwendolyn is."

"Bethany Ann's partial to NCIS." Dove's wife. "She thinks Mark Harmon's a hunk."

"He's sixty years old."

"I think it's his dark smoldering brooding side."

"Opposite the sweet, open, charming, partyboy Zachery Dove who's everybody's best friend and good buddy, always buys the rounds at the bar and who teaches kindergarten Sunday school and coaches youth-league soccer when he's not making s'mores at neighborhood cookouts?"

That wasn't said with any lightness or playful teasing irony. It was a hard jab. Dove lets it go by, pretends to ignore it. Knows where it's coming from. Asks Lieut Caufield, "Is your wife a CSI fan, Matthew?"

"I- I'm not married, Colonel sir."

"I know."

He's read Caufield's file.

And he knows and Washington knows that these metal chunks are the remains of artillery shell casings.

The Zoo didn't shoot artillery into here yesterday.

He knows that, and Washington knows that.

Besides, these chunks would have been complete shell casings tossed as litter around the big guns where they were fired.

Which would have been back on Cop Valley Forge.

They'd have been whole, one solid cylinder.

Shiny brass.

Not blackened chunks and jagged pieces.

Not on site where the projectile part of the arty shells, without the shell casings, would have landed. And exploded into flames and tiny shrapnel.

Again, the casings would be at Valley Forge.

"You'll want to get all that in there," Dove tells Spec Howie, about the litter in the classrooms. To video it.

And he tells Caufield, "Afterwards have your men bag some of it for evidence."

"Yes sir."

Dove allows himself just a moment to imagine that in each classroom there had been a bundle of two, maybe three artillery shells wrapped in C-4 with det cord or a simple blasting cap initiation. Command detonated.

Capt Washington imagines three or four artillery rounds stacked in the corner of each classroom, *That corner that was cratered, blasted close, used as a backsplash to send the thick curtain of shrapnel in a fan upon the women and girls and little babies cowering* in these two classrooms. Maybe some out here in this space here, *As the insurgents in here were firing their RPGs from those windows.* Deaf from the RPGs firing and the Zoo's 20mm grenades bursting and .50-cal clomping the walls, *The terrified, crying, screaming girls would not have had thought about the small stacks of arty rounds. At that moment of detonation they would have had no time even to realize that they were being killed.* Instantly.

"What do you want to bet," Washington says. "There's residue of Willie Pete everywhere."

White phosphorous artillery rounds.

White phosphorous burns at about 5,000 degrees centigrade.

Makes everything it touches burn. For concrete, it scorches.

"Tell me something, Matthew," Dove asks of Lieut Caufield in a quiet disarming manner. "In your AAR you say that your ANA counterparts inspected in here and reported it was empty. No local villagers, no enemy insurgents. But neither you nor any of your men actually set foot inside to inspect it yourself?"

And Dove knows the answer. Privately, minutes after they'd landed, with Capt Cathay and terp Nouri he had talked with the ANA sergeant, who admitted that he himself had not checked the school, but two of the men from the other squad had and they'd said it was empty and they were back on the Cop today, those two, but when the Zoo went back this afternoon he would point them out for the colonel and the colonel could talk to them then.

"The ANA did," Lieut Caufield answers. "They came back, sir, and they said it was empty."

"Understood. But you didn't send even one man with them?"

"No sir."

"You took the word of the ANA without having had your own men's eyewitness verification?"

Washington answers for Caufield. "Isn't that General St Claire's Coin theory? Trust our Afghan allies, our quote coalition partners closed quote."

Dove ignores Washington. To Caufield, "You didn't think it was prudent to act in a supervisory—if not outright but in a subtle way—in a supervisory capacity?"

Again Washington answers before Caufield. "Unless I misunderstand Coin theory, treating our Afghan partners as anything other than equals inhibits and discourages their self-confidence and self-worth."

Again Dove ignores him. Expects an answer. "Lieutenant Caufield?"

"Sir," Caufield admits with hesitance. "Sir, we don't go into schools or mosques."

"Mosques, yes, but whose policy puts schools off-limits?"

Washington answers, "Battalion."

Dove, "I'll need to confirm that. Do you have it in writing? From your colonel?"

"Oh yeh sure I've got it in writing, the B-C's going to put it in writing so his career can be submarine'd, 'See you later, chump, good luck in the civilian job market'. General St Claire says 'hearts and minds', 'respect for the population', RC East commander General Numbnuts salutes him 'hooah sir', brigade commander Colonel Numbnuts salutes him 'hooah sir', and my B-C comes up to Valley Forge and pulls me aside and says 'Stay outta the mosques, stay outta the schools, stay outta the houses and don't you dare kill any non-combatant civilians'. And that's your paper trail, Zach. Sorry, 'Colonel'. There is no paper trail. And if one of my men goes into that school or mosque before he takes fire from it, the next day the imam is screaming up at battalion or brigade that my men have seen their women in the flesh and raped their girls, and he wants ten thousand dollars cash, and my men are brought up on charges and I'm relieved of command for incompetence and the inability to control my men."

Dove, harshly, "Perhaps relieved of command instead for disrespect for your superiors and brazen bashing of those superiors and excessive dependence on a four-year-old's whiny excuse-making."

"The shit rolls downhill not the other way around, which you wouldn't know anything about sitting up there in Never-Neverland Isaf. And not one of those 'superior' numbnuts is ever out here where he's fired upon from a mosque or a school or a compound that he can't go into, and every insurgent from here to Quetta knows that that's our Roe."

Dove again ignores Washington. Turns to Caufield. "Lieutenant, on the word of the ANA, translated through your terp no less, without you yourself knowing whether or not there were civilian non-combatants here, you nevertheless allowed your men to present overwhelming lethal force?"

Washington blows up, "Present overwhelming lethal force? Is that the latest Isaf-speak? You want documentation? You need documentation?" He steps over to Spec Howie and grabs him and pulls him over into the light of one of the windows. And orders, "Film. Here, film!" His face.

And Howie shakes from fear of this man so much bigger and so much more powerful, so passionate, so forceful, and he trains the videocam on him.

Washington, directly into the lens close, in clipped exact militarese. "I, Jashawn Washington, Captain, United States Army, personally on a number of occasions instructed First Lieutenant Matthew Caufield and my other platoon leaders that neither they nor their soldiers are to enter mosques, schools or civilian living quarters unless and after they have been fired upon from said buildings or except under exceptional conditions and only after approval from me. Cut. Print."

He steps away and back toward Dove. "You want a paper trail? That's your paper trail."

Dove does not react, has no response.

Instead asks Caufield, "Explain, Lieutenant, please. How you failed to mention in your AAR that Mr Kyle Wolfe had shot assassination-style two unarmed civilians."

"Ex-excuse me, sir?" Caufield stammers.

"I said, explain how you failed to report that Mr Wolfe had assassinated the two unarmed civilians."

"I didn't see it, sir."

"You weren't aware of it?"

"I didn't see it. Sir."

"And your platoon sergeant, Sergeant First Class Travis Redcloud, he didn't see it either?"

"Sir. You'll have to ask him."

"You didn't ask him?"

"No sir."

"You weren't at all curious?"

Washington interjects, grinning broadly, flippant in his sarcasm, saying, "Don't Ask Don't Tell."

Dove is suddenly angry, "I'm not speaking to you, Jashawn."

"Nah nah nah nah naaaaaahhhhh nah, and I'm not speaking to you. My dad can whip your dad. I'm rubber, you're glue, it bounces off me and sticks to you."

The absurdity is so absolutely irrationally out of place that Dove is caught speechless. *Is this a playground? Are we fifth-graders? Is this entire situation really this insane?* So absurd for a man who was once 16th in the class, Jay-Sire, with an easy promise of one star unbelievably early at eighteen maybe—twenty for certain—*Most likely before me*—so natural in command, so straight-forward with men under his command going all the way back to the Academy and on forward to his platoons and companies, so open-hearted and tough-love honest with them, and Dove knows that this is no accident, it's purposeful, a fifth-grade schoolyard taunting to deliberately rattle Dove, while at the same time, belittle him for his rank.

Because,

He's jealous of my rank, Dove realizes.

He's stewing with envy for my rank, Dove accepts with a bit of pity, and he faces away from Washington.

Calmly asks Caufield, "You didn't think to ask any of your men if they saw Mr Wolfe? Saw his criminal actions? The insurgents were able to film Mr Wolfe shooting two unarmed civilians and none of your men said they saw it or didn't see it, and you weren't at all curious about that?"

Washington again answers for Caufield, "Perhaps their retinas were all burned out blinded after watching a fine young American woman burned alive by those two so-called unarmed civilians. Then again, I wasn't there."

Dove ignores that, ignores Washington. To Lieut Caufield, "And your failure to report the mass civilian non-combatant casualties?"

Caufield hesitates to answer.

"Your failure to report BDA, the mass casualties?"

"We didn't do BDA."

"Say that again, please."

"We didn't do BDA, sir."

"Is that your company commander's own private policy for his battlespace? That his platoons can suppress the enemy with ten thousand rounds fired on one single stationary target and not afterwards perform the mandated and necessary Battle Damage Assessment?"

"No sir."

Dove waits for more. Washington won't interject here. He told Caufield yesterday that he couldn't back him on the *No BDA*.

Caufield offers, "Talon gunship medevac escort had left. We started taking more rockets, and I just didn't think it was worth it, sir, risking my men. Just for BDA. My call. My mistake, sir."

"Taking rockets from where, you started taking rockets from where?"

"Up in the compounds, sir."

Dove knew that already. He's read the AAR. Multiple times. "How many rockets?"

"Three or four, sir. Five. It's in my AAR."

"And you didn't consider calling in artillery support?"

"No sir, not then. Later I thought about it, and I know it wouldn't have been approved, and I guess that's why I didn't consider it."

"Because you knew that it wouldn't be approved?"

"Yes sir."

"And you, Lieutenant, you have the experience and capacity now to read battalion's and brigade's minds and to know what they will approve and what they will not approve?"

"Jesus Christ, Zach!" the anger erupts from Capt Washington. "You think they're going to approve my guns fire-for-effect on civilian living compounds?! What are they putting in the water up there at Isaf that's making its staff officers deaf-dumb-and-blind insipidly stupid?"

Nothing from Dove. No reaction. Not a word.

Now he motions Caufield, Capt Cathay and Spec Howie to leave, get back outside, do what they have to do, out there. Leave him and Captain Washington alone.

A moment, then with just a slight tilt of his head he commands Washington to follow him up the stairs. Just the two of them.

On the Roof

There's a feeling of protection here with the mountainside caving up over so much of it. And the parapet wall that goes around the entire roof. Wide and about two feet high, it's perfect to set the machineguns on and crouch or sit on your ruck behind for cover.

That's what Dove thinks when he tops the stairs.

One guy on the Saw on each of the two front corners.

Saw, for Squad Automatic Weapon. A small, relatively lightweight machinegun. Fires the small 5.56 bullet, same as the M4 carbine. But faster and farther. From canvas pouches of linked rounds. In desperation when you're out of those pouches it'll fire 30-round M4 mags.

Set up on the front parapet in the middle is the big M240-B machinegun. The only 240 the Zoo brought today. The plan called for going in light, fast and mobile, a QRF that would be moving not static, so just one 240 should be more than enough.

Spec Lee Tran the 240 gunner. Pvt Bybee his assistant gunner.

Dove had heard Redcloud tell his squad leaders to make sure the 240 and Saw gunners carried double the combat load. "Sure, they say in-and-out in five hours," Redcloud had said. "But you never know. It's the Army."

Dove had heard that young man with the 60mm mortar tube strapped to the top of his rucksack—

that would be Slurpee

—he'd heard him whine to Redcloud, "In-n-out in five hours, Sarge, c'mon, whaddo I gotta hump this 60 for? Sergeant Utah said we're gettin Apaches." And Slurpee's assistant, big 6-foot-6 Private Leonard, with the base plate strapped to his ruck, echoing the whine, asking Redcloud, "Wanna trade rucks, Sarge?"

GIs always looking for the easy way out, Dove had thought then, and he'd been glad that Redcloud told them to suck it up, "We're bringing the 60. You never know." And glad to hear Redcloud ask, "How many rounds you each carrying?" Three each. And two other men carrying three apiece. Twelve total mortar rounds. *Okay, good,* Dove had thought then. In-and-out, yep, five hours max on the ground, they won't need the 60, he knew. But *SFC Redcloud's right. You never know.*

Redcloud and Mr Kyle Wolfe are at the parapet close to that corner Saw gunner on the stream side. Standing, just looking out.

Dove puts distance between them by taking position at the parapet midway between the 240 and the Saw gunner up at this corner.

He feels the presence now of Washington joining him.

Dove sees below that the two mortar-men, Sgt Slurpee and Pvt Leonard, have the 60 set up and the twelve cardboard-tubed rounds laid out on the dirt ready. You never know. Both of them are sitting on their rucks, each right now cutting into an MRE packet. Men will eat any time, morning, noon or night, when they're just hanging around.

He sees that the ANA and the last of those Tattoo Zoo men who reconned the compounds are near, jumping down off the first terraced wall, with three village males following, and two Zoo soldiers and one ANA in trail.

Out of the corner of his eye Dove sees Washington put one foot up here on the parapet. Rest his M4 atop his thigh.

Dove does not look at Washington here beside him.

Speaks quietly. Calmly. Reasonably.

"Jashawn, you allowed Lieutenant Caufield to submit that AAR," he says. "You had to know it didn't include Battle Damage."

Washington is comfortable with what he sees below. The Zoosters are spread out down there at the rock wall, on both sides. He sees that the overweight video specialist and the Jag captain now meet Nouri, where they'll question those three villagers coming with Staff Sergeant Ketchum.

Washington is glad to see Ketchum and his men returning. Everyone will be here now. Close. He's satisfied that this is a secure spot. This school. *Almost like it was built as a fortress. What was Uncle Sam thinking? Or was it the villagers themselves? Was it they who insisted on this castle fortress design and construction? Just part of their Medieval mindset.*

Zachary Dove was just now asking him something, but he didn't hear, or didn't quite get it, or he just wasn't concentrating.

Again Dove asks, "You had to know the After Action Report didn't include BDA."

"BDA? . . . BDA. What AAR isn't missing something? Every AAR you ever submitted was perfect, Zach? Show me one that's the truth, the whole truth, nothing but the truth, and I'll show you a butterbar lieutenant at

JRTC who doesn't know magnetic north from grid north. And maybe you don't remember, but a hundred things happen to a platoon out on patrol when they're in a Tic and you're just happy to get back with all your men alive and intact, screw dotting every T and crossing every I in an AAR."

That isn't satisfactory to Dove. "One doesn't just neglect to mention a hundred and sixty-eight civilian casualties."

A hundred and sixty-eight? thinks Washington. *One hundred sixty-eight?* He sees the short video playing, the bodies being laid out on the dirt down there, and he focuses through that to see Matt Caufield in real time right now down there alone, apart from that Jag captain and her specialist. Matt looking so alone and lost and weak and unsure. Washington feels sorry for him, *The poor son of a gun.*

Matt, Lieutenant Caufield, it was one hundred sixty-eight. How do you tell him it was one hundred sixty-eight?

"If you think Lieutenant Caufield and Sergeant Redcloud," he tells Dove. "If they had done Battle Dammge and had known there were a hundred sixty-eight women and girls down below here bleeding and screaming and burning—if you don't think they wouldn't have locked this place down and called me up and I'd have been yelling at my B-C to get me a chopper and get himself out here too and get General St Claire out here, everyone, you too, Zach. Because you can't hide something like that, you can't ever hide it. And Lieutenant Caufield and Sergeant Redcloud know that. Caufield's a bright young man. Redcloud's got more sense, more plain everyday common sense than you or I could ever hope to have. But if you think it, if you think that, that they knew it and thought they'd get away with it, then I'll tell you what—. I tell you what, Zach. You just go ahead, arrest me, charge me, charge all of us with murder."

Down the parapet, Redcloud and Wolfe, quiet, and Redcloud asks, "How many you think, Kyle? How many were in that video? Eighty? Ninety?"

"Dresden we fire-bombed twenty-five thousand civilians. Made them all crispy-critters. Intentionally. After even knowing the war was already won." His M4 carbine hanging off his chest where it's clipped to his civilian body armor. Wolfe by subconscious habit checks it to make sure it's on safe. Just a glance and feel, that's all, not even aware of it. "Hundred-forty thousand in Hiroshima."

Redcloud had never known or thought of those numbers.

Which now Wolfe puts into perspective. "Know how many the Rooskies lost in World War Two? Almost thirty million."

"Thirty million? Three zero?"

"Twenty-seven, twenty-eight. But what's a million or two at that number? Soldiers, civilians, men, women and children. Ol' Josif Stalin would send whole armies against the Germans, the troops behind without guns. They were expected to pick up the ones their comrades up front dropped."

But for Redcloud that was then, the long-ago past, not his war. Here now, "They knew doing that to Robyn we'd be all pumped. The guys would be smelling blood. Then firing those RPGs, they knew we'd level this place. And everything in it."

"All so very conveniently captured on video."

A single resigned snicker from Redcloud. "Can't teach these hajj how to tie their boots. How are they so Einstein smart?"

Dove tells Washington, "There's going to be no winners here, Jashawn. In Iraq that morning you were around the corner on the sidestreet and unaware of what your platoon sergeant was doing to that detainee. Yesterday you were on your Cop, but there's no way around Lieutenant Caufield and Sergeant Redcloud failing to report Kyle Wolfe's assassination of those two insurgents. Not with all the women and children mass casualties. If it was just Wolfe and the two insurgents, the lieutenant and his sergeant could walk with maybe a formal reprimand. The problem is that number."

Washington says nothing. Remains simply staring out and down below at the Jag captain and Nouri and the three village men.

"One Six Eight," Dove says. "Whether they knew or didn't know, it can't be swept under the rug with a letter of reprimand and a loss maybe in rank. An investigation is mandatory. You weren't here, Jashawn. Unless they reported Kyle Wolfe's actions to you, you had no way of knowing. Not Wolfe and not the non-combatant casualties."

Washington still says nothing, shows no emotion. It's as if he isn't even listening.

Dove knows better. "Men break regulations sometimes for good reasons," he says. "To save a buddy. To save their platoon mates. Their actions then are noble and are justified, they're defensible. Other times they're not. You weren't here. Unless Lieutenant Caufield reported Wolfe to you, no one's going to blame you. Just as no one blamed you for your platoon sergeant in Iraq. It's not necessary, Jashawn, grace isn't by default granted to one who is quick to hoist himself with his own petard."

Washington says nothing for moments longer. Then, "How'd you make that rank, six years ahead of our peers? Weren't you still just a major last week?"

"How would you know?"

"Gwendolyn would have told me otherwise."

"I wouldn't think that that would matter to Gwen."

"It doesn't. It would to Bethany Ann, she would want her to know. And don't take that as a dis. You know what I think of Bethany Ann."

Dove with a crack of a smile. "That she's too good for me. I married up. And the inverse, she married down."

"I think Bethany Ann would ask that same question. How did you make that rank six years ahead of all the rest of us?"

"The same way you haven't made major, two years behind. I respect my superiors. I know my place and position. Even in those rare instances when they might be wrong. Four years of the best education that money can't even buy, Jashawn, and you brushed off that first lesson from day one. And then you seethe and rage at the injustice that you're still an O-3?"

"Here's how really smart they are," Wolfe speculates to Redcloud. "You're right, Einstein smart. Number One, they know us so well they know the cover-up's even worse than the crime. Number Two, the cover-up makes it a scandal, they know that. Those last rockets they fired, remember?

"From way up there, those compounds?"

"You know what they were for, those last rockets?"

A moment. Redcloud realizes, "They didn't want us doing BDA." He lets that sink in, accepts it. "They wanted us to leave, they knew we'd leave." Another moment. "And we didn't even see it, Wolfie."

"They're the ones, Sarge . . . . with PhDs."

"Even Patton didn't make lite colonel six years ahead of his peers," Capt Washington tells Dove. "Custer got knocked down from general to colonel. What are you, you spit-shining St Claire's boots? Ironing his ACUs? With starch?"

"This isn't about me, Jashawn."

It isn't. Washington knows it.

But can't help himself, just can't let it go. Looks right in Dove's eye, smirks and says, "What's it like up there on St Claire's staff? You all give each other hand-jobs in the air-conditioned breakroom, bragging on who made the best PowerPoint slides that day showing bullet-point by bullet-point how we're winning the war without actually killing the enemy? Without actually 'presenting overwhelming lethal force'? The guy with the best PowerPoint slide gets a gold star? A hundred gold stars and you get punched up a rank?"

"Sun Tzu," Wolfe tells Redcloud. "500 B.C." He stresses it, "B-C, before Christ. The Art of War. Number One: Know your enemy. His strengths and weaknesses."

"That one, Kyle, they got it nailed."

A little laugh from Wolfe. "Yeh, and where's that put us?"

"Court-martialed."

Dove to Washington, "Envy doesn't suit you, Jashawn. Jay-Sire envious of anyone, I never thought I'd see it. You made an impulsive, bad choice once, and anyone today could put that off as youthful idealism. It's a wonder you ever made captain after that. But you don't have to make another bad choice today."

"Maybe I'm happy right here. Company command, captain for life."

"That army went out seventy years ago. You want to carry an M-1 Garand and a wool-blanket roll, wear a steel pot?"

"And it's better today? We have better field grades? Who've done their two years company command and don't see command for another ten years? And then they're so removed from the battlefield they don't even know the guys dying for them by their first names? Can you remember back that far, Zach? Knowing your men by name, first name, the men who might die on our orders?"

"Save it for the book you're going to write. Save that poetic theorizing that'll get you praised on the cover of the *Sunday Times Book Review* and toasted up on the Upper East Side. And giving your guest lectures at the Harvard Kennedy School of Government. Reality is, you can't command a company for life and if you don't come out for major in April you'll be looking at nothing but free time at home with lovely Gwendolyn and the kids. At least she can go back and pursue her music. And you can write that book. Maybe get an article or two trashing the Army in *Vanity Fair*. *The New Yorker*. *Atlantic*."

Washington removes the magazine from his M4.

Slaps it against his thigh. A ritual. Seating the rounds tight.

Puts it back in.

Visually checks. It's on safe.

He nods his head toward Lieut Caufield below. "Matt, the Zoo's his first platoon, but he's not young and he's not stupid. And he listens to his platoon sergeant."

"I've read their personnel files." Dove doesn't need a personnel status report and history lesson from Washington lauding his subordinates.

Washington tries another tack. "In Ranger Batt, go back, our first platoons. Sergeant First Class Barnett, your platoon sergeant, you lucked out, and we would have all traded ours for him."

Barnett. Whose daughter Jennifer years later Dove would present the flag at his funeral. Barnett who died in that chopper crash. Which Washington would know. From the Ranger grapevine. And know that Dove had been his escort officer at Arlington. From Gwendolyn. Relayed from Bethany Ann.

Washington puts it simply. "Travis Redcloud is every bit a match for your Barnett. If Matt Caufield did not see Kyle Wolfe shoot those 'surg, it's because Travis knows it's irrelevant that those insurgents lived or died. If Matt Caufield did not do BDA, it wasn't because they forgot, or neglected it, or just didn't give a shit. It's because Travis did not think it was wise to do BDA. And if he didn't think it was wise, it wasn't."

"You could have ordered them to stay, to complete the mission. Which includes exploitation of the site, BDA."

"They didn't ask."

"You had comms, you knew their up-to-the-minute status."

"It was them on the ground here, alone, not me. Without air cover, and if they call in saying they're taking more rockets from way up there, from there, those compounds, you and I frickin well know my artillery are not going to be given permission to shoot, not into unknown compounds full of non-combatant common everyday villagers, and you want me to order my platoon to stick around for BDA and risk losing a truck and five men to an RPG for a couple of snapshots of another shot-up empty building? I don't go Monday-morning-quarterbacking my subordinates when it's their lives and their men's lives on the line and they're in the shit not me. For what? BDA? A few photographs of a couple of dead insurg?"

"One hundred and sixty-eight. Common everyday villagers. Women and children."

"They weren't supposed to be in here downstairs."

"They were. Reality, Jashawn. Right down below. One hundred and sixty-eight."

Washington says nothing. Then, out loud to himself not to Dove, and it's the opposite of flippant, it's with a deep regret: "That's a lick on us."

It does not escape Dove, Washington said *"On us"* not *"On them"*, on Caufield, Redcloud and the Zoo.

Us. Captain Washington right along with his Zoo.

Later

Capt Cathay is questioning the three villagers through terp Nouri. One, the elder, with a white beard. The other two half his age. Their beards black, one with streaks of henna dye. This elder's sons.

Spec Howie is videotaping it.

Capt Washington, Lieut Caufield, Redcloud and Wolfe are nearby seated on the rock wall, close enough to listen in.

Washington hears Nouri's translation of the old man saying that the women of his household—his compound, that would be—were not in the school building, had not come to the school building, including the wives and daughters of these two sons of his here. Washington has to laugh a little to himself that the old man will be changing his story next week when Washington will have to come back up here with a platoon and a Civil Affairs team to negotiate a settlement with the villagers as to how much each will receive from the U.S. Army as compensation for his women and children killed. Five thousand bucks a head for the women, maybe a thousand per child? This old guy and his two sons, Washington thinks—sure as the sun rises in the east, they'll be singing a different song by then. All their women were killed. Their cows and jackasses and prize roosters too. $500 for a cow? $100 for a rooster? *What am I worrying about that for?* he thinks. That'll be the next Awesome Company commander's problem. Yep, sure as the sun rises in the east, Washington will be relieved of command long before next week. *I'll be at Baf under arrest.*

As in, BAF, Bagram Airfield.

Lieut Caufield hears the Jag captain's questions and terp Nouri's translations of the village elder's extensive answers but isn't listening. Nothing he's hearing is registering. The number 168 stands out in his mind, what Travis told him privately. A hundred and sixty-eight women and children. *How could it be so many? How could we have killed so many? Oh why didn't I have Staff Sergeant Utah or Ketchum go along with the ANA when they checked out this place?* He wishes that he could go back to yesterday and walk through this building himself, and he knows that that wouldn't have happened, that's not what a PL would do, when he has squads and sergeants to do it, and when the ANA is tasked to do it, their job. He imagines that Travis is doing BDA here and Caufield hears his radio call to *Get down here right now, L-T, we got a problem. Ketchum, Utah, get all your trucks down here asap, let's get a perimeter set up down here.*

Instead, for Caufield's part it looks like a disaster. 168 dead. And it looks like a cover-up. Everything points to a cover-up. *168 girls and their mothers. Under my command.* How often in his Officer Basic Course did he hear the warnings about *"War crimes"*? How many anecdotes were told about the officers doing time in Leavenworth right now for the deliberate or negligent civilian non-combatant deaths under their command? *Who doesn't know that higher HQ is always just looking to set an example of a young insignificant first lieutenant platoon leader?*

Lieut Caufield hears but doesn't listen to the question that this Jag captain, this Captain Cathay, is asking the elder. 168 clouds his thinking and mood with the realization that in a few more hours he will no longer command the Tattoo Zoo, that he will be lucky if he spends another hour at Cop Valley Forge, and that will be throwing everything he owns into his duffle bags, and by night tonight he'll be under barracks-arrest somewhere at brigade on Fob Salerno, and *What will I tell my family? What will I tell my mother? What will I tell my father? How will I tell Heather?*—his girlfriend, his ex-fiancée—*168. One. Sixty. Eight.* Life as Caufield has known it is over, he knows that. *I'm a killer. I'll be a disgraced platoon leader. I'll be seen as the incompetent commander whose men killed 168. Girls. Their mothers. Babies.* His girlfriend Heather will be ex-girlfriend, she won't be able to even look at him, to meet his eyes, she'll be ashamed. It would be easier, he reasons, if he could run away, disappear upstream, *Climb those goat trails Travis talked about, end up in maybe Australia, New Zealand, a new life.* Because his life now is going to be under arrest. With lawyers, *And who's going to pay for those lawyers?, how am I going to pay for attorneys?, how's Mom and Dad going to afford for my attorneys?, oh it would be easier if Wolfie had just turned around and shot me with those bullets yesterday. Shot me.*

He'll be fighting for his life. Against *Lawyers like her*, he thinks. Captain Cathay. No, not like her—their lawyers will be lieutenant colonels and full-bird colonels, they'll bring out the big guns to bring down him and Travis. *She's just a kid, she looks like a kid. Can't be older than me. Can be but looks so young.* Now he realizes what's been in the back of his mind and couldn't put his finger on it. *She's small like Heather and has her nice body, probably the same perfect figure under that uniform and IBA, and her soft smooth face and lips that want to smile but know to hold back, and she doesn't look like a lawyer, no one would ever guess that she was an attorney, she looks more the wife and homemaker and mother that Heather will be and, like Heather, with an art history degree, not a lawyer, and not looking to make a career out of art history either.* A wife and homemaker and mother. Except, *She doesn't look like she'd ever punch me with all her strength when I told her I'd joined the Army. She wouldn't cry and wouldn't curse me with those fierce "Screw yous!"* from lips that he'd never heard a *"Screw"* from. *She's in the Army herself, this captain. Probably was Rot-cee and had the Army pay for all her college. Smart, really smart of her, she doesn't have all my student loans which how'm I gonna pay in Leavenworth. And not her, it won't be her, she won't be the one who will be setting an example of Travis and me, putting us away for ten or twenty years or life. Those'll be colonels. Real lawyers. Cutthroat men who know what they're doing—*

He feels a hand on his knee. Squeeze him.

Travis.

And Redcloud makes a fist of that hand, and now just a slight tap on Caufield's knee, telling Lieut Caufield to *Hang in, be tough, it's awright, gonna be okay, all things in their time.*

Caufield makes his own fist. Taps Redcloud's.

Holds it against Redcloud's a few moments longer.

Redcloud taps Caufield's knee again, *Good, settled, done, I'm with you, you got me, we're a team, we're gonna be okay.* He stands.

Looks over the Zoo. The men on the roof. On the veranda. Out here.

Doc Eberly is down a ways over on the other side of Pfc Holloway and Rto Akin on the radios. Seated on the ground against his ruck against the wall. Reading. Earbuds in.

Slurpee is sleeping against his ruck beside the mortar. His assistant, Pvt Leonard—big tall huge teddy-bear of a guy—is cleaning his fingernails with his knife.

Over next to the school building down on the streamside most of the ANA have a little wood fire going, on which their aluminum tea kettle boils water for their chai.

It is the ANA who Kyle Wolfe is watching. *ANA and their chai,* he thinks. *At least they didn't bring their propane tank. Lazy bastards.* But he knows better, he just likes calling them lazy bastards, but they're not, *No one's gonna hump a 40-pound propane tank.* They can make a fire out of anything. Driftwood. Brush. Anywhere. *They've always got those same glass chai cups. Always,* he's seen them pull them out in the middle of nowhere, really nowhere, and get a fire going enough to boil water if only in a pan. Or their helmets, the few who have one. *Gotta boil up their chai.*

One of the ANA is carrying three steaming cups over for the elder and his sons.

Another is bringing over cookies and crackers from their halal MREs.

Sharing? It's the culture, it's the Afghan way. A guy's got two biscuits, you've got none, you've now got one. A guy's got two, there are three guys with none, all've now got a half a biscuit each.

Nick Flowers is down at the stream end of the wall, with Ssgt Utah and a few of his guys. Not shooting video. They can be seen laughing. Must be stories Nick's telling.

On the roof is Ketchum's squad, along with the machine-gunners.

Up there some of Ketchum's guys are sleeping against their rucks against the parapet. A couple sprawled on the parapet, like it's no different than a cot.

Near the middle near Tran and Bybee on their 240, Ketchum and Sniper Rodriquez are seated on the parapet, facing out, feet dangling over.

So much at-ease relaxation because no one's much thinking they're going to be attacked. Not with those two Apaches overhead.

The Taliban know that one shot, two, and the Apaches' infrared can pinpoint the shots, and they'll come down and rain with their 30mm chain guns and rockets instant tickets to those 72 virgins in waiting.

Taliban Rule of Engagement #1: *Do Not Fire When Apaches Are Around.*

Unless you're desperate for a piece of those virgins.

Not likely.

Because, Jihadist Rule of Engagement #2: *You aint getting no virgins unless you take some infidels with you. The more the better.*

Yep, even in the iron-clad socio-political-economic tenets of Jihadist Islam there aint no free lunch. Nuthin free in this world or the next.

The two Apaches on-station high above right now are the third team, having replaced the second which had earlier replaced the first.

Station-time an hour and change, leaving plenty of fuel to return to base on Fob Salerno, refuel and return in rotation.

None of the Zoo noticed the rotations. Who would? From the ground one Apache looks the same as the next. A black mud dauber making lazy circles around up high. The same low droning continuing in the background up there that you don't even notice anymore.

Any Zooster would bet you a thousand-to-one the Taliban won't attack today. They did their thing yesterday, and *Dude, look at em, we wiped their asses all over the place.* Forget the women and children, *That was them, they put them in here to die, the 'surgents did.*

The Zoosters have all got their helmets on. That's the rules outside the wire. Any number with their straps hanging loose. Body armor on, of course. That's the rules. *L-T's got his on, Sergeant Redcloud's got his on, shit, the Isaf staff puke lite colonel's still wearing his.*

Guys on the machineguns up here and Utah's guys down there are on the wall mostly facing out, and Nell's guys are right below here on the veranda, mostly sitting on the wall there facing out, 'cause infantry instinct is to face out, face the threat, even when there isn't any threat.

A herd of deer sitting down or bedding down at rest are always apart a little and facing out.

Instinct.

It's in the genes.

Deer genes and human genes.

Like playing around, goofing off. In the genes.

Like Pvt Finkle right now climbing, handholds and footholds, the mountain ceiling above the roof here. He's a good twenty feet above, and it all started on a dare from Spec Van Louse when Finkle, up here stretched out, his ruck his pillow, staring straight up at the creviced ceiling, guessed that it couldn't be any harder than the rock-climbing wall at the division field house back home stateside. "Yeh," someone said, "except, you're tied in, with a belay man back home."

"You bring ropes, you got your snaplinks?" Van Louse teased Finkle. "You got spikes? You know, pitons?"

"Pitons and ropes and snaplinks, that's for pussies," Finkle laughed and didn't move from where he was lazing beside Van Louse up here.

And Van Louse said nothing. Checked his watch. Then after a while, "Let's see, twenty-five, twenty-six, twenty-seven, going on thirty seconds. At a minute you're officially a wuss just like me."

And Finkle jumped up, took off at a running start, leaped up off the back parapet onto the rock mountainside, hands and feet on ledges. And started climbing, feeling his way up along the curve overhead, and guys started cheering him on, "Go, Finkle! Go, Finkle!"

Ssgt Ketchum and Sniper Rodriquez and others on the front parapet had turned to watch.

"Awright, Finkle," Ketchum orders now. "Enough, enough, get down before you hurt yourself."

More than halfway up, twenty feet high right above Van Louse and their rucks below, Finkle responds, "Aw c'mon, Sergeant Ketchum, how can I hurt myself? I got on my IOVT and Kevlar."

That's Improved Outer Tactical Vest. Body Armor. Just IBA most of the time, for Individual Body Armor, or something like that.

Kevlar, as in helmet.

Ketchum, "Get the fuck down I said. You break a leg, that aint gonna get you a Purple Heart."

Rodriquez, "Art'cle 15. Gonna take two month's pay. 'Struction of gov'ment prop'ty."

Spec Lee Tran, "He breaks a leg, he thinks that's a trip to Salerno and all the Medac babes there in the Cash, isn't that right, Finkle?"

"You coming down, Finkle?" Ketchum orders.

Finkle is stopped cold. Can't find handholds to go further. Kevlar and body armor, he's like an upsidedown turtle clinging to the ceiling. If he falls now he'll land smack on his back. He can't see a way to go back.

Ketchum, "Fuckin I aint joking, Finkle. Down! Now!"

"I can't, Sarge." A note of panic. "I really can't."

"Call the fire department," someone jokes.

"Hook-n-ladder truck," Cpl Sandusky throws in. "On the double!"

"Trampoline!" laughs Van Louse. "We got a jumper!"

Finkle's boots slip out of their ledges, but his fingers grip tighter in their hold, and he dangles, directly above Van Louse, who is up in a flash and yanking aside his ruck and Finkle's ruck and weapon out of the way.

Ketchum is up fast off the parapet, "Finkle, you okay? Guys, let's go, let's catch him"—

"No, Sarge, no! Stay away!"

"You gonna climb down?"

"Stay away, outta the way!"

"Then you climb yerself down, y'hear, right now!"

"I wanna be an Airborne Ranger," Finkle sings the marching cadence. "I wanna live a life of danger. Like you, Sergeant Ketchum."

"You've gotta go to Jump School first, knucklehead."

"Airborne!" Finkle shouts as he lets go, rights himself feet-first, straight down, and lands like a gymnast on the balls of his feet, perfect, and immediately does three backward handsprings, remains on his hands on the third, and it's tough to do with the cumbersome, heavy body armor pulling down off his shoulders, and now he pops back to his feet.

Applause from the guys, and Finkle takes a bow.

Cpl Sandusky jokes, "What'd, you grow up in Ringling Brothers, Finkle? You're a circus urchin? A trapeze artist?"

Someone adds, "His mama was the fat lady."

And another, "His father was the sword-swallower."

"What kind of sword?, if you know what I mean," says Sandusky.

And with light laughter and catcalls from others, Finkle grabs up his weapon and tells Van Louse, "Now who's the wuss?"

"I gotta give it to you . . . " admits Van Louse. And announces, "Hey, whaddaya say, whaddya think, Finkle's nickname is Spidey. Get it, like Spiderman."

Someone, "Naw naw, it's Dinkle Finkle."

Someone else, "Not Dinkle. Dangle. Dangle Finkle. Dangle Fangle."

Sandusky, "Dingleberry Finkle."

Ketchum, "The only nickname you're getting, Private, is Stupid. Capital D-U-M-M-Y. Now don't be doin nuthin stupid like that again, y'hear?" And he goes back to facing out, feet dangling over the parapet.

Rodriquez too.

Finkle takes a standing leap up onto the parapet, both feet. Perfect balance. Impressive. He surveys the landscape, the whole valley, the distant compounds way up there on the terraces. Weapon now slung from around his neck.

He pulls out a pack of cigarettes. Marlboro Red.

Pulls out a Zippo. One you can buy in the PX. With the brigade crest mounted on one side. **ARMY STRONG** inscribed on the other.

He lights a cigarette.

"There was a video you guys saw of yesterday?" he asks Ketchum. "It showed the bodies?"

"Women and little girls, Finkle. Not Taliban."

"I know I know. How many was there?"

"It doesn't matter how many."

"Cuz I heard it was a hundred."

"Who told you that?"

"Louie. Spec'list Van Louse."

Rodriquez, "An' where'd Louie hear that shit from?"

Ketchum, "Don't listen to Louie and don't listen to no one. You listen t'me. If I think you gotta know something, I'm gonna tell you."

Finkle, "I didn't know I was killin women and little girls, Sarge."

"You didn't. Don't even fuckin think that. What'd I just tell you? I'll tell you what to think. You see the shit in there down there? They set off shells—artillery rounds like 155s. They had em rigged to those drums of gasoline. The Taliban did. Not you."

"It's all cleaned up, Sarge."

"What's all cleaned up?"

"Sergeant Nell. His squad, they cleaned it all up." He snaps his weapon to his shoulder, aiming in an arc high.

Lifts the grenade launcher quadrant sight.

Yesterday in the truck he was on the Mk19 auto grenade launcher.

His hand-carry weapon is this M203. A combination M4 carbine with a single-shot grenade launcher attached under the barrel. All called together "203", as in two-oh-three.

"How far's that mosque would you say, Sarge?" he asks.

"The mosque?"

"Yeh. How far you think?"

"Three hundred meters."

Sniper Rodriquez corrects Ketchum, "Closer t'four."

Finkle adjusts the quadrant sight to 400.

"You as fast loadin that," Rodriquez asks, "like on the 19?"

"Yeh, like right. The 19 is the mutha. 19's my baby."

Mk19 is also 75 pounds. Not totable. Rideable in the turret of a truck, not over your shoulders.

"Next time," Ketchum teases Finkle, "we'll have you hump it out here."

"I get a hernia, Sarge, then that gonna get me a Purple Heart? I get to go to Salerno? In-patient at the Medac?"

Rodriquez wants to know, "How many rounds you carryin, or is you slackin off?"

Ketchum warns, "Better have twenty-four."

Finkle, "Thirty-six, Sarge." The distant mosque in his sights, he pretends to pull the 203 trigger, "Ka-plewie."

"Want a target?" Rodriquez says. "There." Pointing to Lieut Col Dove way out there at the charred hulk of the ANA Ranger pickup. "Hun'red bucks says you can't hit him on the first roun'."

"That's the lieutenant colonel," Finkle says.

"Yeh, and whaddo you think he's here for?" from Ketchum. "You think he's here to hand out Bronze Stars and Arcoms for yesterday?"

Rodriquez, "Hun'red bucks, Finkle. Com'on, let's see if you's as good on that as the 19."

Finkle asks, "What's the range?"

"Five hun'red twenty meters."

Ketchum questions that. "Five-twenty, not -fifty, not five-ninety?"

"Five-twenty."

"When's the last time you had those eyes recalibrated?"

"Sniper School. Com'on, Finkle. One roun', hun'red bucks."

Ketchum advises to the negative, "Max range of the 203, four hundred meters."

Rodriquez, "Can't use a hun'red bucks, Finkle?"

Finkle arcs the weapon higher than the sight's max limit of 400 meters.

Rodriquez, "Grenade's a area weapon, 'mano. You don't gotta hit him bullseye in the front plate."

Ketchum warns Finkle, "They can court-martial you just for doin that. You got shit for brains? Put it down."

"What if I aim high, lob it over his head, give him a scare, see if he shits his pants?"

"Put it down."

"I aint gonna shoot, Sarge." Finkle lowers his weapon. "Least not before he gives me my Bronze Star he's brung." He flicks his cigarette out into the air and suddenly leaps straight up backwards, doing a perfect gymnast's flip and landing on the roof on his feet.

Stunned silence from everyone. Then Van Louse starts a slow clapping, and others join in, and Finkle takes an exaggerated bow.

Ketchum asks, "Yeh, squad's now got a bastard born in the circus."

Rodriquez, "Hun'red bucks you do a flip like that the other way." Meaning over the parapet and down below.

Ketchum, "Don't encourage him."

Finkle, "C'mon, Sarge, didn't you-all climb trees as a kid? Up, see who could go the highest? Hang off like monkeys, see who could jump the highest?"

"And I didn't jump offa highway overpasses neither, knucklehead."

"You're a paratrooper."

"Yeh, yer forgettin the oper'tive word. Para—chute. Capital P."

Van Louse, "Yeh yeh yeh, the more I think it the more I like it. Gonna call you Spidey, Finkle. Private E-2 Spidey."

Ketchum, "Don't you have nuthin you can give him to do, Louie, keep him busy?"

"Shit, Sarge, he's ADHD. Forgot to pack his Ritalin. You forget to take your Ritalin this morning, Spidey?"

Finkle, "Holloway made me give my Ritalin to him."

Ketchum, "Dude, Holloway's such a lazy slacker, if he was to took Ritalin it'd put him in a coma. Wouldn't wake for a month."

And Sniper Rodriquez tunes out all the playful chatter. Watches Dove way out there stepping around the burnt pickup truck. *That cur'nel's gonna fuck us all. Gonna 'rest us all, not just Wolfie.* And he sees a video-looping through his mind the short fifty seconds of color film from the briefing earlier, with the charred and dismembered bodies being laid out right down below right here and thinks, *Jesús, María, y San José, cuídanles a las niñas.* Take care of the little girls.

Dove is out here alone just to get a feel. To feel the distances. To feel the ten or twelve RPGs coming this way from the school. To feel the deafening return fire of the Zoo with the .50 and M240-B and Mk19.

He sees that the rocket exploded through the Ford Ranger pickup's door on the side facing the school. Nothing left inside but the bench seat frame and springs and the floor gear shift and the steering wheel column.

Arriving here, after they'd gotten off the choppers, on the way to the school Dove made Caufield and Redcloud walk him around their perimeter here from yesterday, explaining it.

Spec Howie videotaping it.

Staff Sergeant Ketchum's three trucks fired from here. Private Bybee on the 240 and Specialist Tran on the .50-cal fired from here.

Dove hadn't expected to find any spent brass shell casings, that they'd have been policed up by the villagers to sell later as scrap metal, and Redcloud had to kick around in the sand to come up with a few. A couple of 7.62 with a few loose links from the 240.

A couple of .50-cal.

Just one 40mm.

Dove saw where the Human Terrain Team Dr Banks and her terp had been set afire. The dirt still burned black there.

He saw the dried maroon-black blood pooled thick on the ground and splattered like spray paint on the shipping conex where the Bic guy had been killed by Kyle Wolfe. *Assassinated by Mr Wolfe.*

He'd asked Wolfe to describe it in his own words, and Wolfe had just looked at him with scorn and visceral hatred and said, "Film doesn't lie, Colonel. Unless it's been Photoshopped."

"Was it Photoshopped?" he asked.

"Ask the Talib hajj in Salerno Cash who's got no nuts left."

Dove asked Redcloud where he'd been and how he could not see Mr Wolfe so close do the shooting, and Redcloud said he'd been too busy trying to save the HTT Robyn's life and her terp.

Lieutenant Caufield said he'd been up in the door of the Mrap on the radio back to the Cop for a medevac.

That's their story and they're sticking to it. Dove knows, what choice do they have? Unless one of them trips up. *That Mrap gunner Private Bybee, he was right there, he had to have seen it, how could he not have seen Kyle Wolfe shooting the insurgent point-blank on the ground? From the height in the turret, facing the direction there up into the fields, Private Bybee had to have seen Kyle Wolfe shoot the other insurgent first in the back running away then in the crotch lying on the ground already wounded.*

Dove reminds himself that Kyle Wolfe is a *Gnat on an elephant's ass.* Film on the nightly news of Wolfe killing those insurgents won't help the Taliban for more than a day and only until *The story of Dr Banks comes out, and those family pictures of her, and all her friends saying what a sweet innocent wonderful person she was, and everyone the world over will know that Wolfe was justified. Even these Muslims, they can't help but sympathize with a man protecting a helpless woman, even if they won't say so out loud.* That is, Dove is aware, if the media choose to tell Robyn Banks' side of the story or are they *More than content just to stick to the Abu-Ghraib-vicious-evil-torturing-American-GIs side.*

That, Dove feels, is more like it.

Regrets the reality of a media that will do the latter.

But *Lieutenant Caufield, it was his duty to report it honestly. Sergeant Redcloud as well. There was no justification for them not reporting Mr Wolfe's actions. What's the justification for the newsfilm of the 168 bodies of little girls and their mothers?*

The 168 little girls and their mothers, what was the reason for leaving that out of the After Action Report? *Jashawn says they didn't do BDA. Do I believe Jashawn? Why shouldn't I believe Jashawn?*

Maybe the lieutenant and his platoon sergeant didn't know they were in the school, that *It was just poor judgment, trusting the ANA and their lax, typically lax,* or worse, *complicit, typically complicit, inspection of the school.*

And 168 inside.

Dove can't think of a way around that. A way around the bodies of 168 innocent villagers. Women and girls. Those bodies all shown worldwide on TV and the net, over and over and over. . . .

Back at the school Dove interrupts Capt Cathay with the elder and his two sons. "Anything new, Laura? That we don't already know?"

"Sir?"

"The timeline. The platoon arrived here approximately 0930."

"The insurgents showed up the night before, they said."

"Showed up? He"—meaning terp Nouri—"said showed up?"

"That they surprised the villagers, sir. He said they said they surprised them."

"How many?"

"They said, ten or fifteen."

Dove asks Capt Washington, "How did they know the night before that the mission was to here?"

"Ask your General St Claire." Washington jerks his head to indicate the ANA over there. "They're our ally counterparts, aren't they? Our so-called coalition partners? Doesn't St Claire have them reading our op orders up there at RC-East and Isaf? Who knows who's reading them at battalion and brigade."

"Do they attend your Cub briefings?"

"Do I have an S stamped on my forehead for Stupid?"

"What's your lead-time, that you inform them where you're going?"

"When we drive out the gate."

Dove didn't have to ask all that. Unless Washington had turned into an idiot or simply a careless, reckless commander, he wouldn't be giving the ANA a heads-up on the missions.

It was perfunctory for Dove, he had to ask, if only to get the questions out of the way, and heck, maybe Jashawn has become careless.

Even though, no, not Jashawn, and Dove knows that.

He knows the rest. It doesn't take a genius to figure it all out, even if only speculation. The insurgents coming the night before might have just been coincidence. A stopover on their way wherever up or down the ratlines. The minute the Zoo Platoon turned up the wadi to here, the cell phones and the walkie-talkies of the ridge-watchers were humming and the ambush was put into place. The women and children brought to the school. For their presumed safety.

"The night before, they say?" Dove asks Cathay. "Specifically, they said the night before?"

"Yes sir."

They say, Dove thinks. *Whatever they say, the sucker Americans will believe. Insurgents have probably been here for a week. Based out of here. Or just their Rest Stop. A final way-station before crossing that ridge there back to Pakistan for the winter. A good chance they've made this a base, or why else carrying around artillery shells?* The walkie-talkies and cell phones were humming, *And here comes the Tattoo Zoo Platoon.*

Talk about fortuitous.

"Did you get a hard body count?" he asks Cathay.

"They say one hundred and seventy-three."

"One seventy-three? Not one sixty-eight?"

"That's what they said, sir."

Dove asks terp Nouri, "Where are the dead bodies? Have you asked them?"

"It is the custom. Muslim law. Dead peoples they must put in grave in one day, twenty-four hours"—

"I know Muslim law," Dove interrupts. "It hasn't been twenty-four hours. I need to see the bodies."

Dove and the leadership are in a dispersed cluster walking across the stream, following the elder and his two sons. School shrinking behind.

Nouri tells Dove, "They say they know yesterday you are wanting to see dead peoples."

"How did they know yesterday?"

"Taliban they tell them. They say the Americans will come to here in the village in two day-es. Three day-es may be. They say four day-es, you come here in four day-es."

"They said that, they said the insurgents told them?"

"No. Insurgent no. They say Taliban."

The elder and his sons ahead now step single-file onto a goat trail that climbs the steep mountainside in zigzagged switchbacks.

About the three ahead, Dove asks Capt Cathay, "Did they say how many of their women, their wives, their daughters were among them?"

"None, sir, not of theirs. Not all the women came to the school."

"Why not theirs?"

She doesn't know. "They said that they didn't send any of their females with the Taliban to the school. Most of the other families did, they said."

Capt Washington, "Which is why, I'd have to believe, it's why they were willing to come down to your interview in the first place. Without knives and machetes to kill us."

Dove, "Or their 1864 Enfields."

Ancient British rifles.

Washington, "The Taliban's already confiscated those. Gun control."

Given a best guess, Dove would say that those three farmers up ahead there had heard somewhere of *The Taliban's perversion of using women and children as shields. Bait.* And were afraid to warn their fellow villagers. *Afraid for their own lives.*

Along the same lines of Capt Washington's thinking before, Dove makes a mental note to remember that this farmer and his sons did not lose their wives and children yesterday and it will have to be remembered when they will be claiming that they lost all of them when the reparation negotiations take place. When all the dollars to be paid out is hashed over. Naw, Dove knows. They'll just deny it, deny ever having said it. They'll argue that their wives and daughters and granddaughters and nieces were killed, and stick to that, and who's going to call them liars? Who's going to challenge them and say different?

Hey, Dove knows, what's another fifty thousand when you're already making all the rest of them here millionaires?

Figuratively. By their standards, millionaires.

Shoot, billionaires.

There'll be a Mahindra tractor in every compound. 32-inch flatscreen and a satellite dish on every roof. Nope, probably can't get satellite TV down in this bowl. Better, they'll each have a DVD player and watch those Bollywood movies every night.

In the stream still, bringing up the rear, just before stepping up onto the goat trail, Wolfe turns around to look back at the school and the valley.

The Zoosters and those ANA up there on and around the gray concrete school building. From this distance, like toy soldiers on the roof parapet of a solid building that can be a Crusaders' castle. He can almost see King Richard the Lionhearted up there. He knows better, there are no kings and princes in that castle, not among all the joking and bullshitting and teasing of GIs hanging around, everyday goofing off out of sight and out of earshot of the bosses, especially the lite colonel.

He scans the valley all spread out, ringed with the craggily mountain ridges, it's beautiful. Wolfe thinks that it could be paradise. *With a capital*

P, isn't that about what that Ketchum dude would say, isn't that what he's always saying? Capital J for jackshit. Capital A for Awesome Company. P for paradise. *If it was anywhere but this shithole capital A Afghanistan.*

The goat trail ends a good seventy feet up the mountainside on a broad ledge about the area of a B-hut floor.

A cave opening the size of a double front door of a house. A couple of feet inside is an actual wood-plank door. Closed.

No peep-hole little security window.

No brass knocker.

No lighted doorbell.

No colorful autumn wreath.

No welcome mat.

Wolfe steps up from the trail, and the three village men immediately step toward him to leave, but

Capt Washington orders, "Hey hold up, where you going?" and

Wolfe stops them with a hand to the elder's chest, with the same demand snapped in Pashto, "Where you going to?"

The elder gives him a passive look of poorly concealed loathing, says nothing.

Washington tells Nouri, "Tell them, they open the door. Understood? They – open – the – door."

Nouri tells the elder, who now grins innocently and says in English, "No bom."

Washington, "Yeh good, no bomb. Show us."

Wolfe wraps the Afghan scarf he wears up tight around his mouth and nose—for the coming smell. He steps backwards down the trail and stops, his head just level with the ledge, his M4 at ready toward the two sons frozen in place three strides above him.

Experienced in combat, knowing there'd be dead bodies to investigate, Dove came prepared, and now hands to Washington the Vicks VapoRub stick that he'd pulled from his pocket and smeared a single glob under each nostril, and now he ties a drive-on rag—a dust-colored cravat—around his face like a bandit's mask.

Washington does the same, both the Vicks and drive-on rag, and he moves over to against the mountainside on the opposite side of the cave opening from where Dove has now placed himself, both with their backs to the mountain, and

Capt Cathay is scared, and she doesn't know why and knows she shouldn't be and doesn't want to show it to the others, and doesn't understand what they're doing, why the Vicks and the drive-on rags, and

Lieut Caufield has smeared the Vicks under his nostrils and now slaps the stick into Cathay's hand and grabs her by the shirtsleeve and pulls her out of the line-of-fire of the cave opening, over against the mountainside beside Capt Washington.

He motions Cathay, *smear it*. The Vicks. Hands her his drive-on rag.

Spec Howie is stuck frozen motionless with two-ton weights around both ankles, feels like he's drowning, like he's in an incomprehensible dream, everything out-of-focus fuzzy and slowed down almost to a stop, and he senses he should be somewhere else, anywhere. Yeh, he could be having an extra-large latte right now on Bagram at the Green Beans, and

Redcloud shoves him, "Move it, Specialist," to be over protected next to Dove against the mountain, where

Nick Flowers comes over with the Vicks stick and jabs and smears it on Howie like a mustache. "Don't wipe it off, trust me. Leave it on." And he twists the stick two turns and paints a glob under each of his own nostrils, then underhands the stick out to Redcloud, and

Redcloud doesn't use it. Points it at the elder. "You. Mister No Bom." He motions, *To the door, you first.*

Again an innocent grin and "No bom" from the man.

On the roof of the schoolhouse Rodriquez is crouched behind the parapet wall, with his rifle resting on it, and he's watching through the scope.

Sees the white-bearded elder and sees the cave opening which Rodriquez had never imagined nor would have ever discerned was there on the mass of what looks like flat and cragged mountainside. The ledge as well he had never imagined nor could have discerned, and he would have never even seen the goat trail until the elder and his sons first stepped up onto in. *Cabrones Afghans, 'mano,* he thinks. *Slick. Slick as a brick.* There is so much hidden that the Americans can never know.

Ssgt Ketchum is watching through his binos. He's standing on the parapet for a better angle to view. M4 dangling clipped to his vest. He knows what's going on. He can see the cave opening but can't make out the wooden door in the shadows. He knows the enemy puts IEDs on the roads, and they could have that cave *Rigged as soon as our guys step in. Careful there, Travis. Careful, Sergeant Redcloud.*

Rodriquez is thinking the same thing. *Cuidado, Sargento Redcloud, cuidado.* He can see that Redcloud grabs the elder by the back of his dress-up vest to stop him, and can see that Redcloud says something to Nouri, but it's too far even with the scope to read lips even if Rodriquez could read lips, but up there Redcloud is telling Nouri to ask the guy if he's ready to meet his Maker, if Allah is waiting for him with his new young virgin brides. Up there the elder again says *No bom* with a little smile, and Rodriquez can see Redcloud say something to Nouri which Rodriquez has no way of knowing is something along the lines of telling the old man that he'd sure better hope so, that there's no bom.

Ketchum's binos are less powerful than Rodriquez's scope, but he can plainly see Redcloud now indicate to Nouri something that were he up there he'd know was telling him to leave and to tell the two younger men also to leave, to *Go, get outta here, there's no need losing any more of their people,* and Ketchum sees Nouri and the two turn and step down the path, and Wolfe lets Nouri go past but blocks the two young men, halting them with his M4 aimed on their chests.

"Hooah, Kyle," Ketchum says with delight, then quickly centers the binos back again on Redcloud as the elder steps toward the cave entrance.

Through his sniper scope Rodriquez sees that Redcloud does not move. Hasn't put anything over his mouth and nose or put whatever it was, chapstick or something, that those others put under their noses that Rodriquez knows is to block the coming smell of what Sergeant Redcloud had radioed up before was them going to investigate a mass gravesite. Sarge's M4 would be clipped to his vest, it's hanging free, aimed at the ground. *Hijo de puta,* Rodriquez thinks. Sarge Redcloud is right directly in line in front of the cave opening and not moving out of the way.

"Travis Redcloud's got balls t'size of coconuts," Ketchum offers to no one.

"He's Sarge," Rodriquez echoes it. "Numero Uno, 'mano. El sargento don't know no fear."

Up there on the ledge the others are all against the mountainside, with their backs to it, on both sides of the cave opening.

Every eye on Redcloud.

Tic. . . toc, so slow.

Redcloud just standing there.

Every eye on him:

Lieut Caufield sees a man he respects more than anyone on this earth. A man he knows he's so fortunate to have as his first platoon sergeant. A man who has never once set foot in a college classroom and whose wisdom and courage he wouldn't trade for anyone.

Capt Washington sees a man who he knew from the first when he took command of Awesome Company sixteen months ago was every bit as good as the best platoon sergeant he'd ever known, and that was Barnett.

Dove sees Barnett. Sees the flag-draped casket at the gravesite. Sees the folded flag he hands to little Jennifer, and he squints his eyes to see deep into Redcloud's soul to tell him to move, move out of the way, move over to here, and to not get on that chopper, *Sergeant Barnett, you don't have to go, you're senior, you're a sergeant major, you don't need to be on the QRF, no matter that it's fellow Rangers out there who you won't allow to be overrun,* and Dove was ten thousand miles away in DC that night, as far away then as he is now from Redcloud, and could not stop the inevitable then or now.

Spec Howie sees a sergeant first class standing out there and doesn't know why he is and nobody else is. Howie couldn't focus on the words said seconds ago, doesn't know what's going on. Likes the menthol heat of the Vicks firing his nerves all up into his forehead and remembers Mom rubbing it on his chest and pulling his pajama top back down and tucking the blankets back up, *"Sleep tight, Bernard"*, and pecking her lips on his forehead that's becoming intensely anesthetized now, like the Vicks is seaping deep into his brain, and he doesn't realize he's not even blinking, staring at that tall fearsome tough old soldier sergeant first class out there alone all by himself for what reason Howie has no idea and doesn't even realize he's got his paused video camera held upsidedown backwards in his hand at his side.

Capt Laura Cathay sees a man standing in plain line of an explosion that's coming and cannot fathom why he won't move. She knows that there is a bomb. Bomb or bom, it's going to go off. What he's doing it's not rational. It's not reasonable.

Nick Flowers sees a soldier on his viewscreen, an American GI, the most highly trained, most profession, best equipped soldiers in the world, and he now takes two steps away from the mountainside for a better angle in the light, to catch Redcloud in profile and have the cave opening in the frame as well, and he knows the value of this shot and its greater value at that moment of explosion, and still he's hoping there is no explosion, *Please, no, don't,* don't let there be one, no matter that he'd have footage to die for.

In the complete quiet they all can hear the elder yanking on the ungiving wooden door, and

Wolfe, down at the top of the trail, with his head just above the level of the ledge, has his eyes on Redcloud's back, and he sees a man who he will willingly follow to hell. Will volunteer to follow to hell. *Name the date, name the time, my ruck's packed, let's go.* And Wolfe realizes that when the explosion comes in two seconds he too is going to get it, in the face, and he doesn't care and doesn't duck down.

If any of them could read into Redcloud's mind or soul as he's watching the elder yank at the door, they'd see that he knows he doesn't have to stand here, but sometimes you've just got to show the Afghans you're as crazy stupid brave as they are, and any of them reading his mind would hear him telling his wife Brenda that if she never sees him again, that he loves her, oh he does love her, *I love you, I love you, honey. Take care of the boys.* And they'd hear him chuckle to himself, *At least I've got these two seconds beforehand to know I'm dying,* when he's seen so many of his fellow soldiers who haven't, who haven't had even a millisecond to say good-bye and I love you.

The wooden door breaks from its hold and the elder swings it out all the way open.

No blast.

And the elder smiles at Redcloud. "No bom," he says.

On the school roof Cpl Sandusky is crouched low behind the parapet and is watching through binos, and only that upper part of his Kevlar-protected head and the binos are exposed, because he's not stupid and he knows that out here in indian country you never know when the bad guy's gonna pop up out of somewhere behind a rock and put three AK rounds out before ducking back down, and he sure as shit is not gonna have just one of those rounds hit him, no way.

He sees Redcloud up there motioning the elder to go on in there, and he sees Redcloud jump up and down a couple of times. "What's that all about?" he says. "What's he stomping for? Hip-hop Sar'ent Redcloud. You go, Sarge. Like Beyonce."

"Mines," Ketchum says. "Let the old man set off the toe-poppers if they got em in there. Glad it's not me up there. 'Magine the stink. Gag a maggot stuck in the crack of a slut cheerleader the morning after the varsity squad's had their fun. How many bodies you figure, Sniper?"

"Ninety. Hundred," Rodriquez says.

"A hundred sixty-eight," Sandusky says.

Ketchum, "Bullshit, who told you that, where'd you hear that?"

"A hundred sixty-eight. I heard it down there, that's what they said."

"You got wax in your ears, Sandy? Sixty-eight. Six eight. Two digits, not no three. Two. You heard wrong."

"Yeh, well, I heard a hundred sixty-eight, Sarge."

"Hundred sixty-eight?"

"That's what they said."

"Sniper, you think so, you think it could it be that many?"

"I don't know shit no more, Ketch. If it's one six eight, we're gonna be needin Señor Noah here. Build us a big boat."

Sandusky asks, "Noah? Noah's Ark? Sniper, you got frijoles frying on your brain? Who needs an ark, for what, you gonna put goats and sheep and camels on it?"

"What he's saying, Sandy," Ketchum says. "Sniper's a poet, a po—it. Ark's for a flood. Bibbbbb-lical flood. Still don't get it, Sandy?"

"No I don't get it, what's there to get?, it doesn't make any sense."

"You say it's a hundred sixty-eight dead from yesterday?"

"I didn't say it, that's what they say."

"One six eight?"

"Holloway said it, I heard it from Hollo-weird. And Sergeant Akin."

"Akin, awright, he ain't gonna bullshit. Holloway, shit, I'm gonna count em myself twice if he tells me I've got ten fingers and ten toes."

"They said they heard it from the L-T and Sergeant Redcloud talking."

"Like I say," Rodriquez says, and he hasn't taken his eye from his scope this whole time. "One six eight. Us Tattoo Zoo, Sandy niño. Noah's boat. We gonna be up Shit Creek."

Ketchum adds the kicker, "Without a paddle."

In the cave, they all have their SureFire or similar small high-intensity flashlights out, illuminating the long row of white cotton-blanket-covered bodies on the dirt going all the way back where their lights get sucked into the pitch dark.

Redcloud, Dove, Washington, Wolfe.

Nick Flowers filming.

You put a hundred-sixty-eight bodies in a tunnel-like cave, at least half of them burned, all the Vicks VapoRub in the world aint gonna work, not completely. Some of that invisible cloud-thick odor of decay and charring, if only five percent, is going to get by, shimmy in.

Spec Howie had been the first to fold, bending over and heaving his guts not five seconds after stepping inside, and Washington had demanded, "Here, give me!"—for the camera, and booted Howie in the butt, "Get your ass outside!"

Capt Cathay had been next. She'd tried hard, clamped the crook of her elbow over Caufield's drive-on rag she'd tied around her nose and mouth, using her shirtsleeve as a first-line filter, and it worked at first, until Redcloud flipped over the edge of the first blanket, revealing the first two charred bodies—

the woman with half her face untouched, perfect, and that side as well, with her clothes on that side still intact but shredded and blood-soaked, the whole other half of her charred, and the other woman all charred, completely, and a tangle of six or seven severed and mangled charred arms and legs, and lying among those limbs a half-naked, unburned, blood-encrusted toddler girl with half her head missing and a dried ball of her brains spilled out

—and Capt Cathay bent over in half out of control and retched, and Lieut Caufield took hold of her and pulled her outside, and she continued vomiting, her gut empty, but wracked with dry heaves.

And Caufield watched and looked at Spec Howie holding himself up against the mountainside and knew he himself was glad to be outside out of there out of the feel of that smell that, even only imagined, had to be coming from those grotesque women and that infant, and he was glad that he'd had the excuse to escort this female captain out because he knew he'd be next, he couldn't have held it in any longer.

And he couldn't have allowed himself to lose it in there, not with Travis and the captain and Wolfie, all of whom he knows won't lose it, can hold it all in, and most likely the lite colonel too, so *Thank God this small delicate Captain Cathay couldn't hold it* so he could leave by rescuing her, and *She couldn't weigh more than a hundred pounds*, he's humped rucksacks that weighed that much, and she's *Too feminine to be out here where it's an infantryman's world*, and she should not have to see that inside, those *168 bodies torn up and burned*.

And far across the way on the roof of the schoolhouse, watching through their binos or scope, neither Ketchum nor Sandusky nor Rodriquez says a word. Each of them knows that that could just as well be them retching up their breakfast up there, and more than could be, it would be them retching, and they're each glad they're not up there in that cave where they know that stench is something you don't wanna ever smell and are gonna never forget. Worse maybe, 'cuz it's not enemy Taliban, not enemy soldiers, it's mothers and their little girls.

In the cave Nick Flowers films, following the four.

Redcloud lifting the blankets one by one, uncovering the bodies in their tangle and mangle of twos, threes and fours. About a third are women, the remainder girls and little girls and babies. Some infants.

Dove, with his SureFire clamped in his cravat-covered mouth, jotting in his little hardbound pocket notebook. Counting heads and torsos.

Washington next, recording with Howie's videocam.

Wolfe last, pulling each blanket back over the bodies.

And Nick. Filming.

As for Redcloud, there's nothing superhuman about him that he could swim through the smell of 168 bodies and not be affected, and with just a few breaths of it, not more than a whiff or two, while still outside he'd smeared the Vicks under his nose, then flicked the stick to Wolfe, another plain human, who did the same.

The bodies end, and the cave goes on in dark emptiness.

To Wolfe the thin white cotton blankets are familiar from the Taliban and al-Qaeda going way back to the beginning of the war. He's seen them countless times since.

At the third blanket that he'd flipped back down he'd said aloud more with disgust than anything, "I'm looking for the label that says Made In Pakistan."

Washington added, "ISI's single biggest contract purchase matériel item."

As in Inter-Services Intelligence.

Pakistan's CIA.

Initial founder and present sponsor of the Taliban.

Physical protectors in Pakistan of Jalaluddin Haqqani, the head of the P2K branch of the Taliban.

That's Isaf-speak shorthand for the area of three adjoining provinces, Paktika, Paktya and Khowst.

This neck of the woods.

Not that it matters. Those white cotton blankets, you can find them all over the woods.

Wherever there are Talib insurgent jihadists ever ready to be wrapped up tightly on their way to their six-dozen virgins.

Repeat, all over these woods.

In the cave, farther down, midway, Wolfe had said, referring to the horrible wreckage of dismemberment and shredding, "Those are some mighty powerful 40-mike-mike grenades you-all are carrying for your Mark-19s, Travis."

Redcloud didn't answer.

Wolfe continued. "Magic .50-cals and magic grenades to go all the way into those back rooms, around through the doors. Your boy Finkle there must have put a spell on them to make them home in on the classrooms."

"You're assuming, Mr Wolfe," Dove countered. "You are making the assumption that these victims weren't all in the front room."

And Washington answered quickly, "Oh yeh, Zach. You're scared for your life as bullets start flying in from those front windows and you're not going to crawl back behind those thick walls into those two classrooms."

"Tsk tsk, my Captain," Wolfe teased. "You're making the assumption that sweet charming General St Claire won't have them believing in magic grenades and magic bullets, won't put his own spell on them all, the president and on down. Joint Chiefs'll be convening the court-martial board by tomorrow breakfast. DC time."

And no one has said anything the rest of the way. Until now, at the end, when Redcloud looks at Dove with questioning eyes and Dove answers by tapping his notebook and simply reporting, "One-seventy-three."

The villagers' count is correct.

Not the 168 the Cent Com intel analysts had deduced from the intercepted raw video.

173.

Day Two, Morning—Part 2

Outside in the stream, Lieut Caufield is walking back across just behind Capt Cathay and Spec Howie.

Up on the roof of the school Cpl Sandusky has his binos trained on Cathay. "I'd screw her in a heartbeat," he says. "How 'bout you, Sergeant Ketchum, wouldn't you kill to get in her pants?"

Ketchum, "Naw, I like my chicks fat an' ugly an' skanky. With herpes warts all growin down their thighs. Whaddaya think, you got shit for brains, you think I'm not gonna tap that if I got the chance?"

"Fat and skanky like your wife?"

"Ex-wife. That's why she's ex."

Disagreement from Rodriquez, who's following Cathay in his scope as she steps now out of the stream. "She's a fucken lawyer."

Meaning, derogatory, a *lawyer*, you gotta be nuts to want a lawyer.

Sandusky, "She'll make you sign a pre-nup first, Sergeant Ketchum. You give her herpes warts, and then she gets to cut off your dick."

"That aint gonna happen."

Again from Rodriquez, disgust, "She's a fucken lawyer."

Ketchum, "Oh yeh like I'm ever gonna have the op'tunity, lawyer or no lawyer, or hardbody high school chick, a cute blond bobblehead, yeh right, they're linin up for me. I wish. In my next life maybe."

Seeing Cathay turning her head to say something to Caufield, Sandusky admires aloud, "The L-T, he could get him some of that."

Not that it almost looks that way or even could be, but soldiers, when they know they can't have it, they like to think that their platoon leader or platoon sergeant, one of them higher than them, that they can.

Down there Capt Cathay asks, "Have you thought about it, Lieutenant? Are you ready to give a statement?"

"As an attorney, what would you advise?"

"Just tell the truth, what happened. You should have nothing to hide."

"What religion are you, ma'am? If you are a religion."

"Why?"

"Just curious. Are you religious, do you have a steady religion? Do you go to church?"

"How does that matter, my religion?"

"That's what agnostics usually say."

"Latter Day Saints."

"It says Mormon on your dogtags?"

"No. It says LDS."

"Same difference, LDS, Mormon. So you're a practicing Mormon?"

"Why? What are you getting at?"

"Did you do a mission, ma'am?"

"Your records say you're No Preference. How do you know so much about Mormons?"

"Of course, you would have seen my records before coming. . . ?"

Cathay says nothing.

Caufield asks, "Did you go on a mission?"

"Before law school. Mine was in Costa Rica."

"That's not a mission, that's a vacation."

"What are you getting at, Lieutenant Caufield?"

"Do the Mormons say it's all right, ma'am, do they say it's all right to lie?"

"I did not say nor suggest that you should lie. I said just the opposite."

"No ma'am. You advised me I give you a statement. As an attorney you advised it. An attorney working for the other side. The prosecuting attorney. As a Mormon what would you advise me?"

She knows what he's getting at. She knows now and is a little surprised at herself that she doesn't care. Doesn't even care that he adeptly used language, the very first tool of an attorney, to maneuver her so well. This whole thing stinks. No, not the choking stench of that horrible smell in there in the cave that made her throw up her guts, but it stinks on a far higher level of the blackness and corrupt gray of the human soul where she does not even want to venture, and she instantly tries to douse the sparks of those thoughts of the depravity of the soul, such as *The jet black evil of Taliban jihadists leading those girls and mothers into the school knowing from the beginning their intent*, and the flashed spark of *That O-6 full-bird colonel,* Colonel Pluma, *who was with General St Claire there on the roof of the building in Kabul at Isaf when he,* Colonel Pluma, *leaned into the helicopter* for a final word with Lieutenant Colonel Dove who'd then just climbed aboard even as dawn was beginning to lighten the eastern sky to gray, and *The creepiness in that look,* Colonel Pluma's, *the sexual hunger in his smile.* She shivers. *No, not a smile, it was a predatory sneer.* Douse, smother that, the depravity of man's soul, *Get away from there, don't think it.*

She knows that Matt Caufield and Travis Redcloud, sure, they knew that HTT Kyle Wolfe shot those two insurgents in cold blood and they hid it, intentionally did not report it, but they didn't know that those kids were in the school. *They didn't know, they couldn't know.* And they didn't know they killed them. If they even killed them—if, a huge big if—or were even remotely the ones responsible for killing them. *How could their guns fired from so far away kill them all? Bullets can't kill people like that. Bullets don't kill people like that. They don't tear them apart. Into all those so many pieces. Arms and legs. Bullets don't set them afire, incinerate them.* She's been out deer-hunting with her dad and her uncles and her brothers, and bullets don't do to a body what those bodies in there were. This lieutenant walking beside her, Matthew Caufield, he pulled her from there, out from inside that cave there, he had taken her away from those horrible mutilated dead bodies, and she doesn't sense at all that he could ever kill a woman or *That little poor tiny infant baby.*

"I would advise you, Lieutenant. . ." she says now. "And you don't have to tell anyone I said it. But I would advise that you get an attorney before you say anything more."

Lieut Col Dove is ahead of Redcloud, Washington and Wolfe still coming down the goat trail, and he steps into the stream.

Halfway across he stops.

Water running up along his ankles.

He studies the valley ahead all around.

The ridges.

The clouds moving fast.

Big puffy pillowing clouds.

As the other three come abreast to pass him, he stops them with a command of "Sergeant Redcloud, please."

And he asks him, "With all your experience here in this country and with these people, why would you take the Afghan soldiers' word when they told you that the schoolhouse was empty?"

Redcloud just stares Dove down with a look of incredulous contempt that says *If you don't know, you're not as smart as I thought or as smart as a lieutenant colonel should be.*

Dove is not stared down. "It's a simple question, Sergeant. With your experience why did you trust them?"

"Hindsight is 20/20. . . . . Sir."

"You have the rank and position that your soldiers deserve 20/20 from you all the time, Sergeant."

"If that's going to be case, sir, I will respectfully disagree with General Pete St Claire and will respectfully ignore and disobey ninety percent of his useless Coin policy. All my vast experience, sir, telling me that it is pure c-r-a-p. That gets my men killed. And these people killed. If you expect 20/20 from me all the time."

Dove holds his stare into Redcloud's dark eyes. "You respectfully disagree? Is it your belief, Sergeant First Class — is it your belief that your assessment of this war on the micro tactical platoon level and the world-wide macro geopolitical strategic level also is superior to a four-star general's and superior to his far more vast experience and education?"

Redcloud stares at Dove a few more seconds then just breathes out a snort of disgust and turns away.

Wolfe chuckles. Puts his face close to Dove's to tell him, "Are you really this ignorant? Or brainwashed naïve?" He steps after Redcloud.

Just Dove and Washington standing here still. Water swirling around their boots.

Washington now tells him, "This is what you can tell General St Claire. From me, Zachary, and you can quote me. You take this directly to him. If he's saying we can't trust our Afghan partners in even the most basic tasks, I won't permit one of my platoons out the gate with a single ANA soldier along on the patrol. And you tell him, hell, I'll kick every last ANA off of Valley Forge and I'll run it and my battlespace just fine without them. If he wants to push this and make a show-trial of my men, Zachary, and he wants to fry my men. You tell him he's got Jashawn Washington, lowly captain-for-life, who doesn't have a career left anyway to care one way or the another about. And you tell him, you ask him how much he's going to want, just as you said before . . . how much he yearns to see it in the *New York Times* and *Time* magazine and *60 Minutes* and *Drudge*, and them asking what we're fighting this war for and what good are these people if we've got to check and double-check and question their every action, and they're our allies? What's that say for us?"

Washington doesn't want nor wait for a reply from Dove and steps away.

Dove stays, allows all that to settle in.

Watches Washington's back for a moment then looks again at the valley and mountain ridges and is hit with a sudden realization, and commands "Jashawn!", and "Sergeant Redcloud!"

It's an order, loud and fierce, and both Washington and Redcloud stop and turn to look back at Dove.

"Gentlemen," he asks. "What happened to our Apache Talon air cover?"

In them the same sudden awareness. That incessant and forgotten chopper droning high above is gone.

At the low rock wall Capt Washington is on Holloway's sat radio back to Cop Valley Forge. Handset to his ear, only he can hear 1st Sgt Kozak tell him, "Air is Red up there where you are. It turned Amber and they pulled your Apaches and closed the pass."

Washington asks, "Did brigade give battalion a timeframe for when it might be Green? What's Weather Satview look like?"

From Kozak, "Satview shows it coming at you in one big black mass across the mountains. Heading our way too, Captain."

Washington, "How about our 1300 pick-up, they give you anything on that?"

Kozak, "Negative. All we're getting is Air is Red. Red until further notice."

"Talk about risk-adverse CYA. I'm looking, we've got clouds, Eddie, they're at five thousand feet, you could fly a 747 up into here."

Dove on the other sat radio is waiting for Colonel Pluma to come on up at Isaf and hears Washington say that and knows it's a white lie. The clouds moving fast overhead are now obscuring the ridgelines. That's not near five thousand feet.

Capt Cathay thinks it's important to tell Dove, "The elder man said, sir, and the sons as well. They said that the AAF, before they left late last night, they said that the Americans would not be coming today because the weather would be bad."

"They knew the weather would turn, how'd they know the weather would be prohibitive?"

"That's just what they said, sir."

"Did they say AAF or insurgents?"

"Actually, sir, Taliban."

"Gotta love it, Zach, don't you?" Washington laughs. "AAF. The only ones who say that are command staff and gobblygoop like in your op orders. AAF."

As in, Anti-Afghan Forces.

As in, insurgents.

As in, Taliban.

As in, the enemy.

"Anti-Afghan Forces?" Washington continues. "Did General Pete St Claire come up with that all by himself? Or did he empanel a commission, you know, a two-star heading it, to come up with the least threatening wishwashy meaningless word that doesn't tell anyone squat. AAF, sounds like a skin rash. Last year it was ACM, what happened to ACM, did it sound not quite hearts-and-minds enough?"

For Anti-Coalition Militia.

Insurgents.

Taliban.

Washington continues, having a blast, enjoying this. "What, did General St Claire do a focus group and find out that the Afghans don't respond positively to the word coalition, because that includes us

Americans and Nato? Out with ACM, in with AAF. Doesn't it make you wonder? What's in store for next year?"

Dove won't give Washington the satisfaction of a reaction.

Washington digs in deeper. "Down here in the trenches, Lieutenant Colonel Zachary Dove, no one says AAF. Or ACM." And friendly advice to Capt Cathay, "Unless you want the troops to laugh at you, missy, it's just Taliban. Taliban, Talibs, or 'surg."

Dove, "If you ever intend to make that gold leaf, Jashawn, you might consider the futility of your tilting against windmills."

"Which in Isaf-speak, that would make me a what? Let me see . . . I'd be an A-W-C. Anti-Windmill Captain? Aw, Zachary, Zachary, Zachary Dove, Lieutenant Colonel Zachary Dove, who knew it was that easy to be on a four-star's command staff? Where do I apply?"

There's a break of squelch over Dove's handset, and he answers with "Dove here, in Wajma Valley. Over."

His immediate boss Colonel Pluma comes on. "Dan here. I see you've got some nasty-assed weather down your way, Zach."

Only Dove can hear Pluma's end of the conversation.

"Negative," Dove replies, with the same white lie as Washington. "The sun's shining here. I have everything I need, sir, on the ground here. We've got our evidence. If the weather's supposed to be changing for the worse, I request exfil choppers asap."

"Air is Red down there," Col Pluma tells him. "Air status Red that entire third of the country. Roger, Zach?"

Again Dove white-lies, saying, "Clouds are above the ridgelines, it's a milk-run for the F-Models. We're in the low ground, sir, at the bottom of a big cereal bowl, we're sitting ducks down here without Task Force Talon air cover. Over."

"Handcuffs and leg irons, Zach?" Col Pluma asks. "Should we have the parties we spoke about out to meet you when you land at Bagram?"

"Negative. We're going back to Cop Valley Forge. I want to interview all of the Zoo Platoon. The men individually. And some of the ANA. Over."

"Valley Forge? Do you remember what we talked about?"

"I need to do the interviews where the soldiers don't feel threatened, sir. Over."

"They can be interviewed by trained professionals at Bagram," Pluma tells him without subtlety. "Remember the time restraints we talked about? Air is Green up here. Can we tell Air Ops you're going to Bagram and somehow work around your Red down there?"

"I say again," Dove insists. "Request you send the exfil birds. Before we do get weathered in. Over."

"Understand this, Zach. We cannot circumvent around the Red for Cop Valley Forge. Which is Red. I repeat, we cannot ignore the Red for Valley Forge. You read me, Zach?"

"I understand that Air is Green for Bagram and Red for Valley Forge, am I correct? Over."

"It's as green as an Irish spring meadow up here. Is Bagram your destination?, over."

"Negative. Request immediate air exfil for Cop Valley Forge. Over."

"Air is Red," with finality from Col Pluma. "Think about it, Zach. Out."

That *Out* is final, end of conversation, end of transmission.

Dove gives the handset back to Rto Akin.

Nick Flowers is kneeling off to the side, filming up at an angle, capturing it all in a three-shot: Dove, Washington and Redcloud.

Capt Washington asks Dove about the other end of the conversation. "What's that all about, where do they want you to do the interviews?"

Dove covers for Col Pluma. "Air is Red. Weather call."

Capt Washington immediately calls over to Lieut Caufield, "Matt! Let's pull in the perimeter, set up a tight security. It looks like we're going to be here awhile"—

and Washington's head jerks back, his body too, immediately followed by a slight *popping* sound of a distant gunshot in echoes off the mountainside, as Dove is catching Washington in his arms, and Washington's hands are gripping his own neck, with red blood flowing thick between his fingers and covering his satin-sheen milk-chocolate-colored skin with a shine, as his eyes are wide, surprised, and Dove is cradling him straight to the ground instinctively yelling "Medic! Medic!!!"

Eight Minutes Later

The last shell of the eighteen-round artillery shoot from Valley Forge hit about a minute ago and was followed immediately by an even louder explosion of lightning and thunder together that dwarfed the entire artillery barrage and sent down the rain that's falling already in vicious diagonal sheets.

The artillery barrage targeted and silenced the two snipers that Rodriquez had upon seeing the flashes of their second and third shots instantly calculated to be 1150 meters downstream 200 feet up the mountainside in place about 20 meters apart from each other.

Every Zooster is behind cover now.

Ssgt Utah's squad spread out along the entire length behind the low rock wall out front. Each man with his weapon on the wall, helmet and eyes just above the level of the wall.

Ketchum's squad on the roof is behind the parapet, weapons trained.

Ssgt Nell's squad is on the veranda, weapons aimed out. They're lucky, they're out of the rain. For the most part. Except for the sweeping sheets of it that come in between the tall arched pillars.

They're all lucky, inside and out, that the rain is warm.

That is, the ones who can still feel it.

Two can't.

Capt Washington was the first hit.

Within three seconds, even as Dove was yelling his second *"Medic"*, a bullet from the second sniper tore into Rto Akin's face, and Doc Eberly, who had been lazily sitting back against the wall out of the line of sight downstream reading and hadn't seen Washington get hit, saw Akin flop backwards and land on his back on the dirt near Nick Flowers, who swung his camera down on Akin whose face was a deformed mess of streaming blood.

Rules of Combat #Whatever: *Take out the command and the communications first.*

Which Redcloud knows so well that at the first sight of Washington jerking backward hit he'd leapt for the wall and yanked both radios and both antennas from it and onto Holloway and the ground next to him.

Even as the slight *pop-pop-popping* of the second shot was still echoing, Dove was wrenching Washington's hands from his neck to press his own palms there to attempt to stem the gushing of Washington's blood when a third bullet, this from the first sniper, skidded off Dove's Kevlar helmet, swiveling his head in the glazed impact, and deflected into Capt Cathay's belly just below her body armor and sent her spinning and to the ground face-down.

Redcloud was already crouched then behind the wall and plopping the antenna to Holloway's radio back up onto it, quickly from visual memory aligning the antenna exactly to the azimuth it had been on, grabbing the handset from Holloway and then calling very calmly, "Valley Forge base, Valley Forge base, this is Zoo Seven, I repeat, Zoo Seven. We are under attack, I repeat, under attack, over."

If Redcloud had been in the Toc on the Cop at that moment he would have seen the entire op center go silent and freeze, and 1st Sgt Kozak dash to the radio corner and grab the handset from the 2rd Platoon private on radio watch.

At the same time on the schoolhouse roof, crouched at the parapet, with his naked eyes Rodriquez pinpointed that third flash of the third shot way far down there, even as the shouts of *"Sniper! Sniper!"* echoed from out front to up and through the soldiers there on the roof, and Rodriquez then blurred his scope to the area of the flash to see the next flash of the second sniper instantly followed by a bullet clapping right here next to Rodriquez as it smacked flat against the front of 240 machine-gunner Lee Tran's Kevlar helmet and sent him back flat on his back on the concrete, leaving Tran's assistant gunner Bybee frozen in panicked terror, even as

Rodriquez screamed, "240, follow my tracer!", and fired one shot —

the bullet that is always chambered, which, against all sniper protocol, for Rodriquez is always a tracer round, unless he's actually on a specific sniper mission with a specific target, which he's never been on

— with its red burning glow arching far downstream heading upwards toward the mountainside, burning out before reaching it, and

Ketchum shoved Bybee aside and went to his knees behind the machinegun and started sending short bursts and their tracers every five rounds, sweeping across the area on the mountainside where Rodriquez's tracer had been aimed, and in the first few seconds of Ketchum's raking up there a fifth flash appeared, and

below, that fifth sniper bullet hit Lieut Caufield in the collar, nipping the edge of his body armor and angling down through one lung, clipped his stomach and splayed twists of his intestine, tore through his left kidney and stopped somewhere in his thigh, just missing the femoral artery.

Caufield shouldn't have been hit, he could have avoided it, but he had ignored his instinct following the first echo of that first shot to duck down behind the wall and further ignored his officer training to get to the radios to call higher to get artillery or air support, thinking that he should step over to help where the lieutenant colonel was clutching his Captain Washington to the ground, and he next saw Sergeant Akin fly backwards with a spray of blood in the air around his head, and he should go to him he knew, even knowing that no, he should go to the radios and take charge, and that was where he was about to step, but it was the third shot spinning Capt Cathay so near him to the ground to which he had reacted, dropping his M4 to hang from its clip and dropping to his knees beside her, not even hearing then that sniper shot echoing that was the one that hit Spec Lee Tran up on the roof. He'd noted an immediate paleness in the skin of the back of Cathay's neck then heard a machinegun above firing over his head and then had felt something smack him like a ten-pound sledge to his collarbone and burn down through him like his first gulp of white lightning that summer up in the Lakes with his U Wisconsin frat buddies, and he knew at that very instant that it was wrong that he felt being pushed away from pretty Captain Cathay here where he couldn't help her now onto the ground where he now felt himself going and not being able to stop it or reverse it and feeling a whole strip of firecrackers going off down his torso then only seeing the darkening clouds streaming by above chasing out the billowy white ones, and again now hearing that machinegun above so loud, and he knew at that moment that *I'm fucked, fucked really bad,* and heard himself saying "I'm hit. I'm hit", and knew he wasn't even shouting it and was *Proud I'm not shouting it, I don't want to shout it like a wuss. I'm hit and I don't want to be a wuss.*

To that point, the clock running from that first shot to Lieut Caufield hitting the ground was just twenty-four seconds.

The count was bad.

Taliban sniper shots: Five.

Two-thirds of the command taken out: Washington and Caufield.

The one-third left: Dove.

Capt Cathay down.

Rto Akin taken out.

Lee Tran unscratched, as the bullet gouged his helmet but ricocheted off, knocking him out cold, but now eight minutes later he's up, shaking all over still, already with a killer headache like a red-hot charcoal lodged right behind his forehead, but back crouched kneeling behind his 240.

And Ketchum has already laid into Bybee a while ago, slapping him hard across the helmet and screaming right in his face, "You're gonna go dumbshit and freeze-up, you do it on your own fuckin time! I'll put this boot through your face next time, you better fuckin believe it, Bybee! Get your brain outta yer ass!"

In those first 24 seconds, at the first shot Wolfe had acted the warrior on instinct—find cover and watch downrange for the enemy. He'd thrown himself crouched behind the rock wall, M4 and ballcap-covered head above it in time to see, as Rodriquez had, the second flash then the third and knowing they were way way way out of range of the M4 and out of range of whatever M203 grenade launchers the Zoo's brought, and the one M240-B they've got could reach it, and the Saws, maybe, cuz that's pushing it for them with any accuracy at all. And he was up and dashing, seeing as if in slow motion that Captain Washington was down, and that radio guy sergeant too, and the tiny Jag lawyer captain, and now Lieutenant Matt Caufield was going down, but all that would have to wait until later, could be dealt with later, priority now was to suppress the snipers, yeh snipers, because the flashes were a distance separated, and they've got to be suppressed first before anything otherwise others would be going down, maybe even him.

At Second 24 Wolfe was dashing to Slurpee's 60mm mortar.

At Second 31, grabbing Slurpee and demanding "Give me full charges!" Meaning, he wanted mortar rounds with all their charge bags left on them, and yelling the same thing to Slurpee's assistant, Pvt Leonard, "Full charges!"

And Wolfe flipped the 60's bi-pod legs out, dropping the mortar to fire it at a low 50-degree angle, aiming it at the general spot on the mountainside way far down there, with Slurpee and Leonard twisting open the cardboard tubes, and big huge target Leonard was hit smack in his chest in his body armor by the snipers' sixth bullet and pushed back onto his butt on the ground. Three seconds later a sniper bullet cracked right between Wolfe and Slurpee and splattered concrete on the school, and Wolfe yelled up toward the roof for no other reason than to yell because he wasn't going to be heard over the sound of that machinegun barking there, "Suppress them, fire em up!!!"

And Slurpee dropped the first mortar round down the tube and *pooooof* it was out.

At that moment nearby two of the ANA had let loose on their AKs, firing senselessly out over the beach and stream, and that stupidity so incensed Wolfe that he'd screamed in English and Pashto to stop and then grabbed the nearest guy and yanked the AK right out of his hands and flung it toward the wall, and he'd managed to turn his attention back in time to see the first mortar round explode way too high down there on the mountainside. Even as Rodriquez from the roof then screamed down a correction, "Drop it 250!"

Three mortar rounds later, Wolfe and Slurpee found the right angle on the tube, nearly level at about 20-degrees, and they put another five rounds exploding in succession in the area of the two snipers, just as Redcloud then screamed a warning to all from over there at the wall on the radio that "Round out!"

Meaning, Valley Forge artillery just shot their first round.

At Second 24 Redcloud had been telling Valley Forge "We are under attack" and had seen Wolfe dashing for the mortar tube. He knew that his Captain and his Lieutenant were down, hit. Rto Sergeant Akin was down. The Jag captain down. *Doc'll take care of them,* he thought, knowing his own immediate job with Washington and Caufield both down was to get artillery in on that sniper, and he already had his map out of his pants cargo pocket, flipping it open, and he was turning to look over the wall to see where that 240 was hitting, where were the tracers aiming for, heading before they burned out?, and he then transferred that area up the mountainside farther to a spot on the map even as he was simultaneously telling 1st Sgt Kozak over the radio, "Awesome Six: Whiskey. Zoo Six: Whiskey. Request one-oh-fives. Wait one." Then, even as he was seeing out of the corner of his eye Wolfe grab the AK from one of those stupid Afghan soldiers firing wildly like idiots, he was figuring the eight-digit grid for the spot, then he sent it with the barest Fire Mission of *"Dug in sniper. HE. We'll walk you in."*

HE, as in High Explosive.

Walking in, as in sending corrections after each shot.

Back on the Cop, Kozak had repeated the grid back to confirm it, and Redcloud rogered it and told him, "And, Top, we're gonna need a medevac. I've got four Whiskeys. Maybe more."

And Redcloud had known that the arty guys at the first immediate alert of *"Zoo's in a Tic!"* would already be running out of their huts to the two 105s and now ripping rounds out of their crates and just waiting for the arty lieutenant in the op center to get the computer calc for the shoot and to walkie-talkie it to them to set the guns on the correct exact azimuth and elevation for the fire mission.

Darn good thing the guns are preset, he'd thought. Not much adjustments from center-stream and down five hundred meters and up the mountainside.

Redcloud would wait then for Kozak to call back with a *"Round out,"* then wait to watch where it landed to send back corrections. And Redcloud was watching Wolfe and Slurpee send a third mortar out, and *Thank God for Wolfie,* he'd thought. He watched Slurpee's assistant, mountain-big Private Leonard, wobbly back on his feet, and then thrown back onto his butt again as another sniper bullet smacked him in his body armor, and the kid again struggling to his feet and this time screaming in rage above the clatter of the machinegun above, "Leave me the fuck alone!!!"

At the first shot at Second 0 Doc Eberly didn't even know it. Ear buds in, reading, seated back against the wall on this safe side, he only realized something was wrong when he saw out his peripheral Rto Akin flop backwards, and he threw his book down in the dirt and flicked out his ear buds and grabbed his aid bag to crawl to Akin.

Doc had been listening to Tchaikovsky. His *Piano Concerto #1.* In the third movement, at its militaristic finale. Doc had learned long ago that when guys asked him what he had playing to tell them *"Aw, you wouldn't like it,"* and if they persisted, to say *"Alternative shit. Lots of violins and pianos and harpsichords,"* and that would be an instant turn-off and no one would even want to catch a snatch of it. Until that new young medic with 2nd Platoon, Doc Merano, who'd said, "Cool, dude, alternative classical," and forced Eberly to let him try on the buds, and Eberly did, and Merano pegged the piece immediately, *Eine kleine Nachtmusik.* Mozart. And he'd laughed to Eberly that he'd been playing piano since first grade, and he could play some Mozart pretty fair, but not like that guy on the ear buds, he only wished he could. And two weeks ago on that joint patrol with 2nd when the ANA pickup hit the IED and Merano was the first to get to them and took the brunt of the shrapnel from the secondary IED, most of which embedded in his body armor but some ripped open his left thigh and lopped off three fingers of his left hand, and Eberly stopped the bleeding, bandaged it all, got Merano on a short dose of morphine, a bag of blood expander running, and, jogging alongside the litter carried by four others toward the medevac chopper, carrying the IV bag, Eberly caught Merano's eyes as Merano yelled up at him with a wild smirk, "Dude, man, now I'm only gonna be able to play right hand."

In the slow-motion seconds crawling to Akin, Doc Eberly saw Redcloud plopping the sat antenna back on the wall, saw now that his Captain was down, with the big lieutenant colonel shoving his own hands down on his Captain's neck, saw the lieutenant colonel's head swivel a bit, saw that Jag captain twist and fall backwards on her belly, and thought *How'm I gonna get all these?* At Akin he saw a face punctured where the nose oughta be, everything running blood, how was he going to give him mouth-to-mouth if he needed it with all the blood? He himself felt so vulnerable out here in the open, whoever was shooting would see and shoot him next, and he could feel the coming bullet punch him in the back, smack his body armor, he'd be okay, it would hit his body armor, *I'm going to be hit any second, it's coming, it's gonna be now,* and it didn't matter anyway, no way, no how, because he was the medic, he had to be here, he had to do this, he will do this, here, out in the open, and he became aware of his fingers on Akin's throat and feeling no pulse and desperately moving them to find the pulse, there has to be a pulse, and then seeing Akin's helmet that musta been unstrapped, like his own was right then, unstrapped, and Akin's was mostly off and lying angled on the dirt with splatters and globs of blood and brain clumps in it, and Eberly knew then that there would be no pulse, there would never be a pulse again in Akin, and back in the Toc there in the Med Room where Eberly would often hang with Doc Murphy and a couple of the others, and Akin would be a fourth for spades, and he was lousy, Eberly never wanted him as a partner because he didn't know how to bid, and *He'll never bid stupid again now ever again*, Akin sure wouldn't, he would never not take that trick with his king of spades as he should have if he hadn't held it so long and laughed that *Dumb 90 IQ laugh of his*, and Eberly wanted a pulse, still moved his fingers to find it, as he was hearing then the loud staccato of the machinegun overhead on the roof.

As Doc Eberly lifted his eyes from so close to Akin's mouth where he was trying to hear a breathing that he wasn't feeling in the pulse, he saw his L-T from his kneeling position at the belly-down female Jag captain crumple backwards while reaching for his collar, and Doc thought *Oh shit, not the L-T too*, with the machinegun blasting in what he could count were three-, four- and five-round bursts.

For Lieut Col Dove, in those first seconds, when his head swiveled as that third bullet grazed his helmet he saw Laura Cathay twist in the air and flop limp flat on her belly, and his mind already calculated, having just a moment before seen the Rto flying backwards with red blood aerosoled in a halo around his face, that it was all too quick for one sniper, there was more than one of them, they weren't a sniper, they were snipers, and *They're smart enough to aim for the command*, which was him, in the open, naked, with

his hands shining with Jashawn's blood, and he moved one to under Washington's neck where he'd just seen the fast-growing pool, and he felt the big hole of pulverized flesh and bone there just between the shoulder blades, and

Captain Jashawn Washington's eyes were staring up at Dove's face so close then and could see Dove's lips moving but couldn't hear but could read them as *"Hang in there, Jashawn!"* as a shout, a plea, and Washington was then thinking *"Tell my wife I love her"*, but he knew his mouth wasn't moving, there were no words coming out, he didn't hear any of his own words, and he laughed without laughing then at how many times he'd heard others and he himself talk about it, that they'd all always joked about how their last words would be *"Tell my wife I love her"* and they always had good laughs at that because it was so trite and so Hollywood bullshit and everyone always knew it wouldn't actually be them and they'd never actually really have to say it, and here he was now desperate for Zachary Dove to hear him, *Tell my wife I love her, tell her, Zach, tell my wife I love her. Gwendolyn dear the love of my life I love you.*

Dove saw then that Capt Washington's eyes were glossy cloudy and did not move.

He put his lips down right to Washington's ear. "I'll tell her, Jashawn," he said. "I'll tell Gwen. I'll tell her, Jay-Sire...."

Nine Minutes After the First Sniper Shot

The rain is coming down in fiercely blowing swirling sheets.

Dove and Redcloud seated next to each other, backs against the rock wall, just under where both satcom antennas are up there pointing at the same high angle and in the same azimuth into the sky southwest. Dove and Redcloud each with a radio handset to their ears.

"Let's get everyone inside," Dove tells Redcloud. "On the porch there. On the roof. The wounded first. Inside."

A nod from Redcloud.

It was maybe a minute into it after that first shot and Dove had pulled Washington's body over to the protection of the wall, even knowing it wouldn't do any good, too late for any good, but he wasn't going to have the body left out in the open and desecrated by any more shots, however many more of the enemy were out there.

Redcloud had told him that he had the guns back at Valley Forge up and was just waiting for a *"Round out"*, and Dove had heard moments before Redcloud yell for the Pfc here on the radio to get Laura Cathay and Lieutenant Caufield behind cover up against the wall, which Holloway was doing, first pulling Caufield over, then Cathay.

Dove had then turned to look above the wall at the mountainside way downstream in time to see the first mortar round land high, and he turned to see Kyle Wolfe already pulling the bipod legs of the 60 out to lower the elevation angle, and he thought, *Those men are in the open, they're going to get hit*, but didn't have the time to think it further, as he moved away from the cover of the wall to go to the doc there who was giving mouth-to-mouth to the Rto, the center of whose face was gone and the back of his brain in his helmet, and the medic with his full mouth over the Rto. Dove tapped Doc Eberly on the helmet hard and ordered him, "It's no use." Doc pulled away from the dead man's bloody face. Dove told him, "Get the others!"

Lieut Caufield and Capt Cathay. To tend to them.

And Dove pulled Rto Akin's body over against the wall. Next, he would have joined Doc Eberly to tend to Caufield and Cathay, but Ssgt Utah had just sprinted by to help Doc, as were two of his other squad members who were coming from up at the far end of the wall.

Nick Flowers was crawling, filming, passing Dove, camera trained on Cathay on the ground where Doc was going into his aid bag.

The 240 had stopped firing and one of the Saws up on the roof was sending out 3-round bursts, and above that Dove had heard Utah during his sprint screaming at his guys all behind the wall to "Stay behind cover! Stay down!"

The second mortar round had landed lower on the mountainside, and Rodriquez was yelling down from the roof to Wolfe and Slurpee to "Drop another hundred!", and Wolfe flattened the legs of the 60 even more and, as Slurpee dropped another round down the tube and *pooooof* it was out, Dove thought about those three there being the only ones exposed now, along with that crazy sniper sergeant on the roof exposing his upper body to get a better sight through his scope far downriver, as Dove could see just the muzzles of the men on the roof showing over the parapet and just the muzzles of the men up behind cover of the wall on the veranda and all these soldiers, the ANA out here too, were behind this rock wall, just as he saw then Slurpee's assistant take that second hit in the chest and land back on his butt, and Dove got to his knees to sprint over there to help, but the soldier was pulling himself up, shaking, stumbling, to his feet and screaming so loud even above the Saw firing above, "Leave me the fuck alone!!!"

Dove had then heard Redcloud saying into his radio handset right next to him, "Roger that, Top, just waiting for the first round. You know our location, all you need to know for the 9-Line is four Whiskeys. Four critical Whiskeys."

9-Line, it's auto-reflex in any sergeant, lieutenant or captain on the ground, and Dove saw it in his mind then, the nine lines for stats to send back to base to request a medevac, and he knew his position now as commander, his priority, that Air was Red, there'd be no medevac, and there needed to be a medevac, and he plopped the second sat antenna onto the wall, aligned it perfectly with Redcloud's, grabbed up the handset of that radio and called Isaf Kabul.

"Break break break," he'd radioed. "Isaf Command, Isaf Command, this is Major Zachary Dove—Lieutenant Colonel Zachary Dove in Wajma Valley. Mayday mayday mayday, troops in contact. Over."

"What's that call sign again, can you say again?" came the bored voice of the young corporal at the other end.

"Son," Dove had said, "you've got five seconds to put an officer on. Colonel Pluma if he's there."

It took fifty seconds to get Pluma. "Zach, Dan here. What's this, you say you've got troops in contact?"

"Affirmative. Lethal sniper contact. Two snipers. Maybe more. I've got two Kilos, two Whiskeys. Minimum, two Kilos, two Whiskeys."

Killed in Action.

Wounded in Action.

"I'm going to need a medevac asap," Dove continued. "The Whiskeys are life-threatening. I repeat, request immediate medevac."

"Jesus, Zach, how'd you get yourself two Kilos, two Whiskeys?"

"You took our Talon gunships, remember?"

"I didn't take anything, Zach. Air is Red."

"I know Air is Red. Work the medevac around it. Colonel, please."

"I'll get back to you," Pluma ended the transmission.

He did get back. In a couple of minutes. In the middle of the Valley Forge artillery barrage. Sorry, they couldn't lift the Red for a medevac. The weather boys said Wajma and everything north, south, east and west of it down there was about to get hit with some really heavy shit, with no end in sight, and for Zach to hang in, hang tough, they'd get a medevac flying as soon as weather permitted.

A medevac is minimum one Blackhawk and one Apache. Crew of five on the Blackhawk, two on the Apache. Or, minimum, two Blackhawks—crew total ten. Weather regs are clear: the crews and the aircraft cannot be risked.

Which is not unreasonable.

On Cop Valley Forge

The two big 105s have been quiet for the past couple of minutes, their Fire For Effect, FFE, complete and confirmed a success from Redcloud in the valley radioing, *"Thanks, Top, tell the arty guys they've got an avalanche going down the mountain, the sniper threat is history."*

It was true. In Wajma the shells had been walked up the mountainside to high above the snipers' positions then back down, and rock and shale and scrub oaks and dirt was still cascading.

At Valley Forge, the leadership of the other two platoons and other NCOs, like head cook Yglesias, had already made their way to the Toc, and they had some subdued cheers at Redcloud's report. Very subdued. Everyone knew, already the word passed, their C-O Captain Washington was down, wounded, maybe dead. L-T Caufield too. And Sergeant Akin. No one cared about the Jag captain, except it was another with the Zoo who was hit and no one should be hit.

1st Sgt Kozak had already passed on to Redcloud that battalion said brigade couldn't fly the medevac because of the Red Air. And everyone in the Toc thought that was bullshit, the weather was fine outside and Redcloud wasn't reporting weather-lock up there in the valley, until a minute ago when Redcloud came in broken-up and all that they could catch coming over the speaker through the static was his ". . . heckova storm's hitting us . . .", then the comm link went dead. The low-wattage battery-pack radios the Zoo is carrying weren't going to push through the storm to the satellite and vice versa.

That everybody knows.

It's 3rd Platoon today on QRF, and Kozak now tells their leadership, Lieut Paxton and Sfc Northwich, that he wants their trucks ready, the guns ready to mount, and the guys standing by in the barracks, all their shit ready to leave at his word, no one dicking around on the internet, dicking around with other guys from 2nd not on Cop security.

"A hundred-percent in their barracks. Understood?" Kozak says.

Hooah.

But the XO, Lieut Frye, in command in the absence of Capt Washington, reminds Kozak, "Command regs, Top. Can't go outside the wire on Red Air. Not even a Quick Reaction Force. Not until they lift the Red."

Kozak ignores Frye. Tells Paxton and Northwich, "I want you ready. In case they don't lift the Red."

Lieut Frye, "I can't let them leave, Top. I won't."

"You won't know it. Deaf, dumb and blind, L-T. You just remain deaf, dumb and blind."

In Wajma, Fourteen Minutes After the First Shot

Downpour raining like the devil, but no one's outside anymore.

Doc Eberly oversaw four of Utah's men in getting Lieut Caufield and Capt Cathay on makeshift poncho litters and up inside.

Redcloud and Dove wrapped Washington's body in a poncho, and Rto Akin's as well, and Utah's men carried them inside.

Everyone's on the veranda or inside or on the roof.

Four of the ANA have left, deserted.

Their sergeant had tried to stop them, arguing with them, berating them for their cowardice, and when that didn't work, mocking them to *Go, run, go back to your mamas and hide under their burkas.*

It was Wolfe who stopped them, firing two bursts of three from his M4, splashing mud at their heels, and he made them drop their packs and AKs and ammo bandoliers.

If Afghan soldiers want to desert, fine, leave, but not with their weapons. Not guns they can turn around in ten minutes and use against you. Force them to stay, and they're just as likely to turn those same guns on you when your back's turned or in the middle of the night.

Redcloud has a mental count. Lieut Col Dove has it jotted on a page of his little lime green hardbound notebook.

Numbers.

All totaled, they came in this morning with 43 Americans. Including the 2 civilians, Wolfe and Nick Flowers.

Plus 20 ANA. And one terp, Nouri.

4 Americans now out of play. 2 Kilos, 2 Whiskeys.

4 ANA out of play. Walked away.

Isaf, Kabul

In the Isaf Strategic Op Center, Col Pluma is disturbed. How'd it all collapse so quickly? How'd they wind up with two Kilos and two Whiskeys? What, it wasn't even 24 hours ago that he was sending Zach out to inform the general about the Human Terrain Team female Doctor Robyn Banks burned by a rural farmer, and now he himself, he's going to have to be the one to deliver this bad news to the general.

"The status of the commander?" he asks the room.

"C-G's chopper from Bagram is four minutes out," someone answers.

What about Doctor Hutchinsen?, Pluma thinks. *What's the deal, has he worked it all out through Karzai, do they have a deal with the Anti-Afghan Forces?*

Pluma knows that he can only control that which he has control over. And that's about zilch right now.

And he'll climb the stairs on up to the roof now to meet General Pete St Claire's chopper when it lands in four minutes.

What is it, he thinks, *What in Christ's name is it with that fucking Wajma Valley?*

Day Two, Afternoon

Fob Salerno

Seventy or eighty helicopters parked on the concrete pads.

The big CH-47 Chinooks.

Blackhawks.

Apaches.

Small Kiowa scout choppers that don't have the lift to fly up in the altitude of Valley Forge and beyond, even higher to Wajma.

All the concrete pads are connected to a series of straight ribbons of concrete taxiways.

Two Blackhawk medevac birds sit on their own concrete pads beside the road across from the Cash. Two Apache escort choppers on their pads there as well.

Nearby is the crew shed, a B-hut where the medevac and escort crews hang out on their twelve-hour shifts. Perpetual standby waiting on a call relaying the 9-line of a Tic gone bad somewhere or a roadside bomb or taking shrapnel during a rocket attack on a distant outpost.

Lounging in nylon sport chairs on the wooden deck off the back door are three from the medevac crew that went into Wajma yesterday.

The pilot, the crew chief and the flight medic.

On duty again today.

Saying nothing. Just enjoying the sun even as the clouds pushing in fast enmasse from the north are sure to obscure it in a few minutes.

Some old Garth Brooks coming from the small tinny speakers mounted under the eaves.

A soldier comes up onto the deck. No nametag or unit insignia on his uniform. Sterile. A baseball cap—grinning Cleveland Indians' Chief

Wahoo logo—instead of a helmet. M4 carbine spray-painted in desert camouflage.

He's a senior NCO. Since his uniform is sterile, you can only tell by his age and bearing. He's got a short-cropped beard and hair way longer than Army regulations.

Special Forces.

SF for short.

Green Beret medic, and he lets his med ruck drop to the deck and takes one of the empty sport chairs.

He's Doc Boonzmann. If you know him you call him BZ.

He comes over from nearby Chapman Base on these days and weeks when his team's not refitting from a night snatch mission or in rehearsals for one coming up. Drops by the Cash to see what's up, walk the rounds with a doctor, maybe get to watch a surgery, learn something.

An exaggerated greeting from the flight medic, "BZ my man, wazzzzz suuuup?"

"Heard you-all have a mission."

"Air is Red," from the pilot coarsely.

"That's what I hear. Got any idea, think it's gonna be lifted soon?"

"Do I look like a fuckin weatherman?"

BZ isn't offended by the pilot's angry tone. He knows that the medevac crews don't like doing nothing when there's a 9-line they can't go out to, wounded soldiers needing to be lifted out of somewhere. "I heard it's the same place that anthropologist chick got set on fire yesterday," he says.

"We picked them up," the crew chief says. "Her civilian teammate, this real angry-looking dude, I thought he was gonna put a bullet right here tween my eyes when I said we couldn't let him get on board. "

"Did you guys know her?" BZ asks. "I heard she was hot."

"No pun intended," flat and dry from the pilot.

"Cold, sir," from the flight medic. "That's over the line, borderline." And to BZ, "It wasn't a real good day up there. It was her and four LNs. Plus, word was, two Kilos left there with the platoon. LNs."

For Local Nationals. Afghans.

The flight medic adding, "Five casualties, it was packed, we were overloaded, couldn't move 'round. All I could do not to crush their chests crawling over them. Lucky thing, the platoon 68-Whiskey up there on the ground had his shit together. Had em stabilized. Clean. Meds noted. Textbook. And you know how tricky it can be with crispy critters."

"Did you see the 9-line?" BZ asks, meaning today's mission. "Two critical."

"And two KIA."

No one says anything.

BZ, "One of them's female, I heard. I don't know if she's a critical or KIA."

The pilot chuckles a little. "Yeh. Those people up in the hills have this thing about American women."

A thing alright.

And it aint a good thing.

"No trespassing," the crew chief says flatly. "Enter at your own risk. No women need apply."

"Not just in the mountains," notes BZ. "Women's liberation, feminism isn't really high priority anywhere here."

The pilot, "If that isn't the understatement of the year."

Flight medic, "Decade."

Pilot, "Millennium."

Crew chief, "Not that maybe it's such a bad thing. You don't see a lot of divorce here."

Flight medic, "Any divorce, you don't see any. Big zero."

"No kids being brought up in single-parent families," from the crew chief. "Kids tellin their moms 'Fuck off'. Telling their teachers 'Fuck off'. You don't see fourteen-year-old girls gettin knocked up by Tom-Dick-n-José all hanging out on the corner in the 'hood."

"By their uncles and cousins," says the pilot without emotion. "That's who's knocking them up here."

BZ, "Vice is nice. Incest is best."

Flight medic, "You going to put that on your headstone, BZ?"

"No room to fit it. Underneath the Congressional Medal of Honor citation."

Relaxed light laughter.

The pilot, "That's about right. For a CMH. What is it, nine out of ten you've got to be dead?"

BZ, "Yeh but, show it to Saint Peter—it's an automatic entry ticket into the Pearly Gates. And you get the best seat in the house."

"One thing at least you know," says the crew chief going back to the whole broken-family subject. "You know their women aren't getting knocked up by Jody when they're off away in the summer fighting season then come home and find their girlfriend's three months pregnant and says it's yours. Right, yours. Until you do the math, and you haven't been home for seven months."

"Three months pregnant?" the flight medic asks.

"Zero three," the crew chief assures him. "And she's, like I said, like a first-grader can't add it up—three months pregnant and I'm gone seven."

Flight medic, with a laugh, "And she's trying to say no no no it is yours? Honest, honey, honest, honest to God it's yours."

"I'm saying here, what I'm saying, these people here they hate women, but at least their women aren't runnin 'round on their boyfriends or husbands who're off fighting us dressed up in their summer Taliban lightweight ripstop man-jammies."

No one says anything.

Then, "Residual sperm," BZ says.

They all three look at him.

"Yeh, haven't heard of it? Residual sperm."

The pilot chuckles.

"The kid is yours," says BZ. "The little sperms, they hide in the nooks and crannies, all nice and warm and moist in there, then six, eight, ten months later they pop out, swim themselves upstream, and next thing you know she's pregnant. And, howdy-do, it's yours, it is. Got the same big nose and big ears you got."

Flight medic laughs, "And that's your girlfriend's story and she's stickin to it, is that what it is, BZ? Residual sperm, I gotta remember that."

"Fuck me to tears," says the crew chief, shaking his head, resigned, like it's all so suddenly clear. "Residual sperm. Guess I shouldn't of beat the shit out of her then."

Light laughs from all of them.

They know he's joking.

Hope he is.

They're quiet for a while.

Then, "When they clear the Red," BZ asks, "mind if I come along?"

"Be my guest," from the pilot. He tilts his head towards inside. "Put your name on the manifest."

And that's what BZ will do in a minute or two. Go inside where the rest of the crews are hanging and he'll put down his name, SSN, unit, blood type. He'll bullshit a little with the others. From the fridge get a drink—a Coke or Gatorade or something.

And wait for the Red to get lifted. Hope it does. Even though he watches now as the clouds are just about ready to sweep under and cover the sun.

With even blacker ones following right behind that frontal mass.

Across over where all the CH-47 Chinooks sit on their pads, the only two with their tails open and ramps resting a few inches above the concrete are the two that took the Zoo into Wajma early this morning.

The ones supposed to be picking them up.

Like, right about now.

Each crew is hanging out on the ramps or just inside. Waiting for the Red to be lifted.

The sunshine has just disappeared, shadows suddenly gone, and the Chief Warrant Pilot leans out to look up around the tail pylon at the ever-darkening clouds approaching.

He's the pilot from this morning who was wearing the helmet with the **9-11 NEVER FORGET** decal. With the 11 as two silhouette towers. The pilot from whom Capt Washington got the acknowledgement that the Zoo's exfil pickup would be 1300.

His name's Chiarduchi.

Anthony Luke Chiarduchi.

Chief Warrant Chiarduchi.

A Warrant-5. The highest warrant rank.

Mister Chiarduchi.

Mister C to his aircrew. Out of both high respect and the brotherhood of a crew.

Age, forty-five.

He's been flying Chinooks for twenty-one of his twenty-three years in the Army.

Over 7,000 hours. Most don't ever see 4,000.

He checks his watch, which he checked less than a minute ago. The digital readout changes from 12:59 to 13:00.

"We have now officially missed our target time," he says aloud to everyone and to no one.

His 1st lewy copilot checks his own watch. He half-jokes, "At least I have something not to write home about."

"What's that make for you, Mister C?" door gunner Maneosupa asks. "The first time in how many years you've been late hitting the target time?"

Chief Warrant Chiarduchi unwraps a 3 Musketeers bar. Takes a bite. "It makes the Tattoo Zoo wet and cold and a long ways from home."

"It sucks to be them," says the other door gunner, a kid named Rapley.

The crew chief is Staff Sergeant Jarbodie. Thirteen years now crewing Chinooks. Seven months here on this particular bird. It's his helicopter, he's responsible for it, every nut and bolt. It's not by chance that Warrant Chiarduchi, with his senior pilot status, has chosen this Chinook his primary. In his six years in this aviation brigade he knows the superior crew chiefs to the average ones to the mediocre.

Chiarduchi reserving Jarbodie's Chinook says a whole lot about Jarbodie.

In particular, since this is one of the few old C-Models still in the Army inventory. Chiarduchi is tested out certified on the F-Model, but is just as comfortable with the more seat-of-the-pants old-fashioned flying of the C-Model to the E and F, and this Chinook being Jarbodie's, he'll take it to those more advanced hi-tech ones.

Jarbodie has noted to others many times, in jestful respect, that Mister C and the C-Model, it's like hand-in-glove. *"Call him Mister C-Model Chinook. Call this platform Chiarduchi-H-47."*

Jarbodie hasn't said anything right here right now, has just silently waited out this on-hold all-flights grounded.

Like Chiarduchi, he doesn't like missing a target time, especially a pick-up exfil of guys in no-man's land. Guys who've already taken casualties.

He heard the kid door gunner Rapley say *"It sucks to be them,"* and he looks at all that mass of black clouds. Matter-of-fact, plain, he half-mumbles, "I hope they brought their Goretex." Of Warrant Chiarduchi, he double-checks, asking, "Their stat's still the same, Mister C? The 9-line: two wounded, two dead?"

Bare shrug from Chiarduchi. "Medevac's grounded. Could be four dead by now."

"Talk about sucking," Jarbodie says. "Big time."

Isaf, Kabul

In the Dfac, at the close of lunch, Colonel Pluma fills a take-out container with a bacon-cheeseburger, fries, onion rings and baked beans. Fills a smaller one with a tossed salad that he ladles heavily with low-cal Italian dressing. Another small one with a slice each of pecan and lemon meringue pie.

Things are looking a lot better than they were just ninety minutes ago. This whole thing could work out. Doctor Hutchinsen has returned from a personal face-to-face with Karzai, and the good news is that the Taliban are playing ball. Hutchinsen had gotten from Karzai the numbers for two bank accounts in Dubai. Twenty million to go into one, five million into the other.

Unspoken but known to all, the second is for Karzai.

Hey, it goes with the territory.

These people haven't survived for the past how-many-thousand years in a landscape of rock and sand that every other conqueror and empire builder has traipsed through by being stupid.

Karzai's got to feather his nest for when Isaf and Nato and the U.S. loses and leaves, or vice versa, just leaves then loses, and it all collapses around him no matter which. *Shit,* Pluma thinks, *Did I just say when we lose?*

He chalks it off as a Freudian slip that means nothing and doesn't even matter to him.

Win, lose, it's not his war to win or lose.

Take it up with the President. He sitting pretty in the White House.

And hell, the money transfer isn't Col Pluma's problem either, let them deal with it, not him. That would be handled out of Bagram. Transfer deadline: 1500 today Greenwich Mean Time.

That's London Time.

4½ hours behind here.

1500 there is 1930 here. That's 7:30 tonight here.

Plenty of time.

Their worry, not his.

Col Pluma is getting lunch-to-go, late no less, because he wants and needs to be in the op center the moment the weather clears in Wajma Valley to get choppers in there and get Zachary Dove and the Tattoo Zoo Platoon out and up to Bagram.

Under arrest.

Every last one of them.

And get those two Kilos and two Whiskeys out. *Jesus H Christ, how'd Zach allow himself to take casualties?*

Earlier, going up to the roof to meet Gen St Claire's bird from Bagram, Pluma had caught up with Major Vicky Marshall also going up.

Boy did she look good from behind below. Not just good but damn good. They could package her in a bottle just the way she is and sell a million of them.

She would be taking the same Blackhawk after the general and his contingent got off, then she'd have to hitch a lift on another from the military section of the Kabul Airport to get up to Bagram.

"Leaving us so soon?" he'd asked her. "What could be so pressing at Bagram? The hospital's already double-staffed. Stick around. Tonight's the last night of Oktoberfest."

"Too dangerous," she'd replied.

"Dangerous? Here? We've never been hit. Any safer, they're going to take away our combat pay."

"Dangerous for a woman, single and unavailable or married and even more unavailable."

"You're pulling my leg. Right?"

"There's too great a percentage here of O-5s and above to us lowly majors and below. Compared to Bagram where there are thousands to choose from. From pretty pfcs and on up. All young and cute and innocent and they laugh at all your jokes. You can't swing a dead cat by the tail here without hitting an O-6 and above."

O-6 full bird. Like Colonel Pluma.

"Each," she'd finished it, "with the line, 'What's a bad girl like you doing in a nice war like this?'"

"I'll have to remember that," he'd said. She'd said it all playfully, but he'd known what she meant, that it was her friendly, rank-respectful way of saying *Bug off, Colonel, you're not getting anywhere with me.* As if she's God's gift to man. *Which she isn't but thinks she is,* and Pluma would like to wrestle her down onto the bed, and hold her there, he'd show her. *And she'd love it. Begging to be wrestled down. Begging for dominance over her.* Whoever said it was right, *She could be Halle Barry. Except even prettier.* Sexier. More attractive, though that would seem impossible. To Pluma she is the slave girl that he would imagine Thomas Jefferson had taken. That pretty. What was her name? Sally something? Jenny something? Jenny Sally? And nose-in-the-air Victoria Marshall had to be *Half-white already at least, and probably more, three-quarters, and looking like Halle Barry.* A beautiful slave girl who would have never blown him off and so smugly shot him down so easily like that.

Not that he'd been about to give up. "I'm sorry about last night," he said. "Having to steal Zach away from you."

"Oh no, that's nothing. Zachary and I go back a ways, that's all."

"He's never really said anything. That I've heard."

"Not in that way," she'd covered herself. "We're just friends. I heard, someone was saying, I heard that he took a copter out early this morning."

"It's a priority mission for which he is uniquely suited."

"High priority, with a send-off by General Pete St Claire."

"Your sources are well-connected. But no, I'm not at liberty to tell you the who what when where. You heard then, I take it, you've seen that he got his O-5?"

That had surprised her, she hadn't known. Zachary Dove's too young for O-5.

"Before long, Victoria," Col Pluma had then added, still ticked that she hadn't even pretended the slightest tease or attraction to him. "It won't be long, when you swing that dead cat, you're liable to hit Zachary Dove, rising star."

Over at the wall of glass-doored drink fridges, from one Col Pluma pulls a cherry-red Gatorade and drops it into a pants cargo pocket.

From another he takes two Red Bulls and pockets those. Energy for the long afternoon until they can get that Tattoo Zoo out of there. They're already seventeen minutes past exfil time. And the exfil birds not even in flight. Not with Air Red down there.

When the general's Blackhawk had landed on the roof Pluma had updated him on the situation in Wajma while escorting him directly down to the op center, where Gen St Claire had asked for a complete status report, which wound up little more than what Pluma had already told him on the way down. All sat radio comms were down with the platoon in Wajma, which meant the storm had to be clobbering them.

For the general's benefit they'd put over the speakers the live satcom radio transmission from Cop Valley Forge. The company net. With the soldier on radio watch down there at the Cop repeating every 30 seconds, "Zoo Platoon, this is Valley Forge Base, come in Zoo Platoon."

With no answer.

St Claire had broken in and asked to speak with the Awesome Company commander, and when Lieut Frye came on instead, St Claire told him calmly that he did not wish to speak to the executive officer, he wanted the commander. At which point there was hesitation over the radio, then Lieut Frye's voice came over shaky, nervous, saying that his commander was not available.

"Is your commander aware," St Claire then said without emotion, "that this is General St Claire requesting his presence?"

"Sir-sir, he's not here, sir," came Lieut Frye's hesitant reply. "He's-he's-, Captain Washington is in Wajma village, sir."

"Was Captain Washington directed in the op order to go on the mission?" St Claire asked with not even a hint of peeve.

"No sir, I do not believe he was," Lieut Frye said before he realized that he should have just said he didn't know.

St Claire had then asked Lieut Frye who else there at Valley Forge thought it prudent to disregard theater command's operations order and go on the mission, and Frye told him the captain's RTO had gone and also the civilian HTT, Kyle Wolfe, and the civilian embed, Nick Flowers.

In that one moment of quiet in the entire op center, a doubt had flashed through St Claire's mind as to when and how Major Zachary Dove allowed things to get out of control. *Not Major. Lieutenant Colonel. You made him a lieutenant colonel.*

St Claire had showed no break in his calm. "The latest status on casualties, Lieutenant, they would be what?" he had then asked. "You do have that information, don't you, Lieutenant?"

"Sir- . . . . sir. Two wounded, two KIA. That's what we received from the Zoo, sir."

"We need identification, Lieutenant."

"Yes sir," from Frye, then empty air.

"The identities, Lieutenant, did you understand me? Who are they? The wounded and the KIAs. Names and SSNs."

In the ten seconds of blank air that had followed, if St Claire were hundreds of miles away down in the Toc at Valley Forge, he would have seen 1st Sgt Kozak slashing his throat to Frye while mouthing harshly *Don't you dare tell him!*, and

what St Claire and the op center heard next was Kozak's voice coming over the speakers, "This is Awesome Seven. First Sergeant Eddie Kozak, sir. As to the Kilo and Whisky identities, sir, Zoo Platoon did not pass us those identities before we lost radio comms. Over."

And St Claire did not believe him. Knew it was an absolute lie. Knew it without proof, simply from instinct from experience, from the tones of the voices over the radio, he would bet a star that it was a lie. Two stars.

But he had showed no anger, even being lied to, no emotion at all. He told Kozak then that here at Isaf they would be monitoring all Valley Forge satcoms and to hang tough, that they were doing everything possible up here to get the platoon and the dead and wounded out of that deadly valley as soon as possible. "Hang tough, First Sergeant," he'd said. And "Out." End of transmission.

St Claire had then asked for a detailed weather update, and the weather officer put the maps up on the big flatscreens. Real-time from the radar out of Bagram, Kandahar and Salerno. Showing Wajma Valley covered with lightning strikes, color-coded areas of heavy hail. Wind gusts up there in the gorges to seventy, eighty knots. Ground clearance maybe a couple hundred feet. At most.

Everything on the maps heading straight for Salerno. All that same nasty weather.

"Time frame?" St Claire had asked.

"It should hit Fob Salerno, they've got time there, it'll hit approximately 1320 hours local." And the weather officer showed that it would be hitting Cop Valley Forge in less than ten minutes, an hour ago.

St Claire had then asked, "Time frame, duration in Wajma Valley?"

Hours. Two. Three. Five? "It's a weather pattern we've never seen, sir," the weather officer explained. "Out of the Hindu Kush."

Whenever anyone doesn't know anything, they always say *"Hindu Kush"*. That's what St Claire knows, what he's heard countless times, what he's said himself to clueless politicians countless times, and what he'd thought then hearing the weather officer say it. Magic words, say *Hindu Kush* and everyone thinks you know what you're talking about, and it's just the opposite.

Standing away, near the doors, Dr Gene Hutchinsen had thought the same thing. *More Hindu Kush bullshit.* This wasn't his concern, this ops stuff, but he was here because he wanted to know what was going on, what was going wrong down there in that Wajma Valley. *Weather out of the Hindu Kush, it could drop a foot of snow by morning for all we know*, he half expected the weather guy to say next. *We lose this war, they'll blame the whole thing on the Hindu Kush.* The Hindu Kush, the Graveyard of Empires. And *There's not a guy in here who could actually tell you what the Hindu Kush is*, he thought. *Show me on the map the Hindu Kush, suck-butt brown-nosers.*

And he wasn't half wrong.

"Air Ops," St Claire had asked. "Can we get rotary wing in there right now?"

As in helicopters.

"Sir, it depends," the air ops officer hemmed. "On how bad you want to. On how many we're willing to lose."

St Claire finally lost his cool. "Don't give me that George C Scott Doctor Strangelove bullshit! 'Our boys can swoop low in there, bomb the bejeeves outta the pinkos.'"

Sometimes you've got to be dramatic, you've got to kick some ass with your own staff. Put the fear of God in them, let them know you're still a hard-ass like you were as a young eager gung-ho lieutenant.

"Cut the crap," he'd demanded. "Yes or no, can we get medevac and two CH-47s in and back out safely along with gunship fire support?"

"Not conventional, sir, it would be suicide," air ops said. "The 160th perhaps, sir."

The 160th Regiment is the special operations birds.

"But that's iffy, sir," air ops cautioned. "The satellite radios can't punch through that weather, likewise their GPS links. Their infrared's going to be all F-ed up. The 160th would be more or less blind."

Night in the pitch dark is their speciality, not adverse weather.

Col Pluma added the negative, "Getting Spec Ops Aviation approval for an ad hoc mission in that weather.... They're going to defer, sir, and insist on getting approval first from MacDill."

That's MacDill Air Base, Tampa, the Cent Com four-star there.

Pluma adds, "Do we really want Cent Com calling the shots?"

"Let's hear it," St Claire had then asked the room. "Give me something to work with."

"Sir," the air ops officer suggested. "For on-call fire support we can get fast-movers above the clouds, above the storm. Or outside it."

Meaning, F-16s. A-10 Warthogs. Even a B-1.

"Does the platoon have laze capabilities?" St Claire asked.

Hand-held device to paint a target with a laser for the jets' bombs to guide in on.

Unknown, Col Pluma advised. It wasn't in the op order.

Negative from someone else. Conventional line companies like Valley Forge didn't have laze at all, it wasn't in their inventory.

"Are you suggesting," St Claire had asked his air ops officer, clear that everyone in there heard him and understood the rationale for not taking action, "that we drop thousand-pounders without laze capability danger-close to the village compounds there and take that chance of sustaining how many more non-combatant casualties?"

No one said anything.

They'd all heard about yesterday, or knew enough through the grapevine, about those Wajma Valley mass casualties yesterday.

St Claire had then laid down his directive, clear, exact. "There will be no deviation from Air SOP."

Standard Operating Procedure.

Further, "There will be no deviation from Nato Air Safety Guidelines. Air is Red, it's Red. Pass it down. And I want acknowledgements. From battalion on up."

Meaning written acknowledgements. Through Instant Messaging. Get the commanders in writing. That paper trail, even if only digital.

And a final word to the air ops officer. "Talk to the 160th. If they can get weather approval from Tampa and can assure me, in writing, if they can assure me that they can go into that valley and come back out with one-hundred percent of their airframes intact, you let me know."

St Claire was covering his bases.

That Zoo Platoon, they were already in there, stuck on the ground in there, but he wasn't losing a couple of Blackhawks and Apaches and Chinooks, and not the really expensive spec ops 160th ones, not in those mountains in that storm where he could not go in after them and two days from now the Taliban would be parading the dead pilots' bodies through the streets of Quetta or Islamabad. Add to that, the cherry on top, their video footage of $200-million worth of aircraft strewn in pieces incinerated God-knows-where in those mountains.

In Wajma, in the School

Pfc Holloway is sitting against the veranda wall, each radio handset held up near an ear. Both sat antennas up on this veranda wall, pointed up into the southwest.

The rain now coming steady, but not the fierce storm of before right after the sniper Tic.

Just the first terraced wall and field visible through the rain, and the beach out a ways, the now-raging stream and maybe fifty feet up the mountainside.

Out there beyond two hundred meters past the low rock wall it's all rain and clouds, nothing visible.

It's like it's raining hard right here in the clouds.

The handsets are at Holloway's ears because he's hoping to hear Isaf on the one radio and Valley Forge on the other come up, break through all the rain and clouds, make comms.

Yeh, like that's gonna happen. He can't get his satellite TV back in the barracks on post in the states when it's storming, how's anyone gonna get through this thick shit now?

He checks his cheap $25 Timex digital watch. 01:27.

He's had it since Basic, and he'd chuck it and get himself one of the cool Special Ops watches he sees advertised for $500 in those *Soldier of Fortunes* Staff Sergeant Utah's always reading, but this Timex keeps perfect time and just won't quit. He'll get one of those Special Ops watches when he gets back home. Everyone'll think it's cool.

It hasn't escaped him that Wolfe wears one of those watches.

Two, actually. One on each wrist.

He'd heard Slurpee ask Wolfe the other day why two watches, and Wolfe had held up his left arm, "Local time." Then right, "Zulu."

Zulu, that's that Greenwich Mean Time. London. Military SOP.

All times in op orders are Zulu. It puts everyone worldwide on the same sheet of music.

For time purposes everyone pretends they're in London.

Zulu is the same for the guy on the ground calling in an air strike and for the B-2 out of Missouri flying in to deliver it.

It saves a lot of confusion.

Holloway remembers Wolfe then joking, "Afghanistan is so ass-backwards they're a half-hour off everyone else in the world, and you try and get a fat pansy-assed Air Force tech in Nevada flying a surveillance drone here to figure in that half-hour, never mind figuring the ten or eleven hours difference in Nevada. Try, and you're gonna be in a world of hurt."

Holloway couldn't give a shit about Zulu Time.

He lives in the present.

Affuckingstan Time.

Sure, it's a half-hour off everywhere else, but Zulu Time's in England, isn't it?, and his Facebooking and IMing is back with his sisters in California, and how many hours is that different from England, sheee-at, and if it's Daylight Savings Time or not, and he gets a headache just thinking about it, eyes rolled back into his head, who wants to do all that math? Except, remember, radio crypto change is always in Zulu Time, so one push of a button on his Timex gives him that, then another California Time, and another and he's back on local Affuckingstan Time.

That tiny button makes it real easy on Holloway's brain.

He likes it as easy as possible on his brain.

Every couple of minutes now here on the veranda he calls on one radio or the other, "Any station, any station, this is Zoo Platoon, Zoo Platoon, come in, over."

And gets nothing.

Redcloud told him to do it, that's why he does. He knows it's a waste of time and he's going to get nothing. Not in this rain, not through those thick clouds, not through the lightning and thunder.

Then again, what else does he got to do?

And he does it because a platoon without comms with the rear is like being lost out in the woods in Basic and not even knowing which way to turn to head back, cuz you're alone and lost and have no idea where home is, what happened to the other guys?, where'd they go?, where are they!!?, he's all alone, unprotected, that's what it feels like to Holloway without comms to Valley Forge.

Without comms with anyone.

Anyone out there?

Any station?

Holloway pretends disinterest, but he's watching out the corner of his eye Wolfe out here on the veranda seated a few feet away near the doorway, surrounded by a collection of the AKs and ammo bandoliers that he forced the four ANA deserters to leave behind.

He's cleaning the guns. Oiling. Function-checking. Making sure the mags are all full and cleaned of sand and mud and shit.

He had allowed the ANA sergeant to take the four scumbags' knapsacks for the other Afghan soldiers but had argued that the guns and ammo were US-bought and -paid and they were now back with the proper owners, him, and he made sure through terp Nouri that the sergeant understood that in the exact Pashto, not his own see-Spot-run speaking level.

"What you gonna do with all those?" Holloway asks now. "I don't know how you're going to get them back home. They won't let us take home weapons for souvenirs, they won't let us take shit home."

"These aren't souvenirs, what do I want them for back in the States for as souvenirs?" And Wolfe looks Holloway dead in the eye. Squints. Serious. "Don't you smell them?"

"What, who, smell who, smell what?"

"Talibs." And Wolfe sniffs in strong. Yep, "Talibs."

"Wanna know something? You are crazy. Batty."

"Am I? You can't smell those Talibs? Smell. Breathe in deep. Like this. Is it, could be, sure is . . . . Talibs. Haqqani clan. Jalaluddin Haqqani, kid. Ja-la-lud-deen, make a note of it."

Nick Flowers is seated on the other side of Holloway.

He'd had his eyes closed, half fallen into a nap.

He's already gone through his Northface three-day pack, sorting his stash of tiny digital film cassettes and batteries, and he's really glad he threw so many extras in at the last minute, even though it was going to be a simple quick in-and-out QRF, when packing, hearing Slurpee whining to Redcloud, "C'mon, Sarge, do we really gotta take our fart sacks?", and "Pack it," Redcloud saying. "You never know".

And you do never know.

Nick had thought that then and just tossed in a whole bunch of tapes and batteries. He wishes, though, he sure wished he'd stuffed in his sleeping bag. You do never know. *If this doesn't clear and they don't come in for us and pick us up, it could get down pretty cold tonight.*

"Think about it, Holloway," Nick now says. "Why do you think those hajj beat feet?" He means the ANA deserters. "They couldn't get out of here fast enough."

From Wolfe, "Tell the young P-F-C, Nicky. Tell him what Air being Red means."

Holloway, "I know what it means."

Wolfe, "So you know there's no QRF from your Cop coming to pull our asses out, you know that, right? No Quick or Slow Reaction Force. No one, none of your Awesome buddies coming. Not a one."

Holloway didn't. It shows on his slight look of *huh, no?*

Wolfe laughs. "What, you thought the cavalry was in their trucks already on their way to save us? Joke's on you, kid. Air Red means all patrols are axed. Regs writ in stone. Everyone's restricted inside the wire."

"Shows what you know," Holloway says. "They are, they're comin, they're on their way in their trucks." He sniffs in deeply. "I can smell them."

"That's you, that's your own piss when you pissed all over yourself when those snipers started firing."

"Like I say, batty. You are one bat-crazy dude. Jarhead scrambled brains crazy, beat in the head loco-weeds."

"I would have said you shit all over yourself, but your asshole was squeezed up so tight"—in mortified stark-raving terror—"you couldn't get a porcupine quill slid through it."

"Ooooh," from Nick. "Now that's gotta hurt. A porcupine quill, Wolfie? Where do you get these things, come up with these things? I gotta write that one down. 'Asshole so tight you couldn't squeeze a porcupine quill up it.'"

"I'm saving them up for the book I'm gonna write. Everyday Wolfe-isms For The War Zone. Be an Amazon Number One bestseller."

"Wolf-isms, I like it, it's got a nice ring. What other ones have you got?"

"The P-F-C didn't just piss his pants, he pissed in the guy's lying in the dirt next to him."

Nick laughs.

A snort from Holloway. "Crazy jarhead Marine…"

"Former jarhead Marine. Crazy like a fox. I've got all these." Wolfe's extra guns. "And all you've got is that." Holloway's M4. "It's gonna be just us and them, PFC, and if you don't smell em, well, it doesn't matter, 'cause they're out there, whether you want em to be or not. And if Air doesn't turn Green we're going to need every weapon, every last bullet we can scrounge up."

"Look, if you're trying to scare me, I'm already scared enough, you can't get me more scared. Go try someone else. You're the one scared and're just pretending not to be."

"Damn straight right I'm scared. I can smell them." He exaggerates sniffing in. Grins at Holloway. "Haqqani's guys are nothing to laugh about. Underestimate them at your own peril."

And Holloway comes back at him with a cruel thrust that he knows will draw blood. "If you can smell them so good," he says, "how come, what about your nose yesterday, huh? Huh?!"

Which failed Wolfe with the Talibs right here in the school. Worse, failed him with the two hajjis who got Robyn.

The cocksureness wiped clean out of Wolfe for these few moments, he grants temporary victory to Holloway. "That, Grasshopper, you're right," he says. "When you're right, you're right. And that, yesterday, it's a lick on me."

Inside, in one back classroom, Doc Eberly has set up his aid station.

Two patients. Capt Cathay and Lieut Caufield.

Both critical.

If a medevac doesn't come in soon, Doc knows, the L-T isn't going to make it.

When Doc first set up in here, Lieut Col Dove got with Nouri and the ANA sergeant and gave the sergeant an American $20 bill and asked him to take a couple of his men up to the compounds and get an oil lamp or two from a farmer there because Doc was going to need light in here, and he'd need them just until medevac came and then give them back. Rental. Better, Dove gave him another $20 just to be sure, and thirty-five minutes later the sergeant came back with two kerosene lamps, and Dove didn't ask for change and didn't really care that the sergeant and his two soldiers probably took the lamps for nothing, forced the villager to give them up and were keeping the money.

Then, no, Dove looked the sergeant in the eyes, and those eyes said he knew what the colonel was thinking and that it wasn't true. And the sergeant gave one $20 back to Dove.

Fair enough.

Something for Dove to remember.

Way earlier, when Utah's men had carried Capt Cathay and Lieut Caufield in, they'd helped Doc get them into their sleeping bags on the cold concrete floor.

Self-inflating air mattresses under them.

Caufield kept mumbling in his quickly increasing morphine haze, "I'm ca-ca-ca-cold, I'm ca-cold," and Doc used his own sleeping bag to cover him up on top of his own.

He'd put a saline IV into him outside on the ground behind the wall during those minutes of the Tic.

Out there Utah and his men had already stripped their lieutenant of his gear and body armor and had dressed and bandaged the entry wound in his collar while Doc was with Capt Cathay who was conscious and alert when Pfc Holloway had pulled her over to the safety of behind the wall, and she told Doc she felt nothing, no pain, and didn't know what was wrong. But she could not feel her legs or knees or feet, though she was about to push herself up with her hands because she didn't like lying there like she was helpless, and Doc stopped her.

It was after he and Holloway quick-released her body armor and turned her over onto her back that Doc found the pulpy entry wound in her belly just below her belt.

No exit wound on her back.

And he wished, he regretted turning her over and regretted that Holloway had moved her, had dragged her over to there, though he knew that they had to, they had to get her out of the line of fire of that sniper, the same way he didn't want to move her to inside but knew they had to, they couldn't leave her out there lying in the rain in the mud all by herself.

Doc Eberly knew, no backboard, no support, you don't want to move a patient with a bullet lodged somewhere in or around the spine or anywhere close to it.

Cathay was rational and calm out there and refused Doc's offer of morphine, saying she felt no pain and wanted to be fully conscious, to be aware of what was happening, she didn't want to be drugged.

Doc argued it would be better for her, and Ssgt Utah told her the same, and that it would be easier for the medevac crew, and she said "No!", and Doc gave her nothing, and he respected her for it.

And Utah laid firmly a hand on her shoulder out there and grinned wide and nodded, and said, "Ma'am, that's the kind of tough it's all about being part of the Zoo."

Doc Eberly didn't give Lieut Caufield the option of no morphine out there. The LT's face had been locked in a fierce grimace, drools of blood from his mouth and nose, which Doc assumed meant his lung or lungs were hit. Caufield's hands were clenched so tight it looked like the seams of his gloves were going to split open. Through his gritted teeth he was trying to say something, and Doc put his ear close to hear his desperate plea to "Stop it, Doc, can you, can you, please, stop it." The pain.

It was okay for Doc to know, he had to know, he was treating him, he had the morphine, but Caufield didn't want everyone else to know that he was hit, he was weak, he was hurting, that he couldn't endure it, that the pain was too much. He didn't want and couldn't have the men knowing. *Oh God no I can't be weak, I'm their lieutenant.*

And Doc shot him up out there.

Shot him up again a few minutes ago in here. Yeah, it was way too early for another dose, but *Regardless, he's the L-T, and there's not going to be a medevac,* and Doc didn't want him to go out feeling any pain, because when he'd checked just a few minutes ago Caufield's whole left side was red hot to the touch and the hump of a baseball-sized welt was now on his upper thigh. Down there on the top of his thigh. Where there should instead be an exit wound. And wasn't.

And the dribbles of blood from Caufield's mouth and nose from before were now steady streams.

Doc had thought then that they could have saved him at the Cash. He knew they could have. They would have. Real doctors, in surgery. If they could have gotten the medevac.

Too late now.

And he called for Redcloud over his radio and even yelled for someone to get Sergeant Redcloud.

Asap.

Redcloud is here now. On his knees. With Caufield's bare hand clasped tightly between his two.

Redcloud had called the leadership over the Mbitr platoon radios they wear, and the squad leaders are all here. Utah, Ketchum and Nell.

Sniper Rodriquez too, and he's pulled off the second sleeping bag, and all of them are kneeling here with their hands laid on their LT.

A last touching.

A final bond.

He is their platoon leader.

He'd earned their respect even before today.

Dove is over there in the shadows. Standing. Watching. Silent. This isn't his place to do or say anything. Just jot down the time in his pocket notebook.

Capt Cathay knows what's going on.

It's all right close to her.

If she reached her hand out she could touch Redcloud's arm.

She's on the floor level of Caufield and can plainly see his face so pale, with those two shiny ribbons of blood coming down, and she thinks those streaks are so much like the streak of the tear she feels coming down her own cheek, as he treated her kindly, he was nice, *He treated me with respect, when no one else did, he did*, and she's read his records and knows he doesn't have a wife and knows that his SGLI will all go to his mom and dad and knows that he'll never have a wife, never have that wife and kids and family that loves him and waits for him to come home from work every day, and she thinks that maybe that's her too, that she's here now like him and she'll never have the husband and kids and her own family that loves her, and a husband who she likes to imagine she catches is watching her in the mirror as she gets dressed in the mornings, and she can't watch anymore and turns her head away and sees blurred through her tears Lieutenant Colonel Zachary Dove coming close and bending down and taking her hand now, and patting it, and showing just the barest of an encouraging smile, and he says to her quietly now, "It's the infantry, Laura. It's the way of the infantry."

And she thinks that he's saying that infantry's all the sergeants gathered around at death, Sergeant Redcloud and the others, but maybe he's saying, that what he's really only saying is infantry is about death and people dying, your friends dying, and that's the way it is out here in combat.

At this very moment Lieut Caufield doesn't hurt anymore, there is no more pain.

He's floating, and he knows he's floating, and he likes it and doesn't care, he's letting it take him away. There is no pain, there is no feeling of anything, his body is weightless, and he just feels so tired and knows he's falling asleep, and it's so gentle, and Sergeant Redcloud's face is coming down now so close, *Yes that's Travis, hello Travis,* and the rose tatts up Redcloud's neck and along his cheeks come in sharp focus, they're precise rainbow-pretty inkings, and something about this serious man's face now suddenly tells Caufield that he must tell him something, yes he must, *What is it, what do I have to tell him, what is it that he must know?,* and he doesn't sense that he's now wracked with a fit of uncontrolled coughing, and

Redcloud lets the spit blood spray his face, and he doesn't care, as Caufield is trying to tell him something, and his ear now is right at Caufield's mouth as the final cough is just a bare release of spray and he hears Caufield's slow whispers, "Travis . . . get . . . th'Zoo . . . back . . . to Valley Forge."

"Roger, L-T," Redcloud tells him. "We'll get em all back safe to the Cop. Zoo's gonna be just fine."

He sees that there's something else Caufield wants to tell him and is trying hard to concentrate to pull it from his jumbled, fuzzy, fading consciousness.

Moments of full focus in Caufield, "Be . . . care . . . . ful."

"You got it, L-T. Don't you worry about it, careful's my middle name."

And Redcloud detects a smile in Caufield's eyes, or perhaps he just imagines it and imagines the eyes are looking at him when maybe they're not, and he puts his lips down close to Caufield's ear to tell him, "You did awright, L-T. Matt, you hear me? You did good. You're a good P-L, Matt. Proud to have you as my P-L."

He touches with two fingertips Caufield's forehead, as if anointing him, then completes the Sign of the Cross there on Caufield's face.

Rips the IV out of his arm.

Tucks his hands and arms into the sleeping bag.

Zips up the bag, pulling the hood down over his head and zipping it up tight.

He stands and doesn't have to say anything, and Rodriquez and the squad leaders lift the body in the sleeping bag and carry it out of this classroom, and he follows them next door into the other classroom, where the poncho-wrapped bodies of Capt Washington and Rto Akin lie.

Redcloud just now remembers that it was only yesterday that he joked to Matt that he'd better be extra alert because only the good die young and Matt had responded by saying he'd stay close to him, in his shadow, and it's true, the good do die young. Redcloud can't speak for

Akin, because he's only been with the company since deployment and he's kind of a blowhard and not the sharpest radioman he's known, not the sharpest knife in the drawer, but for Matt and Captain Washington, yeh, that's two, two more of the good gone.

"We'll get the medevac in as soon as this storm clears, Laura," Dove tells Capt Cathay. "Is there anything you need, anything I can do?"

She points to her rucksack. "Can you . . .?" Put it behind her against the wall.

"Doc, she wants to sit up."

Eberly, "No no no way. Captain, you can't sit, you know the worst thing for a back injury is movement. The bullet could have only nicked something and it's swelling up and that's what's causing the paralysis."

"Like I haven't been moved around like a sack of potatoes and any damage it's going to do's been done already."

She pushes herself up with her hands, and Dove doesn't consider it of value to fight her and moves her ruck against the wall behind her to lean back against.

"Better," she says, and actually smiles. She no longer feels so helpless, so worthless, so wounded. And about the IV in her arm, she asks Doc Eberly, "Do I really need this?"

And it's Dove who defends Doc. "When the Medevac arrives and that's not in, Laura, they'll Article-15 Sergeant Eberly for gross incompetence and negligent disregard for life."

It strikes Doc that the lieutenant colonel referred to him by name, that he even knows his name, that he said that when he didn't have to say anything or could have just said *"You'll leave the IV in, Captain, and you'll do what the medic says"*. He wonders who this lieutenant colonel is, what's his history, where's he from before, if he's just another Isaf puke, as guys call all those officers up there. Or maybe not. He's got the Ranger regiment combat patch on his shoulder. It was him out in the sniper's lane, not protected behind the wall but out in the sniper's line of fire, just to tell him to give it up on that foolish mouth-to-mouth *I was giving Akin when I knew he was dead already, how stupid of me, what was I thinking?, not prioritizing my patients, you don't treat the dead, you dumbshit, and don't do it again, just learn from your mistakes.*

Learn from your mistakes. Doc now square-roots that, *What was the real mistake?* And knows instantly that he was giving Akin mouth-to-mouth so that he could deny to himself that he could not treat or help all the many others who needed him then—Captain Washington, the L-T, her—they were too many and too much in those few moments and he had not the skills, ability or composure to do it. *I was overwhelmed and denied it by treating Akin who I could not fail because he was already dead.*

Never again. I hope.

And he square-roots that, *Not hope. Never again because you will not allow yourself to be so fearful and incompetent ever again. Ever.*

On the roof most of Ketchum's squad are back against the rear parapet far under the mountain overhang and out of the rain.

In the rain at the front parapet, one man each on the 240-B machinegun and the two Saws. Under their ponchos.

Everybody's already soaking-wet to the skin and have been since the first thirty seconds of the downpour nearly two hours ago, but a poncho always makes one feel dryer and warmer. More comfortable. Less frail. Less insecure.

The ones who are paying attention and watching the rain are beginning to realize that it's coming down easier, less a downpour and seeming to lessen by the minute.

Less rain is a good thing.

Less rain means it's gonna stop.

Gonna stop, Air will be Green.

Green Air means they'll be out of here.

Cross your fingers.

The snipers have been eliminated, what are the chances there are more out there, and how are they going to hit here in the rain and clouds when there's no way they can see through from any distance?

So Redcloud's relaxed the standards. Body armor kept on, but Kevlar helmet off if a guy wants, but kept close at hand.

Guys up at the machineguns on the parapet are wearing theirs under their ponchos, but most of the others, nope, not with the opportunity to take it off outside the wire just because they can when they're not supposed to.

It's a GI thing. Grab any chance you can to do something you're not supposed to do when you aren't going to get slammed for it.

In spite of the fact that no one's talking or joking or playing, too close still to the deaths of their company commander and Akin and just now hearing that the L-T too has died, Pvt Finkle is hopping from puddle to puddle up here stomping, trying to make huge splashes, and from the back parapet Spec Van Louse yells, "Would someone get him his daily Ritalin please!"

No one laughs.

A couple of them, like Cpl Sandusky, are so quiet and staring at nothing, maybe playing in their minds the sight of their captain taking a bullet to the throat if they saw it, or even just seeing Nell's and Utah's soldiers lifting Captain Washington and Akin onto those ponchos, and you couldn't help but see the blood and see Akin's destroyed face. Their captain is dead. Their L-T is dead. It can't be.

Sandusky might be thinking *It can't be. But it is.* He saw it. He's seeing it.

Some see that some of the others here are more disturbed than they themselves are, and can't explain it nor think it's bad. It just is. Don't bother them, don't say anything. *They'll come out on their own.* Yeh, everyone in their own time.

Up front alone on the 240, Spec Lee Tran squints his eyes closed tight to try to get the dull ache in his forehead to ease. When he'd gone downstairs earlier, he'd gotten a Motrin and two ibuprofens from Doc and that's taken the hard screaming hurt away now, and Redcloud had asked him down there if he wanted to switch helmets with Akin's, since his was now structurally compromised and Akin wouldn't be needing his anymore, but "Hell no, Sarge," Tran told him. "This one's good luck."

Slurpee's assistant on the mortar, Pvt Leonard, had been down there in the aid station and he showed off to Tran his chest that already had two purple bruises bigger than hockey pucks from the sniper shots to his body armor. Leonard did take Redcloud's advise to switch out his armor plate with Akin's, since, yeh, everybody knows that ceramic plates are sure-as-shit compromised with a hit, never mind two hits.

Downstairs, Nell's squad is in the front room, scattered about against the walls, some sitting in the windows, on the wide concrete sills.

No horseplay. Guys alone or in twos. At most just whispers between them. They've just seen the squad leaders carry their LT's body in there into that other classroom with Akin's and their captain's.

How do you lose your company commander and your platoon leader both in the same day? In the same minute? What is this, is it Normandy? That's *Saving Private Ryan*, they all know, this is Afghanistan, where maybe you'll lose in the whole company three guys KIA in the whole 12-month deployment. At most, maybe six, with bad luck, and that's, like, really bad luck, and that's not here in their battalion or even in their brigade. Yeah, that might be down with the Marines maybe they're gonna lose eight or ten, but they're jarheads and that's just the way it is in the Corps, it's always been that way. Here, sure, you're going to have a lot more wounded, maybe twenty, even twenty-five, thirty, but that's in the whole country the whole year, and they're wounded, sure, and serious, sure, but the wounded don't die anymore, not with the medevacs and Cashes and those docs there.

Hooah on the medevacs and Cashes.

Hooah on Doc Eberly back there.

Doc knows his shit.

Doc's smart, a brianiac. Cool under fire.

Nell's guys have all checked over their weapons.

A couple of times already since they've come in after the Tic.

Checked their ammo racks, ensured their mags are all easily accessible, ready. Their few frag hand grenades are in their proper pouches like they know they are, easy to reach for.

Nell had told them to. Get their minds off what's happened. Do something, keep busy, "We don't got a six-pack of Bud to take our minds off the Cap'n and L-T and Akin. Get them weapons squared away."

Slit open MREs. "Eat and hydrate," Ssgt Nell had told them. "We don't know how long we're gonna be here. Lighten the load if we have to hump out of here."

Hump out of here? Walk? All the way back to Valley Forge? In the rain? Carrying their dead and wounded on litters improvised out of ponchos?

Lieut Col Dove and Redcloud have already discussed it. The Zoo walking out of here. Briefly. Very briefly.

One more sniper up on the mountainside, or even just a couple of local insurgent dudes with AKs or an RPG or two, and the Zoo's sitting ducks. Would be a turkey shoot.

The Zoo the turkeys.

No one's humping out of here.

This school's a good fortress. Thick walls. Good firing positions. Cleared fields of fire in an open arc. Backside up against the mountain, the only assault can come from direct out front.

If they're hit again, attacked here in the school, who knows if there's an enemy force out there, they all know who the two here among Nell's squad who will stay down here, one to each side window. The rest will go to the roof.

If they're hit again.

Not likely.

'Cuz as everyone knows, you can't see through that rain 'n shit, the Taliban aint magicians, they can't either. What are they gonna do, run through the rain charging here? They'll be cut down like ducks on a pond.

It'll be a turkey shoot.

Them, those enemy Talibs, the turkeys.

Down here also are the sixteen ANA who are left, after the four deserters. They're hanging out together at the bottom of the wide stairway going up.

Chit-chatting. Laughing. A couple passing a hand-rolled cigarette. It smells like weed. Who knows? Who cares? They're Afghans, let em do what they do.

Through terp Nouri, Redcloud had told the ANA sergeant that if an attack came the sergeant could use his men as he saw fit, he wasn't going to order them, but the first line of defense was the rock wall out there out front of the school, and that's where the brave Afghans should be.

To be most effective. Manning the first line of defense.

Since it was their country, he'd said.

Their country. To defend. Fight for.

But it was up to them, he couldn't force them, and he wouldn't force them.

Their choice, he'd said.

If they wanted to show their courage.

Utah's men are all out on the veranda. Only a couple up seated on the wall and looking out. Same thing, no one's going to attack through this rain. Though, granted, it is coming down easier, lighter now.

Anyway, at the first shot, like with those of Nell's squad inside who'll have plenty of time to make it up to the roof, out here on the veranda it's just a matter of hopping down off and behind the wall or getting up, turning and kneeling, gun laid on the wall, and firing.

A matter of a of second or two is all. Plenty of time.

If anyone's foolish enough to attack now through this rain. Coming across all that open beach in the clear fields of fire.

Sgt Slurpee and Pvt Leonard are down at the upper end of the veranda. Mortar tube lying on the wall. All they've got is three rounds left, and Redcloud told them to go minimum charge, fire it hand-held out level and aim for the front line of the enemy. No further than 150 meters. Then it's back to riflemen for them both, back on their M4s.

HQ is set up here on one side of the steps. Where Holloway's got the radios, where Nick Flowers is hanging.

Wolfe's moved his AKs and bandoliers over against the wall right on the other side of the steps, and he's staked that out as his position and told the one Utah specialist there that if he so much as touched his AKs he'd kick the shit outta him, and the guy'd laughed, *"Dude, who'd want that piece a'hajj crap AK?"*

Now, about to step inside, Wolfe has a quick word for Pfc Holloway, advising him to save one final bullet for when they're overrun, pantomiming a pistol to his own temple.

"Ask the Rooskies," he says. "These Muj like to gang-rape butt-fuck you, before they cut off your balls and stuff them in your mouth. Then they gut you alive like a mangy goat. I got that right, Nicky?"

"From what I've read," Nick Flowers laughs. "It's true, Holloway. Russians used to save a last bullet for themselves. The Mujahedeen like nothing more than to capture you alive, it's sort of like their perverse pleasure. A power over their enemies, to put fear into them. And there sure isn't any greater power than forcibly raping another man."

Wolfe, "They line up single-file, take numbers on your soft young ass. The last one castrates you and"—he pantomimes *Stuffs it in your mouth.*

"The Muj? Really?" Holloway asks. "Or jarheads?"

A laugh out of Wolfe, and he acknowledges Holloway's cleverness again. "Wax on, wax off, Grasshopper."

Holloway, "Yeh whatever…" He doesn't get the reference.

And Wolfe spots something out there, at the rock wall, and stares harder to make it out, and realizes "Aw shit!"

In the aid station classroom Capt Laura Cathay watches Lieut Col Dove approach Spec Howie sitting in the shadows in the corner.

Howie silent, his head down, his video camera just lying in his lap.

Dove kicks the sole of Howie's boot to get his attention. "We won't be videotaping anymore, Specialist. You can pack up that camera. Then follow me. And lock and load a magazine into that weapon, son."

Cathay watches Dove stride by and out the room.

Watches Howie fumble with his M4, fumble to get a magazine out of a pouch on his body armor and seat it, and it falls out, clanging on the concrete floor, and he seats it again, harder, and he's at a loss to understand how this all happened, why's he here, why does he have to be here, when right now he could be just getting back from a good lunch and in the media center at his desk where he's already checked his email again to see if there's anything new, and checked his Facebook, and in a little bit he'll get back to editing that video story on the Kiowa chopper mechanics that he's already two days late from when he promised the lieutenant.

Cathay watches Howie shove the camera into his ruck and cinch the ruck up tight then stand, and she thinks that why couldn't it have been him who was hit instead of her, and she immediately doesn't like herself for thinking it. Wipes the thought away, asks *Dear Jesus, protect him, protect all of them.*

She wants her weapon now, can't see it, remembers it last, it was slung over her back out there, out there before, before she was hit, and where is it now, what happened to it, did she lose her weapon, and

Doc Eberly reads her searching, panicked eyes, and he grabs her M4 from the floor beside his and sets it up against her ruck.

Relief. "Thank you, Sergeant."

"Doc. Doc's fine. Everyone says Doc."

"Thank you, Doc."

"As Sergeant Redcloud likes to say. . ." in this instance, about one's weapon always being close at hand. "You never know."

Redcloud's still got his squad leaders and Rodriquez in the other classroom—the makeshift morgue—going over for the second time since they've establish the base here in the school the plan for defense.

That each squad have two or three max on the walls on security, 'cause there's plenty of time to react if an attack's coming, and let the others eat and especially sleep.

Yeh, sleep now, when it's daylight, because if they're still here come dark that means it'll be here all night cuz there aint no choppers coming then for sure, and then it's gonna be 50% alert looking through NVGs.

That's Night Vision Goggles.

Or Nods, Night Optical Devices, same thing—you say potayto he says potahto.

Good stuff, and not cheap, but the Army's done well ensuring each infantry soldier's got one.

They're Nods to most, it's easier—one syllable verses three.

They'll give that 50% on alert the ability to see an approaching enemy before they can even see the big school building.

What you can see at night you can shoot.

The other 50% will be right there at the walls with the soldiers up alert. They'll have their Kevlar on, Nods attached and ready to flip down, gun at hand, they can be sleeping, Redcloud doesn't care, but ready to sit up and turn 'round and start shooting in, like, .05 seconds.

"Beatin their meat," Sniper Rodriquez jokes.

"Whatever rocks their boat." Redcloud.

Ketchum, "Improvised L-S-A for their M4s."

That's Lubricant Small Arms.

And Utah brings up what they're all thinking but don't really want to have to deal with. "What about the colonel?" Utah says. "I don't feel right taking orders from him."

"You let me take orders from the colonel," Redcloud tells him. "You let me deal with the colonel. Your concern's your men, and you've got your jobs making sure they understand, like I say, we're not on the trucks anymore where we've got cases of ammo to shoot through. So I want them counting their magazines, and I don't wanna hear anyone shooting burst unless you've assigned them it."

Rodriquez is gruff. "I aint taking orders from that asshole. We shouldn't oughta neven be here, Sarge, you heard Kyle, he coulda 'rested him right back there at the Cop, And the cur'nel's still gotta bring us back t'this shithole."

Utah disagrees. "Wolfie didn't kill the kids in here."

Rodriquez, "And now yer sayin we done it?! We done it?! Buuuulllllll-shit!"

Redcloud, "It doesn't matter who did it. A hundred seventy-three of them were in here. One seven three. That's going to be investigated, I don't care if the Pope did it. Lieutenant Colonel's just following orders."

Ketchum doesn't want to believe it. "Hundred seventy-three, Sarge? You sure? Hundred seventy-three?"

Redcloud, "You go on across up there and count em. I'll wait."

"We couldn't of known," says Nell. "There is no way we coulda known."

Utah, "Beside the point."

Redcloud, "It's not all-yer-all's concern. You just let me and the colonel deal with that. Hooah?"

Yeh, hooah. Half-hearted. What choice do they have?

Rodriquez, "You say he's jus following orders?" He nods toward the covered bodies of Capt Washington and Lieut Caufield. "Mí commandantes are gonna be gettin CMHes, Sarge. Cuz you say it's jus orders the cur'nel's followin?"

The CMHs he means are Coffins with Metal Handles.

Not Congressional Medals of Honor.

"And you see his Kevlar?" Rodriquez continues. "You see it?! He's got it teared, one small little tear here and what do you wanna bet he's in there right now writin up his own Purple Heart for it."

The slit in the cloth cover of Dove's helmet where the sniper bullet glanced off.

Rodriquez is angry, impassioned, and not through. "Then we're gonna get back and he's gonna court-martial us and they're gonna give him a Silver Star, make him full bird, a full eagle. And Cap'an Washington, they're gonna court-martial him when he's dead and take his rank and aint gonna leave his wife shit. And the L-T, you watch, they aint neven gonna let him have no honor guard at his buryin. Won't have no twenty-one guns an' no taps for him, whaddayou wanna bet."

Done, he's said his piece.

And Redcloud waits now, just staring at Rodriquez as if to say that he can say more if he wants, no rush, continue on, let it all out.

Nothing more, that's it for Rodriquez for now.

And Redcloud looks at each of his squad leaders. "No one is going to hurt the captain, no one is gonna bad-mouth him, no one is gonna charge him with anything. He wasn't here yesterday. About the L-T, what you men have to remember, and lock this in your brain, because this is the truth. I told him, I said, 'L-T, we are not doing BDA'. I was the one who said No BDA, and there's not a court-martial board in all the world's gonna think a lieutenant can go against his platoon sergeant."

"Hooah," from Utah.

"Just remember that," Redcloud says. "I'm the one who ordered No BDA. And you heard that over the radio from me, remember? I called off the BDA. Hooah?"

Hooah from them.

And Redcloud turns to head out of the room, the others following, and he continues his instructions in case of attack. "I don't want anyone shooting at nothin, not one round, he doesn't see a weapon first. If they're more than three hundred meters out you-all hold your fire, I want easy targets, two hundred meters max. Afghans are spray-and-pray, they can't hit anything at a hundred, let's not be wasting ammo out at four."

"Tell me that b'fore," from Ketchum. "They got Tran in the helmet, Sarge. This much lower and his brains are Campbell's Chunky Clam Chowder all over up there."

Wolfe is here in the front area, and he's heard that. "Those weren't Afghans," he says. "The snipers weren't Afghans. Ask the colonel. That right, Colonel Dove, they weren't Afghans?"

For a moment Dove is surprised at that from Wolfe, the direct exchange to him, a sort of opening to a relationship as professional soldiers. But just for a moment surprised, because he's read Wolfe's record and knows Wolfe's history with Force Recon and attached to Delta, and remembers Wolfe putting his face up close down there in the stream before and telling him he couldn't be as ignorant as he was acting. And he's seen Wolfe reacting on battle instinct out there. Wolfe disregarded his own safety, took to the mortar, fought for the unit.

Wolfe asked, Dove will answer.

"Chechen," Dove says. "Al-Qaeda." And he hands it back to Wolfe, further extending an olive branch for a professional relationship. "And why's that, Mr Wolfe?"

Likewise for Wolfe. He saw Dove out there. He knows now that the Ranger Regiment combat patch on his right shoulder is for real. A while ago on the veranda he had said something to the effect of the colonel at least not being just another pansy-assed desk jockey up at Isaf whose only platoon and company he ever led was in some boot camp battalion, and Nick Flowers had taken that as an opportunity to fill him in on the weeks he'd spent with Dove in his 82nd Airborne paratroopers special task force up in Kunar.

"Number One, like he says," Wolfe now says answering Dove, referring to Redcloud. "The Afghans can't shoot worth shit. Number Two, they don't know who to shoot. And Number Three, they don't know how to aim high, above your body armor. For the neck and face."

All of which Wolfe knows that Dove knows already.

And Rodriquez thinks about that, about the snipers knowing who to shoot and is just about to say *Yeh then how come they missed him, huh?*, meaning the lite colonel Dove dude, but he remembers that shot, was it the second or third, it was meant for Dove, it tore his helmet cover, and he holds his tongue now instead of making a dumbass of himself.

Wolfe has nailed it.

The Chechen snipers knew who to shoot. Too far away to discern rank through their scopes, they would have watched behavior from the moment the helicopters dropped the platoon off. Then just waited for the Apache air cover to leave.

Sure as shit they knew who to shoot. Washington, Caufield, Dove.

Two out of three aint bad, and Dove just missed by a hair, as no sniper's going to be 100% all the time.

Sniper #1 would have had a predetermined assignment to take out command leadership personnel.

#2 the comms and any immediate threats, which explains Rto Akin, Lee Tran on the 240 and big-huge-target Pvt Leonard on the mortar.

Redcloud knows that he himself as part of command is alive unhit simply because he got down behind the wall too fast to be crosshaired in the sniper's scope.

He knows that Dove was just plain lucky for the near miss.

Rodriquez realizes that as well. Knows now he'd have really been a dumbass for saying different.

Dove had been just lucky.

And Capt Cathay wasn't.

Wolfe adds, "Plus, it's a well known fact that Haqqani's got the best Arabs, Chechens, Uzbeks, who've been trained by the best and been fighting jihad for years. If those snipers weren't Chechens, they were Uzbek, I'd bet a month's paycheck on it."

Settled.

Dove tells Redcloud, "I've got another gun for you. You take Specialist Howie here and you utilize him how you see fit."

"Chubby," Redcloud tells Howie, "I'll bet you woke up this morning and said I always wanted to be infantry. Now's your chance. You get to be Infantry Blue. You go with Sergeant Rodriquez here, and you do what he says, when he says and how he says. Sniper, you got yourself a chogie-boy, okay? Make sure he knows how to use that thing"—the M4—"and not kill one of us."

"You know which way the bullet comes out of?" Rodriquez teases Howie. "Ay Gordito, gotta put it on safe 'fore you *are* gonna kill us." And Rodriquez himself snaps Howie's M4 to safe.

"You can go out there with your friends," Capt Cathay tells Doc Eberly. "I'm not going to need anything."

"So the minute I leave you can rip that out?" Her IV.

She was hoping he would say something like that. And not leave. If he left, she would be all alone in this room. The only wounded. All those men of the platoon, and the Afghan soldiers too, and she's the only one wounded, the only one so vulnerable, and she'd felt less so just a little while ago when Lieutenant Matthew Caufield was still here alive, and he was worse than her, but she wasn't alone.

It's always better when there's someone wounded worse than you.

But is it better to be dead? Like him.

Maybe it is. Not for just him alone, but them, the lieutenant and Captain Jashawn Washington too. She doesn't know anything about Rto Akin, that he was hit and dead. She doesn't know that. It was all too fast. She didn't see it. She doesn't even know how many shots there were fired at them, she couldn't tell, it was all echoing *crack-crack-cracks*, and one's in her back, she knows that because she can't do anything with her legs, can't feel them, it's not even like when your leg goes to sleep because you've been sitting on it wrong, because then there's that tingling, and now there's nothing.

And her hands shake, she knows they are and can't stop them, and knows she's crying and can't stop it, and is so scared, she is paralyzed and *What does that mean?, how much of me will be paralyzed useless?, how can I live without walking?*, and

Doc Eberly takes hold of her arm to steady it. And feels her face, "You all right, ma'am?"

She is, she can contain it, she can maintain, she knows that when you've got it bad there's someone always with it worse, and Lieutenant Matthew Caufield is worse, and she thinks of those moments out there after crossing the stream after Matthew Caufield outsmarted her with her own lawyerese and had gotten her to admit he should not speak without an attorney, after they'd taken a few more steps in silence he had asked her why she wasn't married and didn't Mormons get married a lot younger, you know, to start having all those babies and that big huge family? "How do you know I'm not?" she'd responded. "Because no ring," he'd said, "and you wouldn't be out here or in the Army if you were married. Because the Church of the Latter Day Saints are all about marriage and family and loads of kids." "How is it," she asked then, "how do you know so much about Mormons? Did you once date a Mormon?" And he'd said, "One would never have dated me. Not me. You know, my whole No Preference thing." But, "No Preferance isn't Atheist," she'd said. And he'd chuckled, "What's the difference?" "There's a big difference," she'd insisted, "an everlasting eternity of difference." "How? I'm serious, how?" he'd wanted to know. "With No Preference," she'd said, "there's still hope. It means you're open to save your soul."

Cathay realizes that this Sergeant Doc Eberly won't leave her and go out there to be with his friends because he's a medic and also because he doesn't really have any friends out there. The whole time before, outside, he was alone over there against the wall farther beyond the radios and reading. With his iPod in, lines running into his ears. By himself. Eyes shrouded, head bent down to the book in hand.

She asks, "Where's your book?"

Just as Wolfe pops in the doorway, "Doc, you left this." Hardbound copy of *Dispatches*. It's what Wolfe had spotted out there in the mud in the rain beside the rock wall. "Books and water, lethal combination, Doc," and he underhands it across, but it's less airworthy soaked than he'd estimated, and it lands flat on Cathay's sleeping bag, on her legs, and he steps in, apologizing, "I'm sorry, I'm sorry I'm sorry, ma'am, I didn't mean it."

Cathay smiles, "I didn't feel a thing."

Doc hefts the book, which is one lump of soggy pulp, dead useless as a book anymore.

And Wolfe is close, bent over Cathay to again apologize, "I'm really sorry," and it hits him hard—

her helmet off, her natural brunette hair short and stylish and feminine, like the soft features of her face, all so very female

—she's no longer a soldier, she's a girl, a woman, and he can't help but think of Robyn, which was only yesterday, and maybe they're alike because they're cute girls way out far in a combat zone where cute girls or any girls or any females at all shouldn't have to be, and he has to get away from her, retreat, and now, fast, just with a couple more gestures *I'm sorry*, and out of here, gone.

"That's too bad," she tells Doc, about the book. "It's ruined. Totally."

A shrug. "I should have listened to Sergeant Redcloud's little voice in my head. You never know. I should have thrown in a couple more in my ruck. Or my Kindle."

The same for her. "I thought about it and didn't. The one I'm reading. We were only going to be gone for just today, just a few hours."

"What are you reading, let me guess. A legal thriller? Romance? Danielle Steele? Jane Austen? Louis L'Amour? *Little House on the Prairie*?"

A smile from her. But no, none of those.

"*Hunger Games? Harry Potter?*"

Again no. Instead, "A beach book. Beach reading. Relationships. Mothers and daughters and sisters. Stuff that guys don't read."

Doc Eberly figures it's one of those romances and she just doesn't want to admit it. He should read a romance novel, and find out what women think, what they want, how to feel comfortable around one, how to talk to them. *How do I act so that one would really like me? What do I say to make one interested in me? How should I be so that one would fall in love with me?* The one time, Cindy from the Subway, in San Antonio, Fort Sam, that *Didn't last but three weeks, she just liked me because it was something completely different,* being with him.

Capt Cathay remembers, "Your music, where's your iPod?"

Oh right, his iPod. Like his book—out there. Gone. History.

And he sees it in her look, her sorrow, that it's unfortunate for him, it's too bad. Genuine sympathy.

Like it doesn't matter, "It's probably floated off," he says. "I'm running a water-immersion test on it for Apple. Water and mud immersion."

She smiles to show him that she appreciates his light humor as his way to cheer her up as a wounded invalid who can't even stand up on her two feet that she can't even feel her toes as she's thinking to wiggle them. *Wiggle! Come on, wiggle. Just one wiggle please.*

He says, "I've got all the tunes on my laptop, so it's not a complete loss. Nothing's irreplaceable."

She looks away. She is a little embarrassed because she senses that his breezy attitude about his book and his music lost is because he knows that, really, in the big picture, his loss is a blip compared to hers, that *I can't wiggle my toes, I can't feel my legs, I'm going to be paralyzed.*

He thinks that she is easy to talk to—and it's just natural, without effort, he's not trying too hard or pretending—because and only because she is his patient and not a woman first. Not first this exceedingly attractive girl that she is. A patient, that's all she can be. His own age, *Maybe even a year younger, or maybe a year older.* Educated, she's an attorney, she's passed the Bar, and she likes to read, *Even if only romance novels, unlike Cindy who read nothing,* there wasn't a book anywhere in her apartment. Nor a magazine. Even with her two other roommate girlfriends, not a book or a magazine, no one read anything. She's prettier, this captain's prettier, more attractive than Cindy, she's so vulnerable, wounded, she is under his care, she is his responsibility, whereas before, outside, when she was with the lieutenant colonel and Captain Washington and Sergeant Redcloud out there, she was an officer attorney captain woman first—

and maybe she was even married already, as he hadn't thought then to check and see if she wore a wedding ring and had just sort of assumed that she was, because she is too attractive, too very female, not to be

—then, earlier, there outside, he could not and would not ever have spoken to her. He would not have had the courage to even let her catch his eye spying her, because then she'd know he noticed her, because he would not have known what to say, and he would have stammered for words, mouth half open, both if she'd caught him watching her or even if she had just randomly said something to him first.

She trusts this sergeant who seems serious and more mature and far less high-school-braggart boyish than most all the rest of them, this Sergeant Eberly who says to just call him Doc, and she is comforted by his protection, that he is her guardian angel until she will be helicoptered to the hospital, and he is here to watch over her that this bullet in her will not lead to more complications before she can be got to the hospital, and if the bullet starts moving and starts being so painful that she can't stand it, *He will give me the morphine.* It struck her a bit ago when he was saying that his iPod floated away that he is good looking, really good looking, strikingly so, she realized, such that, she'd thought then, *He could be in a Gillette shaving commercial.* The sharp, defined face. *Chiseled good looks,* she thinks, *isn't that what they call it? He could be a groom model* in those brides/wedding magazines. His hair is longer than soldiers have, *How does he get away with it?* His sideburns too, they look longer than regulation.

He is turned away, in profile, a few feet away from her now, digging into his rucksack, wondering aloud to her, "Maybe I've got something for us down here at the bottom."

Free to look at him, to spy him these moments without his knowing, she confirms that she was right before, that he could be in that Gillette commercial and could be the groom model, and she's angered for just an instant at him, she's suddenly jealous for Matthew Caufield that this Doc is better looking than he is. *Was,* she thinks. *Than Matthew Caufield was.* A sergeant should not be more handsome than a lieutenant, it just shouldn't be. Than any officer. It's not fair. It seems like the world turned backwards. And *It's not fair that Matthew Caufield is dead.*

Doc Eberly has found a fat paperback at the bottom of his ruck, and he shows her, conceding, regretting, "Sorry, not quite what some might call light summer beach reading."

She reads the cover. *Armageddon: The Battle For Germany, 1944-1945.* Max Hastings.

He adds, "Not exactly your everyday chick lit."

Granted, no it's not. But, "At least you have something to read," she says and feels again an instant of jealousy, that he will be reading—in here still, yes, with her—but in his own world—and she'll be alone.

Nope. "Read it," he says and drops it back into his ruck.

She looks away, down at her hands folded on her lap atop her sleeping bag. She is glad that she won't be alone, but she is not happy with herself for having wanted for him not to find a forgotten book down in his rucksack, and she wishes now that he finds a book in there that he hasn't read and prays that *My Lord Savior* puts a book there for him that he can have that pleasure if only for penance payment for her selfishness wanting him to be here as a medic for her exclusively, and *If I need him, Lord, I know that I will only have to say quietly his name, "Doc", and he will instantly drop his book that I pray that You give to him please. Please, Lord, for him. Amen.*

Cop Valley Forge

Like up in Wajma the weather is easing here, to a rainfall, not the storm and downpour of earlier.

Comms are still out with the Zoo.

1st Sgt Kozak has all 3rd Platoon together in their command hut.

He'd kicked out Platoon Leader Lieut Paxton a minute ago, telling him it wasn't officer business and the lieutenant was too fresh out of West Point and had a whole career ahead of him to be a part of this.

Paxton had argued that it was his platoon, and Kozak told him, "Not today it's not," and had suggested he go do the rounds checking the guard towers or go have a cup of coffee in the Toc with the XO and play Grand Theft Auto or any other game and take the rest of the day off.

Kozak now explains to the platoon that after what just happened here on the Cop means that if Air is still Red and the Zoo is hit again the only support for them will be them, the QRF.

The mission will be to go in and pull the Zoo out.

Kozak wants twelve trucks, and he'll be in his hummer, and if they have to borrow a couple of 2nd Platoon's trucks, do it.

Just a driver and a gunner per truck. Gonna have to leave room to fit in all the Zoo and their two squads of ANA for the return.

Pack heavy on the ammo, meds, water, food, fuel. You never know.

"This is all volunteer," Kozak says. "I can't make anyone go outside the wire with Air Red, and I don't want to. Anyone who volunteers, it's a guaranteed Article 15, possible Article 32, possible court-martial. Minimum, you're gonna lose a rank. I'll take the hit, I'll do the time, but those are our brothers, the Zoo. In or out, you in or out, no shame if you don't want to break regs, a show of hands, who's in?"

Every hand goes up, "Hooah"s all around.

And Kozak tells Platoon Sergeant Northwich it's his choice, two per truck, he can assign them.

Work up a trip ticket just to cover their asses.

As soon as comms are back up with the Zoo in the valley they'll know more.

Plus, wanting to quell all the wild rumors he knows are going around, Kozak now tells them what they've heard is correct. Captain Washington, Lieutenant Caufield and Sergeant Akin are hit, status unclear but most likely negative to the extreme, be free to assume the worst, cuz then if it's not, then that'll make it all that much better later when they know better.

"Then we gotta get em out," someone says, to a chorus of "Hooah"s, but Kozak tells them no, priority is medevac, it's quicker and more direct to the Cash if they can get choppers flying, so cross your fingers for Green Air.

No need rehashing what happened here on the Cop that makes breaking regs for the QRF outside the wire on a Red, as everybody's already been out to see the unbelievable sabotage of the two big 105 howitzers.

It was about a half-hour ago, during the thickest of the downpour, when you couldn't see five feet in front of you and everyone was inside under cover, and even the tower guards could only stare out and see nothing but a curtain of water 360.

The four arty guys of the gun crews hanging out under the roof out front of the ammo bunker retreated into their barracks hut, as they couldn't even see the guns, never mind anyone being able to fire them since you couldn't see the aiming stakes, and, besides, no one had comms with the Zoosters to shoot anyway.

It was about then that two simultaneous explosions rocked the arty barrack huts and the nearby Toc, with reports from two of the guard towers that huge flashes had been seen up around where the big guns sit.

What Kozak, Lieut Frye and the arty platoon leader and sergeant found was two ANA soldiers more or less decapitated, torsos shredded like pulled pork barbecue, with parts of their limbs severed.

Blown splattered against and tossed at random near the Hesco walls.

Along with sticks which had been ash sledge handles and two solid iron 10-lb sledge heads.

Razor-sharp and mangled chunks of 105 brass shell casings all around on the ground.

And both 105s turned to mush.

Their muzzles deformed. Their breeches blown, twisted. Each with a flattened projectile lodged down there with its smashed tip sticking out where the breech should be closed tight.

The best anyone could figure, it was an act of sabotage no one had ever seen before or ever even heard stories about. The two ANA soldiers as undercover insurgents had used the cover of the downpour to get into the gun position, taken two rounds from the open cases under the bunker roof where the four guys had just been before the rain came in torrential sheets, and they shoved them backwards into the muzzles of the 105s. Their instructions had been either to jam the rounds in so hard that the guns couldn't be used—

the harder the better, a sledgehammer would do just fine

—or they were suicidal jihadists who knew well to explode the rounds down into the guns backwards—

a sledge would do just fine

—and either way, their choice, they'd each pushed a round upsidedown into one gun's muzzle, and on the count of three—one, two three, swing!—they'd been shredded by the exploding shell casings.

Yeh, either way, the guns truly are, in a word, fucked up.

The earlier arty barrage from here had eliminated the sniper threat for the Zoo, but there'll be no further fire support from Cop Valley Forge to Wajma.

Not unless someone can get some new guns up here. Fast.

Wajma, 14:15 Local Time

Quiet and still, a relief, there is no rain, not even a drizzle. Just clouds so low that here on the schoolhouse roof you can reach up and run your hands through them.

It's like your head's right up to the ceiling of clouds.

As for the fields of fire here, you can see a little ways across the first terraced field, down along the beach and the stream running fast until it disappears into lower clouds, and along the mountainside across the stream not more than fifty feet up is visible.

Imagine you're in the backseat of a car and the car's cushiony roof that your head's against is these clouds and you're only seeing that limited rectangle visible through the windshield and out as far as until the fog swallows up everything beyond.

Wolfe is standing at the parapet wall scanning with his binos. Surveying a blank canvas empty of any movement except the fast stream eddying and waving and swirling and splashing over boulders.

The couple from Ketchum's squad along the back parapet who aren't sleeping watch Lieut Col Dove coming up the stairs and they do not acknowledge him in any way except with their hard angry stares.

Dove knows they hate him.

He knows they blame him for the deaths of their captain and their platoon leader. And the Rto sergeant.

He knows that they believe that if he hadn't brought them here today Jashawn and Lieutenant Caufield would still be alive and that coming here was only to indict the captain and their LT and Sergeant First Class Redcloud and all of them for yesterday.

Lock-up and immediate prosecution, isn't that what General St Claire said?

For yesterday, which every last one of them believes right down to their core that they had no way of knowing there were any women and girls down below in there and hadn't even thought then that there were Taliban in there either until they started taking rockets from them.

Dove can't do anything about the hate and won't let it bother him, won't let it give them the power of it by acknowledging it or reacting to it. These men no longer belong to the captain or the lieutenant who they have lost. They are his men now.

They are his responsibility.

His along with Sergeant Redcloud's.

His mission now is to get them all out of here alive and back safe on their Cop.

Everything else, General St Claire's mission, all that he'll deal with when they're out of here safe.

Safe. Back to Cop Valley Forge. Every last one of them.

It might be nothing, it might be a cakewalk, the snipers may have been a fluke, just a random chance of the platoon showing up, like yesterday, and a handful of insurgents here who chose to take advantage of it. Cross your fingers.

He is.

But if it's not random, coincidental, accidental, this platoon's going to have to be ready to confront anything that's thrown against them.

Combat.

A fight.

Which means he'll need the experienced warriors to work with him for the unit to fight as a whole, as a fighting platoon. All working together. As one.

Strength not in numbers necessarily, but in unity.

Redcloud first, he's going to need Redcloud. Everything Redcloud knows. The respect Redcloud has of his men. The immediate obedience.

Redcloud and he must be like husband and wife. Equals. With separate responsibilities. Each essential to the command of the platoon. *I will need Sergeant First Class Redcloud.*

It is Redcloud who will direct the three squad leaders.

That Staff Sergeant Ketchum is a Ranger, has three combat tours under his belt already, Dove's going to count on him.

Staff Sergeant Utah, this is his third combat tour, he seems squared away.

We'll have to see about Staff Sergeant Nell. First combat tour. Somehow managed to pull off five-plus years on drill sergeant status. Someone somewhere messed up on that one, but Staff Sergeant Nell sure didn't do anything to correct it, didn't tell anyone. Dove's going to make note to Sergeant Redcloud to keep a watch on Nell, if Nell's going to sham his way here too.

Got to also hope that Redcloud can quiet that sniper sergeant and keep him from infecting the others with his hostility and negativity and misplaced rebellion.

And Dove will need Wolfe.

Like a lone wolf outside the chain of command, *Did you see him taking that 60 before and laying those mortar rounds on the snipers?*

Dove will need all Wolfe's experience.

Those battle smarts.

His knowledge of these people and their culture.

His instincts.

Stuff from the gut that can't be bought or taught.

First thing, level with Wolfe. Let him know that he knows his past, knows his present, and knows his future even better than he does.

He stands beside Wolfe at the parapet now. Silent.

Wolfe scanning with his binos knows the lieutenant colonel has come up and stopped here beside him.

He ignores him. *Lieutenant colonel's come up here, let him say what he's gonna say.*

"Quiet, Mr Patterson," Dove says.

Wolfe remains silent.

"You don't think so, Mr Patterson?"

Wolfe, "I don't know anybody here by that name." He's said it toneless, without inflection.

Wolfe was Kyle Patterson when he enlisted in the Marines, was Kyle Patterson when he was promoted, when he reenlisted, when he was further promoted, and he legally changed his name to Kyle Wolfe only four years ago between deployments to here working attached to Delta.

"A man can call himself anything he wants to, it doesn't matter to me," Dove says. "It's the end product I care about. Who he is. A name is meaningless."

Nothing out of Wolfe.

"We're given our names simply by the randomness of the parents of our birth. Maybe we should wait and we should be allowed to give ourselves the name we choose."

Still nothing from Wolfe.

Dove too says nothing. Waits.

Wolfe, "Dove is your birth name? Or did you pick it out of the Dictionary of Politically Correct Surnames?"

"The randomness of birth. I was just lucky."

"Would you have kept Patterson?"

"It's a city in New Jersey."

A slight chuckle from Wolfe. That's right, a city in New Jersey. *Who wants to be named after a city in New Jersey?*

They're standing at the parapet, not moving, just both looking out.

It's a ballet, they both know it. It's delicate. How much will each give to get what he wants from the other?

What does Wolfe want from this Isaf lieutenant colonel?

Not to be charged, not to be brought up to Bagram Airfield under arrest, but to be let go scot-free, to have Dove exonerate him?

No, that won't happen.

It won't happen.

Zero% possibility of that.

What Wolfe wants, it's simple —

it's the community-of-man, it's esprit de corps, whatever, or just the warrior soul that fights for the warrior next to him

—it's what he knows, that *We're forty-some guys here, and if those Talib enemy are out there like I can smell them, we're going to have to fight not as forty-some but as one.*

"Awful quiet, Mr Wolfe," Dove says. "Too quiet."

"That's John Wayne. In a movie. Where, Number One, they always know the ending ahead of time. Number Two, you know the injuns are already out there watching and waiting because there're always gonna be injuns in a cowboy movie. Number Three, you know The Duke's going to save the day and pull everybody's asses out of the fire."

"Do you think they're out there watching and waiting?"

"You're from Isaf, you tell me, what's the command mindset up there? Will they fly on a Red?"

Dove knows the answer. Doesn't like it. Admits, "Not today."

"If it was anyone but us, us wanton killers of a hundred and seventy-three women and children, not to mention the two Talib insurg at point-blank from some deranged former gyrine contractor civilian, would they fly then on a Red?"

Dove doesn't answer. It's a question he doesn't really want to know, really know, the answer to. He could ask himself, if it were the president shot down out here right now, or just his wife and daughters, would they fly on the Red? If it were General St Claire would they? A handful of senators and congressmen on a so-called fact-finding dog-and-pony-show tour of the war zone? He knows they would. They'd put everything in the air on the Red to get here.

"Are you a religious man, Mr Wolfe?" he asks.

"You know my old name, my record and my history, everything about me, you tell me."

"Baptist."

"Very lapsed Baptist. Even the lapsed won't have me in their church."

"Then your praying for Green Air won't help."

"Unless it's true, what I've always heard. That God turns an ear quicker to someone lapsed just to bring him back into the fold."

"Pray for the Green."

"Mine wouldn't help, not prayers from me. Just the opposite. Even God knows I'm a long long long long way out of the fold."

That's not something that Dove would argue with, not even just to make Wolfe feel better about himself, that's he's really a good man, a good soldier, Marine, a patriot, a man of honor.

All that bullshit.

Dove knows that bullshit doesn't work with Wolfe.

Not today or any day.

"You heard what the insurgents told the locals yesterday?" Dove says. "That we'd be coming back to see the bodies in two or three days. Which would be time for them to edit the video then release it. And then we'd be coming back here to investigate. They didn't know that we'd intercept the video early."

"Or they did, they knew you would, they know their comms are compromised, and here we are. And those Chechen snipers were just the Welcome Wagon. 'Howdy, dumb gringos.' Sun Tzu. Know your enemy. Us. And here we are, the parakeet flying into the mouth of the cat."

Dove is devil's advocate. "Shadow showed nothing. No stationary masses of men, no patrols, no movements, no heat signatures. No cooking fires. Nothing, Mr Wolfe."

"Shadow couldn't see in that cave. Couldn't see those bodies in there. How many more other caves are there up there? Five? Ten? A hundred insurg each hiding in them. Alive. Armed to the teeth."

"If this is as you say the mouth of the cat."

Wolfe, "In which case, I hope you're not a lapsed Baptist. Or lapsed anything. Your praying might actually work. Let me guess. Presbyterian? Lutheran? Methodist? Church of Christ?"

Dove doesn't say. Instead, "We got our comms links back. Isaf and Cop Valley Forge."

"I feel better already. Good news or bad? Give me the bad first."

"There is no good news."

"Now I feel worse already. What's your Isaf say?"

"They wanted to know the IDs of the casualties."

"I wouldn't have told them. Tell them to come and pick up the bodies if they wanna know."

"What makes you think I didn't, Mr Wolfe?"

"You wouldn't still be wearing that rank. They'd be already cutting you orders down to major. Or second lewy. Typical four-star command HQ, they're more concerned with who are the KIAs, God knows why, to keep their status sheets up-to-date up-to-the-minute. More concerned than with these soldiers here. Sorry, no offense, an old broken record, isn't it? Blah blah blah, everyone's always shitting on HQ command. Got worse bad news?"

"Valley Forge says their two big guns have been sabotaged."

"Sabotaged, how sabotaged? Sabotaged?!"

"Made inoperable."

"How, impossible! The 105s? They're behind Hescos ten-foot tall. In broad daylight? Sabotaged?"

"The first sergeant said it was ingenious or just plain dumb luck. An inside job. Suicide saboteurs."

"No 105s?" Wolfe says it to let it sink in, doesn't want to believe it. "No fire support? The first rule of the infantry: Stay within range of the long guns. Air Red on top of that. No 105s and no air cover, what a splendid day to be hangin out in injun country."

Dove had heard the same frustration just minutes ago from Redcloud who was ending his radio conversation with 1st Sgt Kozak after hearing the news of the 105s down. "Next thing you're gonna tell me, Top," Redcloud had told Kozak, "you're gonna say Brigade wants us to do BDA on the sniper squad, so you go ahead and relay, you tell em we're hopping right to it. I'm sending a squad down there right now to pick among the rubble. We'll send up the photos as soon as they get back. If they get back."

Dove now suggests to Wolfe, "If Air doesn't turn Green by nightfall, maybe you'd be wise, Mr Wolfe—you might want to reassess that lapsed part of Baptist."

"Then again, let's look at it this way. They're Talibs, right? Which means they're Afghans, Pashtun in particular, Haqqani or not. As Afghans, that means they're never in any rush to do anything. Their op plan was set for two days or three days from now, cuz that's not until they figured we were going to arrive here. So you say from what those farmers said. So, good, no one's here yet, and the snipers were just a day early, probably sitting up in their cave for a week having chai jerkin each other off up there. Lucky for them, we show up and they get notches on their belts, if they wore belts, and yeh, Chechens, they mighta had on belts. Lucky for us, they're now neutralized and skip-roping up in heaven with their seventy-five virgins. And their Talib and al-Qaeda pals are still two days away. And, lucky us, in the morning this storm'll be gone, the sun'll be shining and we'll all be dancing an Irish jig, cooking up hot coffee and those birds will be coming in, Jesus H Christ, I swear by the soul of Chesty Puller, there's no more beautiful sight."

He pauses. Thinks it over. Smiles, satisfied.

Dove says, "No more beautiful sight? I hope you're right."

Wolfe changes his mind. "Actually, there is one. The blond at the end of the bar, five eleven, shaped like this. When she actually meets your eyes and smiles, and you know, man, you know she's going to fuck your brains out all night."

"All night?" Dove says. "I've been married, it was ten years in June."

"Yeh," Wolfe adds the kicker, "you wouldn't know anymore."

Cop Valley Forge

Like Wajma up the gorge the rain has stopped here, with the ceiling of clouds so low it even obscures the tops of the guard towers.

In the Toc in the TV rec room are Kozak, Lieut Frye and a couple of the others all watching the flatscreen satellite TV feed playing Fox News breaking coverage showing cuts of the video.

Yep, correctomundo, that video, the one the Taliban shot of the Zoo in Wajma yesterday.

Zoo turret gunners blasting away.

Wolfe shooting the Bic guy point-blank.

Wolfe shooting the gas thrower point-blank.

More of the turret gunners blasting away.

Village men carrying the bodies from the school.

Nothing of Robyn Banks burning.

Kozak switches the channel to CNN showing Wolfe putting the two shots point-blank into the gas thrower's groin.

The turret gunners blasting away.

Wolfe shooting Hajj Bic and Hajj Gas Thrower.

Women's and girls' bodies carried from the school.

Nothing of Robyn Banks.

Switches to BBC World showing the bodies being carried out of the school. The same edits. Nothing of Robyn Banks.

Back to Fox News.

"At the risk of sounding pessimistic," Lieut Frye says flatly. "This is not going to be good."

"Not for the Zoo," says 3rd Platoon's Lieut Paxton.

"For all of us," Kozak corrects him. Switches back to CNN showing a loop of the Zoo blazing away, Wolfe shooting, dead bodies carried out.

Lieut Paxton, "Why they'd have to go there in the first place? Why, why, why, why!?"

Kozak, "Why? Why? Why? You sound like my three-year-old."

Isaf, Kabul

In Gen St Claire's office Fox News, CNN and BBC World playing on the three flatscreens. Sound muted. The same loop.

"A moment of weakness, I let my optimism get the better of rational judgment," says Dr Gene Hutchinsen. "I don't know why we should have expected more from Karzai. For Christ's sake, he couldn't even get us twenty-four hours, the incompetent, duplicitous Kandahari pederast. We should pull his personal security and let the ISI assassinate him."

ISI, remember? That's Pakistan's CIA.

St Claire remotes-off the three TVs. He doesn't need to see the loop. Not again and again, not one more time.

Hutchinsen continues, "Spin Boldak backdoor shagger can't get us twenty-four hours and knows that if we call it a draw and pull up stakes and go home he won't last two weeks. It will be 1996 all over again, and he'll be swinging from a lamp post like Najibulla. I'd advise the president, the secretary, Congress—cash it all in, hightail it out of town tomorrow, leave him on his own, just to see him swinging in the sunset."

Col Pluma is seething. "I'll go down there. I'll take two Chinooks into that valley and I'll arrest their asses right now, the whole damn Zoo Platoon, and bring them straight to Bagram detainment, including Zachary Dove. Parade them in front of the cameras and reporters" —

"And what?" Dr Hutchinsen interrupts. "When those two CH-47s find themselves flattened in a fireball against the mountain at what, thirty-five million apiece, not counting their, what, four-, five-, six-man crews. . ." He turns his reasoning to St Claire. "Then it will be you, Pete, you who will be the one who will have a whole lotta 'splaning to do. In front of a wall of reporters and cameras. In DC. Under oath grilled by whichever Senate committee. Not whichever, how many. 'General, what justification can you give us for breaking Nato safety protocol that would so recklessly cause the loss of two CH-47s and all on board?'"

St Claire is serene, flat, emotionless. Silent. Listening.

Dr Hutchinsen, to Pluma now, "Naturally, that will include you, Danny, and your contigent of MPs. Should we notify their families personally, the MPs, a personal phone call from the general? And your wife and kids, do you expect the general to be at your graveside service? Should we have your casket filled with sandbags to give it some weight, since all they're likely to recover of you is at most a tooth or two? A jawbone. Should we tell the lovely wife that you died a hero, a patriotic humble God-fearing hero? Or a blustering overeager gung-ho fool?"

No argument from Pluma.

Hutchinsen offers this now to St Claire. "The story's out, we can't change that. And we can't change Air from Red to Green higgly-piggly and not lose men and matériel that you, General Pete St Claire, you will be made to answer for. Karzai's worthless, and we can't assassinate him and can't allow the ISI to walk in and do it for us. What can we do? We can take what's dealt us and mold it to suit our outcome not the enemy's. Unless we can get the Tattoo Zoo Platoon up here in chains an hour ago, Pete, we've already been out-maneuvered and no amount of explaining and counter-talk and press releases will erase those images the world's already seen and is seeing right now and is going to see for the next two weeks running. There's no way now that we won't be made to look in our hesitance and delay as if we were trying to cover it all up, sweep it under the rug, hide our dirty laundry. That's reality, Pete. Can we get those Tattoo Zoos up here an hour ago, can we turn back the clock, can we get Karzai to take his eyes off the pubescent chaiboy then reach over and squeeze and hold the kid's buttocks and pull him closer? Can we force that faggot bachee-baz, as they say it here, can we force him to actually do something of consequence that requires him to make hard choices against the Taliban enemy who are of his own Kandahari blood? Or, and there's no way to ignore this very fundamental reality—or are we actually better off, all things considered, reality such as it is—are we not better off with that platoon sitting exactly where they are in that valley?"

St Claire, "I don't want to take this in that direction."

A shrug and raised eyebrows from Hutchinsen, *Yeh, who does?, but reality's reality, like it or not.*

St Claire knows exactly what Hutchinsen is saying without actually saying it. "It's off the table, Hutch, it's not an option. The weather will clear by morning, let's assume that, and at that time we'll get the platoon flown directly to Bagram, the entire lot of them, and we'll take it from there." His brain clicking along at light-speed, he orders one of his captain aides, "Get me Colonel Gray-Nance." In his tone, the dichotomy: demanding *Asap!*, asking *Please?*.

Gray-Nance would be Isaf PAO. Katherine Gray-Nance.

Dr Hutchinsen laughs a little. "What, Pete, are you now going Saint Francis of Assisi on us? Bless the beasts and the children, you want to selectively dictate that that sniper was just a lone insurgent who happened upon a target of opportunity? And of course our drones never detected him, and who else down there in that godforsaken valley haven't our drones seen? And let's not forget, what's the latest, Danny?" A smile at Col Pluma. "The report from Cop Valley Forge. That the artillery howitzer guns there have been rendered inoperable, sabotaged, or whatever the artillery term is for howitzers that don't shoot. And of course that's just a coincidence as well, all's honky-dory, peaches-'n'-cream, we'll sing in the sunshine, it's raining lollipops and fudgesicles in Wajma Valley."

Col Pluma to Gen St Claire, "Sir, I think it's reasonable to assume that the insurgents very well know that Zach and the platoon are there and they're trapped. And they know we don't have Predators or Shadow up because of the weather, which makes it highly likely they're coming over the ridges from Pakistan right now as we speak."

Dr Hutchinsen, "Precisely."

Pluma is surprised. Precisely? Precisely?!

Hutchinsen laughs. "Earth to Danny. Earth to Danny, wake up, Danny. I can see your brain hurrying to catch up. What is it with you Nebraskan farmboys? Just can't wash that proletariat evangelical holy-roller goodly godliness out of your hair, can you?"

"Precisely? You want the insurgents coming over converging on Wajma?"

"If you're going to be wearing a star soon, Danny, you'd better start thinking like one. At the very least you're going to have to start appraising situations with far more nuance and begin to understand that the greater good here dictates that the Tattoo Zoo Platoon remain in that valley because our initial opportunity to control the situation was dependent upon a gray-bearded drug-addled pederast who couldn't pour shit out of a boot if the instructions were written on the heel."

St Claire stays silent. *Pour shit out of a boot*, he's heard that before but can't quite remember where.

Col Pluma turns from Hutchinsen to St Claire. "Sir, we can't leave Zach and the platoon hanging out to dry. It goes against every last ounce of the Soldier's Creed."

"No one's leaving anyone hanging out to dry," St Claire insists. "What would you have me do, Dan? Would you have me counteract the Red? Write my own Nato Air Protocol?"

Hutchinsen interjects, warning, "You lose even one Chinook, Pete, on your signature going in there on Red, the Joint Chiefs, they'll be lions circling their prey."

Not that St Claire is not already well aware of that.

Hutchinsen continues anyway. "Lord bless them, one couldn't blame them, what an opportunity to take down the one military commander the American public perceives as Ulysses S Grant, Eisenhower, MacArthur, Schwarzkopf. As it stands today, sure, they're going to try and blame you for the Tattoo Zoo Platoon, but the actions of lowly GI savages recklessly and criminally killing civilian women and children will no more stick to you than anyone holds the Postmaster General accountable when some disgruntled nutjob letter-carrier blows away five of his fellow mail-sorters in a Poughkeepsie distribution center. You supersede the Red, Pete, and lose a dozen, two dozen, American boys, including your MPs, Danny — they'll headline it, 'Negligent Disregard of Regulations'. Worse. 'Negligent Homicide'."

Nothing from St Claire.

Nothing from Pluma.

Hutchinsen, quietly now, to St Claire, as if Pluma isn't here. "Enemy insurgent video of those incinerated bodies in the debris of one or both CH-47s — the lions circling, you won't have a friend anywhere in DC."

Col Pluma to St Claire, "We can get more artillery pieces into Valley Forge, sir. In Salerno they have a 155 battery. We can helicopter in a 155. And enough rounds for fire support."

Dr Hutchinsen, "Air is Red at Valley Forge, Danny. At Salerno as well, as of last count."

Which they all know.

Regardless, St Claire gives Pluma a nod *make it happen.*

"Immediately, sir, for immediate liftoff?"

"When Air is Green. Green at Salerno and Valley Forge."

"Yes sir."

Dr Hutchinsen doesn't back down. To Pluma, "Now ask yourself this, Danny, in all seriousness, and without malice, just for practical purposes. Is the preferred outcome in this present situation eighteen months of court-martials and night after night after night every newscast leading with that same video loop of those same hundred and sixty-eight dead women and children? Night after night, a thousand television cameras outside the courthouse getting close-ups of those hot-dogging My-Lai-killing Tattoo Zoos, juxtaposed with grieving Afghan peasants brought stateside for the trials. Peasants whose wives and mothers and daughters those hundred-sixty-eight were." He turns to St Claire. "The media worldwide will turn it from those killers on trial . . . to your war on trial."

St Claire says nothing.

Dr Hutchinsen smiles. "Then again, most likely, were I a gambling man, I would let it all ride, ninety/ten — that there isn't another insurgent within twenty miles of that valley. And their helicopters are certainly not flying in that weather down there. Good luck on-foot down those slippery mountain trails."

Pluma is stunned. Their helicopters? Whose helicopters? The Taliban don't have any helicopters. That's supposed to be clever sarcasm?

He's angry, incredulous. And he can't put it into words.

Worse, forget the helicopter bit, he knows that Dr Hutchinsen is right. And he shouldn't be.

Hutchinsen smiles at Pluma. No animosity, it's just a competition of minds, of logic, of politics. "The Tattoo Zoo is an infantry platoon, isn't it?" he says. "Part of the finest infantry in the world, the very finest army in the world, is it not? The best trained, best equipped, best paid infantry in the world. Isn't it the infantry's job to fight and defend itself? To take and hold real estate and defend it, by fighting? If these Tattoo Zoos can't deal with a few raghead barefoot insurgents coming across those mountains and beat to death coming down those trails in this storm of the decade, then perhaps we'll have to reassess our training and our overly-generous enlisted pay schedules. Which, Pete," he laughs, turning his argument to St Claire. "Now that, Pete—that points to an entirely different Army command who'll have to deal with their own vindictive Joint Chiefs and duplicitous Senate committees."

In Wajma

Dove and Wolfe have come downstairs from the roof and out onto the veranda, where Redcloud reports to them that he just got more bad news from Valley Forge.

The video's all over the TV.

All the cable news channels.

"Ketch's guys shootin from their trucks." Redcloud says. "All the bodies. You too, Wolfie. You shooting those two hajj. That's what Top says."

"All the plans of mice and men." Dove thinking aloud.

All General St Claire's plans. Lost.

The Taliban releases the video and the media attacks the Army, and St Claire as well first and foremost, for trying to cover it up. No Zoo Platoon already in handcuffs and leg irons to show off to the vulture media.

The plans of the genius Doctor Gene Hutchinsen. Lost.

Everything backwards.

"You tell me, Colonel," Redcloud asks. "You've got the West Point commission, and General St Claire too, and I barely made it out of high school. These hajj can't even read or write and they got me and the L-T to leave here yesterday without doing BDA. And got you and a four-star general to bring us back. We're like the big grizzly sticking his hand in the hive for the honey."

Dove, "They could not have known, there is no way they could know that the weather was going to turn so quickly and make Air Red."

Wolfe, "What, because they don't have Satview and full-bird college-educated colonels for meteorologists on their command staff? Number One, they know every ridge and every goat trail and gully in this unholy miserable land. Number Two, they can tell you the weather tomorrow, the next day and two weeks from now."

Dove won't accept it. "They could not have known this storm was coming to this extent if we couldn't even see it, and, yes, I'll take our satellites and computer models over their Farmer's Almanac old wives tales and old hayseeds sitting around the general store with their rheumatoid-joint-aching forecasting of the weather."

Redcloud, "I don't know, Colonel. Two snipers waiting for us. Chechens no less. Or Uzbeks. They sabotage the 105s back at the Cop. That's not coincidence."

Dove, "We don't do ourselves any favors by giving our enemies mythical powers."

Wolfe laughs. "Maybe we'd be wiser if we did give them mythical powers. Alexander the Great conquered the place and didn't stick around. Same with Genghis Khan. The sun never set on the British Empire, it sure set on them here. The world's number two superpower, nuke rival Soviet Union, ask them about getting their asses kicked here if it wasn't the same goat-herder Afghan with his mythical fighting prowess."

"The mythical Afghan fighter, are you sure, Mr Wolfe? Or is it that after a very short time here all those great conquerors simply realized there was nothing here worth sticking around for? The returns weren't worth the price. If there were gold, the British would have stayed and duked it out. If there were oil, the Russians would have, and if there were a port on the Indian Ocean, no matter the cost the Russians would still be here, full force, they'd have fought this like they crushed Czechoslovakia in 1968."

Wolfe, "Worse, they'd have done it the Roman way, forget PC and Coin. They'd have lined up every male and killed every third one then every third one again and every third again, until the only ones left would have been those who wanted to live more than be Afghans. Except there's no gold and no oil. You're right about that, Colonel. No port on the Indian Ocean. They actually talk about that up in Isaf? They ask what we're here for, why we're still here?"

"Soldiers don't ask why. Marines surely don't, you should know that better than anyone."

"That's why I'm . . ."—in civilian clothes, not a Marine anymore.

"As to your mythical Afghan warrior," Dove has the numbers in his notebook in his pocket and doesn't have to refer to it. "We had twenty ANA this morning and now we're down to ten."

Wolfe dismisses that. "That's just average, fifty percent Awol. The ANA is not the Taliban. Number One, the ANA's fighting for Uncle Sam, and the Talibs, al-Qaeda, the Chechens, they're fighting for Allah. Number Two, the Taliban shoot their deserters."

"Are you saying that our coalition partners are not true believers?"

Wolfe knows Dove's joking, but plays along. "Yeh, in the Constitution, Declaration of Independence, We the People, due process, one man one vote, abortion as a woman's right, the free press, freedom of religion. Las Vegas, Playmate bunnies, strip clubs, Lindsay Lohan, Britney Spears, and not to mention our never-ending support of Israel. If that's not the big one. Israel. General St Claire hasn't put all that up on a PowerPoint slide up at Isaf he shows all the senators and the Sec Def when they come through, about how we're winning their hearts and minds?"

"You greatly underestimate Pete St Claire, Mr Wolfe."

"Do I? I'd love to see him up close. Maybe I'll have to get my lawyer to subpoena him to testify at my trial. Put him on the stand under oath."

"I'll deliver the message."

Wolfe plays it to the hilt, snaps his fingers, "Now we're gettin somewhere, Colonel."

What it was, why they're down from twenty ANA to just ten now is because six more deserted just before Dove and Wolfe came down from the roof.

They'd seen them hurrying down the steps and toward the rock wall, with their sergeant yelling curses after them, and at least this batch had the smarts to already have left behind their weapons and gear.

Wolfe didn't have to fire down at their heels to stop them. Or yell anything.

Dove either.

Nor Redcloud. Nor anyone.

Just let them go, there's no stopping them.

Nouri said that they'd told him that they were just going to lunch with the farmer elder and his sons who'd invited them earlier.

Yeh right.

That and a Brooklyn Bridge.

Not that it matters.

Screw it, twenty to ten.

Six fewer guns now that might start shooting Zoosters behind their backs in the middle of the night.

Six more AKs that the sergeant had brought out here for Wolfe.

About which now Pfc Holloway laughs to Wolfe. "More of the yellow-belly puke wusses' guns you can't take home for souvenirs."

Wolfe, "Yellow-belly, kid?"

"Yeh, yellow-belly cowards. Baaaak bak bak bak bak."

"You go ahead and think that."

"They ran off desertin, what do you call it, you wanna call them brave heroes?"

"It's called hedging their bets, son," Dove says.

Wolfe to Holloway, "And that's why he's a colonel and you"—he playfully smacks Holloway atop his helmet—"that's why you're just a lowly pfc."

Holloway waves to smack Wolfe's hand away, "Watch it," missing. "Don't touch the merchandise."

Wolfe makes a final point to Dove. "Hedging their bets? That's all part of the mystique of the Afghan warrior. Probably Number One. They're always hedging their bets."

Doc Eberly brings to boil a canteen cup of water on his backpacker camp stove.

Rodriquez had been in here a while ago to collect up any empty canteens or CamelBaks from Doc and Capt Cathay on his way with Spec Howie and one of Ketchum's guys with everyone's empties down to the stream to fill.

Do it now when it's quiet. And still light out. And again before dark if you have to.

You can never have too much water.

You never know.

In here Rodriquez had actually met Cathay's eyes, and he felt sorry for her, even though he knows she's the lawyer sent to screw them. "How you doin, ma'am?" he'd asked her just because he couldn't help it.

She tried to smile sincerely. There's something about Sergeant Rodriquez that she doesn't like, that rubs her wrong. Maybe just the coarse cockiness of his face, his expression always a sort of sneer, of anger at something, or maybe he reminds her of the looks she'd seen in the young male fieldhands who came through from spring through fall in her small town of Kamiah in northern Idaho, and she'd catch them watching her in the Dairy Freeze where she worked during high school, and from their looks and laughter she knew they were saying things about her, things about sex, crude ugly things, though she could not understand their street-slang Spanish then.

"Bet yer gonna say you've knowed days they was better," Rodriquez had said. And he'd thought that she's wounded like a drive-by when some little kid gets hit by a stray bullet going through the wall of the wood-slat house on the block and nobody meant to kill a kid. That's her now. Bullet it was for el coronél not her.

No, I'm wrong, she'd thought then. *His face is honest, his eyes are kind.*

Screw that with feeling sorry for her, he'd thought. *She's no little kid, she's no sweet mamacita, more a puta, she's still gonna put us in the slam.* "So's the cap'an and the L-T, they knowed days was better," he'd then said with a gangbanger angry meanness, and he instantly knew he really shouldn't have because it wasn't her fault they were dead. They were dead and she was *Just about as bad as them*. If you can't move your legs, that's right there as bad as them being blown off. *If yer dick can't move neither and y'can't get hard no more is gonna be even worse*. Is it the same for a chica?

"Yer with the Zoo now, ma'am," he told her. "We gonna get you back, and back home's doctors there can do jus 'bout anything, ma'am. Yer with the Zoo."

Rodriquez knew that he should be hating her. But how do you hate *A pretty mamacita like her when she's layin there and can't get up?*

She'd then seen again a softness in his smile, not a sneer at all. *"Yer with the Zoo," he told me, I'm with the Zoo Platoon.*

All the soldiers when they've stopped by in here just to check on her, to ask Doc if everything's okay, if he needs anything, and they're ones she doesn't know, had no need to know, their faces and names don't register, privates and specialists, they've all said the same thing. *"You're part of the Zoo now, ma'am." "Zoo's gonna get you back safe, ma'am."*

Doc Eberly shuts off the flame of his stove. Tears open an MRE packet of cocoa powder and dumps it into the canteen cup. A second. Stirs. Lifts the cup and blows across the top to cool it.

Sips from his MRE spoon.

Not quite right, too weak, no kick to it, and he stirs in two little sugar packets then two packets of creamer.

Blows. Spoon sips.

Good enough.

He offers the cup to Capt Cathay, but she shakes her head.

He knows that you don't give a patient going into surgery anything to eat or drink, and hers is a spinal cord injury, which means surgery for certain. But they're not flying in here to take her out any time soon, or who knows how long. And hot chocolate, just a couple of sips, that warms a person's soul down all inside.

He insists, offering it.

No.

There's something wrong. Both her hands are hidden under the sleeping bag.

"Yeh, come on, Captain, a sip, one sip. It's energy, nutrition."

No, still from her.

Something's wrong. Something, what is it?

She knows he'll stare at her with those intelligent serious eyes until she tells him what it is.

He doesn't stop staring.

She can't meet his eyes.

"I'm . . . I'm . . . I'm . . . wet."

And Doc whips back her sleeping bag, looks and immediately feels, and the crotch of her uniform is soaked. But his hand comes away shiny wet clear, and he flips the bag back over her. Jokes, "A little pee, who cares, ma'am. If it's blood, then, all right, then we've got a problem."

He holds out the canteen cup for her.

She's looking away. Down. She's embarrassed.

"I'm a trained medical semi-professional," he says. "Everybody pees. What, do you want me to carry you like a little old lady in a nursing home, outside and we can dig you a hole out there on the other side of that wall where nobody can see you? We'll hold up a poncho and you can pee in private. Out there."

Still holding out the cup for her to take.

And he knows it's not about her privacy, that's not the concern, that's not what's bothering her. She'll keep peeing, can't control it and won't even know it, won't feel it happening, and he knows that she's thinking that and that it's true, and he's willing to assume that's just something they'll deal with in the Cash and in the hospital in Germany and in the states. All in the future. The doctors who know these things. MD doctors. *Real doctor doctors, not simple basic first-aid platoon medics band-aid dispensers like me.*

"The other option, ma'am. I can radio up a request for resupply, they can chopper it in. Bedpans. And catheter tubes and urine collection bags. Then, of course, they'll have to drop off an RN—female, one each—to do the procedure, respect for your privacy and all, all the political correctness. A female captain RN, and then we'd have two pretty women in here. With all these young Zoosters here with their testosterone raging, and the competition here between you and her would be something fierce. The Chinese symbol for trouble, ma'am, you know what it is? Calligraphy, their handwriting. Two women under one roof. It makes sense, it does, if you think about it. Not that the Ming Dynasty Chinese circa 1500 concerned themselves a whole lot with feminism and gender neutrality— that, no, I don't believe it was high on their list. Binding their feet, that might be an interesting tradition to bring back and to the West. Whoops, me and my stupid mouth."

Binding feet?

Her feet?

You don't need binding to restrict their movement.

"Sorry," he says. "The lips talking faster than the brain processing."

Even so, maybe there's a smile in her, if only a bare trace. But she still doesn't look at him.

He takes a sip now straight from the canteen cup.

Again holds the cup out for her to take. "It's not pure Belgium dark chocolate like you're going to get at Starbucks at five bucks a shot. Homestyle. Like grandma used to make. Close your eyes and it'll remind you of the campout you had in the backyard with your family as a kid. Big bonfire lighting up the whole yard. Roasted marshmallows. With s'mores. Halloween. Pumpkins. Autumn chill in the air. Nothing like a hot cup of chocolate."

She now meets his eyes. Her lips silently say *Thank you*. For his sweet kindness. Really, for his understanding. His lack of pandering pity.

She takes the canteen cup.

Redcloud is here on the roof in confab with his three squad leaders. He's making sure again they know exactly what the plan is, what he expects of them and what they've got to demand of their men.

Dove had just had a private discussion with Redcloud alone in the back classroom where the three bodies lie. Okay, Dove had said, let's assume as given the Afghan deserters' mythical sixth sense of the Taliban out there massing to attack at the right moment.

Conceded.

So, let's have a specific course of action.

COA in military planning lingo.

A staple of those PowerPoint slides.

Redcloud had offered that the enemy knows they've got no air support and no artillery and no resupply and the only ammo the Zoo's got is what they've carried in on their backs. One should assume, Redcloud knew that Dove knew as well, that the enemy would probe and probe again and probe again to get them to blow through their ammo.

Exactly.

Then hit hard with the main attack:

Bamm, all massed, when the Zoosters would be out of frags, down to a mag or two each, that's it. The machineguns down to no more than a belt.

That's what Dove was concerned about.

And what Redcloud is right now making very clear to Ketchum, Utah and Nell.

"I don't wanna see any one of you three firing at all, 'less they're climbing over the walls," Redcloud says. "Your job's to see that your men exercise extreme fire discipline. No more than one out of three of your men fire at any one time. And no one, and I mean no one, on burst. Understood?"

Roger, understood.

"And I don't wanna hear the machinegun and I don't wanna hear the Saws, unless the hajj are comin over that wall down there out there and you can see their pockmarked faces and smell their stinking goat breath."

And the M203 grenadiers, of which Finkle is one of four all total in the platoon, Redcloud and Dove agreed that with their limited ammo carried in, averaging about thirty per 203, they wouldn't fire unless the enemy was massing and no farther out than 200 meters. Period.

Same with the three RPGs and 12 rounds that the ANA carried in.

That's what Dove is telling Wolfe right now.

They're on the veranda.

Dove seated in the entrance eating an MRE.

Wolfe oiling and function-checking his six newly acquired AKs.

Dove has said that he's sure Wolfe is aware of the ANA's habit of firing full auto and going through their magazines before the enemy's even close then turning to their American counterparts and expecting more ammo from Uncle Sam's unlimited supply.

It's different today. There is no unlimited supply. The AK's 7.62 isn't the M4's 5.56 or the same as the M240-B's 7.62, so the bullets the ANA has are going to have to go a long way.

Dove expects first that Wolfe will conserve the deserters' ammo he has for a final last-ditch defense.

No problem, Wolfe will, that had been his intention.

"I'd appreciate it," Dove tells him, "if you'd make the ANA your priority. Fire discipline."

"Can do."

"And their RPGs, if you've seen what I've seen, they'll shoot them off like they're 4th of July fireworks and wonder why they aren't effective and why they've run out."

"Number One," agrees Wolfe. "Number Two, if they haven't already blown their buddy's face off with the backblast."

"That, thank God, I haven't seen yet."

"It isn't pretty."

"So, the ANA is yours?"

"You tell the sergeant, Colonel, 'cause he's sure not gonna wanna hear it from me."

"I already have."

Wolfe is impressed. A nod. The ANA will be his.

Pfc Holloway is curious. "Kyle, where'd you learn to speak Afghan?"

"Pashto, not Afghan. The official Afghan language is Dari."

"Okay, get technical. Where'd you learn to speak Pashto?"

"No one would say that I speak it. I just know the essentials."

Holloway jokes, "Take me to your sister. Can you teach me to say that? How much for a night with your smokin hot sister?"

"Yeh, you say that to some smokin hot babe in a burka, you want every Afghan within earshot to pump you full of lead?"

"C'mon, it's the international language. Take me to your sister."

"You horny, kid?"

"Sheeee-at, I'm always horny."

"Eat some more MREs."

"What's a MRE got to do with it, you get your rocks off in a MRE bag, that how you choke the chicken, Wolfie, in a MRE bag?"

"How many times I told you, kid, it's Sergeant Wolfie. Haven't you ever heard of salt peter?"

"Huh, salt what?"

"Peter. They put it in the MREs. It makes your peter peter out."

"Bullshit. Never heard of it."

"No," from Nick Flowers, "it's true, it is, salt peter. They put it in the meals, at least that's what I've always heard. They double it for the Marines, or so the rumor goes."

Wolfe, "Cause Marines need double. Even triple."

Holloway looks to Dove, who he knows won't play along with Wolfe's and Nicky's bullshitting.

Dove shrugs. "It's an old wives' tale, PFC. Which was true back in World War Two and in Korea. At least as an urban legend."

Wolfe, "Scientific fact, Colonel. Salt peter makes your peter peter out."

Nick Flowers, "Is that your excuse, Kyle?"

"I just don't get turned on by burkas." And to Dove, "C'mon, Colonel, do you really trust what they've got in there?"

Dove looks at the MRE food on his spoon. Looks now at Holloway. "For a young man with hormone levels as high as you'll ever have in your life, son, stuck in these countries where the fairer sex is taboo, you will get shot, PFC, Mr Wolfe is correct. Multiple times. If you're going to be going around asking 'Take me to your sister'. Salt peter's a good thing."

Wolfe, "One thing guaranteed, you know they're not adding it to the chow up in the gourmet Dfacs up at Isaf."

Nick Flowers, "The Dutch and French skirts there, they're all captains and majors, and they don't wear burkas either. You wouldn't want it in the chow, the generals would court-martial the cooks if they found out they were putting it in the chow."

Dove flashes back to Major Vicky Marshall and the thought of almost last night. Almost. Whew, that was a close one. Not even 24 hours ago. Boy how quickly things change.

"You're that horny, kid?" Wolfe asks Holloway. "I heard the Afghan sergeant in there a little while ago telling his buddies he thinks you've got a nice ass."

Holloway, "They'd do it too. Heard of Happy Thursdays? Happy Butt-Fuck Thursdays."

Redcloud coming out, "Aw com'on, clam it, Holloway. Enough with your Happy Thursdays."

"He brought it up, Sarge."

Redcloud, "And I'm bringing it down."

Thursday night's party night for Afghan men, the night before the Sabbath, like Saturday night back home. Except, since women don't participate in anything social and aren't any part of anything, it's men with men, that's the party. Men with men. With boys.

Or so goes the old wives' tale urban legend.

That isn't brought up officially any higher than platoon hang-around-bullshit level.

Maybe whispered among some staff officers in their hang-around-bullshit time. But never among those they don't know and trust.

Never on the record.

"Give you one guess, Nicky," Holloway laughs. "What do you think those puke coward deserters who left are doing right now? Happy Thursday. And it aint even Thursday."

"What'd I just tell you, PFC," Redcloud scolds him.

Wolfe, "Give him a break, Travis. The kid's got dick on the brain. Ketchum told me, he said, Grasshopper, he said you've got a tattoo on your butt, he's seen it, it says Enter Here. With an arrow pointing. How about, want me to tattoo it in Pashto?"

Holloway, "Shows what Sergeant Ketchum knows. I've got Semper Fi tattooed right where I wipe my ass every day." A wide victory grin. "The Holloway Groove," a fist pump, "strikes again. Point, game, set."

Wolfe, "You even know what point game set means, PFC?"

"It means I just wiped your ass all over the floor. Point, game, set." Up yours!

"Southern Cal skateboard dude, you've never even played ice hockey not once in your life. Point game set, that before or after the slap shot?"

Nick Flowers joins the tease, "Kyle, Kyle, Kyle, you've got the wrong game. Ping pong."

Redcloud too, "I thought it was horseshoes. Shuffleboard?"

Wolfe sends it Dove's way, "Colonel, what, what's your guess? Equestrian sports? Steeplechase? The fox hunt?"

Holloway claps the radio handsets tight to his ears, he's not listening. Sneers at Wolfe. "Point. Game. Set."

Paaahumbang from somewhere, dim, distant.

And everyone on the veranda here ducks down, shouting a chorus, Redcloud, Dove, Wolfe, *"Incoming!"*

Guys inside and on the roof too, *"Incoming!"*, grabbing their helmets, ducking, and

the *Faashooowooosh* of the RPG sailing by invisible out front somewhere in the low clouds and fog obscuring everything above fifty feet followed by a dim brightness and a loud *karumph* of the explosion somewhere on the mountainside above the stream.

Fifty feet up is all clouds and it's all those same clouds and fog down to ground-level out beyond the mosque which itself is barely visible. Only the near terraced rock wall is visible, the second shrouded in fog and none of the others or the compounds way beyond in sight.

Another *Paaahumbang* somewhere distant, and

inside Nell's squad is already running up the stairs, while

out here the ANA soldiers exit in a mad dash to take positions out front there behind the low rock wall, with Wolfe stopping the sergeant and in Pashto making sure he understands *No shooting!*, and *Nothing, not until we give the orders!*, while

Sniper Rodriquez and Ketchum's guy and Spec Howie come sprinting up from the stream, each with looped 550-cords of full canteens and CamelBaks slung and bouncing over their shoulders, as

the *Faashooowooosh* sails by of the second rocket, exploding in plain sight this time across the stream.

Redcloud over his pouched radio, "Sniper, get a spot for us when you get up!" And, "Ketch, you got a location?"

"Negative, negative!" the reply from Ketchum on the radio. "Can't see shit through this shit!"

Paaahumbang again,

shouts up on the roof, "Incoming incoming!!!", and

Nell's guys who haven't reached the front parapet hit the deck to crawl the rest of the way, as

a fast *Faashooowoosh* coming this way, then the rocket exploding on the mountainside right above, showering all on the roof below with rocks and shale and dirt.

Redcloud over the radio, "Anybody hurt? Status."

No answer.

Again a demand, "Ketch, Nell, status up there."

Doc Eberly inside has already grabbed his aid bag and told Capt Cathay quickly, "I'm going to have to go, you'll be okay," and is waiting in the classroom doorway, just waiting for a shout of *Medic!*, while

on the roof it's taken Ketchum moments to assess the men, and he leans over the parapet to yell down to Redcloud at the same time keying his radio handset, "Negative! All okay up here!"

Paaaahumbang.

Redcloud asks Dove, "Can you tell where?!"

Faaaashoooo heard coming, and Dove points as the rocket appears out of the fog in a blur heading straight here on an angle from up in the fields and arching downward and burying itself in the mud between the rock wall and the steps, a dud, with just the rear tips of its fins stuck up out.

And nothing follows.

Dead quiet.

Dead stillness all the way out there as far as the eye can see to just beyond the mosque and up into the first terraced field.

Guys subconsciously counting the seconds now.

Since the dud splatted into the mud.

Ten gone.

Twenty.

Maybe that's the sum total of the attack, and it's over.

No one's fired back, not one Zooster's fired, which Redcloud is happy about. No use wasting ammo shooting what you can't see and can only guess where the enemy's at.

The burnt carcass of the ANA pickup now visible, as the fog seems to be rapidly thinning farther and farther out there.

Thirty seconds.

Out at the front rock wall one of the ANA stands and fires off at nothing a full magazine on full auto, even as Wolfe is leaping up shouting in Pashto *"No firing! No firing!"* and the ANA sergeant is grabbing the guy and throwing him to the ground and butt-stock-slamming him with his AK one cheek-bone-cracking smash.

Fifty seconds.

One minute.

Now the conex shipping containers visible.

One minute twenty seconds.

Pfc Holloway snorts a laugh. "They shot their wad. They're done."

"I wouldn't count on it, soldier." Dove, quietly, dryly. "Mr Wolfe, your assessment?"

"If the snipers were Chechen, they've got Chechens for advisors. They're bracketing. Bracketing the rockets."

Dove, "Which would mean spotters. Where?"

"Probably in the mosque there." Redcloud.

Wolfe, "A couple 203 rounds could eliminate that. Can put the last of the 60 mortar rounds through it."

Dove, "No."

Wolfe, "Funny, I knew you'd say that."

Two minutes.

Holloway, a slight tremble in his voice, "What are they waitin for?"

Wolfe, "They're cutting the fuses. Chechens know that shit. For shooting blind from a thousand meters."

Holloway, "Cutting the fuses, what fuses, how?"

Dove, "It means"—he's interrupted by four *Paahumbang Paahumbang Paahumbang Paahumbangs* in quick succession, and

"Incoming!" shouted from everywhere, and

everyone huddles low against the wall here on the veranda, Kevlared heads pulled in close to the shoulders like turtles, faces pressed to the concrete floor, and

immediately four more *Paahumbangs* from somewhere out there!

One second passes.

The ANA out there are all huddled low against the rock wall.

Two seconds.

All Ketchum's and Nell's guys on the roof are huddled low against the parapet.

Three.

The first four rockets explode—two low on the mountainside above the roof, raining rock and shrapnel, and two above the veranda just below the parapet, sending sprays of shrapnel and cement, and

the second four are airbursts out front, exploding low in the cloud overhang, sending shrapnel against the school, into the mud and into a couple of the huddling ANA.

Wolfe quickly snaps to Holloway, "That's cutting fuses, kid," and heads inside, and

Redcloud orders Holloway, "Update Valley Forge," and is right on Dove's tail going inside behind Wolfe.

Inside, all Redcloud has to do while sprinting past Doc Eberly is point back with his thumb *Out there!*, and yell "The ANA," and he follows Wolfe and Dove up the stairs two-stairs-at-a-time.

It took Pfc Holloway more than a minute to get comms. The antennas for both radios had been knocked off the wall by the concussion and flying mud from the rockets, or maybe they'd just been yanked down accidently by Holloway pressing himself to the floor, who knows.

Then he had to set them up and try to get them aligned toward the satellites in haste, and calling on one, *"Valley Forge Base, Valley Forge Base,"* tweaking the antenna to hit the satellite, and when he did get a response it was Isaf Op Center, as he'd switched the handsets accidently and felt like an idiot, and was even standing, in the open, his torso above the wall, and felt again like an idiot, like he should be down in case they fire more rockets, but he stayed standing, switched handsets, got Valley Forge and told them they'd just taken fifteen to twenty RPGs, and sonovabitch if it wasn't right then that he saw way way out there all those dark-clad figures. Men.

"You're not gonna believe this, Awesome Seven," he tells 1st Sgt Kozak back on the Cop on the radio. "Enemy approaching. Too many to count. Holy shit, where'd they come from?"

On the roof Ketchum's men and Nell and his guys are all crouched here, guns up on the parapet, sighting through their scopes.

Standing at the parapet, Dove, Redcloud and Wolfe. All watching with binos.

Sniper Rodriquez crouched, rifle resting on the parapet, looking through the scope. "This is no bueño, Sar'ant Redcloud," he says.

Not that Redcloud needs to be told. Through his binos he sees what all with their binos or scoped sights can clearly make out. Dark figures.

Men in a line from the edge of the stream and all the way up into the first terraced field.

Maybe 700 meters out there. Beyond the conex shipping containers.

At least a hundred of them. More. On line. Each an arm's-length separated from one another.

It's as if they've just materialized out of the thick fog curtain out farther now behind them.

They're coming in a methodical, steady, unhurried, relaxed stride.

"Danger, Will Robinson," Wolfe says. "Set your phasers to stun."

"Stun?" Nick counters. "Don't you mean to kill?"

Dove, "At ease, everyone."

Seen through the binos, every one of them with a full beard.

Dressed in black man-jammie traditional Afghan shalwar kameez attire. Each with a dark wool serape blanket draped like a poncho.

On their heads, each with a black turban, the long wide ends billowing slightly in the easy breeze blowing out.

Most with their arms extended out like wings, the others with them raised over his heads.

Like in surrender.

Wolfe, "Holy Mother of God, Mary, Joseph and the donkeys they rode in on . . . ."

Dove tells Redcloud, "No one shoots, Sergeant. Understood?"

And Redcloud passes the order, yelling, "Hold your fire, everyone! Hold your fire til we say so!" And into his radio, commanding the squad leaders, "No one shoots til we give the order! Pass the word."

And Wolfe yells down in Pashto roughly the same to the ANA sergeant at the wall, where

Doc Eberly is appraising one wounded soldier, who had a chunk of shrapnel go right through his fiberglass helmet liner and lodge itself halfway out the other side. Dead, or should be, and Doc turns to the other wounded guy, who's screaming, even as one of his buddies hoists him over his shoulder, regardless the shrapnel the guy took to the gut and thigh, and Doc yells and motions an ANA to help him carry the dead one, while

Nick Flowers is up here on the roof, leaning over the parapet, filming Doc and the ANA carrying the casualties by below.

Wolfe, looking through binos. "Wanna talk about the mythical Afghan fighter, Colonel. Tell me these guys don't know our rules of engagement better than us."

Rodriquez, "Mo-fos got their weapons slinged behind them, they're hidin em. AKs, RPGs, they got PKMs under them blankets, wanna bet?"

Redcloud, "See the camera?" He points, and Dove swings his binos over to see one of the dark-clad figures slightly ahead of the others walking sideways along atop the first terrace wall filming the others with a video camera.

Wolfe, "Film at eleven. Us shooting innocent non-combatants coming in peace and camaraderie. Tell me these sons of virgin whores don't know our rules of engagement and our media and our panty-waist Pentagon that's gonna court-martial us for opening fire!"

"No one's opening fire, Mr Wolfe," Dove orders.

"Even better for them. For al Jazeera. Film at eleven, them dancing over the entire Zoo Platoon laid out down there. Dead."

"Yeh 'mano," says Rodriquez. "You too, Wolfie."

Sighting through the scope of his 240, Spec Lee Tran says, "I got em in range, I can mow em down, want me to mow em down?"

Dove, "You just hold your fire, son. Does anybody see a weapon, anybody?"

Not a weapon out there.

Not one in sight.

Just the line coming. Dark figures in their black turbans, dark serape poncho-like blankets, black jammies, arms held straight out like wings or over their heads.

Wolfe, "Weapons, we don't need no stinkin weapons."

They're passing by the conex shipping containers. Next distance landmark will be the burnt-out pickup truck.

"I ask again," Dove says. "Does anybody see a weapon?"

Nothing, there are no weapons.

And now way out there at the edge of the fog a second line appears, materializing as if by magic, exactly as the first had.

Same dark figures. At least a hundred. From the stream and all up in the first terraced field. On line.

A hundred-fifty meters behind the first line.

Same dark attire, serape blanket, black turbans, arms held out like wings or raised above their heads.

Rodriquez is amazed. "Where they all comin from?"

Down below Ssgt Utah has run down the steps and now yells up, "Sarge, how long we going to wait to open up on them?"

"No one fires, Sergeant!" Dove calls down. "That's an order!"

And, "Get back under cover!" Redcloud orders Utah.

Of the first line, the ones on the beach are passing the burnt pickup. Next distance landmark ahead, the mosque.

Which is only 450 meters out there.

Redcloud, low, under his breath, tells Dove, "At two hundred meters I'm giving the order to engage."

Dove, "No you're not. Mr Wolfe, let's hear it. Options?"

"We shoot and they're unarmed surrendering, they're willing to go to their seventy-five virgins just to have it on tape. Film at eleven, worldwide, US troops slaughtering innocent Afghani peasants. Guerrilla insurgencies are won or lost in the media, as you know and so do they obviously know. Of course, Colonel, you know you're never going to make full-bird doing twenty-five to life in Leavenworth."

Rodriquez, "I can take out that guy, an' his camera. Easy. He is muerto, jus gimme the word, Sar'ant."

"Hold your fire," Redcloud says firmly.

"Where there's one there are going to be three or more," says Dove, guessing, and he scans his binos up to the far compounds which are now visible through the thinning fog and he can make out figures on the walls and roofs, and one or more could have a camera. Yes, it looks like they do have cameras.

Wolfe scans the same, assumes they are Talibs up there and are probably filming, and knows they're more than a thousand meters out.

"If you can hit them with that M-110 from this distance, Rodriquez," he says, "you win the trophy, put you down in the annals with the greatest snipers living or dead."

Dove, "Option One, again, Mr Wolfe?"

"We shoot unarmed combatants surrendering, you ever heard of the famous Lieutenant William Calley?"

"Vietnam, if I'm not incorrect. My Lai."

"A trophy for the sniper, you get the new Cadillac, Colonel. Calley got life at hard labor. Got clemency and a presidential pardon eventually. But you, Colonel—you don't have Nixon as president. To pardon you."

"Option Two?"

"You stick to General St Claire's hugs-n-kisses ROE and we don't engage them, and pretty goddamn soon, Colonel"—

"Fuck that!" Rodriquez interrupts. "No way, no way, imposible we don't engage them!"

"At ease there, soldier!" Dove scolds him. "You just hold your tongue!"

"Them's got guns under them blankets, Cur'nel!"

"I said at ease!"

Wolfe, "You want to follow the Roe, Colonel, that film of us all laid out dead down there, that's a pretty big victory, there'll be ten thousand new young jihadists joining up by midnight, fifty thousand more in the morning."

As if on cue, from the distant curtain of fog materializes a third line of dark-clad figures.

"Shit!" says Rodriquez. "Chingada! De donde vienen?!"

Dove asks Wolfe, "Option Three?"

"Hell, life is a bowl of cherries, let's sing Kumbaya, they're unarmed, they're turning themselves in, they recognize the superiority of the U.S. military, they recognize the superiority of our way of life, they want to sit down to chai, join the ANA."

Redcloud smirks. "You wanna take that chance, Wolfie? See what's behind Door Number Three?"

"I'm not the boss."

Redcloud, "I say trophies for everyone." And to Tran on the 240, "Sight in on that last group. Ketchum, get your Saws to sight those guys in the middle."

"Negative! Negative!" from Dove. "There'll be no firing I said! Stand down, everyone stand down!"

Isaf, in St Claire's office suite, Col Pluma raps on the doorframe and interrupts a meeting that includes Dr Hutchinsen, PAO Colonel Gray-Nance and a handful of Nato officers.

"Radio traffic, sir," he informs Gen St Claire. "The platoon and Cop Valley Forge. They're taking multiple rockets in Wajma Valley. Enemy insurgents approaching enmasse."

In Wajma, in the school down here on the veranda, Pfc Holloway, like a number of Utah's guys, is standing on the wall to see better.

Standing vulnerable in the open just to see.

And he can't hardly believe that third line out there. *Taliban zombies, where they all coming from?* It's *Lord of the Rings*, where the enemy just keeps on coming. That first line, those guys closest, they can't even be 300 meters now. *Where're their weapons, gotta be weapons? Under them blankets. They got their guns under them blankets, hid under them blankets.*

How many of these guys here are thinking the same thing? *Got their guns hidden, they're gonna pull them out, right in front of that wall there they're gonna pull them out,* and then they'd have good cover of the wall too and just get behind it and fire. From that close.

Ssgt Utah is thinking, *Our Father who art in Heaven,* and that they've got guns under the blankets, and it's just like his all-time favorite movie, it was his dad's favorite as a kid and his dad has it in VHS and DVD, and it's Clint Eastwood, *Fistful of Dollars,* and *they're going to have steel plates hanging hidden under there too, like our body armor, like Clint had, he had that steel plate under that poncho when he kept walking and that Ramon dude kept shooting him, and "Aim for the heart, Ramon" Clint kept telling him,* and dummy Ramon kept shooting the heart and *Clint just kept picking himself up and coming closer toward him, saying "Aim for the heart, Ramon",* and Utah knows now that *I'm not aiming for their hearts, I'm going for their heads and their cocks. Their faces and their dicks.*

It's automatic for Holloway, radio handset up, he doesn't even have to think about updating Valley Forge. "Whole nuther bunch of em just showed up, Awesome Seven," he calls. "Gotta be four, five hundred now, there's hundreds of em, Top."

And hearing back from 1st Sgt Kozak, "Just hang in there, Holloway. You-all hang in there, and you let your Zoo Seven know that the cav's on the way."

Terp Nouri is out there standing on the rock wall shouting in Pashto what Dove from the roof has yelled down to him to tell the approaching Talibs. *Stop! Stop right now, don't come any closer! If you're coming in peace the colonel will meet you out there! Stop where you are! Or they're going to shoot you!*

Deaf ears. They keep coming. Arms out like wings or over their heads.

On the roof at the parapet Dove asks Nick, "Mr Flowers, are you getting all this?"

Filming, which Nick is. Behind Rodriquez now, framed over his shoulder to get the feel of distance, the close distance, with that first line out there coming up now to about 200 meters.

"Gotta tell you, Zachary," Nick says. "I'd much prefer I was on Bagram right now. Saturday afternoon, lots of good-looking honeys hanging out outside the PX there."

"Have you seen a weapon, any weapon at all?"

"Here's what I can do. I can download this to my laptop, zoom in on individual frames, see if there're weapons. And B-gan it up to a buddy I've got at Bagram"—

"And he can get it over to St Claire," Wolfe interrupts. "Who'll send it up to Cent Com and they'll send it to the Sec Def, who'll show it to the President, and then they'll say we can shoot. Or not."

Redcloud, "They hit the wall, we're dead men. Another twenty meters, I'm giving the order, Colonel."

Dove, "No."

"You've already got me for yesterday, what's another life sentence? Ten, nine"—

"No I said, Sergeant! Mr Flowers, have you sent this up by B-gan yet?"

"Laptop and B-gan's back on the Cop," Nick jokes matter-of-factly without humor. "You weren't serious, Zachary?"

Redcloud again, "Ten, nine, eight"—

Dove, "I give the orders here, Sergeant!"

And to Nick, Dove asks, "Do you have me in the frame there, Mr Flowers? For the record."

And Nicky turns and tilts his camera up, framing Dove in profile. "Looking gorgeous, babe."

"Last chance, everyone!" Dove yells for everyone up here. "Anyone see any weapons?!"

"They got em under them blankets!" Rodriquez spits in a fierce angry passion, and

"Shut up, Sergeant," Dove orders him.

The first line is about fifty meters from the rock wall. Close.

Rodriquez, "Es loco, digo que es mal loco!"

"I said, keep your mouth shut! And listen for the order to engage."

Dove drops to his knees, snaps his M4 to his shoulder, support elbow on the parapet.

"Sergeant Redcloud," he advises, "let's hope your squad leaders can keep control of fire discipline."

"You heard that, Ketchum?!" Redcloud orders, and he follows Dove's example, to his knees, the parapet for protection and a steady aim. He sharply demands into his radio, "I wanna see fire discipline, men."

Dove, "Mr Flowers, are you rolling tape? On me?"

"I'm going to make you famous, Zachary."

"You know what they say, Colonel," Wolfe teases, and he too takes a knee to aim over the parapet. "Leavenworth is very pretty..."

"Especially this time of year," Dove finishes it.

He takes in a deep breath.

"Tattoo Zoo Platoon!" he orders, yelling loud enough that even those down on the veranda can hear, while centering his M4's Aimpoint gunsight steady on the close Talib walking the terrace wall filming video.

"Fiiiiiiiire!"

Day Two, Afternoon — Part 2

Cop Valley Forge

First Sergeant Eddie Kozak, geared up in helmet, body armor, ammo rack and M4, climbs into his humvee and pulls the heavy door shut.

Of the three mounted radios he takes the handset of one of the two FM ones, the one which is set to the 3rd Platoon frequency. The freq today specifically for this Quick Reaction Force—QRF. Max transmission, four, five miles, on a good day of clear weather up in the mountains where they're going.

No one's going to hear them from in that narrow gorge but these thirteen trucks themselves today in this weather.

"Button up, we're movin out," Kozak radios the others. "Keep the chatter down. If you've got a prayer, ask that we're not too late already."

He motions his driver, Sgt Dixon, *Let's go*, glances up at the gunner in the turret on the .50-cal.

The second FM radio is set to the Zoo Platoon freq. Nothing there, nothing heard, and he turns up the volume. Nothing but empty air. Which is normal for this far away, they're not going to get the Zoo freq until maybe a mile or two from that valley. Hopefully, when they make it that close.

If they make it that close.

Kozak snaps on the big radio. It's satellite. He turns up the volume. Ensures it's set on the Awesome Company satellite channel, which can be heard and listened to by all.

Everyone.

Battalion, brigade, Isaf.

Hell, the Pentagon, if they knew what was going on. And/or were inclined to curiosity.

Over the sat radio speaker here in Kozak's truck comes a garbled transmission and lots of background noise then Pfc Holloway's voice saying "Here, listen." There follows a crescendo of sharp gunfire that would be Holloway on the other end holding the handset up for the sounds around him.

It's been just over six minutes since Kozak's final words to Holloway on the radio from the Toc to let Redcloud know *"The cav's on the way"*.

Just six minutes, starting with XO Lieut Frye commanding him, "Top, I can't let you go, I can't let you leave the Cop."

And short, stocky, bulldog Kozak, a good eight inches under Frye, pushing himself right into Frye's chin and snarling, "You just worry about keeping the Cop secure."

Six minutes is record time to get everybody in the trucks and Kozak in his humvee actually now rolling, leading the way toward the front gate.

Only his truck and one other are hummers, the rest the big Mraps.

Just a driver and gunner in each truck.

Two each, except Kozak's and the very last, the other hummer, where it's a driver, a .50 gunner and Platoon Sergeant Northwich.

Everybody knows the plan.

Stay off the satellite radio, no matter what, no broadcasting sat, they don't want the whole world to know they're going to be out there outside the wire on the Red.

Sure, anyone in-country can scroll their computer maps to this specific small hundred-square-mile area and find all these thirteen moving dots of the Blue Force Tracker, whose transmitters the Awesome men aren't sure how to shut off without busting them and then the buster's going to have a couple hundred bucks taken out of his pay for the next how-many years to cover what the investigative report will declare *Willful destruction of government property*.

Odds are anyway that no one's going to be looking on the map and no one's even going to be curious to think to look. So don't worry about being seen on the Tracker.

Don't tell anyone you're leaving, stay off the sat radio, the less anyone up the chain knows, the less Kozak's going to have to directly disobey radioed orders for the QRF to RTB.

Romeo Tango Bravo.

Return To Base.

Every driver and every gunner here knows, if a truck breaks down, only the truck following will stop and stay with it, unlike a normal patrol when the unit stays intact, everyone stopping. Today the rest will go on to the village Wajma and the Zoo, then on the return pick up the other two and deal with the breakage.

Priority is Wajma.

The Zoo in Wajma.

Zoosters under attack.

Wajma or bust.

Kozak pulls from one of the pouches of his ammo rack a plastic 20oz soda bottle. Heavily wrapped in duct tape.

Unscrews the cap.

Takes a short swallow.

Driver Sgt Dixon glances over.

"Sorry, Dix, you're driving," Kozak tells him. Screws on the cap. Slips the bottle back into the magazine pouch.

At 26, Sergeant Dixon is Awesome Company head mechanic, boss over the three other mechanics, responsible for keeping all the trucks up and running all the time. He's never outside the wire, that's not his job, but he volunteered today, he wants to be a part of this rescue of the Zoo, and Kozak took him as his driver because he's good behind the wheel and on the return he can fix just about anything if there is a breakdown.

The clatter of gunfire on the sat radio suddenly is cut off. Silence. Dead silence over the speaker.

Kozak looks at the 2nd Platoon guard and his ANA companion manning the open gate, holds one hand up in a wave of departure passing by, looks out there beyond the maze of the serpentine entrance at the wide wadi and the cloud cover and fog not fifty feet up overhead everywhere, obscuring the mountainsides and ridges and the gorge they're going to drive up into.

Water is running deep and fast in the center channel of the wadi. Dixon automatically knows he's going to have to turn and go up a couple hundred meters to where it's flatter and the water is spread out and more shallow.

A spurt of static over the satellite radio, and an unfamiliar voice comes over that Kozak doesn't recognize, and it is quiet and calm and without panic, calling "Valley Forge Base, Valley Forge Base." And, "This is Lieutenant Colonel Zachary Dove in Wajma, I repeat, this is Lieutenant Colonel Dove in Wajma. Over."

Followed by Lieut Frye's voice replying, "Roger, Colonel, this is Valley Forge Base, got you Lima Charlie."

Kabul, Isaf Op Center

Dove's voice coming in clear over the speakers. "Valley Forge, we are engaged in a full ground assault."

Silence throughout the darkened room. Eyes turned toward the speakers, as if just to be closer, to hear better, to make sure you're hearing what you're hearing, that it's real.

Col Pluma up front standing. Frozen in place staring at the one flatscreen showing the map of Wajma Valley.

Dove's voice over the radio, "Enemy strength, estimated, three hundred plus. Enemy firepower, small arms, light machineguns, rocket-propelled grenades. The latter fired in multiple concentrations beyond the range of the single M-240-Bravo we have."

RPGs, multiple concentrations, Pluma thinks, *fired from more than a thousand meters out. Jesus!*

"Enemy has commenced indirect fire," Dove's voice is calmly saying. "Apparent One-Two-Zero mortars. Repeat, indirect fire. One-Two-Zero mortars. Can't get a read on the Poo. I repeat, Papa Oscar Oscar indeterminate."

Point Of Origin. Poo. Where the mortar tubes are.

Mortars, 120-millimeter mortars, Pluma thinks. *Jesus, indirect fire, where they getting mortars?! How are they carrying big 120 tubes?!*

Heavy tubes. Four hundred pounds of thick steel. Each. Not counting the big heavy rounds to shoot out of those tubes.

"Friendly ammo status," Dove says. "Basic plussed-up combat load. What we carried in on our backs."

Fob Salerno, in the Brigade TOC

The same stunned silence throughout as from the speakers comes Dove's sat radio transmission to Valley Forge. "Status, enemy forces, including likely reserves, unknown. Status, friendly forces, including one zero ANA, approximately five zero. Sustaining casualties, Whiskeys and Kilos, number presently indeterminate. Status, friendly location, same as previous. Same grid sent before. In the schoolhouse building."

Standing in the back by the doors, with a smattering of others not on Toc staff but curious, is Chief Warrant Pilot Chiarduchi. His lieutenant copilot with him.

Dove's radio voice, "If you there at Valley Forge Base can get battalion to get brigade to lift the Red and get some Cas up here we'd be mighty grateful, over."

Close Air Support.

And Lieut Frye's voice replying, "Roger, that's a good copy, Zoo."

And Dove's, "Dove out."

Silence.

No one in here wants to make a comment.

Brigade is them. These very officers and enlisted.

"Air!" the brigade commander full-bird asks forcibly. "Status?"

"Red, sir," from the Air Ops officer. "No change."

"Weather in the mountains?" the commander demands.

"Negative, sir," from the Weather officer. "Cloud cover from a hundred feet to above eighteen thousand A-G-L."

As in Above Ground Level, not altitude from sea level.

"Can we get fixed-wing up there, A-10s, F-16s? Can we request Spectre? I want something up there. Now."

"I can request fast-movers, sir," says the Air officer, "but they're not going to approve it. They haven't been."

"Request them. Keep requesting them."

"Yes sir."

"Estimation, time of clearing? Weather?"

"Negative, sir," from the Weather officer. "There is presently no precipitation in the valley itself, but it just keeps getting worse up there. It's boxed in in clouds, we're talking, as I said, sir, to eighteen thousand. It's something I've never even seen models to predict it on."

Silence again.

Everyone in here knows what's going through the commander's mind. He, like them, would love to make Air Green and get Cas up there, have fast-movers approved and up there in ten minutes, or, minimum, they could get four Apaches and their firepower up there in thirty, they could have had them up there already if Air were Green. They'd have never left, the Apaches wouldn't have, if Air were Green.

The commander wants it.

Everyone in here wants it.

No. Can. Do.

It doesn't even have to be said aloud.

In the back, "Come on," Chief Warrant Chiarduchi tells his copilot gruffly and turns on his heels and pushes out the doors.

In Wajma

On the veranda, a minute ago when Dove said *"out"* and ended his transmission he dropped the handset to Holloway seated back tight against the wall here and feeling like everyone's going to think he's a coward because he's not up kneeling firing over the wall, but when Dove had appeared and demanded of him "Valley Forge" and he'd handed him the proper handset, he'd started to rise and put his M4 on the wall, but Dove had forced him down with a hard slap on his helmet, saying "I need you on the radios!"

So he's staying down.

The boss said so.

Handset to each ear.

He's the RTO. The radio guy.

Maybe that's a lucky thing today.

Dove remains standing, back pressed to the wall of the wide pillar on this side of the steps.

He was about to turn a moment ago to raise his M4 carbine and twist around facing out and acquire a target out there, but a mortar round exploded close, between the rock wall and here, sending a gush of shrapnel and mud against the school, lots in the openings between pillars and splattering the walls and through the windows, and

Dove hopes that all the ANA guys have retreated from out there at the rock wall.

He'd seen just moments before after the one mortar round that had exploded out there close but short of the wall, when he was on the radio to base, that Wolfe and the ANA sergeant and one or two of the others were sprinting up the steps here, and Wolfe and the sergeant are across there standing behind that pillar, lucky for them they hadn't been caught taking aim and firing and getting splattered with the shrapnel of the mortar round that just exploded close out front, as have two of Utah's men across down over there, they're collapsed, they've been hit.

Dove had known before while still on the roof that things were going to be really bad, a lot worse than he'd allowed himself to imagine just a couple of hours ago. In those first thirty seconds after he'd open fire, there were two big explosions out of sight somewhere long on the mountainside above the stream that had far more concussion than the RPGs that were hitting close and far, and he knew they were mortars, which was all the more reason it was time he got himself back downstairs on the radios.

What Dove knew then at the very first two explosions was:

Indirect fire.

Way far out of the reach of his guns here.

Could be in the next zip code.

The explosions so close together, there had to be at least two of them. Two mortars.

Not little 60s like the one these men carried in today and now *They've already fired off the last three rounds we had left.* Bigger.

Like our 120s, big like our 120s. Could be, *Soviets have a version, 120-millimeter, theirs or ours, and ours are in the Pakistani Army inventory, which means the enemy insurgent Taliban inventory.* The distant sound of the next two launching, like a 120, too deep throated and strong for an 81, the explosions here big like 120s.

With guys manning them who know what they're doing. Trained four- or five-man mortar teams. Bracketing, with those two rounds following the first two out-of-sight ones hitting still way long, but right on azimuth, exploding high on the mountainside directly above the school.

The next rounds way short, out between the mosque and here, with one even taking out some of their own Talibs sporadically firing behind the cover of boulders on the beach.

The next two closer, but both still more than a hundred meters shy of the rock wall.

The next one just fifty meters shy of the wall, and that's when Wolfe and all the ANA who were out there retreated into here.

And that single round followed by the one just now out front, and the next two, Dove figures, *Are going to be right on top of us here* on the veranda or on the roof.

"You got a ticket for us to your PX on Bagram?" Dove yells down to Nick Flowers crouched on the other side of Holloway and filming Dove.

From framing Dove on the roof just prior to Dove's order of *"Fire!"* and his first shot, Flowers has stuck right to him, figuring he was the story for now, this was Zachary Dove's fight, it would be framed around him, that was the drama, the story arc, until Dove would take a bullet and go down and then it would be Travis or whoever else was left to take command.

There's so much to shoot here, Flowers knows.

Shoot, as in film.

Not 5.56 out of an M4.

Film as in digital HD.

So much going on. He'll have to get back up on the roof eventually, get that bird's-eye perspective. Should go down there at the other end here where those two have just been hit, and in his viewfinder he sees Dove now spin to peer around the pillar,

and Dove sees that there are two ANA who are still out at the wall, they're down, wounded or dead — one's moving, wounded, and Dove steps out to go out there,

but the ANA sergeant shoves him back, as a moment ago the sergeant had shoved Wolfe back, both to stay here on the veranda, as he and another of his soldiers sprint out there, and he must know, as Dove knows, as Wolfe knows, he's got total about thirty seconds between mortar rounds, in the bracketing adjusting, and ten's already been used up, and

the ANA sergeant must also know, as Dove knows and as Wolfe knows, that as long as the men up on the roof and the men here on the veranda keep firing their *clack clack clack* semi at whatever targets they've got out there among the Talibs hiding and firing close behind their boulders and those farther out, the ones with their RPGs way out there at the conex containers which Redcloud up on the roof has the Saw gunners going for,

as long as that firing keeps up, most of the Talibs won't be able to get off a well-aimed shot at the ANA sergeant and his companion who each now shoulders one of their buddies and hurries back this way, as

Nick Flowers swings his camera, panning fast from Dove shooting his M4 *clack clack clack clack* out there just to ensure the Talibs' heads are down and can't shoot, to catch

Wolfe doing the same, then

Nick now swings the camera to aim beyond the steps out there where the ANA sergeant can feel the *thump thump thump* of enemy bullets hitting the body of the wounded man he carries across his back, as

his buddy carrying the other feels a sheer flame of a bullet spearing his thigh and goes down, and

Nick pans in a blur to center on Wolfe hurdling down the steps, to grab both downed ANA soldiers and drag them both bouncing them up the steps, across and in through the entrance, and

Nick hears a whistle-whine in the air high out front and pulls himself tight low against the veranda wall right up beside Dove doing the same, and

a mortar round explodes on the building somewhere close above, between the arched openings and the parapet edge. A little lower and it would have been right through, landing in this veranda. A little higher, on the roof.

Damn good shooting.

Bracketing.

Walking them in.

Dove senses, next is sure to be a bull's-eye on the roof.

On the roof Cpl Sandusky is on the concrete, curled-up tight against the parapet, his arms up covering his head, his eyes squinted closed, he's so terrified and doesn't want to be and knows he can't stop it and doesn't care that everyone can see him and knows he's terrified, he's frozen, he can't get up to his knees, get his M4 up and sight through his A-cog like he should be, he knows he should be, he should be up and shooting, and can't get his body to move.

Before, watching the enemy walk on steadily closer and closer, sighting them in his A-cog, centered on one, he just wanted them to stop, to not come any closer, to stop when the lieutenant colonel was yelling to terp Nouri to yell out there for them to stop and that he'd go out and meet them, and they didn't stop, and he knew he was pissing himself, felt the wet warmth running fast and wide down the inside of his thigh, and he wished he hadn't drank so much water before, hadn't listened to sarge say *"Hydrate"*, he shouldn't have drank so much, and they kept coming, and he wanted to retch, felt his stomach contract hard, tasted the acid bile in his throat, could taste the chicken tortellini he'd eaten before and wished he hadn't eaten anything, his whole stomach screamed to toss his cookies, and he held it, he sighted still through his A-cog, and nobody else would notice, they wouldn't even see how terrified he was because they were all just as terrified as him, they had to be, then *"Fire!"* from the lieutenant colonel and that first shot, followed by the whole clatter of shots, and the

Saws hammering and the 240 right here near going *tatt-tatt-tatt-tatt-tatt* so deafening in his ears that it hurt, and he couldn't get his finger to pull the trigger, told it to and it wouldn't, and when those two rockets exploded on the mountain just above and he saw Bybee twist and saw the blood on Bybee's face and neck and heard someone farther down yell *"Medic! Medic!"*, he yanked his M4 off the parapet and onto the concrete and laid atop it, drawing himself into a ball so tight that nothing would hit him, he couldn't be touched.

He'd felt the kick to his helmet and had heard Ketchum yelling "Get up get up get yer fuckin self shooting! Hear me, Sandusky?", and he didn't move, he wasn't going to, he was dead, Ketchum could think he was dead, and even as Ketchum yanked him up by the body armor and pulled his face so close to him he could feel Ketchum's spit yelling "Puke! Got a rifle, use it!", even with that he wouldn't open his eyes shut so tight that Ketchum, seeing them and seeing the pasty pale of his face, knew it was futile and dropped him with a violent shove.

The mortar round just now a moment ago exploded on the building's concrete just on the other side of the parapet from where he is, the concussion bouncing him up out away from the parapet wall and back down on the roof hard, and he won't open his eyes, he's not going to move, he won't, and nothing's going to hit him, nothing's going to hurt him if he stays right here.

Sniper Rodriquez is really pissed now.

That mortar was too close and it's caused this cloud of concrete dust everywhere and he can't see shit. And they're walking those mortars in now all the way to actually hit here, and *Another ten feet 'levation and it's right here on toppa us and's gonna be the shit*, and *Them's big, gotta be 120s, where'd they get 120s?* This now, because he can't see through the dust, this now's when *They're gonna be rushin us, cept, alright!*, yeh that's an increase in the volume of fire from right below, that's *Utah's hombres on the porch, they're cuttin em down*.

Before, Rodriquez was just pissed, not really pissed like now with all this blinding dust.

Just plain simply pissed before because he couldn't get a good target of opportunity in his scope. The enemy close, the ones still alive and behind the cover of the boulders out close, when they stick up to shoot, they're targets for all the others with their M4s, and the Saws are supposed to be going after that second group further back on the beach behind boulders, and those who've gotten shelter in and behind the mosque and further back, behind those conexes, those're Rodriquez's targets, the guys with RPGs out there, way out there, when they pop out behind the mosque or conexes, he's gotta get them, but they only pop out a second or two, and never in the same place, and just fire off the RPG, and it's not enough time for him to get a good sight picture and get a good clean shot off.

So he's pissed. Pissed at that, pissed at the dust, pissed at everything.

A millisecond after the lieutenant colonel's *"Fire!"* and first shot, Rodriquez put his first bullet into the man just a step ahead of the others, probably the leader, right in the chest, and imagined that he'd watched him in slow-motion stop square as if he'd been hit with a bat swung by Sammy Sosa, even imagining he'd seen the guy's blanket poncho fly up, and when he realigned the scope back on the guy, the guy was on his butt, legs spread open, with the blanket pushed back over his shoulders, revealing the slung AK under there along with an ammo-rack bandolier of magazines, and Rodriquez squeezed the trigger again and, as his scoped view jerked upwards off the guy, he imagined the guy flopping and twisting backwards as the bullet tore through the magazines, absolutely certain he'd hit him without having to see it.

Rodriquez next got a guy moving laterally toward a boulder, got him he knew straight in the side and reacquired his target to aim at him on the ground as he was trying to push himself with his sandaled feet toward the boulder, and Rodriquez shot him again, aiming just below his armpit to hit through to the heart from the side.

And he knew those close guys could be taken by the M4s, so he moved his sighting to the guys just out beyond the burnt-up pickup, most dashing for cover, but two standing in place, raising RPGs to their shoulders, and Rodriquez hit the first too low, in the thigh, then reacquired and managed a quick second shot in the chest, and the guy's launcher flopped skyward and there was a flash and smoke of the rocket shot to the heavens.

Rodriquez got the other guy just after he'd fired his RPG, and could see out of his unscoped eye lots of simultaneous flashes out even farther and knew they were RPGs, so he scoped out there, out at six and seven hundred meters and saw those black-clad figures sprinting for the conexes and others jumping down into trenches or foxholes or whatever they are that he doesn't remember being there yesterday or even today earlier when they'd come in by chopper, which means they were digging them in the rain and cover of the clouds and fog, and *We didn't even know it, hijos de puta hajjis!*

Rodriquez hit one.

Missed another.

Hit him on the second shot.

Missed another.

The rocket grenades started exploding here. A couple too high, on the mountainside above, and rained down rocks like huge chunks of hail and shale like headstones. Others short, in the sand and mud and sending up blinding sprays. Two on the front wall of the school, below and over to the left, and one sailed right through the veranda and in through the window opening and exploded on the wall outside the morgue classroom, which Rodriquez then had no way of knowing wounded Nell's guy on that window there.

When the explosive clouds cleared, Rodriquez scoped way out there, scanning, and there was nothing to hit — nothing moving.

Noticed from the sound *clack-tat-tat clack-tat-tat* that the guy beside him was firing on 3-round-burst.

Specialist Howie.

Chubby.

With both his eyes closed tight.

And Rodriquez then slapped him on the helmet and yelled right into his ear, "No auto! No auto!" and himself snapped Howie's selector to semi.

Yelled close under his helmet into his ear, "Aint gonna hit shit wit yer eyes closed! Open – yer – ojos!"

Noticed Howie's Aimpoint sight wasn't even turned on. Flicked it on. Yelled again, "Open yer eyes, Chubby!"

Howie did, and Rodriquez yelled at him, "Put the red dot on a guy!"

Illuminated red dot in the center of the Aimpoint.

"One shot, one kill! This aint no video game, you aint gettin no more'n those mags ya got! One shot, one kill!"

These few minutes later and *Them ragheads* just walked a mortar round right here, and *If they got more of them 120s*, Rodriquez thinks, *We gonna be in a world of hurt. Chingada, wanna talk 'bout that dude Noah up shit creek wit'out no paddle.*

The moment after that mortar hit so close, Redcloud had been praying *Holy Mary Mother of God pray for us sinners*, and he has just yanked and dragged Cpl Sandusky's stiff tucked fetal-tight body back over up against the parapet, and he kneels over it, sheltering it, and

if you asked him why, since he knows Sandusky is alive and unhit and just terrified, he couldn't tell you now or anytime in the future why, since he should just let Sandusky lie out there in the open, who cares, but don't ask him the why because to Redcloud the whys and the hows and the shoulds or coulds or mights only come when you've got time to think of them and not just react and do.

Do's are what matters.

Do what you do.

He peers over the parapet as the cloud of concrete dust and explosive smoke swirls around, as he's hearing the firing from Utah's men on the veranda below tapering off, which means they're out of targets, which means this closest assault under the cover of the explosions is beaten back, and that's good, Redcloud likes it that they're practicing fire discipline, not just firing wildly, gonna need that ammo.

He hears a spurt from the Saw up at this end and knows the gunner, Garcia, has sight again of a target out at those conexes, firing to keep those RPGs back, as Redcloud had been up there at first when Garcia was firing at the close-in enemy which the M4s could take care of and had screamed at him, right in his face, "No no, get the guys with the rockets! The rockets!", pointing distant to the far-off enemy dashing for the cover of the mosque and conexes.

And he'd seen then that Ketchum was ensuring Tran and Bybee on the 240 were targeting those same enemy far out, and

Redcloud sees now that Pfc Finkle is peering over the parapet, *Brave kid, brave kid there,* M203 grenade launcher raised, *He aint ducking, he knows his job, he's doin it,* as Redcloud had yelled right into his ear just a minute into it, it seems so long ago, to put his rounds on the backside of the mosque, one, two a minute, just to keep them back behind there so they couldn't pop out and fire off their rockets, and

he hoped then that's what Utah'd be telling his 203 gunners downstairs, to go for the backside of the mosque, max range, pushing it, of the 203, and *Don't burn through your rounds, they gotta last!*

A hundred-twenty-something rounds total 203 grenades, that's all the Zoo's brought in. They've got to last.

These mortars landing close, this one right on the wall here, that's bad, and Redcloud knows it.

And knows he can't think about it, can't obsess on it because there's nothing they can do about it, he can't call in artillery, can't call in Cas, might could hit them with the 60 if they had any more 60 mortar rounds, but he knows Slurpee's already fired off the only three they had left, and if if if if if if, always an if, if they knew exactly where those mortars were coming from up there somewhere in those compounds, what, two thousand, three thousand meters away they were firing from, and

oh he wishes he had about fifty more 60 rounds, so they could put them out there at those most distant Talibs, and the ones in between, *How'd by gosh did they get foxholes dug?,* when'd by gosh did they dig those foxholes?, when the fog was in, and *God curse em, if the fog'd stayed longer they'd have had em dug all the way up to the front rock wall right out here.*

It's not difficult, Redcloud knows. You can scrape twelve inches off that soft dirt and sand, maybe eighteen inches, in no time, pile it up out front, and *You've got yourself where we can't see you in there, and if we can't see you we can't hit you and you can just pop your RPG up, fire off a rocket, duck back down,* hug the bottom of the foxhole and who gives a hoot if it hits exact, *It's gonna keep our heads down, gonna keep us scared to death, gonna make the explosions and the confusion blinding for us and you'll get your next rush on us.*

Two or three more rushes, sustained enemy rushes, and *We're gonna be out of ammo.*

Two or three more rushes, and they're Crazy Horse and we're Custer.

He hears a whine, a second, and thinks that it would be better if everyone was firing and they would be deafened and not hear the whine of these approaching mortars, and

he ducks his head down, as he knows everyone up here is going to be doing the same hearing that whine, and he covers Sandusky completely, laying hard against him, and

a mortar explodes on the mountainside above, maybe 50 feet up.

The second even still higher.

Deafened in the explosion and the cascade of dirt, rocks and boulders, Redcloud and no one can hear the whines of the two mortar rounds that follow by ten seconds —

the bare minimum amount of time used between rounds by the expert al-Qaeda Chechens or Arabs or Uzbeks on the two tubes

— and exploded higher still on the mountainside.

Nor can anyone hear the whines of the four in pairs that follow.

Nor the eight in pairs that then land scattered between the rock wall and the building itself and scatter close on the other side of the rock wall.

Redcloud, like Ketchum and Rodriquez up here and Dove and Wolfe and Utah somewhere downstairs, are keeping count.

16 in this first FFE.

Fire For Effect.

Which is when you've got your guns finally set on the correct azimuth and elevation for the target you're aiming at and you start dropping down their tubes shell after shell after shell.

Doc Eberly is busy.

All those mortar rounds and the thundering of whatever came crashing down on the roof just above that made him think the concrete ceiling was going to collapse on him and everyone in here, and

now all that rifle fire, all the M4s firing at once right out there on the veranda,

he knows he's going to be busier.

That it's going to get worse.

And he won't be able to handle it all, and even if he could he wouldn't have enough supplies.

He'll use uniforms, he'll rip up uniforms for bandages.

Each soldier is carrying his own saline bag, they're all supposed to be, in their rucks. Bags and IV needles and tubing. They'll have to gather up everyone's. He knows he's not going to have enough blood expanders for all he's going to need.

Morphine too, they'll have to do without morphine.

Eberly only has two syrettes left. Went through five already, how'd he have to go through so many already?

One thing at a time, bud, one thing at a time, keep the mind clear and focused. *One plus one is two. Two plus two is four. Four times forty-four is 176. 176 X 4 is 704.*

Stop the bleeding.

Clear the airways.

Stop the bleeding.

Clear the airways.

"Just keep in mind, prioritize, Sergeant Eberly," the lieutenant colonel had said to him when he'd come in here before this all began when they still couldn't be sure there would actually be an attack, *What was it?, was it an hour ago?, thirty minutes ago?, five minutes?, when he'd come in to check on the pretty captain,* just checking up on her, cheering her up.

The colonel had pulled him aside, away from Capt Cathay, so she wouldn't hear, and "Keep the ones alive you can keep alive for eighteen hours," he'd told him. "Until morning, if you can. If you need help, we'll get you help."

"I can do it, sir," he'd told the colonel.

He could, he'd thought he could, but he's never been in a mortar barrage like that before, and the ones in Iraq were always when they were safe on the big fobs where they had the huge concrete culvert-pipe bomb-shelters to duck into and there were also always so many medics around. He's never been with so many RPG rockets coming so concentrated, not in Iraq where you'd be in the Strykers all strung dispersed separated and you might see one or two and most missing flying by high or wide, he's never been where *We're all in one so small a location shooting so much in return*, not in the Zoo, it's always, all the times before here in Afghanistan here in the Zoo, it's always *Just been a quick little Tic like yesterday or an IED blowing up a truck*, never an attack like this.

Tic, he thinks, *Troops In Contact. It should be Tuma, Troops Under Massive Attack.*

Tor, Troops OverRun.

Doc Eberly loves words.

He loves numbers.

704 X 4 is 2816.

2816 X 5 is 14080.

Stop the bleeding.

One patient at a time.

Clear the airways.

1 patient at a time.

Keep them alive.

For 18 hours.

The two ANA wounded by the airburst RPG before even the first of the black-clad enemy appeared way out there, he got them in here and immediately prioritized the one with the piece of steel spiked through his helmet-liner and skull as no-chance and treated the other, who's going to live, should at least, maybe lose that leg eventually *If we've gotta keep the tourniquet on 'cause the bleeding can't be stopped with pressure.*

But that was quiet then, treating that ANA, just some shouting from the rooftop and Nouri out there shouting some Afghan Pashto.

It was quiet, it wasn't the attack.

It wasn't even a cry of *Medic!* that got Doc rushing out to the first Zoosters down. It was the rocket exploding inside down at the far end, where Doc knew there'd be Nell's guy Pfc Nuñez at the side window there and ran there, to be stopped by Utah coming through a front window yelling, "Get back, Doc! Gonna bring im to you!"

And Utah dragged Nuñez here into Doc's aid station classroom.

And just a while ago the sergeant and Wolfe brought in the three ANA, and Wolfe immediately assessed the wounded one who'd been shot multiple times carried across the sergeant's back and told Doc to forget it, forget him, "Don't waste your time or his time," and

Wolfe caught Capt Cathay staring right at him, and

she was sitting up straight, had her M4 clutched tight in her hands on her lap.

She told him, "Mr Wolfe, please! Get me out of here, I can shoot."

Wolfe couldn't believe it, couldn't believe what he was hearing, and she had to say it again, more forcibly, "I can shoot, take me out there," and ripped out her IV.

She wants it, she's got it, and he told her, "Hang on tight," and grabbed her up around the legs by the air mattress and sleeping bag and dragged her out of the room, then pulled her up sitting propped against the wall right outside the classroom, and he told her direct close to her face, "You protect Doc! Last line of defense, they come through that door you blast em!"

And Wolfe went back into the classroom and retrieved her helmet and body armor with its clipped-on full mag pouches, and he plopped the helmet on her head, draped her torso with her body armor and told her again, "Hajj get in here, you blast em! And don't let them take you alive!"

That's about when the 90-second mortar barrage FFE began.

Wolfe made it back out to the veranda during the barrage, ducked low there, felt the entire building shake with the avalanche rocks and boulders on the roof, counted the rounds coming in, and

with those last eight explosions out front here he knew if he looked he'd see nothing through the smoke and dirt and sand and mud, and there were no more twin explosions in ten-second sequence after the last two mortars, and in the quiet now, as no one is shooting here on the veranda, they're not shooting above on the roof, no one can see shit, even if they're even looking, and Redcloud's well established the rules, if you can't see shit, you don't shoot, and

in the quiet there's no sound of that approaching whine, and

Wolfe knows in that zillionth-of-a-second flash of thought, *Assholes know what they're doing, coordinated on the mortars with the ground assault*, just as in the same instant

just across on the other side of the steps behind that pillar there Lieut Col Dove is flash-thinking the exact same thing. Like Wolfe he knows the barrage has ended, they're coordinated, the mortars and ground attack, *They're assaulting right now*, and

he lets his M4 dangle on its snaplink, his hands extract two hand grenades from a pouch, yank the safeties, pull the pins and he tosses both behind his back around the column with all his strength, yelling "Fire in the hole!", as

Wolfe is doing the exact same thing, "Fire in the hole!", with his intent, like Dove's, for the grenades to land somewhere between here and the rock wall, and

the moment after the grenades explode he spins on the corner edge of the pillar, rifle up, and starts shooting on semi right into the blinding smoke, as

Dove is doing, spun around on the corner of his pillar, M4 out in the open, he's firing on semi down at the height and distance of where the top of the rock wall would be if one could see it or see anything through the smoke and mud and sand in the air, and

Utah down that way follows their example doing the same, shooting on semi into the smoke, and

Slurpee up the other way too now,

and as the smoke clears from the ground up, bodies appear, black-clad, on this side of the rock wall, on the ground, motionless wounded or dead and crawling wounded, and

more of Utah's men here on the veranda start firing, and

the smoke cleared out more, there are bodies on the wall, there are black-clad enemy charging just twenty meters out beyond the wall, all easy targets, and

still no firing from the roof, as it's not clear up there yet, they still can't see shit down below through the smoke and

On the roof Redcloud knows from the increasing firing below that there must be an assault going on beyond the smoke he can't see through,

and his instinct is to fire off a full magazine on burst out to just beyond where he visualizes the rock wall is, but he doesn't do it because he knows if he fires randomly through the smoke then other guys will too up here and they'll be wasting their limited ammo aiming who-knows-where,

but all that's secondary right now to Redcloud, even as he's yelling "Targets! Targets! Targets!" as a reminder for no one to shoot blind through the smoke as he dashes down to where Ketchum and Rodriquez and Van Louse are pulling rocks and boulders off Zoosters there, he doesn't know how many, two or three, and he hopes not more.

While earlier down below on the veranda, in the still quiet moments before Dove had tossed the grenades then spun around to fire into the smoke, just after the mortar FFE barrage began, Dove had commanded Holloway, "Tell Base to get us the LCMR grid on those mortars!"

Meaning, Valley Forge has Lightweight Counter-Mortar Radar that automatically pinpoints the exact location of the launch tube, on the map, the eight- or ten-digit grid coordinate.

The LCMR pinpoints the Poo. The Point of Origin.

Holloway did it, called Valley Forge and told them.

That's his job. He's the RTO.

On Cop Valley Forge in the Toc, the soldiers didn't need to have Pfc Holloway on the radio pass along a request by the lieutenant colonel out there to get him the LCMR grid of the mortar tubes' Poo.

One of the two big flatscreens is always on a map of Awesome Company's entire Area of Operation, or AO, zeroed in now on Wajma Valley and the surrounding area. With the LCMR always turned on, the launches are automatically picked up, and the computer-generated location of the Poo is indicated by a flashing red dot on the map.

The flashing dots of the Poo today are all in the same spot.

So many right now that they're all superimposed on one another.

A grid coordinate of the spot flashing on the map there.

The spot is on the far edge of the valley, farthest possible from the schoolhouse. Right on the edge of where the map's brown contour lines run together denoting a steep mountainside.

The NCO battle captain in here can bring up onto the flatscreen a Google Earth or military satellite image from a day ago, a week ago, a month ago, a year ago, whatever's most recently available, of the exact same place in black-and-white, and that spot, the Poo, would be in one of the compounds there at the far edge of Wajma plainly seen on Google Earth.

In a compound.

And Lieut Frye knows that Lieutenant Colonel Dove didn't ask for the LCMR grid because he wanted it, that he could use it—he, Dove, didn't have the weapons to neutralize those mortars. Rather, Frye assumes that Dove had Holloway broadcast the request because he knows that battalion and brigade and Isaf are all listening in and, same as earlier when Dove had asked him to request battalion get brigade to lift the Red, Dove is now telling them at the echelons above lowly Awesome here at Valley Forge to get some 500-pounders or 1000-pounders rained down on those mortars.

Dove is asking for Close Air Support.

Cas.

And that only comes from above.

On Fob Salerno in the Brigade Toc, the colonel knows exactly what the Isaf staff asshole lite bird was asking for when he requested Awesome Company get him the LCMR grid.

The colonel knows of Dove. It's the select world of infantry Ranger officers, and wasn't that Dove, wasn't he only recently a junior major, and just before that a heralded Ranger company commander, what's he doing a lite colonel now so quickly?

Screw him, the full-bird thinks. *That rank-hopper knows we can't get Cas in there, screw him.* But this man's not a full-bird because he's vindictive or single-minded or IQ-challenged stupid. He hasn't obtained this rank and position because he's unable to evaluate himself quickly, honestly, on the fly, and he knows that he's not frustrated and angry at that Isaf lieutenant colonel, that Dove, out there in a shitstorm with the Tattoo Zoo Platoon trapped in that valley. Rather, he's irritated at himself—himself, he with seventy-plus helicopters sitting right outside this door and fixed-wing out of Bagram or Kandahar just an IM or satcom request away, and he is powerless to do anything, to get a single one airborne.

Kabul, in the Isaf Op Center, up on one big flatscreen is that Google Earth picture dated twenty months ago of the Wajma Valley, with an overlay in red of the grid coordinates to ten digits and a circle around the exact ten meters at the edge of the vertical mountainside in the compound farthermost from the school building.

Colonel Pluma demands, "Air?"

"Negative negative negative," says the Air officer. "Bagram's got a pair of A-10s on station circling just outside the weather not seven minutes from the target. An F-16 is 12 minutes out."

"Weather?" demands Pluma.

"Red Red Red," says the Weather officer, adding for emphasis, "Candy-apple Red. It's not going anyplace anytime soon. Clouds, fog, drizzle, rain, all the way to the ground. Thunderstorms popping up on the ridgelines and on the other side of them."

The Air officer informs, "The Jdams on the F-16, they shouldn't be affected by the weather, they can launch outside the weather, at least that's what I'm getting assurances."

Joint Direct Attack Munitions.

GPS-guided bombs.

Pluma taps the flatscreen right at the spot of the overlay red-circled spot. "Get them this grid. Two Jdams right exactly here. No deviation. If they can't guarantee a ten-meter radius, it's a negative, no drop. Otherwise, tell them it's a go."

"Careful, Dan," another colonel advises. "That might take a higher call. For a green light on the Jdams."

"My call."

"You're taking full responsibility, are you sure, Danny?"

A British major suggests, "I can run it up to General St Claire first, sir, if you'd like."

Nope. Pluma puts his finger on the spot on the overlay. "Two Jdams. Ten-meter radius maximum allowance. Yesterday!"

On Fob Salerno, in a heavy downpour, the lieutenant copilot hops off the Gator at the lowered tailramp of the Chinook. Chief Warrant Pilot Chiarduchi stabs the gas pedal and U-ies the Gator to head back down the concrete ribbon for the crossroads of the taxiway to race the Gator toward one of the big clamshell maintenance hangers. His shouted instructions to his copilot just before dropping him off were to get Jarbodie to prep for pallets — three, with any luck.

In Wajma in the school, Redcloud comes down the stairs pushing Cpl Sandusky ahead of him, forcibly, a hand on his collar. He's surprised to find Capt Cathay seated right at the door of the aid station classroom, her M4 held firmly.

Spunky, he thinks. *Got spunk.*

He shoves Sandusky in, spins him around and confronts him right to his face. "You don't wanna shoot, you don't gotta shoot, least you can do is save your buddies' lives." He shoves Sandusky so hard that Sandusky trips and falls back on his butt.

On the roof, when they'd gotten the rubble off the others, two were banged up, hurt but okay enough to demand to stay up there, grabbing their guns and facing over the parapet again as the smoke cleared and the enemy who were storming nearer reaching the rock wall were immediate targets for them.

The third man was unconscious, cut and bloody, probably broken bones, and Redcloud yelled close to Van Louse that the man could wait to be brought downstairs until after the assault was beaten back. Shoot now, we'll bring him down after!

They were all firing on the roof then, Redcloud too, all ducking only briefly as a rocket had *pawhooshed* right overhead then simply dudded on the mountainside ceiling just above the rear parapet.

The assault was beaten back, and Redcloud had gone over to where Sandusky was lying curled up against the parapet and pulled him up, screamed into his face, "Open your eyes! Open your eyes!", and yanked him all the way to his feet and rushed him, forcing him, shoving him across the roof to the stairs and down to here, the aid classroom.

He steps out of the aid classroom now and taps Capt Cathay on the helmet in an *Okay, doin good* as he goes by her and heads back up the stairs and does not want to think of all the wounded he just saw down there in Doc's aid station.

Doesn't want to think of the more probably out on the veranda and above now on the roof.

You don't think of that which you can't control.

What Redcloud can hope to control is the men on the roof, and, along with Ketchum, make sure they don't burn through their ammo on the next assault.

Or the one after that.

And he remembers what he meant to remember down there while in the aid station and yells to Van Louse and the other soldier who have just passed him going down carrying the wounded Zooster to get all the magazines off the wounded and bring them up.

With the QRF, in 1st Sgt Kozak's humvee, he checks his watch. For about the tenth time.

Not even seven minutes since they drove out the gate, and they've only come this far, not even all the trucks here in the gorge yet, Kozak knows without asking on the radio or even asking his turret gunner here to look behind, he knows the last one or two should just about now be out of the wadi and in here.

It's too slow, already too slow going.

The running water here isn't even a stream anymore. Seems more like a river. Hardly much streambank to ride up on out of the deep, fast-moving water.

Kozak pinches a thick clump of chew and ritualistically sets it in his mouth between under his lip against his jaw.

Thinks, *Flashfloods, didn't even think of flashfloods.* When it rains up here *It sure knows how to rain.*

"I didn't think about flashfloods, Top," says driver Sgt Dixon as if reading Kozak's mind. "Dudes back home are always getting washed away, Top, it's cuz they're thinking they can drive their 4-by-4s through a flashflood creek."

"Don't worry," Kozak says. "We're all so full of shit we'll float."

In Wajma it's quiet.

Nothing is moving out there.

No targets.

From this side of the rock wall, on it, and on the other side are motionless black-clad shapes on the ground. Scattered. More dense up closer here, far fewer the farther you go out, all the way to 600 and 700 meters.

Of the ones beyond 100 meters, when one moves it gets shot.

Forget mercy, forget your Mother Teresa bullshit, you can debate that shit in your next Modern Ethics graduate seminar over your 24-ounce latte frappuccinos and apple-pecan cream cheese cinnamon muffins.

A guy moves, he's enemy, and unless he's holding up a white flag or a white hanky or white strip of shitpaper, five minutes from now he's going to be shooting at you again.

He moves, he's enemy.

Period.

The ones far out, past 500 meters, Sniper Rodriquez is the one who puts one shot in them. If they move.

If he doesn't see a white hanky.

There are no white hankies out there.

100 to 500 meters, Ssgt Nell on the roof shoots them. With his M4. He's good out to that far. The best. It's all that horseplay free range time five years as a Drill Sergeant. He can put a bullet through a bellybutton at 400 meters, the max effective range of the M4, and he can follow it with two others straight through if he wanted to.

If the dude stood still long enough for the second and third shots after that first jerked and crumpled him backwards.

Close here and out beyond the rock wall to about 100 meters, the ANA sergeant and his four soldiers still unwounded have gone from body to body and put a shot into each head, with Wolfe and four of Ketchum's guys collecting up the AKs and bandoliers of magazines.

All the activity coordinated by the Mbitr platoon radios, rapid commands given, carried out immediately and quickly, Redcloud to his squad leaders, now that it's quiet enough to be actually heard over the radios.

And besides the ANA finishing off the fallen Talibs, no one shoots squat except for Rodriquez and Nell.

Conserve ammo.

Back before all this attack, back just after Lieut Caufield had died, Redcloud had returned to the aid station and taken up the LT's body armor and weapon and had then given Wolfe the LT's Mbitr radio. Wolfe is like a squad leader.

Redcloud had dropped Caufield's gear by his body in the other classroom and thought to do the same with Capt Washington's little Mbitr, to grab it up and give it to the lieutenant colonel.

But it was gone. Off the captain's body armor, pouch and handset and all, gone.

Dove had already taken it.

For a moment Redcloud had been angry. Then he wasn't. Yeh, the lieutenant colonel was now the boss, it's his radio, smart to take it.

Now, after the assault in this quiet, directions and orders can be relayed by radio. Dove would have to be in the loop. He was.

And when Redcloud radioed down to ask Doc Eberly if he needed more help, Doc had replied that Sandusky was catatonic, and Redcloud sent Ketchum down there to the aid station, and Ketchum found Sandusky seated in the dark far corner hugging his knees, and Ketchum yanked off Sandusky's helmet, yanked him to his feet, slapped him in the face once, twice, three, four, five times, screaming at him to get his shit together, if he was gonna be a pussy puke do it on his own time, there's his buddies to try 'n save here, and, dude, if he couldn't do it, if he couldn't even help Doc, well then he'd put a fucken bullet through his brain right now. And Ketchum put the muzzle of his M4 right flat pressed hard to Sandusky's forehead and screamed right into his face to open his eyes!, open his eyes so he could see his brains splattered all over the wall behind him. "Open yer fucken eyes, soldier! Open them, now! I said open them, soldier!" And Sandusky did, and Ketchum pulled the muzzle off Sandusky's forehead and fired a shot right alongside his head into the wall then screamed at him that if he didn't get his shit together right this second and do everything Doc told him to do, if he Ketchum had to come back down here again, then the next shot was gonna be right here, he tapped hard with his gloved index finger, right between Sandusky's eyes.

Nick Flowers would have loved to have been in there then, he'd have loved to film that, to capture that scene forever on digital HD, show the world reality, the harsh reality of cowardice and passion and anger and terror where you know it's real and not some 3D big blockbuster summer release where it's just actors playing tough and all CGI.

But Nick was outside, out front. Filming. Following the ANA sergeant and his four guys making sure every one of these close black-clad enemy bodies was really dead with a single bullet to the brain, and Nick getting snatches of video of Wolfe and Utah's guys gathering up the enemy AKs and ammo and completely ignoring the ANA.

Nick capturing the harsh brutal battlefield reality of the ANA ensuring the enemy is dead.

The Afghans doing it, not the Americans.

At one point Wolfe stepped in front of Nick and raised Nick's camera to aim on himself, speaking right into the lens. "Footnote to the world out there. The Afghans don't do the gang-rape genital mutilation on fellow Afghans. Only on infidel non-Muslim American GIs and Rooskies. Limeys, Polacks, Frog-eaters, Wops and the rest of Nato. Gotta love the culture. Number Two: The Afghan Code — Honor, Hospitality, Revenge. Emphasis on Revenge. End footnote."

Gotta love that Wolfie, no?

You'd think he wasn't in enough trouble for yesterday, but no, now he's got to say all that, and on camera, it can't be erased, taken back or excused away.

A capital offense.

An afterthought. Wolfe added, leaning in close to the lens, "Number Three. Those are just blanks they're firing. You don't think they'd fire real bullets, do you? Only wack-job rogue HTTs coup-de-grâce the bad guys. Not our coalition partners. End footnote. Again."

Nicky missed catching Ketchum with Sandusky inside in the aid station, missed the exclusive it would have been, how that's never caught on tape for real and only showed in movies where everyone knows it's not real, but out here filming he thought about movies and summer blockbusters and how Wolfie and the others collecting up the enemy's weapons and ammo for their own use was never in the movies because the heroes never ran out of ammo.

Forty-two AKs Wolfe and the guys collected.

No RPGs. None carried by the close-assault troops. Smart. Save the rockets for longer-range.

Two little walkie-talkies Wolfe got off the bodies. Both on the same channel, #12. Both silent.

The 42 AKs along with the 10 from the ANA deserters earlier will make almost two for each Zooster still on the walls. That extra weapon for when they run out of 5.56 for the M4s.

And 5.56 belts for the Saws.

And 7.62 for the 240.

Over the platoon radio Redcloud had gotten a rough ammo status from the squad leaders.

M4 carbine, approximately 6 mags per, including all those Van Louse retrieved from the wounded in the aid station.

6 mags per, at 30 per mag.

180 bullets each.

Approximately.

Up here on the roof Pvt Finkle knows he's got 14 40mm grenades left. Wishes he had a hundred.

He's got 8 mags 5.56.

And something to do, anything to do, Finkle took to counting the bodies out there. Starting from close, those that the Afghan soldiers were shooting in the head, how cool is that? And farther out, where he could still see and count plainly, even those in clumps of a couple that could be three maybe. Don't count the legs or arms, they could be under them, could be blown off. Count the solid torsos and the heads, if you could tell that they were still heads.

And for even farther out Finkle used Sandusky's binos which Van Louse brought up when he'd come back up with all the mags off the wounded and Sandusky's rifle and mags and his binos too. Yeh, how cool is that? Finkle's got his own binos now, and didn't even have to buy em.

On the count, Finkle got 127.

When he'd hit 100, he was hoping to get at least to 150.

Just 20-something more. 20-something. Aw, 23, yeh, 23 more.

"Hundred twenty-seven," he told Ssgt Ketchum. "Not even a hundred-fifty."

"Shit," Ketchum said. "There's thirty you can't see and they've already dragged off another thirty."

The other tally, the important one, reported to Redcloud on the radio from the squad leaders: Not counting ANA, 6 Zoosters out of the battle, out of the fight, wounded or dead, no one was asking aloud. Yet.

Not counting from before Capt Washington, Lieut Caufield and Akin.

8 wounded but still on the walls.

Still on the walls, that's important, *We need them all on the walls*, thought Redcloud then.

A couple of minutes ago when Redcloud was with Tran and Bybee on their 240 checking their ammo status, three cans they said they had left. At 200 linked bullets per can.

"Wish I'd carried another six," Tran said.

"I've got two in my ruck," Redcloud told them. A wink to them, "You never know."

And he'd gone downstairs to retrieve them from his ruck on the veranda, and that's when he heard Pfc Holloway tell Lieut Col Dove, "Sir, the Cop is saying they've got a F-16 gonna drop on the Poo two Jdams in one zero mikes."

In 10 minutes.

"Tell them thanks," Dove said.

"I already did. Sir."

"Tell them from me."

And Holloway did. Called back on sat, "Valley Forge Base, this is Zoo Six Romeo. The lite bird says he's got a special thanks for you-all. Sheeeeat, he says he's gonna buy you-all a beer when we get back."

And Dove hadn't corrected Holloway, had let that slide. Not proper radio protocol, not a time for fooling around. But it was clever, kind of, and kind of funny. In a Holloway way. Like there's beer in the AO. Not Awesome Company's AO. Yeah, up at Isaf, sure, that's another thing, another world. *PFC, I couldn't have said it better myself.*

Dove had then put a hand on Redcloud's shoulder, just a solid grip.

A meeting of their eyes.

"Ten minutes," Dove said then almost without sound.

A thumbs-up from Redcloud.

The first he could remember giving all day.

And now back on the roof, Redcloud drops his two machinegun ammo cans at Tran's and Bybee's feet.

"Thanks, Sarge," from Tran. And he really means it.

Utah's guy drops two AKs and a bandolier of AK mags here. He and another are distributing them, one or a couple of AKs each to the guys here on the parapet.

Back downstairs on the veranda Wolfe holds up in his hands for Dove to hear both Talib walkie-talkies broadcasting now some fast Pashto, and he calls for Nouri to come out to translate.

Dove and Wolfe wait for Nouri to break down the Pashto in clear chunks.

Pfc Holloway watching, listening, waiting.

Nick Flowers filming.

"He is he says," Nouri translates. "Allah is watching."

Nouri listens.

Wolfe catches the *Allahu Akbar.*

Nouri, "God is great. Today we have . . . eat, we eat supper . . . with Allah."

Nouri listens. Then, "Warriors of Allah." Pause, listens. "One minute."

The walkie-talkies go silent.

"That's it?" Dove asks. "One minute?"

Back up on the roof Redcloud tells Pvt Bybee, "When we get a chance, you get Doc to look at that." Meaning, the gash across Bybee's face that he's been holding a blood-soaked bandage against. And the blood-soaked cravat tied tight around the gash in his upper arm.

"I'm awright, Sarge," Bybee blows it off. "Aint nuthin . . . ."

"He's just scared if he sees Doc then you won't let him get his tatt," Tran jokes.

Redcloud does a little fist bump against Bybee's body armor, like saying *No sweat, you've got your Zoo tatt, soldier, I approve it, done deal, don't worry about it.*

He hears over his headset Dove advise him and the squad leaders that the enemy's just announced over their walkie-talkies *One minute.*

He looks out there.

Says aloud for everyone up here, "Enemy's saying one minute. Stand by."

They all look out there.

It's so still.

Nothing is moving.

If the enemy's out there hiding, where can they be hiding?

How many of those shallow foxholes and trenches have they got out there?

Where?

Nothing's moving.

One minute to what?

It's so quiet.

Not even a whisper of the easy breeze anymore. Dead stillness.

The clouds hang so low, at most sixty feet up, like a low ceiling of cotton.

It's so calm, peaceful, idyllic. Like a landscape painting.

You can't help but feeling that maybe it's all gonna be okay.

Maybe they know they've been beat bad and they've all gone home.

One minute for their retreat to begin, they're going to retreat.

In the silence out there they all hear the slight but deep-throated *Paaa-thump* that anyone and his deaf senile grandma knows is the launching of a distant mortar.

On Fob Salerno, in the clamshell hanger, over in the forklift maintenance area a specialist is keeping low and out of sight, sitting on a big smashed-in cardboard box used as a makeshift La-Z-Boy lounger, hidden behind one of the three forklifts here.

Totally engrossed in his PlayStation video game.

The forklifts are the huge telescopic-arm types, with tires as tall as a man and as big around as a hot tub.

Chief Warrant Pilot Chiarduchi pulls up to a skidding stop in the Gator and interrupts the shamming specialist. "Hey there, that your's, do you operate that?" he asks.

"That's my job, sir. Why, whatcha got?"

"I need you to get in there and crank it over, and you got the keys to that one?" Meaning, the first forklift.

"Keys are in it. But now Sarge didn't say anything, he didn't tell me nothing, we got something we gotta move? Cuz Sarge didn't say anything, and he's not here and I can't be movin anything without Sarge saying so." And the specialist doesn't even get up, doesn't make a motion to, sure isn't planning to. Not for someone he doesn't know, not in his chain.

Chief Chiarduchi holds out the rank on his sternum, the long straight black bar of a Warrant-5. "Do I look like a sergeant? Get your ass up, I said, and get up in there and crank it over."

The QRF, in the lead truck, 1st Sgt Eddie Kozak spits tobacco juice into his spit cup, which is an empty Dr Pepper can with the top cut three-quarters around and folded back.

He checks his watch. 16 minutes since driving out the Cop's gate.

The Blue Force Tracker map on the mounted computer screen shows they're just about halfway to Wajma.

Making good time.

Could be better. Maybe. But the water's high.

The gorge is wide, maybe seventy meters across here, but the water's running way out of its channel and at times they've got to drive right up to the edge of the mountain and they're still in the water, with it then splashing up in waves across the hood. And, with the flashflood little waterfalls coming in spots off the mountain, the turret gunner here is drenched, Kozak knows, as he himself is pretty much soaked from the water coming in down through the open turret.

Shine it. Relax. Steady….

Sgt Dixon, driving, is doing good, moving fast. Hasn't gotten stuck once. Moving really fast. Throwing all caution to the wind. Making all the other drivers behind do the same.

That's exactly why Kozak wanted him along, was glad he'd volunteered, 'cause he knows how to drive. Knows these humvees. Mraps too. Dixon's a good troop. Runs a tight motor pool. Kozak feels good he's here today. Happy he's not a talker either. Not like some guys, be over there gabbing his mouth off 'bout this-n-that worthless shit, nonstop never-ending about nuthin worth shit. Guys like Sandusky, it was Corporal Sandusky then, was his driver for a week of JRTC, wouldn't shut up about nuthin, it'll drive you batshit. Holloway too. Could be worse, could be Holloway driving him today. Or Sandusky. And wouldn't make this kinda time with either.

They haven't heard anything over the radios for a while. They don't have any sat comms. Can't even receive satcom down in here, and can't get a shot at the satellite to transmit any out.

Not that Kozak's going to transmit.

Not that he even cares to receive right now.

Maybe it's just plain better not to know what's going on up there in that village.

The last he heard, it was eight minutes ago, and it was Cop Valley Forge calling him on the FM company freq, which he could still get back then but the Cop couldn't hear him. Not then, not now. Can't even hear the Cop now. Then, back eight minutes ago, now coming up on nine, Lieut Frye called and said they didn't know if Kozak could hear him, but anyway, whether he could hear him or not, if he could, then he oughta know that the Zoo just reported they were receiving mortars again, a whole fricken barrage. Again.

FFE, Kozak thinks now.

Fire For Effect. Dialed in, rounds coming down one after another.

A whole fricken barrage. Fuckin barrage. *FFE*.

Fire For fuckin Effect.

FF—f—E.

Where're the Taliban gettin so many mortars?!

How they gettin mortars up there down them ridges so steep that the contour lines on the map are all one solid thick brown line?!

Didn't that Isaf lieutenant colonel say Shadow'd showed not shit up there, not heat signatures, not movement, not shit?!

Fuck, *This chew tastes like shit*, and Kozak spits the entire soggy wad into his Dr Pepper can.

Drops down the window a bit. Flicks the can out.

Pulls up the window.

FFE . . . .

He wants to, and doesn't want to, and really wants to, and doesn't do it.

Instead, checks his watch. 17 minutes.

God, he wants to, he wants it, why shouldn't he have it, just a little, yeh com'on he can have a little, knows his driver Dixon will see him and think bad of him, and *What the fuck who gives a fuck?*, he unsnaps the velcro of the pouch, pulls out the duct-taped soda bottle, twists off the cap, takes a good swallow.

Kabul, in the Isaf Op Center, cheers, fists in the airs, *"All right!"* and *"Hooah!"* and *"Thank God."*

Not Colonel Pluma. He's silent.

Granted, subdued cheers were warranted when the F-16 pilot relayed his *Ordnance off*, and these rowdy cheers now at the pilot's confirmation of *Two splashes on target*, along with the near-immediate satellite infrared imagery displayed on one of the flatscreens overlaid on the Google Earth image, showing twin splashes right where the red circle and grid coordinates of the original Poo in the compound next to the mountainside. In that weather down there the satellites can read the giant heat splash of the Jdam bombs but not the humans below the clouds, not the individual AKs fired, not the RPGs fired.

But what Pluma fears, why he isn't cheering, is that they've only Jdammed one mortar, not two.

That much he knows.

One of the two.

And isn't saying aloud.

He knows because he knows Zachary Dove and knows the implication behind Dove's calm words in his satcom back to Cop Valley Forge when that second mortar barrage began. Telling Base the rounds were at ten-second intervals, more or less, and not twin simultaneous launches of two mortar tubes like before.

Repeated, not twin simultaneous launches.

A single tube launching for ninety seconds, more or less.

Eight rounds out.

Eight airburst smoke, Dove reported.

And Pluma knew then, *They've moved the other mortar.*

Even the relayed LCMR POO-launch imagery displayed on that flatscreen over at the end, it showed just one exact mortar-tube POO, not two nearly in the same spot as it had in the first attack.

Confirmed for Pluma when, exactly 7 minutes, after the end of that 90-second single-mortar airburst-smoke FFE, that same mortar, indicated as the same spot on the LCMR POO-launch imagery, fired another 90-second 8-round airburst-smoke FFE.

Reported calmly by Dove to Valley Forge Base as an 8-round airburst of smoke.

About a minute later the F-16 pilot called in *Ordnance off.*

Then the *Two splashes on target.*

But Col Pluma knows they moved the other mortar.

It's still out there somewhere in that damn valley and it's not marked as a gridded POO because it's not firing, and Pluma knows that the enemy isn't going to fire it until they're damned ready to.

On their terms.

And Pluma knows that in the midst right this moment probably fighting for their very lives at an enemy assault coming through those clouds of covering smoke fired from the now-destroyed mortar tube before it was bombed, Zachary Dove has to be thinking that there's another mortar tube out there that those two beautiful Jdam explosions didn't touch.

On Fob Salerno it's raining a downpour.

The two huge forklifts splashing down the concrete taxiway.

A big square pallet on each.

6 by 6 by 5-foot high.

Pallet base is aluminum.

Each pallet covered in dark plastic. Cinched with a crisscrossing of 5,000lb-strength Air Force tie-down straps.

If you could pull the contents-packing-list from its protective plastic cover taped to one side of each pallet, you'd find each titled: RESUPPLY, EMERGENCY, PLATOON, 48 HOURS.

Then you'd find a complete list, including bulk quantity, all in strict military jargon, from specific ammo, to meds, to meals, to drinking water, to snacks, to batteries, to sandbags, to C-wire, to fence stakes, to ponchos and poncho liners, to ballistic eyepro, to chem lights, to LSA, to wool caps, to socks, all the way down to lip balm, foot powder, disposable razors and toothpaste.

That's, Paste, Hygiene, Dental, Individual.

Chief Warrant Pilot Chiarduchi up in the cab driving the first forklift.

Following a little behind, the second forklift, driven by the La-Z-Boy specialist shammer.

Chiarduchi turns at the T-intersection to head straight for the one CH-47 Chinook helicopter out of all of them parked out here that has its tail open, ramp out horizontal. His Chinook.

And there's a soldier sprinting through the rain, chasing the forklifts, taking blurred strides that must be six-foot each, catching up now with the second forklift, then catching up with Chiarduchi's and jumping up onto the step, grabbing the door handle and pounding on the cab's side window, "What the fuck you think you're doin?! Where the fuck you think you're goin?!"

More pounding, more yelling, this guy's older, he's not a kid, he's an SFC, a senior NCO, not just any zit-faced dickweed, he's at least in his early-thirties, and Chiarduchi brings the forklift to a stop.

About fifty yards from the back of his chopper.

The Sfc yanks the door open, demanding, "Where you goin with my forklifts, where you goin with my pallets?! I did not see any paperwork for anything loading out, and I especially didn't see Emergency Resupply pallets on any paperwork!"

Chiarduchi just stares this seething-angry man in the eye.

The Sfc dripping rain off like a busted gutter.

Eyes squinted in barely-contained physical rage.

Chiarduchi calm. Serious, emotionless.

Says, "There's a platoon thirty minutes out about to get overrun. Going to get overrun, we don't get them this. Fifty-plus, Americans and ANA."

"You got the paperwork?"

"American boys and Afghan boys. Soldiers. Fifty-plus."

"Let me see the paperwork."

"You want them on your conscience?"

"What I want, I wanna see your paperwork."

Chiarduchi won't break eye contact.

Neither will the Sfc.

"You just climb back down, Sarge," Chief Chiarduchi tells him. "You walk away. You know nothing. This isn't your concern."

He should, the Sfc knows that, he should climb back down and walk away. He should have never come out here in the first place, should have never chased after them out here. It's their problem, not his, he doesn't need this shit, he needs paperwork, and this old dude doesn't have paperwork, and that's a guar'nteed Article 15 at the very least and cut down to maybe E-5, or shit, specialist if he's lucky, and the wife's gonna kill him if he's stripped down to E-4, how're you gonna feed the kids now on E-4?, and why should he care, he doesn't know those fifty-plus Americans and Afghans, boys, soldiers, who gives a shit, they aint his problem, he really doesn't need this shit.

He takes his eyes off this warrant-five old dude pilot who's probably got more time in and more experience than a brigadier general, and he looks at the open Chinook just down there. Tail open, ramp out level horizontal. Waiting. He can barely make out the figures of two crew members there standing on the ramp waiting for them, one waving now, waving to come forward.

Rain coming down like a squall at sea between here and there.

"Y'know, Air is Red," the Sfc says harshly.

"Aint it a bitch," says Chief Chiarduchi. "Being colorblind."

The Sfc turns back to him. "You ever pallet-loaded the back of an airframe? Any airframe?"

Chiarduchi. "There's a first time for everything."

"Here, get out," the Sfc tells him. "You're gonna put the pallet and the forks through the fuselage walls. Go an' get your rotors turnin."

And he takes Chiarduchi's place in the cab, as Chiarduchi jumps down and sprints for his chopper, and

the Sfc floors it, jerking the giant forklift forward, aiming straight for the rear of the Chinook, expertly moving his hands on the levers to extend and raise the arm a bit and level off the forks carrying the big pallet, straight and true toward that narrow opening that this pallet is barely going to fit through, the crew chief there now clearly visible through this hurricane rain, arms up, hands waving the Sfc in straight and true, the Sfc's mind working as fast as his hands working the sticks, figuring it out, no problem, no problem at all, he'll just tell them later that the pilot said he had the paperwork in the helicopter up in the cockpit and went to get it to show him and *I loaded the pallet and Private Jackson the second pallet*, the pilot said he was coming back and he never showed, never did come back out, *You believe it?, I waited and he never showed* and they buttoned up the rear and the rotors were turning and they were gonna take the fuck off, and *What could I do, you want me to just sit there and have the rear rotor clip the forklift and then you've got a disabled bird with half the rotors gone, and the forklift's crunched, if it's still even standing, or is the best thing, I get our asses outta the way outta there,* and he sure couldn't make the pilot give him the paperwork if he didn't come back out with it and took off to boot, with Air Red, mind you, you believe that old dude crazy warrant-five?

Kabul, Isaf HQ, Media Briefing Room

General Pete St Claire and Dr Gene Hutchinsen are in the back of the room by the doors. No one noticed when they quietly slipped in just a minute ago.

The nineteen media persons take up about a quarter of the plush theater seats here in this media briefing room. Each completely engrossed in the edited-down video of the insurgents' 28-minute satcom-intercepted raw edit of yesterday in Wajma that is playing up front on the big flatscreen.

Among the reporters are AP, Reuters, Agence-France, CNN, Fox, Times of London, a NY Times stringer, Al Jazeera, a couple of Afghan locals, print and TV, and some freelancers like Nick Flowers.

Isaf PAO Colonel Katherine Gray-Nance tells the reporters, "The entire twenty-eight minutes that was captured are there." On the DVD that her captain assistant now passes out, one to each reporter.

"So you can see and judge for yourself that the video put out by the insurgents earlier today is extremely misleading and criminally out of context. You can judge and determine for yourself whether the actions of the civilian contractor were moral or legal, but there is no doubt that they were a response to the horrible, unjustified attack upon his American partner Doctor Robyn Banks. As, in the same spirit, the joint Afghan/American platoon responded with lethal force against the insurgents who were using women and children as their shields in that schoolhouse after, and only after, they had received multiple rocket-propelled grenades and small arms fire from the schoolhouse."

She sees Gen St Claire motion from the back that he'll take over, and he steps forward, "Gentlemen, ladies. If I may."

On Fob Salerno, in the air crew B-hut shed the rain is so loud on the tin roof it sounds like a dump truck is dropping a load of pea gravel on it, a never-ending load.

It's hard to hear the sat radio that's turned up full volume, tuned to the Valley Forge channel, but nothing's come across for a while now, ever since those last reports from the guy in that village Wajma of the commencement of yet another mortar attack and then the ground assault following it.

Most of the four medevac crews are here. Two Blackhawk. Two Apache.

Earlier, when they'd been watching a DVD—one of the *Transformers* movies, which it didn't even matter that you couldn't hear it over the rain on the roof—two of the Apache pilots came back from Brigade Toc and said to put the Valley Forge channel up on the sat radio because the shit was hitting the fan up in the mountains. That's when the Special Forces medic, Doc Boonzmann, or BZ, suggested none too pleasantly that you could see right through the coffee they had made, it was so weak, and he'd buy if someone else would fly. To the Green Beans coffeehouse. Everyone put in their order, they drew straws for who'd have to get soaked going over in the Gator, and the flight medic got the short straw.

Flight medic is back, he comes in right now with all the coffee, and no one heard him even drive up over all the rain, and "Chinook's out there, rotors turning, I think it's fixing to leave," he says. "They got a forklift down there loading a pallet."

"Air change from Red to Green?" someone asks.

"Yeh like, duh," someone else says, pointing above to the rain-pounding on the tin roof.

"That's Chiarduchi," one of the Apache pilots says. "He was in the Toc, he looked pissed. He infilled them into Wajma his morning. Slotted to exfil them."

"BZ," the flight medic says. "That's your guys. In the Tic. In the mountains. Wajma."

Which is what BZ's been thinking, and he grabs up his M4, one-shoulders his aid ruck and he's out the door, sprinting in the rain, and sure enough that's the rotors turning of a Chinook down there, so loud with the engines' whine it can be heard from here, and those are two forklifts heading away, and

BZ is less than a quarter of the way when the flight medic pulls up beside him in the Gator, and nothing has to be said, as BZ hops aboard, and they speed toward the Chinook whose blades are blurring faster, engines louder.

The Chinook is buttoned up in the rear, ramp up, and its whole body lifts up about a foot as it starts rolling forward on its four wheels, and

the flight medic turns the Gator to ride right under the rotors close alongside and up abreast underneath the port door-gunner's open window, with

BZ now standing in the Gator and yelling up to the door gunner, "Wajma?! Wajma?! Going to Wajma!?"

Nothing from door gunner Rapley behind his tinted dark helmet visor, whether he can hear or not or just chooses not to say, and BZ figures what the hey, nothing risked nothing gained, and he heaves his aid ruck up onto the opening where Rapley pulls it inside, and BZ grabs onto the frame and jumps up off the Gator, and Rapley pulls him in.

In the Isaf media briefing room, at the lectern Gen St Claire has outlined for the reporters the events of yesterday in Wajma as reported in the Zoo Platoon's AAR.

He told them that Col Gray-Nance would be answering any questions that they might have dealing with the Human Terrain Team civilian PhD anthropologist Dr Robyn Banks, whose body was at this very moment en route back to her family in Maryland.

He has outlined the investigation that he has personally overseen since the intercepted video was passed down from Cent Com.

"Early this morning," he tells them, "we air assaulted the platoon, and a platoon of their Afghan National Army counterparts as well, back to the village under the command of the investigating officer and his team. The investigating officer is Lieutenant Colonel Zachary Dove, about whom Colonel Gray-Nance will be happy to give you a brief bio, but about whom, should you choose to do your own further inquiry, I am confident you will find that he is above reproach. I am confident that you will find that he is of the integrity to uncover without qualms the truth about what happened there yesterday. As you will see from the highly selectively edited video snippets the Anti-Afghan Forces released earlier today compared with the entire intercepted video that Colonel Gray-Nance has prepared for you, it is as likely—or perhaps more so—that the Anti-Coalition Forces themselves killed those victims either before the joint American-Afghan humanitarian patrol arrived in the village yesterday or after they had left."

The general pauses. He wants that to sink in.

As in, sink in.

As in, do not have your cable channels and networks keep repeating those selectively-edited snippets without at least putting them in context. Don't have your newspapers and websites screaming headlines with photos of those women and children killed by American GIs.

Without him commanding them outright *Don't.*

If it sounds like he's insisting on *Don't,* demanding that they *Don't,* they'll do it all the more.

St Claire's voice is even, without emotion, soothing, certain and gentle. "I gave Lieutenant Colonel Dove just one directive before he left. To return with the truth. Unfortunately, just before noon, just a few short hours ago, the platoon came under lethal enemy sniper fire. Two were killed, two seriously wounded. Severe and unpredicted weather moved into the area at the same time, limiting our ability to support the joint US and Coalition element and to extract them. The adverse weather presently encompasses most of Ghazni, Zabul, Paktya, Khowst and Paktika provinces. Colonel Gray-Nance, is there a weather briefing scheduled for these folks?"

"Yes sir."

Of course, St Claire already knew that.

"Most of you are familiar with Nato protocol, which strictly limits our flexibility to maneuver air assets in such weather as the provinces are experiencing and have been for just about four hours now. Needless to say, because of the weather conditions communications with Lieutenant Colonel Dove and the platoon have been spotty at best. Within the hour the platoon was able to break through on comms, and they reported that they were under a battalion-sized ground assault. Including indirect fire. Mortars. They repulsed that initial assault. Shortly thereafter, according to our intermittent radio communications with them, they have come under a second assault, including again indirect fire weapons. They repulsed that assault, which was immediately followed by a third. Again, accompanied with indirect fire."

He lets all that get absorbed.

Then, "Estimated Anti-Coalition forces are battalion-sized-plus."

Some of the reporters jotting notes, exact quotes, on writers' pads. Most holding up little micro-digital recorders. Two filming, along with a PAO video sergeant.

"In civilian terms, that's four to six hundred men."

Fast note-taking.

St Claire continues. "I was just informed minutes ago that the F-16 air assets that we did deploy, they're standing by on-station just at the edge of the storm. Which is allowable under Nato protocol. Those F-16 assets were able to neutralize the indirect fire mortars with precision guided Joint Direct Attack Munitions. What most of you know as Jdam bombs."

He pauses. Lets that settle. Lets them write it down.

Before the bad news.

"Our last radio contact with the platoon was just prior to our neutralizing the indirect fire threat. We can only assume that the platoon remains under assault by an enemy force in the hundreds. Many multiple times its own—". He pauses for effect. "Including their handful of ANA coalition partners, their present strength is under fifty men."

With the QRF, in the lead truck, squelch and static come from one of the mounted radios.

Followed by Lieut Frye's voice broken up a bit but clearly readable. "Awesome Seven, Awesome Seven, this is Valley Forge Base, how do you read me, Awesome Seven? Over."

Awesome Seven, as in First Sergeant Kozak.

He doesn't answer.

Again, "Awesome Seven, this is Valley Forge, this is Awesome Xray. Be aware, Dragon Six says Romeo Tango Bravo. I repeat, Dragon Six orders Romeo Tango Bravo. Immediately."

Dragon Six, the lieutenant colonel, battalion commander.

Romeo Tango Bravo. RTB. Return To Base.

Immediately.

As in, this very second.

Seems, one of the staff NCOs up in Brigade Toc, with nothing better to do, was scanning around on the computer Blue Force Tracker map curious about what that Wajma Valley looked like on a map and found the thirteen tiny blue dots of Kozak's QRF in the gorge leading up to the valley.

Well, that's not something that a good brigade staff NCO just lets sit. Ignores. Pretends he never saw.

Which of course led to the full-bird brigade commander on the horn yelling to Dragon Six something to the effect of *Just what the hell's goin on up there, you got a renegade company outside the wire in direct violation of orders?!*

Which got Dragon Six yelling to little ol' nobody Lieut Frye at Valley Forge something to the effect of the same thing.

"Do you read me, Awesome Seven?" Lieut Frye asks. "I repeat. Dragon Six is ordering Romeo Tango Bravo. Romeo Tango Bravo."

Kozak doesn't bother to reply.

To his way of thinking, it's just as well *They think we're out of range of radio comms.*

The old saying, *What we don't know won't hurt them.*

Isaf, in the media briefing room, Gen St Claire lets his breath out slowly, silently. Runs his eyes from one reporter to the next, across them all.

Now a deep, silent inhale.

A moment.

Then, "We can rush to judgment and condemn the men of that platoon for a still-as-yet unproved enemy propaganda release," he says in what is just above a whisper that forces the reporters behind the first row to have to lean forward to hear.

"Remember, I just ask you to remember, right this very minute those men are fighting for their very lives.

"Because we have yet to be granted from Command in Brussels permission to break Nato safety protocol, we are not free to send in the aircraft that can give those men fighting alone immediate close air support and to extract them and extract their casualties as well.

"I know that these days it is inappropriate to speak of religion in a public setting, but I would ask that you consider, in whatever religion of your choosing, I would ask you to consider a small prayer for those few handful of men right now."

Fob Salerno, in the Chinook a hundred feet off the ground as it shoots forward above the sitting helicopters through the curtain of rain and out over the runway, banking and climbing to head in the direction of the unseen mountains.

The control tower had just radioed asking what the hell was going on and why was there an aircraft with rotors turning when Air is Red.

Chief Chiarduchi told them hell yeh he knew Air was Red but he had an emergency resupply mission for the minute it turned Green and he had a red light on, a mechanical glitch, the disgrunificator was acting up, and he needed to take it up for a minute just to get the kinks out just to make sure they were airworthy when Air turned Green and they were ordered to execute the mission.

Be back in a minute.

Just a sixty-second test flight.

Just going to take it over the runway, max out the engines, then back.

Sixty seconds.

Just before lifting off, before Crew Chief Jarbodie reported that some crazy dude in the Gator had come up and hopped up in the window, Chiarduchi had run it by one final time with the crew, over the radio intercom, *Gentleman, this is volunteer. If you want out, get out right now. No turning back once we're airborne.*

Not the lewy copilot, not gunners Rapley and Maneosupa and not Crew Chief Jarbodie said anything but *Hooah, let's get this bucket o'bolts movin*, and *What, we aint there yet?*, and *As good a day as any to lose a rocker.*

As in the rocker bar under the three sergeant stripes of Jarbodie's staff sergeant rank.

And Jarbodie isn't happy about the way he's had to do a fast improvisation with the two pallets. Blocked the first with two aluminum stops on the leading edge so it and the second pallet won't slide forward right through him, the doorgunners then the pilots. The second's up tight to the first and is held in place in the rear by the base of the ramp itself.

Bad day to have his spec-4 junior crew chief wake up with the screaming shits and get taken off the manifest. One man short on the morning infil, no problem; short now, no time to strap down the pallets properly. No time on this end right here. No time for unstrapping on that end, once they arrive destination to drop them in flight.

Jarbodie doesn't like it but has unshakable confidence that his pilot is going to take the banking with gentle, precise expertise, knowing that too steep, too hard, too radical and the pallets can tilt over right into the fuselage walls.

And that would be a world of hurt.

Oh, and if the two aluminum stops here break free, the pallets are also gonna go through this dude here whoever the hell he is.

"Emergency resupply?!" BZ yells right up into Jarbodie's helmet to be heard in here. "Is it?!" The pallets. "Resupply?! For the troops trapped in the mountains?! In the village?! Wajma?!"

"Who wants to know?!"

"S—F! Medic! 18—series! I heard they're in the shit! Multiple casualties! Nightingale's grounded! You going to Wajma?!"

"We're not landing!"

A grin, a nod, and a thumbs-up from BZ.

Jarbodie repeats it. "We're! Not! Landing!"

"No prob!"

Isaf, in the media briefing room, Gen St Claire assures the reporters that he's instructed Col Gray-Nance to provide them everything they might need.

He informs them that his weather personnel have expressed confidence that the storm should have passed through by noon tomorrow, and if the reporters choose to stay, the colonel has reserved the VIP bungalow for them, with complete secure-internet access. When flight restrictions are lifted, he assures them, he'll either get them to Bagram for the arrival of the platoon and the investigating team or directly to the scene of the battle in the valley. As the case may be.

In the meantime, he is leaving them in Col Gray-Nance's very capable hands. He has pressing concerns in the operations center.

With the QRF, in the lead truck 1st Sgt Kozak feels good, the map on his mounted computer screen showing that this corner they're moving through—fully in the fast-running water, the hummer's wheels bouncing over the boulders, waves rolling over the hood—opens up into the final couple hundred meters of gorge before Wajma Valley.

The rain started about five minutes ago, light at first and now coming down medium.

Coming out of the corner, Kozak is happy and can't hold back an "Awright!", seeing the gorge open up enough that Sgt Dixon can steer the hummer up out of the edge of the deep flash-flood stream and run along the ground. And there, sure enough, not three hundred meters ahead is the narrow gap between the mountainsides that would be the entrance to the valley. To the village.

It's difficult to make out everything through the rain, the clouds a ceiling less than a hundred feet up, and the inadequate hummer wipers hardly clearing the windshields. And when Dixon can make out more clearly ahead, "Holy shit," he tells Kozak. "I don't like it, Top."

What looks like rapids, a lot of water cascading through that narrow gap going up into the valley.

Kozak leans forward to try and see better. It's way up there, but he can see the water rimming and splashing up, almost like it's going over a dam, that it's dammed-up, flash-flood dammed-up. "Zoo made it through yesterday," he says.

"Yeh but, Top," from Dixon. "It wasn't raining yesterday."

Common sense out of a sergeant E-5 mechanic.

Kozak gets on the QRF 3rd platoon freq and tells the Mrap right behind him to get up here, take the lead, see how deep it is up there. See if they can get through. See if they're gonna hafta maybe blow a bigger opening, a wider opening, let that water through, get it flowing more shallow and slower, maybe, if they have to, blow apart some of the dammed-up shit with some AT-4s.

Anti-tank Weapon.

A throw-away bazooka. The one-time-use U.S. disposable version of the RPG. But with an even bigger wallop.

Kozak tells them to see if it's shallow enough and they can get close and then if they might can pull the shit out of the way with their winch. Tells the entire QRF platoon to come on forward up into this part of the gorge, break it off, every other truck taking an opposite side of the raging stream, get up as tight as they can to the mountain. Get in a herringbone. Half the trucks covering one side of the mountain, the other half covering the other, opposite, across the raging water.

Yeh sure, thinks Kozak, *what are they gonna cover, what are they gonna shoot, who they gonna shoot at, can't see nuthin in this rain and those clouds so low.*

He makes sure the volume of the other radio is up high. Takes that handset and calls the Zoo.

Wajma, on the roof of the schoolhouse, Redcloud hears Kozak's call and lets Lieut Col Dove down below on the veranda answer it.

All wearing a radio hear it. The three squad leaders, Sniper Rodriquez, Wolfe, Slurpee, Doc Eberly.

Some whoops and hollers upon hearing that Kozak and his QRF are so near, just down the stream, at the gap into this valley, just a mile and change, not even two, away, and but for the rain and clouds and fog they could almost be seen.

The word is passed quickly. *QRF's just down there! Top's here!*

The Zoo needs a Quick Reaction Force right now.

Any help at all.

Desperately.

They were hit with three mortar FFEs, each followed by an assault, and they barely managed to beat back the last assault, just barely, as the light rain had begun. If the enemy were sharp they had to have noticed there at the end of that third assault the radical change in the sound of rifle fire from the school as Zoosters ran out of 5.56 and switched to the spare AKs.

Everyone was out of the few hand grenades each had carried in, three or four maybe each. They'd thrown most on the second assault, when the enemy had made it over the rock wall and it looked pretty dire. Only a few had any left for that final enemy rush close on the third assault.

About half of them had to make the switch from empty M4 to AK. Of the half still up on the walls and firing. And mostly missing now on the AKs, without the accuracy of their M4s' Acogs and Aimpoints—with the AKs' iron sights that aren't even zeroed.

Missing, but putting rounds downrange.

Firepower.

A continuous fusillade sent out at the black-clad figures dashing, firing AKs on auto, reaching the wall, over it, closer.

Some were cut down just in front of the steps.

Some reached the veranda walls, six feet higher than their heads, and were cut down point-blank by Utah's guys or Dove or the five ANA left or Holloway who was now up and firing from the instant after that third FFE when Dove slapped his helmet hard and he knew that meant he was through with the radios and being RTO then and it was time to fight for all their lives.

And black-clad enemy cut down close by Wolfe who at one point, on a final M4 mag, quickly retreated inside, stripped Capt Cathay seated guard outside the aid station of all her mags but the one in her weapon, told her this time, "Fire em up when they get in here!", and ran back out, throwing his final hand grenade toward the rock wall and firing his M4 even as he exited at the figures so close just a stride away from the bottom step.

Tally it up, which Redcloud already has, and Dove's heard passed on the radio, and it's not good.

Tran and Bybee on the M240 are down to nine 7.62 rounds on their final belt.

The two Saws are dry. Those two Saw gunners, Garcia and Lantrell, picked up M4s dropped by guys who fell or the spare AKs and fired them in the final minutes.

Pvt Finkle has two 40mm grenades left. One chambered in his 203, one sitting on the parapet wall like a lone sentinel. By the third assault,

Finkle was reduced to firing the grenades at the enemy almost reaching the wall. No more worrying about the RPG gunners way out there. One, it was desperation time up close here. Two, the RPGs weren't flying anymore. *What, what'd, they run out? They're outta RPGs?!!!*

And Redcloud had yelled right into Finkle's ear, "Close up! Close up!"

Finkle's two 40mm grenades are more than the other grenadiers have. Nell's grenadier here on the roof was hit and one of Ketchum's men took up the 203 and fired, like Finkle, grenades at the final rush down there coming up on the other side of the wall.

Utah's two grenadiers on the veranda were hit and their ammo run through by other guys picking up their guns.

It was in the second assault that Rodriquez had realized that this was really the shit, up close, not the hajj way out there, and he swapped out his Knight sniper rifle for an AK to pick off close-range those coming over the wall just right below.

Spec Howie, up here beside Rodriquez, has two full M4 mags and one in his weapon. It takes him so long to get a clear steady sight picture through his Aimpoint, and he's more scared of Rodriquez yelling at him for wasting ammo than of the onrushing enemy, he only fired when he was sure he had a target for absolute sure. Now he's seated back against the parapet, facing away, sucking hard on the CamelBak that Rodriquez gave him.

Rodriquez pats his thigh. "You awright? You hit?"

No, Howie's alright.

"Done good, muchacho," from Rodriquez. "Betcha got infantry blue runnin through yer blood. Jus didn't know it."

A single gunshot down below. Another. Another.

Rodriquez sees it's the ANA sergeant and his four guys doing the headshots to guarantee killed and no playing-possum from the steps and on out to the rock wall. One of the ANA guys has one arm dangling useless, dripping blood from a ripped sleeve tied at the elbow as a bandage.

Rodriquez picks up his sniper rifle. Lays it on the parapet. Gets comfortable and focused through the scope. Time for him. Out 500 meters and beyond if anything moves it's his. Going to be a little tougher in this rain now coming harder. Have to adjust a bit for it. Aim just a hair higher. That's elevation. How hard's the wind now blowing out there? From which direction? Windage.

Ssgt Nell is thinking about the same as he slaps his last magazine into his M4. If it moves from the rock wall to 500 meters out it's his.

Redcloud slaps two magazines on the parapet wall beside Nell for Nell to use. Redcloud has three more left. He'd fired less than the others. His priority had been their firing. Their accurate, controlled firing.

And Redcloud knows now that the enemy had to have noticed the change in the pitch and sound of the gunfire. Your deaf senile grandma in a wheelchair in a nursing home can tell the difference between an M4 firing and an AK. The Taliban know, so *They know we're out of ammo. Almost out. Now's the time I assault again if I'm them.*

Dove knows the same. These enemy would be assaulting. *Who knows how many more are in those foxholes?* They're all out of RPGs. *Must be out of rocket-propelled grenades. That's certain, they've run out. That other mortar isn't set up to fire yet. They're out of mortar rounds.* Maybe luck has turned the Zoo's way.

"Thank the Air Force for those Jdams," Kyle Wolfe tells him. "Thank the scientists for all those years of education they spent that went into inventing them. Taking engineering courses instead of underwater basket-weaving and sociology bullshit and women's studies and minority studies and 19th century Ugandan poetry. Engineering and rocket-propulsion." He heads down the steps, three of Utah's guys following, to start retrieving enemy weapons and ammo.

Dove knows that the enemy saved that other 120 mortar, and if they had shells they'd use them now. They're not, but they saved it, it was important to protect it, which means they know they've got more mortar rounds on the way. *Coming down those goat trail ratlines down the mountain as we speak.*

He calls Nouri out. Out here, to stay with him, to listen to the silent walkie-talkies. If they start talking, he wants to know.

Nouri spent the three mortar barrages and assaults inside. With Doc Eberly. Helping in there, if only to pressure-hold bandages. Nothing wrong with that. Some terps carry weapons, AKs for the most part, and like mixing it up in the actual fight. Others, like Nouri, have soft household hands. Still, he's disgusted by the cowardice of Corporal Sandusky. Such cowardice in battle, and almost useless there to help Doc Eberly that Doc basically told him to take the dead out of here and into the next room and cover them with ponchos.

The dead.

That's a tally no one wants to think about.

Dove knows it, the dead and wounded, and he would send it up to Valley Forge and Isaf, but satcom's not getting through anymore right now in this new rain coming.

For the ANA it's 3 KIA, 3 WIA. 1 of the 3 wounded still on the walls and out there now putting a bullet in the heads of the enemy.

Of the 43 Americans who choppered in this morning, including Dove himself and his two companions and the captain and his RTO and Wolfe and Nick Flowers, 20 are out of the fight.

Of those, 8 are KIA or about nearly so, it's just a matter of minutes or maybe a half hour.

12 WIA bad enough to be in the aid station permanently. Or moved over to the other classroom if the wait for medevac is going to be 18 hours.

Of the 23 still on the walls, only a handful remain unscratched, without a drop of their own blood on their uniforms. Of the wounded still on the walls, some are bad enough—

shot, gashed or cut badly by shrapnel or flying rock or cement or burned by the flaming debris from the few Willie Pete RPGs the enemy included in their assaults

—were this a normal everyday Tic, these guys would have been medevaced already or there would be a medevac on the way for them.

In a normal everyday Tic.

Today they're still on the walls.

You know why.

Nick Flowers, one of those 23, who's shooting only a camera, no guns, hasn't been touched, not even scratched. Nothing enough to draw even a single drop of blood.

Pvt Finkle too.

And Ketchum.

And Lieut Col Dove.

It just happens that way.

Don't ask why.

They know—just as guys who've been there before know, from whatever war—it's called luck.

Nick is inside filming.

Where the unlucky are.

Where three of the wounded are on the concrete floor outside the classrooms, Doc Eberly working on one.

Where they were left because the guys dragging them in from the veranda had to get back out there to repel the last assault.

Where Van Louse is tearing a uniform shirt into strips. For bandages and tourniquets.

Where out here and in the aid station classroom guys are grunting, moaning, crying and don't want to be, except the pain is too much to bear.

Where there is no more morphine.

Where one of Utah's squad, a specialist nicknamed Vampire, feels no pain, and not because of morphine, because he hasn't had any, and not because he's dead or unconscious, because he's as alive and as awake as ever, he knows everything that's going on, he knows that the whole right side of his face and neck and shoulder and down under where his body armor was, down to his waist and thigh is all burned from that blinding flash of that Willie Pete round, and the pain before was so overridingly horrible that he now feels nothing, he's just blocked it, his brain is refusing to recognize it. Nerve synapses refusing to spark. *Yeh yeh,* he tells Sandusky now who's holding a canteen to his lips. *More.*

The number tally that Dove likes is the QRF.

13 vehicles, Kozak reported. Most of 3rd Platoon. 28 soldiers.

"We're loaded for bear," Kozak had said over the radio.

"You're not a minute too early," Redcloud had replied. "We're 'bout down to slingshots and K-bars. I'm kinda surprised battalion gave permission to go outside the wire on a Red."

"You know how that goes," Kozak said. "Better to ask forgiveness than permission."

And Dove, listening on his radio, had said nothing to that, as if he hadn't heard. *What I don't know won't hurt them.* The first sergeant and a near entire platoon out this far isn't just a lackadaisical matter of stepping outside the wire to take a leak or check on some strange sound coming from out there on the other side of the Hescos.

It's not a lackadaisical anything to battalion and brigade commanders who don't like standing orders deliberately ignored or disobeyed.

Or to their generals above.

It's not a lackadaisical anything to Dove and Redcloud and all the Zoosters here who know the QRF is just down there so near. To guys down to their last couple of M4 mags and a disparate collection of AKs.

It's a blessing from God.

To guys in the aid station, like Utah's guy Vampire, when Van Louse announced in a sing-song happy cheer, "Third Herd's just down the river, you can almost see em right now!"

Thank God.

Which is what Capt Cathay is praying. *Thank you, God, Thank you, Jesus, Thank you, Lord.* She sees the joy, the happiness, the lightness in the soldiers coming and going faster now, moving with a positive purpose, as if a weight's been lifted. The QRF's coming. Just downriver. They've arrived. We're going to be rescued.

Might be a challenge getting through right here, Kozak had relayed. The narrow opening into the valley's blocked, like a waterfall. But the guys were checking it out. Should be up there to the Zoo in five, ten minutes max. Soon as they can get through.

"You be careful, the enemy's all over the valley floor," Dove had advised. "They're up in caves, you can't see them. Get your trucks in overwatch position and make the run fast coming upstream. They're dug-in in trenches and foxholes all up the beach."

"Top, we're not going to be able to offer you much covering fire," Redcloud had added. "And nothing out further than the reach of our Alpha Kilos. That's battlefield litter Alpha Kilo Four Sevens we're down to."

"Well, Travis," Kozak said, "we've come to rectify that situation."

"This is Zoo Three Seven," Ssgt Ketchum had cut in on the radio. "Third Herd, I love you guys. Zoo's gonna owe you one bigtime."

Redcloud couldn't quite wrap his mind around it right away when Kozak had said that that opening down there up here into the valley was blocked. Like a waterfall.

How could it be blocked? Yeh, *We've had all this rain from heaven*, but only yesterday Redcloud came through there both coming and going, and he doesn't remember it as anything special, as any trouble. It's no more than twenty, thirty feet wide across, sure, but the water wasn't deep, he doesn't remember it being, and yeh it's gotta be running faster now, but it's not that much deeper right out close here, a truck's gotta be able to get through down there.

Unless it's now blocked by that artillery barrage from the Cop sending half the mountainside there coming down on those snipers. But that was at least four or five hundred meters, maybe a thousand, this side of it, it couldn't be right there.

Redcloud didn't notice anything this morning when they'd flown right over it coming in, but he was in the back of the Chinook and wasn't looking and didn't think to look back over the ramp at the narrow gap, concerned then as they were speeding over the beach, descending, about getting this chopper of Zoosters down and spread out.

What Redcloud has no way of knowing is that last night around ten o'clock an al-Qaeda Chechen or Saudi or Turk demolition squad waited for the end of the dull humming of the Shadow surveillance drone overhead—like the sound of a lawn mower down the street at the end of the block. Five minutes of silence would mean that the drone was gone for sure and it might be a while before it returned, if it did at all, and the demo squad moved out of their cave and blew the four charges they'd planted a couple hundred feet up the mountainsides at the narrow gap.

Which is what Wolfe thought.

He hadn't seen any big huge boulders or trees floating downstream to dam it up. Talibs did it. *Before we came*.

Which is what he told Dove, who had come out to help drag Talib bodies over to the rock wall where Wolfe, Utah and a couple of his guys were placing them.

"Y'know, Colonel," Wolfe had said, "now maybe you might start reevaluating your reluctance to admit to the mythical Afghan warrior." The Americans would be coming back in two or three days, right, isn't that what they told the indig? They wanted the Americans back. Obviously. So, if they dammed it up, they'd be catching the platoon and whoever else in a boxed canyon coming up here, with nowhere to turn around, and then rain an ambush down.

Number Two, Wolfe speculated, they knew the Americans would be coming by air choppering in and be trapped in the valley itself, and Number Three, they know the first-line QRF's gonna be out of the Cop in ground vehicles and are going to be blocked from getting into the valley reaching the trapped platoon. "What do you think, gonna admit that these guys are all War College graduates? They taking West Point correspondence courses online?"

Dove wouldn't give in so easily. "Or, coincidence. This amount of rain this quick, that's just a landslide down there, the consequence of so much rain. A landslide's natural. And breachable."

"That's the Methodist, Baptist, Presbyterian prayer side of you," Wolfe teased.

It's a couple of minutes later, and Kozak comes over the platoon radio, "This is Awesome Seven. Fire in the hole."

Followed by the dim sound of two small explosions way down there too far, too rainy, too cloudy to see.

But everybody is looking that way anyway.

Again over the platoon radio, Kozak, "Fire in the hole."

Two more dim explosions.

Pfc Holloway's got his fingers crossed. Both hands. And knows it.

Inside, Capt Cathay asks Ssgt Nell, "What's that, Sergeant?"

"Top's blastin his way through. AT-fours." Listens, as he now hears over his radio Kozak announce that it's looking good, they've got an opening blown through, be just a minute while they've got to let the river water pour out.

Nell's got a smile and a thumbs-up for Cathay.

Kabul, in the Isaf Op Center

Col Pluma runs it through in his mind one more time. General St Claire's going to come through those doors any second now and the best thing to do is just let the situation speak for itself.

Situations.

For themselves.

If the general wants to speak with the two-star at RC-East, let him call him up and yell at him, demand answers from him, though Pluma knows that St Claire never yells, that he'll know that RC-East doesn't have an explanation, the same as neither does the brigade nor the battalion.

There is no rational explanation.

That sharp sudden quick pain that just hit Pluma in the gut is the realization that Doctor Hutchinsen is going to give him that look, that squint of total scorn, disgust at his ignorance, as if it's he, Pluma himself, who gave the order that put that Valley Forge brain-dead first sergeant and his thirteen trucks out there against all reason. As if it were he, Pluma himself, who gave that hotshot air crew a big thumbs-up, *To infinity and beyond, Go get em boys*, they're flying right now not seven minutes out, and *How in the name of the Father, the Son, and the Holy Ghost are they doing it in that weather?*, Air Ops says not a hundred feet off the ground, and *Alone without wingman cover or Apache gunship cover?*

Screw Doctor Gene Hutchinsen.

Screw that Valley Forge first sergeant, screw those Salerno flyboys. What, they think we can't see where every goddamn one of our hummers and Mraps is in this country at any one time, exact, pinpointed to ten meters? They think we can't put up on that screen a dot for every last goddamn airframe, rotary or fixed-wing, in the air anywhere from the Mediterranean to the Indian Ocean? They think we're blind or stupid? Think they can pull it all over on us?

Jesus, Mary and Joseph, how do they think they can get away with it?

They can't.

That lays there hard for Col Pluma. They can't get away with direct disregard for regulations, violation of standing orders, disobedience of direct orders to RTB, endangering the lives of their men. And equipment. Multi-million dollar equipment.

They can't get away with it, Pluma knows. They know they can't. Know they won't.

And they don't care.

They don't care, he thinks.

This entire room is so quiet. Everyone in here knows that General St Claire's going to be walking through those doors right about now.

All of them on the Quick Reaction Force, Pluma thinks, *the whole flight crew, they don't care.*

"CH-47 approximately six mikes out," one of the Air officers announces quietly.

Mikes, as in minutes.

Everyone in here feels as Pluma knows, that those aviators in that Chinook and those soldiers in those trucks down there in that gorge, they're defying all orders and they don't care.

They don't care.

And everybody in here might be imagining that they're in those trucks, they're piloting that Chinook, that's who they are, that's what they would be doing if they were in that position, if they were stationed in that Cop, if they were an aviator in that brigade out of Salerno.

Col Pluma's heart now slows, his breathing eases, he's enveloped with a warmth, a remembrance of innocence in childhood when there is no evil, just good, just purity of family and security, as if he's at home in Kearney in bed and awakening to see snow falling outside and he's never going to come out from under the down quilt. As if he's nine or ten taking a bath and slides all the way down into the tub on his back with his eyes closed and the warm water rippling over to cover his face entirely.

He's in his mother's womb.

Wet and warm and enclosed secure.

Pure, without sin.

Man as goodness.

The Garden of Eden before the apple, he thinks.

He eases into the sure realization that the first sergeant and his troops and that flight crew don't care, not a hoot, don't give a good goddamn, precisely because they care.

Because they care so very much.

With the QRF

With twenty-one years in, a tour here with the Rangers in 2002, three tours in Iraq and now here again this deployment, 1st Sgt Kozak knows that you can do everything just exactly right, by the book, down to the last detail, and things can still just go to shit on you.

Sometimes the going-to-shit is because there's an enemy out there playing against you, countering your moves, whether yours are pre-planned or improvised, and those bad guys' actions amount to wrenches thrown into your works.

Except the wrenches are bullets and rockets and IEDs, that kind of stuff.

The bad guys here are Talibs.

Or al-Qaeda Chechens or Saudis or Turks or Uzbeks.

Jihadists, plainly. Pashtun or not.

Sometimes it's just bad luck, has nothing to do with the bad guys out there countering you. A guy, one of your men, turns a steering wheel two inches the wrong way. Right instead of left.

Maybe his hand slipped on a greasy spot on the wheel.

Or a bee flew in from the open turret and buzzed his head.

Or a bunch of boulders and rocks slammed the side of the truck.

Bad luck, a wrench.

Which is why if you're Kozak you're right now atop the driver's side of the rolled-over Mrap trying like hell to get the heavy armor door pulled up open.

From the moment driving out the gate of Valley Forge up until now everything had gone just about perfect, better than Kozak could have dreamed. No truck break-downs. None even getting stuck. Movement was fast, considering the high water. Fast on any day. Record time. No RPG potshots coming down from the steep mountainsides.

The first wrench was the dammed opening into the valley. It doesn't matter whether it was a natural landslide or enemy-caused.

It's a wrench, deal with it.

Get the lead Mrap up close to investigate, get all the other trucks in here in a protective herringbone, you've only lost five or six minutes so far, and the Zoosters up there in the valley just a stone's throw away have already beaten back the last attack and are in a lull, they've survived, they're alright for right now, no problem.

Sergeant Cornberger, the man on the turret 240 of the Mrap pulled-up on the streambank right at the blockage, radios back that it looks passable on the right if with maybe an AT-4 or two to blow the big rocks out of the way. Kozak gives a big okay, *Have at it.*

So Cornberger gets two AT-4s out and Kozak's gunner here, Spec Palmer, gets two, and with Kozak's *"Fire in the hole!"* they both fire the anti-tank rockets at the rocks and boulders on the right side, and water and rock spray and boulders tumble down as the half-dammed stream behind pours through.

And if you're Kozak you go *Fuckin-A!*, you see it's worked, and you instruct the Mrap ahead to give it a few minutes for the water to go down, and they do and it does and from your position back a little ways it looks pretty damn clear, shallow enough and running slow enough that even your low-sitting humvee here'll get through.

A-okay, you give the Mrap the word, *Move it on through*, and you feel good 'cause you've batted away that wrench thrown at you.

Pfc Tripp was driving that lead Mrap.

32-year-old Pfc Tripp.

Who goes by the nickname Triple Shot, which goes way back to when he was in Jump School and was known in the barracks as the cool dude who'd do a shot of anything hard—providing you provide it—and follow it with a can of PBR—Pabst Blue Ribbon, his own, he always had at least a case in a big cooler. And he'd do it past midnight, as long as you provided the hard stuff, and, regardless, still he'd be standing tall in formation 0530 for all the physical training the three-week parachute course dished out daily. Would about make the trainees near him puke during those dawn runs from all the stink of alcohol coming off him in sweat, but that wasn't his problem.

The name Tripp quickly became Triple Shot, and that nickname goes a long way in explaining why at 32, in the Army since 19, he, Tripp, is just a Pfc.

He's been busted in rank so many times he's even lost count. Every time for drinking and fighting, and drinking and driving, and drinking and getting punched by a wife or girlfriend for blowing through his paycheck when there were all those kids' mouths to feed, and him never punching back—not a chick, that aint right—but drinking and drinking more and drinking and drinking.

Most recent bust was from sergeant down to Pfc, and that was only a couple of months before deployment here, and he was lucky even just to be allowed to stay in, as his Comanche Company commander said he'd had it with him, Triple Shot was a sodden worthless drunk and would always forever more be a sodden worthless drunk and was a detriment to the United States Army if only for the amount of paperwork generated by all his non-judicial punishments on account of his being a sodden worthless drunk.

But Capt Washington said he'd take him for Awesome, hell, from all he'd ever heard he was a good soldier in the field, overseas, deployed, in the combat zone, where booze was off-limits, outlawed, hard to get.

Well, not hard for everyone; but impossible for Triple Shot.

There's no one who cares enough to send it to him. Those foam-packed mouthwash bottles. Those duct-tape-wrapped soda bottles. Buying the booze, filling the bottles, taping them, packaging them in thick bubblewrap in flat-rate boxes, getting to the post office to mail the boxes, that's just not going to happen with the ex-wives or ex-girlfriends who've all had his who-knows-how-many kids and have to split the meager auto-deducted child-support allotments between them. And aren't all that overly thrilled about it. Or him.

When it gets right down to it, it was those bi-monthly auto-deducted child-support payments which was the reason Capt Washington took Triple Shot into Awesome. Where was that child-support coming from if he was kicked out into the street jobless? Drunk and jobless.

Sfc Northwich, 3rd's platoon sergeant, had put Triple Shot driver of the lead Mrap on today's QRF because here in the war zone he's learned that an always sober Triple Shot is an infantryman's infantryman, with a ton of experience and four tours in combat and a reckless disregard for his own safety and an aggressive motivation to accomplish the mission, any mission, fast, now, the sooner the better, almost as if to just get it done and get back to the barracks where he can start on the shots and PBR, though he's got none of either here and has been completely dry these months, not even a taste of a sip of 3.5 beer wetting his lips.

In fact, Triple Shot had started out today in the turret on the gun, put there by Sergeant Cornberger here who said that he was going to drive, preferring it to being up exposed in the rain on the gun.

Rain, as in, the weather-related H2O type and, more importantly, the enemy-related RPG and 7.62 type.

Not that Sgt Cornberger admitted as much.

Just outside the Cop's gate Northwich could see the first Mrap bouncing and swaying and backtracking trying to cross the wadi behind Kozak's and Dixon's hummer and he called ahead and ordered right there a change—Triple Shot from gun to driver.

Today anyone can be a gunner.

"Get your ass on the gun, Cornberger," Northwich ordered, *"You drive like your granny on Quaaludes."*

Today it's not the gunner that matters, it's the driver, with the bad weather and high water and the speed they'd need to get up to Wajma and the Zoo.

No one would ever blame Triple Shot for overturning the truck.

It was just the opposite.

He was inching the Mrap up into the opening, knowing he was carving the path for the others to follow, even using the V hull to push boulders clear.

At the midway point, he could see ahead of him the beach of the valley under the ceiling of low clouds.

He could see that just ahead to the right was a whirlpool to be skirted.

He would tweak the steering wheel slightly left, that would work fine to avoid it. And he quickly radioed Top, advising of the whirlpool, to warn the others who would soon be following.

At the top of his vision he could see that suddenly lots of black dots were on the beach, black forms, men, the enemy, coming out of the ground, *Are there trenches they've got dug? Are those guns they're carrying?* And he heard over the intercom from Cornberger ready on the machinegun above him, "Taliban! Gonna light em up!!!"

That's when the gorilla-sized wrench was thrown into the works.

Whether it was simply all the rain loosening the earth, or that soaked-soil loosening along with the vibrations from the four AT-4s fired just a few minutes ago, or both combined along with the concussive vibrations of Cornberger firing the 240 machinegun at those black-clad gun-toting forms ahead, it doesn't matter, because this wrench wasn't going to be foreseen or forestalled or avoided.

Triple Shot tweaked the wheel exactly enough to the left to skirt the whirlpool, couldn't hear anything over the engine and the rain and the *clap-clap-clap-clap* of the machinegun just above, then heard Sgt Cornberger's "Oh shit watch out!" over the intercom, and

Triple Shot looked up his side window to see the rockslide slam into the Mrap, and everything went to the right—truck and steering wheel, and the front right wheel into the whirlpool and the truck rolling over onto that side and nosing down into the water.

With a clear view of it all, Kozak would swear that the collapse of the mountainside happened a couple of seconds before Cornberger opened up on the machinegun—before Kozak saw the gun's muzzle flashes and heard its *clap-clap-claps*. Because Kozak knows that at the sight of the mountainside giving way he immediately slapped Dixon's arm *"Go go go!"* to push forward as close as possible to where the Mrap had just been at the edge of the water, and at seeing and hearing Cornberger firing, Kozak radioed the rest *"Tic Tic Tic"* then watched the rockslide smash into the Mrap and the huge truck veer, tilt, slide and topple over.

With Kozak's years and experience so much is instinctual, without conscious thought. Like, slapping Dixon *"Go go go"* to get up close to the coming potential problem, essentially charging the enemy.

Like, knowing without thinking about it, water and heavy armor don't mix.

Whether that heavy armor is a 20-ton Mrap.

Or an individual's helmet and 35-pound body armor.

Before Dixon had even bounced the humvee up the hundred feet or so to the edge of the water, Kozak had flipped off his own helmet and pulled the quick release of his body armor, radioed the others *"Cover us, bring it in tighter"*, flung his door open as Dixon braked to a stop, yelled at him *"Let's go!"*, left his carbine and hopped out, letting his body armor fall off then tossing it back onto the seat.

Kozak was jumping up onto the rear of the Mrap when Dixon—a mechanic, remember, not infantry—up to his knees in the water, keyed in on Kozak and realized *Shit, he's got nothing on* and retreated to the hummer to leave his own M4, helmet and body armor.

Kozak is right now atop the toppled Mrap. Which is the driver's side, the left, port.

He can't get the driver's huge armor door open. It's too heavy to lift straight up against gravity and probably still combat-locked anyway, it's not giving.

Kozak can't see anyone inside through the window, and bullets are *cracking* over his head and *smacking*, ricocheting off the truck, from those black figures running this way, and Kozak gets down to his belly tight against the steel, assesses the whirlpool covering the entire hood halfway across the driver's windshield.

He slides on his belly to look down the other side, the roof, and sees that water is pouring in the gun turret. Sergeant Cornberger is nowhere to be seen. Glancing back, Kozak sees that the truck is actually at an angle, which he hadn't noticed climbing up the back or scampering to the driver's door. The back end is sticking up in the air out of the water, this whole truck is wedged, it aint goin nowhere.

Where's Cornberger, where'd he go?! When Kozak had seen the rockslide hit and the truck topple, he'd lost sight of Cornberger and the turret. *Where's Triple Shot, how'm I gonna get him out?!*

Kozak sees Dixon's bare head peek up over the back end here, and

Dixon sees Kozak lying belly-down and sees those black figures firing what he realizes are these *cracks* going by him, and he's sure First Sergeant Kozak is screaming at him to get this rear hatch open, and he's thankful to get to duck back down and try it, knowing already it'll be in vain, he's tried it already, he's a mechanic and knows these Mraps and knows it's combat-locked and aint going to open.

And Kozak has got to get inside, get Triple Shot out and Cornberger too, he's gotta be in there, and he eases down head-first to go through the turret and freezes in place as he sees inside the most rational, most sane, most logical thing in the face of certain death that he's ever seen and that he will ever see, he knows, however long he lives, if only for the next thirty seconds or thirty months or thirty years or until he's lying on the bed in the nursing home and through blurred vision feels the presence of his grandkids and great grandkids there for his death.

What Kozak sees is an infantryman's infantryman.

It's upsidedown for him, seeing that the front half of the inside of this Mrap is totally submerged and Cornberger's body, unconscious or dead, is on its back on a jumble of ammo crates, held in place by Triple Shot, also on his back, his shoulders with Cornberger's legs over them, and Triple Shot is methodically pulling the pins of a can of thermite grenades and jamming the grenades individually against the radios in their wall rack, which is now the ceiling, and wedging now a couple of others between crates of hand grenades and claymore mines.

Thermite grenades burn through things.

A directed flame at 4,000 degrees Fahrenheit, one can burn through an engine block.

They're designed to destroy things.

Like radios that you don't want to fall into enemy hands.

Like hand grenades and claymores that you want to explode and further destroy the entire inside of an Mrap and everything in it that you don't want to fall into enemy hands.

Triple Shot now sees Kozak and yells, "The rear, rear end!", which Kozak knows means Triple Shot's going to bring Cornberger out through the door hatch there.

And it's only later, if Kozak lives past these next thirty seconds—

with the enemy's bullets smacking the rocks, smacking the truck, something burning across his back

—that he might think it through and imagine what Triple Shot did from the moment that the truck started to topple in a rollover into the whirlpool.

Actually, it began before.

Minutes before, after Cornberger had fired off his two AT-4s and they were waiting for the water to rush though, and Triple Shot was studying the opening to figure how to drive through it safely.

Water and heavy armor don't mix.

Triple Shot had removed his helmet then and quick-released his body armor. Roger that, whaddaya need body armor for when you're inside an armored vehicle?

He had felt for the release buckle of his shoulder harness. Just to be sure. Let muscle memory know where it is instantly if he needs it.

Made sure the door was combat-locked. Can't have it flying open.

Pulled his Army-issue strap-cutting blade from its loop on his body armor and held it in one hand.

When the topple ended, he was out of the harness and moving back to where Cornberger was limp in the harness, his head and torso outside, crushed against boulders. Triple Shot cut him out of the web harness, pulled him in, pushed him up out of the water onto the strewn crates. He then laid on his back to brace and keep Cornberger from sinking into the water and knew he had to zero the radios first and foremost before anything else.

Zero is to erase all memory and crypto from a radio. Wipe it clean. Without crypto a radio is useless to the enemy.

To zero you've got to follow a particular sequence. This button, this knob.

No time for dicking around. The water's rising, he could hear the enemy rounds hitting the truck's thick skin and windows.

He zeroed the four radios, took the necessary extra moments to check them to ensure they were zeroed, then he dug out the can of thermites from the back of the rack where he knew he'd put them when he'd loaded the truck earlier back on the Cop.

If anyone had seen Triple Shot take the three steps to ensure the crypted radios wouldn't fall into enemy hands, they might suggest his nickname be changed to Triple Check.

1: Zero.

2: Check the zero.

3: Thermites.

Kozak would only see the thermites and not Triple Shot's earlier precautions, not his cutting Cornberger out and dragging him inside and not his bracing him and zeroing the radios.

The only one who would ever know all that would be Triple Shot himself, and none of that would ever have meant shit to him as anything important or worth mattering to anyone other than it was just doing what an infantryman is supposed to do.

At the schoolhouse, the gunfire way down there at the gap can be heard as dim pops which echo into a shuffling jumble. It's been going on for a few minutes now. It can't be seen through the rain and clouds. It's been joined by the deeper thumps and the echoes of bigger guns. Have to be the .50-cals of the QRF. And now some echoing *ploom-ploom-plooms* of explosions of Mark-19 grenades.

On the roof, Redcloud had been calling Kozak on the Zoo's freq and getting no response. So he menu-scrolled to find the 3rd Platoon freq, switched, called and got Northwich responding. "Looks like we kicked up a hornet's nest," Northwich told him. "Awesome Seven is taking Whiskey India Alphas. Got a truck stuck bad trying to go through. I'll get back to you."

Redcloud told Ketchum to pass that down to Dove on the platoon freq, and he'd stay on 3rd's freq, monitoring for a sitrep on the Tic down there.

Down below on the other side of the rock wall, Wolfe, Utah and a handful of his men were still dealing with the Talib bodies. They had already gathered up the weapons and ammo, and they had dumped onto ponchos for intel this-n-that whatever little things from the Talibs' pockets.

A couple more walkie-talkies.

Wrist watches.

Combs. Small wads of Pakistani rupees.

Pouches of chewing tobacco. Or marijuana.

A Koran.

A small collection of U.S. Army binos and older-model night vision goggles and compasses and CamelBaks, and Nick Flowers, back outside again, filming, zoomed his camera in on the big surprise, a ragged, well-worn Maxim magazine, last month's edition.

When Dove had been out helping drag bodies over to the wall, he'd told Wolfe and Utah, "I don't really want to look at those bodies."

"I'm with you, Colonel," Wolfe said, and one of Utah's guys came up with the idea of dumping all the bodies over onto the other side of the rock wall and sitting them all up leaned back against the wall, like they'd be a welcoming committee for the Talibs on the next assault.

Two birds with one stone, actually.

A welcoming committee, out of sight, even with arms up waving their Taliban buddies hello.

Dove let that go, pretended he didn't hear it, knew it was wiser not to stop it and understood the wisdom of allowing soldiers their black humor, any humor, in this such situation. He headed back for the veranda, had second thoughts and turned to offer, "No displaying wounds, body parts . . . genitals. If you will."

"Aw, Colonel," Wolfe had said. "You underestimate the high class and sophistication and Quaker morality of these enlightened Zoosters."

Utah, serious and sincere, "Don't worry, sir," reassured Dove.

And Utah and Wolfe stand back now to gaze upon the couple dozen dead enemy the guys have already sat up against the wall, legs stretched out straight, hands laid flat on their laps, and it's easy to visualize the next hundred-plus to be sat down the entire length of the rock wall.

Cool.

Awesome.

Nick Flowers, on his knees for a better angle, pans his camera along the line-up.

"You could get the cover of Time Magazine," Wolfe jokes to Nick.

"I could really get a cover," Nick chuckles, "if, Utah, if you'd get some of your guys to start pissing on them. Wait, put that Koran in their hands and then piss."

It is funny.

Funny, and everyone knows that's an instant ticket to Leavenworth, do not pass Go, do not collect $200.

But awright to joke about.

Three more bodies sat up, it does look good.

"Write your dude up for a Silver Star," Wolfe jokes to Utah about the one who came up with the idea.

"I'm going to put him in for Officer Candidate School. In ten years they'll make him Commandant of West Point."

Their backs are turned, so they don't see the flash of brightness in the clouds down at the valley opening, but they whip around fast at the *kabloom* that follows by three seconds to see the second, larger flash of brightness, followed now by a louder *kabloom*.

With the QRF, the two explosions were the ammo going off inside the Mrap.

The explosions threw off the two Talibs who had been crawling atop the Mrap firing their AKs. The explosions lifted the huge truck into the air, and it settled nose-first even deeper into the whirlpool, its ass-end sticking up at an even greater angle than before.

The turret gunners have stopped firing. There are no more enemy targets appearing atop the Mrap or on the boulders up there and from higher up on the gap's mountainsides.

The Talibs who'd made it atop the Mrap or the boulders and managed to direct their fire on the Americans in the open and that close humvee have all been cut down by the turret gunners.

While all that was going on, Kozak and Triple Shot carried Cornberger's limp body over to against the mountainside, and Dixon had jumped into the humvee and whipped it around and bounced it over to position it close to shelter them.

The Mrap has double exploded, no more black-clad enemy are appearing in the narrow gap, and Palmer, the .50 gunner here in Kozak's humvee, now flops down onto his butt inside, and Dixon turns to him to see his hand and forearm are torn apart bleeding in pulsating squirts, the bad luck of an enemy's bullet, and

Dixon is frozen stupefied until gunner Palmer's scream of "Tourniquet! Tourniquet!" wakes him to search his body armor he's been seated back against for the pouch where he knows he's supposed to have a tourniquet with his first aid kit in one special ammo pouch they're all supposed to have, and

"Here!" Palmer yells at him, holding out his own tourniquet he's pulled from his pouch in the bloody torn-up fingers of his other crippled hand. "Tie it! I can't!"

Outside, Kozak can find no pulse on Cornberger, realizes his head's turned at an angle nearly backwards.

The neck's broken.

It had to be instant, hitting the boulders.

He didn't even know it. Wouldn't have even known it.

Rollovers and boulders don't mix.

Triple Shot is seated back against the humvee tire. Doing nothing. Just sucking in air in huge gulps.

Now for Kozak, in this first free moment of no immediate danger, no one shooting at him, no one else to help Triple Shot drag through the water and rocks and carry over the sand to the safety here, yes now safe with the hummer here sheltering them, it is only now that Kozak feels the burning pain across his lower back.

He feels for it and finds his shirt and tee-shirt torn, and turns to show it to Triple Shot. "Look. How bad is it, how bad am I hit?"

It takes a moment for Triple Shot to focus his eyes to see that Kozak has got a long strip of a flesh-wound of tiny bubbles of blood across the width of his back just above his belt. Like an asphalt burn you get on your hands and knees when you crash your bike in the street as a kid.

"You got another Purple Heart, Top," Triple Shot says. "Bullet jus grazed y'u. Piece a'cake."

Kozak turns to him.

"Piece a'cake, Top," Triple Shot repeats.

Kozak looks him in the eyes. Something's not right.

Triple Shot smiles. "All my gear's in there, Firs' Sar'en," he says. Meaning, in his wrecked, blown-up Mrap. "Rifle, Nods, IBA. Gonna write me out a combat loss?"

"Don't worry about your gear. Got you covered, Triple Shot."

"It's me, Top. They're gonna think I hocked it. For a case of PBR."

And now Kozak sees dark moisture is quickly soaking through Triple Shot's shirt across the belly. Just realizes now that, like him, Triple Shot's not wearing his body armor. No helmet either.

Body armor and water don't mix. *Triple Shot, always thinkin.* The body armor/water thing.

Just one problem: No body armor and AK fire don't mix.

Kozak sees too much dark moisture. Blood. Too fast.

And Triple Shot is not moving. Not animated.

Hands hanging loose at his sides.

Not even a moan.

Not even a grimace.

"Tell me, Top," Triple Shot says. "Just a grazin like yers?"

Kozak yanks up Triple Shot's shirt. Bleeding pulp of three exit wounds. Pieces and flaps of intestines.

The complete opposite of Kozak's own flesh-wound across the back.

Kozak eases Triple Shot away from the tire and inspects his back. Three small neat bleeding bullet entry holes in-line mid-back.

Kozak eases Triple Shot back against the tire, jumps to his feet, yanks open the hummer door, grabs the handset of the platoon radio, and calls, "This is Awesome Seven. I need a medic here asap."

In the very last truck, Sfc Northwich's humvee, no words needed between Northwich and his driver who slaps the gear lever into D and punches the gas.

Except for Northwich and Kozak, everyone here today is either a driver or gunner. This driver is 3rd Platoon's medic. Doc O'Toole.

Kabul, in the Isaf Op Center, Gen St Claire hasn't said a word since coming in. He had allowed Col Pluma to give him the general outline of things, and others added details.

Dr Hutchinsen had asked them to zoom in the Blue Force Tracker map on the big flatscreen to show only the valley and the gorge where the thirteen dots of the Quick Reaction trucks were stationary.

Done. Then on one of the automatic 30-second map resets the forward blue dot had moved to where the brown contour lines are squeezed tight at the opening of the valley.

Okay, they were moving, they're moving through, would have been going through St Claire's mind.

And he recognized that he'd thought *Okay,* and it's not something he would say aloud in here, not *Okay,* though he sensed that everyone in here was thinking it, thinking that exact thing, cheering them on.

Except for Hutch. Hutch wouldn't be. Just for spite, because he didn't conceptualize the Cop Valley Forge-based QRF.

St Claire's got radio comms with the brigade if he wants, and with Valley Forge if he wanted, which he doesn't, and he's got no comms at all with those thirteen trucks there in the QRF.

Playing possum, St Claire had thought. And thinks now. He knows they could hear him if they wanted, they could at the very least talk FM back to their Cop. Though he'd be wrong about that, not having taken into consideration the distance to the Cop and the deep terrain of the gorge. Nor the bad weather.

For a couple of minutes of map resets there had been no movement of that lead vehicle, that blue dot stationary in the valley opening.

Goddamn, there's nothing a commander hates more than knowing something's wrong and not having comms with his units on the ground in the middle of that something wrong.

St Claire then would not allow himself the perverse pleasure of rationalizing that that first sergeant and his QRF shouldn't even be there, as Hutch would be thinking, that they deserve anything they're getting, they broke regulations, ignored and disobeyed direct orders to return to base. He would have loved to have had that pleasure of knowing the orders are correct and moral and the lawbreakers should suffer. Instead, he saw them, those rogues, that first sergeant and his renegade QRF, as being so close to Zachary Dove and that platoon, *Com'on com'on get moving, get up there*, he'd thought.

Though he would never say that out loud.

Then on a map reset suddenly that lead blue dot was gone.

Murmurs among the staff officers.

Pluma told the one on that laptop station to reset it *Now, right now*.

Still no blue dot of that lead vehicle.

Where did it go? It couldn't just disappear?

Count them, the blue dots. 12.

Not 13.

Everyone counted them. 12.

Three map resets later and that new-lead blue dot, the one that had been closest to the opening, behind the now-missing one, it had moved back further and up against the solid brown lines of vertical contour.

Retreat? What the hell's going on down there?

Nothing. No comms. Nothing changed in the blue dots for a few resets.

Then the map reset a minute ago showed a blue dot a third of the way up the line of the herringbone formation, alone in the middle of it.

Two resets later two-thirds of the way up.

This most recent reset now shows it right next to the first blue dot, against the vertical contour lines.

A staff officer who's brought up on his laptop the info stats on all the QRF vehicles announces, "Those are two humvees. The rest, the other eleven are Mraps, the Cougars."

"Eleven or ten?" Dr Hutchinsen asks scornfully.

No one answers.

A map of Cop Valley Forge's entire AO pops up on another flat-screen.

"We've got the beacon and GPS on the Chinook again," an officer announces.

The single tiny red blinking dot on that map.

The rogue, renegade CH-47.

A number of officers immediately look to Gen St Claire to see his reaction.

None.

Not even a twitch of a cheek muscle.

Not a slight squint of an eye.

In the school, Capt Cathay knows that all that distant firing and those two explosions were not a good sign.

She knows it because from her position seated outside Doc Eberly's aid station she's got a clear view out the front doors of Lieut Col Dove at the top of the steps, his back to her for a long time now, staring out down there where she knows all that firing and those explosions came from.

And now the quiet.

No distant echoing firing.

A couple of minutes quiet from out there.

And now she can see Dove turn in profile, and he's talking into the handset of the little radio in that pouch on his body armor.

She stops Van Louse, "Sergeant, please, sergeant."

"Spec'list, ma'am. You okay, you need something?"

"What's happening with the rescue, with your company that's coming, shouldn't they be here already?"

"That's Third Platoon. The QRF. They hit the shit, ma'am."

Now come a quick succession of distant *Pahumbangs*, followed by dim echoes of RPG explosions and a massive mess of distant .50-cal and M240-B firing.

3rd musta hit the shit again.

"You can do something for me, Specialist."

"What's that, ma'am, you want water? Need Doc?"

"Help me. Please." To get outside onto the veranda.

"I have to ask Doc, ma'am. I don't think I can move you."

"Sergeant Rodriquez!" she calls to him just down the stairs.

"Ma'am. Qué pasa, tiene problema, got a problem?"

"I need to get out there. With the colonel."

Van Louse, "I don't think Doc wants her moved."

Rodriquez, "You want in the fight, Cap'n?"

"I – can't – stay – here."

Van Louse, "Doc's gonna say no, no way, you don't mess 'round with a back injury."

Cathay is adamant, "I – need – to – do – something."

Rodriquez, "I don't know, ma'am."

An order from her, "Sergeant." Then, "Please."

"Yer the boss. Let's get ya geared up." And Rodriquez has Van Louse help him get her body armor that's been just draped on her now over her head and on her, makes sure her M4's secure in her arms in her lap, and "Here, 'mano," he gives Van Louse his rifle to carry then lifts Cathay, sleeping bag and air mattress and all, from under her legs and arms and carries her out onto the veranda and sets her down seated against the doorway.

Dove just looks at her. No comment.

Rodriquez, "She wants t'be a grunt, Cur'nel. Can't never have too many guns." He takes his rifle from Van Louse. Tells him, "Ketch says, if yer done helpin Doc to get your ass back up there. Hey, and make sure my boy Spec'list Chubby puts some oil on his bolt, wouldya?"

The 3rd Platoon distant firing is tapering.

Now nothing. Quiet again.

Dove responds to a call on his platoon radio. Listens.

Cathay watches his face. Stern. His eyes staring down there where the valley opening can't be seen through the rain and clouds. She looks at Rodriquez who is also intent listening on his headset that he pushes tight into one ear to hear better. He's also looking down that way.

Cathay hears Dove say, "Roger, Awesome Seven, good copy. Keep us posted. But I'd advise, if it's impassable, Romeo Tango Bravo, and have medevac waiting for you at Valley Forge. Dove out."

Cathay hears him then radio-call Redcloud on the roof, "Zoo Seven, did you get all that?"

She asks Rodriquez, "What's going on?"

"Way down there." He points, "The saddle where the river goes down through, that be where the Third Herd is. 'Bout two thousan' six hundred meters is all."

"Who's Awesome Seven?"

"Top Sarge Kozak. Old Ranger, he knows his shit. Like a pit bull dog. Get his back up in a corner, gonna bite yer leg clean off here at the knee."

A look from Dove, and Rodriquez shrugs, admits, "Hey sir, gotta think pos'tive. Know what they say — neg'tive's for bat'ries, shammers and losers."

Dove, "I'd prefer you not dealing in false positives, Sergeant." And to Capt Cathay, reality. "It's not looking good, Laura."

With the QRF it's looking worse.

The enemy had fired six rocket-propelled grenades from six different positions hidden in the base of the clouds on the mountainside on both sides of the gap.

The turret gunners here had seen the brightness in the clouds along with the *Pahumbangs* and had opened up in that mess of .50-cal and 240 fire into the clouds where the brightness had been.

No more RPGs. No AK fire from there.

But one RPG had exploded on the doorframe of Northwich's humvee parked astride Kozak's, with a good part of the shrapnel going inside where 3rd Platoon medic Doc O'Toole had left the driver's door open.

The steering wheel is shredded, the dash instruments obliterated, the gas and brake pedals gone, and wires cut, killing the engine.

SFC Northwich was spared from most of the shrapnel and probable death because he was faced out his open door leaning out to Doc O'Toole working on Triple Shot to hand him more bandages.

Nevertheless, Northwich was hit pretty good all along his left shoulder and arm and butt and thigh. With the sheer burning pain in his shoulder he had all he could do not to scream *Sons'a'bitches!*, and he'd yanked open the back door then managed to give immediate aid to his gunner who he'd seen collapse inside after taking a good deal of the shrapnel in both legs from the thighs down.

One of the rockets had been high, above on the mountainside, and Kozak had felt down his butt and thighs a slashing of the shrapnel that ricocheted, and he felt down there for the torn uniform and wetness of blood and figured *Later*, he had responsibility for far more right then.

A third rocket had hit short, slamming Kozak's hummer with shrapnel, dirt and rock at the driver's side front, terrifying Dixon half out of his wits, but nothing got through the armor and thick glass, though that front tire was punctured to shit.

The three other rockets were targeted at the lead Mrap across the stream against the mountain on the other side.

One was high, against the mountainside, no kaboom, a dud.

A second exploded off the front bumper.

The third had hit the turret, and the driver reported over the radio that the gunner there was hit bad in the shoulder and arm, and *"I'm gonna need Doc here asap!"*

Kozak had ordered the driver to get that truck *"Over here right now"*, the medic was here.

Now the Mrap next behind the hummers here opens up with a full belt of 240 raking the mountainside at the gap across the way, and an Mrap over there does the same with its 240 on the opposite mountainside of the gap. As Kozak had ordered earlier when the firing had stopped. Every minute or so rake the mountains there, keep the enemy from getting into position up there.

Kozak has just gotten off the horn with the lite colonel with the Zoo up there in the ville. *The colonel's alright, especially for an officer*, he figures, he didn't give him a negative, didn't say they had to find a way through to come to their aid, had to fight their way up into the valley. Didn't even suggest it. Says it's Kozak's choice, RTB or not. Advises yes.

Kozak counts his wounded.

Cornberger dead, nothing to do about it, *We've got the body, we didn't lose it, it didn't wash away, we aint leaving it, and that's a positive.*

Triple Shot, gut-shot, critical, *gonna need more'n we got with Doc.*

His gunner here, Palmer, arm dangling, tourniquet, *Gonna need higher asap or he's gonna lose that arm.*

Northwich, that shoulder and arm hanging useless, a lot of blood there, but he's functioning, helping Doc in the back there and *I know they're gonna have to tourniquet* both legs of Northwich's gunner in there.

The gunner in that Mrap coming across right now from the other side, if he's hit bad like the driver said, *He's gonna need a medevac, and we don't got a medevac here and we aint gettin a medevac here.*

Triple Shot's Mrap up there, it's combat-loss, it's gone, *We aint winchin it, we aint movin it, it's history.* And there's no way of going around it, getting by it, getting through there.

Kozak has already assessed Northwich's hummer, it's undriveable, but he's figured it out, he's got his plan, and he gets on the radio in his truck to tell all the other trucks, "We're gonna move out of here. Gonna move back five hundred meters. Back around that curve back there. Get secure. Assess our next step. Front to back, you-all just follow our lead. Keep the fire up on the hills like you're doing. Australian Peel, front to back."

Here comes the Mrap from the other side, and Kozak hops up on the driver's running board, pulls open the door and tells the driver to get it set to tow Northwich's hummer, hook it up and don't worry about the electrical and air lines, "Ignore all that shit, I wanna be movin outta here in zero-three mikes!"

Kozak hops down, and hears over the headset of his small pouched radio that he switched to Zoo's freq as soon as he'd put his body armor back on something he would have never expected to hear in a thousand years.

An unfamiliar voice saying "Tattoo Zoo Platoon, calling Tattoo Zoo Platoon, this is your rotary air resupply, I repeat, rotary air resupply. We're two mikes out. We're gonna need a smoke where you want these FedEx bundles we've got for you."

Rotary air resupply?

Two mikes out?

FedEx bundles?

Son of a bitch!!!

Kozak can't help it, doesn't even think about how much it's going to hurt his torn-up back, butt and thighs, and he leaps all his five-foot-six stocky self into the air, screaming to the heavens as if he's just won the eighty-million-dollar lottery a guttural "Ahhh-oooo-gahhhhh!!!"

And he snaps one big salute up there to what every U.S. Army Ranger for all time knows is the mythical omnipresent great power, the Ranger in the Sky.

Damn, if Kozak isn't angry-as-hell at himself that he and his QRF has failed and can't make it to the Zoo, but the Ranger in the Sky's taken care of it, the cav's here all the same.

In the Chinook, Chief Warrant Pilot Chiarduchi is running late. He's at least seven minutes slower than he'd wanted to be. Should have been in that valley seven minutes ago.

He'd had no choice but to cut his speed even more once he'd entered the gorge. Until then he'd been able to stay a couple of hundred feet AGL just beneath the clouds, and with forward visibility through the rain maybe three-quarters of a mile he pushed the air speed to max with the weight and loose load back there, taking the turns extra-extra-wide for less bank. In the gorge the clouds are at most sixty or seventy feet off the river down there, and he's had to keep the twin rotors just under them to sense that they wouldn't be smacking the mountain on either side. Constant corners and switchbacks in here as well, and for them he's had to cut forward speed back to what felt to him like a hover to minimize the bank angle because of those two pallets unstrapped-down in the rear.

When he'd had his copilot lieutenant put the radio on Zoo Platoon's freq a minute ago and call them, he hadn't even been sure he would get an answer, whether the platoon had been overrun or not. Jesus H Christ was he elated to hear a voice come up on the other end, "This is Zoo Seven. This isn't a joke, is it? Over."

Zoo Seven, that would be the second in command. *What happened to the first, to the Six?*, Chiarduchi had thought. *Tough times for those grunts on the ground.*

"No joke, Tattoo Zoo," the copilot had responded. "Special delivery. Two pallets. Hot drop." Meaning, not landing. "Give us smoke. Over."

"Roger," Chiarduchi had heard the reply from Zoo Seven. "If you're coming upriver, we're at the far end of the valley. In the school building. We'll give you green smoke. I repeat, green."

The cloud ceiling is even lower, and Chiarduchi's had to cut altitude and he knows his landing gear can't be more than 25 feet off the ground and can almost feel the wheels skimming the river down there, and as he hovers the big bird forward out of this corner then accelerates he sees all those spread-out trucks down below, *Wherever they came from, whoever the hell they are,* five on one side against the mountain, the others on the other side, and black smoke coming out of whatever that is up ahead there where the mountainsides come together—

Holy Toledo!, it's an Mrap, sticking up out of the river, burning!

"Here we go, gentlemen," he announces over the intercom. "Indian country."

And the gap is so narrow there where that Mrap has smoke pouring up out he thinks exactly what his copilot must be thinking, *How're we gonna squeeze through there? The rotor blades are going to hit on both sides!*

Over the Zoo Platoon freq he hears what's got to be that short bald guy with the shiny bare head down there throwing his fist into the air shouting over the radio, *"Cavalry's here, Zoosters! Hear that, Zoosters?! Cav's overhead!!"*

Down on the ground 1st Sgt Kozak is the only one of the QRF on the Zoo freq and the only one to have just learned a minute ago that any chopper rescue was in the air, never mind so close, and every one of the turret gunners turned in surprise hearing the Chinook come around that bend back there, and dollars-to-donuts every last one of them felt that winning-the-lottery instant-jolt ecstasy that their buddies up there in the Zoo were going to be saved.

Hoots!

Hollers!

Fists thrown into the air!

The wheels and the dark belly of the bird, and the blurring twin rotors, all so close screaming overhead that you can almost reach up and touch the tires, and

dollars-to-donuts again every last guy down here watching is thinking *No no no, too narrow!*, visualizing the rotors smacking the mountainside of the gap and breaking apart in a krillion pieces and the fat body of the Chinook jerking and twisting and coming down in a fireball like they've seen a thousand times in movies.

What they see is the Chinook suddenly jump up into the clouds and completely disappearing except for its landing gear—the four sets of wheels skimming the bottom of the clouds right through the narrow gap, out the other side—then the whole Chinook suddenly dropping back down, with its twin rotors now skimming the bottom of the clouds, and it all going out of sight behind the mountain into the valley.

In the Chinook it's a piece of flying that Special Forces medic BZ Boonzmann had never seen before.

Ever.

And that's been as a passenger in a lot of different choppers over a lot of years.

Sure, maybe you can be precise and fancy in a nimble Huey or a Blackhawk, but not in a big whale-like, railroad-tanker-car-size Shithook.

Not just pulled-out-of-your-ass suddenly out of nowhere.

Not so fast, so spontaneous.

Not so exact.

So gutsy.

To jump up into clouds, blind now, not knowing what you're going to run smack into in the next five seconds.

BZ is standing behind the pilots, as he has been ever since they entered the gorge, just to watch the tight flying, trapped in on all four sides—the clouds above, ground so close below, the mountainsides they were gracefully, slowly thundering through.

Seeing that narrow gap ahead, he had held his breath. Yeh, everybody thinks that Green Berets, like their SF counterparts in the Navy, the Seals, are never scared, have no fear, are as brave as they come, but that's just street-talk myth. They've got just as much fear as anyone else. Just know how to hide it, ride through it, not let it incapacitate them, make them worthless, make them wusses. They know how to fake it. Pretend they're better than mere mortals and hold themselves in braggart postures that don't even recognize the existence of danger or its rational fear. That's all just for show. If you're BZ, a Green Beanie, what you know is that when you're like here and now, when you can be killed any second and it's completely out of your hands because someone else is in charge, is doing the driving, you can be scared all you want, but that doesn't do shit, doesn't solve anything, and you've got to trust those whose hands you've placed your life in. Like these pilots. This is their baby here, this is their bird, it's their job, they're the experts, and BZ has to trust them like he expects others to trust him when he's doing his job, he's an SF medic and doesn't want anyone mistrusting him, insecure about him, backseat-driving him.

Jumped up into the clouds by the pilots, blind like them, BZ caught his breath, and he still holds it and imagines that his pulse has slowed, almost stopped, thinking *If these pilots are going to kill us all, so be it.*

He tries now to pierce his eyes through the puffy white of the clouds, feels a thump-thump-like jerk, darts his eyes down to the pilot's hands on the sticks and sees just easy tweaks, feels the bird level itself, exact again, feels a slight lightness, like an elevator starting down, looks ahead through the windshields again, and they're out of the clouds, just below them, and this is that valley, the river so close right below and all those clumps of black figures on the beach, and now rifle flashes from them, and he hears the *twack-twacking* of bullets hitting the thin skin here.

The lieutenant copilot had an adrenaline-rush at that thump-thump-like jerk, knew it's a feel that you never want to experience because it's the rotors hitting something, and if it's a mountain that's the end of it, goodnight Irene, sayonara señorita.

Which is why, for Chief Warrant Chiarduchi, when his hands immediately twitched to adjust for the thump-thump jerk and the bird responded beautifully, just as he wanted, he knew it was all right, that the tips of the blades hadn't been broken off, the blades remained in balance, and he knew the thump-thump wasn't the mountain, it was just a rock, they'd nicked a couple of rocks, they'd chopped a couple of branches of a tree, he should have ascended another foot, maybe two, he'll have to note that on the return, five feet higher.

Neither Chiarduchi nor his copilot could imagine that the thump-thump was the forward rotor blades encountering two Talibs who'd been making their way down the mountainside with the intent to pop under the clouds just long enough to fire off an RPG each at the trucks down on the other side. The lead guy, forward and a little lower, had the blades hit him just a hair above the chin, and he never knew it.

The second guy was sliced at the waist all the way through just shy of the spine. He knew it for about three seconds, as his body tottered, leaving his legs standing and his torso and head back perpendicular against the rocks, like a Ponderosa pine cut in half in a windstorm.

Had a sarcastic joker like Kyle Wolfe not been down there somewhere at the school ahead and instead been up here on the mountain to see it, he'd have had a laugh and thought the virgins couldn't catch a break in heaven today. Now seventy-five are gonna have to be happy with a guy without a head. Another seventy-five with a guy with nothing but a butt, dick and two legs.

You try hugging a guy with no torso.

Not even a long, scraggly, lice-infested beard to finger aside to find the scaly, chapped lips to kissy-smooch. For both guys.

Whoa, rethink it, maybe that's a good thing, no head, no torso. From a virgin's point of view.

An irreverent fellow like Kyle Wolfe is gonna pat himself on the back that he can always find the positive side to things.

Or maybe that's Sniper Rodriquez. Yeh, if Rodriquez had been up there on the gap and seen it, he'd have thought just about the same as Wolfe.

Except, Wolfe would bring it along one step further. *Count em up*, it's not looking good, *they're gonna run out of virgins up there today. Where they going to find all the virgins?*

Which is why a wise professional warrior like Kyle Wolfe isn't a civilian adjunct professor at any of the military academies teaching Religious Tolerance in 21st Century Warfare.

Crew Chief Jarbodie wouldn't be teaching it either.

Put him in the Wolfe school of thought.

He's extra mad right now, extra hateful, because of the *thwack thwack thwack* of bullets hitting his airframe.

Enemy bullets.

And not because they might hit him, hit one of the pilots, cut hydraulic lines.

Because they're hitting his airframe.

This is his bird, he's responsible for every square inch of it, and he wants it perfect, and bullets don't make it perfect.

If you were to ask him right now if for every hole put into the skin of his bird would he himself put a hole in the head of one of those virgins, tit for tat?, he'd just frown at you like *Are you kidding?*, and you'd know that he'd put two holes in every one of those virgins' heads for every one in his airframe. Just for spite. *They're gonna shoot up my chopper, their heavenly virgins are fair game too, target practice.*

Door gunners Rapley and Maneosupa in here have opened up, and their swivel-mounted M240 machineguns is music to Jarbodie's ears.

You can't hear the *thwack thwack* of the enemy's bullets over these machineguns, so maybe they're *No longer splintering my airframe.*

He's back on the ramp now, as the Chinook has dropped down out of the clouds. When Mister Chiarduchi had said over the intercom that they were entering Indian country, he'd moved down along the sides of the pallets to here where he knew he'd have to be to see out below to drop the pallets. On the port side. He's got his safety harness strapped in above, has it stretched tight to keep it from drooping and have a pallet catch it on its way out. He himself is tight as far close to the edge as possible as he triggers the ramp to drop, announcing it over the intercom and immediately feeling the ship dip down up front, this rear up slightly at an angle, as the pilot adjusted to keep the pallets from sliding out.

Jarbodie leans out, twisting to look forward, his head tilted down to keep the wind from whipping under his helmet visor.

He wants to see ahead, to see if there's going to be anything that'll cause him to call *Abort abort abort!* and raise the ramp.

Otherwise it's the pilots' show now. It's the pilots' skill, experience and instinct now to know the exact moment to drop the rear, feel the ten-feet minimum off the ground there, while trimming the rotors at just the right cut to jump the helicopter up and forward to send the two pallets dropping out below.

Behind the pilots, through their windshields SF Doc BZ makes out the thin wisps of green smoke ahead, and *What's that behind? The mountain? Yeh it's a mountain, and there's a gray building there,* that's the destination, the green smoke, *right there at the base of a mountain, son of a gun if the platoon's not holding up in Fort Apache.*

Time for action.

He one-shoulders his med ruck.

M4 carbine in hand, without body armor or helmet or even any ammo but the magazine in the weapon, he feels naked.

More so, as he strips off his Cleveland Indian's ballcap and stuffs it down under his shirt.

At ease, relax, no time for rational thinking.

He steps to the rear behind this second pallet.

He'll follow it. He can't see anything out back there right now, but he'll have time as it falls off, he'll be on the ramp and he'll be able to judge if they're too high to jump off.

What's too high? No fret, he'll know.

Ten feet? Fifteen? Twenty? No way twenty.

I'll know it, I'll feel it, I'll know it, too high I won't go.

No time for rational thinking.

But his med ruck is one-shouldered because he knows he's going to have to drop it free and riding it on his back would just weigh him down on that side and a man *Can break his back that way.*

No time for rational thinking.

But his M4 isn't clipped to his belt because he's probably going to have to drop it mid-jump, *Depends how high I am,* and *Clipped to you, dude-a-roo, it hits the ground first and you've got the muzzle going through your belly and out your spine.*

His belly and his spine.

Not a pleasant image.

He's thinking, *Hurry up hurry up hurry up.*

His stomach is a tight knot. He's aware that his asshole's squeezed shut, you wouldn't get an electron of light through it with a 50,000 candlepower police spotlight. He purposely breathes fast. *Oxygenate, get oxygen to the muscles, to the brain, maximize the 0-Two.* Alert the adrenal glands, have them on standby.

In here in this Chinook, standing, holding onto one of this pallet's tie-down straps, with the door gunners' machineguns deafening even above the twin engines screaming right above, *Why oh why'd I get on this?,* he regrets being here, just for this moment, for these moments. He has parachuted out of choppers dozens of times, rappelled out a hundred times, fast-roped out a thousand times, but he's got no parachute here, there're no ropes hanging down, it's a freefall, but he'll know if it's too high to go and he won't.

Too high, you hit the brakes, buddy.

He repeats it to himself, *You hear me? Too high, you stomp on the brakes.*

No time for rational thinking.

He'll know to hit the brakes. By sight. Looking down. If it's higher than the roof of mom's house he'd jump off of as a kid, he'll back off.

One step at a time.

He'll know what to do at the edge when he can see below.

Leaned way out, Crew Chief Jarbodie watches that concrete building and the mountain it's under getting closer, even as he's seeing the nose of this helicopter pointing downward, descending, then holding right above the river at not fifteen feet, and the mountain closer and closer, they're heading right at it, off the water and over the beach now, the green smoke dying there just ahead of that wall there, and Jarbodie would fear they would be running right into that building and that mountain, smack center on that building, the front rotors are going to chop into the roofline and the mountain, except that he knows it's Mister Chiarduchi flying this thing, and there aint no one better than Mister C, and—

—On the schoolhouse roof Ketchum, Pvt Finkle, Van Louse, Tran, Bybee and the rest up here could swear that that fearsome bug-like huge screamingly loud Chinook is going to crash right into them, those blurring rotor blades are going to cut their heads off, and most duck down below the parapet, but

not Finkle and not Ketchum, they're watching, and see the Chinook suddenly stop flat-out on a dime in the middle of the air, they'll swear later that those blurring front rotor blades were so close that if they reached their hands out they'd have all their fingers cut off right at the knuckles.

They see the Chinook jump back and start to pivot mid-air, the nose lifting and the tail dropping, now even, level, and the rear rotor blades now blurring around to them and now so close that both Ketchum and Finkle would later swear that if they didn't have their eyepro on they'd have had their eyelashes trimmed, and

they see a guy hanging out the tail there, bug-like himself behind that helmet visor, free arm waving like *Down down down!*, and the rear of the chopper dropping, the edge of the ramp's not five feet off the ground, and the shiny black-plastic-covered pallet just slides right off, lands in a splash on this side of the rock wall, and

they watch the Chinook jump forward, up, and damn if a second black shiny pallet doesn't come sliding off, higher, maybe at twenty feet, and it lands on the other side of the rock wall, then

"For real, you won't believe it," Finkle's going to tell the guys back on the Cop, he just knows he's going to have to tell the guys from 2nd and 3rd. *"Here comes this dude, steppin offa there, it's gotta be thirty, forty feet in the*

air, it's higher than we was there," on the roof, *"swear to you, dude, it's higher. And here he comes, and I see his ruck's goin out this way, his weapon's goin this way out over here, dude, and he's flapping his arms like this, just awesome like, gettin his balance, y'know, and that wind, from the chopper blades, it just twists him, bro, and his hands are fannin 'n flappin like crazy."*

Down on the veranda, seated in the open against the doorway, Capt Cathay had a perfect view of the approaching Chinook coming straight in, so near and so fast it looked like it couldn't stop, and

she caught her breath, then the chopper did, it suddenly stopped, jumped back, started to pivot, and it was so loud and frightening here so close, now throwing up a hurricane of water and mud and pebbles.

Without eyepro Cathay might have been blinded, pelted scarred, except for that sniper, Sergeant Rodriquez, who threw himself down over her like a blanket covering her, his own body-armored back absorbing the pelting.

Cathay and Rodriquez didn't see the pallets dropped nor BZ coming out at forty feet.

Lieut Col Dove, Redcloud, Wolfe, Pfc Holloway and others here, all tight against the veranda wall, each so curious with just one protected eye sneaked out to peek, did see it all.

Saw the two pallets dropped close, perfectly, land flat on their bases.

Black-plastic-covered emergency resupply pallets.

From the sky.

The Lord's gift.

And they saw that lone bare-headed soldier come out from so high and let his rucksack go from one hand, his weapon from the other, and they saw him twisting and flailing his arms for balance in the jerking, buffeting rotor wash, down all the way and out of sight somewhere behind the second pallet on the far side of the rock wall.

Day Two, Afternoon—Part 3

The Village Wajma, In the Schoolhouse

The pallets have been broken down and everything carried inside. Wooden crates and steel cans of ammo distributed upstairs and down.

Famine or feast, they've gone from being down to a mag or two for the M4s and half the guys on AKs to almost two thousand rounds of M4 for each guy still on the walls. Thirty thousand rounds total for the Saws. Ten thousand 7.62 for the M240 machinegun. A hundred-twenty M203 rounds each for Pvt Finkle and other grenadiers.

The four wounded of the air crew are back in Doc Eberly's aid station.

Door Gunner Rapley is under a poncho in the other classroom.

There's a calmness and quiet from the roof on down. Even in the aid station now, where the morphine from the ample medical supplies from the pallets has been a blessing.

Out on the veranda near the doorway Nick Flowers is seated beside Capt Cathay. He's playing for her on his camera's viewscreen the Chinook resupply drop. What she'd missed.

When Redcloud radioed down from the roof that choppers were *"Inbound, two mikes out, resupply drop, they want smoke"*, Wolfe and Ssgt Utah and the rest of the Zoosters out there sitting the enemy dead up against the rock wall had raced back for the shelter of the building.

Not Nick.

On film, for honest realism, Nick has learned from experience, a resupply drop should show in one take both the choppers delivering it and the soldiers receiving it.

No cuts, no edits, pure straight-through untouched action, the story told in that single framing.

Which meant that Nick would have to shoot from a position and angle that got the school in the frame too along with the choppers.

Which is why he went the other way. Out another hundred feet or so beyond the rock wall. Up onto the first terrace rock wall where there just happened to be three dead Talibs who he could lay one atop another and lie behind as a shield and as a support for his camera.

Does it sound callous, stacking enemy dead as a shield and tripod? Sound gross?

This isn't Nick Flowers' first rodeo. He's been up close too many times to choppers coming in low and fast and all the shit debris their rotor wash throws up can put a flat rock or a chunk of driftwood upside your head and you're left with a crater you can put goldfish swimming around in. Like that twister coming at Dorothy in *The Wizard of Oz*. Better, like all those twisters in *Twister*, buses tumbling, trees shooting like arrows, Guernsey cows flying in the air.

Not Guernsey cows here in Afghanistan.

Goats maybe.

Emaciated goats. Ribs bulging like a washboard.

The two choppers had come in earlier this morning from downstream down there, and Nick figured these would as well, and he'd zoomed the Canon HD that direction, not running tape, not wasting it. He only turned it on Rec when he first heard the deep, cutting *whooomp-whooomp-whooomp-whooomp* telltale sound of a Chinook, which he'd known it was even before it suddenly appeared sinking down out from the cloud ceiling. He had actually just kind of assumed it was going to be a couple of Blackhawks, small and agile, and coming in and kicking out crates of ammo, like something like in that old black-and-white 16mm stuff from Vietnam, with the Huey crews throwing out wooden ammo boxes to shirtless sweating GIs on some barren jungle hilltop.

A Chinook's better. Bigger, more awesome, terror-inspiring. Like a huge semi-truck, a gasoline tanker, madly driven by that T-1000 cyborg in *Terminator 2*, coming straight down the shiny wet avenue, flames haloed in the background, it's going to clobber Arnold Schwarzenegger, flatten him like a pancake.

A Chinook's three long wide rotor blades both front and back are ominous scary just by the sound, and double that for the Kansas twister of deadly debris they can throw up at a low hover.

Awesome, Nick had thought then. *A Chinook coming in on a hot LZ.*

He'd checked the sound bar to make sure he was picking up that distant AK fire which was immediately drowned out by the Chinook's machineguns replying in kind.

And he'd realized then that he sure hoped the door gunners up there wouldn't mistake him for an enemy fighter, his camera a gun aiming at them and them blasting him when they came overhead. Those three stacked bodies were *An effective shield from the shit that Shithook's going to kick up, not necessarily from the bird's machinegun bullets.*

Nick breathed a little easier when those machineguns had quit firing, and he realized that he should have thought of that, that there was no enemy up this far in the valley for them to shoot.

Now, playing for Capt Cathay the video that he's seeing himself for the first time, he couldn't be happier, seeing that as the Chinook drew nearer, its wheels and belly not ten feet off the ground, he'd reverse zoomed the camera back out just right and not too quickly, filling the frame with the helicopter and its front rotors cutting through the rain, nose dipped downward, tail just slightly raised.

He's very pleased now seeing the way the camera caught that aggressive *whooomp-whooomp-whooomp* and even the change in tone to a throatier, guttural *whoomp-whoomp* as it stopped, pivoted, leveled off then lowered its rear end.

Hot damn, it was near perfect. He'd managed to frame the entire chopper, tips of its front rotor to tips of the rear, and had the school as a backdrop. Even more scary action with mud and stones sprayed out shooting by the camera lens, like it's flying right at you and you want to duck to not be hit.

And Nick's happy as a clam now that he was behind those stacked enemy bodies for shelter. And for a steady hold on the camera.

A tripod, if you will.

Three stacked bodies—one two three—a different kind of tripod.

A six-legged tripod, if you will.

Call it manmade.

As in, made up of men.

The viewscreen shows first one pallet then the second coming off as the chopper jumps forward and up, and Nick likes what he's shot, could only be more pleased if he'd shot it with a half-dozen Cinemascope 3D cameras on dollies and cranes.

"Watch," is all he says now to Cathay.

The soldier comes out off the ramp.

His rucksack dropped free that way, M4 flung this way, and it's caught in the rotor wash and comes spinning toward the camera to smack with a *metallic/plastic clack* below out of sight where the wall would be, while the soldier fights for his balance, brings his legs together like he's making a parachute landing and hits hard on his feet on what looks like a boulder.

"I'll edit this out," Nick says of the video getting all jerky and out of focus, as the camera was then swinging wildly when Nick had gotten up, jumped off the wall and headed for the soldier on the ground.

"That's all right," Capt Cathay tells him, and looks away.

She doesn't want to watch anymore, she knows what happened next. She'd heard at that point the *whooomp-whooomp* of the Chinook receding and Rodriquez had gotten up off of her and the *clacks* of AK fire way out there had then started up again, with the overriding sharp staccato of the helicopter's two door gunners then blasting over them on their machineguns.

Someone had yelled right above her *"Doc, out here right now!"*

Redcloud.

And Wolfe and the ANA sergeant and a couple of Zoo Platoon soldiers were already heading out down off the veranda, and she'd heard Dove telling Redcloud quickly, *"Better break them down, get them inside fast,"* meaning the pallets. Which she could see in Redcloud's expression wasn't something that he had to be told, nor appreciated. Which didn't matter anyway, because things changed fast, as Cathay then saw way out there the first of two near simultaneous flashes on the Chinook, followed in two seconds by the arrival of the actual *booorump* of the explosions.

Just before those two rocket-propelled grenades hit his Chinook, Crew Chief Jarbodie had felt real good.

It had been a perfect pallet-drop. *Mister C is something else.* Any closer and those pallets would've been sitting right smack in those ground-pounders' laps, literally in their laps.

Actually, on approach Jarbodie had sworn that they'd come too close, that he was about to see the three front rotor blades start chipping cement off that building and then digging deeper and the blades disintegrating and the whole ship would go right through that wide porch there, and when they'd stopped so suddenly and started to swivel, Jarbodie'd felt it was like those dancers on *Dancing With The Stars*, when they're twirling and running and suddenly stop and twirl and go back running the other way. A thing of beauty. And he'd looked back, above, and could have sworn that now the rear rotor blades were going to chip the building, they were blurring so close and were gonna then start shaving right down the gray wall right down through the big openings of the huge wide porch. But as the pilot dropped the rear they didn't shave anything, didn't hit anything. Those rear blades just slapped the air and rain, giving Jarbodie's helicopter lift, and the edge of the ramp wasn't three feet off the ground when that first pallet came off. *Three God-blessed feet! Doin it blind.*

Not exactly blind blind. Jarbodie had been Mister C's eyes, shouting over the intercom *"Down down down down STOPPPPPPPP!"*, and before even the end of his *"STOPPPPPPPP!"* Jarbodie had felt and heard Mister C pitching blades for forward and upward thrust, and the only glitch of the entire beautiful *DWTS* ballet had nothing to do with the pilot, as

stepping right behind as the second pallet dropped off the ramp had been that SF dude, and Jarbodie stopped him with a hand to his chest, "No! Too high!" And the guy had looked down there which a blind man wearing a welder's mask at midnight could see was at least 35 feet up and yeh *Too high!*, but the guy just slapped Jarbodie's hand away with his rifle and stepped off, and

Jarbodie had thought then, watching him let go of his ruck and toss aside his rifle, as everybody knows, *It's not the fall's gonna kill you, it's the confrontation with the ground.*

Sort of exactly like the thought he'd had in about another 90 seconds, when it would instead be *It's not the little 7.62 Kalashnikov rounds that're gonna kill you, it's the RPGs.*

In those 90 seconds he'd raised the ramp, buttoned it up, unhooked his safety strap, was striding the length toward the front where he'd either watch the flight behind one of the gunners or from behind the pilots, and the *twack-twack-twack* of AK rounds striking the skin had started, with the gunners opening up with their 240s, then the terrifying *Kabaaaams* and jerks of what could only be explosions of two near simultaneous rockets hitting up front, one high, the second lower.

The moment before the two RPGs hit, Chiarduchi had estimated it to be about 20 seconds to safety on the other side of the gap. He knew that his blades were already in the clouds, another few seconds his entire ship would be, hidden up there, and he'd calculated to give it at least ten more feet of altitude this time through to guarantee they wouldn't be skipping the blades off the mountain like last time. The instruments read the exact reverse azimuth, the rest was feel, experienced instinct, and he'd felt he was level and true, just 20 seconds to safety, then he'd be able to drop it back down out of the clouds, and they'd be over all those trucks there on the other side beside that river.

Safe.

Home-free.

How much wood would a woodchuck chuck if a woodchuck would chuck wood, Chuck?

How much cents could your senses sense if your senses could sense cents . . . . Chuck?

How much sense can your senses sense in a couple of seconds?

Two rocket-propelled grenades blurring by missing right in front.

Explosive sound right overhead.

Ship yanked one way.

Controls twisted in Chiarduchi's hands and under his feet.

Explosive sound below, flash, flame, blur of debris flying past, copilot's scream over headset *"Jesus!"*, instrument panel explodes, searing burn on the calf and knee and through gloves and torn sleeve all the way to shoulder, buzzer and flashing red lights on head panel, ship's nose in sudden dive, blood spraying in pulsating squirts from copilot.

The mind can put 2 and 2 together fast when it's had over 7,000 hours flying these things.

First hit was the gear box right above, the front rotors.

Controls turning to mush, ship banking to port.

Second hit near the copilot's feet and up through and longways across the instrument panel.

All systems going No-Go.

Catastrophic failure.

Fob Salerno's a million miles away.

Chiarduchi had a thousandth of a second to decide they were now suddenly too low and wouldn't be able to get lift and couldn't make it through the gap.

A thousandth of a second to know that the ship wanted to go to port, was pulling hard to port, and if he set it down here, which he could, right now right here, he could bring it level on its wheels to the ground, and if he did they were mincemeat in the middle of the enemy, with the mountain and gap between them and the safety of those guns of those trucks just on the other side.

A thousandth of a second to know that setting down here was 180 degrees back the other way and almost two miles from the safety of the guns of the Tattoo Zoo Platoon.

A thousandth of a second to reject landing right there.

A thousandth of a second, all that one single second, to know he had to turn that 180, get back, set her down as close to that building and that platoon as possible, *If I can get 90 seconds lift out of her, can I get 90 seconds lift out of you, honey?*

He managed to get 82 seconds out of her.

He'd let it bank port the way it wanted to, hard, barely missing the mountain, nearly perpendicular at the deepest part of the bank, then door gunner Rapley had watched the blurring rotor blades appear to be disking the beach, and the black-clad enemy right here, like you could reach down and shake hands with them, so close that Rapley could see the blood splash from the exit wounds from his machinegun as its bullets struck them, and he watched one get sliced by the rotors right through from one elbow, through the torso, through the other elbow, and

Warrant-five Chiarduchi had fought the controls to right the ship out of the bank that wanted to send it veering into the ground, he'd gotten it righted, fought to keep it level, give it some lift, any lift, the gray building was way across up there, and he didn't hear but felt a rocket hit the rear, had felt in the controls that it had taken out an engine, nothing left of the control panel instruments to tell him anything, instinct had told him shit had gone through the rear rotor box, he was losing everything, and he'd thought, *If I can just make it to the field*, the first terraced field, near, close enough to the building and the platoon, *Set her down there in that field*, he'd be needing lift, more lift, he could feel the front wheels weren't more than six feet off the beach, couldn't force his ship from listing to port.

He didn't make the first terraced field.

The front port landing gear had hit the beach, the front rotors chopped through the three Talib bodies that Nick had stacked and lay behind on the terrace wall, and then chopped into the wall itself, breaking up, flying wildly, and the rear rotors hit the ground and shattered and flew wildly.

End of flight.

The big awesome Chinook lying on its port side, Rapley's gunner window crushed on the terrace wall.

One could say that the cockpit had made it to the first terraced field. Just the cockpit. Bent there at the wall.

All the rest, the entire fuselage lying back on the sand and rocks.

A beached dead whale of a big black bird.

Flames now licking out of the engines and that blown-away rear gear housing.

Wolfe and Rodriquez had reached BZ by the time the Chinook nearly out of sight way down there was banking hard and just missing the mountain.

BZ's immediate demand of them had been *"Get my ruck! Get me my ruck!"*, with his right leg from the knee down at an unnatural angle and the foot angled the other way, and blood already soaking his pantleg at the bulge of a compound fracture.

Rodriquez raced over to retrieve the ruck, but Doc Eberly came up fast carrying the sum total of the medical supplies he had left—strips of ripped uniform. BZ grabbed them straight from Eberly and tied his own tourniquet even as they watched the Chinook then closing in, flying crooked, so low to the deck, single engine at a horrible whine.

The black bird looked like it was coming straight into them, that it could not veer off, could not correct, steadily dropping and going to crash into the close pallet and the rock wall. Then somehow it appeared to be banking, forcing itself away, up toward the terraced rock wall, and *"Down! Down! Down!"* was shouted by everyone as they all hit the dirt on their bellies—but not BZ tying a second tourniquet above the first and watching out of the corner of his eye the Chinook manage to veer at an angle for the terrace wall and almost make it there when its rotors smacked the wall and the ground and all went flying.

Right now in the aid station classroom Doc Eberly has deferred to BZ, letting him take charge and direct him in the woundeds' care.

BZ is seated on a couple of wooden ammo crates, with his splinted leg stretched out straight on another crate.

From the moment the Zoosters had carried him in he had been scooting and dragging himself along the floor from one wounded to another assessing them. He'd tried to put from his mind the hellfire pain from his own ripped-apart knee and ankle and from the compound fracture, knowing he wasn't going to inject himself with one of the six syrettes of morphine in his ruck that he'd checked to find that all six, packed carefully in foam in a small Pelican case by himself as standard operating procedure, remained intact. Oh was it a temptation, the six fentanyl lollipops he also carried, sweeter than morphine even.

No, he'd just have to charge through the pain, he'd told himself, as he tells himself now, making it a challenge, converting the hurt, the actual screaming-out continuous wrenching pain itself that demands an end, that demands that he find release from it—

that he can convert it to a pleasure, pain is pleasure, pain purifies

—knowing, *These soldiers need me rational, need me at my peak, don't need my mind all slurred-up on opiates, whistling and humming old Grateful Dead tunes on the lollipops.* And knowing that these soldiers come first when it comes to the dope he's carried in.

Earlier, he'd checked the bleeding under his compound fracture bandage, found none, it had held, and he'd loosened his tourniquets slowly, making sure it still held, which it had, and he'd removed the tourniquets completely, because he knew no one was coming in and flying him and the rest back to the Salerno Cash in twenty minutes or an hour or two hours, where they could save a tourniqueted limb.

By the time Doc Eberly and the others carried in the air crew, BZ was as ready as he could be. He knew what he had in his ruck, had already gone through Doc's depleted med bag, had asked a soldier doing nothing but just mixing drink powder into his CamelBak what he was doing, what was his job, was he a medic too, and the young blond guy, a corporal whose nametage on his body armor says SANDUSKY, kind of mumbled no, he was sorta kinda just down here helping Doc.

BZ told him to *Get your butt out there and get the pallets broken down and get the med supplies in here asap!* But Sandusky didn't move and showed no signs of moving. "Didn't you hear me?" BZ demanded of him. "You had your eardrums blown out?".

No, his eardrums weren't blown out, Sandusky told him. But Doc had told him, he said, Doc'd said he didn't have to go outside. And wounded Vampire piped in, with no small amount of bile telling BZ that Sandusky was a chickenshit, he'd pussied out, he had shell shock, Post Traumatic Stress, battle-rattle fatigue, after only thirty seconds of bullets flying.

And BZ felt like telling Sandusky *If you give that CamelBak one more shake and don't get out there I'm gonna hop myself over there and put this one good boot I still have so far up your ass you'll be flossing with bootlaces for a month,* but instead just told him calmly that *There's a helicopter that just crashed out there* which he had to have heard *and there are five guys on that helicopter and they're going to be bringing them in here any minute and hopefully all five of them are still alive and they're going to need whatever medical supplies are on those two pallets out there,* and he'd personally, and his platoon medic doc as well, they'd both *Really appreciate it if you could go out there and help bring the medical boxes in right now, that would do a lot of good for everybody. Please.*

And Sandusky had just kept shaking up his CamelBak. Didn't meet BZ's eyes. Kept looking down at the CamelBak, mumbling in a repetition about *"Doc says I don't gotta go outside. Don't gotta go outside. . . "*

Earlier, outside on the ground just after the Chinook crashed, with the rain suddenly increasing to a downpour, BZ had spread open his ruck Rodriquez had dropped beside him, and Doc Eberly had grabbed up two of the Sam splints in it and quickly shaped them. BZ assumed this sergeant might be a medic and asked, and Eberly said *Yeh* and noted BZ's sterile uniform lacking rank and unit, had seen the sophisticated medical contents of BZ's ruck, and asked if he was a doctor from the Cash. *Nope, 18-Delta.* And like all 64-Whiskey combat medics, Eberly knew what 18-Delta is—a Special Forces medic. And he'd then followed BZ's lead getting a tight bandage over the compound fracture and the Sam splints secured and got some of Nell's guys to get BZ and his stuff inside.

Then Eberly ran over to the Chinook where Wolfe and Rodriquez and Dove and Utah and a some others had gone.

When the first two rockets had hit, Crew Chief Jarbodie had known by the jerk and dive of the helicopter that it was catastrophic, hoped that it wasn't, but he'd snapped his safety harness into the airframe just where he was, beside the port gunner, Rapley, and he'd pulled the strap tight.

Tight, his back to the fuselage wall.

Unstrapped, when you crash-land you bounce off everywhere.

Everything everywhere in a Chinook is metal.

Bouncing is catastrophic.

Jarbodie knew the sounds of the engines, the sounds of the gears, the sounds of the rotors.

They were all wrong.

He knew the feel of flying, banking, could tell change in direction and bank angle blindfolded.

They were all wrong.

Two wrongs don't make a right.

That many wrongs make a catastrophic.

Beside Rapley, back to the wall, Jarbodie was looking across out starboard gunner Maneosupa's window, over his shoulders. He could see nothing out there but the whiteness of the clouds in the near-vertical bank to port, facing the starboard side straight up into the clouds, and Rapley right beside him facing out straight to the ground and now blasting his machinegun.

Jarbodie imagined his helicopter viewed from the ground from a distance, and it was like when in *DWTS* the professional male dancer twirls the female star away and the star stumbles and trips, and if she picks herself up and regains her composure and continues on like nothing happened, returns to her partner and steps off fast, sharp and confident, the audience applauds, goes wild.

They would be applauding, Jarbodie knew, as the ship had righted, applauding like crazy. He visualized his CH-47 C-Model Chinook level and flying straight, and inside he could now see the terraced field across outside Maneosupa's window and knew they were heading back for the infantry platoon and the safety there at the building with them and *We're going to make it*, he knew, *We're going to make it*.

Until the rocket hit the engine.

Until that loud explosion, the vibrations.

The sounds of an engine whine of catastrophic failure.

Sounds of metal in gears.

Rockets in engines mean fire, and Jarbodie had mentally cataloged the locations of the fire extinguishers for after the crash after unstrapping.

God save me, help me, he'd prayed. *Help me put out the fires that there will be, help me save the others, God, please, I have been a good person, I hope you see that I have been good and will you please help me and I'll help them.*

He'd felt the port landing gear right beneath him hit the earth.

Felt the blades encountering the earth.

Then nothing.

When he came to he'd heard nothing in a relief of silence and felt a hard rain on his face and was seeing the gray-black of clouds straight up out Maneosupa's window where the downpour was coming in straight down on him and Maneosupa was suspended by his safety strap on the floor which was then perpendicular to the earth.

The floor like a wall.

It's the floor, not a wall, it's not supposed to be a wall.

The floor was a wall.

The ceiling next to his head the other wall.

Jarbodie with his back tight on the fuselage wall which was now a floor.

Rain rain rain coming down on him like he was under a fire hose on full blast, *Let it rain rain rain*, he'd glanced back to the rear and there was no fire from the engines and all the fuel lines, *Let it rain*, then a dark figure filled Maneosupa's window across above him, silhouetted, and *That's funny*, Jarbodie had thought, *The Taliban don't wear baseball caps*, then he recognized the unique shape of an M4 hanging straight down off the figure.

Now, more than an hour later Jarbodie knows that that figure was this mysterious civilian here who they call Wolfe or Wolfie on whom he's leaning, who's got his free arm around him, slowly making their way away from the Chinook and toward that rock wall where those dead enemy Taliban are seated up against, *I wonder who thought of that*. He'd missed that before, hadn't seen them, when the soldiers had carried him from the Chinook before on a poncho. Things still hadn't been exactly clear then. But he remembers now, he remembers what he told this Wolfe in the helicopter there the first thing when Wolfe had asked *"Are you alright? Where's it hurt? Where's it hurt?"*

"God works in mysterious way," he'd told him.

"Say again?" Wolfe had said.

"Rain rain rain," he'd said, and remembers now that he really should have explained it, but hadn't thought to, that all that rain then, it's stopped now and it's good to be walking not in any rain at all, but then all the rain was God's blessing.

Lots of rain, no fires.

Every bone, every muscle, every joint hurts now. It hurt in the school building there, it hurts now walking back.

Nothing broken. No major lacerations. In the school building, when he could feel that most of his dizziness was gone he'd said he had to get back to his helicopter, and that staff sergeant had assured him that it had been stripped, that all the sensitive items—the guns, the ammo, the radios, the navigation boxes—had been removed and were inside here safe from the enemy insurgents, and that lieutenant colonel assured him the same thing, but he'd insisted, and this civilian Wolfe had offered that he'd take him back out there to check again.

And they did, the two of them.

There had been nothing left that the enemy couldn't have. *Let them drag the whole airframe off, the whole carcass of an airframe, and make a Winnebago out of it. Turn it into a mobile taco stand. Goat tacos. Tear it up, blow-torch it to pieces and sell it for scrap.*

Jarbodie is content. His aircraft is not his anymore.

It's dead.

And he thinks of Rapley dead. Rapley, whose body he'd seen half-in half-out, with the half-out bent in half at a unnatural angle against the smashed wall.

And the lieutenant, the copilot today, he lost a lot of blood, *Can he survive until we can get medevacs in here?* Yeh, medevacs, the plural, he knows it's going to take more than a couple of Nightingale Blackhawks to bring all those wounded in there back to the Cash.

And Maneosupa, who'd hung unconscious on the floor that was then the wall, can they keep him alive?

And Jarbodie's PIC—his Pilot In Command—*Mister Chiarduchi, please God don't take him, don't let Mister C die.*

Jarbodie stops, can't go any farther, and Wolfe holds him up steady so he won't collapse. Wolfe sees he's closed his eyes, that it's something inside that's stopped him cold, that he's struggling with.

And Wolfe is in no rush, he'll stay out here just ahead of the rock wall with this crew chief and let him gather his thoughts, compose his physical strength, for as long as it takes.

Kabul, Isaf HQ, In the Op Center

In this semi-dark amphitheater, the staff officers at their workstations on the four tiers of long curved polished mahogany tabletops.

Quiet. Maybe a murmured question and answer between a couple.

Colonel Pluma is seated in a swivel chair in the back on the highest tier. Legs stretched out, boots on the tabletop.

Fingers interlocked of his hands in front of his face, he's twiddling his thumbs.

Literally.

Watching them go around. And around and around.

He takes his eyes off them and focuses directly on the one flatscreen down there that displays the Blue Force Tracker map of Wajma Valley.

He zeroes in on one spot. Where there's nothing, no blue dot or red dot, but where he knows was the last spot that blinking red dot had been and stayed blinking there and didn't move for at least twenty minutes.

There's been nothing there for nearly two hours now, and Pluma doesn't know why he looks there, he knows that nothing's going to magically appear, that that helicopter is crippled. No, not crippled, he knows, as Zachary Dove had reported when they'd finally gotten sat-comms back with the platoon, *"The CH-47 is an irretrievable loss."*

Gen St Claire was here before, earlier, and they'd all watched in silence as the map showed the blinking red dot of the rogue Chinook near the twelve blue dots of the rogue QRF trucks. Thirty seconds later on the map reset the blinking red dot was in the valley, midway up it. On the next three map resets the dot was approaching the black rectangle that represents the school building, then right at it, then a few hundred meters away from it, heading back for the valley entrance.

Okay, the movement away from the building answered the question whether the Chinook was going to land and pick up the platoon and go well over its max weight trying to ascend with all of them or was it dropping a resupply pallet or two or three.

It hadn't lingered, so it had to be the latter, and there had been quiet cheers in here, *"All right!"*, *"Awright!"* from officers who couldn't help it, and clenched fists shaken aloft, and Col Pluma had been aware of his own fist clenched, though hidden down at his side.

There was an even louder, more enthusiastic *"Go go go!"* from someone as the next reset had the dot almost at the narrow saddle there where the river channeled between the steep brown map contour lines.

And someone shouting his elation, *"The son of a bitch has made it!"*

And another, *"Fuck ! In ! Hooahhh !"*

Col Pluma's eyes, like Gen St Claire's, like everyone's in here, had settled on a spot on the map where the twelve dots of the QRF trucks were. That's where the red blinking dot would be on the next reset.

It wasn't. It was nearly heading back up the valley in line with that distant black rectangle.

"What gives?!" from someone.

What gives is right, Col Pluma had thought and would have thought that the general was thinking the exact same thing.

"Can't you, can't you, can't you get comms with them?!" someone had asked in frustrated anger.

And *"You try and call em if you think you can!"* had been someone's reply, and Gen St Claire had held up his hand to demand the end of it, no argument, no fighting in here.

On the reset the blinking red dot was short of the black rectangle.

On the next reset it was in the same spot, short of the black rectangle.

And the next after that.

And all the next for the next twenty minutes, when on that reset it just wasn't there anymore.

That was when, Col Pluma knows now after comms had been reestablished with Zachary, they learned that the platoon had ripped all the electronic equipment they could from the chopper and had burned with thermite grenades whatever they thought was electronics but couldn't tell one way or another.

And when he learned, of the air crew, 1 KIA, 3 critical WIA. 2 walking wounded.

A 6-man air crew didn't jibe with the aircraft's manifest of 5 for its original infil and exfil missions, and Zach wasn't relaying names of any of the Kilos or Whiskeys, period, not of the platoon, not of the air crew, not until air medevac showed up, only for them would he have a roster.

Pluma could have pushed it, would have if St Claire had still been in the room, and probably still wouldn't have gotten the names, from the tone of the attitude he was getting from Zach over the radio.

Imagine telling General Pete St Claire no, he thinks, and he immediately knows better, knows that newly minted Lieutenant Colonel Zachary Dove would have given the general the names, all of them, along with the ranks and service numbers and blood types and religious preferences. Hell, he'd have given the general their wive's maiden names, number of kids, and ages, the casualties' favorite color, favorite food, secret sexual fantasies, yeh with the wife and mistresses, both. *If Dove would have had to make it all up. If General St Claire were here and demanded it of him.*

The brigade down there found out who the sixth member of the air crew was and passed it up. Some Special Forces 18-D medic had gotten aboard the chopper at the last minute. Guy named, *what was it?, Booner?, Boonman?, Boonzmann. Yeh, BZ someone said brigade reported everyone called him.*

One dead, five wounded, a thirty-five million dollar helicopter turned to scrap, at least Zachary had said that the two emergency pallets were dropped intact and were *"Very very much appreciated by the men of the Zoo Platoon."*

Pluma has seen a copy of the pallet packing list and knows that Zach's got enough ammunition now for a full platoon for a week, which is Christmas-morning for the half-platoon Zach had reported were all that were combat-able. *Almost half dead or wounded bad enough they can't fight. Why did we have to send them into there today?* And he can't remember the weather paragraph in the operations order, *Where was the weather, what'd it say?* With access to *The most sophisticated weather satellites in the world, and no one saw that storm coming? That homely fat girl with the overbite and the bangs,* who used to do the weather for the local channel in Lincoln, Nebraska, *Even she could have seen that storm coming.*

And Col Pluma would after all these years almost welcome seeing her on one of the three flatscreens up front always on the news channels — BBC, Fox, CNN.

But they're black. Pluma had had them shut off just after St Claire and Doctor Hutchinsen left. Who needs to see the same loop of the same video over and over and all the so-called experts coming on to tell everyone exactly what they're seeing of this video of American troops massacring Local National peasant women and children?

Maybe they're already running clips of St Claire's press conference earlier, but Pluma doubts it. Too soon, it'll take them this long just to edit what they like. Hopefully St Claire will have won them over with his seriousness, compassion and charm that Pluma has seen often with whore reporters acting like his vassals as they themselves have exalted him to near-celebrity status as a future powerful politician Caesar.

That's not Pluma's concern. The media is Katherine Gray-Nance's, let her worry about them. When the news channels start playing St Claire, *The bitch'll come in here all excited,* and they'll turn the TVs back on.

Goddamn reporters. *Can't go to war without them, can't make them walk point, make them ride in the lead truck, can't shoot them.* Pluma remembers one story they wrote on St Claire. *The Compassionate Warrior it was called,* that's impossible to not remember. In *GQ* or *Esquire*, one of those two. Or the *New Yorker*. Talk about sucking up.

Pluma hopes the general will be compassionate with him when he learns that not ten minutes ago he gave the brigade down there the option, they could ignore the Red Air and send a Blackhawk Nightingale medevac to Cop Valley Forge for the four seriously wounded of the Quick Reaction Force. It had been only then that the QRF had reestablished comms with their Cop and had told them they had one killed and four seriously wounded needing immediate medevac and they were about twenty mikes away and requesting Nightingale.

Pluma chuckles right now as he thinks of them calling in their 9-line for Nightingale. *What, next thing, that Awesome Company down there's going to be putting in all those law-breaking QRF wounded soldiers for Purple Hearts?* He doesn't know the answer, but should, and wonders if men who get wounded or killed in combat while wantonly disobeying orders, do they still get Purple Hearts?

Again a chuckle, as he thinks *I'll Google it.*

Even better, he'll ask Jag.

Better still, *That cute little young petite Jag captain from Bagram who went out with Zachary this morning. Cathay. Laura Cathay. Captain Laura Cathay.*

He'll ask her when she gets back with Zach. *Look at her, if that's not a virgin rose ripe for the picking I don't know jack about women and my lovely and gracious and fat obese, grossly obese wife is a Sports Illustrated swimsuit model. Yeh, back in the day she was. Was, past tense. And don't say it, I don't want to hear it, it's not because of "The four children I bore for you, and you expect me to have the same body I had at twenty-five, yeh then you stay home and raise them," nag nag nag nag nag. It's because you can't keep your damn pie-hole shut from stuffing in Cheetos and chips and ice cream and all that crap. Captain Laura Cathay, that tight little body, that's present tense. Wow, and doesn't even look twenty-five, a gen-u-wine hardbody, it'd be like doing a sorority girl at a Christian college like Oral Roberts or, even better, at a nunnery, woohoo!*

Yeh, he'll ask her. Soldiers breaking orders, do they get Purple Hearts? When she gets back with Zachary Dove.

How easy it is to divert the mind when you don't want to think about General St Claire finding out you've ignored the Red to let Nightingale fly to that Cop.

Nightingale flying in that rain under those clouds not fifty feet off the deck. On a Red Air.

It had been line-of-sight FM comms between Kozak's QRF and the Cop, not satcom, so Isaf didn't hear the call and the 9-line request.

But Valley Forge had then satcommed battalion with the 9-line, and battalion then called brigade, and the full-bird brigade commander is a RotCee classmate and longtime close friend of Pluma's and called him direct with the 9-line, knowing that Isaf would have already heard it listening in, but hoping that he could catch a break from the friendship and they could all pretend the Red was about to be lifted and thus skirt around it.

Pluma had figured if a Chinook could make it in that weather down south there and all the way in to Wajma Valley then a Blackhawk should damn well be able to make it to Cop Valley Forge and, *What the hell, permission granted from here.*

And Pluma had been exact in stipulating that anything beyond Valley Forge was Red and was remaining Red and there would be no aircraft risked flying up that socked-in gorge to that insurgent-crawling Wajma.

There'd be no more $35 million aircraft turned to scrap metal in that damned village.

Pluma looks up now at the Local Time clock on the wall in line with eight clocks of different Times.

6:13.

It's going to be dark soon down there in *That hellhole bastard Wajma sonovabitch Valley of Death.* It would make a hellova *Horror movie. Late night TV, Vincent Price, Bella Lugosi. The Valley of Death.*

He'd much prefer thinking about that *Cute tight little hardbody virgin Jag lawyer Laura Cathay. With no ring on her finger,* he didn't see one, and *She's so cherry she didn't even know you're supposed to wear gloves going outside the wire.* First thing he would do, first thing, he'll *Pull the quick release of her body armor, let it fall off, and I know those little titties there are going to be firm and standing straight up and the nipples pink and hard as marble, land ahoy God Bless America!*

With the QRF, in 1st Sgt Kozak's Humvee

Sgt Dixon is driving. Kozak motions with a hand hurriedly *Go go go go!* to go around and pass the only truck ahead, the Mrap towing the crippled humvee.

They're out of the gorge, midway across the wide wadi, with Cop Valley Forge in sight ahead.

The nine trucks behind are doing the same, like Kozak's, speeding up, tightening it up. Home's just ahead. You can't help but punch the gas when you can see home.

Kozak wants in front of the Mrap because he wants in the Cop first, right now. Because the medevac bird's not there, and it should be by now.

Just a couple of minutes ago, coming out of the gorge, on higher ground where you can see across the wadi and over the Cop's Hesco walls, he'd hoped to see at least the rotors of a Blackhawk spinning at idle on the LZ and maybe an Apache flying cover in wide circles low over the

Cop, or better yet still, two Blackhawks on the LZ for all these many wounded and dead.

Nope, neither, nothing.

A call across to the Cop, and Lieut Frye there said he didn't know where the medevac was, that they said they were coming, and nothing's been radioed since, and they can't be reached on the Nightingale freq, and maybe they had to turn back because it was getting dark.

Kozak knows it's getting dark, and he knows no one is flying no way no how in this rain under these clouds on a Red at night, you can forget that, it aint happenin.

And he's got three badly wounded in the Mrap they're passing now. Three badly wounded he's got to get medevaced to Salerno now, today, asap, before it's dark and too late.

In here in the seat behind Dixon is Cornberger's body, wrapped completely in a poncho and strapped in.

In the other seat, right behind Kozak, is Triple Shot, strapped in, wrapped in a poncho. Except the poncho has slipped down off his head which hangs bobbing against his shoulder.

Back just over two hours ago Kozak had quickly reorganized the patrol when he'd gotten all the trucks out of that lethal four-hundred meters of gorge and back around the first curve safe from the enemy who'd attacked from the other side of the narrow gap at the entrance to the valley.

Dixon and a couple of men from the other trucks changed the blown tires on Kozak's and the crippled hummer.

Dixon checked and made adjustments to the Mrap's tow bar to the crippled hummer.

Kozak and the medic, Doc O'Toole, got the two badly wounded gunners into the back of that Mrap where O'Toole would keep them stabilized for the long bouncy ride home.

Platoon Sergeant Sfc Northwich, himself wounded and with a shoulder and arm heavily bandaged and non-functioning, got up on the .50-cal in the turret of the Mrap, to Kozak's adamant protestations, but it was *"Either me or O'Toole or you, First Sergeant,"* Northwich argued. *"And Doc O'Toole's needed with those two, and you've gotta run this patrol, so it looks like . . . me."*

Kozak had tried to convince Triple Shot that they could put him on a litter and set him up into the Mrap where O'Toole could care for him on the return, but Triple Shot said he was comfortable right here in the seat behind Kozak's where they'd put him hurriedly for the ride out of the kill zone back there. *I feel pretty good,* Triple Shot told Kozak. *Just strap me in tight here and I'm gonna be awright.*

The whole reorganization and repair had taken all of about twenty-five minutes, and Kozak got on the horn one last time with Dove to make sure they shouldn't stick around in case they could break through and lend a hand now that the chopper went down up there in the village.

Dove told him to move it out, to get his own wounded back to Valley Forge. *"Face the facts, Awesome Seven. The reality is you can't make it to us and we can't make it to you. Take care of your soldiers who you can take care of."*

The QRF had headed out then. Toward home.

The Mrap carrying the two wounded gunners and towing the humvee was in the lead because of the old adage in the infantry: *You can only go as fast as your slowest man.*

The trip was slow. And uneventful. The enemy obviously didn't really care about the QRF now that it wasn't rescuing the stranded platoon, and if they were gathering anywhere, it would be up in that Wajma Valley for the grand prize. The Zoosters.

It wasn't until about two miles still from the Cop that Kozak could finally break through on the radio to them, and he sent in his 9-line and told Lieut Frye that it was urgent, four seriously wounded, and "Beg em for a medevac, I don't give a shit about Air bein Red."

It wasn't but a few minutes later, above all the noisy clanging and shaking in the truck that Kozak heard, *"Firs' Sar'en."* Again, *"Firs' Sar'en."*

It was Triple Shot. Trying to hold his head up. Eyes creamy with a thick glassy glaze. *"Firs' Sar'en."*

Kozak shouted for Dixon to stop! *Call Doc O'Toole!*

And he was out, pulling open Triple Shot's door, taking hold of his head, "Triple Shot! Triple Shot, what is it, Triple Shot? What can we do, Triple Shot?"

"Firs' Sar'en?"

"Right here, Triple Shot, what do you need? We're ten minutes away, Triple Shot, just ten minutes."

"I know you got it, Top." Triple Shot talking oh so slowly, oh so quietly, with oh such extreme difficulty. Between soft shallow slow breaths.

"What, Triple Shot, what?"

"You . . . got . . . it . . . ."

"What? What do you want, Triple Shot?"

"You . . . your . . . "

"What do I got, Triple Shot, what is it do I got?"

"Your . . . your . . . sody . . . bottle . . . ."

And Kozak took his duct-taped-wrapped soda bottle from its pouch.

Could feel by its weight it was still at least a third full.

Twisted off the cap.

And Kozak spent the next couple of minutes holding Triple Shot's head and holding his soda bottle to his lips, letting him sip. Slurp. Gulp. Not giving a shit that most of the sharp warm Dewar's was spilling, dribbling out the corners of Triple Shot's mouth, wasted.

Kozak knew that for these months deployed here Triple Shot, in a warzone, in combat, knowing he can't stop at one drink and can't perform at max drunk, had not tasted a drop, had not even asked for a sniff from one of the other guys' duct-taped soda bottles and secreted Listerines.

And Kozak let him finish his. He imagined that it was a taste of Heaven for Triple Shot. A sight ahead of him of the Gates of Paradise, a return to all those wild, carefree, happy days and nights of his life from which he got his name.

Kozak tilted the soda bottle up at the end for the last few drops just to wet Triple Shot's lips, as his eyes were already focused off far away nowhere and his head was limp in Kozak's hand.

Kozak tossed the bottle away outside.

And O'Toole helped him pull Triple Shot out, and they wrapped him in a poncho then set him back in the seat and strapped him in.

Dixon now whips the humvee past the Mrap and jerks the steering wheel this way and that to take the rivulets and gullies with the least bouncing, aiming for where he's seeking the most shallow spot of the raging flood water running down the center channel. He sees what he likes, and he floors it, because he knows that the First Sergeant wants to get on satcom in the Toc right now and start demanding of battalion where the Sam-hell their medevac birds are.

Dixon warns Kozak to *Hold on!* and gets the humvee airborne above the channel, and it lands on the huge flat boulders in the middle just under water, then zips forward, splashing through and up the embankment and airborne again, and he floors it again now even before the rear tires hit the dirt.

Damn, he's one hellava driver! Helluva mechanic and helluva driver!

Kozak is tempted to check behind to see if the bodies of Triple Shot and Cornberger have been bounced out of the safety straps, but he doesn't.

He won't look back. He knows they're there, what's it matter if they're strapped in still or not? Two bodies, it's just two bodies. Two dead bodies lost on a mission that failed. *We didn't reach our objective. We failed. I failed.*

Two dead bodies.

And he knows in a day or two on the Cop, if he's still there and hasn't already been arrested, he, as first sergeant, it will be he who will call their names at the memorial they'll have for them.

"Sergeant Cornberger, Kevin Whatever," he'll call three times, and there'll be no answer three times.

Then, *"Private First Class Tripp, Gerald R,"* three times and no answer.

No, not *Tripp, Gerald R*. He'll call instead, *"Private First Class Triple Shot."* No answer. *"Private First Class Triple Shot."* No answer. *"Private First Class Triple Shot."*

Awesome Company will be in formation, at attention, and everyone will be looking at the two sets of combat boots with an upsidedown M4 stood up planted straight between each set, and hanging from one will be Cornberger's dogtags and from the other M4 will be Triple Shot's.

And how many more for the guys up in that valley?, Kozak thinks. *Captain Washington. Lieutenant Caufield. Sergeant Akin. How many more, what others? How many more pairs of boots, and more M4s, and their dogtags?*

Out of everyone, everyone and whoever else, he is going to miss most Jashawn Washington. *Jashawn, you can't be dead, Jashawn. You can't be.* Why does he want to be a first sergeant if he doesn't have Jashawn Washington as his company commander.

It's not a question.

I'm gonna hang it up. If they don't throw me out, which they will. Put me in prison, which they will. I'm going to hang it up. Time to go fishing.

A break in squelch on the radio, then a yell from one of the trucks behind, *"They're here! They're here!"*, and Kozak instinctively looks out his window downstream and sees it, or doesn't he?

He drops the window, and sure enough it's there, it's a moving dark shape just below the clouds not three-fingers'-width above the wadi. And another, close behind and a little higher than the first.

They're black birds, fast-approaching really big black birds, they're Blackhawks.

It's Nightingale.

In Wajma it's just enough daylight that you can see with a struggle, but that's going to be gone in about five minutes, and Redcloud tells everyone to call it quits, stop filling any more sandbags and get these last few full ones in a chain upstairs to the roof.

The resupply pallets each had four bundles of 250 sandbags, and the Zoo's gone through three-plus bundles, which is a lot of sandbags filled with wet dirt by so few guys in these short few hours.

Not to mention carried up onto the veranda and stacked into more protective fighting positions on the wall. And carried all the way up to the roof for good fighting positions on the parapet. Plus thick stacks on the front steps, basically narrowing and protecting the entrance.

Each pallet had six entrenching tools, which the guys used. Not that they needed to. Every soldier in a Redcloud-led platoon knows to carry his entrenching tool always on the outside of his ruck.

The guys worked fast in the rain, and now a drizzle for the past hour or so. It's one thing filling sandbags back on the Cop for another bunker or a supply conex or even your own hooch—who really gives a shit?—but when you're filling them for a fighting position you might be behind in five minutes or later tonight or tomorrow morning and two never-ending days from now however long you're gonna be here, you do it huffing in a constant sweat.

Anyone who's ever filled sandbags knows that you work in a team. One guy on the entrenching tool, another holding the bag open, a third to tie the bag and toss it up to the top of the stairs onto the veranda.

The teams today got into contests, who could fill ten bags fastest. Then twenty. Fifty.

Lieut Col Dove filled them. Redcloud too. And Rodriquez, everyone who could did.

Nick Flowers filled sandbags.

The only guy Redcloud left on security was Spec Lee Tran on the 240 on the roof parapet. If the enemy came close or even looked like they were going to come close, even just appear out there just beyond the crashed Chinook, which was about as far as you could see when it was still full daylight, Tran could blast them and everyone would have time to get back on their guns.

The only ones still on the wall who didn't fill sandbags were the two wounded who could fight but not get down in the dirt with an entrenching tool or seated holding a bag open. And Capt Cathay. And they filled 30-round M4 magazines. All the guys' empties and the ten cases that came on each pallet. And they broke open crates of claymores and trip flares and hand grenades.

Doc Eberly and BZ remained inside in the aid station, but they had more important things they were doing. Like BZ showing Eberly how to tie off arteries so a guy maybe wouldn't lose a limb later because it was tourniqueted for eighteen hours. Or more. And redressing wounds, stuffing gauze in tight down into the muscle to the bone. Again, to stop bleeding-out.

On the sandbags Ssgt Ketchum was in a lather, soaked to the skin from his sweat as much as the rain, competing with two of his guys against Ssgt Nell and two of his guys, two out of three, 25 bags each set each team, who's faster, when Ketchum had noticed *"Where's Sandusky? How come he's not out here filling these?"*

"In the aid station," someone said.

"Fucking bullshit!" from Ketchum.

"Naw," from someone else. "He says Doc says he doesn't have to come out."

"Not 'less he's doing open-fuckin-heart surgery," Ketchum said, and he stormed inside, found Sandusky sitting on the floor in the aid station against the wall just staring at the glow of the cigarette in his hand on his lap, and Ketchum controlled himself, checked his wrath and bent down to Sandusky and pulled up his chin and said very gently, "Sandy, you wanna come out and help us fillin sandbags?"

"Doc said I don't hafta go outside," Sandusky said.

"Yeh but you wanna help all yer buddies in the Zoo, doncha?"

"Doc says I don't gotta go outside."

"C'mon, they're yer buddies, dude, we all gotta pull our share, make it safe for all a'us."

"Doc says I don't gotta go outside."

"It's safe. The bad guys, they're hiding. We whipped their ass. Maybe they're comin back later, but it's safe and quiet right now. They're all way down at the other end, you can't even see them. Come on, come with me, we'll just take a little peek, I'll show you."

"Doc says I don't gotta go outside." And Sandusky took a long draw on his Marlboro. Hadn't once raised his eyes, hadn't once met Ketchum's.

"Yeh, well, Sandy, guys worse off'n you are out there, all yer buddies are doin something. Everyone's helpin out."

Sandusky let the cigarette smoke just come out of his mouth and nose in passive fluffs. "Doc says, Sarge, he says I don't" —

And Ketchum lost it, grabbing him by his body armor and yanking him up to his feet and pulling him out of the room, outside, with Sandusky whining all the way, "Doc says! Doc says! Doc says!", and Ketchum threw him to the mud at the empty sandbags. He picked up an entrenching tool and threw it at him blade-down. "Fill! Start filling!"

And Sandusky started crawling away, and Ketchum stomped his boot on his back, "Where you goin, where you gonna run off to?"

Sandusky punched Ketchum's leg away and kept crawling, and Ketchum let him, laughing after him, "Yer goin the wrong way! That's where the Taliban is, you lookin to join the Taliban, desert to the en'my? That's the wrong way, dickwad!" And Sandusky crawled straight head-first into the rock wall. Got himself huddled against it, shoulder to it, face cradled in his hands.

"Look at yerself!" Ketchum yelled out. "Look at yerself, Sandusky! Coward, fucken fraidycat puke coward!"

Neither Dove nor Redcloud said anything. Pretended not to see it, not to watch. It's a squad leader's job to discipline his men. An officer doesn't interfere, and neither does a platoon sergeant, unless it goes too far, unless it's violent.

The others didn't want to watch, but couldn't help it, and pretended not to be seeing it. Even Nick Flowers didn't feel right filming it. But picked up his camera and did from a distance. It's uncomfortable, embarrassing, seeing someone so nakedly afraid, so nakedly a *Fraidycat puke coward*. Someone who just yesterday you were joking with. This morning. Who, when the brigade and battalion commanders came to the air terminal for a pep talk to the company the night they were deploying, it was he who raised his hand when they said *"Any questions?"*, and he said, *"I just want to get over there and kill those ragheads who killed our brothers and sisters on 9-11."* Some of the guys would have thought about

Sandusky not having his tatt yet, and some of those would have tried to think what he'd done in the Tics in the past. Where was he yesterday? The others in his truck, if they're not wounded right now today, they'd have remembered that Sandusky had stayed in the seat, had slammed the door shut, hadn't gotten out. What had he done a couple of weeks ago when the ANA were IED'd? Stayed in the truck buttoned up.

"Look up there!" Ketchum mocked Sandusky. "We got a female, a female Jag captain lawyer's got more balls than you! Look at her. Division headquarters staff puke female's got more balls'n you! Go ahead, what you waitin for, go over the wall, Taliban's waitin for you! You can suck em all off t'night. You can let them pork you in the ass t'night, cuz that's the coward pussy cunt fucken pussy you are!"

"At ease, enough, Ketchum." Redcloud.

"Fucken coward pussy with a capital P, Sand-dusk-Pussy!"

"At ease I said! Enough, Ketch! Drop it, leave it!"

And Ketchum went back to filling sandbags, working more feverishly. And no one said anything else.

And Sandusky remained huddled at the rock wall. In the rain. One cigarette after the other, trying to light them, and each getting soaked, and none lit, and his Zippo continually getting extinguished. Going through his whole pack and left with nothing but soggy crumbly broken cigarettes littering his lap and the mud.

A little while later Redcloud had tasked Ketchum to get a couple of his guys inside and get the ponchos and poncho liners from the resupply hung up over all the windows. Two or three thick, he didn't want any light going out tonight. And they'd be using light inside, if only for the docs in the aid station.

Kyle Wolfe and Ssgt Utah spent most of the two hours before losing all light setting up an exterior defense. Stretching out the rolls of C-wire from the first terrace wall to the stream in a single row. Setting out trip flares in front of the wire, in it and behind it. Setting the claymore mines that came on the pallets on the enemy side of the rock wall, all along it, from the terrace wall to the stream, about four feet apart, using the dead enemy they'd sat up to screen the mines, planting the claymores right between their legs, tight to their groins, hidden camouflaged under their garb. Yeh, under those dark serape blankets. You can't even tell they've got claymores clamped tight on them like jockstraps.

"Howdy Doody," Utah had said. "Now this is going to be some welcoming committee." And when Ssgt Nell had come over to have a look, Utah'd lifted a serape and the dead Talib's jammie top to show the claymore, and Nell'd laughed and said that it was a lucky thing those fellas had already gotten to heaven and gotten their "Legs-wide-open vir-gines, cuz when we blow them claymores there's gonna be nuthin left of em" from their knees to their necks.

The backblast of a claymore'll do that to a fella. That's the backside, curved in, with the C4 on it. The front, convex, curved out, that's where the near-thousand ball bearings are that, when the C4's set off by the electrical blasting cap screwed into the top of the mine, shoot out in a sweet arc that, when aimed properly at about waist-level out twenty feet will pretty much stop a bunch of charging soldiers . . . . permanently.

On the backside the explosion and the stones and pebbles and debris thrown out by the backblast will cause trouble for any of the friendlies dumb enough to be within 10 or 15 meters of it, which is why the rock wall makes for an excellent backblast shield. The dead Talibs too. Plus, the explosion is better funneled forward. "Super awesome," is what Van Louse had said when he'd come over to check it out. "Oughta get Nick to take a picture of this."

"No way, are you crazy, Louie?" Utah told him. "Do you want to get us all thrown in jail?"

Van Louse, "Aw com'on, it's a defensive perimeter, you gotta set up a defensive perimeter, there's no law against that."

"It's called desecrating the dead, Louie," Utah'd said. "What, did you sleep through all the Roe classes? It's a war crime."

"Yeh," Wolfe had said. "If ever there wasn't an oxymoron."

What's more, Wolfe and Utah had rigged the claymores far more complexly than Redcloud had expected. Every sixth one was daisy-chained to one another all the way down the wall. That is, the first wired to the seventh to the thirteenth to the nineteenth, and down the line. The second to the eighth, etcetera. With six command wires buried in the mud back and up onto the veranda where Utah would control three initiator clackers and Wolfe the other three. That way, in an assault or multiple assaults, you can blow a lethal arch of body-shredding ball bearings out the entire length of the rock wall six separate times, six claymores going off each time. Thirty-six all totaled.

The complex rigging of the daisy-chain, Redcloud knew, was a pure Wolfe thing. Utah wouldn't have thought of it, nor would have Nell. Ketchum maybe, but he wouldn't have considered it worth the extra time. For Wolfe, this is an art, Redcloud thought. And wouldn't have a way of knowing that for Wolfe it was also an homage to the grunts of that war that he wasn't even born yet for and that he's read so much about, Vietnam, when, from what he's read, daisy-chaining claymores was everyday commonplace.

Well, maybe not all of thirty-six, in chains of six.

Each cushioned separately concealed in the crotch of a dead enemy soldier.

That's art.

And for Wolfe it sure beats filling sandbags.

Which in a sense is kind of like the ANA pulled off.

The only Afghan who helped fill sandbags this entire time was the ANA sergeant.

The other five still here are inside—the 3 dead and 2 badly wounded.

The four who hadn't deserted before the assaults and fought in the assaults? They're gone.

It was after the air crew and the electronics had been brought from the downed Chinook and they were breaking out the sandbags and entrenching tools, and out of nowhere, totally unexpected, gibberish had started from the four-pack loudspeakers mounted on the distant mosque's roof, which you couldn't even see through the fog. The sentiments of some of the Zoosters was to *"Just shoot them, move up closer where you could see em and put some 40mm grenades on the roof and blow them sky high"*, or even *"Use the AT-4s"* that came on the resupply, *"just one's enough, blow those speakers up, blow the whole roof off the place"*.

Dove had ordered *No*, you don't fire upon a mosque, not on his watch, not unless you're taking direct fire from it and can see the muzzle flashes coming from it.

And particularly not during a call to prayer.

How would that go over worldwide, with the cameras the Taliban surely have pointed on the mosque right now, the United States Army blasting away on a mosque with anti-tank rockets during call to prayer?

And that's what it was, Wolfe had confirmed, just from the words and phrases he understood. And which Nouri said yes it was a call to prayer, which he then loosely translated.

Wolfe said that he wished they'd thought about it when they'd arrived and had the ANA go into the mosque and liberate the little Honda generator that's always in these concrete mosques in these tiny villages.

Liberate, as in take for their own. ANA are famous for that. From compounds. All the time. Food, money left out, a gun, a radio, and even a twelve-year-old boy once in a while, but only to borrow, just for the night.

But not from mosques. No liberation there; some things are just sacred.

Not one of those farmers up in not one of those compounds probably had a generator, Wolfe had said. But the mosque, a mosque's always gotta have a generator. For the loudspeakers. For the call to prayer.

In the compounds they'll burn kerosene for light, cow patties for cooking and they'll huddle under blankets around a small tin coal stove all winter, but their mosques are always going to have a little Honda generator and always enough gas for those calls to prayer.

Five times a day.

It was when the tone of the voice coming from the loudspeakers down there had changed and Nouri had stopped translating that Dove became concerned. Redcloud too.

And Wolfe could pick out enough words of the Pashto, in particular names, like *"Nouri"* and *"The province of Nouri, Ghazni"*, and *"The family of*

Nouri". And the names of the ANA soldiers alive here. The ANA sergeant's name. Names of towns, districts, provinces.

Nouri refused to translate. Refused Dove's demands that he translate. Moved away from Dove and the others. To cluster with the remaining ANA listening intently, some jittery.

Wolfe had translated what he could. That the Talibs out there knew Nouri and the ANA still here, alive or wounded. By name, family, hometown.

They were saying something about *To live to return to their families.* Something about *Allah will see that their families are safe.*

That there was now a *kandak* in the valley here. A *kandak.*

Wolfe knows that word well. So does Dove. They've both worked with kandaks before.

Battalions. *Kandak* is battalion in Pashto.

A *kandak of Soldiers of Allah*, the voice over the loudspeakers was saying. Here in this valley.

Talibs in battalion-size massing for attack.

A kandak against one small American platoon.

And *How many of our brothers of Allah* remain alive with that platoon? Five? Six? Seven? *Come out and join us.*

Come out and rejoice with us as we will fire upon the American platoon our recoilless rifles.

Come out and celebrate with us the arrival of our recoilless rifles.

Even Dove and Redcloud and others listening carefully understood *recoilless*, as it is the same in Pashto as in English. Said repeatedly over the loudspeakers, *Recoilless blah blah blah, Recoilless blah blah blah, Recoilless blah blah blah*, and Wolfe translated the word for *Rifles* used as well and said that they were indeed saying the plural as far as he could tell.

There isn't an ANA soldier anywhere who doesn't know of the mighty power of a recoilless rifle, having heard since he was a kid the stories from a father and grandfather and uncles of all these years of war since the Russian invasion and the death and destruction from afar brought by the recoilless rifles of all sides.

The sing-song Pashto continued from the mosque's loudspeakers. A repeat, which Wolfe could translate, for *Our Afghan brothers to come out* and they would tomorrow join with them in *Walking on the graves of the infidels.*

Ketchum said to level the mosque with a couple of the Laws that came in the resupply. He could hit it easy from here. Wipe out the loudspeakers.

Law, as in LAW, as in Light Anti-Tank Weapon.

The man-pack version of the bigger AT-4. Like the RPG, shoulder-launched, but throw-away. All-in-one. A tube about two-foot long, you extend it out about double, plop it on your shoulder, flick up the sight, pull out the safety, trigger it and watch the small rocket fly. Smash the tube on the ground to bend it and make it unusable for enemy for anything, and toss it aside.

"Two Laws for those loudspeakers," Ketchum said, "One AT-4 straight in through those windows, that prayer hole is history."

No, from Dove.

And coming from the speakers, a repeat that *Your families, fathers and your children should live a hundred more years.*

A repeat that *Your families will thank you to Allah for whom we all serve.*

And the remaining four ANA left. Nouri too. All but the sergeant.

They knew enough without being told to drop their weapons and gear.

Nouri apologized humbly to Dove and Redcloud, telling them he was sorry, very very sorry, but he must go, he must, for his family, he could not cause harm to his family.

Not Dove, nor Redcloud, nor Wolfe, nor the ANA sergeant nor anybody said anything to stop them from leaving. Just watched them hop over the rock wall and head down the beach toward the mosque.

Dove and Wolfe have seen the destructive power of the recoilless rifle in the first month of the war here when the Northern Alliance and the Taliban still had them to rain upon each other. Redcloud and some of the others know the weapon from Iraq, when the al-Qaeda insurgents might manage to get off two or three shots before the Apache gunships would send rockets into their positions.

They all know the weapon as a "tank killer".

It fires an artillery shell, unlike the smaller, less powerful rocket round of an RPG or a Law or an AT-4 or a mortar. And it is far more accurate than all those.

Far more accurate on the first shot for a guy who's trained on it.

It is a tank killer.

From a long way off.

It makes the AT-4 and the even-smaller Law look like peashooters.

From a long long way off.

Can't launch as far away as a 120mm mortar, but a lot easier to get the aim more accurate and spot-on.

Which Dove had thought then and is thinking right now, as almost all the light has gone and everyone is heading inside. That if the insurgents have big, tripod mounted recoilless rifles, the 106mm, even one, they can fire it from halfway far across the valley and *We can't reach them.* Even the smaller, shoulder-fired one, they can shoot it *From out about a thousand meters, and even if it's not real accurate that far, how hard is it to hit this building?, and the only thing we have that we can touch them with's the M240-B, and no lightweight machinegun's anyone's preferred weapon at that range.*

Anti-tank guns accurately aimed, by Chechens what do you want to bet, if they've got a 106 they can put rounds right through the windows here. Maybe the sandbags will help. *If they've got flechette rounds*—air-exploding in a supersonic shower of 2,400 little razor-sharp darts that shred, anti-personnel, you don't want to be caught in the open, not even an arm or a hand out in the open—*I don't want to see it, let's just pray they don't have them, that Uncle Sam never sold the Pakis fletchette rounds.* Good thing for the sandbags, against flechettes they will help. At least it's something.

Recoilless rifles were a motivation for the men getting them filled faster.

Dove has thought it through already, is thinking it through, and he knows *We're going to have to do something.*

And he's interrupted by Redcloud now stepping away, a lit cigarette in hand that he got from Ssgt Nell, out toward the rock wall, and Dove calls to him, "Sergeant Redcloud!"

Redcloud stops. Turns his head.

Dove knows what Redcloud is about to do and was just a moment ago intent on stopping him. He changes his mind. Waves it off to Redcloud, *Never mind.*

Redcloud goes to Cpl Sandusky still huddled against the rock wall staring blankly into the dead Zippo in his hands.

Squats down and puts a hand on Sandusky's shoulder.

"Corporal," he says. "Sandusky. Sandy. Come on, let's go inside, Sandy, it's getting dark out here."

Nothing from Sandusky, he doesn't look away from his Zippo.

"Can you hear me, Sandy? Do you know who this is? Do you know who I am? Sandy, come on now, snap out of it. Sandy, do you know who I am?"

Nothing, then a slight nod from Sandusky.

"Who, Sandy, who am I? Tell me who I am. Who do you think this is, Sandy?"

Nothing. Pause, then slowly, "Sergeant Redcloud."

"Good. Good. Here, here's something for you. Here"—

The cigarette, which Redcloud places in Sandusky's lips, and Sandusky lets it droop there for these few moments then draws in on it slowly. His eyes still locked on his Zippo.

"Okay, see? It's all cool now, Sandy. Now we're gonna get up, and we're gonna go inside, okay? We're going to go inside, we can't stay out here. Okay? Come on, stand up."

Nothing from Sandusky. Just letting the cigarette smoke drift out one corner of his mouth.

"Yeh now, Sandy, you can do it, you can get up, and I'm right with you, we'll walk up inside. Ready? Okay?"

Nothing. Just another slow draw on the cigarette.

"We're gonna go to Doc's room. We're going to the aid station, and you don't have to leave the aid station. You just stay in there and you help Doc, do what you can, okay? You're gonna help Doc, in the aid station, and that's it, you don't have to leave the aid station. Okay? Com'on com'on let's stand up now."

Nothing.

"Sandy, do you hear me?"

Sandusky takes the cigarette from his lips. Moves his eyes from his Zippo to its glowing tip.

Redcloud says again, "We're going inside, where you can stay safe in the aid classroom, okay, Sandy?"

And Sandusky now slowly moves his eyes to focus on Redcloud's lips.

"You'll be with Doc," Redcloud tells him. "I know you trust Doc Eberly."

"I'm not . . ." Sandusky says, his eyes on Redcloud's lips. "I'm not . . . I'm I'm I'm . . . Sarge, I'm not gonna get my tatt now am I? I'm not gonna get my Zoo tatt, am I, Sarge?"

"We'll talk about it when we get back to the Cop, okay? Don't you trouble yourself about that now, we'll talk about it back on the Cop."

Redcloud doesn't know it, and it wouldn't matter to him anyway, but Dove has already told Ssgts Ketchum and Utah and Nell, *"Not a word. Not one word. Put it out to the men."*

Meaning, tell their men that no one's to say anything to or about Sandusky. He's a casualty, not to be harassed, berated, mocked or laughed at.

Redcloud could have saved Dove the trouble. If he thought about it. He knows that his men, just seeing his actions now, that they would know it all already, know to stay silent, to now leave Sandusky be.

And he walks just behind Sandusky now, one hand just barely touching Sandy's back, and what he's thinking about, he's thinking, *If they've got recoilless rifles we're really gonna be in a world of hurt.*

If they've got recoilless rifles. It's still an if.

Was that a recoilless rifle that hit the Chinook? Recoilless rifle or RPG?

It was too far away to tell.

If they've got recoilless rifles they can take out any chopper flying into here.

Sandusky starts up the steps, Redcloud right behind him.

Just one recoilless rifle, Redcloud thinks, *and guys who know how to shoot it, a couple dozen rounds, they'll control the Air, and they can pretty much level this place.*

Day Two, Night

In Gen St Claire's office suite.

Just he, Dr Hutchinsen and Col Pluma.

Seated at his conference table. He at the head, Hutchinsen to his left, Pluma his right.

St Claire is eating dinner made special for him, as most evenings.

Salmon salad tonight. Double portion, as usual.

In a 24oz tumbler a protein shake.

In another an orange-tinted Gatorade.

When St Claire had motioned the cooks to enter with his meal, that signaled the end of the evening Cub, and all the dozen staff officers stood at once to leave, dismissed, but St Claire indicated for Pluma to stay along with Hutchinsen.

Being dismissed from a Cub is a good thing. Asked to stick around means you've done something wrong or the four-star is going to task you with some problem you really don't need added to an already overflowing problem box.

The Cub this evening had been quick, as they always are with St Claire.

The morning one at 0700 sharp, the evening at 1900 sharp.

No PowerPoint briefing slides. St Claire wants to hear it from you and considers the time your staff is spending making the slides to be time better spent running their tiny spoke in the big wheel.

Right, time better spent empting that problem box.

St Claire wants the big picture, precise and exact, and don't give him nit-nat bullshit just to try and impress him with your hard work and hard charging go-get-em spirit that's going to win the war single-handedly.

And if it's charts or diagrams or maps that you think he absolutely has to see on a slide, give it to him on a hardcopy print-out and let him review it at his choosing.

Essential to know about St Claire in a Cub or any briefing:

Don't waste his time.

Give him the bullet points, and he'll ask questions if he needs to know more.

Don't bring something up unless it's an issue that cannot be resolved with 100% finality without the general's direct input.

Do not bring something up unless the potential military and/or political ramifications might be from mildly to extremely devastating to the war and/or this command.

When in doubt, bring it up in a concise bullet point and let the general wave it off or ask questions.

This evening's Cub dispensed with everything countrywide, with the exception of Wajma Valley, by 1907hrs. Including the change in the upcoming Secretary of State's arrival at Bagram Airfield from Wednesday 1453hrs to Thursday 0850hrs. And included Dr Hutchinsen's off-hand remark that Bagram had better secure the runway's perimeter to ensure that the Sec State wouldn't have to dash across the tarmac under a hail of insurgent machinegun fire.

Everyone laughed, knowing the Sec State's heralded past as First Lady landing under fire once in Bosnia.

Supposedly under fire.

But not really.

Which is why it was clever.

Even more clever said by Doctor Hutchinsen, because everyone wants to laugh when he says something clever.

Or when General St Claire says something that's always even more clever.

And that little mockery of the Sec State is a joke that St Claire himself would have said, had it just been he and Hutch together, just the two of them in private. Not here, not around this conference table with all these ears whose voices might someday appear next month in *Vanity Fair* or *The Atlantic* or *Rolling Stone*.

Countrywide the Cub took all of seven minutes.

Wajma Valley and the Tattoo Zoo the rest of the time, a bit longer.

Even without any rehash of facts and stats that the general already knew. Those were skipped. Presented were the latest status updates.

Including:

Lieutenant Colonel Zachary Dove's report that he has 26 there available who are capable of carrying arms, carrying on the fight. Individual status of personnel unknown. And that's counting the two civilians who Cop Valley Forge reported were on the morning infil, the Human Terrain Team contractor Kyle Wolfe and the embedded journalist Nick Flowers.

Status on the embed Flowers? *Unknown, sir. Dove refuses to send up specifics on the casualties.*

In addition, of those 26 available to fight, 2 could be the non-combat-arms Division Staff personnel who infilled with Dove. The Jag captain, Laura Cathay, and the Public Affairs specialist, Bernard Howie. *How useful they'll be, sir, there's no telling, sir, if either one knows which end of an M4 the bullet comes out of.*

There was light laughter at that.

Status of the flight crew of the CH-47? *Three critical, one dead, two walking wounded which, sir, we assume is part of the 26 available to fight. Of those six, sir, there is no status on the individual who is not on the manifest. A Special Forces 18-Delta medic from Chapman Base. The details, sir, all the rosters are in there.*

The thin three-ring binder of important stats. Which St Claire had already scanned. Which Dr Hutchinsen was just then going through, quickly flipping the pages, snapshotting each into his photographic memory.

Individual clean white sheets of pages with nothing but the straight facts. Courier New or Times New Roman font, 12pt, and nothing else. Include a fancy multi-color pie-chart PowerPoint slide, and the general will tear it out and just flick it across the polished table. And you won't do that again. If it's not 12pt font, it had better be an important Excel spreadsheet, a map, a photo or essential satellite imagery.

Individual status? *No sir. Again, Major Dove won't give us any specifics by name and SSN.*

Afghan Nationals, how many do we have left? *Of the 21 Local Nationals from Cop Valley Forge who were on the initial airmobile assault into the village, sir, including one civilian contract interpreter, 5 are dead or wounded and 15 have deserted.*

"Dog bites man. Give me man bites dog," St Claire had said then, and everyone laughed.

Yeh, tell us something everyone doesn't already know. The high rate of ANA desertion aint news, Jack.

Latest weather for the AO? *Cleared up by tomorrow afternoon, sir. From all indications. Unless something unforeseen comes up.*

Present status, near term, long term for the Red? *As we learned today, sir, our computer models aren't quite as precise as we'd thought. Concerning this geography. The Hindu Kush, sir. It's got its own peculiar random weather characteristics. Needless to say, we've been haranguing the civilian contractor stateside and they're pleading innocence, lots of backtracking, blame-shifting. They're working on it, they say.*

Status, your best Swag? *Swag, sir? Sir, we're hoping for Amber by maybe mid-morning. Green by noon, sir.*

Swag, for SWAG.

Scientific Wild-Assed Guess.

Satellite imagery? *Depends on the weather, sir.*

Drones? *Negative, sir. The weather.*

AC-130 Spectre gunship? *Dedicated, sir. Special Ops up in Kunar. And the Germans, Operation Stein Garden in Logar. As we discussed previously.*

160th airframes? *Again, sir, dedicated, Special Ops, Kunar, Helmand, Zabul, Kandahar, the Germans for Stein Garden.*

Fast-movers? *F-16s on-station outside the weather, sir, ten minutes from the valley. Just need grid coordinates for their Jdams, sir.*

On-station time? *Continuous, sir, they're rotating in and out. Again, sir, they're blind in this weather. We just need solid confirmable ten-digits for the Jdams.*

Status on A-10s? *Available on-call, sir. Weather-dependent, sir.*

Primary tenet of Coin is protection of the civilian population. I do not want any air ordnance released on any of those civilian non-combatant compounds or anywhere near those compounds, is that understood? Unless you have the data showing the Poo right there in the compound, and you will record that data, is that understood? *Yes sir.*

I trust the battle commander's judgment, especially when sixty seconds can be the difference between life and death for the platoon, such as was the case earlier this afternoon with the Jdam launches, but there will be no further airstrikes without Roe Attorney-Judgment Approval, signed. Understood? *Yes sir.*

I want to be perfectly clear on this. Roe Attorney-Judgment Approval. *Yes sir. And, sir, if the platoon calls in a Status-Black-Emergency ten-digit center-of-mass for Troops In The Open?*

Your recommendation? *It's Major Dove, sir, I think we can trust his judgment.*

You would be confident in Lieutenant Colonel Zachary Dove's ability to differentiate enemy combatants from non-combatants, when half his force is dead or wounded and when he's down to just twenty-six men with the capacity to fight? *Aw, sir . . . .*

Have you considered that that Status-Black-Emergency Troops In The Open will just as likely be the enemy insurgents dressed as civilians and appearing very much to be non-combatant Afghan locals in the footage we see on CNN and the BBC and in full-color above-the-fold in tomorrow morning's *New York Times*, if only by their shredded bodies left by the thousand-pounders? *Sir?*

Are you aware that "Troops In The Open" is a call to Mecca for our adversaries for whom dominating the battle on the media front is essential to their victory? *Yes sir, of course, sir.*

Everyone in here should be old enough to remember the shooting gallery in Desert Storm with Saddam Hussein's retreating tanks and trucks and troops up the Highway of Death? *Sir?*

It played great on CNN for about twenty-four hours, with gunsight footage straight from the cockpits, the triumph of America. But you ask General Schwarzkopf today if he'd have instead passed the order not to fire upon those retreating Iraqis and do you know what he would say? *Understood, sir. No airstrikes without precise Poo data and that data recorded, along with Roe lawyers' stamp of approval.*

Fire support? The guns at Valley Forge? *Negative, sir. One 155 is ready for airlift to the Cop as soon as the weather clears there and at Fob Salerno.*

Rangers? *On standby, sir, at Salerno. One company. Three CH-47s standing by for the air assault. Just waiting on the weather, sir.*

And General St Claire was given the latest update from the Salerno Cash. The QRF's three wounded were serious but stabilized and not in need of immediate transport to higher. The two dead were still dead. They had names now—Sergeant Cornberger and Pfc Tripp, which meant nothing to St Claire.

It's all in the binder anyway, those specifics.

Prior to the Cub, St Claire had learned of the medevac for the QRF after the fact of its return without incident to the Salerno Cash and had let it ride, pretending ignorance. If Colonel Pluma knew that St Claire knew, it didn't matter. Not right now. St Claire would deal with Pluma's overreaching and questionable authorization of the medevac on Air Red later—tomorrow perhaps—depending on the overall outcome of this unwelcome and potentially devastating situation in that valley.

Devastating to the war.

To this command.

To the Zoo? In St Claire's mind?

Sorry, that's small potatoes.

As for that Awesome Company unauthorized QRF, St Claire received assurances that he would have a copy of the After Action Report direct from the battalion as soon as they received it from the company, and that battalion had been directed to forward it in the original form without its or brigade's input.

He received assurances that Major Zachary Dove or Lieutenant Colonel Zachary Dove, whichever, would be ordered to send up the specifics on his wounded and dead, by name and SSN, but St Claire asked if it wouldn't be more prudent to wait until the casualties were officially identified by Graves Registration, rather than risk a premature error and the wrong word prematurely getting back to a family, even just one family.

He didn't have to say it, but everyone thought of that Pat Tillman fiasco and the media battle it caused the Pentagon and the careers it shot down.

Yeh, all right, okay, specifics can wait.

Nothing without Graves Registration's signature.

St Claire received assurances that the brigade was presently investigating how that lone CH-47 managed to take off without authorization and without any resistance with two pallets of emergency resupplies and a crew of five and the one un-manifested Special Forces Green Beret medic, and the results of the investigation were to be passed forward asap.

St Claire gave assurances to Colonel Katherine Gray-Nance that her efforts today under such extreme time constraints had been better than the general could have hoped for.

The evidence of her exemplary work was in fact at that very moment on the three muted flatscreens on the front wall playing cable news channel loops of the insurgents setting afire anthropologist Dr Robyn Banks and highlights of the general's informative, open, heartfelt and emotional press conference.

Col Gray-Nance assured the general that she realized the importance of this Battle of Wajma Valley, she called it. That she realized that it could be a defining moment in this war, how the American public and the worldwide audience would perceive the war as right or wrong, ethical or immoral, simply from the actions of the players in this dramatic moment. She said that she hoped that *The others here in this room would realize its importance, sir, when they offer you their own advice from the wisdom of their previous experience*, with an eye as much or more on winning the PR war as on the actual fighting on the ground.

St Claire assured her that he well understood the significance of both, of winning both, but that he would be disappointed to learn that any of his trusted staff in here believed that both victories be given equal priority.

Realizing her mistake, "Yes sir, that's what I meant," Gray-Nance had then said, and St Claire brushed off her apology with something about him very well understanding that for her, as his public affairs officer, his eyes and ears and heart and brain of the media, she should prioritize this as a media battle first, and that he not only wanted her to do so but he expected her to, as he expected and wanted the others here to advise him on the battle from the combat rifles-bayonets-and-Jdam perspective that is their expertise and should be their primary focus.

Anything further?

Nothing from anybody.

No? Are you certain? Come on, let's have it, if you think it's important. Anything?

Nope.

And he waved the cooks in with his dinner, and everyone knew without his saying *End of Cub* that they were dismissed. And relieved.

He indicated for Col Pluma to stay put along with Dr Hutchinsen.

And right now a few minutes later still silently playing on all three muted flatscreens is the same forty-five seconds of St Claire in the press conference but three or four seconds off-sync from one TV to the next to the next.

Hutchinsen sucks on the fat rubber straw of his 48oz Nalgene cooler cup he usually fills for the evening at the Dfac with a mix of crushed ice, Pepsi, Mt. Dew and a can of Rip It.

As for Pluma, he figures that he'll eat something after he leaves here. He has a little chuckle to himself, now watching the three TVs showing the same St Claire speaking the same thing but out of sync, each one just slightly off the others, and the third now cuts to the BBC anchor talking. Now immediately it cuts to the video of the insurgents throwing gasoline on Robyn Banks and her bursting into flames.

Doctor Hutchinsen was right, Pluma thinks. *The Anti-Afghan Forces shouldn't have left that in their edit they B-ganned.*

And he gets another little chuckle to himself, thinking about Gray-Nance blowing it with that *Propaganda is more important than bullets*, her *Schooling all of us as if we're morons*, and the general catching her on it but pretending that it's perfectly all right that she thinks it, but not really, and the *Fat bitch should have known that's exactly what he'd say, and she didn't, and she's supposed to be the media wizard who knows what they're all thinking*.

Pluma figures that now it's his turn to get the schooling from the general. *Going to take me to the woodshed. Bend over, Daniel*, and down'll come the general's wooden paddle. For sending Nightingale to Cop Valley Forge. Pluma can hear St Claire very calmly asking, didn't he *Know the consequences of the medevac crashing in the Red?*

"Dan?" St Claire is saying to him. "Your thoughts, Dan. You pull any punches, I'll find someone else for the job."

"Sir? Specifically? Exactly what aspect?"

"Broad-based, as a whole. From this seat." His position of command.

"You know my gut instincts, sir. I'd order the Rangers in right now. They're ready, they're Rangers—." A shrug, *What more needs be said?* "If that Chinook could get in there once, then they can get in there again."

Hutchinsen chuckles a snarl, "Did the Chinook get back out?"

Pluma does not hide his displeasure with Hutchinsen. Pretends he's not here, presents his argument solely to St Claire. "Not to pull any punches, sir, but we both know that Operation Stein Garden is just a throw-away mission to make the Germans feel good, feel like they're actually fighting. We can postpone it for twenty-four hours and get Spectre on-station and move the 160th assets to Salerno for the Rangers."

Hutchinsen, "Air is Red at Salerno, Danny."

"Not necessarily for the 160th." Pluma just can't help confronting Hutchinsen as wrong. "They thrive flying in challenging conditions and dangerous circumstances."

"Challenging?" Hutchinsen smiles. "Hmmmm. I wonder if that helicopter flight crew crashed there in the valley would consider that an appropriate euphemism. Challenging. Dangerous? Is that your euphemism for lethal?"

"That Chinook was conventional. Nighttime is Special Ops' strength, it's actually their advantage. They're called, you might be aware, the Night Stalkers. Night, not Day Stalkers. You ought to go out with them on a mission some night, Doctor Hutchinsen, and see exactly what their capabilities are."

Hutchinsen gives him an innocent look that says *How do you know I haven't?*

Pluma continues his argument directly to him, not to St Claire. "That Chinook flew in there in broad daylight, and still they made it all the way in and almost all the way out before they were shot down, and maybe that was just a lucky shot for all we know. Nighttime, the enemy's blind. 160th's not."

He turns to Gen St Claire. "The point is, sir, they made it to the school building. Conventional, sir, and not Special Ops."

And back to Hutchinsen. "If you've flown with the 160th, you already know that they can fly blackout on a moonless night straight down a coal miner's shaft. And come back out."

Hutchinsen, "Did you miss the latest word from your buddy Zachary Dove? Something about, what was it?" Playing innocent. Playing stupid. "Recoilless rifles? Whatever those are. I'm not a military man, what do I know?"

Hutchinsen knows what they are.

Pluma knows that he knows what they are.

When Dove's report had come in, to refresh his memory from blips about the use of them in all those books about the war with the Soviets he's read over the years, Hutchinsen had immediately looked it up on Wikipedia—*Recoilless Rifle*.

He adds, "I wouldn't imagine they're hauling the big ol' monster two-hundred-ten kilogram M40s down those mountain trails, with their hefty 106-millimeter ammunition. Normally vehicle-towed or vehicle–mounted, I don't suppose so, no, not the M40s, not down those slippery footpaths, not tonight. But if they're bringing into that valley the nine kilo 90-millimeter shoulder-launch M67 recoilless rifles, you don't think, Danny— you don't think that they also might have some twenty-three ounce night vision goggles?"

To see those Spec Ops birds flying blackout on a moonless night right down a West Virginia coal miner's shaft.

Hutchinsen continues. "As I say, I'm not a military professional, but I have heard those in-the-know talk about the recoilless rifle being up there with Stingers and ZPUs and ZU-23s when it comes to a copter pilot's worst nightmare. Unless those 160th fellows are more than mere mortals."

No response from Pluma. Just an angry stare at Hutchinsen.

Who continues, "How many Rangers are there in a Ranger company? A hundred and twenty? Forty per MH-47, since you want to utilize the 160th? Plus air crews? Danny, you're awful brave with other people's lives."

He sucks in on his drink.

What he knows Col Pluma doesn't know. What he knows no one here at Isaf knows but for Gen St Claire with whom Hutchinsen shared the information.

What he got from a close Agency source. Then confirmed from another close Agency source.

Satellite imagery from eighteen hours ago and up until the weather moved in just before noon of unusually heavy vehicular traffic on the Pakistan side of the border not twenty miles from Wajma Valley. Jingle trucks going to the farthest turn-arounds on the dirt roads up into the mountain passes and disgorging crates of matériel and clusters of moving human forms.

Activity that was confirmed after the weather blinded the satellites by eyes on the ground who were saying even as little as two hours ago when the info was passed to Hutchinsen that the trucks were still arriving.

The Agency's analysis clearly speculates that it's an operation of the other agency, the Paki one, the ISI.

Information that Col Pluma doesn't have a need to know.

And a blabbermouth public affairs wench like Gray-Nance would never need to know, if only to remain naïve of such Paki operations.

Information that cannot be made public knowledge, can only be guessed at but never proved, when that government—Pakistan in this instance—is an ally of the one at war with those it is actively arming.

The kind of geopolitical knowledge of extremely serious and deadly hijinks only privy to a select few, like Dr Gene Hutchinsen, PhD, who now gets his own little chuckle to himself, thinking what he has known since he was about in third grade: *Politics aint beanbag.*

St Claire has gentle eyes for Pluma, and Pluma feels the general's empathy for him, that he too would like to send the Ranger company in to save Zach and the platoon, he would, and use the lower-risk 160th MH-47s to do it, he really would, if only the risks were not still so damn high against those 120 Ranger soldiers and the air crews. Forget the weather, yeh the 160th loves the night, say the G-Model MH-47s can glide right through the pitch dark and the negative weather, but it's tough to slip around a couple of recoilless shells flying at your fat naked flanks viewed through night vision goggles. Even one bird of the three lost, that's more personnel than already on the ground there in that cursed valley.

Better to move the conversation along.

"Your gut feelings," he asks Pluma. "On authorizing airstrikes there in the valley for troops in the open."

"I think you're right, sir. There's a difference between artillery and thousand-pound GPS-guided bombs from aircraft fifty miles away. If we can get that replacement howitzer to Cop Valley Forge, cross our fingers. And you're right, sir, that grunts shooting rounds from a big tube is not what the media likes to play as much as we're the big bad wolf when we're carpet-bombing arc lights with B-52s on lonely little civilian-dressed soldiers carrying nothing but AKs. AKs and a copy of the Koran. For the media, you might as well dress us up in Hitler masks, as the Texas Chainsaw murderer."

From Hutchinsen a smile and laugh, "Good, very good. You do know the difference, Danny."

"I'm not completely stupid, Doctor."

"There's a difference between stupidity and naïveté. And in your case it's not even naïveté as much as it is your allowing your emotional bond, your attachment to Zach Dove as both friend and subordinate, mentor and protégé—allowing that relationship to get in the way of battlefield practicality and your extensive military understanding of what it takes to win at the most minimal price. The further removed one is emotionally, the easier life-and-death decisions are to make. Your close friendship with Zachary Dove is noble, even moral, and to be respected, but it should not be relevant here."

And now it's St Claire who has a little chuckle to himself that he hides. He knows that Dan Pluma not only does not have an emotional bond or friendship with Zach but that he doesn't even like him. He knows that Pluma is envious of Dove's intellect, his matinee-idol looks and bearing. That Pluma covets Zach Dove's years of platoon and company commands in actual on-the-ground combat, and he distrusts the false humility Zach uses to hide his own vicious ambition for rank. That Dan Pluma recruited Zachary for his staff here only because he knew of no major better for the job and because Zach would make him look good.

What's more, the deeper chuckle that St Claire now hides is that he knows that Hutch knows all that and is simply playing Pluma with false praise, and for no reason other than as a game, mind games, toying with Pluma. Because Hutch doesn't need Pluma for anything. Not his regard, not his acceptance, not his respect.

Unless. . . .

Unless, St Claire realizes, *Hutch isn't sure that I'm on his side. Isn't sure that I won't be swayed by Dan,* that Pluma might just touch St Claire's soft spot, that spot that holds dear what he clearly remembers his father telling him, that *On your deathbed, son, you won't think "I could have made full-bird or I could have had another star." You'll regret that "Why are there so few people here?" Or you'll rejoice that so many have come to say goodbye. You'll know you made the right choice, son, when the room is full and you can see that there isn't a one in there with a dry eye.*

Another chuckle inside that St Claire does not reveal. That Hutch, for all his genius and confidence and swagger, thinks that St Claire might be convinced by Pluma of the righteous virtue and unimpeachable morality of Pluma's pedestrian way out of this total quagmire that this Tattoo Zoo Platoon incident has turned out to be.

St Claire eats his salmon salad, drinks his protein shake, and shows not the least expression that he's listening, that he hears Hutch now do a pivot on Pluma to obliterate any forthcoming counter of Pluma's to the argument Hutch has made already earlier in private to St Claire and to which St Claire has yet to show approval or even given to Hutch an indication that he might favor.

"From what I gather, Danny," Hutchinsen is saying, "and it is noble and perhaps it's the Christian thing to do, and I respect it, I truly do. All that forgiveness and all, all that choirboy 'turn the other cheek'. I suppose that you would be of a mind to forgive, to turn the other cheek, or just ignore that reckless insubordinate mutinous First Sergeant Edward Kurt Kozak down there at Cop Valley Forge who broke regulations and countermanded direct orders to return to base. That you would forgive and forget, chalk it off, let bygones be bygones, the entire platoon that willingly joined him or were coerced or shamed to join him, and nonetheless broke the law. Should our hearts go out to a first sergeant who not only put every one of their lives in jeopardy, but, remember, who lost some? What were their names? Cornberger, Kevin Randal? Tripp, Gerald Russell? Forgive, forget? And what will you tell their families, Danny? 'Eh, shit happens'?"

"As a matter of fact, Doctor Hutchinsen—"

But Hutchinsen interrupts him with a palm raised. He's not through.

As Gen St Claire knows that Hutch is not through, as he knew what he was going to say, as he knows what's coming.

Which is why he's had Col Pluma stay after the Cub in the first place. *Hear the argument, Dan, and give me the counterargument.*

"The same goes, I suppose, for that helicopter flight crew," Hutchinsen continues. "Who took to the sky against all regulations, which, maybe you'd like to brush them all away and ignore the fact that Warrant Officer Five Chiarduchi, Anthony Luke, had to be aware of them. Warrant officer five, Danny, not warrant officer one. Not private first class, who one would not expect to know regulations by the book. Nato Air Safety Regulations, who needs those stinking Nato regulations? Thirty-five-million-dollar Chinook helicopter, who needs another stinking Chinook anyway? Give that Chiarduchi, Anthony Luke, a Distinguished Flying Cross for valor."

Done, Hutchinsen leans back in his chair. Sucks up on his drink. *Ball's in your court, Danny.*

Pluma doesn't take it. Perhaps he senses he's being set up.

St Claire looks at him. He expects the counterargument, and says so with his slightly raised eyebrows, *Well?*, to which

Pluma raises his hands, palms up. Smiles back, as slight as St Claire's expressions. A shrug. Concedes, "Mark this day down on the calendar. I agree with the brilliant Doctor Hutchinsen, PhD. Seriously, I do."

St Claire's response, his eyes ask, *How?*

Pluma to Hutchinsen, "I'm actually surprised. This isn't the State Department, staffed to the brim with nothing but Ivy League civilians and their free-thinking Henry David Thoreau intellectualism anti-militarism and their superior attitudes of moral irrelevancy and their dogma of man's individual rights verses the compulsion of a tyrannical state. I'm surprised that you would accept that this is the military and the entire institution of the military is built on the foundation of strict discipline—a sort of tyranny, if I may—that one must obey lawful orders. And if those who do not obey lawful orders are allowed to get away with that disobedience and there is no discipline, then the entire structure collapses."

Hutchinsen, "Chiarduchi, Anthony Luke, and his flight crew? That First Sergeant Kozak, Edward Kurt, and his platoon? Those?"

Pluma takes his argument to Gen St Claire. "At the very least, sir, there are going to have to be Article 32s. We should lock down Cop Valley Forge asap. Get the MPs in there as soon as Air clears. With Jag prosecutors. We'll have to put into custody the Chinook flight crew when Zach brings them back to Bagram with the Tattoo Platoon."

Hutchinsen, "If he brings them out alive."

Death rays shoot from Pluma's eyes to Hutchinsen's.

Hutch just slurps on his drink. *What, did I say that? If? Whoops.*

Pluma again takes his case directly to St Claire. "I don't see a way around formal investigations and obvious prosecutions, sir. Everyone knows what happened, from the company at Valley Forge to the battalion to the brigade staff to the chopper task force they all know about First Sergeant Kozak's Reaction Force and the flight crew and what the Tattoo Zoo did yesterday, and there's no way of hiding it. And when soldiers learn that they can break serious regs without cost or negative consequences, there's an old saying"—He directs it at Hutchinsen now. "An old saying that perhaps they teach at Princeton in their ethnic studies course. The Oakies and Other Dumb Hick Great Plains Folk ethnic studies course. That we Nebraska farm boys learn when we're just yay high. You make your bed . . . ."

Dr Hutchinsen can't help but grin. He'd known that Pluma would make that exact case, that in spite of his desire for compassion for soldiers simply trying to help other soldiers *We must adhere to the strictest interpretation of regulations and proper military protocol blah blah blah.*

"I have to admire you, Danny," Hutchinsen says. "At least you're consistent. Earlier this afternoon you wanted to take two Chinooks down there personally and arrest Zachary Dove and the entire lot of that psychopathic platoon. Who, lest we forget so quickly, only killed one hundred and sixty-eight little girls and their mothers and their sisters and their grandmothers. Earlier this afternoon you were quite adamant about bringing those psychopathic killers straight away up to Bagram and lock them up and throw away the goddamn key."

Pluma responds quickly and fiercely, "Earlier this afternoon, correct me if I'm wrong, you were willing to leave the lot of them there in that valley in hopes that they would be overran and massacred. Poetic justice, wasn't that your reasoning? Or, better, because that would be a lot tidier than a year's worth of nasty trials and news reports and defense attorneys in front of microphones on courthouse steps making this command look incompetent and hypocritical and perhaps even criminal?"

Aw, but Hutchinsen knows he's won the day. In an even tone, slowly, almost didactically, like a high school teacher explaining to Johnny why he only got a 73 on the test, he says, "It wasn't not five minutes ago, Colonel Pluma, that you were making the case to Pete that you believed we should send in an entire Ranger company in three how-many-million-dollar super-secret MH-47s to rescue those very criminals. You're willing to throw away the lives of one-hundred and twenty elite Rangers and three more Chinooks just to put under arrest and lock up in Bagram detention the three-dozen oddball Charlie Manson groupies who started this entire nightmare, this potential political disaster?"

Nothing, no answer from Pluma. His expression hard.

Gen St Claire, "Is that still your position, Dan?"

A moment. Pluma breathes in, releases it. "The very heart of the Soldier's Creed, sir. You don't leave your buddy behind."

Hutchinsen, "Of course, Zachary Dove, your good buddy."

"Buddy is a euphemism. For a soldier, any soldier. And those three-dozen oddballs, you call them, they're soldiers. Soldiers first."

"And the hundred-twenty Rangers, they're soldiers, but expendable soldiers? They're expendable? And who are you going to send in to pull their bodies out? Who else then becomes expendable?"

"Ask them, go down to Salerno right now. You interview them, ask every last one. You don't know soldiers and you don't know Rangers."

If Hutchinsen now had time to think about it, he would not have allowed his eyes to jump to the Ranger Tab on Pluma's left shoulder. Too late. He did.

"You can ask them," Pluma continues. "But I'll save you the trip and the trouble. I'll tell you what you'll hear from every one of them. 'Send us in.' 'What are we waiting for?' 'Hooahh, let's go!' They're sitting in that hanger right now and they're pissed to the max they're not in there in Wajma Valley already. Just like that First Sergeant Kozak and Warrant Five Chiarduchi and his flight crew and that SF medic Boonzmann."

"Ah-ha!" Hutchinsen's eyes light up. "So they're heroes?"

Again death-ray eyes from Pluma. Is he walking into a trap? *Fuck this motherfucker.*

Again from Hutchinsen, "They're heroes? Anthony Luke Chiarduchi and Edward Kurt Kozak and Marcus L Boonzmann are now heroes?"

Pluma wants to answer, wants to scream it to this Doctor Gene Hutchinsen PhD who he knows is setting a trap for him. *But what trap?*

Hutchinsen is relentless. "And Sergeant Kevin Randal Cornberger and PFC Gerald Russell Tripp, you will personally sign off, Danny, you'll put your own signature on their Silver Star paperwork when it comes through here? Silver Star minimum, right, at least?"

Pluma knows that General St Claire did not invite him to stay because he wants him to be silent.

Hutchinsen, "Heroes get Silver Stars, don't they?"

Pluma feels St Claire's eyes on him now.

Hutchinsen, "At least a pat on the back, a handshake, an Army Commendation Medal, don't you think? For heroes?"

Pluma turns to the general. "Men can be heroes and at the same time criminals. We can laud their bravery, sir, we can even envy it, but we don't have to condone their behavior. We don't have to and we cannot condone their behavior, sir. General Stonewall Jackson, General George Pickett, they are true heroes by anyone's light. And criminals by their actions of taking up arms against their country."

Hutchinsen, "Make up your mind, Danny. They're heroes and you want to lock down Valley Forge with MPs and prosecutors? You want to put those hotdog hero flyboys into custody the minute they get back here and start their Article 32 proceedings two minutes later?"

Pluma won't answer. Wishes Hutchinsen were gone, out of here, or at least shut up.

Hutchinsen, "Heroes or criminals? You can't have both, not in today's celebrity media world, it just doesn't work that way."

Pluma remains silent.

But St Claire is waiting for an answer.

Hutchinsen, "Come on, Danny, it's not that difficult."

Pluma will not even acknowledge Hutchinsen's presence here now, will not look at him.

Hutchinsen, "Heroes or criminals?"

Pluma draws in his breath. Relaxes himself.

Feels St Claire's eyes on him.

Again from Hutchinsen, "Heroes or criminals? Simple question."

Pluma now to St Claire, "If we're going to be by-the-book on Air safety regulations, sir. If Air being Red means Air is Red and we can't change it, then we have to be strictly by-the-book the whole nine yards."

St Claire, "Leave them out to dry in Wajma Valley?"

"It's not my preference, you know that, sir. My spirit is with the Rangers down there waiting at Salerno, the same as theirs. Which I know you understand as a Ranger yourself. As if you were a lieutenant with one of those platoons or the commander, Captain Haas. Damn the torpedoes, sir, you'd be begging higher HQ this very minute to send your company in for Zach and that platoon."

"Yet you will have me prosecute First Sergeant Kozak and his men and the flight crew?"

Hutchinsen interrupts, "Danny wants to have it both ways. An old saying from the Princeton grad seminar Marie Antoinette and the French Revolution. You can't have your cake and eat it too."

St Clair's hand goes up to silence him. This is between himself and Pluma now. He waits for Pluma's answer. Prosecute Kozak and the flight crew or not?

The answer?

For which Pluma chooses his words carefully.

Coldly.

Quietly.

"We cannot pick and choose the by-the-books we agree with and serve our purpose and like and not those we don't like, that challenge us. If Air is going to be Red, you are correct, sir, then we cannot by any rights or with any good conscience, then we cannot send in the Rangers."

Unspoken, that all three know, is that Gen St Claire has the power and the authority to make Air any color that he wants. As 4-star theater commander, unless the 4-star at Cent Com or the Sec Def or the president specifically stipulates the color of Air, St Claire can color-code it Green or Amber or Red, or fucking Chartreuse, if he wants to.

St Claire knows it.

Dr Gene Hutchinsen knows it.

Colonel Pluma knows it.

And isn't afraid to say it.

He pulls from his thin briefcase satchel a single piece of paper.

Isaf Command letterhead.

A single typed paragraph.

General Peter St Claire's signature block.

Pluma pushes it across the table toward St Claire.

"We simply need your John Hancock, sir."

To exempt the Air as Green in Wajma Valley and Fob Salerno and all points in the 30-minute balls-to-the-wall flight-time between them.

This is why St Claire sought Pluma's counsel to counter Hutch's. He would have expected nothing less from Pluma. For he knows that for all of Pluma's shortcomings, for all his brusque un-likeability, for all his small cheats of character, he knows that Pluma is a subordinate who is not afraid, nor will he hesitate, to tell truth to power when he knows that truth is more valued to that power than a thousand pleasings of obliging yes-men.

St Claire does not pick up the sheet of paper. Just a bare glance tells him what it says. With but the tips of two fingers he pushes it back across to Pluma.

"You hold onto this," he tells him. "For now."

And he pushes away from the table and stands.

He drains the tumbler of Gatorade.

"Gentlemen," he says. Meaning, they are to join him.

Wajma, in the Schoolhouse

The aid station classroom is lit with the battery lanterns that came in the resupply.

Both Doc Eberly and BZ wear their bright LED headlamps.

Eberly had discarded his helmet and body armor long ago when he first established this as the aid station after the sniper attack.

BZ got onto the helicopter and jumped off wearing neither.

They have all their wounded as stable as they're going to get them.

Eberly is greatly relieved that BZ is here. A combat medic on the platoon level is trained and expected to keep a soldier or two or three alive and stable until a medevac arrives, when the flight medic will take over. A half-hour, hour max, wounding to medevac.

It's been eight hours since the initial sniper attack.

There are fifteen seriously wounded in here, including the ANA and the flight crew. Not counting Sandusky.

Eberly believes that he could not have dealt with it all, even considering the resupplied meds, without BZ. Without those ten more years of SF training and experience that BZ has. Eberly imagines that if BZ hadn't arrived he'd be over there sitting in the corner next to Sandusky. He'd be slumped over there staring at his thumbs like Sandusky. He'd have given up. How much could he do? He just doesn't know enough.

BZ wouldn't believe that, not for a minute. He sees a line-dog platoon medic with just months of training compared with his own years who only has to be shown once how to do something, and even then he's doing it, and doing it right, before you're even finished telling him how. From when BZ was carried in here and first crawled from patient to patient in a quick initial assessment, he'd remarked later to Eberly, and he's told him several times since, how impressed he was, amazed really, by how much Eberly had done with so many patients with so little for so long.

And that first time that BZ had said it, Eberly replied with something about BZ should go and have a look at his failures in the other classroom. And BZ had assumed that meant they'd established a temp morgue there in the room across the way and he'd said in return something about *No thanks. It's too long a crawl.*

Just a few minutes ago, watching Eberly insert a clear plastic chest tube higher into the abdomen of the pilot than the one that BZ had shown Eberly where and how to insert earlier, and the empty 2-liter water bottle immediately starting to fill with blood, BZ had said, "When you get out of here, you put in for 18-Delta, man. I mean it. You put in for 18-Delta. I'm gonna look you up, run you down, make sure you do."

Before that, they'd done an inventory of the remaining morphine, including that which BZ had carried in, and it took Eberly about a half-second to do the calculation: at present usage they had enough to last until four in the morning, and the word from Isaf was that the weather wasn't clearing until maybe noon at the earliest.

"That's if the bad guys hiding all over these hills don't attack again between now and 4am," BZ had half-joked. "They weren't scared of the helicopter, who knows how many are up there."

They'd agreed to save the six fentanyl lollipops and their super glorious pain-abatement for any fresh casualties only, the ones conscious enough to be able to suck.

"Aw heck," BZ had joked. "I might just decide it was a dumb idea getting on that chopper, what's the use, and suck em all down myself. In your calculations, enough til four, did you figure in them two?" He'd nodded toward one ANA soldier and the pilot, Warrant-5 Chiarduchi.

Eberly had.

"You're an optimist," BZ had said. "That's good, it's fan-tas-ta-rif-fic. A medic should be an optimist. Yessir, I see 18-Delta written all over you."

And BZ feels, as Doc Eberly kind of feels but chooses not to accept yet, that neither the ANA soldier nor the pilot are going to make it until 4am. BZ doesn't think the pilot is going to make it another hour.

Either way it doesn't mean morphine or a lollipop for BZ himself. A triple dose of Motrin has taken most of the sharp pain away from his busted knee, leg and ankle. If he were in the Cash already, heck yeh *Shoot me up, put me into la-la-land* while he waits for the more serious guys taken into surgery first, and heck just *Ship me like this up to Landstuhl* where a team of orthopedic surgeons can take their time in big operating rooms and pin his bones all together and make him like brand new.

Not that he thinks he'll ever be brand-new brand new.

No, he knows his SF days are done. No more parachuting, no more Halo, no more rappelling down buildings, kicking in doors, he'll be lucky if he can even meet the minimum 2-mile-run time standards anymore. Even run two miles. More like hobble. It's *Time I guess to go PA.* No more excuses. Physician's Assistant and an officer commission, *Your glory days as an SF operator are over, BZ bud.*

It could be worse, he knows. Of the five crew on that Chinook only one's walking, and that's gotta be just pure luck. One gunner's dead, the pilot's gonna be dead, the other gunner's got who-knows-how-many broken ribs and it pretty much sounds like that lung's punctured and xrays at the Cash'll show where his back's probably fractured. That young copilot lieutenant's going to be lucky if he keeps both legs at the knees. If.

The smartest dumb-ass thing he's ever done in his life, BZ knows, was stepping off that ramp and not staying aboard. If he'd have stayed up there *I reckon I'd of curled myself up and held on tight to something* and he'd have been *Bounced around in there like a rubber ball on a fistful of methamphetamines.* Without a helmet on or body armor. Then, after they would have pried all the parts of his body *Impaled by metal piping and struts and shit,* they would have poured his liquid brains out of his skull busted up into about a hundred pieces then they could have just grabbed his sleeves and pantlegs and jostled all of him into the center of his uniform, tied the sleeves and pantlegs together tight and toted him off that bird like a small sack of smashed tangerines. Then dumped it into a body bag, and he'd be just a big round lump at the bottom.

BZ had asked that crew chief, that Jarbodie, how he was walking, how come he wasn't turned into peach cobbler when they crashed? "Strapped in," Jarbodie told him. "Held on tight. Prayed."

I wouldn't of thought to pray, BZ knows. *I'll have to remember next time.*

Yeh well, probably not, or definitely not, there's not going to be a next time. His action days are through. For the knee alone. You blow a knee, kiss the action shit goodbye. He'd known it from the moment he hit the ground. Just the flame of pain. Knew it a moment before hitting, off-balance, bringing his legs together for a parachute landing and seeing that below, what is it, a rock? Aw shit!

He knew it when he immediately sat up and saw his leg all bent the wrong ways into a Z.

He'd thought it had a nice ironic twist of fate to it, that it was a sure sign his days as an action operator were over, when that reporter, that photographer, they call him Nicky, he came in here with the busted pieces of his M4 he'd figured had been blown to the kingdom come, and the dude had laughed, *"The thing came this close to scalping me."* Then the dude acted real serious-like and appraised the damage to the gun, saying, *"Guess you can put a splint on it, give it two aspirins and tell it to call you in the morning."*

What a motley crew this is. They've got a reporter, Nicky, and *His camera's always up in your face or you see him filming on the sneak.* That civilian, his name's Wolfe, he's the partner, Doc here says, of that lady anthropologist got burned yesterday right here. They've got a lieutenant colonel commanding a platoon. *Lite colonel commanding a platoon! Got a female, Doc says she's a Jag captain, and she's sitting out there, with a gun in her lap*, she's paralyzed in her legs and Doc says it's a sniper's bullet he hopes is just close to the spinal cord and hasn't severed it in one neat cut. And that wild-eyed dude, always got a half-grin half-snarl, *Was the first to me out there, retrieved my ruck*, that Chicano sniper dude, and *He tells me in here, he says "That there what you done, 'mano, unreal. Tienes cajones like sandias. Watermelons." And he goes, "Hombre, bienvenidos al Zoo."*

It was Nicky who explained to BZ what that meant. The whole *Tattoo Zoo* thing, and showed him the actual tattoo on one of the wounded soldier's chest, that burned one there, they call him Vampire. And Nicky told him what he was doing here, making a feature-length documentary he hoped. And BZ had said, "What are you going to name your documentary, A Trip to the Zoo? And get it on Animal Planet?"

Bigger than that, Nick had told him. Feature length. Maybe two parts. Going to go for the big time. HBO. Sell them worldwide rights. Make a ton of money. Win an Emmy. "Don't have an ending yet," Nick had admitted. And shrugged and laughed a little.

BZ's very first sight of Nick had been out there first thing after he'd sat up and seen his leg bent like a pretzel with that compound fracture bulging under his pantleg, and here was this civilian-dressed dude coming running through the rain right toward him, hunched over, with that camera held out in both hands in front, aimed right at BZ who yelled at him for *No pictures, no pictures, I'm SF!*, but the other guys were arriving and Nick kept filming, coming closer, and when BZ ordered him again, "No photos, no photos, I'm SF!", Nick told him, "Don't worry, I've worked with SF before. I'll pixilate your face."

That didn't last long, because of the AK fire and the Chinook's machineguns drowning it and then the dim explosions of the rockets hitting the bird, and Nick was zooming in down there and holding on the Chinook coming straight up this way struggling not to crash then managing to veer at the last moment then its rotors hitting the ground and it crashing on that wall and pieces of the rotors flying, with some coming this way right over Nick and BZ's heads within arm's reach, and *That crazy-assed reporter all the time on his knees, with that camera pointed, and didn't even hit the dirt on his belly.*

Yeh, crazy-assed Nick Flowers could have been decapitated by one of those rotor pieces. Just like BZ sitting up exposed.

By the time Nick had come in for a few minutes of film of BZ and Doc working to save the copilot's legs, BZ had accepted that his SF days of no identity and no photos were over and didn't care what Nick filmed of him.

The lieutenant colonel had already gotten the stats of the flight crew from Jarbodie. Name, rank, unit. Entered into his little hardbound notebook. And he'd come in here to get the same from BZ. Name, rank, unit. Who sent him here. Why'd he jump off with the chopper so high. Sergeant Eberly has to be happy to have some help. And from the lieutenant colonel, *Thanks. Sincerely. Thank you.* You probably won't get a medal for it, though. And by the way, *"The civilian fellow with the camera, you can trust him, you have my word on it. He has free rein, and he won't compromise your SF status."*

The colonel seems like he'd be true to his word, BZ thinks, while watching now Nick position himself at a low angle aiming his camera on Dove bending close over Warrant Pilot Chiarduchi.

BZ can see Nick pull himself closer, his camera tight on the pilot's face as his glazed, slow eyes follow Dove's face coming up close to him, then BZ's view is blocked by that crew chief dude Jarbodie kneeling at the pilot's feet.

Just a couple of minutes ago Wolfe had been in here. Just to check up again on Chiarduchi specifically. Doc Eberly motioned that his pulse was bare, if at all, and Wolfe listened with Doc's stethoscope and felt the pilot's cold cheeks and watched his eyes try to focus on him. "That was an awesome piece of flying, sir," Wolfe told him, not even sure that the man was conscious enough to hear. "Nicky's got it on tape. Gonna get ten million views on YouTube."

Wolfe went out, and quickly returned with Dove and Redcloud, and Nick following. Now Jarbodie is here too.

The rocket that had hit the Chinook at the copilot's feet, mangling his legs, had exploded through the entire instrument panel and had sent pieces of everything into the right side of Chiarduchi from his toes to his chin, shredding that foot, entire leg and that arm. How he'd managed to work the pedals and the cyclic and fly for nearly another minute-and-a-half is known only to God.

But those injuries alone to the extremities don't kill a man.

The stuff embedded deep in his gut, from his hip up to his chest, can.

Stuff tearing into the liver and kidneys and intestines and arteries and lungs, and maybe a sharp piece cutting across the heart muscle.

That stuff can kill you.

If you're not medvacced to a Cash in that first golden hour.

Which was hours ago.

Near, his eyes locked on Chiarduchi's, which move just enough for Dove to know he perhaps can hear and understand, Dove quietly entreats him, "Tony Chiarduchi. Mister Chiarduchi. Do you know where you are, Mister Chiarduchi? You're in Wajma, the Wajma Valley. You're with the Tattoo Zoo. You're here with us. The Tattoo Zoo."

Dove can see a slight jump in both his eyes.

"Listen to me, Tony. Tony, I know you can hear me. Listen to me."

Again that slight jump in Chiarduchi's eyes.

"These men here, Mister Chiarduchi. These men of the Tattoo Zoo . . . . you've made it possible for them to see their wives again. And their children. And their moms and dads. You made it possible."

There, again, was that a jump or not?

"The men of the Tattoo Zoo . . . they thank you. God bless you."

The eyes are frozen.

Doc Eberly hears nothing on his stethoscope pressed to the neck.

Dove puts his ear close under Chiarduchi's nose and hears no breath.

Dove takes hold of the head-end of the poncho and Jarbodie the feet-end, and they lift Chiarduchi's body.

Redcloud unfolds a brand-new poncho liner and spreads it over the body, and they carry Chiarduchi out of this room.

From his seat on the ammo crate, watching and unable to get up and help, *A hundred choppers sitting there on Salerno,* BZ is thinking. *And no one would have thought a thing about it if he'd done the proper thing and hadn't taken off on Red Air.* The pilot and all his crew could have by now had a big dinner in the Dfac. He could by now be watching a DVD back in his room. On the internet, on Skype with his wife. If only, *If only he'd done the proper thing and hadn't taken off on the Red.*

BZ's mind goes completely blank for a moment. Then it hits him, *It depends what the meaning of proper is.*

Isaf, in the Officers' Dining Facility, walking through the kitchen is Gen St Claire, flanked by Dr Hutchinsen and Col Pluma.

Hutchinsen is saying, "It is absolutely essential, Pete, that we have that film, whatever he's shot. I'd imagine it has to be the best footage he's got in all his years bopping around in these war zones. Like he's smack dab in the center of Agincourt. Saratoga. Gettysburg."

Pluma, "For all we know, Nick Flowers might be one of those dead or wounded and there is no film video."

Hutchinsen, "Then we'll have to put our faith in Specialist Bernard Howie, won't we? And if he's wounded or dead, it's more than just the gods against us, it's fate written in the stars, a story Shakespeare would write about, we're not meant to win this war. Forget Agincourt and Gettysburg, it's Little Big Horn. I'll just shuffle off to the next one, if you don't mind."

St Claire, "Easy enough for you to say."

On the walk over St Claire had allowed Hutchinsen to make his argument that Pluma had not heard yet. One for an entirely new direction for L' Affaire Wajma, as Hutchinsen called it.

First, they would have to throw all their previous thinking out the window. Starting with By-The-Book.

The insurgents hadn't been playing By-The-Book from the very get-go.

The Tattoo Zoo Platoon had ignored The Book when they'd lied in their AAR and didn't report Battle Damage.

Karzai can't even read The Book.

Zachary Dove had tossed out The Book when he'd refused to bring the platoon straight to Bagram, thus kyboshing his own exfil.

Kozak and his QRF and Chiarduchi and his flight crew were so insubordinate you'd think they'd been throwing all The Books onto a bonfire at Fahrenheit 451.

Forget The Book, Hutchinsen contended. It's time to not just think outside the box and not just into the next dimension but beyond the power of the gravitational forces that bend light. Throw out any thought that Kozak and Chiarduchi and even the Tattoo Zoo Platoon are criminals, no one in America wants anymore to have their good guys made criminals, they already have enough criminals and cowards and hypocrites in their presidents and senators and sports athletes and movie stars and minimal-talent pop celebrities and even the local mayor and dogcatcher. The last thing Americans want any longer from this lousy war they don't understand or know much about or even care about is to have the young man who dated their daughter and took her to the junior prom, was second-string on the bench on the basketball team, mowed lawns all one summer just to buy that '91 Ford Escort and hotrod-bling it up, cut tobacco in the August heat to lock down on layaway at the pawnshop that Fender Stratocaster for the garage band he was forming—they don't want that boy turned into a killer zombie. Boys you played Little League with on the same team. Flipped burgers with in the McDonald's. What, you're going to bring them back here in chains and bring the wrath of the entire military judicial courts-martial system down upon them? Boys who knew the possible adverse repercussions from their behavior, yes, granted, and knew the very real chances of their getting wounded or killed and knew also their getting court-martialed, and they still climbed into those Mraps and into that helicopter and went to help their buddies. Boys who, regardless their welfare or careers, wouldn't leave their buddies behind.

Heroes, Hutchinsen gladly conceded. Heroes, just as Pluma had said they were.

And you don't put heroes in chains.

Including those boys of the Tattoo Zoo Platoon.

Nobody in America wants to believe their sons and grandsons, their brothers and nephews, the young man next door with the wife and three kids and every Saturday afternoon he's out there in his driveway washing his car—nobody wants to believe that he would fire upon a school full of women and children and infants if he knew they were in there. Women and children like his own wife and kids. And everyone understands that a ruthless jihadist enemy like the Taliban would do just that.

But Americans don't want to read words, they just don't read in-depth news analysis anymore. Don't even read newspapers anymore. Don't buy them, don't read them. Not even the headlines. They won't listen to speeches from lying politicians and ass-covering generals. No offense, Pete, present company not included.

Forget all that crap yakity-yak bullshit words, Americans don't want to read or listen to all that jammering and yammering and he-said/she-said/no-he-said/no-she-said.

Visuals.

Americans want visuals.

Americans get their news from visuals.

Americans form their opinions from visuals.

From a thirty-second video on Facebook and Twitter and on Drudge.

If a picture says a thousand words, a video clip says a million.

Video of the anthropologist Robyn Banks on fire burning alive drowns out anything negative the video of her partner Kyle Wolfe killing her killers says. Drowns it out ten times to Sunday. Turns Wolfe's actions into superhero status.

Americans are right now rooting for Kyle Wolfe.

Read the blogs, you'll see.

Google it. Count the number of hits Robyn Banks gets ablaze.

It's going to be linked right into Kyle Wolfe blasting those savages.

It's all going across cyberspace at light speed.

Robyn Banks on fire. Kyle Wolfe firing.

Kyle Wolfe, talk about a poster-boy. The avenger.

Visuals.

Video of a lone American platoon surrounded by a thousand suicidal jihadist Bronze Age warrior savages who'll light afire all our Robyn Banks from sea to shining sea if they have the chance.

Video of that lone platoon fighting for their lives against that scraggily-bearded horde. Fighting in their own Battle of Little Big Horn.

Actual footage of American boys standing shoulder-to-shoulder against an onslaught of wild-eyed jihadists in their own Battle of Ulundi, a single lone platoon against fifteen thousand Zulu warriors.

That's what Americans scream for in his lousy war.

Their soldiers as heroes not villains.

Their boys as heroes.

Which is where Nick Flowers comes in. His video.

If there's just one man left standing when the exfil choppers can finally get in there safely or when the Rangers can be assaulted into there safely, it had better be Nick Flowers.

Or, if nothing else, at the very least his cameras had damn well better be intact.

That's Hutchinsen's argument.

And Pluma's counter. "So, for Nick Flowers' film you are now willing to accept the risks of losing a company of Rangers and their three Chinooks, conventional or special ops?"

Hutchinsen, "I'm not willing to accept any such risks. I do not authorize risk-taking. I'm simply presenting the options. A, B, or C. If we don't do anything and the insurgents retreat because the platoon has now been resupplied and our choppers go in there tomorrow noon when the weather clears and pull them out, we have the film and we have our heroes. If the insurgents retreat and don't attack."

Hutchinsen and St Claire both knowing, remember, about the trucks unloading on the Paki side of the border.

Pluma reminds him of the other possiblility. "Or, worst case scenario, they are attacked, and Zach's firepower overwhelms them, beats them."

He doesn't know about those trucks unloading.

St Claire stops at the ice cream freezers and pulls out two boxes of Klondike bars to carry back.

Again from Hutchinsen, "I'm simply presenting the options. All the better if Zachary Dove pulls off the great victory. With Nick Flowers' video then we'll really have ourselves heroes. If not, if the platoon is overrun, however grim and repulsive that is, and there is no Nick Flowers video, there are no visuals, except what the enemy will be broadcasting of dead and mutilated and pathetic bodies of American aggressors, then we must settle for reality. There will be no heroes. Just dead bodies. And in its own way the perpetrators of the civilian mass casualties of yesterday are dealt with, end of that story. And we march right along by-the-book on Eddie Kozak and Tony Chiarduchi and their lame-brained puppet followers and throw the book at them all."

Silence between the three going back through the kitchen and midway through the near-empty dining room.

Then from St Claire, "Let's hear it, Dan. Don't go wet-noodle on me."

Pluma, a resigned shake of the head. "Heads he wins, tails he wins."

St Claire stops before the closed doors marked **RESERVED — ISAF COMMANDER**, with four stars.

"Your reasoned objections?" he asks Pluma.

"How can I object, sir? It's a win win. The only one who loses is Zach and the platoon if they're wiped out. It would seem, it's up to you, sir. Your priorities. It's your command, everything will ultimately fall under you, accountable to you. What are they, sir, your priorities? Getting the film and making heroes out of everyone, including those who are bound to die going in to secure it? Or crossing off Zach and the platoon as expendable. Leaving them to fate, as Doctor Hutchinsen says. In the hands of the gods. I'm sorry if I offend you, sir. You asked me not to pull any punches."

A smile and a nod from St Claire. He had indeed asked that of him.

Now he sets the boxes of Klondike bars on the table while motioning Pluma to *Get that paper out of that briefcase satchel.*

Of the three pens and one mechanical pencil in his left-shoulder pocket St Claire selects the Mont Blanc fountain pen that was his father's.

Pluma sets the single sheet on the table.

St Claire writes some bullet points amending it.

Says, "No time like the present, Dan. . . ."

Signs it.

". . . .To learn of the true weight of playing God."

He caps the fountain pen and pockets it, and he picks up the boxes of Klondikes and goes through the VIP doors where all the journalists who were at the media briefing earlier are having dinner.

Pluma and Hutchinsen both can hear St Claire give a little laugh coming from in there, *"Evening folks. Just a little dessert for you from the chef's private stash."*

Pluma reads what St Claire has added to the exemption of Red authorization.

Doesn't show it to Hutchinsen.

But figures Hutchinsen knows already.

Wajma, in the Schoolhouse

Out on the veranda, seated against the wall on radio watch, Pfc Holloway feels alone.

No one to talk to.

No, not on the radios, he doesn't want to talk on the radios. As he just did ten minutes ago, as Isaf calls every half hour wanting a sit-rep, and Holloway told them exactly what Colonel Dove had told him to tell them and what he's been telling them every time they call. *No change in status.*

"If Colonel Pluma calls me direct, or General St Claire," Dove had told him, "then you come get me. Otherwise, if there's a change in status, I'll call them."

Holloway hopes that General St Claire doesn't call, what's he gonna say to a general? *Hey, dude, cool, how you doin, General, how's things shakin up there at Isaf? You got the Holloway Groove up there?* Yeh right, *Then I'll be busted down to Private E-1.* No, if General St Claire calls, he'll just say, *"Sir, I'll get Colonel Dove, sir. Wait one, sir."*

Calls from anyone isn't who Holloway wants to talk to. You can't really *talk* talk on the radio, it's all business. Boring military business. Not buddy talk, bullshit, that shit.

So, right, no one to talk to for Holloway because there's no one out here anymore. Oh yeh, Utah's squad, and a couple of Nell's. Pfc Inhelder right here near him, but he's sleeping, or *Pretending to be asleep so I won't talk to him, so I can't talk to him.*

Holloway misses the colonel out here, and Sergeant Redcloud and Wolfe and Nicky. Even the hot captain's not here anymore. She's inside there too. *Yeh she's hot. Chicks like that, they look like they've always got their noses in books, they never go out, not to clubs or dancing or partying, and they wanna give it up, they be beggin to give it up, get em on the living room floor, we're talkin rug burns and ass burns and muff burns, they go crazy wild, chicks like that who look and act like bookworm librarians.*

That's not fair, he knows. Not fair to think that. She's got a sniper bullet there in her and she can't move her legs, *That's gotta suck. Suck suck, like really suck.*

He misses them being out here not because they talk to him or they even want him to talk to them or even listen, but because he gets to be a part of what they're saying. A part of the plans. The running-things.

Like when First Sergeant Kozak called up on satcom from the Cop when they'd just gotten back there and told Holloway to put his Zoo Seven on, then Holloway could tell by what Sergeant Redcloud was saying that First Sergeant was telling him who died and who was wounded in 3rd Platoon. Then Redcloud told it quietly to the colonel so that Holloway couldn't hear, but he could tell they didn't want anyone here to know the names, because Redcloud said, "No use everyone troubling over it here. They've got enough to think about."

And Holloway knew there'd been a medevac to the Cop because after talking to the first sergeant, Redcloud had told the colonel in private, but then he'd said, and Holloway'd heard, "Thank God they got them a bird. But then you've got to think, y'know, they can fly one up to Valley Forge but not into here?" And before Dove could answer, Redcloud answered it himself, admitting, "Right. If they had RPGs and recoilless rifles up in the mountains surrounding the Cop, there wouldn't have been any medevacs either."

That's the kind of stuff Holloway likes being a part of. Being right there near all the important things goin down.

And after, when they'd all left, Holloway had sneaked a satcom in to the Cop, cuz he knew his buddy Frankie was on the radio there and would give him the gory details. Sergeant Cornberger and Triple Shot dead, and *Cornberger's an asshole, who cares. No, that's not right, he doesn't deserve dead, and he's got his wife, oh man she is hot. At the Memorial Day picnic, in those cutoffs?!* Talk about memories. *Whoa there*, in the air terminal the night they were deploying over to here, she was *In those fuck-me tight jeans, sheee-at, and in cowboy boots with at least six-inch-high heels, FMPs, fuck-me pumps, what do you wanna bet she's shacked-up with someone from Club Gemini right now, and that captain and that master sergeant in their starched uniforms with creases you could cut your fingers on are coming up the walk to the front door right now about to ring the doorbell and tell her, Mrs Cornberger, sorry but your asshole husband's dead.*

Aw c'mon, Holloway, that aint nice, they aint gonna say asshole.

Triple Shot, now he was cool. A cool dude. Ace. Everybody likes Triple Shot. Gotta be the oldest pfc in the Army.

Sitting out here alone, with both radio handsets resting on his shoulders up close to his ears, doing nothing, talking to no one, no one to talk to, Pfc Holloway can't clear from his mind the image of Cornberger's hot wife in those fuck-me tight jeans in there in the air terminal and Cornberger bending her over backwards for that one huge final kiss and Holloway and his couple of young buds hanging together cuz they don't got wives and girlfriends there to see them off, they hoot and catcall over and would all like to jump those bones in those fuck-me skin-tight jeans, and Holloway knows now that he shouldn't think bad of Cornberger, because he's dead, but he'd sure like to get a piece of that wife of his and knows she is *Gonna be part-tee-ing with that 400 grand SGLI she's gonna get.*

She, yeh, she is going to be in the Holloway Groove. If he didn't have another eight months stuck here. By the time he gets back *She'll of blown through all that 400 grand sure as shit.*

And Holloway thinks that he'd better stop thinking of Cornberger's sizzlin-hot wife cuz he's gonna get a hard-on and that Wolfie's gonna come out here and see it and make some stupid joke and say it's *Gonna give that Afghan sergeant somethin to grab onto when he fucks me in the ass.* And Holloway thinks he catches the sergeant looking at him sitting across on the other side of the steps where he knows Wolfe's got all his AKs, and all he can see is the dude's eyes in this darkness, and kind of thinks that they smile at him like as if he knows exactly what Holloway's thinking of.

"Enchilada," Holloway tells him, then looks away, and he gets a sudden impulse that something is out there approaching and jumps to his feet, swivels and looks out and can't see a thing.

Flips down his Nods. Turns them on, and his vision all brightens to a greenish haze.

He can see to the bottom of the steps just a few feet down.

Can see a scattering of unused sandbags and a couple of entrenching tools stuck straight up in the mud.

And nothing further out. Can't even see out to the rock wall.

Nothing but a fog of clouds right here.

They could be coming through that right now and *We wouldn't even see them. No, wrong-o, Holloway. There's the trip flares. Trip flares and that razor wire and them claymores, those pilots were aces bringing it all to us. Aces.*

It took balls flyin to here. Through clouds so low, they couldn't no way no how know they weren't going to run straight into the mountains.

The 3rd Platoon too. First Sergeant and them, *Third Herd's aces coming out here for us.* And Frankie had told Holloway that Northwich and Palmer and Hererra were all medevaced real serious. Sergeant First Class Northwich, they're not supposed to be able to get to the platoon sergeant, *Your platoon sergeant's like Superman or Iron Man. They're not gonna get Sergeant Redcloud, no way no how.* Palmer, Holloway doesn't really know him. But Hererra, him and Holloway went through One-Station Unit Training together, *Hererra's an awright dude. Hope he isn't wounded too bad. That would suck.*

It would suck, except, Hererra's gonna get to see all those nurses back there, gets to flirt with all those nurses back there. Unless he's had his nuts blown off. *Now that would really suck.* And Frankie didn't say. Said he didn't know.

Aces, Herrera was. Palmer too. All of the 3rd.

We'd of did the same for the Herd, we'd of came out here for them if it was them here.

Yeh, the Zoo would have.

Gotta believe, yeh, *We'd of QRF'ed for them.*

Holloway checks his cheap Timex digital watch.

8:17.

Only about 10 more hours until morning.

Choppers're gonna come get us in the morning for sure.

On the roof Redcloud has carried up a case each of 8oz Red Bull and a case of 24oz Gatorade.

Really, Redcloud came up here just for a few words with the guys on the parapet. To get a look himself at just how well they can see out there.

They can't.

The night's black as a charcoal briquette already. If the moon's out, you can't tell and aren't going to see it anyway through this fog.

Even with Nods on, it's nothing but fog you see, leavening thick, you can't even see the rock ceiling right above. Can barely see the guy just five feet away from you down the wall. Just his shape. With Nods. Without, nothing. Just black.

Redcloud came up because he'd wanted to make sure that Ketchum had his guys on the Saws squared away on where to shoot if a trip flare went off or if they heard the jangling of the pebbles in the empty ammo cans that Wolfe and Utah had hung along in the C-wire.

He wanted to make sure that Specialist Tran had squared away Bybee on the one functioning M240 they salvaged from the wrecked Chinook, fully comfortable with the twin grips and the butterfly trigger.

He kinda just wanted to reassure himself that, yeh, now they've got two 240s. And plenty of ammo to go with them, even the full cans from the chopper.

He wanted to make sure that Ketchum's guys would get some sleep. 50% alert, guys've gotta get sleep. Nerves are going to be bad enough frayed on edge.

"You too, Ketch, you get some shut-eye," he tells him. "We've got plenty of time to react if the trip flares go off."

"What about you, Sarge? When you gonna sleep?"

No problem. "I'm getting into my jammies down there. Going to curl up, dream about Swamp Phase." Ranger School. "Going to make the colonel stay up all night. Remind him of the Ranger standard. Patrol leader's got no time to sleep."

From Ketchum quiet laughter. "Tell him it's the final exam, last patrol. He falls asleep, he gets recycled."

"Yeh, there you go," a chuckle from Redcloud. "That's gonna fly with a butterbar, not so sure with a O-5. I mean it now, you get some sleep too."

"Roger that, Sarge."

The next guys down are Spec Van Louse and Spec Howie seated together. Van Louse chowing down an MRE. Nods on to see to do it.

Redcloud asks Howie, "You get something in your belly yet, Specialist?"

Van Louse answers for Howie, "Chubby's too scared to eat, Sarge. Scared if he eats he's gonna blow chunks next time when they come charging and he looks down and sees his arm's blowed off."

"He's just yanking your chain," Redcloud tells Howie. "You eat somethin. It's going to be a long night. You're infantry now. The tip of the spear. If nothing else, infantry fights on its stomach. Get something in you, Specialist. And get shut-eye when it's your turn."

Van Louse, "Too scared to sleep, Sarge. Thinks the Taliban's gonna sneak down, rappel down the mountain up above right here, gonna cut his throat when he's sleeping." He laughs at his own teasing.

Redcloud realizes that Spec Howie could move a few feet down the parapet away from Van Louse and not even be seen by him, let alone have to listen to what must be a constant ragging, and that Howie is beside Van Louse because it makes him feel safer. More secure. Far less alone.

A hand to Howie's shoulder, Redcloud tells him, "I'd be worried about that too. Cept the Taliban don't have ropes. Would hafta use their turbans, tie them all together. Like sheets. Like climbing down breaking out of jail."

Van Louse chuckles at that.

Redcloud with a last reassurance to Howie, "The thing is. Taliban law, if you take off your headgear, when you get to heaven, if you've got no cover, no virgins for you."

Next down, Redcloud likes the way Pvt Finkle's got ammo crates stacked as a seat where he can lean forward on the parapet with his 203 up on the sandbags. A couple of dozen 40mm grenades stood up on the parapet, ready to grab and chamber. And shoot.

"Sergeant Ketchum showed you your fields of fire?" Redcloud asks.

"Yes, Sergeant."

"Don't go all John Wayne now. We don't need a hero. Not a dead hero. Keep your head down."

"Can't keep it down if yer gonna see, Sarge. Can't aim if you can't see."

Good point. *Good kid,* Redcloud thinks.

"Sarge?" Finkle's just itching to know. He whispers. "Third Herd made it back they're saying, right? They have anybody get hit? I mean, serious?"

"They ran into a pretty good buzzsaw down there. Don't worry about it. I'm sure they're gonna wanna be filling our ears with nothing but how they hung their butts out there for the Zoo when we get back tomorrow."

"Any of them, Sarge, you know . . . ?" Die?

"Nothing for you to worry about it." A pat on his helmet. "Plenty of time for those things when we get back."

Downstairs in the big open area up front two and three layers of ponchos and poncho liners drape all the window openings and the entrance doorway, effectively blocking the light of the kerosene lanterns and various flashlights and headlamps from showing outside.

A few moments of quiet and rest, Lieut Col Dove is sitting on two stacked cardboard boxes among the litter of remaining resupplies here.

His LED headlamp light on low-intensity, on his forehead.

Helmet and body armor off and lying at his feet. A bad example sure, but the men of the Zoo have experienced this day's deadly combat and know what's pretty well certain to come again soon enough before they leave here, and they can make that choice now when and where and how to wear their helmet and body armor. Their choice, they know the odds. Some with their helmets off, he's noticed, but no one's shed his body armor. No, not so, the doc, Sergeant Eberly, has. Smart of him.

The body armor and helmet, it's all been just too uncomfortable for Dove after wearing it all day since O-dark-thirty to get on that chopper at Isaf. How many hours ago was that? Like, seems a year ago. He's not used to it. He's been on staff too long these many months—more than a year now, going on two, both the Pentagon and here—and at Isaf in Kabul your body armor and helmet just hang on the wall in your cubicle room. How long ago was yesterday? Last night? About this time last night, every night, it's about time right now to video-Skype with Bethany Ann and the kids. *Not even twenty-four hours, there she was, that Major Vicky Marshall, wow, what coulda woulda shoulda glad it didn't . . . .* Like, another world away from here, this Wajma Valley.

He hadn't even thought about it, but he'd just pulled out his little hardbound notebook and looked at the picture of his wife Bethany Ann.

They're going to miss the call tonight. She's going to wonder why.

Tomorrow night. For sure *Tomorrow night we'll Skype.* He hopes.

Honey, you're so beautiful. You're so good, so kind, you're an ideal mother, you're as good a woman as I could ever want, as I should ever want, I'm lucky you love me so much. He thinks that last night he cheated on her in thought, in desire, for Major Vicky Marshall, and knows that that is as much animal hormonal urges and compulsion going back to caveman days, pre-history, and *We should be more civilized to control it now,* to not betray the *Trust and faith of Bethany Ann,* and if he weren't married *I could fall in love or at least in full fast joyous lust with Vicky Marshall,* oh that would be so easy, he's certain of that, but *I hope I am forever in the future strong enough never to do it again. I'm sorry, Bethany Ann. I'm sorry.* And he feels a hope that she would accept and forgive him—forgive him for the temptation but not if he'd fallen into it further. *I didn't, I was saved by this mission. In the future I know now how I can be weak, how I can fail, and would fail, and I won't. I won't ever again. I had better not.*

He slips the notebook back into his pocket.

He cracks the cap of a plastic 24oz Frosty Blue Gatorade and downs half in one long swallow.

Tears open the wrapper of two Nature's Valley granola bars and eats them between sips of the rest of the Gatorade.

He throws a glance, his headlamp spotlighting Capt Cathay lying back against her ruck just inside the doorway. Her chin's on her chest, her eyes look closed, she didn't respond to this sudden illumination, maybe she's asleep, yes she must be asleep. Best for her if she is. He should have never brought her here. *I didn't bring her, they assigned her, at random, or perhaps she volunteered. I should have known better, you don't bring a woman out to a place like this, a staff officer, a non-combat-arms staff officer.* She had no idea what she was walking into. *I had no idea what we were walking into.*

He's glad to see that her hands hold in her lap a bottle of Gatorade resting on the receiver of her M4. She hasn't eaten a thing. He knows why. As *Mr Wolfe might say,* "Number One, cuz you don't know if your bowels are even going to work when you're paralyzed, and Number Two, you don't eat before surgery and she's wishing and hoping medevac's going to arrive any minute now and whisk her away."

It's not fair to her, you don't send a woman out here *Where they can get shot in the spine or killed for no good reason. Or Doctor Robyn Banks, burned.*

That hothead sniper, Sergeant Rodriquez, breaks open a box of MREs. "There one you want *especiál?*" he asks Crew Chief Jarbodie. Nope, anything. The first one he pulls out he tosses over to him. Next one, he checks it, calls to Wolfe coming out of the aid room, "Wolfie, your favorite," and tosses it across to him.

Wolfe checks it. Yep, chili mac, and thumbs-up *Thanks* to Rodriquez.

Wolfe has been in with the docs. He'd gone in to see if they needed any help. You know, changing bandages, hanging IV bags, anything.

Naw, they were okay, thanks.

And he'd stuck around talking with BZ. Force Recon to SF, that sort of thing. In Wolfe's time in-country attached to Delta they'd worked plenty of times with SF, and maybe he and BZ knew some of the same people.

Yep. One, a master sergeant named Tongason, who Wolfe worked with in '06, and BZ said Wolfe probably hadn't heard, but Tongason'd got blown up in a jeep in Ethiopia last year and he's still a year later in Walter Reed right now, last BZ heard. The other two in the jeep, BZ didn't know them, but he'd heard, they had to scrape up their pieces and you could fit their like sum total in like two little Pelican laptop cases.

"The Horn of Africa," BZ had said. "The shit is starting to happen down there. And you never hear about it. Teams are deploying there all the time. We know about it, cause it's other guys in the battalion, but no one else does. Sort of the secret war."

"I can only deal with one war at a time," Wolfe said. "Gotta learn a whole new language? Ethiopian? Kenyan, Somalian, forget it. What we got here's wacked enough, I can't imagine down there."

And in high praise Wolfe told BZ, "Dude, when I saw you come off that tail I thought, he forgot to hang the fast rope. Like the 34-foot tower, I was waiting for your count. Y'know, Jump School. One thousand, two thousand, three thousand."

"Pretty lame-brained, wasn't it?"

"If we wind up stuck in here like for two more weeks," Wolfe told him, and referred to his chop-suey'd leg, "the bones are going to half-heal up and they're going to have to cut into there and re-break everything all over again."

"You're telling me," BZ had said and laughed.

"If we wind up stuck here for two more weeks," Doc Eberly added his two cents quietly. "Kyle, you're going to have to go up to the village there and steal all their opium paste they've got stored, and we're going to have to distill our own morphine derivative."

"Two weeks?" BZ said. "By tomorrow. Breakfast."

Wolfe laughed. "You kidding, aint none of us going to make it to breakfast, going to be around still by breakfast. Hey, not that I'm a cynic. You guys just save one shot for me. One, that's all I need, just set aside one for me. I want to go out high as a kite, fly so high I can sail right over Saint Peter, way over his head, over his Pearly Gates, he won't even see me, won't know I've snuck in, I've snuck right by him."

"The very definition of God," Eberly said then, deadpan as if this were a late-night dorm-room philosophy session, though he was joking. "He's all-knowing, all-seeing, you can't sneak by God, that's not the way it works."

"He'll be too busy welcoming you guys," Wolfe teased right back. "Heroes like him"—Jarbodie. "Jumping out the back of a chopper without a rope just to think he's going to save a handful of grunts. And you, Doc, God's going to be too busy handing you-all out medals and slapping you on the back, 'Good job, good job'. He won't even see me floating right on by overhead."

And eventually Wolfe got to another thing he'd come in for. He wrote down three numbers on a torn piece of wrapping. *12, 20 & 5.* Gave it to Doc Eberly and told him that was another book he had to read. He didn't remember the author, a doctor and his time as battalion surgeon in Vietnam. Like that other one he'd told him about, that *Home Before Morning*, except that was a nurse and this is a doctor. Something Eberly would want to read. What are the numbers for? Call over the radio from the chopper pilots to the Mash—it was Mash back then, Cash now—how many litter-borne wounded, walking wounded, and dead.

And that was it. Wolfe doesn't know why he thought he had to give Doc the name of that book. As if there aren't hundreds of other books too.

Right now out here in the main area Wolfe sits himself down on the floor against the wall. Slits open his MRE bag.

Sees something among the litter of supplies on the other side of Dove. Tilts his head. Squints. *Huh?*

"Don't tell me, no." He's up. "Can't be, no way, can't be."

He moves some boxes. "Hallelujah, eureka, the Tooth Fairy's come! Where's this been hiding? Shoulda known we had these before."

An unopened crate. Flashlight illuminates it for Rodriquez. "Sniper, you want to help me?"

Clearly labeled in military stencil, MINE, ANTI-PERSONNEL, M18A1. CLAYMORE. 12 EA.

Rodriquez, "Yeh sure. What you gonna do, where you wanna put em, 'mano?"

Wolfe, "The Maginot Line."

"Say again?"

"The Maginot Line. Trust me."

"Line of maggots, who maggots, what maggots, insurg maggots?"

"Maginot Line. What'd you do in high school history, you sleep through all your history classes?"

"History class? High school? Like, Jorge Washington? Pablo Revere? Poncho Villa? Cristoból Colón, all that crap? High school? I got my GED, all it costs me, a tatt of a dolphin here"—on the calf—"and a lizard, a Gila monster here"—the other calf. "The puta works Department of Educación, is a sexy-tary, Departmento de Educación Especiál. Cap'n ma'am," he asks Cathay who's awake now. "You know this maggot line he's talkin bout?"

"That's before my time. World War One."

"Post World War One," Nick Flowers throws in. "Between the wars. Brilliant theory, barring the front door."

Dove, "If you're not going to leave the side doors open. The Maginot Line, Mr Wolfe? Are you sure you want to go that route? It didn't work out too well for the French."

"Number One, Colonel—that's the French. Number Two, we're not French."

Rodriquez, "Yeh 'mano, an' Three, where we gonna put those? Can't see shit out there."

At Isaf Kabul, a Blackhawk helicopter ascends straight up from the roof of the HQ building.

All its exterior lights are out.

Interior too.

Pilots flying on NVGs.

The helicopter continues straight up to altitude AGL at 2,000 feet then shoots forward.

Inside, doors closed, Col Pluma looks out down at the speckles of lights of the city. The climb in a straight ascent is familiar to Pluma. Getting up while still over the expansive Isaf compound to an altitude safe out of small-arms fire, not that there ever is any here in Kabul. Someday, he thinks, *The day the Ruskies or Chinks or Iranians give the muj Stingers we're goners, we can kiss ruling the skies goodbye, the war is over. Lost.*

Just two other pax with him aboard. Two of the journalists from the press briefing. A Reuters guy and a Getty photographer, or *Videographer, or whatever the hell they're calling themselves these days, they've all got video-cams along with those normal Nikon photo cameras.*

He can't remember their names. Should have thought to force himself to remember them when that fat bitch Colonel Gray-Nance introduced them to him down there on the roof as the helicopter was coming down to pick them up.

He shouts over the engine and rotor noise to the Reuters guy seated across from him, "Lucky the Russians aren't giving these mujahidin their version of the Stinger. Like we supplied the muj with in the Eighties. In their war. Would put a whole new spin on the war."

The Reuters guy just smiles, nods. Too much trouble to try to talk in here over the deafening noise.

"A whole new spin," Pluma repeats, this time pantomiming a missle flying straight, then a tremendous explosion, this very copter exploding, and he again gets just a smile and nod from the reporter.

Pluma had said it all just to see if he could get a rise out of the guy. A tease to get a sign of fear in him, make him nervous.

Nope, nothing.

Okay, all right, so the guy's been plenty of time here in war.

Pluma looks back out at the sparser lights of the city thinning near the outskirts, and he looks ahead at the black darkness of the empty landscape of dark hill-forms they're heading toward.

Kevlar and body armor on, and his M4 carbine stood between his knees, muzzle on the floor, Pluma has the feeling of the past, of younger days doing soldierly things, being a soldier. A soldier soldier.

A little touch of the thrill and anticipatory fear of going into combat.

Being a soldier soldier again.

At least for the next twelve hours maybe.

Wajma, in the schoolhouse, Redcloud turns off his Nods and turns on his headlamp as he comes down the stairs.

Takes off his helmet and drops it atop a box.

Stacks two empty wooden ammo crates and sits.

Dove hands him a plastic 24oz Gatorade bottle.

Redcloud twists off the cap. Thumb-and-middle-finger snaps it all the way across where it bounces off the poncho drapes of the side window.

He drinks it down, empties the bottle.

Drops it into his helmet.

Dove offers him a couple of granola bars, but he declines.

Reaches into a large cardboard box of packaged snacks and comes up with a store-countertop box of Slim Jims.

He pulls open the box and takes out a handful.

"Breakfast of champions," he tells Dove. "And lunch. And dinner."

He pockets the handful and grabs another couple then stops Spec Lee Tran who's come down from the roof to bring up another couple of cases of MREs, and Redcloud plops the box of Slim Jims on the MRE boxes. "See if they upstairs don't want these," he tells Tran.

"Any candy bars in there?" Crew Chief Jarbodie asks. "Hersheys or Mounds or Pay Days? Anything?"

"Help yourself." Redcloud swings the box around. "You're in the Zoo now," and kicks it across the floor near to where Jarbodie is sitting. "You-all brought it, shoot, we owe you."

Redcloud bites off about half a Slim Jim. Savors it on a slow chew.

Dove hands him over another Gatorade.

"I don't think I've pissed but once all day," Redcloud says and screws off the cap. "Dang it, I forgot to tell Ketch and Utah to use em for piss bottles."

He takes a long swallow, then "Hey, Sergeant Nell!" he calls loudly toward the front.

"Yeh Sarge?" comes Nell's answer from out on the veranda.

"Pass it on. I don't want guys going out to piss, don't want em pissin on the wall, in the corners. Use the Gatorade bottles."

"Hooah, Sergeant," unseen from Nell out there.

And Holloway's remark from out there, "Just don't drink the yellow Gatorade." Followed by his own laughter. Then, "When we run out of ammo we can throw piss bottle bombs at the enemy." More of his own laughter, and some other voice out there that says, "Holloway, if you can't say anything funny, don't say anything at all." And "Yeh? Yeh?" from Holloway, "look who's talkin."

Dove motions Jarbodie that he'll take a couple of the Kit Kats from the box Jarbodie's come up with, and Jarbodie flips him over one. Another. Another. Another. And another. Enough.

"Laura," Dove calls softly to Cathay. And he underhands a Kit Kat which she catches. Another, and she catches it.

"It's nothing but sugar," he tells her. "It won't hurt you. Nothing to digest, it goes straight into the bloodstream. Pure energy."

Redcloud drains the rest of the second Gatorade.

Dove meets his eyes.

Moves his legs to show him the military stenciling on the sides of both the cardboard boxes he's sitting on.

Asks, "Ready?"

The boxes are labeled: **BAG, BODY, PLASTIC, ZIPPERED, BLACK, 12 EA.**

From Redcloud hesitancy, and he tips the Gatorade up to get the last drops from it. Screws the cap back on. Drops the bottle into his helmet with the first.

Now a nod *yeh, let's do it.*

Dove stands. Lifts both boxes.

Redcloud gets up, tears with his teeth the wrapper off another Slim Jim and follows Dove into the morgue classroom.

Bagram Airfield, on the tarmac, the back of the C-130 is open, and dark shadowy forms of a few people can be seen inside in the dim red lighting.

Outside, standing on the concrete just off the tailramp, the Air Force crew chief calls out a warning, "Engines turning!", to Col Pluma out about fifty feet away.

Pluma waves back a *Got it, be right there,* and says into the radio handset, "I'll call you again in an hour, maybe ninety minutes, Zach. Out here." He jerks the handset to the soldier crouched over the rucksack from which the handset cord extends, ordering him, "Pack it up, let's go."

The soldier, Sergeant Lachowicz, on temporary loan from division signal company, who during his first tour here two years ago and now this tour also has never spent a moment outside this huge, safe, 20,000-person base, throws the handset into his ruck, cinches up the ruck, lifts it over one shoulder, bends to grab the flip-out sat antenna, and his M4 drops off his shoulder and rattles to the concrete. He manages to grab it up in hand and the antenna in the other and has to run to follow Pluma up into the airplane, as the first prop engine kicks over and revs in a harsh whine, killing the quiet that had been out here.

Wajma, the schoolhouse, on the veranda, Dove gives the radio handset back to Pfc Holloway and tells Wolfe with just a nod *Go ahead, move out, it's all yours.*

"Semper fi," from Ssgt Utah. "Good luck."

"Walk in the park," from Wolfe in reply.

Through Nods, Utah, Dove, Holloway and Redcloud watch Wolfe lead the ANA sergeant and Pvt Finkle down the steps and all three disappear a moment later into the thick fog and dark.

Dove checks his watch. 21:27.

Holloway checks his. It jumps from 9:25 to 9:26.

If Redcloud had to read minds, he knows that it would be easy-as-pie reading Finkle's. The young private is thinking right now he's special. Feeling special. He's selected to go on this special mission with this experienced, mean-talking, hip civilian dude with all that Marine Corps special ops action hooah shit like *Call of Duty*, *Wolfenstein*, *SoCom*. And with this big strong Afghan dude who looks like he'd as soon cut your throat as shake your hand. Finkle's got a chance to shed his Kevlar, just wear his ballcap he's got in his ruck like everyone carries. Ballcap on backwards, like Wolfe the special ops guy, so his headstrapped Nods can be on the front and turned on now, just like Wolfe got. And no body armor, how cool is that? *Don't gotta wear body armor. Cuz we've gotta move too fast, too quiet. Like injuns. Sneaking like injuns.* Redcloud knows that Finkle's feeling like he's all those soldier heroes from all those old World War Two movies he's seen on TV after midnight, and he's sneaking off like them on a special mission to blow up those German guns, like that cool flick *Guns of Navarone*, that was awesome when they blew up that whole mountain to smithereens, and Clint Eastwood and those guys in *Kelly's Heroes* and best of all *The Dirty Dozen*.

Yeh, Finkle, right you are. How cool is that?

'Cept, Finkle's probably never seen those flicks, wouldn't know nuthin about those flicks. But he does know *Call of Duty*, *Wolfenstein*, that's, like, guaranteed for sure.

Redcloud knows that Wolfe has by now allowed the ANA sergeant to take the lead and has put himself behind Finkle, because he'd heard Wolfe's last-minute instructions to Finkle. To not lose sight of the sergeant in front of him not for one second, not in this dark and not in this fog, no matter if he had to jog to keep up.

Redcloud knows well why Wolfe would have the sergeant on point. The sergeant seemed to understand their destination from the map, but maps don't matter to Afghans. He doesn't need a map. He knows where they're going. Even with his very limited time here in Wajma yesterday and today he would have the lay of the land. Know the feel of where the compounds are. Know where he might have to skirt any villagers in their compounds or out by chance tonight. As an Afghan he can use the language and his cultural familiarity to neutralize any surprise confrontations. More, Redcloud knows, just as Wolfie knows, that as an Afghan the sergeant can feel his way around to avoid any of those confrontations. 'Cause he's Afghan. It's his country, they're his people. He feels it, he feels them. Americans can't.

Dove had known ever since that second assault this afternoon when only one mortar fired, not two, and had assumed the second had been moved and thus hadn't been taken out by the Jdam, he knew then that they were going to have to do something about it. Eventually.

First things first then, and that meant getting through the assaults and then getting through the recovery and through the resupply and the Chinook crash and getting the sandbag fortifications done, ammo distributed and stacked at each position, and prep for long night waiting.

He'd known from the first that they couldn't deal with that surviving 120 mortar in the daylight anyway, they'd have to wait for the cover of night.

When he and Redcloud had zipped the last KIA into a body bag he mentioned it to Redcloud, and Redcloud said that he'd been thinking along the same lines, that they were going to have to eliminate that 120, or else the next attack, especially if they've got recoilless rifles, it would be lights-out, you could close the books on the Zoo.

Redcloud said that he figured to make it a Ranger patrol, two or three men at the most. Cross the valley, find the mortar and destroy it with C4 or thermites or, if they couldn't get close, with 40mike-mike from the 203, or even a Law. That's what he'd thought at first. With all the black dark and the fog making it impossible to see, the next best option was just to get close enough to know where it was and get a grid for it then call up to get the fast-movers to drop a Jdam on it.

He said he'd lead the patrol.

Dove agreed that it should be a Ranger op but said no, Redcloud was out, the mission was too risky, chances too great of the patrol not making it back and he was too valuable here, that the Zoo needed its platoon sergeant more than any other leader. Let's get the leadership together and hash it out, Dove suggested.

The three squad leaders, and Wolfe included. Rodriquez too.

The only other Rangers besides Redcloud being Ketchum and Dove, Ketchum insisted it be his mission, he wanted it, man, he breathed this kinda shit.

But Redcloud nixed it. Said he wanted Ketch on the roof with his squad, needed Ketch on the roof with the big guns. "I can't be everywhere at once, I'm going to need a strong leader up there on those machineguns."

That was final. Ketch was out.

Leaving the only other Ranger, Lieut Col Dove.

Who smiled, said, "I guess I drew long straw. I knew there was a good reason I came along."

No, not so fast, Redcloud said. That the colonel had the rank, he could give the order and go if he wanted to. But that rank was exactly why the colonel couldn't go. Not on a suicide mission. That Dove was the only one who General St Claire and his ring-knockers up there were going to believe about what happened here yesterday and what's happened today. "We lose you, sir," Redcloud said. "The Zoo, Captain Washington, my L-T......there's no sayin what they're gonna do to them. Drag them through the mud, court-martial my privates and specialists."

"Funny," Dove had said then. "Somehow I knew you were going to say that."

"The Zoo's going to need your word. The weight your word's gonna carry."

And Ketchum and Utah and Nell all agreed.

And Dove knew it was true. Had known it was true. Had known he couldn't go, though he'd have loved to lead the patrol, would have been honored to, that he could order it that he go.

He knew that Redcloud was right about Staff Sergeant Ketchum, that he was more valuable on the roof than probably dead out there. Knew that when Ranger Ketchum was nixed that there was only one other who could lead the patrol. Not a Ranger, but with all the skills of a Ranger. And more experience.

He looked straight at Wolfe. "Mr Wolfe?"

"Just waiting for you to ask." As if anyone would even need to ask? Like Wolfe wouldn't jump at a patrol to find that one-twenty mortar?

Just give him two guys, two requirements:

Number One, they gotta be quick and mobile.

Number Two, fearless.

He wanted, one, the Afghan sergeant. Cuz if Afghans are one thing, they're quick and mobile, they were born quick and mobile and they can run these mountains barefoot in the darkest part of midnight. And they're fearless. They'll hedge their bets and desert when they're on the losing side, but it aint from fear, and this sergeant, he hasn't deserted, so that's another plus in his column.

And, the second guy, Redcloud knew his men better than Wolfe did, let him pick who he thought best for this type of mission.

"Hands-down," Ketchum spoke before Redcloud could. "Finkle. Trust me, dude, you want Finkle. Yeh, Finkle. You want quick and mobile, he's a acrobat. And he aint just fearless, he's fucken reckless fearless. With a capital fucken R-F."

Agreement from the others, except for Dove who had feigned offense and said, "Gosh, guys, I was kind of thinking of volunteering Specialist Howie for it."

It took everyone a couple of seconds, then they laughed, and howled even greater when the double-meaning of it hit.

Yep, not just the absurdity of Howie being quick and mobile or fearless, but that the lieutenant colonel may have been volunteering Howie as totally expendable, worthless as a warrior, who cares.

Dark jet-black humor. From the colonel.

"That one, Colonel, good one," Ketchum had said still giggling. "Specialist Chubby humpin a Ranger patrol? I'm gonna take it to my grave."

Bagram Airfield, in the C-130, as it taxies to the end of the runway.

This is the same Air Force Air Evac C-130 that went to Fob Salerno yesterday afternoon to pick up Robyn Banks.

Inside, a dozen Air Force doctors, nurses and medical techs belted in on the web seating along both fuselage walls.

And the two journalists and Pluma's radio sergeant, Lachowicz, seated closest to the rear on one side.

Across on the other side, Col Pluma.

Also here is the Army nurse who Pluma intentionally sat himself down next to when he came aboard after the satcom call to Dove. Someone he was completely surprised and had never expected to find aboard here.

Major Vicky Marshall.

"What are you doing here?" he'd asked her.

"I'm a nurse anesthetist."

"Yeh sure, but what are you doing here?"

"I know people."

"This is an Air Force crew. Air Force tasking, what are you doing here?"

"A little birdie told me that the place that you sent Zachary Dove to this morning, the numbers we got in Hospital Ops, that Zachary at last count has something like a 14, 8, and 10."

"And I know hospital terminology?" Pluma had said put-off.

"14 litter-borne. 8 ambulatory. 10 dead."

"I can assure you, Vicky . . . . I can assure you that Zachary Dove is perfectly all right."

A pleasant, forced smile from her then, *Okay, assure me.*

"I just spoke with him two minutes ago out there."

"Zachary?"

"The one. The only."

"And the others? 14, 8, 10?"

"I don't remember the exact numbers. It's not good. That's why this." This Air Evac plane. "If I didn't care—. If we didn't care at Isaf Command, the weather's all socked in down there, the fog's pea soup—. Command would not have authorized this flight."

Vicky said nothing, offered no thanks.

"Thick as pea soup down there," Pluma repeated to scare or at least worry her. "Going to be touch-and-go. The pilots aren't even sure if they're going to be able to land."

"I guess it's lucky I brought my lucky rabbit's foot."

"Where?" And he couldn't help raising one eyebrow saying it, suggestively, flirting.

"Oh, I'm not telling," she'd returned as if jousting, but ringing false. Then conceding politeness, "That's what makes it lucky. It's like a birthday wish. You don't get your wish if you tell anyone it."

"Remind me on your birthday."

And she hadn't answered that, wanted to end it. Looked away to pretend interest in what the crew chief was doing nearby checking some hydraulic fluid level at some gauge or something.

Spurned twice in one day by her, Pluma threw his own dart. "You sure it's a rabbit's foot? Not a bear's claw?" And adding, with a lilt of a joke, but cutting, "Or rattlesnake fangs?"

Vicky gave him an innocuous smile and shrug *Who knows, could be, who cares?*, and has not said another word to him in these few minutes since, and Pluma let her be.

The plane maneuvers a tight 180 that Pluma figures is the end of the runway.

Pluma gets a slight comfort of pleasure thinking that for Victoria Marshall he'd find it a hoot if Zachary Dove had his dick shot off, was one of the litter-borne, just to see the expression on her face when she saw him dickless. *So much for your roll in the hay with him, sweetheart.*

The plane jerks to a hard stop.

Experienced hands go up to grab onto the seat-webbing above their shoulders.

She wasn't even surprised by the pea soup, Pluma thinks.

The engines rev.

Must have already talked with the crew, got the status, knows it'll be a pure instrument landing. Flirted with the crew. Batted those eyes. Smiled.

The engines rev stronger, and everyone can feel the caged surge against the brakes that restrain the plane from rushing forward.

Women in the war zone. No fair. You can get anything you want with some nice firm tits and a tight ass and the whiff of a wet cunt. And if you're Halle Barry gorgeous, except more so, double that.

Brakes released, the plane lurches forward, and everyone holds on as their bodies are sharply pulled to the rear, and Vicky thinks that the colonel's thigh pressed tight against hers is intentional, that it's forced, that he's using the forward thrust as an excuse to touch her.

Yeh well, and she forces her own thigh away from his. *Too late now, slimeball,* she thinks. He can't do what she'd expected of him. *He can't kick me off the plane now.*

Wajma, on the schoolhouse veranda, Dove checks his watch. 21:35.

And he knows it's ridiculous to check the time, that just seven minutes have passed since they left, and what, are they supposed to be coming back by now, mission accomplished?

Perhaps he's a little anxious that they would be coming back, mission aborted, it's too damn dark out there and you can't see your hand in front of your face in this fog, *How are they going to cross the valley and find one mortar tube hidden where, a needle in a haystack? In this fog?*

No, Kyle Wolfe won't quit. Not Mr Wolfe. Not his nature.

Young Private Finkle, he'll go where Wolfe tells him, do what Wolfe tells him.

The Afghan NCO, he won't quit. It's his pride, it's his country, and he's going to show Mr Wolfe, he's going to show Finkle, *He's going to show Sergeant Redcloud and me, show all the Zoo that's he's an Afghan soldier* and they may not have NVGs and M4s and encrypted Mbitr radios and GPSes and even CamelBaks, but *They'll fight you tooth and nail, literally tooth and nail,* and show you that you've got nothing on them in bravery.

Dove knows that it's do-or-die for the three of them out there and Private Finkle doesn't even know that. The Afghan NCO's not giving up until they find that mortar and destroy it, and neither is Mr Wolfe.

Wolfe was going to leave his Mbitr platoon radio behind. Said he didn't need it, what was he going to do, call for help? Who's the cavalry? Number Two, if they got caught or killed and he hadn't had time to zero it, the Talibs would have the radio, which means they'd have all the freqs, all the encryption, could listen to you all night long, can wake you up to the morning call to prayer on it.

Nope, Dove had insisted. If you find the mortar site and you can't get hands-on to destroy it, you get a ten-digit grid on the Garmin, and if you're compromised and know you're not making it back, you call it in to us and we can call up Cas and a Jdam.

Wolfe took his radio with them. Told Dove, though, he was going to leave it off, so don't bother calling checking up all the time.

Agreed. The patrol was on its own.

Dove turns his Nods off. Speaks softly in the pitch black to where he knows Pfc Holloway is just below sitting against the wall. "If Isaf or the Cop calls, unless it's something vital or it's Colonel Pluma personally, tell them it's No Change in Status."

"Roger that, sir. You told me, sir."

Yeh, right, that's right, he had. Before. *Kid's pretty sharp.*

Something else is troubling Dove, and he pushes through the hanging ponchos of the entrance doorway, inside. He's going to have to speak with Nick Flowers. It's what Colonel Pluma had said when he called not ten minutes ago. About *Command attitude's done a one-eighty. The Tattoo Zoo are all heroes now. The key element is going to be that video your Nick Flowers there is filming. Flowers, he's not out of the play of the problem, I hope, is he, can you assure me he's not one of your casualties, Zach? Great. Now listen, I can't emphasize enough, Zachary, General St Claire has put the highest priority on getting Flowers and his film out of there. Intact, both of them. That film, Zach, it's the whole enchilada here we're talking about.*

Enchilada, Dove thinks as he seats himself inside on a box beside Nick. *Now where have I heard that before?*

Wolfe calls out in Pashto to the sergeant whose form he can barely make out through his Nods, *Stop, Wait.*

They do.

Wolfe has got some quick points to make with Finkle. It's too late now to try and teach him the compass here that Wolfe is following or the Garmin GPS he also holds, so Finkle's going to have to pay attention to the feel of where they're going, cuz if he winds up out here alone he's going to have to find his way back to the school on his own.

"You know what this place looks like, from being up there on the roof all day. You know where we're going. Picture it. We're gonna be movin there with mountains on which side? Which side?"

"Left."

"So on the way back you keep the mountain on your right. Rub your shoulder against it. You'll bump your head right back into the school."

"Got ya. Easy."

"Not so easy when you've got a bunch of pissed off true-believers on your ass who want your hide. You just pay attention, get the feel where he's going." The sergeant. "Stay up tight and move as quiet as he does. Put in your brain and keep thinking it, if you gotta come back on your own, you're doing everything the opposite."

Wolfe's hand goes to the arm of the sergeant who's not wearing Nods in this pitch dark. A slight tap *Move,* and they're going again.

Wolfe feels comfortable, he feels good. Travel light, move fast. Each carries only his weapon and seven magazines in an ammo rack. First aid pouches. Finkle's got a dozen 40mm grenades also pocketed in his vest. Wolfe and Finkle both have a Law slung over the small knapsacks that all three carry. The same in each knapsack, including the sergeant's: two blocks of C4, two thermite grenades, a handful of frags, two smoke grenades, a poncho, some 550-cord. Added in Wolfe's, a spool of det cord and a coil of timing fuse.

All three dropped in bottles of water and Gatorade and quick-energy snacks.

Redcloud's advice, of course. You never know.

Now, Wolfe thinks, *we've only got to cross this whole valley the long round-about way and not be seen or heard.*

In sh'allah.

Day Two, Night—Part 2

Wajma, in the Schoolhouse

Now this is the Holloway Groove, and Pfc Holloway doesn't know why he didn't think of it before.

He's back in the swing of things, this is the way he likes to roll, he's back in the gang, back where the action's gonna be, back amongst the big shots, the Vips.

VIPs, but Holloway just calls them Vips.

Not Veeps. Vips.

Hey, this is Pfc Holloway afterall, don't argue with it, it doesn't have to make logical sense.

He's inside. He is with the Vips.

In here.

Where there's those lights, those lamps, and you can see.

He's seated against the wall at the entrance. And that's that Captain Beautiful Cathay just across from him so close. Captain Fine Specimen of a Chick Cathay. *Chick Cathay, cool, like Chick-Fil-A.* Even sleeping she's beautifuler than that lawyer who was Reese Witherspoon in that dorky chick flick *Legally Blonde*, she's way more prettier, and without no fake blond hair and painted long fingernails and that stupid poodle she always carried around with her everywhere, even sticking his stupid little head out of her purse.

There's Sergeant Redcloud.

The lieutenant colonel.

Sniper asshole thinks he's God's-gift-to-everything Rodriquez.

Asshole in fact sitting there on the other side of the captain, close to her, thinks he's gonna get a piece of that, *I know he thinks he's gonna turn his Mexicani homie-boy charm on her, and he aint. Thinks the tatt's gonna give him the edge, he can slip it in her. Good luck with that, homie, cuz it aint just you, I've got the tatt too.*

There's Nicky. On that computer, looks like a tech nerd gone wild, who knows what he's doin. Who cares?

There's that sergeant from the helicopter. Jar-something. Jar-head. No. Jar-booty, yeah Jar-booty. Booty. Booty awright. *I seen the way he's been sneaking looks at the captain, thinkin he's gonna get himself some of that booty.* Yeh right, him and Rodriquez. That Wolfie was still here, what do you wanna bet *He'd be sittin there right in her lap thinkin he was gonna get some of that booty himself too.*

Jeez now, if only someone in here would say something.

Say something, do somethin, someone talk. C'mon!

Holloway didn't come in here to be part of the Vips just to have nothing happening.

The Holloway Groove, it was the ultimate Groove-elicious moment when it had hit him that he could be in with the Vips if he could just get these two radios in there. Antennas gotta be outside, yeh, with a clear shot to the satellites in the sky, but the radios can be inside, but the 6-foot cables aint gonna reach that far. Six foot of line, need about twenty. *Wish I'd brung the kitbag, got a 25-footer in it.* Then it hit him, wasn't there one in the bottom of his ruck, didn't he leave one there, a 25-footer, cuz doesn't Sergeant Redcloud say you never know when yer gonna have to set the antenna out away from you so you can get behind cover and still make comms?

Yessireebob, and Jack and Jill and the hill they tumbled down on, the cable was there just where he hoped for, at the very bottom of his ruck.

Yeh, well, two antennas, two radios, one cable aint gonna cut it.

Two antennas. Two radios. One cable.

That aint gonna cut it.

Two antennas. Two radios . . . .

When his brain's working high-speed, there's no stopping the Holloway Groove.

Akin!

He's a real radioman, MOS to prove it. He's gonna have another in his ruck!

"Sppppt, Inhelder," Holloway had called to the guy he couldn't even see. "Here, watch the radios."

"Huh?" was the voice Holloway couldn't see.

"Watch the radios. Only be a minute, gotta do something."

"Gotta do what? I don't know what to say on the radio."

"Inhelder," came Ssgt Utah's voice from farther down. "Watch the radios. Holloway, what you got, you have to take a dump?"

"Yeh, Sarge, gotta take a dump. Be right back quick."

"You know the procedure? In the MRE box in the back room back there."

"Yeh Sarge, I know."

"And you don't urinate on top of the excrement, it turns it all into a soggy mess. You piss into a Gatorade bottle."

"Got it, Sarge."

All hyped-up in the Holloway Groove, he went inside and acted like he was going to take a dump and went straight into that one back room where with his SureFire on bright he could see all the black body bags that were bulging and laid out all perfectly in line, and he could see back in the corner where they have the MRE box shitter covered with a poncho to keep the stink in if anyone's even shitted in here, *Who'd want to shit where all these guys are? I aint never gonna take a crap here with Captain Washington and the L-T just there, sorry, dude, no thank you.*

He found the ruck with Akin's nametag on the flap, and sure enough Akin didn't just have the 25-footer cable but had the whole sat radio kitbag. Sheee-at, Akin, *You da man, you come prepared, you musta been a Boy Scout,* maybe he had something else in his ruck that *We can use, might come in handy,* but no, *You don't rob from the dead, that aint right,* and Holloway left it, didn't look further in Akin's ruck, didn't take anything, though he'd seen a *Hot Rod* magazine and a *Four Wheeler* too and a Victoria's Secret catalog which he sure could use passing the time. All three of them. Especially the Victoria's Secret.

But you do not steal from the dead, and he didn't take them.

Out on the veranda he'd switched the cables, and Inhelder had asked him how it was taking a crap in there with all the bodies.

Awright, Holloway had said. "They got em in body bags, and they're not gonna crawl out and watch you."

"Yeh but it's not right, it don't feel right," Inhelder had said solemnly. "I gotta go right now, I gotta take a dump something fierce, it's crowning, but I am not going in there."

Utah's voice from down in the dark, "I've got a better idea for you, Inhelder. I give you permission, you can go out on the other side of the wall out there and do your business."

"Don't forget to wipe," came Slurpee's voice from down the other way.

And Utah's voice again, "Inhelder, I can't guarantee you that Tran up there isn't going to mistake you for Taliban and open up with the two-forty."

Slurpee's voice, "Tran's gonna wipe your ass clean spic-n-span, Inhelder, with a stream of seven-six-two."

Utah's, "The tracers alone, ooooh, that is going to burn."

Slurpee's, "Oooooohee mama, gotta love those tracer rounds! It's like eating chilidogs you dumped like a whole bottle of Tabasco on and later when you gotta shit it comes out burning something fierce, like you've lit up your ass on fire back there!"

"You can all shove it," Inhelder had said. "Say what you want. I'm holding it in til morning."

But Slurpee was on a roll, his voice singing from down there, "You say yer crowning, Inhelder? Yeh, you hold it in til morning, they medevac you with a gunshot to the leg and the nurse there at the Sal Cash she's a ten, useta be a Oakland Raiders cheerleader. And she goes to cut off your pants and what's sitting there? A big turd. Right there in her face. A big turd. Then what you gonna think, Inhelder? Gonna be so shamed, yer gonna wanna die."

A laugh came from a new voice. Ssgt Nell. And, "Where do you come up with that shit, Slurpee? Bro, you got one sick sick sick sick i-mag-gin-ation. Where do you get that shit?"

"I don't know, Sarge. Just natural, man, like breathing. I know that Raiders cheerleader nurse, when she cuts off my pants, she's gonna see this giant raging hard-on stickin right up in her face."

And there was laughter all up and down the veranda at that.

And Holloway had wished he'd come up with that. Knew he was going to have to remember that. *Hard-on stickin right up in the nurse's face in the Cash.* Was gonna have to remember it and use it someday.

Oakland Raiders cheerleader nurse. Put that image in the Holloway Groove. Those little white shorts so short and so tight. All her waist bare naked skin tan and smooth, and her bellybutton, sexxx-eeeeeee. And her *Boobs, they be 'bout poppin outta that bikini top* . . . .

He kinda sorta really wished he'd took that Victoria's Secret catalog of Akin's when he had the chance.

And then he'd pulled the two radios into the doorway and dropped a couple of sandbags on the cables so no one's boots would snag the antennas off the wall, then set himself and the radios completely inside.

Inside.

With the Vips.

If only they were doing something, saying something.

Redcloud thinks there's something he should do but doesn't know what it is, can't think of anything.

What's he forgotten? Something? What? There's got to be something. Maybe there isn't.

They're set up as good as they're going to be. What more can they do? Thank God for that resupply. *Thank God and the pilot, God rest his soul, and his crew, thank God for them, if we didn't have that we'd be stuck with what?* They'd be stuck with, what was it Pfc Holloway had said before earlier tonight? *We'd be stuck throwing piss bottle bombs at them when they storm us.*

If they storm right now, Redcloud knows, *We've got the advantage.* Not in numbers, he'd love to have the whole company here, all of Awesome Company tonight here, but in that fog out there, where if there's a moon out tonight you can't even see it, making it dark as the devil's soul out there. *Yeh we can't see, but we've got NVGs and they don't. We can see them before they can see us.*

If you can see, you can aim.

If you can aim, you can shoot.

If you can shoot, you should be able to stop them.

Redcloud checks his watch. Analog. A couple of minutes after eleven.

It's been an hour and a half since Wolfie left. They should be across the valley over there by now. How they going to see to find that mortar out there when you can barely see Finkle walking right in front of you and Finkle can barely see the Afghan sergeant right in front of him? Unless you trip right over the tube, and then you're gonna have yourself a little firefight. Or a big firefight. Firefight, Tic, whatever you want to call it, if they get into one *We're gonna hear it from here, and we'll know it.*

As long as Redcloud doesn't hear gunfire, so far it's a good thing. What he wants to hear is a big explosion, which is Wolfie and them blowing up that tube and hopefully all the mortar rounds too, and no gunfire at all, which means no opposition, no pursuit, the perfect textbook Ranger Handbook raid.

Without thinking, Redcloud makes a quick sign-of-the-cross shortcutted just in front of his chest.

The 4 of Lieut Col Dove's watch changes to 5.

23:05.

Passed ninety minutes now and Dan Pluma still hasn't called back.

Ninety minutes, Dan had said, he'd get back in ninety minutes.

Dove hopes that Murphy's Law hasn't gone into effect.

He glances over at Pfc Holloway seated just inside the doorway. Okay, he's got the handsets up on his shoulders close to his ears, he's listening.

Holloway meets Dove's eyes and gives a slight nod, *Nothing here.*

A slight nod back from Dove, *Sure, no problem.*

Smart young man moving in here. No need to be out there in the dark. Took the initiative to figure it out. Safer for the radios in here. Though, the Achilles heel are the antennas. The antennas get blown up, you can use the radios for boat anchors.

Doves looks at Nick Flowers on the laptop burning DVDs copying files. When Dove had told Nick about Isaf putting a high priority on Nick's tapes, he warned him that that probably meant that General St Claire would absolutely be looking at everything first and then restricting Nick's own usage of what the general did not like.

"Naw," Nick had said. "That's not the way it's done. They can't confiscate an embed's equipment or his work."

"So, what happens," Dove had told him, "when they come and pick us up and an MP says, 'Mr Flowers, I'm going to have to secure all your cameras and your tapes'? What are you going to do? When he has three other MPs behind him, and they all carry sidearms and their M4s. And you're not getting on the chopper without rendering everything to them. Render unto Caesar. Do you imagine you can simply tell them 'No thanks' and you'll be free to be on your merry way, stroll out of here? Catch a taxi? A Taliban cab, a Toyota Corolla flying the white Taliban flag?"

"They can't do that."

"I'm not saying that you'll lose your work. I'm saying that General St Claire is going to determine what you can use and cannot use. What you cannot, you're not keeping, you'll never see it again."

"He can't," Nick had insisted. "Nobody can. I'm a journalist."

And Dove had let that settle, let Nick think about it for a bit. Then said, "You're here courtesy of the United States Army and Isaf. Nato. They'll take everything, and if you start screaming and yelling they'll give everything back, and all or some of your tapes will be blank, erased. Just by coincidence only the video that they don't want released and anyone ever seeing. Erased. And they'll say, 'Oh goshdarnit, it must have been the electronics on the helicopter, some magnetic field, the radio interference, it works funny that way. Sorry.'"

"Okay, I hear you," Nick said. "But you're my witness, Zachary."

"No, don't trust me, I work for General Pete St Claire, remember?"

"No one's ever asked to see my stuff first before. Not in Iraq and not here. No one."

Granted. But, "You've never filmed a hundred-seventy-three dead women and children collateral damage before. Or—" Dove indicates the ones in the morgue room.

"What am I supposed to do? What would you do?"

"Go along, what can you do? General St Claire's a reasonable man. He'll let you oversee the editing. He'll probably let you keep seventy-five percent of it, ninety percent of it, to do what you want with."

"That's unacceptable. No journalist would accept that."

"Many would."

"Well, I can't, Zachary. Can't. No way."

"You did. You did, you accepted the restrictions when you were with us when I allowed you to film my task force."

"Beforehand, that was agreed upon beforehand, I knew what the terms were. And you didn't demand, remember?, or ask, to see my film afterwards, you didn't, Zachary."

"I trusted you. If I had thought that you had broken the restrictions, even one restriction, I would have confiscated your tapes."

"You said earlier, you said on the chopper, you said I could shoot what I wanted, that I was free to shoot anything, that I had free rein, I believe those were your exact words."

"And I said, I remember, that General St Claire had already asked that he see your film first. And General St Claire outranks me. By a long ways."

And Nick knew then that it was hopeless, that he was going to lose this one. Even if he could keep ninety percent, it's not right, it's still not right, even ninety-five percent, it goes against the very grain of the First Amendment, you don't let the generals or the senators or the corporate CEOs or the police chiefs or any of them tell you what you can show and what you can't.

"What I would do, Nicky," Dove had then said. "I'd make a copy of everything I had shot today. And I'd give it to Mr Wolfe or to one of these men who you trust, and I wouldn't tell me who. That's what I would do."

"Yeh, if I'd brought my laptop. S-O-L again."

"You can't do it on your camera?"

Nope.

"You need your laptop?"

"I need to go from my camera into my laptop. And I don't suppose you brought one, did you? A laptop?"

Yes. But, common sense, Dove can't be a part of it. And you can't trust him anyway.

No difference, Nick said. Dove wouldn't have the right cable anyway.

Resigned, Nick had known then that he really really really was S-O-L. And yeh, might just as well add, without a paddle.

Until, "You might check with Specialist Howie," Dove said. "He might have brought a laptop. And the cables."

Not only had Spec Howie brought his laptop and all the proper cables, but he had in his ruck a brand-new unopened pack of ten recordable DVDs, and he also had three brand-new still-in-the-plastic 64-gigabyte jump drives.

"That Howie, you gotta love him," Nick had said to Dove when he'd come back downstairs with his new-found treasure trove. "The kid came prepared to shoot *Gone With the Wind*."

And Dove had made it clear one more time to Nick. "Do not tell me who you give your copy to."

Crew Chief Jarbodie aches all over, but it's a dull ache, almost soothing. The Motrin has taken away all the sharp persistent pains.

This wasn't part of his plan for the day. To be here in the middle of nowhere Wajma Valley in a school building, with these twenty, twenty-four, twenty-five, is it thirty soldiers max?, surrounded by who-knows-how-many insurgents out there just waiting for whatever they're waiting for to attack.

He remembers them, he remembers seeing them, in their black clothes and those black turbans, flying in here *When they were shooting at us*. Black jammie clothes and black turbans and AK-47s. *They were like beetles under us, scurrying*. Shooting. Beetles with AKs and RPGs.

How many are out there massing now?

Unless they went home.

Over the hills to Pakistan. Good riddance.

Jarbodie wonders that it was what, 1300hrs, that they were supposed to come back in here and pick up the platoon? Ten hours ago. And look at him, here he is now. Who'd a'thunk it? Here they all are now.

He remembers ten hours ago they were sitting on the ramp of his CH-47 and the pick-up time, 1300hrs, went by, and what did he himself say about these soldiers stuck up here? Yeh, it sucks to be them.

Sucks to be me.

Sucks worse to be the others. Mister C . . . . Sorry, Mister C . . . .

He's glad to feel the dull ache. It means he's alive, he's got feelings, he's got all his body parts. Maybe he'll wake in the morning and nothing will hurt, he won't be able to feel his legs, he won't be able to feel his arms, his fingers, and he'll be a quad cuz something's in him and he doesn't know about it now, but his spine's really broken but isn't quite yet but will be by morning.

Like her.

Poor girl.

What's a female captain doing out here?

Do they let females command infantry platoons now? *I don't think so. Maybe in a year or two. Probably in a year or two.*

Jarbodie doesn't remember her on the flight into here this morning, doesn't remember seeing her. But maybe she was on the first bird.

She's kinda cute there sleeping. Her head cocked to the side against her rucksack on the folded poncho liner that he had watched that designated marksman so-called sniper slip under her head without her waking.

She's gotta be exhausted. Drained. Who wouldn't be? Emotionally. Just thinking, am I ever gonna walk again?

Her thigh's covered now there under the sleeping bag, but Jarbodie can visualize what's under there, under where the colonel had very carefully slit with his knife her uniform pantleg at the seam and up it, cutting high and low, making a wide flap, and without waking her.

Jarbodie had heard enough of the whispers when the Hispanic sniper sergeant dude had come over and talked with the platoon sergeant, and the platoon sergeant had agreed, and the two had talked it over with the colonel, and he'd said it was okay by him, but the platoon sergeant said the colonel'd have be the one who'd have to cut her uniform because he was an officer with enough rank over her she couldn't get mad and who-knows-what, but she wasn't going to argue with a lieutenant colonel.

And Jarbodie had watched the colonel carefully pull away the sleeping bag then make his cuts. And carefully lift the flap of the uniform, revealing the sleeping captain's angel white thigh.

Jarbodie had watched the sniper guy take the colonel's place, then with a black Sharpie pen he took his time, a professional at work, an artist, and he drew the tattoo.

Tattoo Zoo.

The same tattoo that Jarbodie had seen on that guy's chest in there wounded. Which the platoon sergeant now explained in whispers to him was this platoon. *The Tattoo Zoo.* And he told him that stateside the Jag captain could visit them at their post or they'd cut orders for Sergeant Rodriquez to go to her wherever she was and he'd ink her permanent in full color. If she wanted it. On any part of her body she wanted it. Thigh or anywhere. Or nowhere. Rodriquez was drawing it on her thigh then because they didn't want to wake her and knew she couldn't feel it and they'd figured it would be a surprise for her.

"The tatt's like a mark of distinction, right?" Jarbodie had asked.

"You might say that," Redcloud answered.

"What'd she do? Your doc says she took a sniper round."

"It's not that easy. You don't get the tatt by just getting hit."

"Something heroic huh?" Jarbodie looked at her and kept his gaze there.

"She wakes, you ask her," Redcloud said.

"Naw. You know, then she's going to think I'm hitting on her."

"My Zoosters won't let you do that," Redcloud said lightly. "She's part of the Zoo now." And he'd left it at that.

In the C-130 in flight, they're over a half-hour late in landing, and Col Pluma had wanted to be with the Rangers by now.

At fifteen minutes late Pluma was angry and went up front to find out what was going on, what was the problem.

Fob Salerno was right below, the flight engineer explained. They were circling, in a holding pattern. Burning excess fuel. Ceiling under a hundred feet down there, fog was like cotton candy down there. On the airfield down there they were putting out water bottles to mark the runway.

Water bottles?

Yeh. 2-liter bottles with IR chemlights in them. Infrared. Pilots would be coming in on NVGs, it was the only way to do it. IR chemlights in full bottles. Concentrated the light and the weight of the bottles kept otherwise naked chemlights from flying off in the prop wash.

Your choice, Colonel. IR chemlights in 2-liter water bottles, or divert to Fob Sharana or Kandahar Airfield. Go back and buckle yourself in, Colonel, we've got control of this.

Now a painful *whine* of hydraulic motors or gears, a sudden deceleration, a change in the *growl* of the engines, deeper, more angry, and a roar of the props reversing thrust, and the entire airframe is shaking, shuddering, and Pluma wonders how many of these doctors and nurses here and those two reporters have any idea that they're going to be landing with runway lights made of 10-cent chemlights in 30-cent water bottles and the pilots looking through Nods and in the next sixty seconds *We could be plowing into some Godforsaken goatherd's poppy field a mile off the end of the runway.*

He has to scream to be heard, and "Hang on tight, Victoria!" he tells Maj Vicky Marshall to try and make her as unsettled as he himself is. "Say your Hail Marys! This could get ugly!"

He has a death grip on the seat-webbing at head-height, and he's got his eyes squeezed to narrow slits, his whole face now in a clenched grimace for the crash that's coming.

Wajma, in the schoolhouse, it's been an hour and forty-five minutes since Wolfe left, and Dove assumes they have to be across the valley near the farthest compounds by now and probably have been for a while, moving quickly behind the experienced Afghan NCO. They'll have to be sneak-n-peeking to find that silent 120 mortar.

What Dove had suggested to Wolfe was to Kiss it.

KISS. Keep It Simple Stupid.

With the proper punctuation:

Keep it simple, stupid.

That the Chechens or Uzbeks or Iranians or whoever was operating those mortars were smart enough to move one before a Jdam could be dropped on the Poo, and they're not even going to think that just dumb GIs of a lone platoon taking fire would even notice the second had been taken off-line and moved away to safety. It will probably be close still, in the very next compound or even out in the open, because they're smart enough to know that we're blind in this weather, that our satellites can't see them.

Kiss it, Dove had suggested. Chechen, Uzbek, Talibs, they're soldiers, which means they're going to be shucking and jiving, eating and smoking and talking. Making noise.

Look for the noise.

Wolfe had said that he'd been thinking along those lines and had been wishing the Pentagon had come up with some NVGs for the ears. Nods for the ears.

Call them NLDs. Night Listening Devices. That you could wear.

And Redcloud had shown Wolfe his own palm. Then held it up cupped behind his ear. An NLD.

Redcloud had his own suggestion. Advantage yours, Wolfie. No one out there is going to think anyone's stupid enough to be out looking for them when they can be safe and secure sitting in here behind these thick walls.

And that is the key, Dove knows. That Mr Wolfe has the element of surprise on his side.

Which he hasn't lost yet. No dim distant gunfire from way out there yet. Yet.

Dove has to wonder if the patrol was worth it. A mortar is invaluable for long ranges on a target not in direct line-of-sight. Like, across the valley hidden behind the high walls of a compound. On the other hand, a recoilless rifle, lightweight shoulder-fired, can be pretty fairly accurately engaged from 600-700 meters, and its shell is going to hit this school building head-on, easier to hit than a 120 mortar round and a mite more lethal than a rocket-propelled grenade. If they've got recoilless rifles, or even just one, and *Keep loading it with fletchette rounds, then holy smokes, it'll be like pumping out 12-gauge No-5 shot at birthday balloons.* Then again, *If they lay in again another thirty-six rounds, forty-eight rounds, of 120 on us, and they already know their general elevation and deflection, they won't need the recoilless.* Then again again, *With the 120 they can smother us with those smoke rounds and effectively cover their own massive assaults and will be right on top of us before we even see them.*

He checks his watch. 23:22.

Nothing from the enemy out there since this afternoon when they shot down the Chinook. Oh sure, they took some potshots with RPGs way out there at the Chinook when the Zoosters were getting the wounded out and gutting the crippled bird. A couple of rockets actually came close enough, exploding near the terrace wall and sending shrapnel into the helicopter, and Dove took same shrapnel in his calf and thigh when he was tourniquetting the lieutenant copilot right there in the cockpit. The fragments were shallow, minor, and Dove dug them out himself when he got back in here, rinsed the gashes with bottled water and wrapped quick bandages around them. No need to bother the busy doc with nothing.

Nothing, right, the same sort of nothing not coming from the enemy out there for a long time.

Dove checks his watch again. 23:23.

It's going to be a long night.

A *kaaruuumppp* comes from far out there at a distance, and both Dove and Redcloud immediately whisper "Recoilless!", and Redcloud orders quietly into his handset to the squad leaders, "No one fires. Lay quiet, remember."

Everyone waits.

The temblor vibration felt as much as heard of the explosion.

Slurpee's voice calls in from the far covered window in a near silent hush, "Left of us. Up high. Hundred, hundred-fifty meters left."

Everybody waits again, says nothing.

That answers the question, at least from Dove's and Redcloud's point of view, whether or not the insurgents have a recoilless rifle. Or two. Or three.

One good thing, in this thick cloud of fog the flash of the explosion would be so diffused that, if the enemy could see it at all from the distance, they couldn't tell where it was. They would know the compass direction to the school building, but they're likely to be off a few degrees in aiming blind, and off a little from a great distance means off a lot at the point of impact—wide of it, left or right. They would know the ground distance by rough estimation, but without a sight-picture of your target, it's hard to get an accurate trajectory of the shell just on a best guess, which means your shells are going to most likely be too long or too short.

If the enemy can't see the explosion or pinpoint it in its flashed diffusion, they can't adjust. Can't make their aiming corrections.

Which is what Dove is thinking and Redcloud is thinking.

And why no one here is to fire. Don't allow the enemy out there in this blind night and fog to use your own muzzle flashes if they can see them to get an exact fix on you. More so, to use the sound of your firing to get a fix on you.

No one here is to fire, period, even if muzzle flashes can't be seen out there. No firing. Don't give the enemy your clatter of weapons to target you. Or the clatter of your mouth.

Shut completely up. Period.

And that means, if a shell hits up here or near out there, you don't scream, you don't shout, you don't make a peep.

That means, if a shell comes in here and tears off your arm, you shut up, you don't shout, you don't call for your mama, you don't yell medic, and if you do, then the others are gonna jump on you and clamp your mouth shut, if they gotta shove the buttstock of their rifles into it.

That's what Redcloud had instructed the squad leaders. And for them to hammer it into their men's heads.

No firing. No yelling. No shouting. No crying. Not a peep.

Unless the trip flares out there close go off.

Or you hear the pebbles rattling 'round in the ammo cans hanging on the wire out there.

In which case Ketchum's men know to throw frag hand grenades. Out beyond the rock wall. Change in plans, no firing the 240s or the Saws. Throw frags. They'd practiced with rocks earlier after it was dark when they'd all settled into place, Redcloud putting a single green chemlight on the wall for the guys to know the distance to throw, to give the guys a visualization of distance to remember. Throwing rocks in practice to get the muscles to remember the distance, so that without the chemlight as a marker, without any sight of the rock wall, if and when they'd have to throw grenades they'd get them out to beyond the wall to the C-wire.

Trip flares go off, or noise in the wire, throw frags.

Finally, Redcloud had told his squad leaders, "You follow my lead. And the colonel's."

Redcloud knows that he's improvising here, it's all a crapshoot. Enemy's probably got some hajjis out there, spotters, *Just on the other side of our C-wire laying there and watching and knowing exactly where we are, they can hear us cough and sneeze in here, could throw a rock through the front door if they wanted,* just waiting to walkie-talkie back when the diffused flash of the recoilless shell explosion is brightest, right in front of them.

Naw, Redcloud thinks different. Taliban couldn't throw a rock or a frag through the front door because Afghans don't know how to throw. American boys grow up throwing footballs, baseballs, you name it. Accurately. Afghans, naw.

Again a distant *kaaruuumppp*.

One thousand one, one thousand two, one thousand three, one thousand four —

The temblor vibration greater than the first, some flash brightness seen in here also this time.

The sound and vibration of rocks hitting the ground out there.

Slurpee's voice softly from the veranda reporting, "Right next to us. High. A couple hundred feet."

A bit of chatter on the little walkie-talkie radios taken from the dead Talibs. Just a sentence or two. Pashto? Chechen? Uzbek? Farsi?

No one to translate. Yep, Nouri's deserted. Wolfe's on the patrol.

It doesn't matter. Redcloud can guess what was said. Fire corrections from one of those 'surg spotters laying out there watching close just on the other side of the razor wire.

Quietly into his radio handset Redcloud says, "Ketch. Move the men away off the walls up there."

"Roger," comes Ketchum's whispered voice back over the handset.

Redcloud thinks he can hear the boots of the guys stomping across the roof above, retreating, but he knows that's impossible through the thick concrete and that it's only his imagination, knowing that they should actually be doing it right now.

Nick Flowers has already set aside the laptop, and he's over here filming. He's got both Redcloud and Dove framed and can easily rack-focus between them, whoever the action's on, which is right now Redcloud. Even in this low light and these deep shadows Nick can get expressions and reactions, and he knows the camera is picking up the sounds of the explosions and the rocks falling out there.

Another distant *kaaruuumppp*.

Everyone waits through the one thousands, instinctively all a little hunched, scrunched, with chins on their chests, eyes squinted shut. Which Nick captures in Redcloud and quickly focuses on Dove for the same.

The temblor vibration and flash now on the other side of this building. Louder and closer.

Utah's voice over the radio this time. A whisper, "Utah here. Over on this side. About a hundred feet up."

There's a muffled cascading of rocks there on that side.

Now Utah finishes, "About twenty feet off."

Again a quick few sentences jabbered in whatever language over the Taliban walkie-talkies.

Redcloud, over the radio and loud enough for everyone in here to hear, "If you're not behind cover, get there." He goes completely to the floor, between a couple of empty ammo crates.

Nick swings his camera around and moves closer to Capt Cathay seated against her ruck and very much awake as Rodriquez crawls to her and holds a spare body armor over her from her chest up and flops down on the other side of her, pretending the shield is as much for himself.

Kaaruuumppp.

Wait.

Wait.

Wait.

The explosion somewhere above.

A thunder of rocks on the roof.

Silence.

Jabber jabber jabber on the little walkie-talkies.

Wait.

Redcloud over the radio, "Utah. Ketch is off the walls up there. Keep your ears peeled for sound in the wire. Your squad with the frags."

"Roger, Sarge. As we speak."

Wait.

Wait.

Kaaruuumppp.

Wait.

Wait.

Wait.

Explosion and flash brightness out there down Utah's way, farther out.

Utah over the radio, "Missed. Short. Down by the stream."

"Roger."

Jabber jabber jabber.

Wait.

They don't know where we are, Redcloud thinks. They're off. Maybe the next one'll be even farther off. *I'm gonna have to get Ketch back on the walls if they start charging.* Going to have to risk the avalanches of rocks.

Kaaruuumppp.

Wait.

Be off. Miss. Miss. Miss. Please Lord I pray to You let it miss.

The explosion not more than a *plop* high up the mountain, then some boulders hitting on the roof on Slurpee's side.

Where that Saw is, *That's Garcia there where his Saw is, rocks woulda hit him.* If they'd all still be on the parapet. *Hope Garcia took the gun with him* back to the back wall.

Jabber jabber jabber.

What Redcloud doesn't know, at this very moment in the stairwell where all Ketchum's guys are huddled just below roofline, Spec Lee Tran pushes by Ketchum at the top who pulls him back, "Where you goin? That you, Tran?"

He'd be blind without his Nods.

Before the first shell was fired, Tran had been asleep, his helmet off, with Bybee alert behind one 240. He was still groggy and not all the way awake when Bybee had grabbed hold of him and told him Sarge says to get back, back in the stairs, and he'd clutched firmly to Bybee racing back to here, pitch black, his Nods still on his helmet, and his helmet-

"My helmet, Sarge, I left my helmet."

"Fuck your Kevlar, Tran. You don't need your Kevlar."

"It's my lucky helmet." Tran breaks free and goes straight ahead, blind, until he hits the parapet wall. Feels around. Not quite at the gun position. *Where?* Feels along the wall. To the 240. Feels around below-

Kaaruuumppp.

Ah-ha, yep, his helmet. Plucks it up, blind.

One thousand.

Plops it on his head.

Two thousand.

He gives the finger to whoever they are out there.

Three thousand.

Flips the Nods to on and turns on his heels.

Four—

Downstairs, Redcloud knows this explosion is right overhead, near the roof, maybe even it hit the wall up there.

It was loud, yeh it hit.

But there are no sounds from up there. No one calling medic, no one screaming. Silence.

Which is good. Means no one was hit.

Wait, hold still, guys, another's coming, just hold still.

Jabber jabber from the walkie-talkies.

Still no noise from above on the roof. Cross your fingers no one was hit. Lucky thing they were off away from the front wall.

Quietly Redcloud radios, "Ketch. Status up there, Ketch?"

"We've took some flak. Nothin serious. Blind up here. Bright as shit. Night-blind, give us a sec."

The NVGs would have auto-adjusted at the close explosive flash, but everyone's night vision would still be half-washed-out, if only from all the peripheral flash.

Ketchum's voice continues over the radio, "Took a shitload in my plate. Feels like I've been smacked by The Hulk."

Redcloud, "You okay?"

"I'll tell ya in the morning," from Ketchum, whose voice sounds still too shaken to remember that a couple of seconds before the shell hit, Bybee had stepped up in front of him onto the roof, saying to him, "Tran prob'bly can't find his Kevlar."

Kaaruuumppp again way out there.

After the last hit on the roof, everyone down here inside has got their heads down low as they can, in tight as they can like turtles, bodies curled tight if they can.

Except for Nick, who's flopped himself down against the wall on the other side of Rodriquez, now framing Rodriquez's face in a close-up.

"You volunteered for this shit, Nicky, comin out here," Rodriquez jokes. "Betcha wished ya stayed back on the Cop."

The explosion is away from the building, somewhere out there.

Slurpee calls in quietly, "Out this way. Short."

They don't know, Redcloud thinks. *They don't know exactly where we are.*

Dove quietly calls over, "PFC Holloway. Get Valley Forge. See what they have for an LCMR reading on the Poo for the recoilless."

Jabbering now comes from the walkie-talkies, and it doesn't end. Extended, it goes on and on, in a staccato that sounds like directives.

Right now Redcloud sure wishes they had Nouri here to translate. Into his radio handset he orders, "Ketch. Get the men back on their guns in position. Utah, Nelly. Eyes sharp. Frags first, men. You know the drill."

And he's already heading for the veranda. Dove right with him, saying, "Let's hope Mr Wolfe neutralizes that mortar."

Redcloud, "I'll settle for his three guns back here right now."

From way out there, a *screech of backfeed* of the mosque loudspeakers turned on.

That's not what Redcloud or anyone expected.

Pashto or Arabic now coming from the loudspeakers in rote singsong.

Nods on, Redcloud goes down a couple of steps, behind the maze-like sandbag walls on them, looking out over them as if to pierce the dark and fog to laser in on the mosque.

"Funny time for prayers," he whispers.

Dove, "There's always time for prayers in Islam."

"The Religion of Peace."

"Let's hope."

"Yeh 'mano," Rodriquez's whispered voice right behind them. "Y'put hope in one hand, shit in th' other."

Redcloud finishes it, "See which fills up first."

"Sergeant Rodriquez," Dove asks. "Check if Holloway's got a confirmation on the Poo."

"Negative, sir," immediately Holloway's voice comes from behind. "Cop says the computer didn't show any Poo launches."

Must be the overcast, Dove thinks. Concussions absorbed in here. Or the computer's registering it as thunder.

Redcloud, "Which makes which hand filling up, Sniper?"

"Shit one, Sarge. You gotta ask?"

The rote praying over the mosque's loudspeakers abruptly ends.

Silence.

Redcloud rests his M4 on the sandbags, flips it from safe to semi, expects to see forms of the enemy suddenly appear, thinks better of it and expects trip flares to go off, to hear the pebbles rattling in the ammo cans.

Instead, a *clang* on the mosque loudspeakers.

A voice in English, saying, "A-ten-shun – in – the – school. A-ten-shun – in – the – school. Sar-gen – Red – Cloud – you – please – listen."

The voice is familiar. Recognized.

"Please – you – listen – also – Ker-nel – Duve."

"That's Nouri," Redcloud says. "Son of a gun." And Nouri continues broadcasting for *"All the Zoo Platoon"* to know that the Soldiers of Allah are powerful, with *"A thousand jihadist warriors"* right now coming down the mountain paths to *"Join with their brothers"* in this valley.

The Soldiers of Allah have powerful weapons, Nouri says. Such as the *"Recoilless rif-fel-les you my friends the Zoo-es-ters have saw tonight explode in the school, no?"* But do not to be afraid, my friends, for the Soldiers of Allah do not want to come to you the hurt. They would make peace with you, for you also are much brave warriors. They say the captain female there with you must have medevac helicopter. They say helicopter is to come. Helicopter is to take captain female to Cash at the Fob Salerno. They say they do not shoot RPG to helicopter.

"Clemente, over here," Redcloud calls softly. "On the double."

"Sarge?" a voice comes from down the veranda Slurpee's way.

"With a pouch of forty-mike-mikes." And into his handset to his squad leaders, "Everyone stand fast. No frags. No shooting. Stand fast, I'm movin out to the wall."

Nouri's calm voice from the loudspeakers tells the Zoosters that the warriors of Allah want peace and friendship with the brave platoon.

Quickly to Dove, before Dove can order him *No*, that *Mosques are off-limits*, Redcloud advises him, without room for that *No*, "Taliban's own Nicky can't film in this pea soup. No video, no one's the wiser."

Nouri's voice says that they want for the Zoo warriors to return to their families and their country, and they will permit that they can return now to Cop Valley Forge.

Redcloud leads Clemente between the gap in the sandbag walls and down the steps, then zagging their way over the holes and mounds of their sandbag-filling, to the rock wall, where they crouch, and Redcloud exchanges his M4 for Clemente's 203 and whispers, motioning for Clemente to set out all the grenades from the pouch on the wall here.

And Nouri's voice out there just soothes with talk that Allah's warriors wish to have a shura with Sar-gen Red Cloud and Ker-nel Duve. That they must come to the mosque. The shura is to be at the mosque. All will be to speak about and plans will be to make about for the Zoo Platoon to leave Wajma tonight and walk to Cop Valley Forge and be no harm to the Zoosters.

Elbows on the rock wall, Redcloud uses the launcher's quadrant sight for max distance, no target to see and aim on, but forcing himself to remember the angle of elevation to repeat it, and he's pretty sure that he's got the right direction to the distant mosque from the angle to it using this rock wall as a reference.

All will be safe, Nouri is saying. The Zoo Platoon will be going home to the Cop.

On the veranda, Dove might have ordered Redcloud *No* simply by rote ROE habit, and he's glad that Redcloud hadn't given him room to. What, come on, what are the chances anyway that anyone can actually hit the mosque with a 203 blind like now? From this distance. And true enough, if *We're blind even with our NVGs, the insurgents, if they're filming, they couldn't be filming. Good luck, Travis Redcloud.*

Pfc Holloway calls out quietly, "Sir, it's Colonel Pluma on the radio," and Dove heads inside to take the call.

And Nouri is saying for Sar-gen Red Cloud and Ker-nel Duve to do not take their guns, to leave their guns in the school and to come to the mosque now.

Plooop, Redcloud fires a grenade. Immediately loads another and just after the first explodes somewhere out there he fires the second. Reloads, and just after the second explodes he fires. The same with the next four grenades.

And Nouri's voice warning, *What are you doing, Pri-vit Finkle?* Do not shoot your tiny grenades, when the Soldiers of Allah have many RPGs and many recoilless rifles. Big artillery shells. Not small grenades.

Redcloud fires again, and it and the next three explode with Nouri's voice calmly saying that shooting your small forty mike mike does not say that you want peace and does not say that you want to return to your families, and Redcloud puts out another.

And another.

Waits.

The first explodes and Nouri's voice screams over the loudspeakers, and the next explodes and is followed by *backfeed*, and the loudspeakers go dead.

Redcloud fires three more, *plooop. . . .plooop. . . .plooop.*

After the dim explosions, silence out there.

Just silence.

Redcloud stands. He's already loaded another grenade.

He's half night-blind from his own muzzle flashes, as his NVGs adjust back to normal, and he senses something and turns his head and sees through his Nods a dark form of a Talib soldier not six feet from him on the other side of the wall, who without Nods hasn't seen Redcloud yet, and Redcloud instinctively fires the launcher before he even has time to reason *How the heck did he get through the trip flares and the concertina wire?*, and the grenade punctures the guy's chest, right through it, right at the heart, throwing him backwards and out of sight in the darkness and fog.

Needing the spin of about 20 feet outside the muzzle to arm itself, a 40mm doesn't explode at such close distance, but at 250 ft/sec velocity it's like a gunshot billiard ball punching through a body and out the other side.

Through the heart, chalk it down as pretty darn quick death.

"Shit, Sarge," Clemente says, having seen it through his Nods. "Lord shit, how'd he get through the wire?"

It's not worth asking yet for Redcloud. He's already reloaded, and his eyes are searching straight ahead and to the sides, as if there might be more coming. But there aren't.

And he's listening, listening for the loudspeakers to come again, but they don't.

Listening for a karuumph of a recoilless firing, and there isn't any.

Now come new sounds from way way way out there and up in the direction of the distant terraced fields and the village compounds. A combination of a loud explosion followed by an AK firing on auto and a couple dim explosions of grenades, and now a distinct second loud explosion and more of the AK on auto and then the sound of an M4 on 3-round burst . . . then it all ending.

Nothing up there through the dark and fog, not a sound. Redcloud has his head turned, his ear turned that way, as if begging to hear something if only to visualize what's going on.

He knows that it's got to be Wolfe and his patrol, that had been an M4 for sure.

No more firing; they're hiding or retreating.

Whatever's happening up there, whatever Wolfe's doing, Redcloud knows that he is powerless to do anything.

Just hope it's good.

Cross your fingers and hope it's going Wolfe's way.

Now a dim crescendo of a few AKs firing.

M4s returning fire, with more AKs, maybe six or seven.

But at least the M4s are still firing.

Nope, no more, just the AKs.

No more M4s.

Fob Salerno, on the tarmac, the ground fog is considerably less than up in the mountains in Wajma, and portable mobile floodlights illuminate the area behind the open C-130.

Col Pluma tells his Rto, Sgt Lachowicz, to hurry it up and get the sat antenna and gear packed back up and get up into the Mrap here that's to take them over to wherever the Ranger compound is.

The two reporters are already up inside the Mrap.

Pluma is late and wants to get over with the Rangers and work out all the details with Captain Haas about the assault into the valley. Then from there he can get back on the horn to Zachary, as he just informed him he would, and nail the specifics from Zachary's end to get the Rangers into the valley.

Antsy, Pluma watches Lachowicz throw his ruck up into the back of the Mrap then climb up inside, and, before following, Pluma takes one look around to see two military passenger vans pulling up to the C-130's lowered tailramp where the flight crew and all the medical personnel wait and will get in the vans for a ride over to the Dfac serving midnight chow.

All is Pluma's doing. Part of his quick outline to his Isaf staff in arranging all this, and they've made it happen. The Air Evac crew, flight and medical, will eat and can freshen up, then be brought back to the plane, where they'll remain in place on standby for when the lead infil Chinook returns from Wajma as a medevac. That chopper is to land here, where triage will be established by the Air Evac docs and the Cash personnel, and the most seriously wounded who can be better treated at the far more extensive facilities at the Bagram Airfield hospital will be loaded straight aboard the C-130.

Pluma's goal, known by the Cash here and the entire Air Evac crew: No more than 30 minutes on the ground here from that Chinook medevac arrival to C-130 ramp up.

Pluma's directive was clear: *It will have been as much as twelve hours since some of these men have been injured and I don't want another minute wasted until they're in a trauma center.*

In Pluma's last glance he hopes to see among the Air Evac personnel Vicky Marshall looking at him, at least for no other reason than because he's important, it has been his orders that have made all this possible. His planning. His orders. His mission.

She's not. She is in fact laughing with a couple of the doctors, male doctors, who Pluma remembers were both lieutenant colonels.

Up inside the Mrap now, Pluma sits beside Lachowicz, across from the two reporters, leaving the hatch door open because neither he nor Lachowicz knows how to close it, and it's the Reuters reporter who gets up out of his seat and slaps the auto-open/close button.

Pluma makes note of the button. Hopes the Reuters reporter and the Getty photographer watching will think that he didn't close the door because he's a full-bird colonel, and full-birds leave that little nit-noid stuff to others beneath them, not because he didn't know the button.

Next time, Pluma figures, he'll push the button, and that'll give others he's riding with in one of these steel monsters the impression that he's familiar with this ground combat equipment, that he's just another soldier at heart, and if they're enlisted in here with him, he's one of them, and if they're General St Claire or other generals, he, again, is ground-battle wise.

Not the very next time, but now, when they get to the Ranger compound. Nope, he'll let Reuters or the Getty guy do the opening, or this sergeant Rto. Because he's got to keep the act going that he didn't do it this time because it's beneath him. Not because he didn't know.

Minor, what's he nagging himself with all this minor shit for?

What's really bugging him, though, and underlying this impatient foul mood, is that tight cunt Major Victoria Marshall, who thinks she's got all the gold in Fort Knox between her legs.

Laughing with those doctors. Contrasted with the smirk he detected behind her faux smile after that three-bounce landing and finally coming to a stop and him saying to her with his own laugh, "Like the Whirly-Twirl at the county fair," and her with that faux smile, saying, "And the date who's brought you is all pale and pukes all over himself, and there goes his chances for even a good-night kiss."

And Pluma knew that she was talking about him. That she was laughing at him, that she'd noted how pale he'd been, that he'd been scared and she hadn't. Not that he'd puked, but he'd sure felt like it. And she must have known. Oh she knew it. She did, because then she'd said, with her own laugh this time, "Then what really gets the guy, you tell him right when the ride ends, you say 'Oooh oooh let's do it again!'"

Bitch!

And he'd thought he'd gotten a semblance of his superiority back when, as the ramp was going down, he called across to his Rto, "Sergeant, get set up out there. We've got comms to make." And added to her, "Would you like it, Victoria, should I tell Zachary you say hi?"

He remembers her words exactly, including her lilt of playfulness, as if she were jabbing a dagger into his chest. "Tell him that when Major V Marshall sees him next time I'll be wearing nothing but a smile."

Royal grade-A stamped certified bitch!

Hurry up, let's get over to the Rangers. That's what Col Pluma wants right now. Get with the Rangers, dictate the final op order, get on the three CH-47s his staff's ordered ready here, get into that valley, and when he's brought Zachary Dove back to Bagram, she'll see that it was he who did it, it was Dan Pluma who pulled loverboy Zachary Dove's frightened ass out of there and got that whole stinking platoon out just in the nick of time. If Zachary Dove and all of them are going to be heroes back at Bagram, then what's that going to make the man who orchestrated their rescue?

A rescue that is inherently a suicide mission.

Orchestrated by Colonel Daniel Pluma.

Orchestrated . . . .

and Led.

By Colonel Daniel Pluma.

Soon to be General.

That'll show that bitch.

Wajma, on the school roof. The distant gunfire of the patrol's firefight ended a few minutes ago, except for an occasional AK shot, distinct even from this distance from the sound of an M4.

Dove has not heard from Wolfe over the platoon radio and will not insult him by initiating a call. When Mr Wolfe wants to call, when he has to call, he will, he'll call. That's the way he laid it out before leaving, and Dove respects that. What can Dove do anyway? What can Sergeant Redcloud do? Can't send out a patrol to rescue them if they're in deep trouble. If Wolfe can't radio because he can't because he's dead, there's nothing Dove or anyone can do.

If Wolfe found the mortar tube and got a grid and he's running for their lives right now, he'll put a little distance between themselves and the enemy and between himself and the mortar site and then call in the grid, and Dove will request directly to Isaf for Cas and for a Jdam strike.

If.

When.

Dove is standing at the parapet and came up here not for the purpose of getting a higher and clearer perspective of what had been the sounds of Wolfe's firefight. He came up for something else. Worse.

He had just gotten off satcom with Col Pluma, Redcloud had finished his grenade fire on the mosque, Wolfe's Tic began, and Staff Sergeant Ketchum radioed down calmly to Redcloud that it was a *"Shitload worse"* than he'd thought. Two Kilo India Alphas. Dove had cut in before Redcloud could answer, saying he'd take it, he would handle it, and he directed Chinook crew chief Jarbodie to grab up two body bags, please, from in there, in the morgue room.

At the parapet Dove knows what's going on behind him. He hears them zipping-up the second body bag, and he turns away from the parapet, finds Ssgt Ketchum's dark shape in his Nods' view and tells him, "Here, allow me," to lift that end of the bag to carry it with Ketchum downstairs. "This one is?" he asks.

Ketchum, "Specialist Tran, sir."

Specialist Lee Tran, Dove knows is the full name, because he's already taken down the stats from Ketchum in his notebook when he first came up. Specialist Lee Tran and Private Aaron Bybee.

Jarbodie is going to stay behind, stay up here on the roof. He's manning the 240 taken from his chopper. Ketchum had said that Tran and Bybee were on the machineguns, and Jarbodie had said he'd take one, no problem, he wanted something meaningful to do. Put himself to use. The 240's second-nature to him, he knows the weapon in his sleep. Can break it down to the tiniest pin in the trigger housing . . . . drunk.

Ketchum put Van Louse on the platoon's 240. Told him and Jarbodie they could switch out, act gunner and assistant for each other on their guns, 'specially if it got to be they was both burnin through their barrels. He himself, he'd act assistant for both of em when he could. Hope to hell it don't come to that.

What Ketchum had told Dove, he feels responsible because he shoulda held Tran back from coming out looking for his Kevlar with the recoilless shelling going on like it was. Bybee was the same way, Ketch shoulda kept him back at the stairs. But shoot, what Ketchum figures, Tran probably saved the whole squad and didn't even know it.

When Redcloud had ordered Ketch to get his guys back on the parapet wall, you couldn't see shit, even through Nods, like now you still can't hardly, and Ketchum had gone right by Bybee's body and didn't even see it and then tripped over Tran's.

The guys behind him found Bybee's. Van Louse thought he was just laying on his belly, face down on the roof, *Y'know, for the incoming*, and he wouldn't answer him, so then he went to turn over his head and the *Whole thing came right apart from like the nose on up*. Two parts. *You seen it, Colonel.* Big chunk of flak, a chunk of the shell musta cut right through it. Right at the rim of the helmet, just sliced right into the skull and straight through, like halving a honeydew melon with a machete. Probably didn't even know what hit him.

Same with Tran. His body was way over here, that means it was throwed. Guys are finding bits and pieces of the head. His jaw with all his lower teeth, and there's an ear. *You seen his Kevlar, Colonel, all's left is the rim, part of it, and his chinstrap. Figured, Colonel, if it hadn't a'hit him straight square in the Kevlar*, it was comin straight back there, woulda hit like right there on the mountain wall *Where we were down low on them stairs. Woulda wiped us all out.*

Tran *Saved my lily-white ass, saved all our asses up here* and he don't even know it.

And Bybee, poor kid, Bybee was jus goin out to help him look for his Kevlar. *Lucky helmet, Tran said.* Lucky helmet.

Yeh, lucky for us, I reckon.

Down in the morgue classroom Van Louse and Doc Eberly carry in Bybee in his body bag, and Redcloud takes one corner handle and guides it over to lay at the end of the row, tight to the one beside it, all on line straight and even.

"It's Bybee," Van Louse tells Redcloud.

No response from Redcloud, who looks Eberly in the eye now, and Eberly just shakes his head a little, like to say, *It was just nothing anyone could do.*

Eberly knows he shouldn't think it, but he does regardless, that he had been relieved when he first ran upstairs and went to where Van Louse was calling him to Bybee's prone body and close up he saw Bybee's head half sliced off, sort of surreal in the Nods' green glow, but immediately clear a hundred percent certain that he wouldn't have to do anything, not even seek to find a pulse, he wouldn't be dumb enough to try mouth-to-mouth or CPR, and he wouldn't have to try to tourniquet and bandage all Bybee's four limbs that he'd quickly assessed as mostly shredded, if they were even still attached.

He felt the same kind of cynical relief with Tran's crumpled body. Head gone, there wouldn't have to be any futile waste of effort and hope. There was nothing left of Tran's shoulders or upper chest, but the rest of him was like brand-new. *Guess there won't be an open coffin,* he thinks as Dove and Ketchum now carry in Tran's body bag. *Like his mom and dad didn't see enough bad stuff in Vietnam when they were little kids.* He wonders if they'll insist on seeing the body, *If in their culture they have to see the dead body for proof.*

Ketchum just shakes his head to Redcloud like he wishes it wasn't so and it's his responsibility.

"He went out up there, Sarge, cuz he'd left his dang stupid lucky Kevlar there at his gun," he says.

To Redcloud the past is past, deal with the present and the future. "Who you got on the guns?" he asks.

"Chopper dude, crew chief, he's on his. Said he'd take it. And Van Louse."

Earlier Redcloud had given Jarbodie an M4 and Sandusky's Nods, and he's glad now that Jarbodie has got himself a job and place here. It'll make him feel like he's doing something. Take his own mind off his chopper buddies who've got it worse.

"Awright. Make sure he knows the scheme. Frags, and no shooting unless you hear different from me or the colonel. Get back up there, make sure your men don't let this all with Tran and Bybee mess with their mind, rattle em scared."

"Hooah, Sarge. What do you think 'bout Wolfie and Finkle? Sounded like they got themselves a shitstorm out there. Think they're gonna make it back?"

Who knows?

Time will tell.

Tomorrow is another day.

Cross that bridge when we come to it.

And Redcloud remembers the little 45 record his grandfather used to play all the time on his turntable when he was a kid and lived with him, and it's Chuck Berry singing, *Say la vee say the old folks, it goes to show you never can tell.*

He knows it's not say la vee, it's some French words which he can't spell, but he knows it means *such is life*.

Say la vee.

Yeh, if those Frenchies were here right now, what would they say, how do you say *such is death*?

Lieut Col Dove checks his watch. 23:51.

Not even thirty minutes since it all began. Since the recoilless barrage began. Seems longer ago.

He sits atop one of the deads' rucksacks in here and motions that Redcloud should too. Time to talk briefly in private.

Dove clicks on his SureFire and shines it on the last two body bags.

The bright spot of Redcloud's headlamp follows.

Dove, "I remember them on the gun up there this afternoon. Neither of them looked to be more than sixteen."

"Tran just got married not a couple months before we came over. High school sweetheart. Small town somewhere in Minnesota. Funny, isn't it like the goverment, his parents were boat people, he said they were teenagers when they came over. The goverment takes people, it's never colder than 85 degrees in Vietnam, and they take and set them down in Minnesota. 'Here, have some mittens and a snow shovel, on us.' I can hear the social worker. 'Here's a hundred pounds of salt. It's not for your food, it's for the sidewalks.'"

"First generation. Patriotic. There's a sense of obligation in first generation. To fight for their new country."

"No hooah speeches, sir. Tran just liked bein a soldier, said he always wanted to be a soldier, since he was a little kid. Had a GI Joe, played with little toy soldiers, said he had a whole army. Was good too. I was looking forward to him getting sergeant, give him a fire-team."

"Aaron?" Dove asks.

"Bybee?" Redcloud thinks a moment. "He came to the company after we got here. Just out of Basic. He was with the Third. He's only been in the Zoo a couple of weeks, three. You know how sometimes two people just don't get along? And there really isn't a reason for it? Teddy, that's Northwich, Third's platoon sergeant. Just didn't like Bybee, from day one. Riding him, riding him, always riding him, sayin Bybee couldn't do nuthin right. Even if he did it exactly right. You know how that can be. Had all the other guys in the Third ridin him too. Captain Washington, he asked me. Said Teddy said Bybee was a piece of you-know-what, wouldn't never make a soldier, wasn't worth feeding, wasn't worth beddin-down. Would I take him? That's the C-O. Would I try and make a soldier outta him? And if not, then they could put him on permanent ash-and-trash detail there on the Cop."

"Jashawn knows people," Dove says softly. "He does. He did."

Moves his light onto the first body bag, nearest the doorway. Washington's.

Redcloud says nothing for a bit. Then, "Bybee was doing alright. Was gonna be alright. All he wanted . . . . You know, all he wanted, Colonel . . . All he wanted was his Zoo tatt. Wanted to earn his tatt. And not just so Teddy and the guys in the Third who rode him would see. To be part of us. One of the Zoo."

Dove lets that sit. Doesn't say anything. He'd heard a break in those last words of Redcloud. Emotion, breaking, perhaps choking up. And Dove knows that Redcloud doesn't break, doesn't choke up, won't, and won't allow himself to.

It's best to leave it. Best to get to the topic you indicated Redcloud to stay in here to talk in private.

Before, after the first call from Col Pluma, Dove had told Redcloud about how Isaf had now changed course and intended to hail the Zoo Platoon as heroes. If they survived this.

No longer war criminals. Heroes.

Time now to discuss this most recent call.

Dove explains that Col Pluma is at Fob Salerno, is on his way over to the Rangers there. An Air Evac C-130 is already staged there at Salerno for the wounded. The tentative plan is to air assault the Rangers into here as reinforcements. A full complement. Full company.

"How air assault?" Redcloud asks.

"He said Chinooks. Conventional."

"When?"

"He didn't say."

"They got an idea when Air's turning Green?"

"He didn't say. He's calling again when they finalize the op order. With the Rangers, the flight crews, all together. Also, they have two conventional platoons from a line company stationed there on Salerno on standby as secondary Reaction Force. Air assault, conventional air frames. As backup to the Rangers. If need be."

"Who's the Ranger C-O? Do you know him?"

"Captain Mike Haas. Senior captain. Moved over from the 173rd. He had a Ranger platoon in a sister company down south in Helmand when I had my company here. So far his men have been executing some very effective ops. Mostly night snatches. He inserted the entire company on a two-week border sweep. I've seen the AARs. He's doing some good stuff."

"So he's not looking for a Silver Star, Medal of Honor?"

A shrug from Dove, *Who knows?*

"First sergeant?"

"John Hockaley. You remember him, you should, don't you? I think the only time he's left Regiment was recruiting duty."

"You know the platoon leaders, platoon sergeants?"

No, not really. They're Rangers, it shouldn't make much difference.

"I guess . . . ." noncommittal from Redcloud. "I guess we wait for your Colonel Pluma's next call."

"Suggestions?"

"That's above my pay grade, sir. I'll let you colonels hash it out. I will tell you this. General St Claire, him wanting this hero stuff . . . " He shakes his head.

Dove says nothing.

Redcloud stands up from the ruck. Says, "I don't want to be a hero, sir."

"General Pete St Claire won't give you a choice."

"It's all too college-smart for me, with all due respect, sir. A baby-killer one day, a hero the next?" Redcloud can't accept either. "There a third option?"

"Dead?"

"And a hero don't matter then when you're dead. Not to my wife. Maybe my kids, it'll comfort them. Make em proud." Redcloud's head-lamp sweeps over the neat row of black body bags across the wall. He shuts it off. "Let's get out of here, this room gives me the creeps."

Me too, Dove thinks. *It should*, and he stands to follow him out.

In the front room, both Dove and Redcloud are lying back against their rucks, and Dove makes note of the time, 00:14, as there's a surprise break in squelch over all their platoon Mbitr radios, followed by Wolfe's voice:

"Zoo Base, Zoo Base, this is Zoo Recon, Zoo Recon, over."

Dove answers, "Zoo Recon, this is Zoo Base, this is Dove, over."

"Gettin close, not sure exactly how far. Don't want your killer marskmen shooting us. Breaking an IR chemlight. I say again, I'm carrying an IR chemlight. How read me?, over."

"Lima Charlie, Recon. We're looking for an IR chemlight."

"Don't shoot the fucking chemlight."

"Roger, Zoo Recon, we won't shoot the chemlight."

"Or the fucking former jarhead carrying it."

Dove laughs. "Roger, Recon."

One more thing from Wolfe:

"Heads-up to Doc Eberly. Naptime's over."

"Roger."

Redcloud calls out, "Doc Eberly?"

Unseen, from the aid classroom, Eberly, "Heard it."

And Redcloud motions Dove that he'll take the veranda and Dove the roof, and Dove grabs his helmet, is on his feet, and he clicks on his Nods as he sprints up the stairs.

Day Two, After Midnight

Wajma, in the Schoolhouse

This is exactly why Pfc Holloway used his brains to figure out getting the 25-foot antenna cables to be able to set the sat radios inside so he can be inside too.

Inside where the action is. Not action action, but in-the-know.

He's right in the center of where everything goes on.

That is, he gets to hear about everything that goes on.

He's like the Secret Service agent standing next to the president, he gets to hear everything first.

Yeh, he could be a Secret Service agent someday. After the Army. Maybe he should do a couple years a MP first, that's the career they sorta want, that would sorta grease the skids for him. A couple years in the MPs then get out and join the San Bernardino Sheriffs, be a deputy cuz that shows you've really got law enforcement, which they wanna see on your application for the Secret Service. His cousin is a San Berdoo County deputy sheriff, he made it. He's in the jail still, still working county jail, but everybody's gotta do that the first couple years. Of course, his name is Lopez, and that didn't hurt him gettin on, since Holloway's aunt married Tuco Lopez and changed all their names, so his cousin's really only Latino by name—a red-haired Latino, like if that isn't wacked. But the name's really all that matters, and you almost hafta be Latino to get on the force, so maybe Holloway should change his name to something like Hollowaypez. Geraldo Hollowaypez. Get some gang tatts for the backs of his hands, for his arms, a coupla teardrops comin down off his eyes. Be one of the chicos on the block. Be The Head Cholo walkin the block in Colton. He could like bebop into the Sheriff Department tomorrow, they'll say *Welcome aboard, Deputy Geraldo Hollowaypez* and give him his badge and a gun and the keys to a cruiser, and he'll have Lake Arrowhead his area of patrol, and *Sheeee-at, those college honeys on summer break up there in the mountains all tan and shiny with Hawaiian Tropic in shoestring thongs with their string bikinis and cups so small their tits are flopping all out of them.* Oh yeah, the Holloway Groove. Nope. Hollowaypez Groovo. *Sí 'mano, the Hollowaypez Groovo, and don't you never forget it.*

Here they come now, down the stairs from the roof, coming back down. Colonel and Sarge and Wolfie.

They're going to come over to here, Holloway hopes, and sit back down. Cuz that's where Lieutenant Colonel Dove moved his ruck before and was sitting, being close to the radios. And Sergeant Redcloud and Wolfe too sat here, after when Wolfe got back, and Holloway was right there in the center of it for Wolfe explaining the whole recon patrol. Until Holloway got the call from Isaf, *"Bombs away"*, and got to tell the colonel and them "Isaf says bombs away", and they all three ran up to the roof. When they could have seen all they were going to see just as good from down here on the porch. Like Holloway had. Just stepping out, flipping down his Nods and whispering to all the guys out there who he couldn't see but knew were there, "Bombs away."

When you're in-the-know like Holloway you get to be the one to share the word.

And he knew all the guys out there would then be looking out into the dark and fog, all with their Nods down, waiting.

Then there was a flash of light, like heat lightning dispersed in the clouds on the horizon, and a couple of seconds later a sharp *carrrumpth!*

Five seconds later there was another flash — a double flash actually, with another just a second after — and all two of them together even brighter then the first, then the *carrumpth!* and an even louder *babbbooompt!* and Holloway thought the whole building shook at that and would swear he felt the skin on his face tingle and singe in what he thought was a concussion wind from those last two blasts.

When the blast and sound passed and it was quiet, "That's gotta be the truckload of one-twenty mortar shells Wolfie and Finkle found," he whispered, proud to be the one sharing the knowledge with everyone he couldn't see out there.

It was Holloway who'd got to call up to Isaf the grid coordinates of the location for those two Jdam hits. It was Holloway who'd got to tell the staff officer there that it was Lieutenant Colonel Dove requesting two Jdams on enemy insurgent active indirect-fire weapons and a ammunition depot.

Holloway knew he wasn't telling the whole truth when he said the target was active indirect-fire weapons, and that it wasn't really a depot depot. But Dove had told him to say that. And it was only a white lie. A recoilless isn't really an indirect-fire weapon, but it is crew-served. And Wolfe had said that wagon of mortar shells were like a depot.

In fact, Wolfe had reported that they found that the indirect-fire mortars had been damaged in the afternoon's Jdams. Made inoperable. Both of the tubes. Worse than just inoperable, for the enemy—the only whole pieces of either of the tubes were their baseplates.

Those bombs this afternoon had taken out both the mortars, and probably the crews as well, though their bodies had most likely already been carried off, because Wolfe's patrol hadn't found any body parts, but the compound itself was pretty much still standing whole.

If anyone survived, they didn't stick around. Except for one old guy. And he was still kind of delirious from the bomb. A villager. Old farmer. It was his compound, and "I say old," Wolfe had explained, "because you know how it is. Thirty-five, forty is old here. Looks ancient here."

The Afghan sarge was able to get information out of him. The sarge, according to Wolfe, was invaluable. He was walking around in that compound, without NVGs no less, *Like he was a bat in his own bedroom*, and he's the one who found the old man, back in a room, back in a corner, prob'ly smelled him out. And got him to reveal that the Talibs had stored mortar rounds in the next compound over.

"Did you let him live, the old man?" Holloway had asked before he could think that it wasn't his place to talk.

"Now what would you have done, wise Grasshopper?" Wolfe had said and didn't wait for an answer because he didn't want one, not from Holloway.

Holloway knew then that he'd better shut up and stay shut up. That they could just as easy take their conversation somewheres else, and then whatever he learned he'd have to get from someone else.

Holloway likes to be, if nothing else, the first to know.

After Wolfe had called up on the platoon radio on the way back, Holloway had stepped out onto the veranda to watch, and in a couple of minutes he could see through Nods the IR glow of the chemlight. No one shot at it, but Slurpee had called out to the glow, "Sppppt, that you Wolfe?"

"It aint Santy Claus," came Wolfe's voice. "It's General St Claire, come to see if you boys need another gun."

Redcloud and Utah met Wolfe out front of the steps and each took a corner of the poncho that Wolfe and Finkle were carrying the Afghan sergeant on, both breathing really hard and really smoked.

They'd carried him at least three miles, zigzagging across the rough terrain of mud and ditches and walls and rocks. Tripping, falling. Wild AK fire reaching out for them at random looking for a lucky hit.

The way the story came out, as Wolfe would soon after be telling Dove and Redcloud—with Holloway right there listening—when the sergeant was hit and went down, Wolfe told Finkle to grab up the sarge's AK then grab him under the one shoulder, as Wolfe was his other, and they dragged the sergeant, Wolfe no longer firing, not wanting to give away their position in the dark and fog.

At a hundred, hundred-fifty meters they tripped into an irrigation ditch, and that's where Wolfe worked on the sergeant.

He told Finkle to make a litter. To get the poncho and 550-cord out of his ruck and tie up the poncho ends, one to the AK, one to Finkle's own 203. They'd be the carrying handles, the AK and 203. And he treated the sergeant, starting on the worst bleeder, a through-n-through in his thigh. Quick gauze stuffing then a tourniquet, that's all for now. The other calf torn open with another through-n-through, a tight bandage did it there. Gunshot in the left lower gut, the docs will have to deal with that. The sucking chest wound over the right lung, a plastic bandage to keep it airtight for the time being.

All the while, the sergeant wheezing in the pain and managing to get out in Pashto for Wolfe to leave him. Wolfe could understand that, *To go, to leave him.* And Wolfe kept telling him back, in Pashto, *No way, my friend, no way.* And in English he said a couple of times, "Americans don't leave their buddy behind," and tried to form it in Pashto and probably wound up with something close enough. "We're not leaving you, my friend, don't even think it," Wolfe said in English, and if nothing else he knew the Afghan sergeant, like all ANA, knows the English *friend. Dost.*

On the roof, Dove, Redcloud and Wolfe have just left for downstairs, as the Jdams hit, so that excitement's all over. And Pvt Finkle and Van Louse were close enough to hear Wolfe saying after that biggest explosion, "That's gotta be the ammo." And Redcloud said, "We won't know if they got the recoilless, until they fire it again. Or don't fire it again."

"We took out the recoilless," Finkle said. "Wolfie hit it square-on with the Laws, Sar'ant Redcloud, I could see it. And my grenades, I know I hit it too."

And, "I'm glad you could see it, I sure couldn't," Wolfe said. Finkle was seeing it, Wolfe teased, with his wanna-be's. His hope-to-be's. "I'm placing my bets on that satellite-guided thousand-pounder."

Then they left, and now Finkle is finishing his story, whispering to Spec Van Louse, with Ketchum invisible in the dark but close enough to hear. Telling of that run back to here being the hardest thing he's ever frickin done in his whole entire life. *That Afghani sarge is heavy, I didn't know he was gonna be so heavy!* And Finkle still can't hardly feel his fingers from gripping the weapon carrying him on that poncho litter he made. He musta thought he couldn't go no farther a hundred times, and he'd fall and wouldn't wanna get up, and that Wolfie, *That dude's tough. Tougher'n woodpecker lips.* He'd say, that Wolfe was always cussin, *Goddamit Finkle, goddamit keep up your end!*

And Finkle tells Van Louse that he doesn't know how many times he was sayin *I can't, I can't, I can't go no more,* and Wolfe would say, he kept sayin *Can't aint in the dictionary. A Marine don't know the word can't,* he said. Musta said it a hundred times.

Finkle tells Van Louse that he doesn't know how Wolfe did it, cuz he was like carrying his end with just one hand, and Finkle could just see him in his Nods switching hands, cuz Wolfe had to be navigating, with his compass and his GPS, and Finkle just can't believe how he did it. Himself, he was all twisted around, didn't know if they was comin or goin, coulda sweared they was headin straight for the mosque or even them truck conexes, thinkin any second they was gonna run right into a whole bunch of insurg.

"I aint never gonna forget it," Finkle whispers to Van Louse. "I aint never gonna forget him sayin 'Can't aint in the dictionary'. Y'know?. . ."

"I couldn't of done it, no way. I'd of left the hajj wounded," whispers Van Louse. "But you're Spidey, Finkle. You're superhuman."

"No way. I woulda left him, I woulda. Swear t'you, I woulda."

Ssgt Ketchum's voice comes softly from the dark. "No you wouldn't, you wouldn't of left him."

Finkle, "Who's that?"

"Yer squad leader, knucklehead. And you wouldn't of left him."

"Yeh, Sarge, I sure wanted to."

"But you didn't."

"That's cuz of Wolfe, he made me. He made me, Sarge."

"Yeh, he made you this time, and next time yer gonna make someone else."

"I don't know, Sarge. I sure didn't think I was gonna make it."

"You made it, didn't you? You know why? Know why?"

"Why, Sarge?"

"Cuz none of us is alone, Finkle. That's why we got each other."

Van Louse has already told Finkle about what happened to Tran and Bybee and how it was lucky for them-all that Tran came back out for his lucky helmet 'cause otherwise the shell woulda probably got them all. As it was, Van Louse has a bunch of rips in his uniform, his *Arm and shoulder that was facing that way,* and cuts, but they aint bad, and he *Aint goin down to doc 'bout them just to be laughed at.* Van Louse told Finkle that he didn't know if it was flak from the shell or chips and bits of rock or cement, and it felt like when your runnin buddies all at the same time flick a spoonful of peas at you in the cafeteria at lunch. *But you oughta see Sarge,* Van Louse said. *He took all kinds a'shit in his I-B-A,* body armor. *Big hunk of it about this big,* the size of a pie tin, *got stuck right here,* right over the heart. Ketchum already traded in his IBA plate, Van Louse told Finkle, *For one of them others down there,* in the morgue room. Y'know, *Cuz they aint gonna be needin em.* The important thing,

Van Louse said, was that if it wasn't for Tran and his freakin lucky helmet that shell was gonna hit right above where they was all huddlin there in the stairs, and it *Woulda been lights-out, angels playing harps up in heaven,* that's a fact, Jack. Tran and his freakin lucky helmet, who'd a'knowed.

Finkle is a lot more calmed down now than he was when he first got back and got up here. He was super hyped-up then, and he knows it. Just from the first, the patrol going out there, following that Afghan sergeant and in so much dark and not knowing where the shit he was goin, and then finding he'd climbed on top of a whole ammo dump of mortar shells and 106 recoilless shells too, then attacking that M40 recoilless he couldn't even see at first but's sure he hit it with the three grenades he shot just like Kyle Wolfe had said to, then retreating and having all those shots coming at him, and the sergeant gettin hit, and when he's draggin him with Wolfie there's all those bullets still cracking right by him he just knew he was next thing gonna be chopped up, a hundred bullets tearing him apart in a bloody spray of splatter like the alien monsters in those movies. Then, he'd never made a poncho litter before, and not out of rifles and 550-cord, and he knew he had to make it strong cuz the sergeant is taller than him and taller even than Wolfe and has gotta weigh a ton, and he had to make it whilst in water up to his knees in that irrigation ditch. Then, a'course, the run back, carrying that Afghani, and thinking all the time his lungs were gonna burst and his fingers were gonna catch fire and burn off, if his arms weren't gonna first.

Yeh, when Finkle got back he was hyped-up. He could have flown to Mars and back at the speed of light. He really couldn't concentrate then on what Van Louse was telling him about Tran and Bybee and that recoilless bombardment, cuz he really wanted to tell Van Louse and everyone all about what he'd done. What they'd done out there. Him and Wolfie and the sergeant.

He has now, to Van Louse, in whispers. And he's a lot calmer. The hype is gone, mostly.

Now he can wrap his mind around Tran and Bybee. Tran was cool, didn't never boss you around. Bybee, in the little time he's been in the Zoo, he was alright, he was a nice guy, wasn't no show-off, wasn't no big-shot know-it-all bullshitter always had to pop in poppin off with his own story to one-up yers, talkin over you, not listenin. Bybee wasn't like that. Quiet, really, more'n anything just quiet.

"Y'know," Finkle whispers to Van Louse a little sadly. "Bybee aint gonna get his tatt now."

"Not a real one," Van Louse says, and they both know that Sergeant Rodriquez will draw up the tatt on some thick artist paper and they'll all sign it, and the L-T will write a note and the C-O will too, and they'll put it all in a big manila envelope and mail it to the family.

Naw, Van Louse thinks, *There is no L-T*, Lieutenant Caufield is no more. *There is no C-O*. Captain Washington is no more. Sergeant Redcloud will have to write the note. Maybe get the lite colonel to write one too.

Van Louse knows one thing. That he doesn't want to go down to that morgue room anymore. He doesn't want to carry no one down there and he doesn't even want to be in there. Not even now, still, that it's better, he knows, they're all in them body bags. That way you don't have to know which one's which. It's somehow easier that way. They're just bodies. Maybe not even your runnin buddies, your platoon mates, your fellow Zoosters.

Van Louse knows that he's always going to keep his Kevlar on, that's for sure. Chinstrap tight too. Knows that Finkle must be thinking the same thing, as he watches Finkle through his Nods now blindly remove the headstrap from his own Nods and snap them back onto his helmet. Yeh, Finkle's gonna wear his Kevlar too.

What Van Louse would like to think about, it's the recon patrol with Finkle, as if he was there with Finkle. To visualize it the way Finkle told it. With him there too. Cuz Finkle, dude, he did some awesome shit out there tonight.

The same way that downstairs Pfc Holloway was picturing it when Wolfe was telling it. Before they all went up to the roof after the radio call of *Bombs away*.

The three have just come down and Wolfe went into the aid station, probably to see how the docs were doing with the ANA sergeant, maybe to tell the Afghan guy that those explosions were blowing up the mortar rounds and the recoilless rifle they'd found with the bombs dropped from a F-16 or maybe a F-18. If the sergeant is even conscious still now, since Doc musta pumped him full of morphine. *Hooah, morphine, gimme some morphine!*, Holloway thinks.

Dove and Sergeant Redcloud have sat back down where they were, but they aren't saying nuthin. Except, the colonel just asked Holloway if Colonel Pluma'd called again yet. Nope.

It's the same as before, except Wolfe's in the aid station. Sniper Rodriquez back sitting where he was before, and Captain Cathay still the same, always right over there. What's she gonna do, where's she gonna go?, it's not like she can move anywhere. Both listening before to Wolfe and not saying nuthin.

And Nick's now back getting back on that computer, whatever he's doing. He was filming then when Wolfe was telling what happened. Mostly filming on Wolfe, but also swinging the camera to get the faces of Dove and Redcloud in close-up listening.

Holloway had wished that Nick would get a close-up of him, and he was holding the radio handsets up near his ears to look important, but he knew the recon story wasn't about him at all. Nick had already been in Doc's aid station in there to film Doc and the other doc, that SF dude who's got one knarly set of balls jumping outta that chopper so high up off the ground, when they had to a'been working on the ANA sergeant, and Holloway knew that the patrol, no matter all his Holloway Grooveness, wasn't his at all, but was about Wolfe and Finkle and that wounded Afghan sergeant, the way Wolfe explained it to the colonel and Sergeant Redcloud how it all went down.

It was about how the hell the Afghan sergeant knew where the next compound over was without even thinking, maybe just following some path in the mud that a Afghan just grows up knowing, knowing without being conscious of knowing, it's learned instinct, a dog goin home.

The big steel gates of the next compound over were open. The Talibs had a campfire going inside there. For light, cooking, talking around. Wolfe counted eight. In sight around the light of the fire. He had to stop the Afghan sergeant from charging in with his AK blazing. There could have been another twenty in the rooms. Another ten or so on top the walls. You couldn't see. The eight around the fire, you know how Afghans are gonna have their chai, gonna spend the night chatterboxing like a bunch of church ladies at an afternoon ice-cream social. That's how Wolfe put it.

The next thing Wolfe knew, there was Finkle climbing up on this tractor parked right against the wall, then up onto the high tarped load on the farm wagon hooked to the tractor. Finkle's idea, to get atop the 15-foot hard-packed clay compound wall to see better. Not a bad idea, until the Afghan sergeant flipped up a corner of the tarp to reveal a ten-stack high of wooden ammo crates that Wolfe could read with his Nods the markings, 120MM, which is all he needed to know, confirmed by some others marked CARTRIDGES 106MM FOR RIFLE M40A1. *Down, Finkle, now.*

First thing, Wolfe marked the spot on his GPS.

Off with the knapsacks and out with the blocks of C4, spool of det cord, coil of timing fuse.

No time to be high-speed textbook, no time to do it right and break open a couple of the crates to put the C4 directly on the half-dozen rounds that would explode the whole wagonload.

Just three big flattened clumps of C4 wrapped separately with det cord and placed right against the outermost crates, is how Wolfe explained it. And daisy-chain the three with det cord, rig it to initiate with timing fuse that you unloop and cut off five-minutes of and lay out and fire up and get the hell out of there following the ANA sergeant fast for the next compound, to hide behind its wall protected from the tremendous concussive blast and debris forthcoming. Boom, ammo cache gone. So, when the Talibs arrive carrying a brand-new 120 tube or tubes down the mountain, they aint got nuthin to drop down them tubes. If they've got a M40 recoilless hid someplace here, sorry pals you're outta luck, *No shells for you.*

As Wolfe told it, both Dove and Redcloud thought it was about as good as you can get for improvised demolitions in a real time-crunch situation in the pitch dark and fog, with the enemy not fifty feet away just on the other side of that tall compound wall.

Wolfe said he'd have preferred stepping away a couple hundred meters and just blowing up the whole wagonload with one Law, but you couldn't see three feet, never mind a hundred meters, so how you gonna aim?

Second best, adapt to the situation you're given and improvise C4 and det cord and timing fuse and slink off fast far enough away out of the big massive blast a'coming.

The best laid plans of mice and men . . . .

Who are the mice and who are the men?

Lying on the ground tight against the next compound's far wall, fingers pressed into the ears for the coming big bang, and five minutes go by, and nothing. Six minutes, nothing. Seven. And Wolfe knows he can measure off five-minutes of timing fuse six ways to Sunday, exact, so maybe the fuse was crimped or broken inside or just old and wet from being maybe, what?, Korean War vintage?, leftover stockpiles from a Seattle warehouse when Vietnam ended? Or, did some Talib drift away from the comforting glow of that campfire to wander outside to take a leak and smelled the fuse burning and pulled apart the whole thing just in time?

Whatever. Wolfe told Finkle and the sergeant they'd give it a safe ten minutes then go back and re-rig it. Which is about exactly when they saw a flash of light and heard the first firing of the recoilless. Not far either, from near somewhere close, and priorities changed that quickly—the immediate threat to the Zoo was the recoilless, while the cache was GPS'd and could be dealt with later by Cas.

Wolfe and Finkle followed the sergeant straight in the direction of the recoilless, with Wolfe making sure that Finkle was close on the sergeant's ass, with his own hand on Finkle's knapsack, pushing.

Dove had stopped Wolfe in his recounting then, wondering, if one were to check the drone surveillance footage since yesterday, one is going to see that tarp-covered wagon. Which begs the question, how could the ANA checking out the compounds yesterday and today miss so much munitions right in plain sight? Don't they look underneath a tarp?

Redcloud, "Because my men didn't go in the compounds, sir."

"I refuse to believe that so many ANA would be so complicit."

Wolfe, "They wouldn't see it if it was hidden in tunnels. Or in rooms behind barred doors they've got hid behind stacks of sacks of grain and rice and beans."

Redcloud, "You know the ANA, sir. When the Americans aren't around watching them, they mosey into the compounds and the farmers offer them some chai and some dried little cakes and pistachios and almonds and a bowl of little wrapped candies, and that's it, that's the sum total of their search."

Which is entirely possible here. Was.

Which Dove could not disagree with.

Which is probably the case with the M40 recoilless rifle itself.

Which they found was firing from the compound two over.

At least that's what it sure sounded like to Wolfe, close, from the distance across the compound from the big wide steel gates that were open. A U.S. M40, by sound, because you sure couldn't see it through the fog and black dark. A tried-and-true M40, probably part of the billions of dollars of military aid given to Pakistan over the decades. An M40 here an M40 there, who's keeping track.

The M40 is sixty-year-old technology that's near perfect in its design and manufacture and still produced today and sold by international arms traders, whose salesmen the Taliban buyers meet in London or Vienna. Those salesmen showing full-color brochures, *Hey, you could use one of these M40s, be quite the bang there in Afghani-land, how about a couple gross? Cheap today, just for you, my friend, special discount, two for one. How 'bout, we throw in these shoulder-launch M67s also? Half off, just today.*

The M40 was in the compound three over from the wagonload cache. From the brightness at each shot, Wolfe pictured it on the roof of the housing area. If it was an M40 and not some third-world knock-off, it'd have to be tripod-mounted, with at least four or five guys manning it.

Best guess, the gun had probably been hidden down below under piles of loose hay, and the ANA going through the compound wouldn't have even bothered to look, distracted easily by the offered chai and the candy dish brought out by the 9-year-old boy whose head they playfully pat and leave their hands on his tight little young butt.

The Talibs aint stupid. They probably had three boys with trays of candies and pistachios in that compound alone.

Local boys, right here from the village.

What choice would their fathers really have?

You going to be the one to tell pesky insurgents no?

Ha ha ha ha.

The least you can say for the Talib insurg, they're going to slip the family elder a couple hundred rupee for the candies and almonds, a couple hundred more for hiding the guns and ammo, and a grin and a wink for the diversionary use of his grandsons.

The ANA leave the compound, join their American coalition partners outside and trudge on over to the next compound, leaving the Americans outside again, and so on and so on and eventually down all the way to the school building.

You ask them if there's enemy or weapons or ammo or anything in the compounds, and they just shrug *No, Nope, Nuthin, M-tee*.

And up in that compound later in the day the Talib gunteams show up and move that huge heavy M40 and its heavy tripod mount up there on the roof and move the rounds too. And just wait.

"To be more fair to the ANA," Dove had said, and Pfc Holloway couldn't wrap his mind around anyone wanting to be fair to the soldiers most all of which walked out of here deserting.

"Let's be fair," Dove said. Even assuming the recoilless rifle was right there in the compound, all that wagonload of rounds in the other, the village elder would have told the ANA that the insurgents had left them weeks ago just for temporary storage. And they'd be coming back to get them sometime maybe next month. And don't tell the Americans please, because you know how they are. They'll take everything here, tear the place up, arrest us and leave our women to starve. Then, Dove said, add it all up, and those were the same ANA who first left here after the initial sniper attack. "Because they knew what was in the compounds and knew then when the snipers attacked, they knew what was coming next."

"I don't know which is worse," said Wolfe. "Or better. That excuse, to blame it on their lame-ass stupidity and their deceit. Or on them and their thing with little boys."

"Which," Redcloud said to Dove, "is why Coin saying we've got to stay out of the compounds is back-asswards."

That now Pfc Holloway could wrap his mind around.

Coin back-asswards. ANA's back-asswards.

That makes sense to Holloway.

And with Wolfe's telling, Holloway wished he'd been there, like Finkle, that he'd been Finkle and been the hero of the day.

It was about right then, Wolfe said, when they'd got to the compound with the recoilless rifle firing, that was when, just after the last recoilless shot, Nouri's calling in English over the mosque loudspeakers started. It wasn't real loud or clear way up there in the farthest terrace, but Wolfe could make out a fair part of it. All that *Soldiers of Allah* and *Jihadist warriors of Allah* shit.

Again the ANA sarge had wanted to charge in with guns a'blazing and Wolfe had to hold him back, cuz it was suicide and the idea was to take out the recoilless and put it out of commission, and bullets weren't going to do it. The Laws could. And Finkle's 40-mike-mikes, maybe.

Mark it with the GPS first and mentally note that the gun is actually about 30 meters away on an exact 297 magnetic heading. To later with a map plot the exact ten-digit grid of the Poo to send up for a Jdam strike.

The three moved away from the open entrance, just in case a Talib or two wandered out to take a piss and bumped into them. The plan became the Laws to be the primary weapon, and Wolfe would fire both, from the open door, initiating the action with the first, at which time Finkle would be the secondary with his M203 grenades, firing at a straight-on-level height from atop the compound wall, hopefully hitting low on the gun, at the base, to also take out the crew. In the entrance with Wolfe, the Afghan sergeant would rake the compound with two mags of AK, Wolfe would fire off the second Law, and Finkle was to get three grenades off and a full mag on burst then drop down off the wall, and the three of them would beat feet out of there, melting away silently into the dark and fog.

Before they could boost Finkle up the wall, the Afghan sergeant pushed them both back against it and clamped a hand over each one's mouth.

Voices of men approaching, and the sergeant had heard them first, or felt their presence, and if he hadn't, they'd have been heard themselves and found out, as Wolfe and Finkle could see through Nods five Talibs walking by so close you could almost touch them. AKs and one with an RPG. They headed right in the open gates.

A very close call, but for the Afghan sergeant's sharp ears or his Afghani sixth sense.

Last-minute instructions to Finkle: No firing until Wolfe himself fires off the first Law, and Wolfe was going to wait for the recoilless to fire again to give him a clear exact spot to aim for in the brightness of the launch blast. For Finkle, at Wolfe's first Law, quick, three grenades then a full mag on burst, aiming always low on the brightness of the recoilless' twin launch blast—the muzzle and the breech. *It aint foolproof, but it's the best we've got.*

They boosted Finkle up on the wall, where he straddled it, and Wolfe tossed him up the 203.

They could hear Nouri's voice dimly over the loudspeakers, and then came the first dim explosion and the series that followed of what Wolfe assumed was the Zoo firing M203s or Laws at the mosque and its loudspeakers that continued yammering on with Nouri's voice.

Wolfe and the ANA sergeant separated, one to each side of the open entrance gates.

Wolfe silently snapped open both Laws.

Un-saftied both.

Left one on the ground, shouldered the other.

Across the fields, the sound of single grenade explosions and Nouri's loudspeaker voice.

And the recoilless here didn't fire.

Wolfe could only force his imagination to visualize it in place and distance from its firing before.

Aimed the Law there.

Waited for the recoilless to fire and give him an aim point he could be confident of.

Heard another distant grenade and Nouri's wounded cry over the loudspeakers and another grenade, and the loudspeakers screeching and dying. Then in sequence three more grenade explosions.

Complete quiet from the distance.

Men's voices. The gunners, across there, from a height, the roof, that's where the big gun is, a little to the left of where Wolfe'd been aiming, and he adjusted, felt a tinge more confident.

Figured that with their talking, it was tranverse and elevation instructions relayed and now the big gun would fire again.

He waited.

It didn't.

He couldn't be sure he was going to hit it if he couldn't aim right on it, and he couldn't aim for certain if he couldn't see it, and *C'mon, you'd think the gun crew they'd shine a flashlight,* he reasoned, wishing, that they would need a flashlight to see what they were doing, *C'mon c'mon, give me something to aim on! Light a cigarette at least! Something!*

Nothing.

For Chrissakes, you're Afghans, fire up a joint! Pass around a doobie!

Nothing.

Just a sec, what's that?, not nothing, there were now men's voices approaching from close right in front of him, coming this way, and Wolfe knew it was now-or-never, a couple more seconds and he was toast, and he shouted *"Eyes on, Finkle!"* and shot off the first Law, and was elated that the loud bright explosion was close, just across the inside here, the rocket hadn't disappeared high to sail away and explode who-knows-where worthless, and he grabbed up and fired the second Law, hearing the Afghan sergeant nearby firing his AK on auto and Finkle's grenades exploding then his bursts of M4, and they all fell back and joined up and took off, and that's when AK fire started behind them, the cracks of wild bullets streaming past and the brightness of the fog lit up back there, and it's an instinct to return fire, even when you're about ten seconds too late to realize you're giving away your position in the dark and the fog.

And then the ANA sergeant went down, hit multiple times.

In the aid station classroom the ANA sergeant knows that it's the morphine that has eased him into a painless gentle relaxation. He knows his body wants to just fall into sleep, but he won't allow it.

This face close above him, he likes it, it is kind, it is friendly. It is the man that the terp Nouri had said they called the animal wolf. *Leewe* in Pashto.

He is speaking a bad, chopped, basic Pashto.

Saying *You live my friend.*

Saying *Morning. Helicopter. Cash. Fob Salerno.*

Saying *Medics saying you are good. A-okay.*

Saying *Cash Fob Salerno they for you are the American doctors.*

Saying *You to be strong, Sergeant.*

Saying *Must to be you strong, my dost.*

The sergeant didn't understand the English of the two medics explaining to *Leewe* that he should make it until morning, and that they had tied off the bad bleeders in his thigh, the sucking chest isn't going to kill him by morning, and the two gunshots in the gut, they're a different story, who knows?, they're not bleeding, really, not bleeding out and you've got to hope not much inside, but they're for the trauma surgeons at Salerno to deal with. Knock on wood, BZ told Wolfe, we can keep him alive through to morning. Percent chance? Eighty, maybe, depends on what the two gutshots have butchered in there. If the liver's turned to mush, no one at Sal or Bagram hospital's gonna save him.

But the sergeant, even as he was easing into the peace of the morphine, did feel the compassion of the young medic, the one who helped his own men yesterday, yes it was only yesterday, and *He came to us and helped us and helped to carry them* to the helicopter. The sergeant felt the optimism in this young American's constant reassurances that *You okay, You okay.*

And the other medic, with the strong hands, the rough hands, and the strong voice, and the sure hands, his confident hands, and that shattered leg that *They are surely going to amputate at Cash Salerno and he will be the rest of his life with a wooden leg.* This older medic who he cannot think he can remember having ever seen anybody ever do something so brave as he did when he came out from the back of that helicopter from high up in the clouds.

And this man they call *Leewe* now saying *Strong, Sergeant.* Saying *Sleep, dost,* and putting his hand now on the sergeant's face, and the sergeant knows that he is going to leave him now, and he doesn't want him to leave, *Don't leave me, stay here,* because he wants to tell him *Thank you,* he wants to say. *Thank you my friend. Thank you for carrying me for so far and so long with that short small boy soldier you call Finkle.*

He doesn't know why they carried him for so far and so long. He didn't want them to carry him. He told them to leave him. They would not leave him. He does not know why. He feels that maybe those are wet tears welling in his own eyes, but they can't be his own eyes because the tears feel so distant, like they belong to another man, as he thinks now that maybe the *Leewe* and the boy soldier carried him because he was the same as one of their American soldier comrades. That he was one of them. That they treated him as they do their own comrades.

And he does not believe he deserves it. He knows he doesn't. Because he knows what this man they call *Leewe* and the rest of them do not know. From before noon, from before the snipers, he knew that those farthest-most compounds across the valley held the potential for bad. For terribleness.

They were not the compounds that he and his two squads checked out. Farid's squad had. And when they were all here outside the school he had noticed something wrong in Farid and his four men, and he'd pulled Farid aside and gotten him to admit that they'd come across a couple of Taliban weapons caches. A couple of mortar tubes and lots of shells and the surprise of all surprises, what they knew, and couldn't hardly believe, was the weapon their fathers and uncles and older brothers had all talked about from the war first against the Russians then later against each other. A recoilless rifle.

There were no Talibs anywhere, Farid said, and the old farmers said that they were afraid that the Americans would bomb their houses and destroy their lives, and the Afghan sergeant knew that to be probably true and knew that they were only going to be here in this village a couple more hours, so the mortars and that deadly recoilless wouldn't matter, not really.

Then, with the snipers, Farid and his men, they were the ones who deserted then right after. Even then the sergeant didn't say anything to Nouri to tell the Americans because he knew the helicopters were coming very soon to take them away.

The helicopters didn't come, but they would, as soon as the rain stopped, but Farid must have told someone else earlier, because that's when the other squad deserted, and that was before the big attack by all those Taliban.

Little by little it had now become too late to tell Sergeant Redcloud and that stranger colonel. Pride, embarrassment, being forced to admit a lie. By then, by the time the Taliban commandant called out over the mosque loudspeakers for the rest to join them and save their own lives, Nouri and the others all knew the futility of fighting such a well-prepared foe. They all knew what was being said over the loudspeakers about recoilless rifles was true. They left.

And the sergeant had wanted to walk away with them. Just to save his own life. But he could not. He had betrayed these Americans once, he would not again.

Leewe and the small boy soldier carried him so far. How many times did he smack against the ground when they tripped and fell? How many times had he wanted to cry out in agony and did not? How many times did he hear in their English language, in their tones, in their anger, that they wished they could leave him?

Yet they did not.

And these two medics now are *Giving me everything of themselves just for me as they do for their own American companions.*

I have betrayed them all and they still give all to me.

And the ANA sergeant allows himself to fall into a jumbled drunken morphine sleep with a last sure thought of *I will give them back in payment with my life for them someday. . . .*

On the roof Ketchum's voice calls out softly to Pvt Finkle, "Hey, Spidey. You gotta be whooped. You go 'head catch some Zs."

"Shit, Sarge, I feel I can run a marathon and swim the Mississippi and then eat out a lesbo nympho all night then eat out her lesbo roommate too."

"You get some sleep. That's an order. Specialist Chubby, you take Finkle's watch, you hear? You got your eyes peeled over the wall?"

From Van Louse, "Got his eyes in another MRE, Sarge. Chowin down again. Says chow takes his mind offa being scared. Gonna go back to Bagram ten pounds heavier."

Ketchum's voice, "Turn 'round, Chubby. Get your eyes 'n ears out there."

Van Louse jabs Howie with an elbow, which is his own prod *C'mon, do it.* And he's known every move, every breath of Spec Howie since before the recoilless firing and especially since, what with Tran and Bybee buying it, Howie's been sitting even tighter against Van Louse, he won't let his shoulder not touch him. And he's been following everything Van Louse has done. From strapping down his own Kevlar tight, to double-checking his body armor is straight and tight, to removing his magazine from his M4, slapping it against his thigh to ensure good seating of the bullets, slipping it back in the gun, visually checking the gun's on safe, to constantly fiddling with his Nods over his eyes, to listening to every word Finkle said of his spooky terrifying patrol out there right in the midst of the enemy, to digging out another MRE from the box, didn't matter which, and now eating again.

Van Louse doesn't look at it as bad, Howie doing everything he's doing, imitating him.

He figures Howie's just trying to do what's right as an infantry grunt which he knows nothing about. Thinking that doing what Van Louse is doing will help save his own skin. No different than if Van Louse was stuck somewheres in a public affairs office on some big base, and he'd be copying whatever the photographer or reporter writer dude there was doing. Looking at him and copying him. And hoping that no one would notice that the most he's ever written's been a book report maybe, and that would be mostly copying from someone else's, and the most now he ever writes, if you could call it writing, is texting, with nothing but a letter or two for whole words and no periods and no caps —

2 for to and 4 for for and LOL for lots of laughs or laughing out loud or whatever it s'posed to mean

—and even he knows that that isn't really English English.

Ketchum's voice, "Remember now, Chubby. It's frags, not firing your weapon, y'hear? And throw em out the other side of the wall, if you can 'member where that is. An' don't forget to pull the pin. Half the time Remfs are always forgettin t'pull the pin."

Rear Echelon Mother Fuckers.

Staff pogues.

Like Spec Howie.

Who Van Louse defends, whispering down Ketchum's way, "Yeh Sarge, he knows. Been through that with him a'ready."

Ketchum's voice, "You throw like a girl, Chubby, the 'surants see you throwin your frags like a sissy, gonna think the sissy frag-thrower's a fag, be a good chance they're gonna spare you and're gonna wanna turn you into their bitch boy."

Again Van Louse defends Howie. "Shoot, he says he played baseball in high school, Sarge."

"Warmed the bench. You warm the bench on junior varsity, Chubby? Were batboy, wasn't you, admit it, wasn't you?"

"Center field, Sarge," Van Louse says. "Got the most ground to cover in center field. Longest throw to home."

"I know what center field is." And moments pass with nothing more from Ketchum. Then, "What'd you let yerself get all fat 'n pudgy for, Specialist? You want to stay in the Zoo, go infantry, you get yerself back in shape, you score yerself three-hundred on the PT test—shoot, move 'n communicate, I'll even send you to Ranger School. Wanna be a Ranger?"

"My ass, Sarge," from Finkle. "Not before me. He aint goin to Ranger School 'fore me."

"What'd I tell you 'bout gettin some sleep?"

"How'm I gonna sleep with you-all yappin over my head?"

Van Louse, "Close your eyes, Spidey, and think about all that sweet snatch you say yer gonna eat all night."

"When I get home I'm gonna."

"With your girlfriend? Chantelle?"

"She's not my girlfriend, I've told you."

Ketchum's voice asks, "That that black chick sister at the Memor'l Day picnic? Nice rack on her, nice tight ass, gotta be a really nice piece, Finkle."

"She's not my girlfriend."

Van Louse, "So you aint eating that out?"

"Who said that? I didn't say that."

Van Louse chuckles, "You aint cuz she's a sister and sisters don't know cuntee-lingus cuz the brothers don't ever go down on em. Black guys don't eat pussy. Black guys don't munch on the fur burger."

Ketchum's voice, "You believe that bullshit, Louie?"

"It's true, Sarge. Ask any black guy. Black guys don't eat pussy. Ask Sergeant Utah. Ask him, he'll tell ya."

"Utah don't eat nuthin. It aint cuz he's black, it's cuz he's that holy roller shit. Church of the Fellowship of the Naz'rene John the Baptist Mary Mag'lene Cross of Christ ghost rider in the dark, all that shit. I know, cuz his wife talked my ex into goin to church with them one time, and, y'know, if yer not goin to church with yer wife, if you tell her you aint goin on Sunday, you aint gettin any Saturday night and you sure aint gettin it again twice Sunday morning. We go, and they're all that speakin in tongues bullshit. And hosanna, hal-eee-luye-la, people fallin on their knees. Singin, stompin their feet, loud, Christ A'mighty, you coulda raised the damn roof on that place. Brung down the rafters. Those folks, Louie, they don't eat no pussy, got laws 'gainst goin down on the whisker biscuit. Don't hardly ever fuck even. It's all the sin of the devil. Sin of Bee-ellll-zee-bub! They don't never drink, not so much as a beer, and don't smoke, even chew, cuss, spit, and they sure aint eatin pussy, and fuckin's once every blue moon. And then when they do, they gotta fall down on their knees right after and pray and beg God for forgiveness for their evil ways. On their knees on wood floors. An' they toss gravel down on em first, and you know how that feels on yer knees? Hurtin for Christ for their sinnin ways."

"Sergeant Utah's got like four or five kids, Sarge. So you know he musta done it plenty if he's got all those kids."

"Yeh, Louie, sure, an' you know the way they fuck? It's gotta be all the lights out, like pitch dark, can't see your hands in front of your face. Like right now here. And you don't got Nods. He's gonna have all his clothes on. Just his zipper down. She's on the bottom, and she's all dressed like a Amish schoolmarm, and she's under the covers, the big quilt her great-great-granny made back when they come across in a covered wagon. And all's there is, there's just this little hole cut in the quilt bed coverin, and that's where he sticks his little thingy in. Wham wham wham, three strokes, he's done. Put a warm cow's liver under that hole, he wouldn't know the diff'rence."

"Yeh well, Slurpee says," Van Louse answers, "I've heard Slurpee sayin he don't eat pussy. He don't and he never would."

"Slurpee laps at the cooch. Slurpee tricks his tongue down in the bone zone. He's jus sayin that cuz he can't let his black brothers think he's a wuss, got himself pussy-whipped. Don't want them thinkin he's a white boy cracker, cuz only honky crackers eat that nasty tuna-smellin snatch. He don't want them thinkin his dick aint big enough, it aint all his dick doin the talkiin, cuz his dick aint ji-normous enough to be drivin the sisters wild. The brothers, they're tellin theirsefs it be the white boys who only eat the tuna taco cuz white boys don't got dongs big 'nough to give a woman a piece a'real lovin. Louie, a word from wise ol' Sarge Ketch. Take it from the old man got a tongue can play Charlie Daniels on the fiddle. They all eat pussy. They all go down, take a ride downtown. Ringing that bell ding ding ding. Capital Ding Ding Ding. And, Finkle. I know yer still awake, Spidey. You go 'head, you go down on that sister babe, that Chantelle. She won't never be forgettin it. Whooeee. Flick that tongue, Finkle, that good-lookin sister aint never goin back to the brothers."

Van Louse, "You get a rep for it, Spidey. Word's gonna be texted from all the black sisters. On Facebook and Twitter too. Spidey's got the tongue of a octopus. Spidey sucks you like a Dyson vacuum, will clean you up even on the rag."

"Aw c'mon, dude," from Finkle. "That is dis-gust-ting."

"You get the rep, gonna have to live up to it. Be saying 'bout you, that Spidey, he's got the Finkle Groove."

"Shit, that's Holloway, that's Holloway, and the only groove he's in, Holloway is so gay. Aint that right, Sarge? Holloway's gay."

"I wouldn't know about that," from Ketchum. "He been crawlin into yer rack when there aint no one lookin? Not that I'm judging now. You can work that tongue a'yers, Finkle, keep it in shape. On Holloway. For cuz when Mister Baseball Mister Center Fielder Chubby there pulls the pin on his frag and lets it fall outta his hand and it goes down 'tween yer legs in yer crotch there, Finkle, yer gonna be needin that tongue, that's all yer gonna have."

Laughter.

Invisible, unseen up on the other side of Spec Howie is Jarbodie on the second 240, listening to all that.

Him here.

Howie, Van Louse and Finkle together.

Ssgt Ketchum down from them.

Jarbodie can't see the middle three or Ketchum farther.

Ketchum can't see the middle three or Jarbodie farther.

And Jarbodie is thinking that GIs are the same everywhere. Doesn't matter where, everywhere. Doesn't matter when, what the danger out there waiting for them is, they're like this. There's enemy out there right now that shot down his helicopter this afternoon and totally destroyed it and killed his pilot and killed the kid Private Rapley, and the other two are down there right now and God-only-knows if they're going to make it, and this Sergeant Ketch and this Louie and this Finkle or Spidey and this Chubby, they've got their friends down there dead in those body bags and laying in that other room there wounded and who knows if they're going to survive, and they can talk about eating pussy and shagging anything in a skirt, they wish, they like to imagine, and none of it matters, and they know that none of it matters.

An enemy out there who two hours ago fired those recoilless rounds this way. Who knows what they're setting up for next? Who knows when? Five minutes? Ten? Just before dawn? And these guys are joking and jiving. Maybe it's partly the confidence from those two fast-mover bomb strikes. Yeah, the recoilless is taken out. And those bombs give them assurance that there's help available, so close and ready. We're not alone here. And they talk and laugh and joke about pussy.

Laugh and joke about Finkle getting his dick blown off.

It's awright to laugh and joke. Talk. Takes away from thinking about what's still out there.

Jarbodie likes the talk. Likes hearing them. If he knew these guys, if he were their friends, if he were in this platoon, he would be doing it with them. Like with his chopper crew.

They're like GIs everywhere, he guesses. Soldiers in Patton's army in the freezing cold of the Bulge talking about their gals waiting for them back home. Bragging on the nookie they had waiting. Guys really freezing in the Frozen Chosin, teeth chattering even more in terror of the Chinese hordes massing just over the ridge. Draftees lying in some swamp in the Mekong Delta, a million mosquitos and leeches all sucking their blood, they're talking about sucking pussy back home or on R&R in Thailand, and buying that cherry-red '68 GTO when they get to the USA.

His own dad, he couldn't have been a day older than this kid Finkle here there then in Vietnam. Had to be talking about the same thing. Hadn't even met his mother yet, it would be years before they met. Never did talk about his Vietnam days, not at home, not ever with his son, not until after his son came home from his own first tour of Iraq.

Then they could talk, father to son, they were equals, they'd both gone to war when their nation called, and Jarbodie could hear some bits of random stories about Dad in the Mekong. Dad and his days like this. Nights like this.

Jarbodie thinks he feels a drop of rain on his face. No.

Yes, there it is again.

He raises his face up.

Yep, another drop. Another. More.

He thinks, *Shit*, the last thing he wants is rain.

Rain means wet. Wet means cold. Cold hurts.

"Someone got a spare poncho they're not gonna use?" he whispers.

Ketchum's voice, "Yeh, just a sec."

Jarbodie hears some rustling down there where he's been hearing Ketchum's voice and it must be Ketchum going through his rucksack.

Now, "Here, catch."

A folded poncho hits Jarbodie right in the shoulder.

Nice throw, he thinks.

"Thanks," he says.

And he thinks that Sergeant Ketchum probably played high school baseball or a lot of Little League. A pitcher. Throwing a perfect strike tonight up here essentially blindfolded by the dark and fog.

Downstairs, Capt Cathay would like them to start talking again. Everyone's been too quiet since they came back down.

Her Casio Ladies G-Shock shows 01:26, and she's checked it too many times since they came back down, and the time is going by too slowly. When they talk time goes quicker. It's too many hours still until morning.

It was just what, twenty-four hours ago that they were waking her and telling her that she'd better get her rucksack packed and she'd have to draw a weapon and magazines and ammunition and NVGs from the arms room because she had a helicopter she had to be on at 0400. And she'd been excited because she was going somewhere, she was doing something adventurous, she was going to see some of Afghanistan, she was going to see some soldiers on a small base somewhere, on a Cop, a firebase, in danger, where the insurgents were.

If she thought that they'd listen to her or that they'd care that anything she had to say was important or relevant or that she could talk about combat and the insurgents and what might happen next, she would say something just to start a conversation.

But she's an outsider. She's from Division HQ. She's a Remf—yes, she knows what that means. And she's a woman. And she's not infantry. Lieutenant Colonel Dove, he's staff, Isaf HQ, but he's a Ranger, and he's a man, and he knows combat. And he got wounded. His leg is messed up and he's been favoring it, and she can see even in this dim shadowy light of the lamps the dark of the dried blood on his uniform pants. *Why couldn't I be wounded like him?* And only still be limping. Be walking.

She feels an anger at him, that he's the rough tough Ranger and it's she who is wounded badly, and it should have been him. The bullet, didn't he even say, didn't it ricochet off him and hit her? It's his fault, and she should hate him for it, but she does not want to go there, she does not want to degrade herself to that ugliness and evil that is anger and hate and vengence, and she will instead think of her family, of going home, and of her being strong for her sisters and brothers, her being stoic and brave and happy for her younger sisters and brothers and show them that life is not what *You the Lord sends our way but what we make of it*, in the way of *Goodness in the reflected glory and love of Jesus Christ Your Son.*

Take me away from evil thoughts, please take me away from the evil in man and allow me to see the beauty, to see the peace that is in Your love, Lord.

She had hoped that their conversation would start a while ago when the Pfc on the radio got a call and said to Colonel Dove that it was Colonel Pluma's radioman saying that he wanted them to switch to the Ranger satellite freq. Channel Number 273. Leave the radio on the Isaf channel, Dove had said, and put the other on the Ranger one. They wouldn't be needing to talk back to Cop Valley Forge anyway. Everything would be coming from Isaf or the Rangers at Salerno from now on. Call Valley Forge first and inform them they were vacating the freq.

The Pfc established communication with Colonel Pluma's radioman on the other channel, and now everyone's waiting for Pluma to call again. And that was a while ago. And no one said anything since.

Capt Cathay had thought a conversation would start when Sergeant First Class Travis Redcloud got up and shed his body armor then pulled off both his shirts, and she'd never seen so many tattoos before. His whole torso, front and back and both his arms are covered in them. She'd seen before those parts on his neck and up his chin, but she'd had no idea someone could be so tattooed. Or would want to be. Except, those bikers in motorcycle gangs and felons in prison, they've all got tattoos all over their bodies. She would never get one tattoo, would never want one tattoo, not to mention that many, her whole body painted like a carnival merry-go-round.

Something was bugging Sergeant Redcloud. Something up around behind his neck between his shoulders where he couldn't see but could feel. Wet and bloody and a long broken scab. Mr Wolfe inspected it up close with his flashlight and said it looked like he'd taken some frag under the skin. Had to be this afternoon during the attack, what took him so long to notice it? Take it out is all Sergeant Redcloud told him, and Mr Wolfe did. Just dug it out with his knife, and Capt Cathay doesn't think she even saw Sergeant Redcloud flinch. And Mr Wolfe handed him the frag piece, and Sergeant Redcloud just tossed it aside, litter. Mr Wolfe poured peroxide to wash the blood running from the cut, then taped a bandage over it, and that was it.

And it was the first that Capt Cathay saw of the Zoo tattoo.

On the back of Sergeant Redcloud's shoulder.

Frightened, she diverted her glance away—it was ugly, that skull. And looked back. From this short distance inspected it.

Yes, full of violence, the skull and that bullet hole in the forehead. But the colors, the roses, *They're pretty*, she thought. Strong and firm, not frail, and beautifully rendered, the roses are real. And the script for the name, Tattoo Zoo, is perfect, just as soldiers see themselves. The skull too, that's what soldiers want. That violence, that proximity to death, their enemy's and perhaps even their own, yet the skull is flanked by roses, of course, the romance of roses. She thought that as a logo, a corporate name, that it announces powerfully and literally exactly what it is. The Tattoo Zoo. A line platoon of infantry soldiers.

"Is that how your platoon got your name?" she asked in a whisper of Rodriquez who is always just happening to be sitting next to her.

Rodriquez held up two fingers. "My secon' I done."

"You? Yours? You drew it?"

He shrugged a humble *Yeh sure no big deal*.

"It's your design?"

Again Rodriquez just kinda shrugged it off as nothing.

"You're an artist, Sergeant," she said. "That's art."

Another shrug from Rodriquez. "Jus a tatt."

"The roses are beautiful. Really pretty."

"Pretty, ma'am? S'posed to be muy macho. La guerra. War. Never thought of pretty."

"Everyone in the platoon has one?"

No, Rodriquez shook his head, *No, not hardly*.

"So, it's if you get a Purple Heart?" Cathay asked, and she imagined that Sergeant Redcloud would already have ten Purple Hearts.

Again Rodriquez had shaken his head *no*. "Don't nobody get it jus for that," he said. "Purple Heart, I know guys've got one cutting theirselfs shaving. P'atoon knows. Dudes they know. If you's one be gettin the tatt."

And Cathay didn't know what to ask next. Or sound stupid asking it. The tattoo must be gotten for doing something brave. Like what Kyle Wolfe and that young boy private and the ANA soldier did tonight. For being brave. Super brave.

Before she realized why she wanted to know it, she asked, "Does Lieutenant Caufield have one?"

Rodriquez pointed to the back of his own shoulder, the same spot as Redcloud's tatt. "I got jus the green and the blue still I gotta do," he said. "L-T was a numero uno L-T. Numero uno." And that's all he said about it, and he might have wanted to say something about her own temporary tatt that he drew but he didn't, and he'd just leave that for her to find on her own whenever she did.

And Capt Cathay was glad that Matt Caufield had the tattoo that said that he was one of the few selected and honored as brave in his own platoon. He had the tattoo, of course he has the tattoo, he is the type of man and leader whom she would give the tattoo and whom she would know would without question deserve the tattoo, and she would prefer right now that it was Matt who was sitting next to her instead of Sergeant Rodriquez. And that isn't fair, because Sergeant Rodriquez has been kind, after he'd been so hateful and seething with anger at her at first. He's been kind and gentle and polite and protective, but she knows that he sits near her only because she is a woman, that she's female, and if she were a man he wouldn't care about her. She feels that it is his maleness wanting her as a female, that he on his Cop is so far separated from any women and this man really loves and needs the presence of women around him. Which is what he wants from her. As a woman. For sex or just for love or just for that missed motherhood. That is what is drawing him to her, and even with her zero experience with men and sexuality and not even one single kiss for passion other than Josh McAllen on the mission in Costa Rica when she had to slap him away, she knows that it is sexuality that Rodriquez feels for her and it is the total absence of it that she feels for him.

And wishes he were Matt Caufield.

And that will never be.

But she is glad now at 01:27 on her Casio G-Shock that nearly ten minutes ago she had made herself take hold of Sergeant Rodriquez's hand, knowing that he would want that, and she whispered to him then, asking that if another attack came would he first, please, before he went out there or up to the roof, would he please help to bring her around outside, to move her to set her up on the other side of the doorway. So she could shoot, she said, *Direct and point-blank*, the first insurgents *coming up those steps*.

"Cap'm ma'am, yes ma'am," he told her. "You got it."

And she'd felt him squeeze her hand and she knew he didn't want to let it go. So she left it in his for a little while longer.

She's thirsty now and knows that fluid intake is important when you're on a high level of fear and stress for so long, but she's afraid to drink because she's embarrassed that she's wetting herself and can't control it. She hasn't wanted to feel herself down there but has anyway, because she has the urge to know the truth, however unpleasant. So, she just won't drink anymore.

The same way she's not eating anything. Not really. Not since those Kit Kats that the lieutenant colonel tossed over. And only those because she knew that she needed the sugar energy. And the yellow packet of M&M peanuts from the MREs that Sergeant Rodriquez had nonchalantly dropped into her hand as if it was nothing. Then when he'd seen that she'd left a collection of just the peanuts on the floor, having sucked the chocolate off each one separately one at a time, he'd gone out onto the porch and then come back with three more packets he must have gotten from the other soldiers there, and he just laid them in her lap, without saying anything, as if it were no big deal. Plus he added a packet of MRE Skittles. Pure sugar. At least it's some energy.

Capt Cathay raises her eyes now at the *squelch* coming over on all the handsets they all have in here clipped up near their shoulders close to their ears. Sergeant Redcloud, and the lieutenant colonel, and Mr Wolfe. Sergeant Rodriquez's headset close on this side, half out of his ear, and she hears clearly, "Ketch here. Sarge, stick your head outside. Startin to rain again."

A nod from Redcloud to Rodriquez, and Rodriquez gets up and goes outside to check.

Wolfe says, "I'm not a weatherman, but does rain mean the fog goes away or gets thicker?"

Nobody answers.

Then Dove says, "I wouldn't imagine it could physically get any thicker. That's about as great a maximum density of water vapor just shy of rain, snow or a block of ice."

Wolfe, "Cotton candy. Wouldn't maximum density be more like cotton candy? So thick you feel it stick to you when you try and walk through it."

Redcloud, "Wolfie, rain would melt cotton candy."

"Point taken. Like a snow cone, then. Shaved ice all in a giant lump filling this entire worthless valley."

Redcloud, "Sounds like you've got a fixation on the carnival midway, your cotton candy and snow cones."

Dove, "Funny, but I don't remember, Mr Wolfe, anything in your background about a summer stint huckstering on a travelling roadshow."

Wolfe plays along, "Runs in the family. Uncles on my mother's side. Played all the cons. Shoot the balloon, win the big teddy bear. In the DNA I guess. Rumor has it, it's gypsy blood running through both sides of the family. So what's better, what do we want? Rain? Or fog?"

Pfc Holloway is quick to throw in. "Who cares?" A chuckle. "As long as I'm here dry inside."

Wolfe, "Aw, from the mouth of babes."

"Look who's talkin. What makes you the only one who thinks he can say something funny, Wolfie?"

"It was a compliment, ye my not-so-wise Grasshopper."

Rodriquez comes back in. Indicates to Redcloud *so-so*, nothing real bad out there, *jus regular rain.*

Dove, "Your question is really, Mr Wolfe, whether the rain is better because it's making those mountain trails raging mudslides for the enemy coming down them loaded with weapons and gear. Or the fog is better because the insurgents can't see this building until they bump their noses right into it."

Nick Flowers pipes in, "Beards, Zachary. Bump their beards."

"I stand corrected."

Wolfe, "I'll take Door Number Three. The rain and the fog."

Holloway, again, for a laugh, "As long as I'm here dry inside."

Wolfe, "Famous last words of Davy Crockett and Jim Bowie."

Redcloud, "Door Number Four, Wolfie. No rain, no fog. Visibility out to three miles. Air is Green."

Dove, "From your mouth to God's ears."

Wolfe, "Leave me outta that. God's not listening to my prayers. He's got me on His Do Not Call List."

Capt Cathay is bold enough to say quietly, "I'll pray for you, Mr Wolfe."

They're all surprised she spoke up.

Wolfe, "I wouldn't if I were you. It'll automatically put you on His Do Not Call List. Express train to hell. You don't even get a rest break in purgatory. I'd pray for you, Captain, but it'd just do the opposite and get you on the list too."

"How her if it's you doing the praying, Kyle?" Nick asks.

"The Friend of My Enemy is My Enemy. And you don't want God as your enemy. Believe me. I appreciate it, Captain, the offer, I really do. But better if you pray for yourself. That'll help everyone here."

Pfc Holloway answers the sat radio. "Zoo Platoon, this is Zoo Six Romeo, over." Listens. Says, "Roger, out." Tells Dove, "Colonel's RTO, sir. Radio check."

That's it, just a radio check, no word, no news.

Wolfe makes the sound of radio squelch, and mimics a radio call, "Davy Crockett here, Crockett calling. Will you take a collect call from San Antonio?" Sings, "Davvvyyyyy, Dave—ey Crockett, king of the wild frontier."

Holloway, pissed, as if it's he who's being mocked, "What's that supposed to mean?"

"Never heard of the Alamo, Grasshopper? Davy Crockett, Jim Bowie, William B Travis? Surrounded by two thousand of General Santa Anna's finest? You flunk out of seventh grade history?"

"I know the Alamo."

Dove, "They didn't have rain or fog at the Alamo, Mr Wolfe."

Redcloud, "Or a M40 recoilless or RPGs."

Wolfe, "They had cannon, lots of cannons. Santa Anna had a thing for big round cannonballs."

Redcloud, "One RPG equals ten cannons."

Nick, "You guys are depressing me."

Wolfe, "You want depressed, how about this for depressed? One word: Thermopylae. Number Two, Saragarhi. Three, Roncevaux Pass. Four, Shiroyama."

Dead silence.

Holloway's lost.

Rodriquez too.

Redcloud's got the gist, though but for the first one he doesn't know the names.

Dove adds, "Cameron, Mr Wolfe. Number Six, Karbala."

Rodriquez asks, "What's all them, Sergeant Redcloud? Them like Call of Duty games?"

"Losing games, Sniper Sarge," Wolfe says. "The side that always loses."

Dove, "One more, Mr Wolfe. The crème de la crème. The M word."

"Of course," Wolfe replies. "The best for last. Masada. If we get to Masada, I'm bailing. I'm walkin out of here, right out there, going to look up a Talib recruiter, join the winning side. Ask where the Haqqanni recruiting station is. Where do I sign up."

Nick, "I'm with you, you can forget Masada. Time to grow a long beard, put on man jammies."

Rodriquez asks Capt Cathay, "Ma'am, you know what they're talkin 'bout?"

"History Channel stuff."

Holloway, "Geek Channel you mean."

Wolfe, "I figured you for Lifetime, Grasshopper. Hallmark. HGTV. Home Shopping Channel."

"Up yours. Geek jarhead."

Redcloud, "At ease, Holloway."

"Sarge, he's the—"

"I said at ease, PFC! Chill. Just chilllllllllllll oooooout. Kyle likes yankin your chain. You encourage him. Chill."

Wolfe, "Actually, I was kinda hoping Grasshopper had the freq and could call up Papa John's there and get us a couple of pizzas delivered. Pepperoni, sausage, mushrooms, what else you guys want?"

Holloway, "If there was someone named Grasshopper here maybe he could."

Redcloud, "Don't you know who Grasshopper is, Holloway?"

"How am I supposed to know who his Grasshopper is, Sarge? I'm supposed to know some jarhead Marine Corps comic book Road Runner the jarheads've got for their their football mascot? A wonder they don't got Porky Pig. Even better, Sponge Bob."

Capt Cathay, "I thought everybody knew Grasshopper."

Nick, "Everybody does."

Holloway, "Yeh now, like I'm stupid. Yer all now yankin my chain. There is no Grasshopper. No offense, ma'am. I'm talkin"—him, Nick.

Redcloud, "From TV, Holloway. The TV show. There is a Grass-hopper."

"What TV show?"

Wolfe, "Wax on, wax off, Grasshopper."

"That's Mr Miyagi, I know Mr Miyagi."

Redcloud, "Same thing."

Capt Cathay, "Yoda too."

Nick, "Grasshopper, you want to be Yoda instead?" He does a Yoda, "Yoda I am. Wise I am."

Holloway, "Cool, it's cool. You-all wanna pull my chain, be on his side"—Wolfe's. "It's cool, I'm cool with that. You say I'm Yoda, cool, I'm Yoda, I can be Yoda. If I'm your Grasshopper, whoever your nerdo TV show is, then yer Fonzie, Kyle. Yer Fonzie."

Wolfe, "Fonzie?"

"Yeh, Fonzie. If the shoe fits . . . ."

"Fonzarelli, Arthur Fonzarelli?"

"Fonzie from *Happy Days*. At least you try 'n act like him. Or think you do."

"Oh yeh yah, that Fonzie, sure, Grasshopper, Fonzie from *Happy Days*. Which would make you what, Ralph Malph?"

Nick, "No. Chachi. Better yet, Richie Cunningham's little sister, what's her name?"

"Joanie," Capt Cathay says.

"Ha ha ha ha ha," says Holloway. "Just for that, you know what? I am gonna order a pizza. I'm gonna call up and order one jus for me and Sergeant Rodriquez. What do you want on it, Sniper?"

"Pizza? Gotta be, 'mano, gotta have chorizo, cesos y lengua."

"In English?"

"Inglés? Aint nobody speakin no English in here. Fond Zee and Grass Hopper, and Yo Dee, I aint never heard a'none a'them."

Nick, "Rodriquez, you don't know Yoda? Not Fonzarelli, and Chachi, and Mr Miyagi? I suppose you've never heard of Sergeant Schultz? I see nothing. I know nothing." He does Schultz in Spanish, "No veo nada. No sé nada."

Wolfe, "You don't get none of those shows on Univision and Telemundo? We're talking the very essence of twentieth century Western culture you're missing out on, Sniper. We're talking classics up there with the *Odyssey*, *Hamlet*, *Macbeth*."

Nick, "All stuff, Wolfie, they're going to put in a time capsule, wait and see. *Happy Days*, *Hogan's Heroes*, *Get Smart*, *The Brady Bunch*, *90210*. *The Real Life*, *Who Wants to be a Millionaire*. Along with rap and hip-hop and Happy Meals and fruit roll-ups, and they'll dig it up in a thousand years and know exactly how this civilization collapsed."

Wolfe, "Sounds like you've given it quite a bit of serious thought, Nicky."

"I've got a list, it fills about six pages in a notebook. Double-sided. The decline and fall of the American civilization."

Redcloud, "I've got something you can add."

"What's that? I'm game."

"General St Claire's PowerPoint slideshow. Hearts and Minds. With all due respect, sir."

Dove, "It's not my PowerPoint presentation."

Wolfe, "Come on, Colonel, admit it, tell him, tell Nicky that even St Claire doesn't believe his own bullshit."

"A field-grade officer should be careful what he says in the presence of a journalist."

Nick, "And that's first on my list. Political correctness. A-Number-One root of all evil. Root of our decline."

Wolfe, "I thought *Happy Days* was first."

"I take it back. PC is third. *Happy Days* number two. First on the list, Adam Sandler."

They all laugh.

Not all. Holloway doesn't. It took him a couple of seconds to get it, that it's a put-down of Adam Sandler, who he thinks is great. He loved *The Waterboy*. Loves *Mr Deeds* and *Big Daddy* even more. Has a DVD of *Zohan* and the others back at the Cop. Man, dude, can't nobody ever beat *Happy Gilmore*! Especially that part where he punches the old guy from that game show, *which one?*, right in the face. Bamm! Kaplowee!

Rodriquez laughed only because Capt Cathay did and the others did.

Holloway pretends like he's about to make a radio call. "Sniper, what'd you say you wanted again on your pizza?"

"Chorizo, cesos, lengua. Doble jalapeños. Double."

"Double jalapeños, you sure? Sheee-at, I sure wouldn't wanna be holdin yer shitpaper when it's catchin fire burning up when you wipe your ass in the morning."

No one laughs, and Holloway expected a laugh at that, like Sergeant Slurpee woulda gotten, but he catches the look Colonel Dove sends his way, and he knows he's meant to see it, to see that he's gone too far, that the lieutenant colonel disapproves, that Holloway can't be talking that way, not now, not in here now, not with a female present, not a female officer, not a gentle one like her there. And Holloway knows it was wrong, that he was wrong, that his words were crude and gross and not the language or topic that the pretty captain would want to hear.

A subtle nod back from Holloway, and Dove accepts it, drops it.

And Capt Cathay got a sense of the look the colonel had for the Pfc and confirmed her sense in the Pfc's quick glance over to her, and she feels a pang of guilt that these men can't be really all themselves because she is here and it is only because she is a female. Her presence is holding them back. They are all conscious of her, not having all the camaraderie and horseplay joking that they would without her. And that joking is going to be crude and uncultured and nasty and full of *shits* and *fucks*. If Matthew Caufield were here now he would be the same as Lieutenant Colonel Dove is being. He wouldn't be talking like that, like he probably talks when it's just the guys around. He would have maybe said something to the Pfc, not just the reprimanding look that Dove gave him. But even Sergeant Rodriquez right here, he's not talking with all his foul tongue that *I know he does, I've heard him doing before.* Same with Mr Kyle Wolfe. They aren't saying *fuck.* Not here now. Or *shit.* Only *Because I'm here.* It is a respect that she is a female, that she is a female officer, that she does not use that language herself, that *I am me, they sense who I am and they respect me and they want to protect me.* These men are very aware that she is here, even the Pfc now, and she feels a comfort knowing that in spite of her not wanting to be singled out because she is she, their instinct to do just that, single her out man-to-woman, that it is part and parcel of their instinct to protect her. Of that she feels fortunate. She isn't a woman alone here. They will instinctively protect her from whatever horrors the insurgents bring should they attack again.

Capt Cathay says a silent prayer now thanking the Lord that she is not alone, that He has provided these men here in this dangerous place in this day and night of peril and that He has created men in His own image to protect women.

She says another prayer. For Mr Kyle Wolfe there. That he believe in his own good, in his own capacity for good and for loving and for seeing the *Love You have for him, Lord, and that You will protect Mr Kyle Wolfe also.*

She sees Mr Wolfe check his watch.

Sees the colonel check his.

"All kidding aside now, PFC, I'm not yankin your chain," Wolfe says. "If you had the freq of Mohammed's Pizzeria in Khowst City, we could call them up and order a couple extra large with goat entrails. Nan breadsticks stuffed with sheep eyeballs. I'm not kidding."

Redcloud, "That what they were eating up in the ville, the 'surgents?"

"As a matter of fact, halal meals. The ones you-all pass out for hearts-and-minds. Your tax dollars at work."

Nick, "Feeding the enemy. That's not even a news story, Wolfie."

Wolfe, "The folks back home don't know it."

Nick, "They don't care."

"Good point. I don't know what I was thinking. A moment of optimism. An informed public should know that their tax dollars are feeding the enemy. So much for optimism."

Redcloud, "The soft-hearted HTT in you showing. Sign of weakness."

Wolfe, "Sleep deprivation. I'm not thinking straight."

"There's an easy answer to that."

"I know. Sleep. Too wired-up on this here." Another Red Bull he's drinking. "That your Army was so generous stocking a year's worth on that resupply. Wouldn't wanna miss the action, y'know."

Dove, "No action. Think optimistically. There isn't going to be any more action. They've gone home. We've taken out their recoilless. We've taken out their indirect-fire weapons and munitions. They've seen us get our resupply, so they know they'll be walking into a shooting gallery. They can't see their own noses in the fog—or beards—and the rain's now making them wet and miserable. Discretion is the better part of what, Mr Wolfe? They're climbing back up their ratlines back for Pakistan as we sit here thinking they're massing for an attack."

Holloway says quietly, "Enchilada."

Which gets chuckles out of Dove, Wolfe and Redcloud.

Dove, "See, PFC Holloway, that's why you're Grasshopper."

"You too, Colonel, sir?"

"It's a compliment, PFC."

Silence. Holloway believes Dove, but just wants someone to explain it.

Nick, quietly, "Google it."

And Wolfe challenges Dove's argument. "And how much of that, Colonel—how much is just your own wishful thinking, or do you really believe it? They've gone home?"

"It's entirely possible. In sha'allah."

"That's what William B Travis was telling Davy Crockett too the night before the army of Santa Anna appeared on the horizon. Option Two: They're still comin down those goat trails right now. Barefoot. Or in knock-off Nikes, two dollars a pair. With four-dollar Kalashnikovs. Every other one totting three RPG rounds, a dollar-twenty-five on the open market. Platoon leaders talking on those little walkie-talkies, fourteen-ninety-five at Radio Shack on sale. They're wet and they're cold, but they aint miserable, because the wet and the cold are gifts from Allah to make them strong and to make us wet and cold and miserable. And weak."

Dove, "Are you saying that the tenth century beats the twenty-first?"

"They're firing at us our own recoilless rifles we give to Pakistan as foreign aid. They're eating our halal meals we manufacture and pass out free by the gazillions. You tell me."

"We have the watches, they have the time?"

Nick, "I've always thought that should be carved in stone."

Wolfe, "Their four-dollar AKs are more effective than our billion-dollar B-2 bomber if you're not going to use it. If you don't have the cajones to use it. Who's Santa Anna here and who's the Alamo?"

Redcloud, "We lost that one, Kyle."

Sniper Rodriquez throws in, "Whoa there, hol' on. Whaddo you mean we, Kemosabe?"

Nick, "Sniper, you don't know Sergeant Schultz, but you know Kemosabe?"

Wolfe, "I know you didn't flunk seventh-grade history, Rodriquez. I know you gotta know the Alamo."

"Alamo's a national holiday in Méjico. Only war, one time they whopped ass on the United States."

"Technically no, it wasn't the United States, Texas wasn't part of the United States. Was still Old Mexico."

Rodriquez, "Like you say, Holloway, you nailed it. Geek History Channel Beee-eSsssss."

Holloway, "You got that, Sniper. Booooorrr—reeeeen."

"Pop quiz," Nick says. "Who said, Those who don't learn history are destined to repeat it?"

"I know who didn't say it," from Redcloud. "No offense, Colonel. General St Claire. We came here yesterday and sure didn't learn because we're here again."

Dove, "The circumstances were radically different. Those one-hundred and seventy-three bodies. There was no way that we couldn't come back."

Quiet.

Then, from Nick, "Really, I wasn't just asking it, I want to know. I don't know who said that, 'Destined to repeat it'. You hear it all the time, everybody says it, but they never say where it's from."

Wolfe, "Groucho Marx probably. No, wait—Yogi Berra. Déjà vu all over again. When you get to the fork in the road, take it. And, PFC Grasshopper, that's Berra, B-E-R-R-A, not Bear."

Holloway, "He on the Geek Channel, got a show on the Geek Channel?"

From Capt Cathay quietly, "George Santayana. The exact quote: Those who cannot remember the past are condemned to repeat it."

Nick, "Of course, I shoulda guessed it. Santayana. One of those old dead philosophers."

Redcloud, deadpan, "Is that the same Santa Anna of the Alamo?"

"If they had wireless out here we could find out," Nick says. "What kind of a school building is this, without wireless?"

Wolfe, "Yeh, that's the first thing the Taliban are going to install. Internet for all. These schools especially. Double for girls' schools."

Everyone freezes at the *whistle* outside of a trip flare going off.

A second one immediately following, and

Redcloud's fingers start counting, One, Two, mainly a showing to Capt Cathay to calm her sudden wide-eyed fear, to Ten, and the first frag hand-grenade *blast* out there is heard, followed by about eight more.

Silence.

Redcloud on the radio, "What you guys got? Report. Ketchum?"

Ketchum's voice over the radio, "Stream side and 'bout in the middle. I think we got em, Sarge."

Redcloud, "Utah?"

Utah over the radio, "I hear something, Sarge. It sounds like the fella is calling for his mama. Whatever mama is in Afghani."

Nell over the radio, "Sarge, I've got some Allahs over this way. Either Al-lahs or Aw-shits, sounds 'bout the same to me."

Redcloud, "One more frag each."

"Rogers" from all three squad leaders.

Wolfe to Dove, "I guess they didn't go home back over the mountains after all."

On the roof dimly through the light rain can be heard out there a moaning in Pashto from two separate spots. Ketchum can see Finkle, Van Louse and Spec Howie through his Nods and calls out softly, "Van Louse, you throw one where you think that's comin from and you too, Chubby, throw it where you think it is. One each."

Ketchum stares out through his Nods and thinks he can make out the form of the rock wall. The light rain that started a while ago has seemed to thin the fog.

In the flashes of the explosions of three frags from downstairs out from the veranda and now from Van Louse's and Howie's, Ketchum has clearly seen the rock wall and has an exact sense of how far to throw his own grenade beyond it to reach the C-wire. He listens.

There, still out there low is a gurgling of a struggle for breath and a few spat words with the tone of a plea, and Ketchum imagines a black-clad Talib is out there beyond the wall, just across the invisible C-wire, holding a catcher's mitt, and Ketchum twists out the pin of his frag grenade, holding the spoon tight to the grenade's body, getting a clear imagined visual of the worn wrinkled oiled-shiny center crater of the mitt, and he lets release the spoon of the frag which he holds another couple of seconds then zings a fastball straight for that imagined mitt, hears the thud of it hitting, then there's the flash and bang of the explosion.

After the momentary blindness and deafness, he lets his eyes and ears readjust. Listens. Is there anything out there? He can't tell.

But he knows there's something out there, lots, farther out, and these that came close and set off the two trip flares were probers. There will be more probers, if there haven't already been. Who says there were only two? Maybe the frags killed or badly wounded all of them. Most likely some have gotten back. And they're telling now of the trip flares and of the C-wire, and the enemy is now changing their plans. They'll send more probers forward. With long tree branches to trigger the trip flares and to snag the concertina wire and tug it away hard, peeling it away, dragging it off down to the stream perhaps, as those American soldiers throw their grenades and shoot their rifles at the rattling pebbles in the empty ammo cans to no avail.

Ketchum feels a sudden presence beside him.

Redcloud.

Ketchum gets a sense of Redcloud's approval without words from him. Whispers to him, "Where there's one, Sarge, you know there's gonna be more."

Redcloud is surprised that out there is the dark form of the rock wall that he thinks he can make out. *The rain has done us good*, he thinks. *Wanna bet it's the captain lady's prayers*. He knows that if he can see the rock wall then these men up here will be able to see the dark shapes of the enemy as they come over the wall and try to cross the open ground to the building. He knows that the men on the veranda will see them even more clearly, closer.

"How many more hours til dawn," Ketchum says. Not asking, just stating a fact of the obvious.

He doesn't look at his watch, and neither does Redcloud.

"It's gonna feel like ten thousand minutes," Redcloud says.

Ticking by ever so slowly.

Second by second.

An eternity between seconds.

Redcloud goes to each firing position up here and spends a couple of minutes.

With Pvt Finkle he tells him that he did real good out there on the recon patrol. Way beyond his short time here in the Army. Shy of a year, and he did what most guys with twenty in wouldn't and can't do. The colonel himself said he was going to write Finkle up for a Bronze Star with a V.

The V's for valor.

Having the colonel on his side, Redcloud tells Finkle, that's a real plus. The colonel's known and well-respected in Ranger Regiment, can pull the strings to get Finkle when he makes Spec-4 into Ranger School, if that's what Finkle's gonna want.

Redcloud asks Spec Howie how he's doing and if this one day with the infantry here isn't full of more thrills than ten years sitting behind a desk in the rear. He tells Howie, "You just listen to Specialist Van Louse here, do what he says, keep your head screwed on straight, you'll be alright. We'll have you back to the PX and Burger King and the USO on Bagram 'fore you even know it."

Redcloud asks Van Louse if he's sure he's going to be comfortable on the M240 machinegun. Yep. And to watch it, make sure he's not going to get carried away and burn through a barrel. "You need a barrel swap, it starts to glow on you, Louie, you call me over." Roger.

With Jarbodie on the second 240 Redcloud doesn't say anything. Just crouches here, looking out with him.

After a minute, Jarbodie admits, "When those flares went off, I almost let loose here." On the machinegun. "In the air you just shoot. Everyone already knows you're there, they can hear you and see you, you don't got to worry about giving yourself away."

Another minute of silence between them.

Jarbodie, "Been one long day. Even longer for you, huh. 1300 we were supposed to be picking you up here. Now look at us. Both of us. Puts a whole new spin on that goose-and-gander thing."

Redcloud doesn't say anything for a bit. Then, "You-all didn't have to come. If I don't get a chance to tell you, it's because I don't know enough words to say it."

Silence between them.

Redcloud, senior professional NCO to slightly less senior equally professional NCO, "If you hadn't of come . . . We were about down to throwing rocks. Every one of my Zoosters . . . We all know it couldn't of been easy taking that chopper up."

"They'd've all done the same. You'd've done the same."

In this dark an imperceptible nod agreement from Redcloud, *perhaps so.* Then on second thought, a shake of his head *no.* "That's why there's regs against it."

Regs against it, Jarbodie thinks. *Rightly, yeh, regs against it,* and he would rather not be here, in this dark and this light rain and thick fog through which you can barely make out that wall out there, if it really is the wall, beyond which there are how many hundreds if not thousands of Taliban enemy waiting to storm up and overrun this place. He could be asleep warm and dry and safe in his room on Salerno right now. If Mister C'd just never said *"Who's in, who's with me?"* and the crew'd just never gotten on his helicopter this afternoon. Never took off breaking every kind of reg on a Red just to help these fellow soldiers out. *There's regs against it.* If they'd just never took off. But that isn't even a question, Jarbodie realizes, knowing with a calm sadness that he would get on his helicopter on a Red tomorrow or the next day or the day after and would always get on his chopper on a Red. With regs against it, and he can't really tell you why. He can't put that into words.

"Save the frags for the others," Redcloud tells him. "We're countin on you on this—" the machinegun. "Nothing sweeter than the sound of it singing steady 'n true."

Yeh. Nothing sweeter.

Just one more thing from Redcloud. "I'm going to be set up up here. You need a hand with a barrel swap, you just yell."

Dove is on the veranda, standing, looking out. It's reassuring that now with Nods you can at least kind of make out as far as the rock wall. *We've got a chance now,* he thinks. A hundred feet between here and there is a long way when you're running through the hail of bullets these men will put out. Running, tripping in those potholes from the sandbag digging.

Wolfe goes down between the sandbag walls on the steps to stand out a little, just enough to get a little closer sight and sound of the wall and beyond it.

Rodriquez is right behind him. Whispers, "They was gonna attack, shoulda came when couldn't nobody see shit."

Which is what Wolfe has thought. That maybe that had been the plan with that English crap about Soldiers of Allah going on the loudspeakers, and maybe his patrol had thrown them off when he'd surprised them at the recoilless. Maybe they couldn't figure where that other group of Americans came from and how many there were and were they attacking from the flank. Did the Americans come in by parachute in the dark? Or maybe the Jdam hit on the recoilless also took out their command leadership. They'd planned for a midnight full-out attack, first with that early prep with the recoilless they shot, and *The loudspeaker shit to demoralize us,* then more recoilless, maybe a couple dozen shells, then a couple of probes, then full attack 12 o'clock midnight straight up. They could have made it all the way to here without being seen. Now they're late. *Now we're gonna see em.*

Or maybe they're not late, they're on schedule. They're just waiting for more of their hajj brothers to get down those trails. They're waiting for another mortar tube. For a couple of lightweight shoulder-fired recoilless, the 90 millimeter. Attack'll be at first light, it's always at first light; that's one of the cardinal rules of the infantry, to be up and ready and psyched before first light. Stand-to before first light.

Dove is thinking that too.

He wonders if he has enough guns. 9 on the roof, plus the sniper and Sergeant Redcloud. The 2 Saws and the 2 big 240s up there are the real firepower.

11 on the veranda here, and that includes himself, Wolfe and Laura Cathay. And his Rto, Pfc Holloway. And, no way around it, he'll have to be a shooter too. And Dove may just have to talk to Nick Flowers and see if he's adverse to taking a weapon and taking sides. He might not have a choice. Life or death, he won't.

Dove doesn't have to pull out his little hardbound notebook to know the numbers in the two rooms back there. Don't count the two medics, their primary function is in that room. Sergeant Eberly is mobile, the other isn't. Eberly can respond to the calls for medic.

Dove knows the numbers in the rooms. 15 in those shiny black bags, including 3 ANA. Across the way 17 who he hopes won't need bags. 3 of those 17, ANA, including the sergeant.

Redcloud is in the aid station classroom. Just to check on things. A few words to the wounded men conscious. *Night's halfway through, not long til morning. Weather's clearing. You just hang in there. Choppers'll be here before you know it. Try and get some sleep. The men have your back. Upstairs and down, we got you covered.*

He crouches in front of Cpl Sandusky seated in the shadows in the corner staring into empty space at his hands in his lap, an unlit cigarette drooping in his lips.

"How you doin', Sandy?"

"Doc won't let me smoke, Sarge."

"You just do what Doc says. Can't smoke in here, Sandy, 'cause there's men here who can't hardly breathe. They need clean air, Sandy, you understand?"

Hesitant nod from Sandusky.

"You do what Doc says, okay? You just sit tight right here, okay? Just a few more hours til morning. A few more hours is all."

Redcloud goes over to Eberly and BZ.

Quietly he asks if there's anything he can get them, do they need anything?

"Morphine," BZ says. "If you've got a private stash someplace."

"You hurtin pretty bad?"

No, not for him. BZ indicates the wounded men.

Eberly holds up five fingers.

"Five hours?" Redcloud asks. "Enough for five more hours?"

Nope. "Dosages," Eberly tells him. "We'll be dry before morning. We won't have any for . . ."—new casualties, the men out there on the walls.

Redcloud asks BZ, "Rangers, Special Ops. Medics always carried those fent'yl lollipops," doesn't he have any?

BZ shows four fingers, that many left. Jokes, "Was figuring on holding them for my own personal use once the cavalry arrives."

Redcloud smiles, he assumes better.

BZ, serious, "Five liquid syrettes," for, he indicates, these wounded in here. Again, four fingers, "Lollipops. The conscious ones. Plop the pop in their mouth, watch the pain turn to smiles." A wide grin, "Lucky first four fresh conscious ones get the pops."

Redcloud shows crossed fingers, *let's hope no fresh ones, no more casualties.*

Eberly asks, "What's the word on Air clearing? Do they know our status, our manpower? By my count, there are 23 trigger-pullers left."

BZ, "You countin the Jag lawyer captain and Steven Spielberg out there?"

Yep, Eberly is. But not themselves, BZ and him.

From Redcloud, a finger to his lips, *now keep this quiet.* A whisper, "Brigade's got a Ranger company standing by. Aboard their choppers."

BZ, "No shit? Hot damn. I'll go out there, you give me two chemlights, I'll bring em in," moving both arms in the air like he's an airport guy directing a plane to the gate waving green-coned flashlight markers.

Eberly, "Right, if we had a wheelchair for you to roll you out in."

BZ, "I'll hop on this," his one good leg. "Hippidy-hop here comes BZ cottontail."

A hint of a smile from Redcloud, and again he puts a finger to his lips, *don't say anything,* don't get all the guys' hopes up. Not yet.

When Redcloud comes out of the aid station, he sees Holloway answering the radio, "Roger, wait one."

Holloway calls softly to outside between the ponchos covering the entrance, "Colonel Dove, sir. It's Colonel Pluma."

Fob Salerno, Ranger Compound

Floodlights turn it into day under the cloud ceiling no higher than 100 feet, illuminating the three CH-47 Chinooks, tails open, dim red lights on inside, enlisted crews there in each waiting.

A cluster of Rangers behind each helicopter. Sitting or lying propped back against their rucks on the pierced steel portable-runway mats that make this helicopter pad next to the fenced Ranger compound.

Soldiers doing what soldiers do when they're just waiting. Sleeping or trying to. Eating, bullshitting, reading. Rearranging their gear.

The compound is through the open double-gate of the 12-foot chain-link fence that, mesh-covered, you can't see through.

Inside over the fence the nearest building is a hardened brick-and-mortar B-hut for staging, where inside it's a scattering of old office chairs and a long counter-top plywood table in the center around which the command congregates, standing over maps and print-out imagery.

Ranger company commander Captain Haas and his first sergeant. All his platoon leaders and their platoon sergeants. His Rto and his company medic.

The pilots and copilots of the Chinooks also.

And the two reporters who Col Pluma brought along—the Reuters guy and the Getty photo-videographer. An unusual allowance embedding them with Special Ops, let alone letting them in here in the briefing, especially on such short notice, but Col Pluma has assured Capt Haas and his commanders that the journalists know that if they fail in their trust and present the Rangers in an prejudicially negative manner, neither they nor their organizations will ever again be granted a Spec Ops embed.

Standing at the head of the table is Colonel Dan Pluma.

Holding the radio handset near his ear. A small external speaker also cabled to the satellite radio and on the table for everyone to hear the conversation.

Just waiting these few moments for Dove's voice getting on the radio.

Dove will be the final word to put the plan into motion. Pluma has fulfilled the first three of the four stipulations that Gen St Claire had handwritten as bullets amending the authorization to suspend the Red Air.

In order:

— Fixed wing air evac to be forward staged at FOB Salerno;

—All Ranger & Aviation to be volunteers, without negative notation or repercussions for those who choose not to volunteer;

— COL Dan Pluma to infil on the first chalk;

That third one had struck Pluma, and still strikes him, as a particularly Doctor Hutchinsen devious inspiration. Probably Hutch's idea. There'd be no free ride for Pluma, he'd have to put his money where his mouth was, there'd be no sending in other men — the hundred-twenty-some Rangers plus the three flight crews — to do the dying or potential dying while Pluma would remain safe in the rear to bask in their glory should they succeed while suffering neither injury nor death in the battle, success or failure.

Pluma had figured it out long before getting on the Blackhawk chopper to fly to Bagram to meet the Air Force air evac. Hutchinsen had him nailed, could read him right down to the lines in the palms of his hands, to his very soul, and knew that Pluma would come up with an authorization around the Red to stick in front of the general, and he'd prepped the general, and it had probably taken him less than the blink of an eye to come up with that #3 stipulation.

Ouch! Let's just have a looksie what kind of balls Danny-boy's really got.

Make Danny-boy get on that first chopper flying into those mountains in that zero-visibility.

Into that boxed valley where recoilless rifles will be aimed straight at the chopper from level-on on the mountainsides.

Surprise, Danny, Talibs've got NVGs too!

Surprise, Danny, those big lumbering Chinooks 200 feet off the ground look like giant Macy's Thanksgiving Day Parade balloons through NVGs in a recoilless rifle gunsight!

Ride em cowboy, Danny-boy!

You're to infil on the first chalk!

Check your balls, Danny, go ahead, feel for them. How far up into you are they hiding all scrunched-up shivering?

Pluma can just see Hutchinsen's conviving brain a'click-click-clicking. Make Danny-boy, if the chopper's lucky enough to even get in there in one piece and land — make him dash out with the first Rangers right into the blazing guns of the how-many insurgents are still right now coming into that valley from Pakistan that, actually, unfortunately, poor sonova-bitch Danny-boy has no earthly idea about.

As for the last stipulation, the fourth bullet, Pluma is sure that it was General St Claire's own, that he would not have needed Hutch's inspiration to come up with it. It's called Natural Preservation. Something any four-star general has running through his blood. In his genes. And forged into a black obsidian diamond starting at West Point. It's something that Pluma has known about since he was a kid, talked about every Easter — the whole story about Pontius Pilate washing his hands.

Pete St Claire washing his hands.

Put the whole thing ultimately laid on newly-minted Lieutenant Colonel Zachary Dove.

Bullet #4:

—Contingent upon witnessed request for immediate Ranger QRF from the ground commander in Wajma Valley, LTC Z Dove.

The "witnessed" part specifically ordering that Col Pluma's word alone of Dove's request would not stand.

The request would have to be witnessed by these Ranger commanders and flight crew and the rest in here and anyone else who just happened to be listening in, by purpose or chance, on the Ranger sat channel. All total, enough of them that their stories would have to match in the investigation and criminal proceedings that would follow the disaster that even just losing one chopperful of men would be.

Enough to say as one voice, *Yes sir, we heard Lieutenant Colonel Dove formally request the QRF.*

"This is the Tattoo Zoo Platoon in Wajma," comes Dove's voice over the radio, plainly heard by all on the external speaker. "Dove here. Over."

"Zach, Dan Pluma here. How you holding out? Over."

"It could be worse. Over."

"Any change in the enemy situation?"

"We had some trip flares a little while ago. So we know they're out there still. Probers."

"I'm here with Mike Haas here. Mike and his leadership. And the three flight crews. Mike and his men are just waiting for word from you, Zach. Give us the word and we're right in there with you. Over."

"Is Air Green down there? Because it sure as heck isn't Green up here. Over."

"It's Green if you want it to be Green, Zach."

"It's pea soup up here. Ceiling's maybe thirty feet. Forward visibility, fifty, hundred feet max. With NVGs."

"CH-47s, Zach. Three. F-models. The pilots tell me they just about fly themselves. The pilots all assure me it's a doable. Flying on NVGs is second nature to them, they assure me."

Pluma knows that Dove knows the capacity of the F-Model and its terrain following radar that maps it for the pilots on their heads-up displays like it's high noon. They won't even need the NVGs, the F-Models do fly themselves. Just plug in the coordinate data and so-on and so-forth and let the computers take you there, hands- feet- and eyes-free.

"They assure me, Zach, that they can hover and descend straight down blind in zero-zero into an empty lot in midtown Manhatten. Between the skyscrapers. Midnight in the rain. Zero-zero."

Dove, "Two Talibs with one shoulder-fired M67 90-millimeter recoil-less rifle can bring down an F-Model same as a B- or C- or D-Model."

"They say it's well within the parameters of acceptable risk, Zach."

From Dove, "The flight crews say they're equipped with onboard counter-measures for the 90-millimeter?" Sarcasm; the F-Models all have hi-tech doodads to throw off heat-seeking surface-to-air missles, but there's nothing been invented to divert simple 90s or RPGs or 7.62.

Which Pluma knows as well. "I said, Zach," he's testy, "we're all well aware of the risks."

Passionless, businesslike from Dove, "I say again, the ceiling's max thirty feet. Ground-level visibility is a hundred feet max. It's been raining now too with the fog. How copy, over?"

Of the faces around this table, from Haas and his platoon leaders and platoon sergeants to all the pilots, none shows emotion. Flat. Serious. If anyone is scared, if anyone thinks the weather report from the lieutenant colonel on the ground there in the valley is far too dangerous to ignore, none shows it. Same with the lethal threat of recoilless rifles.

From Pluma, "We've got you, Zach, we hear you, we understand. The weather there is challenging, we read you. Possible enemy AA fire could be challenging. Roger, understood, over."

"Roger. Nothing further, over."

"We can be wheels-up in ten minutes. Another thirty to you. You just tell us you're under assault or that you feel that an attack is imminent. I say again, tell us an insurgent attack is imminent, and we're on our way. The big man needs to hear it from you, Zach. Request Quebec Romeo Foxtrot. Say the word, and we'll see you in forty minutes. I'll call you en route to give you our maneuver plan. Over."

From the radio, Dove's voice, "Wait one. Over."

Silence.

Everyone in here knows what that means.

Give me a minute. Be right back.

Wajma, in the schoolhouse, Dove lowers the handset.

Both Redcloud and Wolfe are standing close, and Dove's been holding the handset up in the middle of all their ears to hear.

Wolfe asks, "Who is he, what's he talking about? Three F-models, with what, who's this Mike Haas?"

Dove, "Ranger company."

"A whole company?"

Yes.

Wolfe, "Three big birds coming in here dropping off a whole company when you can't see shit, and flat in the middle of a what, a kandak of Taliban? A whole insurg battalion they won't see til they're shot down right on top of them?"

That sits. Lays there.

All three know it.

Redcloud tells Dove, "Sir, we don't have that many body bags."

Wolfe, with a grin, "Unless they bring their own bags."

Redcloud, "Then we'd still have to police up the pieces. No thank you."

"Oh yeh like we're going to be around to be policing up anyone's pieces."

Dove holds a stare on Wolfe, wanting a yes or no, request the QRF or not.

Wolfe, "We'd be fools to turn down the cav'ry riding in to the rescue. F-Models, they can use this weather to their advantage, the pilots don't need to see to come in, don't need to see to hover at three-feet. If the pilots can't see, neither can the bad guys."

From Dove, his look, so that's a yes?

Wolfe, "But they've got ears, and we know some of em's got our NVGs, and a monster Chinook from fifty feet away, it's pretty hard to miss with an RPG when you're standing in the downwash and aiming at the sound. I don't want to think what one guy carrying a recoilless"—on his shoulder— "could do."

Is that a no, then?

Wolfe, "Which brings to mind Desert One. Iran. 1980. Multiple airframes maneuvering in a tight space, that's an engraved invitation to ol' Mister Murphy. Hit one and you've got the domino effect."

Enough with the hedging. Simple, yes or no?

Wolfe, "Oh come on, I'm just a civilian HTT. And not even that, not much longer. You're the O-5, it's your position to make those big calls."

Still not a yes or no.

Wolfe, "What's it matter, it's not as if you're gonna do what I say because I say it anyway. Anyone would be a fool to turn down a company of hooah US Army Rangers. Ask PFC Grasshopper, he'll tell you I was born a fool and I'll die a fool."

Which means?

Blank neutrality from Wolfe, he can't decide.

Again, Dove insisting, which means?

Wolfe, just a bare shake of his head . . . *No.*

Redcloud too, his answer to Dove is just a slow *wish-it-wasn't-so* shake of his head, *No.*

Dove raises the handset. "Ranger Command QRF, this is the Tattoo Zoo, over."

Fob Salerno, in the staging B-hut, Col Pluma answers, "This is Dan, go ahead, Zach."

Dove over the radio, "We appreciate your offer, but tell Mike and his men and the air assets that if they can stand by we'll give you a call when the weather clears up here. At which time, when we're Green here, I would recommend extensive AH-64 gunship prep to clear out likely Alpha Alpha threat. Repeat, best to initiate with Apaches. Over."

Pluma gives the handset to Capt Haas. "Zachary, this is Mike. Congrats on the O-5, the colonel told us. Look, the company wants a shot at this, Zachary. Every man here's a volunteer. Give us the word, it's your call, we're at your disposal, what do you say? Over."

A moment of silence from the other end.

Then Dove's voice, "I checked with my platoon sergeant and he says that we don't have near enough body bags for your company, Mike. Leave it at that. Air is Red up here. We'll call you when it's Green. Out."

Col Pluma grabs the handset back from Haas. "Zachary Dove, this is Dan, you hear? Dan, over."

Dove's voice, "This is Tattoo Zoo. Dove, over."

Pluma, "Don't you goddamn 'Tattoo Zoo, Dove over'. Say again why you're refusing our reinforcement."

Dove, "Roger that, Colonel. Sorry for the misunderstanding. Over."

"Does that mean you're requesting our QRF, you're requesting reinforcement, that you're under threat of imminent attack?"

"Negative, sir. I say again, negative. We are not under attack. Over."

"Are you threatened with imminent attack? Answer that."

"Visibility status, one hundred feet. Negative verification of present enemy status. Neither personnel nor equipment. Over."

"Cut the bullshit! Are you about to be attacked?! Over!"

"Negative. Over."

"One more time, Zach. Do you request immediate Quebec Romeo Foxtrot? Over."

"Negative. No Quebec Romeo Foxtrot at this time. As I told Mike Haas, sir, my platoon sergeant has advised that we don't have enough body bags for Mike and his men. Nor, he informs me, do we have enough ponchos to wrap the body parts in when those F-models auger in. Over."

"I heard what you told Mike! You're on speaker here, Zach."

"Then you'll understand, sir, if you think back to your days as a lieutenant. A good platoon leader knows to listen to his experienced platoon sergeant. We'll call you again when Air is Green. Out."

The *Out* said as a final *No more talk, period*.

Pluma wants to yell. Wants to scream. Wants to throw the handset. Wants to demand of Dove that he say yes, that he request a QRF right now. Knows that every man in here is looking at him and that every one of them knows that Dove is correct.

Yes, Pluma knows that every man in here knows that there aren't enough body bags for them.

That no one carries that many body bags.

Enough for both them and the men of the Tattoo Zoo Platoon up there right now in that deadly valley.

Every man in here knows that the ranking officer on the ground up there has determined that it would be one or both of them zipped into those bags, no question about it, one or both.

And that he is choosing just the one, himself and his soldiers.

Giving all these men in this room and those men in those three chalks behind the helicopters a reprieve.

A reprieve.

Which is what everyone in this room feels. Because in spite of the terrible risks that everyone in this room knows come with their going into Wajma Valley right now tonight, there is not a man in this room who would not right this minute be going outside and hustling with the others out there onto those three choppers.

If the decision is theirs, these men are all wheels-up airborne in ten minutes.

It is Dove's. Has been Dove's.

Col Pluma wants aboard the lead chopper. Wants wheels-up. Wants tomorrow's glory of combat brilliantly executed and bravely survived.

Is relieved that the choice has been stripped from him.

Thinks that St Claire knew all along that Zachary Dove would say no to a suicidal QRF.

Slams both fists on the table and kicks a swivel chair away to crash into the wall!

St Claire knew all along.

But, Col Pluma reasons, St Claire wants that video footage the embed Nick Flowers has. He needs that footage. To make the Tattoo Zoo Platoon heroes. To counteract the 168 dead women and children, little girls.

Or not. Not heroes.

The dead bodies of the American soldiers of the Tattoo Zoo paraded in front of the al Jazeera cameras do just as well to counteract those 168.

General Pete St Claire: *Heads I win, tails you lose.*

Col Pluma again slams his fists on the table.

Sweeps his eyes across the faces around the table.

"Everyone outside," he says. "Tell your men to piss and shit and be ready. Get them in stick order right at the ramp. Reverse stick order. I don't want any hesitation 'Where's my place?', when the word comes in. I want radio checks with the platoon every fifteen minutes. The moment Zachary Dove requests a QRF, that very moment I want rotors turning. Understood?"

Subdued *Rogers* and quiet *Hooahs* around the table.

Wajma, in the schoolhouse, Dove, Redcloud and Wolfe are back seated on the floor against their rucks.

Silent. What's there to say?

Pfc Holloway couldn't hear Col Pluma's end of the radio conversation but has figured out what it was all about. That there was a Ranger company they were going to send up here and Lieutenant Colonel Dove here said no.

Sheeeeeeee-attttt!

A whole company of Rangers here with the Zoo, nothing could be sweeter to Holloway. *Tell em yes. Sheeee-at yes.* Sure, it wouldn't be easy flying into here in that fog out there, but they're pilots, that's what they do, what they're paid to do. That's what they're supposed to know how to do. And Holloway remembers that time that him, Brad and Cory were going up to Big Bear after that big snow up there, and Cory was going to show him how to 'board, and there was all that fog up at the top and it got so thick that Brad couldn't see and ran the car into the guardrail and right through it and they were hanging off, one wheel off, that when it all cleared up later you could see was just a straight drop-off a thousand feet down. That was a close one.

Wolfe quietly says to Holloway, "PFC, when they call again you tell them the colonel is already engaged elsewhere. Tell them he's out negotiating a truce with the bad guys in the black turbans."

Holloway, "What's that s'posed to mean? I'm s'posed to lie, for what?"

Wolfe to Dove, "Tell him, Colonel, turn off the radio. Or better, just don't answer it, PFC."

Holloway, "If I took orders from you. Yeh, aint happening in this life."

Redcloud, "What if I told you to, Holloway?"

"Why, Sarge? Turn off the radio, why? I don't get it, it don't make any sense, Sarge."

No one says anything.

Dove knows what Redcloud and Wolfe are saying.

Temptation.

He's aware that both Redcloud and Wolfe are watching him to discern his reaction to gauge whether or not he has the strength to resist the temptation.

He nods to Holloway, "You just keep monitoring." The radios.

Wolfe acknowledges to Dove, "You're a stronger man than me."

"Oh I doubt that, Mr Wolfe."

"No, really, give me the radio. If I could do your voice I'd be telling them, 'Ranger boys, come onnnnn downnnnn!'" Like *The Price is Right.*

Dove has Holloway pass to him the handset. He extends it out toward Wolfe.

Who declines. "I said, if I could do your voice."

Dove offers the handset to Redcloud.

Who declines. "I'd of made a lousy officer." Then changes his mind and takes the handset. Pretends to depress the push-to-talk button. "Ranger QRF Six, this is Zoo Seven. We've mutinied on the lieutenant colonel, so go ahead and mount up an' fire up your engines, we're waiting on you. Tell your medics to bring a boatload of morphine 'cause we're down to our last doses. And you'll be needin plenty for your own. Out here."

He tosses the handset to Holloway.

Dove asks him, "They're down to how much?"

From Redcloud, "A while ago," he holds up five fingers. "Unless they've used them."

Dove had not known that.

"I tell you, sir," Redcloud says quietly. "Don't tempt me." To call the Rangers up for real.

Fob Salerno, outside the fence, the floodlights are all off. The dim red lights inside the Chinooks are the only illumination. Just enough from those lights here in the dark and fog to see inside the back of a single helicopter at a time and the soldiers sitting on its ramp and those seated on the steel runway-planking against their rucks in two sticks from the ramp.

Rto Lachowicz, with Col Pluma and Capt Haas on the ramp of the first Chinook, keys his handset and calls, "Zoo Six Romeo, this is Ranger Six Romeo, radio check, over."

In the three cockpits the pilots can hear over their headphones Holloway's response, "This is Zoo Six Romeo. Lima Charlie, over."

And hear Lachowicz's, "Roger. Out."

On the ramp of the first Chinook, Col Pluma checks his watch. 03:15.

Wajma, on the schoolhouse roof, Ssgt Ketchum knows that it's probably been only ten minutes since, but he checks his watch anyway.

Quarter after three, and that's only seven minutes, not ten, since that racket of the pebbles in the empty ammo cans and then the trip flare going off, and he'd tossed one frag and knows his other throwers up here did too. Then when the racket of the pebbles continued, moving, he'd tossed another and told the others to too.

If only he could have seen out as far as the concertina wire he'd have known what they were doing. If he could see out that far now he'd know if it was even still there. Or did they drag it off?

He's down to sixteen frag grenades and figures that's about all anyone else has too. It'll have to do. He'd be down to none, they all would be, if that Chinook hadn't come this afternoon and resupplied them, that's for sure.

Down to none.

They were down to none after the second or was it the third assault.

They'd be in sorry shape.

In a world of hurt.

If they were even still here.

Would be here, yeh, but dead here.

Enemy woulda attacked again 'fore nightfall if they hadn't of got that Chinook resupply. Would of knowed they were down to shooting the en'my's own AKs. Down to a couple magazines each.

Wanna talk about a world of hurt. Put yer head between yer legs and kiss yer ass adios muchacho.

Quarter after three. Just three more hours. No, less'n that. Two and a half maybe 'fore first light.

Everything changes with light. Turn off the Nods and flip them up and really see. A new day starts with light. Even if this thick fog is still here, dude, it's light and you can at least see something. See.

Less'n two and a half hours.

Downstairs, Pfc Holloway has both handsets balanced on his shoulders against his ruck close to his ears. His head back on his ruck, his eyes closed because they're so so so very verrrrryyyy heavy. He wants nothing more right now than to slip off into sleep.

These radio checks every fifteen minutes are killing him. Just when you start to drift off, *Zoo Six Romeo, Zoo Six Romeo, radio check, over.*

It's a bitch being the rto.

Yeh, it's a bitch sometimes bein rto.

Be a whole lot worse up there, above here on the roof, like Sergeant Ketchum and Finkle and them guys. If it's still rainin, that's now gotta be a real bitch.

Poor suckas.

Who he wishes he could tell right now what he knows, that they had a company of Rangers coming here but the colonel and Sergeant Redcloud turned it down. He'd love to tell all the guys that, but if the colonel or sergeant wanted that out they'd tell the squad leaders, and they haven't, but when they make it out of here and back to the Cop and they've whipped those Talibans' asses, he'll tell the guys and everyone in Awesome Company that Sergeant Redcloud knew all along *We could do it without them bullshit Rangers cuz if for nuthin else the secret weapon we got, the Holloway Groove.*

Naw, not really. Not the Holloway Groove part, but he sure is gonna tell them-all about the colonel telling the Rangers to kiss off.

Lieut Col Dove checks his watch. 03:41.

He pulls out his hardbound pocket notebook.

Before he opens the notebook, he draws one of the pens from his pocket and clicks it down. Not that he's going to write anything. Just to look like he's writing, to pretend he's making a note of something. In case the others see. The pfc, his eyes are closed now, but he can open them at any moment for the radio. Sergeant Redcloud and Mr Wolfe, they both have their eyes closed too. Nick Flowers finished his DVD burning a while ago and is lying on his side on the floor asleep, as his relaxed snores tell.

Dove opens the notebook.

Stares at the snapshot of his wife acetated to the inside cover.

That's all he does.

Love you, honey.

Bethany Ann, I love you.

He regrets that he didn't think to fold into this notebook one of the snapshots he has back in his room of her and the children too. *Who'd have thought this little five-hour excursion into here would lead to this?* . . . .

He lays the tip of his finger on her face. Just to touch her.

Five hours in and out and you don't even know I'm here . . . .

He closes his eyes.

Please, Lord . . . Please make her strong, make them strong, make them not suffer, make them know that I love them, that I will always love them. Protect them, Lord. Shepherd them without me when I'm gone and not coming home.

He slowly folds the notebook closed on his finger still inside.

Wolfe's eyes are closed, his chin is resting on his hands cupped over the butt of his M4, but he isn't asleep. He doesn't know what the lieutenant colonel is doing, doesn't care, for it wasn't but just a few moments ago that he cracked his eyelids just enough to spy the captain. She's asleep, for sure asleep, with her head canted against the poncho liner bunched up as a pillow on her rucksack, and he has that image in his mind now, of her face . . . so . . . pretty. So young. Just a girl really. She should be somewhere, not here, somewhere else, *Somewhere fun and carefree and full of hope and the possibility of romance and stumbling into love,* tonight's Saturday night and she should be with her girlfriends, at a wedding shower for one of them, or a baby shower for herself, for her for her first baby, and her face radiating joy and the purity of the laughter of a three-year-old, and *She shouldn't be here, shouldn't have had to come to here, shouldn't be slumped back against a rucksack on a cold concrete floor wearing a dirty smelly uniform and body armor weighing her down, with her legs frozen with a bullet in her back. A bullet in her back, She'll never walk again, she won't dance at her wedding, maybe she won't be able to conceive or carry a baby all the way to term, if she can even feel to make love, to have slow tender whisk-me-away intoxicating sex with the man she loves, to have their baby,* she probably won't, ever, never, all only *Because she was sent to this nowhere nothing shitty fifth-world village because a former Marine named Kyle Wolfe killed two scumbag enemy soldiers dressed as civilians who deserved to die for setting Robyn afire in flames.* And also because, he allows, *These innocent soldiers of the Zoo returned fire into this building and didn't have even the slightest idea they were killing the women . . . . and girls . . . . in here.*

He cracks his eyelids again, just enough to watch her without being seen. To spy. *Sleep, pretty woman. Sleep, cute lady.* To lock into his memory this vision of her. *Sleep in peace, little girl. Find your peace, you will, because I know your God is going to bless you. Anyone here in this building, it's going be you first He blesses.*

He closes his eyelids.

Scrunches both tight. Draws in an inaudible sniffle. Raises one finger to press firmly against the corner of one eye, before a tear might certainly break free and slip down.

Like Wolfe, Redcloud has his eyes closed, and he almost appears asleep, he could be, but he's not, and he knows what Dove was doing, that Dove was secretly looking at a picture of his family.

If Dove had been more cautions, he would have remembered that Redcloud's blood runs Ranger red and Rangers can see everything even with their eyes shut, can see by hearing, can see by sensing motion, can see through their eyelids, and to fall asleep is to miss, and to miss is to err, and to err is to fail, and to fail is to harm the men you are responsible for.

Redcloud is not going to sleep. He cannot allow himself to. He's the platoon sergeant. These are his men here. Those on the walls still. Those back there with the docs. Those bodies back there in that other room that must still make it home to their families.

Sure, he's aware that Lieutenant Colonel Dove was talking to his family telling them he loves them through a photograph or two. He himself has snapshots of his wife Brenda and the boys in a pocket of his rucksack. In a zip-lock baggie. An embroidered hankie of Brenda's smelling of her perfume folded with the photos in there. He won't pull out the zip-lock and look at the photos until tomorrow whenever they get back on the Cop and all his men are taken care of and he's got a few minutes to himself. Sometime after he's personally packed up L-T Matt Caufield's belongings and made sure Ketch and Utah and Nell have done the same for their men dead and wounded.

Sometime tomorrow.

He figures.

Actually, today. It's long after midnight, today is tomorrow, technically.

That's when he'll think of Brenda and the boys.

He knows without thinking it that she knows he loves her more than anything.

He knows without thinking it that she knows that she is and always will be the only one woman and wife forever for him. He knows without thinking it that she knows everything about him, that he has no secrets from her, that she knows him for all his unassurednesses and self-doubts and knows that he believes he was lucky to have ever even met her and knows that he fell in love right off, even when she didn't, she didn't want a soldier, would not love a soldier, until she trusted to her core that he would love no other woman, as he could not even imagine there ever being someone so much as one to him as she is.

He knows that the boys will be fine without him, that Brenda has done well with them in all the time that he has been away, and that they'll manage without him also because they are well-behaved and disciplined and polite and caring and considerate today, and that they understand that their lives are theirs to make of them what they will, because the older ones have learned already that they and they alone are responsible for their behavior, good or bad, loving or hateful, with the consequences theirs to benefit or suffer from. And he feels confident that in his absence, if he never returns, that they will teach the younger ones who have so many years of growing-up still.

He knows for certain that if it is God's will he will be with Brenda and the boys when this deployment is over.

If it is God's will.

If it is God's will he will return to the Cop with all his soldiers who are alive now.

He knows that God has given him the physical and emotional strength to face and fight an enemy that wants to kill him.

He knows that God has given him skills and talent superior to theirs in the fight.

He knows that what is God's will is God's will but that God expects of him that he use his physical and emotional strength and his skills and talent as a force of good for these young soldiers who are under his care.

In Your name, Lord, I pray for them.

In Your everlasting love I pray that You give these men strength to overcome whatever happens now in these coming hours and that You show them, even those who do not believe in You or do not accept Your love... That You show them that Your compassion for them is without bounds, endless. Amen.

Day Three, Morning

In the Lead CH-47 Chinook In Flight

The copilot radios on the Zoo platoon freq to tell the platoon that the Ranger element is two minutes out, but there is no response.

These three Chinooks are in tight formation speeding up the gorge just under the cloud ceiling, about 700 feet above the ground. A good safe altitude compared with the rogue Chinook flying in here yesterday.

It's daylight, but still in the gray range, as it'll still be a while before the sun comes up hidden behind the high clouds that drape well below the ridges.

The copilot switches channels to call, "Apache One-Four, this is Charlie Hotel One. Do you have comms with the platoon? Over."

The reply comes, "This is Apache One-Four. Affirmative. Platoon is in the building. They can hear you Lima Charlie, and they asked us to relay that you can park your big black Bluebird school buses as close to the building as possible."

In Wajma, one AH-64 Apache gunship flies just under the cloud ceiling in a wide figure-eight over the compounds of the farthest terraced field.

It's the front-seat weapons officer on the radio, answering the Chinook copilot's question now as to the Apaches' status. "One-Eight is swinging in to execute his second run. Enter the valley on your approach at minimum five zero zero A-G-L and you're good. I repeat, minimum five zero zero Alpha Golf Lima."

The other Apache is at about 400 feet above the ground, banking over the stream at the school-end of this valley.

It's flying nose-down, and as its tail comes around facing the school it hovers over the rock wall that is now mostly a blasted, crumbled ruin. The gunship powers forward, swaying left and right, its belly-mounted 30mm

chain-gun pivoting independently with the weapons officer's eye movement and firing at the occasional black-clad figure scurrying in or out of
the shallow trenches dug the width of the beach from the stream to the
terrace wall—the first about a hundred feet from the rock wall, the last out
past the conex containers.

Each Apache made its initial run three minutes ago when they
arrived, then the first made a second run, expending all its ammo, 30mm
and rockets. Now this is this Apache's second run.

The chain-gun goes dry before the Apache reaches the far end by the
gap of the valley's entrance, and it fires its last few remaining rockets at
the fleeing enemy trying to get to cover up the sides of the mountain and
those seeking safety up across the fields.

The Apache now banks hard to head up to join its partner in a wide
looping figure-eight, just as the three CH-47s come in through the gap, so
close behind one another that their rotors seem to be overlapping.

Behind them are two more Apaches, and one now goes right, the
other left, they're the gunship support to replace the first two.

Thirty seconds behind them are two Blackhawks.

All part of Col Pluma's revised plan that struck him at about 0345
when he realized that Zachary Dove really was not going to request
support until weather cleared and the ceiling lifted and Air could be
declared Green. Pluma figured that if that were the case, with Air Green,
as Dove had suggested, it would be safe for Apache gunship prep of the
battlefield ahead of the Chinooks and continued gunship cover for the
actual Ranger assault.

Hell, Pluma ordered, let's get some medical personnel in there too—
doctors, a couple of nurses and trauma medics, all volunteers. That's
what's in the two trailing Blackhawks. And all the folded-up litters, med
supplies and portable oxygen bottles they could fit aboard before taking
off from the Salerno Cash.

On the school veranda, without even looking around outside, Dove
recognizes the deep-throated *wruump-wruump-wruump* as rotor blades of
Chinooks approaching.

"You hear that, Laura?" he tells Capt Cathay, whose eyes are glassy
and unfocused and trying not to be, as she holds her bloody hand up
against the patch of skin left of his cheek on the side of his face that is
singed red and oozing bubbles of blood.

"That's our medevac, Laura, they're here," Dove tells her. "You just
hang on, it's just going to be a couple of minutes, a couple of minutes,
that's all. Hear them?"

He's cinched a tourniquet up high on her left arm that two AK rounds
mashed through, and another at her knee on her left leg that a few more

pulverized. He grabs a roll of gauze dressing now from Slurpee to wrap her arm to try and keep it all together. He knows she was shot up by the one Talib here who he himself put two 3-round bursts into as the Talib was already splayed back against the sandbags shooting at Cathay even after she'd just hit him with a burst as he'd come up from the steps.

He tries to get it all straightened in his mind and thinks that that was soon after the RPGs and the recoilless shells and doesn't know which it was, the rockets or shells, or both, that was the explosion that wounded him too.

And which was it that got Mr Wolfe?

Maybe it was the same one, had to be a recoilless round since it was so big, or two rockets together, since it must have first wounded Wolfe over there and then him too, even knocking his legs out from under him and putting him to the concrete, he knowing even as he was going down that he was losing it, and he had, he'd lost it, for how long?, was it ten seconds? Fifteen? Twenty? A minute?

And his first vision coming back to consciousness was of Wolfe, or what was left of him.

Mr Wolfe. Just a blurry image of peeled flesh and bared bones and muscles and tendons for legs, just one arm whole, the other showing nothing but torn dangling muscle and a jagged bone.

Dove had then watched Wolfe throw himself over against the wall to be able to reach that clacker, and then Wolfe's look right into his own eyes, that crazy bright delightful smile he had for that moment, and time seemed to warp down to a near-stop at that very instant, as Cathay was firing into the Talib appearing between the sandbag walls on the steps, slamming the Talib back against the sandbags as he was firing back at her, and Dove then was firing two bursts into the guy's henna-streaked beard, and then trying to refocus on Mr Wolfe over there clawing up to see above the tattered sandbags on the wall, and a moment, two moments later, Wolfe was squeezing the clacker, and the concussion of that explosion bounced Dove, and he knows that he lost it again, for maybe longer than twenty seconds, remembering now distinctly seeing Pfc Holloway's boots as he was thrown limp down near them.

He can remember then first hearing again, he could hear, and still hear gunshots, and he remembers that he forced himself to his knees, willing himself to reject the pain screaming from both legs as a hindrance, and forced himself to his feet, supporting himself on the wall, and he had realized that his M4 was still in his hand, and he faced out then and had to squint and search to find two black-clothed figures coming over the rubble of the wall out there, and he fired at them and they didn't go down, and he kept firing and they did, and he slapped in a new magazine, and he could then hear a machinegun firing above from the roof, and a couple of M4s too, and he watched the few more enemy

Talibs reaching the rock rubble go down, then there were no more Talibs charging forward to aim at and shoot.

It was then that he had thought that he heard some voice from his radio handset saying something about *Tattoo Zoo, this is Apache One-Four, we've got your location in sight, hi ho Silver,* and an answering voice in his handset, *Roger, welcome to the fuckin party,* and he'd known that the answering voice it couldn't be Sergeant Redcloud because of the cursing, and had known that it couldn't be Mr Wolfe because that was impossible, and had known that it couldn't be Utah because he was covered in jagged blocks of concrete and brick, and had known that it couldn't be Nell because Uath had yelled to him just after an earlier assault that Ketchum'd radioed from upstairs that Nell was down, and maybe it was Ketchum on the roof, it had to then be Ketchum on the roof, he was still alive.

Then he'd thought that was the sharp clipped sound of Apache rotor blades nearing, and his eyes slowly focused out farther to see the two gunships that looked like mosquitoes coming fast, and then the lead one was swooping in a hover bank just above out front, then its chain-gun blazed, and that's when Dove knew that he could let his M4 hang and turn his back and see if he could save the bloodied body of Captain Laura Cathay.

"Hang on," he tells her now five minutes later. And to Slurpee he has to yell to be heard over the sound of so many helicopters coming in and setting down, telling Slurpee to stay with her, to make sure they know that *She's got a spinal injury also!*

And he stands, getting his balance on the wall, and he forces himself to move his wounded legs to step forward to go down out there where the first Blackhawk is just setting down on this side of the crumbled rock wall, rotors seeming to be spinning below those of the center and closest CH-47 Chinook of the three that have set down in a V on the far side of the wall, tails facing this way, Rangers streaming off.

On the top of the ramp of that closest Chinook, Colonel Pluma hesitates. He can't believe the horrible wreckage of the school building beyond the blurring rotors of the two Blackhawks where the crew chiefs are tossing out the folded litters to the Cash medical staff trying to find footing among the litter of enemy bodies on the cratered ground.

Smoke billows out from the stream-side of the building where that quarter of the veranda is all collapsed. It's hardly better up the other side, mostly collapsed. The walls are crushed hollowed concrete, with jagged brick showing and in places bucket-sized holes all the way through. The entire veranda roof looks like it's going to come crashing down. Most of the parapet is crumbled or missing. *Jesus Christ,* Pluma thinks, *how did anyone survive?* Did anyone survive?

A soldier, a wiry little guy, has leapt up atop a solid part of the parapet up there and is holding his weapon up above his head in both hands, thrusting it back and forth rapidly in a primeval scream of triumph, and he maintains his balance up there even as the first Blackhawk jumps up to ascend out, its rotor-wash hurricaning back against the building and him.

Pluma knows his own plan. Both Blackhawks will circle with the Apaches—air-cover for the Rangers of the other two Chinooks who should right now be pushing out and establishing a perimeter, killing any enemy still a threat, ignoring the wounded ones, leaving them be, to live or die on their own, they don't exist this morning, there's no time nor empathy for them nor cameras to record evidence for tomorrow's global condemnation and eventual court-martial convictions for this deliberate criminal breach of the laws of war.

Pluma's directives to Captain Mike Haas following that midnight briefing, privately, away from the ears of the two tag-along reporters, had been point-blank regarding the Taliban insurgents: See No Wounded, Hear No Wounded, Speak No Wounded.

And Pluma had then had a chuckle to himself, as he thought that it was Doctor Gene Hutchinsen's flippant sarcasm he remembered from sometime yesterday that he borrowed then, telling Haas, "Let the Taliban break their own Air Protocol regs and fly their own medevac choppers in to get their own goddamn wounded." Haas expressed doubt whether they could trust the two tag-alongs not to film the enemy wounded, and Pluma right then scratched them from the manifest, they were no longer welcome, Mister Reuters and Mister Getty, sorry, fellas, change in plans, security issues, appreciate your flexibility; they could get themselves back over to the C-130 air evac and hang out with the medical personnel there, perhaps get an interview, do a soft-news feature with the *Lovely nurse Major Victoria Marshall who thinks her shit don't stink*.

These Rangers from Pluma's central Chinook here are already securing this immediate close perimeter and are to assist the medical personnel in getting the most-seriously wounded onto this Chinook as quickly as possible for its flight back to Salerno. The Blackhawks will be backup medevac for those with less life-threatening injuries.

The second Blackhawk lifts off, straight up, and Pluma can now see a civilian-dressed man with a camera, who he assumes is Nick Flowers, filming the Cash docs and medics trying to hurry between the mosaic of grotesquely sprawled black-clad bodies and limbs that litter the upturned ground from that rubble of rocks all the way to the building. A tall soldier behind Nick Flowers, right at the foot of the concrete steps, is saying something forcibly, motioning the doctors who zero-in on him to *Get away from me, go up there inside, take care of the wounded inside*, and goddamn if that isn't Zachary Dove. His uniform is more blood red than any color.

Blood red and dust gray/dirt brown filthy. *What happened to his legs?,* with his pants mostly shiny-crimson strips of cloth.

And Pluma sees that Nick Flowers is now aiming his camera out this way, seemingly right on Pluma himself, and sees that Dove takes a step forward and slaps a hand onto Flowers' shoulder to grip for support.

With neither envy nor venom Pluma thinks, *Another son of a bitch Purple Heart for Zachary Dove,* recognizing reality and nothing more.

Nick Flowers brings to mind General St Claire, about whom Pluma thinks, *At least he's going to get his precious hero film,* with nothing but a feeling of venom.

He grabs Rto Sgt Lachowicz to pull him near to yell to be heard over the whining-down of the engines and rotors right above. "Set up and get me the general on his bird in-flight!"

The attack had come after six-thirty, but everyone was up and on the walls by 0500. Dove knew that first light would be around 0530 or so. That's the very first indication of a lightening, just barely, the almost imperceptible beginning of a new day.

It would be an hour or more until the sun would rise, and above those ridgelines even later, and with all this weather and clouds you probably wouldn't even see the sun. But it would be light. Starting to lighten at 0530, 0540 at the latest.

The rain had stopped a while before. Even then the fog appeared a lot thinner, which meant the ceiling was rising. With Nods you could see out beyond the rock wall, and no one could see the concertina wire. Which was a bad sign. It should have been there. Was it farther out, beyond visibility? Or had the enemy dragged it off?

Dumb question. It sure didn't move or walk off on its own.

That's sort of a play on it that Slurpee had thought. That the bad guys dragged off the C-wire, folded it back up and carted it off, cuz that's all they really wanted, those long rolls of concertina, and they themselves have diddy-bopped off, happy as clams with another freebie from the Americans.

Yeh, not likely.

When Slurpee had whispered that to his buddy Pvt Leonard, Leonard had said, "Hooah, let's call the choppers and get our butts out of Dodge," but knew all along even saying it, *That aint happening.*

Dove had thought that the insurgents might have decided to attack even before first light, that could have been entirely possible. Maybe 0515. They knew where the school is, they could rush forward and count on the dark for concealment. Except, they would know that the Americans had Nods and could see them way before vice versa.

No, most likely they'd wait for light.

Regardless, Dove and Redcloud had everyone in place early. Get ready, get psyched emotionally, relaxed, get comfortable, make sure all your frags and magazines and ammo cans and extra weapons are right there beside you at hand.

Everyone on the walls.

That meant Redcloud and Sniper Rodriquez on the roof where they'd be the ones to fire off the ten remaining Laws that came in the resupply.

The Light Anti-Tank Weapon.

Remember? U.S. version of the RPG. Except, one-shot, throw-away.

Ten aint a lot, but you gotta take what you got.

Redcloud and Rodriquez on the roof would use the Laws on RPG gunners behind the conexes or in the mosque and on any concentration of men charging out to 300 meters.

Down below, Holloway would be back outside out on the veranda with the radios, beside Dove. A rifleman primarily in an assault, rto secondary, this time around with so few defenders left.

Rodriquez had already carefully moved Capt Cathay to her position against the doorway facing the steps.

Wolfe was in his position beside the pillar on the other side of the steps from Dove.

Nick Flowers could do what he wanted, Dove had told him, but if worse came to worst he should be prepared to grab up a weapon that one of the men drops. "I'll play it by ear," Nick had said.

Doc Eberly and BZ were in the aid classroom. Their plan was for Eberly to bring any of the seriously wounded back in for BZ to tend to. Worst case scenario, if they were going to be overrun, Eberly would take up a weapon in the doorway above Capt Cathay, making it two guns getting any enemy coming up the steps between the sandbag walls. BZ had an M4 as a very last line of defense for the wounded in the classroom.

Cpl Sandusky was lying in the fetal position in the farthest corner.

No one cared about him.

No one even thought about him.

All lights inside had been extinguished, and Redcloud had had a couple of Nell's guys rip down all the ponchos and poncho liners covering the windows and the entrance.

When the 100% alert was started at 0500, Wolfe and Ssgt Utah went out to check on the claymores on the other side of the rock wall. After the enemy had pulled away the C-wire and it was still too dark and rainy and foggy to see the wall, a couple of the enemy could have covered themselves in mud and slithered up and cut the claymores' electrical wires and the daisy-chaining det cord. Or they could have even taken up the mines and set them on the other side of the wall, facing the school, in which case, when the Zoosters would set them off, the shredding force of about eight hundred ball bearings in each would be coming right back at them, lethally greeting them, *Good morning to you, infidel suckers.*

Nope, the claymores hadn't been tampered with.

Just exactly as Wolfe and Utah had implanted them, all 36, in six daisy-chained series of six. Each tightly tucked between the dead Talibs' legs in their crotches.

Now all everyone had to do was just wait. And watch.

And listen.

Redcloud on the roof had one working Talib walkie-talkie.

Dove on the veranda another.

Both were silent.

They had been silent for hours.

Still were by 0600 when it was light enough to see out as far as the mosque.

In that 0600 radio check from the Rangers, Dove reported that everything was quiet, dead, you couldn't see a soul out there and the cloud ceiling looked to be about two hundred feet, and *Cross your fingers it keeps burning off,* but it could just as easily come closing in again any minute. *Be advised,* he'd ventured, *you might want everyone in place on the birds, if the ceiling keeps rising fast like it is.*

At the 0615 radio check the Talibs still hadn't come up on the walkie-talkies and Dove reported that ground visibility was now out to a little beyond the mosque and there were no enemy in sight. Plus, the ceiling was now maybe three hundred feet.

Dove didn't tell them that Redcloud had passed down to him on the platoon Mbitr radio that from the higher advantage of the roof they could make out that the rows of shadowed low berms of mud appeared to be the front edges of trenches about every fifty feet out as far as you could see. Even with binos Redcloud couldn't see behind the berms into the trenches. Couldn't see any movement at all. He said that it looked like moles or gophers had burrowed perfect straight-line stripes along the width of the beach.

"That's easy enough," Wolfe joked over the radio to everybody with an Mbitr. "Call Bill Murray from *Caddyshack.* He'll put C4 in all of them and blow the shit outta everything."

"Gonna need 'bout ten Bill Murrays," Ketchum corrected him from his vantage point on the roof.

"Good luck with that," said Utah.

"What's he gonna do?" said Nell. "Shape the C4 into gophers like in the flick, or into Talibans?"

Ketchum said, "Stick the blasting caps in their turbines."

"Com'on, enough, men," from Redcloud. "Keep the channel clear."

Which ended it.

No more playful radio banter.

Just peer out and watch and listen.

Nothing moving out there, there wasn't a human being.

Some of the Zoosters started thinking that maybe the bad guys had picked up and left.

Even Wolfe, who called softly across to Dove, "The better part of valor?"

Dove mouthed back, "In sh'allah."

Exactly. One could hope.

At the 0630 radio check Dove had Holloway report that the status was the same, no enemy in sight, and visibility was about five hundred meters, the same, just out past the mosque, and the ceiling maybe four hundred feet.

Just so there'd be no misunderstanding thinking Dove was saying it was safe to come in, he took the handset from Holloway to advise the Rangers directly that if they took flight now they *"Might fly through the weather on instruments, piece of cake, but all indications point to a well-dug-in enemy force, and as soon as you drop out of the ceiling you'll be big slow-moving targets for rockets shooting straight up right under your bellies. Not to mention, recoilless rounds from the village compounds and/or the hillsides."*

And everything remained perfectly still and quiet.

Dove's watch showed 06:37 when across both his walkie-talkie and Redcloud's upstairs on the roof was barked a two-word command, *Allahu Akbar*, and three RPG launchers plopped up onto the berm along the length of the first trench, with three turbaned heads immediately up and aiming and firing, then back down, launchers down too, and three in the second trench popped up the same and fired just as the first trench's RPGs exploded.

On the roof, Jarbodie and Van Louse on the 240s and the two Saw gunners opened up on the first trench too late, and were thrown off aim and blinded by the explosions of the first three rocket grenades then the second three and couldn't even see the three enemy that popped up from the third trench and fired their RPGs.

Which was just enough time for the three in the first trench to slide another rocket into their launchers and pop up again and fire.

And the three in the second to do the same.

Likewise for the three in the third trench.

Of the eighteen initial rockets fired, half were high, hitting the school building or the mountainside above it. Five were short, exploding or burying themselves in the mud ahead of the rock wall. Four hit the rock wall, the target of all eighteen.

The Talib thinking was simple. It's one thing for a jihadist to go collect his half-gross of virgins in heaven, but he's supposed to do it while taking out infidels, as many as possible, and charging into three dozen claymore mines planted there at the rock wall would be futile suicide that accomplishes nothing and leaves the enthusiastic jihadist without any notches on his rope belt.

The Talibs would have preferred to have stolen the claymores, or turned them around facing right into their dead buddies and the rock wall, or faced them into the mud or cut their wires during the night, but their efforts had failed, and the slithering warriors they had sent forward had been killed or wounded or chased back by the Zoosters' frag grenades. Next, as backup they'd have blasted the wall with the 120mm mortar tube brought down during the night, except, they hadn't carried down any rounds and all the already in-place rounds had been destroyed earlier by the Americans' big bombs. Backup to the backup, their third option was that initial RPG barrage, to blast the rock wall with rockets and hope to render the claymores useless covered in rocks facing straight into the mud or into the sky, or better yet, set them off with the RPG explosions.

For a little added insurance to that backup, they included a fourth option, to have a PKM machinegun pop up out of the first trench and rake the wall with a belt of nothing but tracer bullets to set off one or more claymores with their flaming slap, then the resulting daisy-chain setting-off of the others through the instantaneous explosion of the det cord links.

Whether it was the rocket-propelled grenades or the tracer bullets, it worked.

There was a multiple-blast of claymores going off that was so loud and the concussion so great that the Zoosters in the school were knocked off their feet or bounced, as were the Talibs in the first two trenches. And the cloud of smoke and debris was a thick opaque curtain between the trenches and the school for almost two minutes.

About one minute into which the Talibs launched their first human-wave assault.

With two separate shoulder-launched recoilless shells fired blindly from the area around the conexes and Talib warriors rising up unseen through the smoke out of the trenches.

As chance would have it, at the firing of the first three rocket-propelled grenades aimed for the rock wall, Dove had grabbed the radio handset from Pfc Holloway and he had it pressed tight to his ear calling *"Ranger element, this is Zoo Six"*, and was thus not knocked temporarily deaf in that ear when the claymores went off, and just moments after those tremendous explosions he was able to hear the response, *"Come in Zoo Platoon, come in Zoo Platoon"*.

He told them, "Sit-Rep update. Weather remains adverse. Enemy Alpha Alpha threat likely. We are under attack." He didn't wait for a response or *Roger* and did not request a QRF but simply repeated, "Ceiling and visibility limited. Massed enemy attacking. Out."

Dove dropped the handset and motioned Holloway to ignore it and take up a position to shoot, and he would have no further outside radio comms with anyone until thirty-eight minutes later when he'd thought he'd heard on the earpiece over his platoon Mbitr radio net some voice calling all broken-up in staccato *"Tattoo Zoo Platoon, Tattoo Zoo Platoon, come in Tattoo Zoo Platoon"*, which he'd thought sounded like it was coming from a helicopter, but everything was exploding all around him and later he would not be able to remember whether that was before he went down unconscious on the concrete the first time or after that second time with Mr Wolfe's massive blast, and anyway, none of that mattered then, because that wouldn't be for another 38 minutes, that initial helicopter radio call, if there'd even been one.

After another 38 minutes of battle.

After the start of that first assault and the six assaults that followed.

As chance would have it—luck for the Zoosters—the wind aloft was blowing into the mountainside above the school and caroming off and pushing the explosive claymore smoke cloud out away from the school and rock wall toward the trenches.

As chance would have it, those first two hastily shot-off recoilless shells were wide of the school and exploded on the mountainside.

Because of those simple elements of chance the Zooster defenders' vision was not obscured by blinding smoke sweeping toward them nor were their nerves shattered by two direct-hit recoilless shells, and, as they'd recovered in the moments following the terror and disorientation of the RPGs and claymores exploding, they were able to see the leading wave of enemy coming through the smoke out just beyond the rock wall.

As chance would have it, only five of the six daisy-chained claymore groups were exploded by the four RPGs and the PKM fire that hit the rock wall, so when Wolfe and Utah each pressed their three clackers in hopes that some of the claymores remained, one of them, and they would never know who, set off the last set of six in place the length of the wall, devastating in a hail of shredded black clothing and limbs the first human wave about to reach the wall.

As the attackers' plan would have it, their advance called for them to leapfrog from trench to trench, and as the battlefield quieted and grew still, with the cloud of smoke drifting out over the middle trenches, there were moments which seemed like minutes to the Zoosters on the walls who wanted to believe they'd won, they'd driven the enemy off, until the sets of three RPG gunners in each of the first three trenches in turn rose up and fired, as they had prior to the first human wave assault.

This time with the intent, even firing recklessly and hastily, of aiming not at the rock wall but higher, beyond it, at the big gray concrete structure that was the school building and its handful of infidel defenders on the roof and the veranda.

At Fob Salerno, on the lowered ramp of the Chinook where all the Rangers were seated aboard, as they were on the other two, there had been no randomness of chance in Col Pluma's immediate reaction to hearing Dove over the radio saying they were under attack.

He'd circled his arm above his head, the universal symbol for the crew chief here and the other two on the ramps of the other Chinooks to *Crank her up!*

He hadn't allowed himself even a moment to hesitate and think it all the way through rationally, knowing that Air wasn't Green down here and sure wasn't up there in Wajma. It might be Amber here in ten minutes, they were saying, and Amber up there in maybe thirty minutes or maybe an hour, but it was still Red.

His *Crank her up* order given, Pluma would take his chances.

That's right, there were American GIs out there being assaulted and about to be overrun, *Screw my star they'll take away from me*, if General St Claire was making him God for this one moment, *Not that if it even matters that dead I won't even know that I didn't get my star.*

At least an hour earlier, in private conversations with the Chinook pilots here and over the radio with the pilots of the Apaches and Blackhawks across the Fob on their concrete pads, he'd told them that if at any moment any one of them felt that during the flight it was too risky, that the danger to themselves and their pax was unacceptable, they were to abort the mission, singly or together, no questions asked. Further, he demanded that the lead Apache pilots, who would arrive in the valley five minutes before the Chinooks, understood that if they determined that it was too dangerous due to the weather conditions there or due to the overwhelming enemy force on the ground, they themselves had the authority to call off the forces following, to order them to abort, to turn around and head back to Salerno.

At 06:40 on Col Pluma's watch the Chinook's engines whined fiercely starting up.

Thirty-eight minutes later, give or take, in flight, up front standing right behind the pilots of the lead Chinook, headphones on the entire time to hear all the radio traffic, Col Pluma would hear the Apache pilots report that the ceiling in the valley was *"Six-hundred-thirty feet, ground visibility unlimited, enemy resistance nonexistent."*

He would hear from the Apaches, *"We're just gonna mop her up for you. Just to be on the safe side."*

In Wajma, during the thirty-five-plus minutes of concentrated, systematic attacks, the Taliban came in six more assault waves following that first.

Each assault was preceded by a couple of minutes of complete silence, calm and stillness out there beyond the rock wall, then by a single command over the walkie-talkies, *Allahu Akbar*, then an RPG barrage. Rockets launched from all the trenches, two or three in each, even those out as far as the conexes. By the final attack the Zoosters had managed to whittle the RPG launches to just four, from the more distant trenches.

Each assault was also preceded by two shoulder-launch 90mm recoilless rifles fired from around the conexes, *karuup karuup* immediately after the last RPGs would explode. Not much more than the muzzle of each 90 would appear from the corner of a conex, fire then disappear. To appear before the next assault from around a different conex. Near impossible for Jarbodie on one M240 and Van Louse on the other to get them. Same with Redcloud and Rodriquez on the Laws they would fire toward where the muzzle of the recoilless appeared and shot and they would hope that the Laws' detonations on the conexes would kill the gunners hiding behind them. It didn't matter that most of the recoilless and RPG rockets missed the school long or short or wide, they were meant to terrorize and distract the Zoosters, to get them to keep their heads down and to send up an explosive cloud curtain to conceal the following human wave assault.

The counter-plan that Dove, Redcloud and Wolfe had worked out well before dawn was two-part simple.

Part One: The men on the veranda were to use their M4 carbines primarily and most importantly on any enemy who got this side of the rock wall. Secondly, frag hand grenades and M4s out just beyond the wall.

Part Two: The men on the roof with the Saws were to reach out beyond the wall, into what Dove and Redcloud had assumed would be the shallow foxholes of yesterday afternoon's battle. Same with Pvt Finkle and Ssgt Nell on their M203 grenades launchers—get the enemy at a distance. Jarbodie's and Van Louse's M240 machineguns were to go for the distant targets, primarily the more lethal ones, the RPGs and recoilless rifles. As with Redcloud and Rodriquez, with their limited number of Laws that they would end up depleting by the third assault, targeting the ones out there with the RPGs and recoilless 90s.

With each successive pre-assault barrage and then the human wave assault itself it became simply a matter of who would run out of men first.

The twenty-odd Zoosters on the walls?

Or the four-hundred-plus Talibs?

Through six barrages and assaults, on the roof both Saw gunners had been taken out, neutralized wounded, and Ketchum was then behind the only still-functioning Saw.

At the end of the second and the fourth assaults Redcloud helped Van Louse change out the red-hot 240 barrel, and Jarbodie changed his out at the end of the second, then burned his palms through his gloves changing it out after the third, dropping and losing the hot barrel over the parapet, and it didn't matter much anyway, because in the next assault the feedtray cover and the feedtray of his 240 were wrecked with a stream of enemy PKM bullets that also severed his hand at the wrist and tore through his elbow, and he immediately tourniquetted his arm above the elbow, shuddered to get the image out his mind that if he looked again he'd see that he had only shredded flesh and blood and bone where his hand should be, and he tried to make sense of the deformed steel of the 240's feedtray and tried to find the belt of ammo that was supposed to go there, and knew he wasn't thinking straight, and Redcloud swept the 240 machinegun off the parapet and slapped an M4 into Jarbodie's good hand, and Jarbodie tried to control it but was clumsy and unsteady lying it on the parapet, all wrong left-handed, but still he thought he could acquire a target and pull the trigger, until a bullet tore into that left shoulder and sent him onto his back on the concrete roof.

On the fifth assault Nell was wounded, out of the fight, and Redcloud had fired off Nell's last 203 40mm grenades at the enemy coming out of the second and third trenches.

By that sixth assault, Finkle was out of 40mm grenades and was now solely a rifleman.

Van Louse was on the platoon's 240, the only one left, with Howie beside him firing methodically his M4, and Van Louse would be wounded on that sixth assault, Rodriquez taking over the 240, and Howie doing what he'd seen others doing earlier—including Van Louse saving Jarbodie's life by stopping the bleeding only minutes earlier between one of the assaults—giving Van Louse first aid, a tourniquet and bandages, gotta stop the bleeding, can't let Louie die.

Nick Flowers was on the roof. He'd run up from downstairs between the third and fourth assaults. He wanted to film the guys up there, needed especially to get Redcloud in action. Plus, he wanted a bird's-eye view of the human-wave assaults. He'd wound up at first less filming and more aiding, assisting Van Louse with bandaging Jarbodie and helping Finkle carry Saw gunner Lantrell in a running hurry downstairs.

He still hadn't taken up a gun, and in the pause after the sixth assault Redcloud asked him if he needed any remedial training on the M4. *Nah,* he chuckled. *Just put it on burst, aim down at the turbaned fellows coming across the wall down there and keep on pulling the trigger.*

Not counting Nick, it made six guns on the roof for the coming assault.

On the veranda it wasn't really any better. Down on the right side looking out were Dove, Holloway and Utah. The other side, Wolfe, Pvt Leonard and Slurpee. Capt Cathay remained seated at the edge of the doorway, and so far she'd had the opportunity to fire just once, and that happened during the sixth assault when she put two 3-round bursts into the Talib who made it between the sandbags up the steps.

She would have to do it again during the upcoming seventh assault.

Inside, BZ put an IV into Jarbodie. Worked on Lantrell. Stop the bleeding, clear the airways, go to the next one, what's his name?, doesn't matter, Garcia, you say your name's Garcia?, okay all right you're gonna be alright, and an IV into him, get those blood expanders filling him up, hell yeh it hurts, hurts like hell, here suck on this lollipop, last lollipop, shit!

He knew that Doc Eberly himself had at least two wounded and maybe even three right outside the classroom who he was trying to save, and BZ was scooting himself toward the door to go out there to help when the final barrage began, with RPGs hitting out there on the veranda and a recoilless shell coming through a window and bursting on the other side of the aid classroom wall, exploding it inward, showering and pelting with concrete and brick BZ and the wounded.

On this seventh barrage the recoilless and the RPG gunners were either getting better with practice or just more lucky.

For one, the recoilless shell flew clear through the window and exploded inside. Two, the other exploded on the archway down above Utah, collapsing that section of the building on him, crushing him, and up above on the roof Ketchum had to scramble up the concrete slabs falling underneath him, and he was yanked up to his feet to safety by Finkle.

Just moments later two rocket-propelled grenades exploded in the veranda up the other way, and they're the ones that wounded Pvt Leonard, lacerated Dove's legs with shrapnel and ran a 52-inch lawn mower up and down Wolfe's arm and leg.

Add to that the two RPGs that exploded on the mountainside just above the roof, crashing rock down, disrupting everyone up there except for Rodriquez, who, at the first sight and sound of the two recoilless rifles popping out from behind the conexes and firing, had opened up with the 240 on them then instinctively moved the gun down to shoot where even through the explosive clouds of the 90mm recoilless shells and RPGs then going off he knew was the first trench, raking it, giving a precious twenty-five seconds time for the guys up here and whoever might be alive down on the veranda a chance to recover and get back up on their guns, pinning in that trench the next Talib human wave that he could not see but knew was there . . . . until his belt ran out.

In the twenty-six seconds it took Rodriquez to find among the empty open ammo cans one with a belt and to load that belt, the Talibs had risen up out of the first two trenches and charged. At least fifty in the first trench, half as many in the second.

In those twenty-six seconds most from the first trench had already crossed the rubble of the rock wall, all firing their AKs.

With almost no resistance from the Zoosters.

From the veranda just a lone shooter popped away on semi with his M4 resting on the sandbags, his eyes as big as saucers, looking through a slit between the bags at the black-clad enemy coming at him. Pfc Holloway.

On the roof Redcloud fired his M4 blindly aimed down at where he imagined the rock rubble to be, spraying on burst, trying to blink out of his eyes all the concrete dust painfully pinching him blind.

Ketchum had lost the Saw in the collapse of his section of roof and in all the strewn rubble around him couldn't find his M4, desperate for any discarded M4, he couldn't see one, none within reach.

Finkle fired his M4, raising himself on his elbows on the parapet to see straight below better and was thrown back onto his butt with an AK round right smack in the sternum of his body armor.

Spec Howie had Van Louse under him against the parapet, just the muzzle of his M4 atop the wall, his helmeted head exposed enough for one eye to try and steady an aim at those vicious enemy wild men charging, one at a time, *clack*, steady on another, *clack*, faster than he'd ever done anything in his life before just a few minutes ago blurring through treating his friend Louie who he's shielding with his body now, as he rapidly snaps the trigger *clack . . . clack . . . clack.*

By the twenty-sixth ticked-off second when Rodriquez had slapped the feedtray cover shut and was about to pull the trigger, he could see that down there straight below the leading Talibs were not more than ten feet from reaching the steps, and over their deafening AK fire Rodriquez would never hear Wolfe's yell from down there, *"Fire in the hole!"*, but Rodriquez would hear the explosion of the twelve-claymore Maginot Line that he and Wolfe had set up and be thrown back off his gun by its huge concussion.

Just before Pfc Holloway dimly heard a scream *Fire in the hole!* from whomever he didn't know who, he had slipped a new magazine into his M4, flicked the selector to burst and held his breath in fear at what in even his limited vision through the slit between the sandbags showed so many black-clothed forms and ugly screaming bearded faces and turbaned heads of the charging Talibs so very close, just three strides away, and there was the massive boom of the claymores going off and he'd later imagine that he saw for an instant those chests and beards and faces and turbans exploding into a multi-colored mist before he was lifted and thrown hard against the building wall by the concussive force.

On the roof, when the machinegun had gone silent, Nick Flowers had swung his camera to frame Rodriquez going through the cans of ammo in a rush, and he kept himself on his belly, hidden as much as possible behind what was left of the parapet wall, and in a few seconds came the *clack-clacking* of AKs firing, and it became a crescendo, and he knew that there was an enemy charge coming and willed himself to raise this camera over the wall and to pop his head up far enough to see the viewscreen to aim, capturing the wild horde of Taliban coming over the rock rubble below, closer and closer in an insane victory rush, when suddenly everything went up in a massive explosion down there, and he knew as he was bounced back and onto his side on the roof that that had been the Maginot Line that Wolfe had joked about setting up with the extra case of claymores.

Yeh, the Maginot Line, Wolfe's last line of defense, twelve claymores planted in the mud at the base of the building, strung along it, daisy-chained, their concave backs right against the concrete, their bases in the mud, the convex fronts aimed up at about a 30-degree angle.

Four things happened within the few hundredths of a second after Wolfe screamed his *Fire in the hole!*

Two AK bullets hit him center-of-chest in his civilian body armor, weakening the structural integrity of the ceramic plate.

A third bullet went straight on through the plate and mush-roomed into his chest where it severed the aorta where it comes out of the heart.

He pressed the claymore clacker he held.

An AK bullet hit him on an upward trajectory in the left temple and tore off an Egg McMuffin-sized chunk of his skull and brain.

Wolfe had sensed the certainty of total disaster for the first time in his life when he'd felt the rush of air of the recoilless round sailing by and through the window and at near the same time the two RPGs exploding on the wall near him, and he'd felt a thousand degrees of burning from flesh and muscle and bone shredded that was so overwhelmingly excessive that his brain could not process it and he was aware that he was feeling no pain in a physical numbness as he was shoved flying toward the concrete floor and he had for one unrealistic moment of wistful thinking the knowledge that he'd yet to have been wounded in all these years of combat, just like Wyatt Earp never being scratched in all his gunfights on the frontier, and Wolfe was also yet still unscratched, but no he wasn't Wyatt Earp after all, he was wounded, his lucky streak of invincibility was over, and he felt an instant of peace, the enticement to collapse into a guiltless release of no further need for action because it's all over, nothing else matters, that he could close his eyes and accept this final turn of fate and not care as he was flying and smacking the concrete, except, he could not close his eyes, would not, could not command them to close, even as his mind realistically and truthfully processed the optic signals that showed his right arm just a nub from which hung muscle and bone from the shoulder spurting blood, and he realized that the claymore clacker that had been in that hand was no longer there, gone along with the hand and arm, and he envisioned that the enemy would then swarm up and overrun this entire school and this Tattoo Zoo and kill and desecrate these Americans his comrades, and he knew that he had to find that clacker and had to set off his Maginot Line and hope that it was still intact where he and that sniper Rodriquez had set the twelve claymores slathered in mud right below tight against the base of the building, which is why Wolfe scanned the floor and saw the clacker and pushed himself over to reach it, then caught Dove's eyes locked onto his, and grinned right back at Dove, imagining himself saying *Fuck these hajj assholes and the horses they rode in on*, then he pulled and pushed himself up because he knew that he would have to see the charge of the hajj enemy to be able to time the explosion of his Maginot Line at exactly the right moment to blow them away.

Which is why he was chest-high above the single layer of punctured sandbags remaining on the wall, seeing for a brief moment the wild charging Talibs so close, almost here, about to reach here, then yelling a primal caveman scream of *"Fire in the hole!"* while consciously willing his left hand to squeeze the clacker.

At that very instant he would feel three hard punches to his chest then nothing more.

Nothing more.

He would never know anything more.

Not the past, not the present, not the future.

Wolfe was no more.

Not even to be able to recognize that that was the exact way that he would have chosen to go.

If he had had time to choose.

Which perhaps in those moments clawing at the floor to reach the clacker, grinning at Dove, pushing himself up to his one leg, watching the coming enemy, squeezing the clacker, he had done.

And knowing exactly at that last instant the very last thought that he would ever have was his sensing in utter certitude that his choice was faultlessly correct, unquestionably moral, what God Himself would do.

Then knowing nothing more.

Ever.

Inside the building, when BZ recovered his senses after the recoilless shell had hit just on the other side of the wall, he heard the machinegun above blasting for a few seconds then quit.

In the relative silence that followed, he thought that he would have to go out to the big room because the explosion would have been there and that's where Eberly and some wounded would be and would need him.

He grabbed his aid ruck to drag along with him, but hearing the rise of so many AKs then firing on auto outside out front, he was overcome with helplessness, a hesitancy, weakness, from the sudden debilitating terror, sheer fear, natural fear, of what he visualized as a swarming assault coming up the steps right then, and he wished to flee, oh how he longed to flee, but knew that there was no place to run and he had only one leg to run on, and he let go of his aid ruck, discarded it, picked up his borrowed M4 instead, and in spite of the pain he swung his splinted leg out the doorway then propped himself in the jamb, facing out enough to observe the front entrance, expecting at that moment to see those swarming hordes entering with their AK rifles blazing muzzle-fire.

The flash of Wolfe's Maginot Line going off temporarily blinded BZ and shook the walls and jerked the M4 out of his hands and knocked his head back against the jamb. When he gained his senses again, all he heard was one single M4 firing selectively *clack . . . clack . . . clack . . .* out on the veranda, and from the roof he heard the *spppppt . . . spppppt . . .* of the lone machinegun interspersed with the dim *clack . . . clack . . . clacks . . .* of three distinct M4s firing up there. He heard no enemy AKs firing. He blinked his eyes clear and saw no enemy Talibs storming through the entrance.

He figured it was over. Just one gun firing out front, a machinegun and a couple of gunners on the roof, meaning only three or four were alive enough to fight, and when the Taliban would be charging again in a minute or two it would be the end.

He picked up the M4, pulled it tight to his shoulder, sighted through the Acog, magnifying his view of the entrance doorway.

He heard no more firing out front.

No more machinegun above.

Just a single M4 up there plinking *clack . . .* and *clack . . .* then *clack* again and a couple more times.

In his Acog he saw a figure go to his knees in the doorway, and it was the lieutenant colonel tending to the captain lady with a bullet in her low back. He wondered why the colonel would be bothering to waste his time, that he should be on his gun, for the last stand, as he himself would be, as he was right then, and as he'd be taking out as many of the enemy who would be coming through that door until he ran out of bullets in these other six magazines in the bandolier he'd dragged with him when he'd come out here.

A hand on his shoulder jarred BZ out of his thoughts.

Redcloud. Asking, "Where's Doc? Send him upstairs if he can." Then lightly pushing downward the muzzle of BZ's M4, telling him, "It's over. They're running. Choppers just radioed. They're three mikes out."

Then a crescendo deafening everything, the scream of an Apache approaching, then its guns firing.

And Redcloud found Doc Eberly over where the three men he had been treating were, and they had all been showered with the shrapnel from the recoilless round. Eberly was alive, seated slumped against the wall. And conscious. Having chosen to work unencumbered, protected within the concrete walls, he hadn't worn his body armor since yesterday afternoon, and, facing away from the point of impact, he had been chopped from mid-belly and down, his arms scorched.

BZ joined Redcloud to help him rip off what was left of Eberly's shirt and help him push Eberly's intestines back into his belly and tie the shirt over it all to keep it as one.

Eberly unable to move but watching it all.

And BZ folded over Eberly's arms that were charred from the elbows down to rest on the knot of the shirt.

"No morphine," Eberly managed to say in a breath.

With compassion, "No. We're all out," BZ told him.

"No morphine," Eberly repeated with no more than a whisper. "Write it."

And BZ knew what he meant.

In the wee of the night, just a few hours ago, in the stillness and quiet of the aid classroom, they'd spoken of it. He and Eberly. Of pain and getting wounded. Of how much pain a man could endure. Would it be better to go out all drugged up and feeling nothing and not even knowing who you were? Or, skip the morphine, no morphine—ride with it, the agony, ride the bucking bronco, *Feel the intensity,* Eberly had said, and *Be totally alive at that last moment so that you can see for yourself and be conscious yourself whether or not there is anything beyond.* And if there wasn't, *Poof, it's over, gone, there'll be no pain anyway, there'll be nothing, just like before you were born.* And if there was, if there's a beyond, *I want to be conscious, I want to be me, to see it, to see that instant transformation into the afterlife. Into heaven,* he'd said. *Or hell,* BZ had corrected him with a chuckle.

Naw, Eberly had rejected that. *Heaven,* he simply said, because he knew there was nothing evil in him that would warrant hell. Flawed and deficient, yes, and pocked and speckled with all the petty envies and little sins of man, of living day-to-day, but not evil. *I want to be one-hundred percent alert,* he'd told BZ. *I want to watch what's coming.* He said he wanted to catch a passing glimpse of *Truth and Beauty. The absolute infinite perfection of the endlessness of pi stretching out forever. To the twelve trillion digits a computer has counted it down to.* He said that he wanted to see *The Higgs field. To see the particles in the Higgs field, the subatomic boson, the God Particle. To watch electrons and quarks and to slow them down to the gait of a horse trotting a racetrack. To watch them like racecars circling in slow motion a Nascar track. With each Higgs particle no bigger than a pebble on the track, and to see them separately in the blackness they swim in, like watching the sky on a cloudless, moonless night out in the desert. And to see between the stars, between the pebbles that are the Higgs boson, inside that empty black space between them and to discern the blips of shiny dots that are particles that are even smaller. And give them a name. The Eberly boson. The ocean in which the Higgs boson swim.*

And BZ had chuckled. *You sound like a poet,* he'd said.

And Eberly had said nothing more, and was kind of surprised at himself that he'd spoken his imagination so freely. He thought that he must have sounded too intellectual, condescending, and had barely caught himself in time, on the verge of rhapsodizing like it was 3a.m. in the dorm room with a couple friends playing around in a game of mental gymnastics to break down pi, which everyone knows never ends, that when multiplying the diameter by pi, whether one digit or three or nine or twelve trillion, you can never get an exactly true circumference, the ends of the circle's arc never meet, can't meet, if only leaving an infinitesimal gap between them, a gap on the atomic level, the space between the atom's nucleus and its electron, which *You take a frag grenade set on the concrete floor here, it's the nucleus, and the electron is going to be one single claymore ballbearing—one ballbearing—out 4,000 meters away, twice the length of this valley.* One hundred times the distance anyone can even throw a grenade. All empty space, the Higgs boson, *Which we can't see and even know if it's there. Knock on wood this valley is right now as empty.*

Which Eberly didn't say aloud and was relieved then that he'd shut up. Who was *This Green Beret medic BZ to care about pi? Who cares? Who should care? The ends never meet, they can't, period, and who can see into the atom anyway? Nobody, and nobody's ever going to, not that small, so small that it takes a million atoms stacked one-atop-each-other in just the thickness—the micron thinness—of that discarded litter plastic field dressing wrapper.*

And again he'd repeated, just *No morphine* he'd said to BZ then in the wee just a few hours before.

In the quiet in there immediately after the battle was over, Redcloud was punching an IV into wounded Pvt Leonard, and BZ wiped clean Eberly's chest.

He took out his Sharpie.

In block letters he wrote, **MORPH: 40MG.**

And an approximation of the time, **07:20L.**

It would inform the medics and docs at the Cash that Eberly had already been administered twice the max.

BZ had granted Eberly his wish.

Wajma, the Final Hour

The clouds are high, about even with the ridgelines now and washed out bright white by the sun that's crested the ridge behind them.

The center, lead Chinook left thirty minutes ago, just twenty minutes after landing. On board were the litter-borne wounded as well as the Salerno Cash staff who had come on the Blackhawks. The two Blackhawks had then landed and taken aboard the walking wounded, including BZ, who insisted on being the last of the wounded to leave and only was able to walk to the chopper with the help of a Ranger under each arm.

Cpl Sandusky went on the second Blackhawk.

Shepherding Sandusky out to the helicopter, Redcloud had felt some pity for him. Sandusky's arms were limp, his head was down, his eyes afraid and staring at his boots. Redcloud knew that Ssgt Ketchum would tonight pack up all of Sandusky's gear and personal belongings, just as the surviving men would do for the other Zoosters dead or wounded bad enough that they wouldn't be coming back.

A realistic, cynical part of Redcloud thought that he could imagine Sandusky down the line in a month or six months or a year talking big and loud, boasting about his heroic exploits in that war in Afghanistan, in particular these days in Wajma, to family and friends and mostly to loser dudes in any dive beer-joint, anywhere, everywhere.

In spite of that, Redcloud felt a sadness for Sandusky, who will always know himself as a failure, and will be one, as a coward. And Redcloud as quickly snuffed out that sadness, conscious of those so many other soldiers here who fought despite their fears and have been wounded for real physically, most with injuries that will always effect them and change their lives, make their everyday living that much more challenging, and that much more challenging for their families and kids and wives and future wives and kids. Sadness for Sandusky? No, not when there are those still inside there who were as terrified but still stayed on the walls and are silent now in the black bags, and

Redcloud gave Sandusky a hand up into the Blackhawk and turned away and would be content to never have another thought of him, bad or good or indifferent.

As for wounded Lieut Col Dove, Colonel Plum and the colonel trauma surgeon had argued with him to get him to board the Blackhawks, and he'd simply refused. The medics had cut away most of both of his pantlegs and had wrapped both legs from thigh to ankle in white gauze dressings that now are showing large blots of seaped-through blood. *Look,* Dove told them, *I can walk just fine.* And, regardless, the Zoosters were his responsibility and he would not leave this valley before his men.

Rangers are carrying into the Chinook nearest the stream the last of the gear of the dead and wounded Zoosters, including their weapons and rucksacks.

Inside the Chinook, Sniper Rodriquez and Spec Howie are stacking it all to be securely strapped down for the flight. Along with the soldiers' gear are a few boxes that remain of the resupply.

Rodriquez knows that among the body armor of the dead and wounded are also those of the Zoosters left here. Including his and Dove's. Everyone's but Redcloud's. *"No use being burdened with the extra weight,"* Dove had told Redcloud. *"Have them shed them if they want to."*

Helmets too. Everyone knows that every GI in the bush has always got stuffed down in his ruck a favorite civilian ballcap for just in case there's a chance to shuck the helmet and wear it. Dove dug out his, Bethany Ann's alma mater, Liberty University.

Redcloud has kept on his body armor and helmet for no other reason than that's just what he does working outside the wire, what's normal for him, Army regs and all. He wouldn't feel right otherwise.

Rodriquez waves the Rangers in who carry the three body bags of the dead ANA, and the crew chief has them set them along with the gear, to be strapped down with it all.

"Don't you go gettin no loco ideas, Chubby," Rodriquez tells Spec Howie. "Yer respon'ble for all this shit. You let one thing go missin, it's gonna be comin outta yer pay, and I don't think yer gonna wanna be knowin what a M4 costs and you don't wanna even dream 'bout what it's gonna cost ya if you lose some Nods here I know yer gonna wanna put into yer ruck and carry off. You get to Valley Forge, the only dude you let neven get close to this shit, that's Firs' Sardent Kozak, y'got that, 'mano? Top Kozak. Hooah, Chubby?"

"Why, where are you guys going to be? You're not coming too?"

"Cur'nel's got other plans."

Howie is scared to be separated. "You're not coming back to Cop Valley Forge?"

"You don't worry 'bout us or the cur'nel. You worry 'bout not letting nobody, ya'hear me?, not nobody, you don't let nobody touch nuthin til you get Firs' Sardent Kozak in here sayin he's takin charge of it. That be all you gotta be 'memberin up here"—in his noggin.

Howie is even more scared. "Is Colonel Dove going to go back to Bagram without me?"

"Cur'nel says you gotta wait for him at the Cop. You aint never leaving Valley Forge, Chubby. Yer in the Zoo now. Gonna give you the tattoo. Yer a Zooster, 'mano." Rodriquez laughs at Howie's even more frightened apprehension at that. "Aw chico, that be somethun you gotta be proud of. Don't wanna be a Zooster?" And he gets serious and tells him, "You done good up there. Done good." He means it. "You done buen buen buen good, Spec'list."

Rodriquez hears someone outside yelling *"Sergeant Rodriquez!"* Finkle's voice. *"Sergeant Rodriquez, it's time, it's goin down!"*

And he tells Spec Howie one more time, "Ya'sure now you can han'le all this? Zoo's countin on you."

A nod from Howie, and Rodriquez gives him a grin and an index finger laid for a moment on Howie's cheek, sort of an anointment, then turns and runs off and down the ramp to join what's left of the Zoo.

Colonel Pluma knows that this isn't his place to interfere any more than being the very first in the rank, standing right at the foot of the steps, where he is the first to render a salute. That position is appropriate and fitting simply by being the ranking officer here in the valley.

He'd done his active part, his duty, hours earlier in the middle of the night when he made certain that the Rangers were bringing with them two cases each, body bags and American flags.

It's deadly silent here now. Not a peep from anyone. All work has stopped. Even those other two Ranger platoons on patrol spread out down the beach and up in the terraced fields are frozen in place, they've all taken a knee, notified by radio minutes earlier, *Everyone, hold it up where you are. Fallen Comrade.*

The Rangers had cleared a wide path of the enemy dead from the steps all the way to the Chinook sitting on the high edge of the beach just this side of Chiarduchi's and Jarbodie's crashed Chinook.

Now from the base of the steps, starting with Col Pluma and Ranger commander Captain Haas, Rangers here line the path, facing inward in two ranks.

Farther out, the Zoosters are in a single rank from the rubble of the rock wall to the Chinook's ramp that is raised level waist-high.

Pvt Finkle.

Pfc Holloway.

Sgt Slurpee.

Sgt Rodriquez.

Ssgt Ketchum.

And at the ramp, Redcloud and Dove.

From the school two Rangers come down the steps, one on each end of the body bag they carry. An American flag drapes the body bag.

Col Pluma and Capt Haas snap and hold a salute, and the Rangers in the ranks do the same as the body passes.

Same with the Zoosters.

And the bearers set the body on the ramp then sprint back for the school where a second set of bearers exit with the next body.

At the ramp, Redcloud quickly lifts the flag and unzips the bag just enough to confirm for Dove the identity against what Dove has previously entered in his hardbound little notebook.

This first body is "Staff Sergeant Jacob Utah" Redcloud tells Dove low. And he zips up the bag, folds back down the flag, and Dove and he render a salute and hold it as the flight crew lift and carry the body into the cargo hold.

The process is repeated over and over, with the two sets of Ranger bearers maintaining a proper interval between bodies. They could be the Old Guard at Arlington.

Nick films it from different angles, moving and stationary.

It's one body after the next.

Those of the platoon we don't know by name.

And:

Rto Akin.

Door Gunner Rapley.

Chief Warrant Pilot Mister Chiarduchi.

Spec Lee Tran.

Pvt Bybee.

Lieut Matt Caufield.

And Capt Jashawn Washington, for whom Dove motions Redcloud to pause, not zip it up yet. Washington's face is frozen in that last moment of life yesterday not even twenty-four hours ago. Eyes open, staring, but empty, without movement, lifeless. Almost as if Dove feels he can reach in there with his words and Jashawn will hear him, but knows different. Knows that he himself will get back stateside, his wounded legs be damned, maybe as early as tomorrow night, two days at most, this war can go on fine without him, and he will have Bethany Ann and the kids join him for the burial which he hopes Gwendolyn will insist is West Point, the cemetery there. And Dove will find some quiet moments in private with Gwendolyn when he will tell her Jashawn's last words, and tell her that Jashawn gave his life not fighting a Taliban enemy, nor a War on Terror, and not defending a president, nor the Constitution, nor the United States—but defending the men of his company, the men under his command.

Dove will tell Gwendolyn that her husband died where he did not have to be, had been ordered not to be, protecting his men.

Three simple words:

Protecting his men.

No higher calling.

No prouder honor.

Redcloud zips up the bag, and he and Dove each snap a salute and hold it as the air crew carry the body inside.

The quiet is now broken by three Blackhawk helicopters coming in above the gap downstream, and Col Pluma knows it's Gen St Claire and his media entourage.

They had departed Kabul sometime after 0630, about the time the attack here began, and with at least one stop to refuel it's a long flight.

Pluma was hoping this ceremony would be finished before they arrived, and he'll deal with the recriminations for having allowed it rather than having postponed it so that the general could lead it and luxuriate in the glory with all those cameras of his media there aboard who would be centering their coverage on him, as if he were the focal point of this Fallen Comrade.

Pluma quickly tells Capt Haas to get the three Blackhawks to land out there as far away as possible, *Now!*

Which Haas does, breaking rank and moving away to give orders over the radio for his lieutenant platoon leader out there with his men on the beach to get on the horn with the choppers and bring them in way out there beyond the conexes and the farthest-most trenches.

Dove and Redcloud don't pay any attention to the helicopters' noisy intrusion, care nothing about their arrival, ignore it, and Redcloud pulls the flag halfway off the final body. Unzips the bag.

It's Wolfe.

Again a motion from Dove for Redcloud to give it a moment longer.

Wolfe has his now-tattered Sig Sauer ballcap on his head—someone must have found it among the litter and rubble and placed it there— probably Redcloud, maybe Sergeant Rodriquez—and pulled it down low on his forehead to conceal where Wolfe's skull is missing.

Someone, probably that same someone, cleaned Wolfe's face with water, wiped away the blood and dirt, giving his appearance a purity and making his open eyes stand out, alive, aggressive, in that final triumphant yell *Fire in the hole!*

Dove knows that he and Redcloud and these few Zoosters standing here and all the wounded who have been flown out, they would all be dead if it hadn't been for Mr Wolfe's last line of defense that he'd had the audacity to call the Maginot Line and it actually held and worked in spite of the name. *Rewrite the history books, Mr Wolfe.*

Dove would wish *Godspeed* to Wolfe but instinctively assumes that heaven would never be Kyle Wolfe's destination and he would never be at-home comfortable up there even if he were to manage to sneak in or con his way in.

Dove thinks that he should regret Wolfe's death but knows that if not here and now it would be next year somewhere in-country here working off-line in black ops six-times removed from the U.S. Government, due to the hard evidence video of him wasting those two Talibs right here just . . . what? . . . hardly two days ago.

If not here and now, Wolfe would have been off-line killed in two or three years in northern Africa somewhere, maybe Sudan or Somalia or Mali or Kenya. He would never have put himself safe in a comfy stateside job instructing tactics and weapons on a military base or on a personal protection detail for some corporate CEO or Hollywood mega-celebrity or hip-hop mogul. There are some men, and very few in this modern era, Dove thinks, whose nature is war and who embrace rather than reject that nature, and Wolfe is, or was, one of them. Such is today's instant media culture, Kyle Wolfe will be remembered for those two assassinations which will havetens of millions of views on YouTube, if they don't already, but, Dove wonders, who will be the Homer to tell the world of his carrying that wounded Afghan NCO through the gunfire and fog and rain and mud? Who will be the Virgil to tell the world of his Maginot Line? Who will be the Kipling to tell us of a man who with an arm and leg threshered to shreds pulled himself up to be able to see the charging horde to best time that Maginot Line?

Dove silently whispers *Godspeed, Mr Wolfe*, and he brings his hand up precise and rigid in a salute that he holds as Redcloud now zips the bag tight and re-lays the flag then he too holds a granite salute.

And two of the flight crew lift the bag and bring it up aboard.

A motion from Redcloud, and the Zoosters hustle over to their rucksacks and weapons and quickly saddle up.

Redcloud sees out there far that the more anxious few media are hurrying here, and he raises his binos to make out farther away that it is Gen St Claire coming, striding like a conquering king, with other media flanking him. Redcloud knows that Dove wants to get moving and keep moving, and he motions Rodriquez, *Lead out!*

Single-file, two strides spacing between them, it's:

Rodriquez

Slurpee

Finkle

Ketchum

Holloway

and last, Redcloud at Dove's elbow.

Redcloud notes that every stride of Dove's is shortened and stiff and jerky, difficult and painful because of his wounded legs. He calls ahead, "Rodriquez! Lighten it up a bit!"

Redcloud knows what's up, what exactly is to happen.

He had been beside Dove after the two Blackhawks with the walking wounded had departed and Col Pluma had then told Dove what was on the agenda. Namely, the coming arrival of Gen St Claire and the media. The general would meet the platoon there in front of the school, a salute and handshake for each one of them, the platoon's soldiers. There'd be a walk-through, with Zachary detailing for the general and the media the heroic stand of the greatly outnumbered platoon.

Pluma had not mentioned that earlier immediately upon landing when he'd talked to the general's chopper when it was about 75 minutes out still, St Claire's captain aide had specified that the general did not want the wounded and dead to be exfilled before he and the media arrived. Pluma hadn't had to be told the why. As for the wounded, Pluma ignored that order, allowed them to be evaced, because there are some things for which you have to draw the line, and delaying the departure of wounded is one, even for a man like Pluma, very much conscious that his first star that awaits him just two months away can always be axed.

No matter, he would tell the general that the trauma surgeon colonel had been adamant that some of the severely wounded would die with more delay, no further explanation necessary, as General St Claire would not have to be reminded about the Medical Corps' disregard for rank or protocol—four-star general or SecDef or senator or president be damned, they have no say when a soldier's life is in jeopardy.

With the wounded then gone, Pluma had told Dove of the general's clear instructions via his captain and that he, Pluma, would take the hit on the wounded, but the dead would be held here until the general arrived to spearhead the Fallen Comrade ceremony.

No wiggle-room, Pluma emphasized. The captain aide had made it clear: General St Claire would spearhead the Fallen Comrade.

Had Dove already left on the medevac Blackhawk, there wouldn't have been a question, but Dove drew his own line and told Pluma harshly, "I'm not having General St Claire's media vultures photographing our dead."

"You will do as the general and I say you will," Pluma told him. Further, Pluma said, these few survivors and General St Claire and the media would all return to Cop Valley Forge so that the media could get a look at the platoon's everyday home in this desolate land, as well as to be introduced to the first sergeant and his heroic Quick Reaction Force from yesterday. The men could get shaved, showered, in clean uniforms, then it would be up to Bagram then Kabul for the Zoo survivors, where a heroes' welcoming ceremony awaited in both locations.

Dove had remained silent for a few moments, had said nothing, then he turned to Capt Haas and asked, "Mike, can you have your men hurry it up in there, I want to get the bodies aboard asap."

"You didn't hear me, Zach?" Pluma said.

"Perfectly," Dove said, and again asked Capt Haas to have his men ready the bodies now, and

Capt Haas was caught in the middle, where he'd have liked to do what Dove asked and had do what Pluma ordered, and

Redcloud would have just turned away and gone inside and gotten with the Ranger first sergeant, a friend from long ago in his own days in the batt, and gotten him to get the men hustling the bodies out and aboard, forget the formality of a Fallen Comrade, no matter how much Colonel Pluma would have protested.

He didn't have to.

Because Dove faced Pluma and said quietly and simply, "Colonel, sir, these men did not die for a photo op for a four-star general. Nor for a lieutenant colonel with two days in rank." Himself.

And Pluma said nothing. Didn't say no, didn't say yes. Nothing. Then, quietly, he made it clear, "That chopper does not leave until the general arrives." And he stepped away, toward the rock wall, heading for the Chinook as if that was the business he had, to tell the flight crew that even once the bodies were aboard they were not to depart.

Understood by Dove and Capt Haas, Pluma was washing his hands—if Dove wanted his ceremony now without the general, it was on him.

"I ordered you, Mike," Dove told Haas. An out for Haas, Dove would take the hit.

Then Dove stepped aside in private with Redcloud and told him to have the men get their rucks out here, and they could shed their heavy stuff, including their body armor and helmet and get it loaded on the gear helicopter to take back to Valley Forge. Dove told him to tell them to keep it quiet, and told him his intentions.

Redcloud had his Zoosters stage their rucks at the rock wall, and that's where Dove dug out his ballcap and pulled from the bottom of his ruck the extra uniform he always carries as emergency backup and right there he stripped off what was left of his pants and put on the clean pair, hiding all the bloodied dressings.

And Pluma didn't think anything was unusual or out of the ordinary. Soldiers shedding their heavy body armor and donning favorite civilian ballcaps when they're soon going to be boarding the CH-47 Chinook and fly twenty minutes back to their safe, comfortable Cop. Let them have that luxury, they've been in combat for the past twenty-four hours.

That was before the ceremony. Now Zach Dove and these so few of the platoon have rucked up and are moving off, and Col Pluma is at a loss to quite understand it. Where are they going? What are they doing?

He and Capt Haas are a couple of strides behind Redcloud and Dove. He can see that ahead Nick Flowers has settled into the first trench and has supported his camera on the berm, aiming it skyward to film that sergeant with the sniper rifle now stepping on the berm and leaping over. One, two, three strides and that black sergeant is going over.

Pluma calls ahead, "Zach, where you going? The general's going to want a walk-through, may I remind you. It's going to be hard enough explaining no Fallen Comrade ceremony."

"He doesn't need a walk-through," Dove answers without turning around. "Nicky's got it all on tape. The soldiers want to get home, sir." He steps up on the berm, and Redcloud puts a hand on Dove's elbow just in case, for support, as Dove makes the short, awkward, painful leap across the trench.

"Another half-hour won't kill them," Pluma says and leaps across the trench. "For these other journalists, a walk-through for them. Remember, Zach, we have to counter a hundred and sixty-eight dead women and children on tape."

"A hundred and seventy-three, sir."

"Say again?"

"A hundred and seventy-three. Nicky's got it. Everything General St Claire needs, sir, he can get it from Nick already."

"What, you want to take the Blackhawks back? The Blackhawks aren't for you, Zach. I told you, the CH-47 is yours. Everyone's going to the same place."

Just a hand wave acknowledgement is all from Dove, and the men keep striding, over the next berm and trench.

Pluma doesn't get it. Why would Zach want to insist on flying on the Blackhawks instead of the Chinook? Just to show that he can do it?

Pluma says, "Maybe you'll get away with it with the general, Zachary. You're his golden boy. The Fallen Comrade and now this? That O-5, you know, Zach"—meaning Dove's new lieutenant colonel rank. "It's easy-come easy-go."

Up and over the next berm/trench. Rodriquez in the lead showing no indication of stopping or that he's aware of the general approaching just a couple dozen strides ahead.

Still, Redcloud calls forward a reminder, "Rodriquez. Drive on. No salute."

A hand wave acknowledgement from Rodriquez. It's all part of the plan, gone over before, Rodriquez and the others all know what's happening. They know Lieutenant Colonel Dove's instructions. They know to ignore the media who are now fluttering around them like pilot fish.

Ignore them completely.

Ignore the camera shutters clicking, video cameras thrust forward and swinging by panning.

Ignore the questions shouted, *Are you the Tattoo Zoo Platoon? Are you the survivors, the only ones left? How many enemy was it that attacked you? You killed all these? Are these all Taliban? These trenches, did the insurgents attack you from them? That helicopter wreckage over there, is that the helicopter you came in on and crash-landed in here?*

Rodriquez ignores everything and looks right past Gen St Claire who now halts in place as this seven-man patrol of Dove's draws near him, and Rodriquez can't help but grin to himself, recognizing that the general has three Blackwater-type civilian personal security dudes cloaking him, which is exactly what Rodriquez would expect.

And Rodriquez strides right by the general, right on past.

Gen St Claire does a double-take.

Slurpee strides right by.

Another double-take from St Claire.

Wiry little Finkle next, with a lit Marboro hanging from his lips. With quick eyes that dart everywhere except on St Claire, deliberately ignoring him. And St Claire is certain something's up, this is a travesty, it's a charade or a joke, especially the cigarette—no one flagrantly flouts a cigarette dangling out of his mouth so blatantly disrespectful of a general officer, any general officer, and particularly not a zit-faced kid who can't be but a week out of Basic. But St Claire doesn't let it rattle him, automatically shuts off the surprise, beams a smile, knowing the cameras are turning to him, and he sees that behind Zachary Dove two officers break off—Dan Pluma and a Ranger captain. And he locks his eyes on Dove nearing, ignores the next two Zoosters passing, Ketchum and Holloway, expects that Dove, following military protocol that establishes that the senior ranking non-com or officer of any group of soldiers like his small patrol going by is obliged to render the single required salute to a higher ranking officer encountered or passed—he knows that Dove will salute and stop, and

Dove does raise a salute. Saying, "Good morning, sir", and Gen St Claire returns the salute, sharply, and holds it . . . . and Dove just strides right on by.

Son of a bitch!

No one strides by a general officer, not a four-star general officer, and not one who just the other day gifted you that lieutenant colonel rank!

The insolence!

But St Claire holds his anger, hides it, maintains his smile, and cannot have these cameras so close record that he is dumbfounded, insulted, not in control of the situation, and as he turns to watch Dove's patrol stride on and cross the next trench he senses the presence of his personal protection team automatically, instinctively holding off the media, backing them away.

At St Claire's side, Colonel Pluma hurries to tell him, "Zach said the boys just want to get back to their Cop." He's making it up. "I think he thinks, sir, he thinks that the Blackhawks are going there first."

"I'm told you sent the casualties off?" St Claire asks less a question than a subtle reprimand. He lets it drop. For now. "They get on board, you have the pilots lift off and bring the ships up and set down in front of the building." The school. For the walk-through and the ceremony.

Pluma, "Zach said he didn't want to make this a dog-and-pony show, sir."

"I don't give a good goddamn what Zach wants."

Pluma knows his marching orders: Get the bird which Zach and his men climb aboard back to the school. He'll deal at that time with the general learning there would be no Fallen Camrade.

St Claire turns away, grins and holds out his hand to meet, "Nick Flowers? Pete St Claire. Good to finally meet you, you've been bouncing around my theater for so long. Are you ready to get back to Kabul and make yourself quite famous?"

"I need my computers, and all my personal gear's all back at Valley Forge."

"No problem, young man. We're stopping there first." His hand now to Nick's shoulder, to walk together toward the school.

And quickly, as a throwaway, explaining away Dove and his soldiers, St Claire to the media close with a chuckle, "The men just want an aerial view, a God's-eye view of the devastation they rained down. They'll be meeting us up there—" at the school building.

Pluma remains watching Dove's patrol heading for the three Blackhawks. He asks Capt Haas if he's got the pilots on his radio, and Haas gives over the handset. Pluma waits to see which helicopter Dove will get on.

He can see that the flight crews are out of the three helicopters. Can see that they're watching the seven soldiers approaching in single-file. Can see that the first crew all snap to a salute as the lead soldier comes abreast, and he can understand the salute, as the crew members would recognize the torn and filthy and bloodied uniforms of the soldiers and surely the large splotches of glistening wet blood already soaking through the pants that Zachary Dove changed into not all that long ago, and know that these are the men who were in this battle in which all this landscape littered with enemy bodies is testament to.

Pluma sees that the first soldiers walk right on by the first Blackhawk, and it's obvious that Dove isn't going to take the first one, and Pluma is a bit relieved that Zach at least knows enough not to have the impertinence to get on the general's chopper. *Always a class act, that Zach*, Pluma thinks. Willing to defy and piss off the general, but only so much.

Dr Hutchinsen, sitting in the general's Blackhawk, reading on his Kindle, knowing better than to be out there with the general where the cameras are, was distracted by a soldier walking by, and a second one, in a uniform filthy and bloody, and he stuck his head out to see what was going on, and recognizes that it's Zachary Dove and the few remaining of the Zoo Platoon.

As Dove nears the flight crew here, he snaps a return salute to them, and Hutchinsen calls out, "Zachary Dove. Soon to be on the cover of *Time* magazine, *People* and *Family Circle*. Congrats, ol' boy."

A nod of recognition from Dove and that's all, and he continues right on past.

That wasn't right. Not to Hutchinsen, who is struck that that's not the obedient, submissive, brown-nosing Zach Dove who he knows, and he now steps out of the helicopter to watch Dove and his men moving along away.

He asks of the pilots, "What's going on? What's the deal, where are they going?"

Shrugs from the pilots.

A shrug from the crew chief.

Aloud on the radio speaker from the cockpit comes Col Pluma's voice calling the Blackhawk pilots and telling them that when Dove and his soldiers get on the second or third helicopter, they are to fire up and deliver the soldiers to the schoolhouse where the general will be waiting.

Hutchinsen and the crew watch the patrol where right now Dove returns the salute of the second Blackhawk crew and walks right on past.

On toward the third Blackhawk.

Pluma's voice over the radio, *"All right, you in the third Blackhawk, you're to deliver those soldiers to the school building."*

There it's the same. Dove returns the crew's salutes and goes right on past.

Dove and his men aren't getting on any helicopter. They're headed in the direction of the gap there downstream, the entrance to this valley.

"Son – of – a – bitch," Hutchinsen growls. He knows the general's plans, the whole honoring and celebrating the heroes, starting with the general saluting Zachary Dove and the other survivors, meeting the wounded and honoring the dead. The walk-though of the battlefield, Lieutenant Colonel Zachary Dove escorting the four-star, all cameras rolling. He knows the plans because they were his also.

And there's Dove right now, walking away, heading in the opposite direction. Leaving. Without so much as a *"So long, see you later"*.

"Take a good look, gents," Hutchinsen tells the pilots here. "That is a man there with one enormous pair of—as they say in Méjico—él tiene cajones gigantes." Pronounced, exaggerated, syllable by syllable, *cah-hone-ays hee-gan-tays.*

Col Pluma and Capt Haas are sprinting. Not toward the Blackhawk helicopters. Toward the school, to catch up with Gen St Claire, who is just now crossing the first shallow trench and has no idea what's going on behind him back down the beach with Dove, until Nick Flowers reacts to seeing one of the media guys jerk his video camera away from the general to aim it far behind, and Nick spins and sees Pluma and the Ranger captain sprinting close and sees way down there that the Zoo patrol is past the third Blackhawk, in their casual march away.

Nick feels the presence beside him of the general, and he flicks on his camera, flips up his viewscreen and zooms it in on the backs of the Zoosters down there.

Gen St Claire watches Nick's viewscreen. His expression a frozen mixture of disbelief and rage.

Which he quickly morphs to bland neutrality. Feigned amusement, really.

And quietly asks with false easy playfulness, "What in the name of Samuel Hell Jackson are they doing?"

Nick, "Beats me. Out for a Sunday stroll? It is Sunday, isn't it?"

To Col Pluma coming up St Claire asks, "Dan, did you know about this?"

"No sir, not at all, sir. I can't say what's gotten into him."

St Claire holds out his hand, a universal sign, and Capt Haas puts his radio handset into it.

St Claire motions his civilian protection detail to get the media away at a distance. This isn't for the media to see, hear, nor record.

He calls on the radio, "Zachary Dove, Zachary Dove, this is General Pete St Claire, over."

A moment passes.

Over the handset only St Claire can hear Dove's answer. "Roger, this is Zoo Six, over."

St Claire, "What's going on, where are you going, Zach?"

"This is Zoo Six. Zoo Platoon is going home. Over."

"Who directed you that you had permission to leave?"

"This is Zoo Six. Mission in Wajma accomplished and complete. We have not been advised as to change in Air status. I repeat, have not been advised as to change in Air status. Zoo Platoon is returning to base overland via Lima Papa Charlie. Over."

As in, LPC.

Leather Personnel Carriers.

Boots.

St Claire, "I have a Chinook here that will take the platoon back to Cop Valley Forge. Understood, Zach?"

"This is Zoo Six. Roger. Over."

St Claire's eyes glued to Nick's viewscreen. The image zoomed in, all that's seen are the backs of Dove and Redcloud and the other Zoosters moving away.

St Claire into the handset, remaining perfectly calm and cordial, "Did you hear me, Zach? We have a Chinook that will take the men back to their Cop."

"This is Zoo Six. Roger. Out."

Out?

Out?!!!

On Nick's viewscreen, and even with the naked eye, one can see Dove's soldiers not changing direction. Angling down the beach straight toward the distant valley opening.

Out?!!!!

You don't *Out* a four-star. A four-star *Outs* you.

Outing one, that's enough to make him go ballistic.

St Claire doesn't.

Says quietly into the handset, gently, "In case you do not understand, Zachary. Lieutenant colonels do not command platoons. Over."

And Dove's response, "This is Zoo Six. Roger."

Still, viewing from way up here, it can be plainly seen that Dove's patrol does not stop or turn around and change course.

St Claire, "Are we clear on that, Zachary? Platoons are commanded by O-1s and O-2s. Am I clear, Lieutenant Colonel Dove?"

"This is Zoo Six. Roger, Lima Charlie."

Loud and Clear, my ass; right there on Nick's viewscreen, no change in direction of the patrol.

"I'm not sure that you do understand, Zachary. Platoons are not commanded by O-5s. Nor by O-5s returned right back down to O-4."

"This is Zoo Six. Roger, sir, understood. Out."

Out?!!!!!!

St Claire watches, and they all watch here, on the viewscreen or with their own eyes, and the distant figures of Dove and his six soldiers do not stop or change direction.

A slight chuckle from Col Pluma. Even from only hearing St Claire's side of the conversation, it's easy to guess Dove's side. Lightly, he half-jokes, "I wonder what Doctor Gene Hutchinsen, PhD, would advise in this situation."

"Shut up," St Claire tells him.

And the problem solved in the quickness of his analytical genius, he orders one of his two captain aides here, "Get these reporters rounded up and back on my birds. We're done here. We'll do the Fallen Comrade at Bagram."

He steps off in long strides to head back for the Blackhawks. Pluma and Capt Haas abreast but both an inch behind, and

without even looking at him St Claire orders Pluma, "I want those two Apaches a hundred feet over Zachary Dove's inflated head right now this very moment, and I want minimum two gunships shadowing them all the way to Cop Valley Forge, I don't care if it takes Dove two days or a week to get there."

"Roger, sir."

St Claire waves his arm above his head, motioning the distant Blackhawk crews *Crank em up!*, that even from the distance they will recognize.

He orders Captain Haas, "Get a platoon with them, I want them in a protective cocoon." He's not about to have Zachary Dove survive all this only to have his head and the heads of those Tattooed Zooers stuck up on stakes two miles downriver under Taliban flags flying high. "You police up all these weapons and ordnance"—the battlefield litter—"and destroy it in place. Same with that helicopter"—the crashed Chinook. "Order in more demo if you have to, I don't want one usable speck of it available." *Not for these peasants,* he thinks. "Then you take the remainder of your company and you hustle yourselves down there and join up with Zachary Dove and his Cub Scout troop. It looks like a nice day for a hike."

Capt Haas, "Yes sir."

"Flown in with the demo, have them include an SF medic, drop him off with Zach." St Claire is not about to have soon-to-be-crowned war hero Zachary Dove bleed out on his little Sunday stroll, then have to answer to the president and the Joint Chiefs all laying the blame all on him, tossing him under the bus. Or tank. "And when you join them, if you don't think Dove's in good enough shape to make it back to Cop Valley Forge, you call in an exfil bird, you understand?"

"Yes sir."

A motion from St Claire, *That's all*—

and Capt Haas breaks away.

Col Pluma too.

St Claire lightens his mood, lets out a guffaw. An arm again now around Nick Flowers' shoulders. To pull him close.

To tell him with a scent of cynical delight, "For Zachary Dove's sake, I hope you have on that camera *Pork Chop Hill, The Longest Day, Platoon, The Great Escape*. Combined, rolled into one. Hero stuff—clear as day, the good guys verses the bad. White hats verses black."

Black, like the dress of these dead Talib bodies they're walking past strewn over this beach.

Nick shrugs. "You know what they say, General. Art is subjective. Art's in the eye of the beholder."

"Who's talking art? Since when has art ever won a war?"

A stride. Another. St Claire draws his arm away from Nick. Likes it that he hears the engines of his Blackhawks ahead in their tenor whining of start-up.

Nick probes. "Winning, who's talking winning? Are you confident of winning this war? How do you define winning, if it's even possible to define winning?"

St Claire grins. Is neither dumb nor reckless enough to get cornered by a disarming, play-dumb journalist. "You don't mind," he says, "if I reserve my judgment until I see what you've filmed that is usable. If you've shot *Pork Chop Hill* . . . or . . . *Porky's*."

"Usable, what do you mean? Usable how?"

St Claire doesn't answer. Just winks at Nick—one little playful wink—and assumes that Nick knows exactly what he means, but has no idea that Nick gave one set of DVDs that he burned to Redcloud. Gave a second set to Wolfe, and it's in Wolfe's Marine Corps rucksack right now aboard the Chinook with all the excess gear. Nick returned Spec Howie's computer to him with everything copied into a password-protected folder. Has hidden in an MRE Reese's Pieces wrapper down at the bottom of his own small 3-day pack a 64-gb thumb drive on which everything is copied.

And earlier he'd slipped into an outside pocket of Dove's rucksack a second 64-gb thumb drive hidden in an M&Ms wrapper. Without Dove's knowledge. In the rucksack on Dove's back right now.

An Apache flies crossing patterns five hundred feet above Dove's patrol, behind, rear protection. The other Apache glides toward the gap to scout ahead.

A fireteam of Rangers sprints past the patrol to join the fireteam who is already out front to make a wedge leading and protecting the Zoosters.

The others of this Ranger platoon are behind sprinting to join up, to make a flanking and rear protective envelope around Dove's patrol.

The Ranger lieutenant catches up with Dove and Redcloud. Tells them that his platoon has been assigned to accompany them wherever they're going, even if it's all the way back to Cop Valley Forge. He asks if there's anything he should know, or anything particular they need from him and his men.

Redcloud tells him they're welcome along for the movement but that he should remember that this is the colonel's patrol and the Zoo would set the pace, and suggests that the point element disabuse themselves of the notion that this is a forced speed march in Ranger School, "Cuz they're not impressing anyone, they're not being graded this morning."

No problem.

And Redcloud suggests that the lieutenant have hia point-man maneuver on the high ground, make a trail up along the mountainside and keep out of the water to navigate through the gap. Keep the bandaged wounds of the colonel's legs from getting soaked.

No problem.

And, Redcloud tells him, have them get it secure on the far side of the gap and park themselves there, because Redcloud's plan is to take a breakfast break there. "If they really want to make the colonel happy, they'll already have some coffee heated up when we get over."

No problem. And the lieutenant asks Dove, telling him that he doesn't want to sound condescending and like he's kissing ass, but if the colonel wants, seeing as he's wounded, the lieutenant and his men will be happy to carry his rucksack.

Nope. "Coffee," Dove says. "That would be appreciated."

Yes sir!, and the lieutenant hurries forward and now sprints past Slurpee then Rodriquez to get up with the leading Rangers ahead.

Every step is difficult for Dove. Stabs of wincing pain.

Which does not escape Redcloud. "Sir, it's a pretty good hump back."

Just a nod acknowledgment from Dove.

"Rodriquez!" Redcloud calls ahead. "Notch it back a bit."

Rodriquez raises his rifle, *Roger*, and he shortens his stride.

"You know, sir, lesson's been taught," Redcloud coaxes Dove. "There's only so much crow a four-star's gonna eat. We really oughta get those"— legs, Dove's wounds—"cleaned and tended to. The gear bird, one quick call, they'll pick us up here."

"Sheee-at yeh!" from Holloway just ahead. "Ten minutes to the Cop. Hot showers, hot chow, see what my hos've put up on Facebook for me! Gonna be a good night for Rosie Palm tonight"—

"Clam it, Holloway," from Redcloud.

"Aw, Sarge, com'on, in ten minutes we can"—

"At ease, clam it I said! Just once, PFC, just one time let's try 'n see if you can't zip your lips and drive on keeping them zipped. Cuz nobody really cares about you or your hos or your Facebook. Think we can have that for today, the rest of the day? Just once?"

From Holloway just a wave of his hand back, *Yeh right, whatever.*

From Dove, "All day, Sergeant Redcloud, all the way back? Not one word? This is PFC Holloway we're talking about, after all. What would Mr Wolfe say?"

"Wolfie?" And Redcloud shakes his head.

Yeh, he thinks. *What would Wolfie say?*

A few more short strides, then it hits him, he knows. "Enshallah," he says.

Dove offers the option, "Enchilada."

"Sheeee-at yeh!" from Holloway. "Saaaaa-weeeeett!!! Colonel's rolling with the Holloway Groove!"

"PFC!" Redcloud taps the muzzle of his M4 against the top of the frayed, dirty In-N-Out Burger ballcap Holloway's wearing. "What'd I just tell you?!"

"Yeh, Sarge, but"—

"Clam it!" Redcloud isn't kidding. "C-L-A-M-I-T! No buts!"

Just ahead of Holloway, it's Ketchum who laughs. "In what world you dreamin of, Sarge? Gonna have better luck tellin Holl-o-weird not to breathe."

Redcloud, "What I might just do, I'll make Finkle RTO. Let you have Holloway. Y'hear that, PFC? One word in the next twelve miles, your days of shamming are over, turn in the radio, you're in Ketch's squad."

Dove likes hearing this banter. Knows that it's good. Good for the men. Good for right now. At the end of the twelve miles, whenever that is, this afternoon, tonight, no rush, when they're back on their Cop they'll have plenty enough days and weeks and months for each to deal in his own solitary time with *Having lost so many of their friends, their platoon brothers.* There are going to be all those nights in the weeks and months and years coming when *Most of these men here, these six, and me,* and the wounded who have been flown out, when *We'll all wake shaking from our dreams,* and some few won't be able to shake those dreams asleep and awake even long down the road when *The stronger of us have cleansed them of painful feeling,* and there will be those one or two or three of the weak who will use them as an excuse for their alcohol and drugs and wife-beating and child-terrorizing and perhaps even suicide, and *All of us in our own time will have to come to terms with these twenty-four hours through which we have survived simply and unfairly by sheer random- ness,* and each one will have to overcome the fear and vulnerability and helplessness and guilt and self-loathing and rage and hate or become miserable and pathetic and vicious and dishonorable, and that man *I might pity, will feel that I should pity,* but for whom *I know myself enough to know I will mostly feel only scorn* . . . but now is not the time *For us to judge others, or even ourselves,* that's not for now, not right now, there will be plenty of time later, and time itself, the endurance day to day through it, will eventually fade this very real and internalized horror of these hours into a remembrance to be proud of, something fondly recalled as a high point of challenge and accomplishment in a man's life, and *Something we are comforted in our longing to return to, knowing that we don't have to, remembering only the triumph, dimming the horror,* like men have always done from the wars they've fought for the last five thousand years. Survived and overcame.

We'll get over on the other side there, of the gap, Dove thinks. *Have some coffee and breakfast, allow the men to let out their breath,* sit silently, each to begin to take measure and comfort that it is safe now, to *Catch our breath secure in the protection of these Rangers,* and in the protection of the Apaches. *We'll have our coffee* and let the sun come over the ridgeline, and Dove recognizes only now at this moment that it's foolish to put these Zoosters' lives in further danger these next twelve miles to home in a patrol of which *I myself am the wounded, I am the slowest one, I am the weak link,* and he knows that General St Claire and his troupe all will have flown out and be long gone heading back to Kabul by then, and he decides that when he has poured his second canteen cup of coffee and Sergeant Redcloud his, he'll give Redcloud a nod to radio up a request for exfil, have choppers come in and take them all back to Cop Valley Forge, and choppers for the Rangers as well to return quickly and safely to Salerno, and so be it.

"PFC," Dove calls to Holloway's back just two strides ahead. "Perhaps I can see about getting you a position on comms staff or as a runner up at Isaf. It's a plum, clean, safe duty."

Silence from Holloway, he won't break Redcloud's *Clam it* order. But he raises a hand to the back of his ballcap to pretend to straighten it, with only his middle finger exposed to Dove.

And Dove smiles at that. Pushes it, an added inducement, "Lots of pretty E-3 and E-4 clerks stationed up there. Brit, Dutch, French."

Holloway's middle finger remains up on his hat, pressed hard, slowly pumping up and down.

Dove can't help it, his whole face grins. Holloway isn't gesturing an angry, disrespectful *Fuck off* to him, but just responding to Dove's obvious tease of a cushy job and sexy girls with his own counter, an affirmation that aint none of that's worth giving up the Zoo for.

Aint the same, aint as special as a warrior in the infantry.

In the Zoo.

From Redcloud also a rare and ever so slight smile. No need to say anything.

While up ahead, Slurpee turns his head to call back, "Colonel, sir, that offer stand for me? Hooah on a sham job in the rear with all that Isaf muff. I'll take it, sir, put me down for it!"

Air-Evac C-130, In Flight

About twenty minutes after take-off from Fob Salerno. Heading for Bagram Airfield.

Triaged in Wajma by the Cash medical personnel and quickly again at Fob Salerno on the tarmac with the addition of the C-130 medical staff, twenty wounded are aboard. Twelve remained at Salerno for treatment.

The twenty in here on litters stacked three-high on both sides of the metal rigging down the center of this fuselage.

Major Victoria Marshall bends to check Capt Cathay in a middle litter.

Cathay's eyes closed, she's well-drugged asleep, and that's good. She's not feeling any pain.

Vicky glances at the digital monitor.

Respiration, heartbeat, blood pressure. The numbers are okay.

The captain looks okay. Fragile. Delicate. But okay.

Pretty features. Wholesome young pretty, though smudged with dirt and blood and black soot, and without make-up. Her lips, without lipstick, even under the distorting clear plastic of the oxygen mask, they're feminine and pink-red and sensual.

Vicky knows without checking the chart again that Cathay was given morphine there in the village, and she instantly calculates an estimate of the combination of dosages of the drugs she will use if she is to be her anesthetist for the surgery to clean and debride and re-dress her arm and leg at Bagram and, as the doctors have already determined, to get her immediately on the air-evac jet up to Landstuhl this afternoon.

To the major military med center at Landstuhl specifically for the bullet buried in her back.

Which Vicky hopes hasn't severed or gravely damaged the spinal cord.

They'll know at Landstuhl.

Vicky lifts aside the edge of the sheet and puts her fingertips just lightly on the slightly smudged Sharpie inking of the Zoo tattoo on Cathay's bared thigh. It's just in black, unlike the multi-colored real ones she saw back there out on the tarmac, like on the chest of the soldier up front here, what's his name?, Van-something? Van Lowry? Van Louie?

On the tarmac someone from the Cash had said that the tattoo was what the platoon called themselves. Someone else had said that they awarded the tattoo like a medal, for courage. And that wounded soldier Van Louie had corrected him. Had said, *"You jus gotta do yer job."*

That's what Vicky remembers he'd repeated. *"Jus do yer job is all."*

She sensed then that that was false humility, and she wonders what Captain Cathay had to do to earn it. *I could have never done it. Oh how brave you had to be. How brave you were to make these rough, hardcore infantry soldiers honor you.*

And Vicky realizes now that she has her hand lying on Cathay's cheek and doesn't remember putting it there.

She realizes that her own eyes are welling up, and doesn't know why they should, then knows it's because this young delicate Captain Laura Cathay must know of her bravery and the respect shown in their giving her this tattoo, even temporary, simply inked in a black Sharpie, though Vicky has no way of knowing that in the village when the Cash medics had scissored off her pantleg Capt Cathay first saw the Sharpie tattoo and was surprised and didn't know when they'd drawn it on her and couldn't imagine why they'd draw it on her, then knew why. Had remembered them saying before, how many of them had said it?, that she was one of them, that she was part of the Zoo. No, she thought then, not just in the Zoo, but this meant that they thought she was brave, that she was a warrior like them. Like Sergeant Redcloud and Sergeant Rodriquez and Sergeant Ketchum. And Lieutenant Matthew Caufield.

Capt Cathay had cried then. Sobbed, with her tears flowing freely. And the medics thought it was out of pain, her suffering through the pain of her grave wounds.

It was just the opposite.

But Vicky Marshall cannot know that. She was not in the village, but at Fob Salerno on the tarmac behind the open C-130 where they were waiting for the casualties. She only knows that whatever this captain, a sole female among these fighting men—whatever she did, she may never walk again, may lose half her leg, may lose all her arm, but will always have in her spirit the knowledge that she was awarded their tattoo.

Vicky Marshall cannot know that in the village when Cathay was carried into the Chinook and her litter set on the floor, in the slow-motion slurry vision of the morphine enveloping her, Cathay knew they were setting down a litter beside her, and she forced herself to focus on the face of the man on it, and it was the good-looking medic, Sergeant Eberly, and his face was unscratched, *Oh maybe he isn't wounded,* she'd thought, and she saw that his eyes found hers, then his lips were telling her something that she would never be able to hear over the screaming whining of the engines and rotors, but his lips were smiling, she thought, and she thought that she could hear him saying something like *See, I told you that you would make it. You're going to be all right.* And in her blurry vision she could then see that he was bandaged—his arms, his belly, his waist—and she chose instead to look again at his lips which were then saying something that she imagined was that *We could have maybe been friends, Captain. I could have maybe borrowed from you one of those romance novels you read and I could learn what makes an attractive smart woman like you tick.* But hands came down and hid his lips under a plastic oxygen mask, then a mask was as quickly clamped over her mouth and nose.

Vicky Marshall can't know any of that. But she somehow feels in this peaceful sleeping young female captain an essence of glory, though *I would not trade me for you,* she thinks now, and she would not want these grievous injuries Cathay has, but she envies and wishes for herself that same glory, though she reasons that she will never have the opportunity that this Captain Cathay has had, to *Know that I myself could ever be brave enough and unselfish enough to step outside of myself* and outside of her own self-interest for others, simply primarily for the benefit of others, *To give my life or be willing to give my life for others I don't even know,* and as such to gain their respect and their love. *As you have.*

Vicky senses that she is being watched, being stared at, and she finds the intense eyes of the soldier on the litter on the other side of the rigging staring right into hers.

She smiles a nurse's automatic reassuring smile, and immediately regrets it, realizing that he is the strikingly handsome, ruggedly attractive man, younger than she, who is aboard because they determined that he would be dead already and could not have been saved at the Salerno Cash and cannot be saved at Bagram and is expected now to die in flight, with his entire lower gut, the doctor had said, looking like all the organs had been put through an industrial paper shredder, with that shredder's broken, fragmented chunks of gears and shards of blades embedded scattered in there, and they're the only things holding him together.

The woman is beautiful to Doc Eberly.

In her wide-open eyes he sees compassion. Knowledge. Wisdom. Certainty. Aloneness.

Now pity.

No, don't feel sorry for me, he thinks. *I don't even feel sorry for me. A week ago I would have been too timid, too afraid to look at you, to stare at you when you looked back. I would have been afraid to say hello. I would have been afraid to tell you that you're beautiful. Afraid to tell you that you're what God would create as His woman. That you are lovelier than His imperfect perfection of the never-ending beauty of pi. I would have been afraid to tell you I want to fall in love with you.*

Her head moves up, out of sight, then she's gone.

And Doc Eberly is reminded of that last breezy, tossed-off, joyous and meaningless *"Bye, see you around"* from Cindy from the Subway and then he'd never seen her again, and he knows that it was because he was and is too intellectual for her, he was and is too serious for Cindy from the Subway, who just wanted every day to be like — oh how he wishes now for those times, if only one time more — to have every day like when she's atop him, hands pushing down on his chest, she's bouncing, laughing with such playful free abandon and child delight, and he remembers her as being then the *Most beautiful, the most pure, the most innocent, the most wonderful girl in the world who trusts me so completely that she can be so open and translucent, lighthearted and unafraid to give herself to me, with no care whatsoever of my judgment of her.* He envisions that he had let go then of who he was, that he was laughing with her, released from his own self-restraints of perpetual control to be as sprung-free as her, to laugh like her without thinking, laugh and call her name aloud *"Cindy!"* and later giggle then laugh again as he now mounted her, his hands pressed down cupping her naked breasts, and now hearing that laughter from then, hearing it as real, a perfect memory, he's fascinated at laughter, that there is laughter, and he can't pinpoint where it's from, where does laughter come from? Where is it born? From two cells forming as one in human life, and where among these 23 chromosomes and those 23 chromosomes is that impulse to laugh hidden? Where is the directive to laugh written? *What part or mystery combinations of each of the adenine, cytosine, guanine and thymine of our DNA allow us to know to laugh, allow its unchecked release, and allow it without us even being conscious that we should laugh?* So many molecules that are so many atoms of electrons in a cloud around nuclei that are protons and neutrons that are quarks and empty space, all energy so inanimate, invisible, uncatchable, of nothing but chemistry and physics, and *Where does that laughter come from? Where is the laughter in the electrons? Where is the crying in the protons? Where is the love in the quarks?*

How is it that my brain, which is but a hundred billion cells transferring chemical-electrical charges through a hundred trillion synapses, how is it that it can discern to now shut down or reroute those that should be warning me of the pain that must be going through me in all the chemical-electrical messages sent up on my nerves so that I can feel only a dull numb emptiness? How do those cells know to go quiet, when they should be clang-clang-clanging with red lights flashing and sirens wailing? Where in the light-speed spinning of the path of the electron is the conscious decision to shut down, turn off, and how is it passed to the septillions of atoms along the way and how do the particular atoms who are purposefully and selectively charged with igniting me to think right now that I am Eberly, they call me Doc Eberly, how do they know to ignore that order to shut down?

I am, we know, my DNA. Where is that in my DNA?

Where am I in my DNA?

How does my DNA know how to laugh? How does it know when to laugh? How does it recognize love? Where in my DNA does it sense love?

He feels a hand on his forehead.

He feels it is warm.

It is smooth.

He focuses on a face close.

Her face.

Major Victoria Marshall asks him, "Do you need anything?"

She feels a cold shiver of tenseness through her hand on his forehead. As if it's sparking inside under there, like a thousand severed live electrical wires dancing erratically on an ice rink.

"We can give you something for the pain. Do you want something for the pain?"

More than the barely perceptible shake of his head *No* she can see the immediate fear of *No!* in his eyes.

"Are you sure?" And she remembers, "I know you've had a maximum dosage already, but that was more than two hours ago and we can give you more. You don't have to suffer, we can get rid of all the pain."

Again, more than the shake of his head, his eyes are adamant, *No!*

"You're some tough boys," she tells him. "You Tattoo Zoo. You're some tough men. Tough men to go through all that."

She sees that there's something wrong. What? A wiggle of his oxygen mask, it's familiar to her, when patients want it off.

"No. We need to leave this on here. We need to leave it on so to make it easier for you to breathe."

His eyes demand *No!*, and before she knows what's happening, his bandaged arm jerks upward and his bandaged hand punches the mask askew. And "No!" comes the whisper from his lips. And "Please?" the whisper pleads.

She doesn't know what to do.

Again, a nearly silent plea, "Please?", from him.

"Tell me," she asks. "What is it? Is there something you want to say?" She pulls his mask down completely. "Do you have a message you want me to pass on for your wife?"

From him, barely, in a hush, "No."

"Do you have a wife? Are you married?"

. . . . "No."

"A girlfriend?"

. . . . "No."

"Your parents? You want me to tell your mother something?"

. . . . "No."

"What? What is it?" She glances at his chart. "What is it, Sergeant Eberly, what would you like? What is it I can do for you? Tell me."

. . . . "Kiss . . . . me . . . . please" . . . .

She smells like she's just stepped from the shower, shampooed in a strawberry gel, fresh and sweet and clean and feminine, perfumed just lightly enough to entice and draw him closer.

Doc Eberly wants to run his fingers through her hair, over her ears, to caress the back of her neck and gently pull her face to his, as he's seeing in her eyes staring right at him a glistening moisture that softens their maturity and seems to be saying *Yes I will kiss you forever, Sergeant Eberly.*

And her eyelids lower and close completely the moment he feels her lips touch his.

And he closes his eyes.

Her lips are soft.

Smooth.

Warm.

Moist.

They taste like just-picked raspberries in vanilla bean ice cream.

His lips are hungry and press into hers to bite hers to keep her here, and hers press back and lay gentle, as if to say be calm, that they're not leaving, they're not going anywhere, and

he smells the burnt flesh as he feels the hardened, charred, oozing bloody muscle of her arm to push the IV needle into the pretty anthropologist Robyn who just a few hours before on the drive up to the village filled the humvee with the smell of some jasmine honeysuckle soap, and

he can hear the near-silent words that Sergeant First Class Travis Redcloud is whispering as he bends his face low to tell his dying lieutenant *"You're a good P-L, Matt"*, and

he sees through the distorted green of his Nods the headless body of Specialist Lee Tran belly-down on the concrete roof, and

he sees Kyle Wolfe on the roof of the Toc building brusquely wipe off the streak of a tear from his cheek, and

he sees Lieutenant Colonel Zachary Dove press his palms down over the pulsating spurts of blood geysering from Captain Washington's throat and a pointed 7.62 bullet approach in a slow-motion spin then glance off Dove's helmet, splitting in half down its length, and

he sees one shard tumble off to splat into the dirt near Sergeant Redcloud's boot treads, and

he sees the other tumble lopsided and tear a shredded hole through Captain Laura Cathay's uniform at the waist not a centimeter below her body armor, and

he sees the scope's crosshairs set dead-on center-of-mass on the dark-seraped Talib and Rodriquez squeeze the trigger then reacquire the Talib and put a second bullet through the olive-green ammo bandolier across the man's chest, and

he sees First Sergeant Kozak leaned into the backseat of the humvee holding his duct-taped soda bottle to Triple Shot's lips, tilting it, letting him sip, slurp, gulp, and

he sees Kyle Wolfe in the half-dark in the school in the quiet of the deepest part of night espy Captain Cathay and think *Sleep in peace, little girl*, then scrunch both his eyes closed tight and draw in a concealed sniffle, and

he sees Sergeant Redcloud and Colonel Dove on foot, the last of the departing patrol, now about to cross over the gap and disappear, and both stop and turn for a final look at Wajma Valley below, and

he watches Redcloud's eyes slowly sweep the valley that is empty of all Americans, abandoned, with just a few dying flames licking from the exploded wreckage of what once was the Chinook, and Redcloud's eyes pan the shallow trenches that have been filled with the black-clad bodies and limbs of the enemy Taliban that have been dragged and dropped into them, leaving a clean rocky beach, and Redcloud spots up on the farthest terraced field a single farmer exit his compound and two boys exit after him, and Redcloud thinks what he's reminded now that he said aloud only a day or two ago and knows he's thought countless times before— *Just leave them in peace out there, what are we bothering them for?* —which he knows is futile to ask, and he turns away to crest the mountainside, and

Doc Eberly watches Lieutenant Colonel Zachary Dove holding his stare on this panoramic picturesque Wajma Valley and imagine that it is summer and the terraced fields are all richly colorful in wheat and corn and four boys are running barefoot splashing in water up to their knees in an irrigation ditch, and Dove understands with a tinge of sad regret that the bittersweet reality is that he is the last American to ever again look upon this valley, and

Doc Eberly sees Zachary Dove turn away and step over the ridgeline to follow Travis Redcloud, and

he feels her lips press quickly into his then pull away, off.

He opens his eyes, and her face remains close.

It is so perfectly angelically beautiful.

Her eyes gleam. They're happy. They're confident. They are kind.

"Thank . . . . you" his lips say without sound.

A smile, her lips closed . . . . and she brings them down and lays them against his cheek, and

he feels their slight pucker and feels them stay and not leave, and he is calmed into a single slow breath that he draws in deep as he experiences a profound peacefulness knowing he is blessed to be sent on his way with a kiss from this most perfect woman in an imperfect world that is like the perfect imperfection of pi, which he visualizes now as thousands of numbers streaming by, and

he starts to pick them out in order one by one

3

.

1

4

and releases his breath

1

5

aware that as he counts to the last of the 1000 digits of pi that he knows by heart for absolute certain from memory since 5th grade

9

2

6

5

the gap between the circle's unjoined ends shrinks ever smaller

3

5

8

and he accepts that somewhere in these numbers his voice will be heard no more by any living human

9

7

that they may know him as Doc Eberly or Doc or Sergeant Eberly or just Eberly and may know his many thoughts and imaginings from before

9

3

2

but from this time forward as he counts down pi no one here on earth alive will be able to hear him and can know any more of what he knows or imagines and might have one day written

3

8

Cover soldier portraits, L-R: *Ssgt Marcus Vasquez, 1Lieut Kevin Bell, Spec John Phillips, Pfc Anthony Overby, Sgt Thomas Travis*

Made in United States
Troutdale, OR
10/02/2023

13350946R10342